KU-215-295

THE GAME OF KINGS

They had reached the door to the Hall. One hand on the standpost, he turned, and the kitten's eyes were bright blue. 'Watch carefully. In forty formidable bosoms we are about to create a climacteric of emotion. In one short speech – or maybe two – I propose to steer your women through excitement, superiority, contempt and anger: we shall have a little drama; just, awful and poetic, spread with uncials and full, as they poet said, of fruit and seriosity. Will they thank me, I wonder?'

Mariotta, collecting her wits, produced the only deterrent she could think of. 'Your mother is in there.'

He received it with tranquil pleasure. 'Then one person at least should recognize me,' Crawford of Lymond said, and pushed the door gently open for her to walk through.

Also in Arrow by Dorothy Dunnett

QUEENS' PLAY
THE DISORDERLY KNIGHTS
PAWN IN FRANKINCENSE
THE RINGED CASTLE
CHECKMATE

THE GAME OF KINGS

Dorothy Dunnett

ARROW BOOKS

Arrow Books Limited
20 Vauxhall Bridge Road, London SW1V 2SA

An imprint of the Random Century Group

London Melbourne Sydney Auckland Johannesburg
and agencies throughout the world

First published in Great Britain by
Cassell & Company Ltd 1962
First paperback edition published by Century 1984
Arrow edition 1986
Reprinted 1990 and 1991

© Dorothy Dunnett 1961

This book is sold subject to the condition that it
shall not, by way of trade or otherwise, be lent,
resold, hired out, or otherwise circulated without
the publisher's prior consent in any form of binding
or cover other than that in which it is published and
without a similar condition including this condition
being imposed on the subsequent purchaser

Phototypeset by Input Typesetting Ltd, London

Printed and bound in Great Britain by
Courier International Ltd.,
Tiptree, Essex

ISBN 0 09 994950 4

The Game of Kings is jointly dedicated as may seem fitting to an Englishwoman and a Scot

FOR
ALISTAIR MACTAVISH DUNNETT
AND
DOROTHY EVELINE MILLARD HALLIDAY

CHARACTERS: *These are some of the Scots who play a part in this story:*

RICHARD CRAWFORD, third Baron Culter of Midculter Castle, Lanarkshire
SYBILLA, the Dowager Lady Culter, his mother
MARIOTTA, his wife
FRANCIS CRAWFORD OF LYMOND, Master of Culter, his brother

SIR WALTER SCOTT OF BUCCLEUCH, a Border landowner
JANET BEATON, his wife
WILL SCOTT OF KINCURD, younger of Buccleuch, his heir

SIR ANDREW HUNTER OF BALLAGGAN
CATHERINE, his mother

AGNES, Lady Herries, a young heiress
JOHN, Master of Maxwell, brother of Robert, sixth Lord Maxwell
THOMAS ERSKINE, Commendator of Dryburgh Abbey and Master of Erskine

LADY JANET FLEMING, widow, of Boghall Castle, the Queen's aunt and governess
LADY CHRISTIAN STEWART, her goddaughter
MARGARET GRAHAM, her widowed daughter

ARCHIBALD DOUGLAS, sixth Earl of Angus, ex-husband of King James IV's widow
SIR GEORGE DOUGLAS, his brother
SIR JAMES DOUGLAS OF DRUMLANRIG, his brother-in-law and uncle of Maxwell

JOHNNIE BULLO, a gypsy
TURKEY MATTHEW, a mercenary soldier

Court:
MARY OF GUISE, widow of King James V and Dowager Queen of Scotland
MARY QUEEN OF SCOTS, her daughter, aged four
JAMES HAMILTON, second Earl of Arran and Governor of Scotland
HENRY LAUDER OF ST. GERMAINS, Lord Advocate to the Queen
ARCHIBALD CAMPBELL, fourth Earl of Argyll, Lord Justice-General

And these, by birth or adoption, are the English:

EDWARD, Duke of Somerset, Earl of Hertford, Viscount Beauchamp, Lord Seymour; Lord Protector of England and Governor of his nephew, King Edward VI, aged nine

The Lords Warden:
SIR WILLIAM GREY, thirteenth Baron Grey de Wilton, Lord Lieutenant of the North Parts for England
THOMAS WHARTON, first Baron Wharton, captain of Carlisle and Warden of the Western Marches
HENRY WHARTON
SIR THOMAS WHARTON } his sons
SIR ROBERT BOWES, Lord Warden of the East and Middle Marches

MATTHEW STEWART, Earl of Lennox and Lord Darnley, Franco-Scott turned English

LADY MARGARET DOUGLAS, his wife, and daughter of the Earl of Angus

Former officers of the Royal Household:
JONATHAN CROUCH, prisoner of war
GIDEON SOMERVILLE OF FLAW VALLEYS, Hexham
KATE, his wife
PHILIPPA, his daughter
SAMUEL HARVEY

Minor Commanders and Officers:
EDWARD DUDLEY, captain of the King's castle of Hume in Scotland
ANDREW DUDLEY, captain of Broughty Fort on the River Tay in Scotland
THOMAS WYNDHAM, captain of the English fleet on the River Tay
SIR JOHN LUTTRELL, captain of the King's fortress of St. Colme's Inch on the River Forth in Scotland
SIR RALPH BULLMER, captain of the King's castle of Roxburgh, in Scotland
SIR THOMAS PALMER, soldier and engineer

Contents

THE GAME OF KINGS

OPENING GAMBIT:
THREAT TO A CASTLE

First of ye chekker sall be mēcioune maid
And syne efter of ye proper moving
Of every man in ordour to his king
And as the chekker schawis us yis forne
Richt so it maye the kinrik and the crowne,
The warld and all that is therein suthlye,
The chekker may in figour signifye.

'Lymond is back.'

It was known soon after the *Sea-Catte* reached Scotland from Campvere with an illicit cargo and a man she should not have carried.

'Lymond is in Scotland.'

It was said by busy men preparing for war against England, with contempt, with disgust; with a side-slipping look at one of their number. 'I hear the Lord Culter's young brother is back.' Only sometimes a woman's voice would say it with a different note, and then laugh a little.

Lymond's own men had known he was coming. Waiting for him in Edinburgh they wondered briefly, without concern, how he proposed to penetrate a walled city to reach them.

When the *Sea-Catte* came in, Mungo Tennant, citizen and smuggler of Edinburgh, knew nothing of these things or of its passenger. He made his regular private adjustment from douce gentility to illegal trading; and soon a boatload of taxless weapons, bales of velvet and Bordeaux wine was being rowed on a warm August night over the Nor' Loch which guarded the north flank of Edinburgh, and toward the double cellar beneath Mungo's house.

Among the reeds of the Nor' Loch, were the snipe and the woodcock lay close and the baillies' swans raised their grey necks, a man quietly stripped to silk shirt and hose and stood listening, before sliding softly into the water.

Across four hundred feet of black lake, friezelike on their ridge, towered the houses of Edinburgh. Tonight the Castle on its pinnacle was fully lit, laying constellations on the water; for within, the Governor of Scotland the Earl of Arran was listening to report after report of the gathering English army about to invade him.

Below the Castle, the house of the Queen Mother also showed lights. The late King's French widow, Mary of Guise, was sleepless too over the feared attack, for the redheaded baby Queen for whom Arran governed was her daughter. And England's purpose was to force a betrothal between the child Queen Mary and the boy King Edward, aged nine, and to abduct the four-year-old fiancée if chance offered. The burned thatch, the ruined stonework, the blackened face of Holyrood Palace showed where already, in other years, invading armies from England had made their point, but not their capture.

Few civic cares troubled Mungo Tennant, awaiting his cargo, except that the ceaseless renewal of war against England made a watch at the gates much too stringent; and the total defeat by England thirty-four years since at Flodden had caused high walls to be flung around Edinburgh which were damnably inopportune for a smuggler. And for Crawford of Lymond, now parting the flat waters of the Nor' Loch like an oriflamme in the wake of the boat. For where a smuggler's load could pierce a city's defences, so could an outlawed rebel, whose life would be forfeit if caught.

Ahead, the boat scraped on mud and was lifted silently shoreward. The rowers unloaded. Burdened feet trod on grass, crossed a garden, encompassed an obstacle, and were silent within the underground shaft leading to the cellar below the cellar in Mungo's house. The swimmer, collared with duckweed, grounded, shook himself, and unseen followed gently into, and out of the same house. Crawford of Lymond was in Edinburgh.

Once there, it was simple. In a small room in the High Street he changed fast into sober, smothering clothes and was fed two months' news, in voracious detail, by those serving him. '... and so the Governor's expecting the English in three weeks and is fair flittering about like a hen with its throat cut.... You're gey wet,' said the spokesman.

'I,' said Lymond, in the voice unmistakably his which honeyed his most lethal thoughts, 'I am a narwhal looking for my virgin. I have sucked up the sea like Charybdis and failing other entertainment will spew it three times daily, for a fee. Tell me again, precisely, what you have just said about Mungo Tennant.'

They told him, and received their orders, and then he left, pausing on the threshold to pin the dark cloak about his chin. 'Shy,' said Lymond with simplicity, 'as a dogtooth violet.' And he was gone.

In his tall house in Gosford Close with the boar's head in chief over the lintel, Mungo Tennant, wealthy and respectable burgher, had invited a neighbour and his friend to call. They sat on carved chairs, with their feet on a Kurdistan carpet, ate their way through capon and quails, chickens, pigeons and strawberries, cherries, apples and warden pears, and noticed none of these things, nor even the hour, being at grips with a noble and irresistible argument.

At ten o'clock, the rest of the household went to bed.

At ten-thirty, Mungo's steward answered a rasp at the door and found Hob Hewat, the water carrier.

The steward asked Hob, in the vernacular, digressing every second or third word, what he wanted.

Hob said he had been told to bring water for the sow.

The steward denied it. Hob insisted. The steward described what instead he might do with the water and

3

Hob described in detail how he had ruined his spine raising the steward's undistinguished water from the well. Mungo, above, thumped on the floor to stop the racket and the steward, cursing, gave in. He led the way to the apartment beneath the stairs where lived Mungo's great sow, the badge of his house, the pet and idiotic pig's apple of his eyes, and waited while Hob Hewat filled its water trough. He then sat down suddenly under an annihilating tap on the head.

Hob, who had done all he had been paid to do, disappeared.

The steward slipped to the floor, and stayed there.

The sow approached her water dish, sniffed it with increasing favour, and inserted both her nose and her front trotters therein.

Crawford of Lymond tied up the steward, left the stye, and climbed the stairs to Mungo Tennant's apartments.

In the gratified presence of their host, Sir Walter Scott of Buccleuch and Tom Erskine were still hard at it. Buccleuch, beaked like a macaw, was a baroque and mighty Scots Lowlander with a tough mind, a voice like Saint Columba's, and one of the biggest estates on the Scottish Border. Erskine, much the younger, pink, stocky and vehement, was a son of Lord Erskine, who was head of one of the families nearest the throne, and captain of the Queen's fortress of Stirling.

'Just wait,' Buccleuch was roaring. 'Just wait, man. Protector Somerset will get his damned English rabble together and march into Scotland up the east coast. And he'll tell off his commander, Lord Wharton, to get his Cumberland English together and invade us at the same time up the west coast. And half the west coast landowners are pensioners of the English already and won't resist 'em. And all the rest of us'll be over here at Edinburgh fighting Ned Somerset – '

'Not all of us,' said Erskine neatly.

Buccleuch's whiskers promenaded. 'Who'll stay in the west that's worth a docken?'

'Andrew Hunter of Ballaggan?'

4

'Christ. Andrew's a nice, gentlemanly lad, but his estate's been bled dry; and as for the ill-armed crew he calls followers – Man, they'd lay on a battlefield like dandruff.'

'The third Baron Culter?' suggested Tom Erskine, and Buccleuch got the derisive note and turned red at the wattle.

'I know fine the cheeky clack of the court,' shouted Buccleuch. 'They say Culter's not to be trusted.'

Tom Erskine lifted the broad, brocade shoulders. 'They say his younger brother's not to be trusted.'

'Lymond! We know all about Lymond. Rieving and ruttery and all manner of vice –'

'And treason.'

'And treason. But treason's not Lord Culter's dish. There are those that want to take time and men to hunt down Lymond and his band of murderers; and those that demand that Culter should lead them as proof of his loyalty. But if Richard Crawford of Culter won't interfere; says he has better business to attend to and refuses flatly to hound down his brother baying like the Wild Jagd, that still doesn't make him a traitor.' And inflating the great chasms of his cheeks, Buccleuch added, 'Anyway, Culter's just got married. D'ye blame him for keeping his shield on the hook and his family blunders all tied up at the back of the armory?'

'Damn it,' said Tom Erskine, annoyed, 'I don't blame him for anything. It isn't my fault. And if it's that black Irish beauty he married, I don't expect he'd notice if the Protector knocked on the front gate at Midculter and asked for a drink of water. But –'

The large red face had calmed down. 'You're dead right, of course,' said Buccleuch cordially. 'In fact you've given me a wee notion or two I can use to the fellow himself. If Culter's going to be in credit at court at all, he'll need to bring himself to capture that honey-faced de'il.'

Mungo Tennant, the silent and flattered host, was able to make respectful comment at last. 'Crawford of Lymond,

Sir Wat?' he said. 'Now, he's not in this country, as I heard. He's in the Low Countries, I believe. And when he'll be back, if ever, God knows. . . . Bless us, what's that?'

It was only a sneeze; but a sneeze outside the door of their chamber, which dislimned every shade of their privacy. Tom Erskine got there first, the other two at his heels. The room beyond was empty, but the door of Mungo's bedroom was ajar. Taking a candle like a banner in his fist, Erskine rushed in.

His hair soft as a nestling's, his eyes graceless with malice, Lymond was watching him in a silver mirror. Before Erskine could call, Buccleuch and Mungo Tennant had piled in beside him and Lymond had taken two steps to the far door, there to linger, hand on latch and the blade of his sword held twinkling at breast level as they jumped, weaponless, to face him, and then fell back.

'As my lady of Suffolk saith,' said Lymond gently, 'God is a marvellous man.' Eyes of cornflower blue rested thoughtfully on Sir Wat. 'I had fallen behind with the gossip. . . . Nouvelle amour, nouvelle affection; nouvelles fleurs parmi l'herbe nouvelle. Tell Richard his bride has yet to meet her brother-in-law, her Sea-Catte, her Sea-Scorpion, beautiful in the breeding season. What a pity you didn't wear your swords.'

Rage mottled Buccleuch's face. 'Ye murdering cur. . . . You'll end this night – '

'I know. Flensed, basted and flayed, and off to hang on a six-shilling gibbet – keep your distance – but not tonight. The city is not full great, but it hath good baths within him. And tonight the frogs and mice fight, eh, Mungo?'

'Man's mad,' said Buccleuch positively. He had managed to pick up a firedog.

'Mungo doesn't think so,' said Lymond. 'His mind is on fleshly lusts and his treasure.' And certainly, the jennet fur at his neck warped with sweat, Mungo Tennant was gaping at the intruder.

Lymond smiled back. 'Be careful,' he said. 'Pits are yawning publicly at your feet. O mea cella, vale, you

6

know . . .' And suddenly, it came to Mungo what he was threatening.

'Don't linger, I pray you, cuckoo, while you run away,' said the sage. Mungo Tennant said nothing. He rushed toward Lymond, collided with Tom Erskine on the way, and falling, sat on the candle. There was a moment's indescribable hubbub while the three men and the firedog blundered cursing into each other in the dark; then they got to the far door and wrenched it open. The corridor as far as the stairhead was quite empty, and the light feet running downward were already some distance away. They hurled themselves after him.

They were three floors above the ground, and the staircase was spiral. The spilth of Buccleuch's bellow rattled the pewter in the kitchens; Tom Erskine shouted and Mungo piped like a hen-whistle. The servants on their pallets heard and started up; tallows flared and a patter of bare feet began on the rushes below.

Mungo's sow heard it too. Drunk as a bishop, she hurtled stairward as the first of the servants arrived. Great blanket ears flapping and rump arched like a Druid at sunrise, she hurled herself at them as Lymond and his pursuers fled down. She bounced once off the newel post, scrabbled once on the flags, trotters smoking, then shot Mungo Tennant backward, squealing thickly in a liberated passion of ham-handed adoration. Mungo sat down, Buccleuch fell on top of him and Tom Erskine swooped headfirst over them both, landing on the pack of unkempt heads jamming the stair foot like stooks at a threshing. Winnowing through them, utterly unremarked in the uproar, was Lymond.

Screaming, squealing and grunting, the impacted cluster swayed on the stairs, torn and surging like rack where the pig unseen hooked the bare feet from under them. Buccleuch was the first to get free, grey whiskers overhanging the swarm like a Chinese kite at a carnival. 'Lymond!' he shrieked. 'Where's he got to?'

They scoured the house in the end without a trace of him, although they found Mungo's steward mute and

7

bound in the pighouse. 'Damn it!' said Buccleuch furiously. 'The windows were barred and the door lockit – he must be here. Where's your cellar?'

Mungo's face was spotty under the pig-spit. 'I've looked there. It's empty.'

'Well, let's look again,' snapped Buccleuch, and was there before Tennant could stop him. 'What's that?'

It was, undoubtedly, a trap door. In bitterest necessity, Mungo Tennant held them up for ten minutes protesting: he claimed it was sealed; it was ornamental; it was locked and unused. In the end Buccleuch stopped listening and went for a crowbar.

It opened with a hissing, fairly oiled ease.

Mungo need not have worried. The lower cellar, the cavern and the long underground tunnel to the Nor' Loch contained no contraband at all. But, because tuns of Bordeaux wine make hard rowing, all the wells of Edinburgh ran with claret next day; and on this, the eve of the English invasion, the commonality of the High Street were for an hour or two as blithe as the Gosford Close sow.

Late, the laminated sheet of the Nor' Loch held a faint chord of laughter.

> *'There was a lady lov'd a hogge*
> *Honey, quoth she*
> *Won't thou lie with me tonight?*
> *Hoogh, quoth he.'*

And, long since ashore with his men and his booty, Crawford of Lymond, man of wit and crooked felicities, bred to luxury and heir to a fortune, rode off serenely to Midculter to break into his new sister-in-law's castle.

> *'Won't thou lie with me tonight?*
> *Hoogh, quoth he.'*

* * *

In the Castle of Midculter, close to the River Clyde in the southwest lowlands of Scotland, the Dowager Lady Culter had reared three children of whom the youngest, Eloïse,

8

died at school in her teens. The two boys remaining were brought up variously in France and in Scotland: she had them taught Latin, French, philosophy and rhetoric, hunting, hawking, riding and archery, and the art of killing neatly with the sword. When her husband died, violently, in the field the elder boy Richard became third Baron Culter, and Francis his brother received the heir's title of Master of Culter as well as taking name from his own lands of Lymond.

Until Richard's marriage, Sybilla Lady Culter had lived alone at Midculter with her older son. What she thought of Lymond's activities she did not say. She welcomed Mariotta, Richard's new bride, with warm arms and dancing blue eyes, and today, in the late summer of 1547, had dismissed her son to his eternal local meetings and had invited the women of the neighbourhood to meet her daughter-in-law. And thus, in Richard's absence, forty women clacked each to each on plush chairs encased by the barrel vaulting, the tapestries and the carving which made the Great Hall of Midculter famous.

Mariotta, black-haired and beautiful, walked on air decorated with compliment and envy. Richard's mother Sybilla, small and splendid, with cornflower eyes and fair skin, effaced herself as well as she could, controlled the household machinery with half her mind and kept her own counsel about the other half.

'And how's Will?' she said rashly to Janet, third and most formidable wife of Wat Scott of Buccleuch, and Janet, big-boned and handsome and heartily florid, thirty years younger than Buccleuch and the cleverest of a diabolically clever family, fixed an unwinking eye on the ceiling and groaned.

In Sybilla's mind, Buccleuch's heir by his first wife was a pleasing, red-haired child who, losing his mother at five, had been gently reared by Sir Wat's then chaplain. Then Buccleuch had sent him to France, where he had attended Grand Collège until this year. Nevertheless, Sybilla was able to put her own accurate interpretation on Janet's groan. 'Religion or women?' asked Lady Culter expertly.

'Women!' It was a cry of despair. 'Can you see Buccle-uch turning a whisker about women! Not a bit of it. Moral Philosophy, that's the trouble,' said Janet with gloomy relish. 'They've taught poor Will moral philosophy and his father's fit to boil.'

'It *is* theology then,' said Sybilla uneasily. 'I suppose he might manage if he sticks like Lindsay to the vulgarities in iambics; but if he's developing into a Calvinist or a Lutheran or an Erasmian or an Anabaptist it isn't very healthy: look at George Wishart and the Castillians.'

'He isn't quoting Luther. He's quoting Aristotle and Boethius and the laws of chivalry and the dreicher speils of the Chevalier de Bayard on loyalty and the ethics of warfare. He's so damned moral that he ought to be stand-ing rear up under a Bo Tree. And he won't keep his mouth shut. I grant,' said Lady Buccleuch with a certain grim amusement, 'that the pure springs of chivalry may be a little muddy in the Hawick area, but that's no proper excuse for calling his father an unprincipled old rogue, and every other peer in Scotland a traitorous scoundrel.'

Sybilla pulled herself together. 'Wat knows how to argue, heaven knows. Why not explain?'

'Because Buccleuch isn't a plaster saint and Will would drive the Archangel Gabriel to lunacy and drink,' said Lady Buccleuch with candour. 'Wait till you hear him on the subject of perjury, patriotism and divided loyalties. The last time he trailed his coat Wat and he were shrieking at one another in five minutes like the Ghibellines and the Guelphs. Damn them both,' she said thoughtfully, 'for a couple of sumphs,' and paused, her gaze suddenly sharpening.

Sybilla, her smile unimpaired, caught her daughter-in-law's eye smartly as Lady Buccleuch spoke again. 'You've heard Lymond's back.'

For an instant the clever blue eyes focused. Then Lymond's mother, turning, said, 'Oh, Mariotta, my dear. The gypsies. I expect they've finished supper below, and it might be safer to send them away before Richard and the horses come back. Although they looked very honest. Could you . . . ?'

Between Mariotta and the Dowager Lady Culter there was perfect rapport. Mariotta laughed and instantly took herself off to see the gypsies dismissed.

'So fortunate that they came,' said Sybilla, ' – with the extra musicians being held up; although acrobatics are not my favourite entertainment. And what do you intend to do about Will?'

'We weren't discussing Will,' said Lady Buccleuch with brief exactitude. 'As you perfectly well know, I was talking about Lymond.'

'Yes,' said the Dowager. 'Yes, I remember; and yes, I know he's been seen about. So they say.'

With difficulty, Janet transfixed the wandering blue eyes. 'Sybilla. What about this marriage of Richard's and Lymond?'

'It makes no difference. None at all. Lymond never could be Lord Culter as things are. Even his own estate of Lymond was forfeited when he was outlawed. There isn't another heir. If Richard and Mariotta both died, the whole fortune would go to the Crown.'

'He couldn't succeed Richard now, certainly,' said Janet. 'But if the English took over? Criminals at the horn with the right kind of politics have died in silk sheets before now.'

'So they say. Perhaps it's lucky then,' said Sybilla, 'that this criminal has cheated his way out of favour with every party in Europe. Did you try some brazil on your curtains?'

And this time, Lady Buccleuch took the hint.

Mariotta was returning from her errand by the wheel stair when she heard the horses in the courtyard and guessed that Richard and his train were coming in. The requirements of dignity fought with a wifely desire to scamper below. She was hesitating still when footsteps turned the stair corner below and an alien and unknown yellow head rose from the serpentine depths, a nautilus from the shell.

Young and exhibitionist by temperament, Lady Culter gathered her skirts, darkly glowing, and just missed a simper. 'Can I help you, sir?'

Norman fairness recognizing Celtic darkness howled like a cluricane. 'I've got the servants' stair again. This place was built by mouldiewarps for mouldiewarps, and to the devil with lords and gentlemen. Jennie, m'joy, where is thy master? The traces d'amour? The path to a Culter? Any Culter: old Lady Culter, young Lady Culter, or his middle-aged lordship . . . ?'

If she thought the mistake genuine, it was only for a moment. Then: 'A rather primitive sense of humour, surely?' she said pleasantly. 'My husband has not yet arrived, but his mother the Dowager is upstairs. I shall take you to her, if you like.'

A crow of delighted laughter answered her. 'A Culter, and bad-tempered, and black. Come dance with me in Ireland.'

'I,' said Mariotta firmly, 'am Lady Culter. I take you to be a friend of my husband's.'

He came to rest two steps below her. 'Take what you like. Yellow doesn't suit you, and neither does angling for compliments.'

'I – really!' said Mariotta, roused. 'There is no excuse for rank bad manners.'

'Richard doesn't like me either,' said the fair one sorrowfully. 'But that's unmannerly rank for you. Do you like Richard?'

'I'm married to him!'

'That's why I asked. You don't believe in polyandry by any chance?' He rested a shoulder and elbow against the newel post, staring at her cheerfully. 'It's difficult, isn't it? I might be a distant cousin with a quaint sense of humour, in which case you'll look silly if you scream. I might be a well-known cretin to be kept from your guests at all costs. Or I might be – oh no, my angel!'

Quick fingers, closing on her wrist, wrenched her up from a head-long plunge to the lower floor, to the servants and her husband.

12

'– Or I might be annoyed. Don't be a fool, my dear,' he said. 'These were my men you heard entering below. You are not being badgered; you are being invaded.'

Held close to him as she was, she found his eyes unavoidable. They were blue, of the deep and identical cornflower of the Dowager's. And at that, the impact of knowledge stiffened her face and seized her pulses. 'I know who you are! You are Lymond!'

Applauding, he released her. 'I take back the more personal insults if you will take back your arm without putting it to impious uses. There. Now, sister-in-law mine, let us mount like Jacob to the matriarchal cherubim above. Personally,' he said critically, 'I should dress you in red.'

So this was Richard's brother. Every line of him spoke, palimpsestwise, with two voices. The clothes, black and rich, were vaguely slovenly; the skin sun-glazed and cracked; the fine eyes slackly lidded; the mouth insolent and self-indulgent. He returned the scrutiny without rancour.

'What had you expected? A viper, or a devil, or a ravening idiot; Milo with the ox on his shoulders, Angra-Mainyo prepared to do battle with Zoroaster, or the Golden Ass? Or didn't you know the family colouring? Richard hasn't got it. Poor Richard is merely Brown and fit to break bread with . . .'

'The poem I know at least,' exclaimed Mariotta, chafing her wrist. 'Red wise; Brown trusty; Pale envious –'

'And Black lusty. What a quantity of traps you've dropped into today. . . . If you wish, you may run ahead screaming. It makes no difference now, although five minutes ago we were in something of a hurry . . . the servants to be tied up . . . the silver to collect . . . Richard's personal hoard to recover from its usual cache. A man of iron habit, Richard.'

He had wandered absently past her and ahead up the stair when Mariotta, fully alert and aghast, started after him. 'What do you want?'

He considered. 'Amusement, principally. Don't you think it's time my family shared in my misfortunes, as

13

Christians should? Then, vice is so costly: May dew or none, my brown and tender diamonds don't engender, they dissolve. Immoderation, Mariotta, is a thief of money and intestinal joy, but who'd check it? Not I. Here I am, weeping soft tears of myrrh, to prove it.'

They had reached the door to the Hall. One hand on the standpost, he turned, and the kitten's eyes were bright blue. 'Watch carefully. In forty formidable bosoms we are about to create a climacteric of emotion. In one short speech – or maybe two – I propse to steer your women through excitement, superiority, contempt and anger: we shall have a little drama; just, awful and poetic, spread with uncials and full, as the poet said, of fruit and seriosity. Will they thank me, I wonder?'

Mariotta, collecting her wits, produced the only deterrent she could think of. 'Your mother is in there.'

He received this with tranquil pleasure. 'Then one person at least should recognize me,' Crawford of Lymond said, and pushed the door gently open for her to walk through.

* * *

Meanwhile Sir Wat Scott of Buccleuch was riding westward from Edinburgh, free at last of the Governor's councils, and leaving behind him his good friend Tom Erskine, a distraught smuggler, and a depressed pig.

Buccleuch was accustomed to war. Since the golden age before Flodden of a dynamic kingship and culture, it seemed that he had been governed by children, or by their elders and so-called protectors locked in civil struggle for power. And always the nobles who fell out of power were able to look for help to England's Henry VIII, who as a matter of personal pride and pressing European politics meant to conquer Scotland for himself, and to take the child Queen Mary to England, there to rear her in English ways and marry her in due course to his son.

Henry had sent force after force over the Border into Scotland to harry them into submission. He had taken hostages; offered inducements; granted pensions; offered

14

high positions to the discontented, impoverished great and, in the very month of Mary's birth and her father King James's death, had snatched as captives to London half the Lowland Scottish peerage at the disastrous battle of Solway Moss, and had there extorted from them as the price of their freedom a written promise to help him achieve the marriage between his son Edward and Mary.

Now Henry was dead, and a child sat on the English throne too: Edward VI, for whom ruled his uncle, Edward Somerset, Protector of England and avid adherent to Henry's policy for the marriage, who also burned and pillaged and put to the sword, and seduced the Scottish nobility for other weapons; for King Henry in marital and concupiscent frenzy had severed his country's church from the Pope; and there were many in Scotland, who looked away from the French Queen Mother and their old ally, Catholic France, and toward the Reformed Religion instead.

None of that, however, concerned Buccleuch who was little troubled, if ever, with matters of right and wrong. He thought occasionally about religion when it appeared to be taking too close a grip on politics and therefore on the future of the Scott family, but this latest upheaval was nothing to him. The Bishop of Rome was no paragon, but old Harry of England had damned nearly overrun Buccleuch's home of Branxholm, and that put him anyway in the bottommost pit with the heretics. When your nation has no standing army, there is nothing for it but to defend it yourself, with your tenants at your back, and hired swords and foreign mercenaries to eke out, depending on what the privvy purse can afford. Buccleuch liked fighting. Having received his orders, he turned westward ready to explode into military activity, and digressed on his way home to call at Boghall, a castle placed on its malodorous peats in the centre of Scotland and owned by the Flemings, a family uniquely loyal to the Queen, whose head Lord Fleming had himself married a lively and illegitimate daughter of the royal house.

Lady Fleming, who was governess as well as aunt to the

15

baby Queen, was away, but the honours of Boghall were done by her goddaughter Christian Stewart.

She was a favourite of Buccleuch's. Comely and tall, with hair of fine dark red and a decisive air to her, she was pleasant and positive to talk to, and it was impossible to tell that she was blind from birth. Familiar with every inch of Boghall, she stood chatting to Sir Wat after his necesary talk with Fleming, and it was she who told him Lord Culter was upstairs.

'Culter?' said Fleming, overhearing. 'I thought he had left?'

'Not yet,' said Christian unemotionally, and followed slowly as Buccleuch, losing no time, took the stairs for all his fifty-odd years like a sheared ram.

Richard, third Baron Culter and Sybilla's older son, was not only upstairs; he was on the roof. On the main parapet the sun slapped at the face off turrets and battlements, and far below, the castle rose from the bog like a lighthouse on its circling strands of barmkin, park and moat. The great dusty apron of the courtyard, the outbuildings and stables, the bakehouse, the brewery, the barns, byres and domestic offices seethed with foreshortened life. Buccleuch walked forward and the girl followed, sure-footed, the red hair lifted about her shoulders with the wind.

Lord Culter watched them come. There was about him none of the mad abandon of the bridegroom. A sober, thickset figure with brown hair and reliable grey eyes, Richard Crawford in his thirties was a man of wealth and tried power. He waited, his face stony, and before Buccleuch opened his mouth, he spoke. 'If it's about Lymond, don't trouble, Buccleuch.'

'It's about Lymond,' said Sir Wat grimly, and let fly.

As Mungo Tennant had listened, so Christian Stewart heard the argument in silence, but with a concern and understanding which Mungo Tennant applied to nothing.

Buccleuch ended roaring. 'Man, you might as well be in league with Lymond as let others think you are, and the army that fights on suspicion is a whacked army. Look

16

at what's happening! Five years ago your brother Lymond was found to have been selling his own country for years: he's been kicked from land to land committing every crime on the calendar and now he's back here, God forgive him, with filthier habits and a nastier mind than he set out with.

'All right. Meanwhile, what's left of a national entity struggles on. Half a million folk. And three million English are trying their damnedest for the overlordship of Scotland with the hairy natives like you and me kicked out, and the land parcelled out to the Dacres and the Howards and the Seymours and the Musgraves. And in between the raids every landowner between Berwick and Fife is courting England like a pregnant scullery-maid. God knows, I don't blame them. I've taken English money myself to protect my house and my tenants. You promise food and horses and nonresistance and when they invade, you do or don't lick their boots according to the thickness of your walls and the kind of conscience you have.'

He got up suddenly from his seat on the parapet, and began to pace. 'Then we've got the Douglases, the beauties, and others like them. They're the folk who're accepted as go-betweens with the English in London; who've got a kistful of gold, a family tree back to an acorn, and too many men-at-arms to need to tolerate a rough word.

'They get respect from both sides, and money comes pouring to the purse because each faction thinks it's bought the man's ultimate loyalty. But Sir George Douglas's loyalty is to his own house and the devil, and if the devil doesn't see the Douglases up there at the top of the dynastic dungheap, then to the Pope with the devil. Are ye with me?' asked Buccleuch.

'Yes, I'm with you,' said Lord Culter. 'Go on.'

'Right. We've all those, and we've the rest, like yourself, who carry the throne on their backs from generation to generation – maybe just because you've so much at stake in Scotland that there's no other game worth the risk; still you do it . . . We think the Protector's going to invade. We hope to put an army in the field to stop him at Edinburgh. It won't be a very good army because it'll have

17

one eye on the Lothian lairds and one eye on the Douglases. And by God, Richard Crawford,' ended Buccleuch with a growl that lifted the pigeons off the turrets, 'if they've got to watch you too, there'll be a wheen of skelly-eyed Scotsmen at the Golden Gates in the next few weeks.'

There was silence, and wily choleric eye stared into bright grey. Then Christian said sharply, 'Richard! I smell smoke!'

He had gone in a moment, running across the slats and up, higher, to the battlements. Buccleuch, caught mopping his face, gaped at the girl and at Richard's vanishing figure. Christian spoke fast. 'He came up here because he thought he saw smoke coming from Culter direction.' In a moment, Buccleuch was with Richard on the highest rampart.

The August sun mobilized against them the last furious heat of midafternoon, beating from the crowded roofs and turrets, the grained corbelling and cherry-caulked flanks. To the east lay the roofs of the barony town of Biggar, smoking in the socket of Bizzyberry Hill, and the Edinburgh road. On the south, the horizon was jumbled with hills; footstools before the greater furniture of the English Border. To the north and northwest the roads for Ayrshire and for Stirling girdled the crag of Tinto.

To the west, springing from the base of the castle, the bog rolled, jellied green and shimmering between an avenue of hills, to dip three miles distantly into the bed of the Culter burn, where stood the village and the castle of Midculter.

For a moment, nothing was to be seen, and Buccleuch became jocular. 'Smoke! Never worry, man. My chimneys were in mourning for a month before my first wife and the cook got the hang of the ovens . . .'

The wind patted their faces, and turned. A great column, black as the onset of night, rose from the west and hung wavering on the horizon.

With an undreamed-of turn of speed Lord Culter reached the stairs with Buccleuch after him, yelling bills and bows for the castle to hear. Left alone, Christian

Stewart herself found the stairs and descended, with debate in the unseeing eyes.

*　*　*

When the door opened, the women in the Hall at Midculter were not surprised. They expected to be fed; and Lady Buccleuch, for whom pregnancy spelled food, had already taken strategic foothold by the windows, where the cold dishes were ready laid. Sybilla, standing by the hearth, was in the middle of a long, grave story provoking much mirth. As the door opened she said happily, 'Now we can eat. Janet will be so pleased.' The blue eyes smiled at her daughter-in-law, ceased to smile, and then simply rested, thought suspended, on the still-open door.

Lucent and delicate, Drama entered, mincing like a cat. Leaning on the door, Lymond shut it and without looking turned and took out the key with one hand. In the other a naked sword point, descending, was poised among the slit lavender stems. At his side, Mariotta stood perfectly still.

After the first moment, every trace of expression left the Dowager's face; her white hair shone like salt. Moved by her stillness, the sound of the key, the blaze of the sword, the first heads turned. A murmur grew and expired. Dumbness, flowing among them uncovered like a crocus in the snow the lost reprise of a hornpipe, pursuing its scratchy but dogged course in the musician's gallery. Then that also died.

Back to the door, the newcomer spoke indolently, slurring his words. 'Good evening, ladies. The gentlemen now entering behind you are all fully armed. I am Francis Crawford of Lymond and I want your lives or your jewels – the latter for preference; both if necessary.'

Through the rustle of shock came the first cries of horror: from those rose a storm of exclamatory fright and abuse, and from that an orchestration of outraged feminine frenzy that tortured the very harp strings in the gallery. Someone, losing her head, plucked at the small, stately figure. 'Sybilla! It's Lymond!' And fell back, frozen, before the Dowager's stony face.

The room was lined with armed men. Some, working efficiently, stripped each woman of money and jewellery; others searched and denuded the room, and with cocked weapons encouraged resistance with a leer. There was none.

On them all rested Lymond's peaceful blue gaze, quite at random. But long ago instinct told Mariotta he was fully aware of one thing. Bent urgently on exposing some frail nerve, she spoke. 'Why not look at her? Your drama wants dialogue.'

He turned on her the vague survey. 'Oak of linen and pole of jewels, I've decided on pantomime.'

'What a shame, now. I was all ready for buskins, and it's nothing but socks.'

'Mine doesn't always mean comedy, my dear; far from it.'

An approaching voice, of the self-same timbre, answered him. 'Farce, then,' said the Dowager composedly. 'My son is not very complicated, Mariotta, although the artifice glitters. He's afraid – '

'Afraid!' Blue eyes, dead of feeling, looked into blue. 'Afraid of what? Damned by the church and condemned by the law: what possible capacity for fear can heart and head still find? Oimè el cor, oimè la testa . . . After five years of villainy, I promise you, I have the refinement of a cow-cabbage.'

'– Afraid I might puncture the cocoon of Attic detachment. What we see is acting, isn't it, Francis?'

'Is it?' he said derisively. 'You won't get your diamonds back, I fear, when the curtain comes down. And the name, please, is Lymond: a new medal: choose the trussell or the pile. My present face is the provident, forbearing one.' The smiling eyes turned on her were empty. 'De los álamos vengo, madre. From the stews and alleyways of Europe with a taste for play acting – yes – and killing and treason and crimes, they say, nameless and enticingly erotic. Haven't I been worth five years' excellent gossip to you? Are you not all waiting agog to see me seize my sister-in-law by the hair? When I think of it, damn it, I'm a public benefactor.'

'Chattering ape!' Lady Buccleuch took a hand in the game, full of rage and pity for Sybilla and hatred for the black-bearded ruffian who had just seized her emeralds. 'What's poor Richard ever done to you except get himself born first?'

The blue eyes were speculative. 'Ill-calculated,' he agreed. 'But not necessarily final.'

Strophe and counterstrophe reached their epode. The Master was out of her reach, but not the grinning thief at her side. 'Final as far as I'm concerned, ye petty-souled slug, ye!' shrieked Dame Janet with ear-cracking clarity, and seized and hurled a cold pudding into Blackbeard's face. As the big man, cursing, scraped at blancmange with both hands, Janet filched his own dagger and made for him.

But not fast enough. Lymond, watching from the door, had no mind to lose one of his men. Good humour and indolence tittered into the shadows, and as Dame Janet began her lunge, Lymond drew back his own arm and threw.

In the silence of the room Janet screamed, once; and her right arm dropped on to her side, the knife slipping from big, relaxed fingers. Then slowly and disjointedly, Buccleuch's wife fell, and Lymond's dagger, thrown with accuracy across the width of the room, glittered in her gown, stained and sticky with blood.

'Afraid?' said the yellow-haired man and laughed. 'Forgive me, I should have warned you: I have a tendency to be bloody-minded. Bruslez, noyez, pendez, ompellez, descouppez, fricassez, crucifiez, bouillez, carbonnadez ces méchantes femmes. Matthew! When you have digested your windfall will you kindly report progress below? Now' – as Blackbeard, red with shame, disappeared through the screen door – 'come along, ladies. Leave your female Telemachus alone for a moment; she's not dead.'

He surveyed them pleasantly. 'Epilogue,' he said. 'We

have heard sweet-voiced Calliope busily shrinking me like a sea worm and calling me play actor. And the lady of Buccleuch taking heart therefrom to give us a roaring, a howling, a whistling, a mummying and a juggling, with sorry results. And Mariotta, trying to wring shame from the unshamable.'

He turned his head, and the girl's heart jumped. 'Qu'es casado, el Rey Ricardo. Weel, weel, sister, what shall we do with you, Mariotta?' He watched her thoughtfully, and then looked beyond her and smiled. 'Observe,' he said. 'Their eyes lit like corpse candles. I beg, under the circumstances, to be original. . . . Yes?'

Blackbeard had reappeared. 'All finished, sir; and the horses are ready.'

'All right. Get them out.' The men began to leave, and the reports came in: 'All doors barred, sir. Valuables loaded, sir.'

With careful and porcelain tread, Crawford of Lymond walked to the screen, and the women fell back before him. At the door he turned. 'We've had a deal of bad poetry, haven't we? Suggesting the climax to this thrilling and literary spectacle. The Olla Podrida, my sweethearts, will now be set on the fire. I regret Richard isn't with you. No matter. God hath a thousand handēs to chastise and I have two – how can Richard escape us both?'

He scanned them all, and they gave him back contempt for reflective stare. 'I don't suppose,' he said regretfully, 'we shall meet again. Goodbye.'

The door shut behind them all, and locked. The women stared at it, mesmerized, and observed across it the wavering shadow of an uncanny cloud. Behind the chamfered windows the sun was obscured by drifting wreaths of grey smoke, and the silence filled with the crackling of flames. The youngest surviving Crawford, in leaving, had deftly set fire to the castle.

* * *

The bonfires stacked against its walls were blazing merrily when the party from Boghall shot down the incline toward the castle. Behind Richard came every able-bodied man from Lord Fleming's garrison. They tore away the faggots and, using hatchets, broke through the main door and again through the door of the Hall.

Richard, gripping his wife, looked over her head at his mother. 'Who did it? What happened?'

But Mariotta answered. She shut her eyes; the darkness showed her a cool blue gaze, and she opened them again. 'It was your brother. He must be insane.'

'Not insane, dear.' Sybilla, speaking gently, contradicted. 'Not insane. But magnificently drunk, I fear.'

I listened to what they had to tell him; he dropped beside Janet as she lay nursing her shoulder wound and spoke to her, and came back with an unseeing face to his mother's side through the babble of relief and hysteria. Through white lips he said, 'I appear to have made a fool of myself. But not again, in that way, I promise you.'

Buccleuch's hand was on his arm. 'By God, when we come back . . .'

'Back?' said the Dowager.

Sir Wat's beard folded; a sign of concern. He said flatly, 'You've not heard the news?'

'*What* news?'

Without looking at Mariotta, Richard answered for him. 'We heard at Boghall. It's open war, and sooner than we thought. The English have collected an army and are on their way north. We are all summoned instantly to the Governor to fight . . .

'. . . So Lymond – dear God, Lymond must wait.'

* * *

Only eight months had gone since Henry VIII of England had been suspended in death, there to lie like Mohammed's coffin, hardly in the Church nor out of it, attended by his martyrs and the acidulous fivefold ghosts of his wives. King Francis of France, stranded by his neighbour's death in the midst of a policy so advanced, so brilliant and so intricate that it should at last batter England to the ground, and be damned to the best legs in Europe –

23

Francis, bereft of these sweet pleasures, dwindled and died likewise.

From Venice to Rome, Paris to Brussels, London to Edinburgh, the Ambassadors watched, long-eared and bright eyed.

Charles of Spain, Holy Roman Emperor, fending off Islam at Prague and Lutherism in Germany and forcing recoil from the long, sticky fingers at the Vatican, cast a considering glance at heretic England.

Henry, new King of France, tenderly conscious of the Emperor's power and hostility, felt his way thoughtfully toward a small cabal between himself, the Venetians and the Pope, and wondered how to induce Charles to give up Savoy, how to evict England from Boulogne, and how best to serve his close friend and dear relative Scotland without throwing England into the arms or the lap of the Empire.

He observed Scotland, her baby Queen, her French and widowed Queen Mother, and her Governor Arran.

He observed England, ruled by the royal uncle Somerset for the boy King Edward, aged nine.

He watched with interest as the English dotingly pursued their most cherished policy: the marriage which should painlessly annex Scotland to England and end forever the long, dangerous romance between Scotland and France.

Pensively, France marshalled its fleet and set about cultivating the Netherlands, whose harbours might be kind to storm-driven galleys. The Emperor, fretted by Scottish piracy and less busy than he had been, watched the northern skies narrowly. Europe, poised delicately over a brand-new board, waited for the opening gambit.

PART I

The Play for Jonathan Crouch

1
TAKING EN PASSANT

The gardes and kepars of cytees ben signefied
By the vii Pawn. . . . They ought . . . to enquyre of
all thynges and ought to rapporte to the gouernours
of the cyte such thynge as apperteyneth . . .
and yf hit be in tyme of warre, they ought not to
open the yates by nyght to no man.

1 · THE ENGLISH OPENING

On Saturday, September 10th, the English Protector
Somerset and his army met the combined Scottish forces
on the field of Pinkie, outside Edinburgh, and smashed
them to pieces in a defeat as dire as any the Scots had
suffered since Flodden. They did not, however, capture
the baby Queen or take the fortress of Edinburgh, but
remained outside its gates burning and wrecking while, as
Buccleuch had predicted, a second English army invaded
Scotland on the south-west, and ensconced itself in the
near-Border town of Annan on its triumphant way north.

On the same day, quite near Annan, a man rode a
broad-faced pony into a farmyard and stopped, a pike at
his chest. Sitting still, he hissed through his teeth, brown
eyes judicial over inquisitive nose. 'Colin, Colin! You're
not doing yourself justice! It's as smart, ye ken, to let
Lymond's friends in as his unfriends out.' And as the
pikeman answered him with a bleat – 'Johnnie Bullo! I
didna ken ye, man!' – the rider clicked his teeth and the
pony moved on.

It carried him gently through a rubble arch and up a
long alley to a yard crowded with men. Saddlebags, rugs,

weapons, tenting and food sacks lay piled against the house wall; and the reek of a boiling pot over an open fire fought weakly with the odours of sweat, leather and horse dung. Johnnie Bullo entered the yard through a gate, and dismounting, addressed the air.

'Turkey in?'

A man passing with a bonnetful of eggs jerked his head across the open yard and grinned, showing two sets of bereaved gums. 'Over yonder, Johnnie.'

Turkey Mat, professional soldier and veteran of Mohacs, Rhodes and Belgrade, sat against an upturned barrel, hauling off his boots and bellowing orders. Forty and liverish, he had done nothing for his looks by growing a curled black beard in the Assyrian style. The men in the yard admired Turkey.

Johnnie Bullo approached gently. 'Man, you've a fire there you could lead the Children of Israel with.'

Turkey Mat was emptying river sand from one boot. 'Hey, Johnnie! No harm in a lowe with the farm bodies at home.' And as Bullo wordlessly turned to survey the planks nailed over doors and windows: 'That's the farmer, not us. He's got six lassies and says he pays us for protection, no' for stud fees. . . . We're moving on tomorrow anyway; and I hope to God it's to the Tower: my stomach's declared war on my elbow. Have your brought the dose?'

The gypsy brooded. 'What d'you suppose? I've had it a fortnight. It's begun to grow whiskers like your own. What you want is a cross between an apothecary and a bloodhound.'

Flinging down the other boot, Turkey swore. 'There's been a war! Do they no' tell you anything in these parts?'

Johnnie grinned, dropping to the ground beside him. 'I thought you went east?'

'So we did. I never saw so many weel-kent faces all in the one place; the most of them chowed off and in no state to give the sort of snash you get from half of them when they're upright. It was better,' said Matthew, 'than a front seat at the Widdy-Hill the day after the Assizes.'

'And profitable?'

'Oh, aye.' A smile winked in Turkey Mat's beard. 'There was Arran, biting his nails to the elbows at Mussel-burgh, wanting men and food and powder and intelligence (and wanting the last more than most); and Protector Somerset coming north hung over with booty and wee gifts from the Lothian lairds, with a trail of tumbledown castles behind him . . . man, the moneybags were fleeing here and yon like cockroaches on a biscuit. Mind, that was last week,' he added with belated caution, watching Bullo bounce a small leather bag in one hand.

'Twelve crowns,' said Johnnie agreeably.

'*Twelve crowns*! Twelve crowns for a teazle o' Tay sand and chopped henbane and a week's rakings from the doo-cote! It's robbery!'

Nevertheless the transaction was completed, the gypsy derisive. 'What's money to Lymond's men? I hear Governor Arran's thinking of calling him in to finance the next expedition.' He waited a moment, then added lightly, 'And I hear you got yourselves a new prize up-by into the bargain?'

Turkey registered surprise. 'Not us. We fell in with an English messenger with a dispatch from the Protector to his commander at Annan; but Lymond wouldn't touch him.'

Bullo raised an eyebrow. 'So the Master's money is on England, is it? Now *that*, Matthew, is interesting.'

The other shrugged and bawled an order across the yard. 'God knows; but he sent Jess's Joe after to make sure the message reached Annan safely. Did you want him? He'll be back directly. He turned off with Dandy-puff for a minute just before we came in.'

Bullo showed his teeth. 'And in drink, maybe? It would be nice to have him civil, for once.'

There was no chance to comment. As he spoke, three riders passed through the gate and drew rein: two were the Master of Culter and the man Dandy-puff, while the third was a stranger, a young man, tied to his horse and wild about it. Johnnie Bullo's smile widened. 'Hell's hell again: the de'il's back.'

Francis Crawford of Lymond, Master of Culter, was neat as a pin and stone sober. He dismounted, emitting a feu de joie of explicit orders: the prisoner was unhorsed and unbound, the animals led away, and the muddle in the yard cut up to shape instantly. 'God!' said Matthew in simple admiration. 'He's got a tongue on him like a thorn tree.' And they watched him approach, the stranger trailing sulkily behind.

As at the sack of his mother's home, Lymond was lavishly dressed. The knowledgeable gypsy eyes scanned the dairy-maid skin, the gilded hair, the long hands, jewelled to display their beauty while the Master, serenely smiling, returned the compliment under relaxed lids.

'Johnnie, my night-black familiar. Civility's nearly as dull as sobriety and I cannot – will not – be labelled dull. I have peper and piones, and a pound of garlik; a ferthing-worth of fenel-seed for fasting days, but dullness have I none: nor am I overfond of being discussed, my Johnnie.'

'You've quick ears, Lymond.'

'But yours, like Midas whispering in the hole, are closer to the ground. . . . What do you think of our new recruit?'

If the gypsy found the question surprising, or the reference offensive which it undoubtedly was, he showed nothing of it, but simply turned and bent an admiring glance on the tall young figure behind Lymond.

'My, my. He's a bonny blossom to be let away from his nurse.'

The stranger flushed. He was a graceful creature, with fair skin and a thatch of carroty curls. His clothes, of a thoroughly expensive and unostentatious kind, were a credit to tailor and souter: his scabbard and accoutrements were inlaid and ornamented with a little more *brio* than the rule.

'– And his fancy hat!' breathed Matthew in awe.

The newcomer addressed Lymond with dignity. 'I must confess to disappointment. Do you mete out this kind of treatment to every gentleman who offers you his sword?'

'Big words, too!'

Turkey Mat was silenced by the Master's hand.

Lymond, his back to the stone dike at one end of the yard, crossed his legs gently before him and instantly the yard, led by curiosity and its hope of a rough-house, deployed itself. Turkey and Bullo, grinning, ranged themselves on either side of the Master. The young man, stranded perforce in an open circle, stood his ground.

'Oh, Marigold!' Lymond spoke plaintively. 'A silken tongue, a heart of cruelty. Don't berate us. We're only poor scoundrels – vagabonds – scraps of society; unlettered and untaught. Besides, we didn't believe you.'

'Well, you can believe me now,' said the young man belligerently. 'I didn't ride all the way from – all this way to find you just to pass a dull Tuesday. I'm taken to be a fair fighting man. I'm prepared to join you; and I'd guess you need all the swords you can get. Unless you're over-nervous, of course.'

'Terror,' said Lymond, 'is our daily bread in the Wuthenheer. We eat it, we live by it and we disseminate it; and not only between Christmas and Epiphany: there is no close season for fright. So you want to join us. Shall I take you? Mat, my friend, awful and stern, strong and corpulent – what do you say?'

Turkey was in no doubt. 'I'd want to know a good bit more about the laddie, sir, before I had him next me with a knife.'

'Oh,' said Lymond, 'would you? And what about you, Johnnie?'

Johnnie Bullo regarded his fingers. 'If I were yourself, I would perhaps give him his head. He looks a meek enough child.'

'So did Heliogabalus at an early age,' said Lymond. 'And Attila and Torqueinada and Nero and the man who invented the boot. The only thing they had in common was a cherubic adolescence. And red hair, of course, makes it worse.'

He considered, while the boy watched him steadily; then said, 'Infant, I can't resist it. I'm going to put you to the proof; and if you impress us with your worth, then quicquid libet, licet; as was remarked on another,

31

unsavoury occasion. Are you willing to be wooed, sweet Marigold?'

Redhead was not charmed. 'I'm willing to give you reasonable proof of my talents, of course.'

'Proof of your talents! . . . Oh, little Peg-a-Ramsey, we are going to do well together. Come along then. Gif thou should sing well ever in thy life, here is in fay the time, and eke the space. Your name?'

'You can call me Will.'

'– Sir,' said Lymond affectionately. 'Surname and parentage?'

'My own affair.' A rustle among the onlookers gave credit to this piece of bravura; Lymond was undisturbed. 'Never fear. We're all runts and bastards of one sort or another. Do you swim? Hunt? Wrestle? I see. Can you use a crossbow? Your longest shot? Can you count? Read and write? Ah, the sting of sarcasm – Have we a scholar here? Then produce us a specimen,' said Lymond. 'What about some modest quatrains? Frae vulgar prose to flowand Latin. Deafen us, enchant us, educate us, boy.'

There was a pause. The examinee, dazed by mental gymnastics at top speed, at first boggled. Then he had a pleasing idea. Lowering his lashes over a malicious sparkle he recited obligingly.

> *'Volavit volucer sine plumis*
> *Sedit in arbore sine foliis*
> *Venit homo absque manibus . . .'*

Flat incomprehension informed every face. He halted.

There was an uneasy and deferential pause. Then Lymond gave a short laugh and capped him in German:

> '. . . *un freet den Vogel fedderlos*
> *Van den Boem blattlos . . .'*

'You appear,' said the Master, 'to have left your studies at a very tender age? Don't trouble to explain: tell me this instead. What about Pharaoh's chickens appealed to you? Why did you decide to join me?'

'Why . . . ?' repeated Redhead, needing time to think.

'Word of three letters,' said Lymond. 'Come along, for God's sake: no need to let me have it all my own way. What was it? Rape, incest, theft, treason, arson, wetting the bed at night . . .'

'. . . Or burning my mother alive,' said the other sarcastically.

'Oh, be original at least.' The Master was undisturbed. 'Why are you here?'

Silence. Then the boy said slowly, 'Because I admire you.'

An appreciative titter ran round the audience. 'You shock me,' said Lymond. 'Explain, please.'

'All right,' said the boy. 'You've chosen a life of vice, and have been consistent and reliable and thorough and successful in carrying it out.'

Lymond considered this with every appearance of seriousness. 'I see. Thus the baseness of my morals is redeemed by the stature of my manners? You admire consistency?'

'Yes, I do.'

'But prefer consistency in evil to consistency in good?'

'The choice is hypothetical.'

'Lord; is it? What an exciting past you must have.'

'I despise mediocrity,' stated the young man firmly.

'And you would also despise me if I practised evil but professed purity?'

'Yes. I should.'

'I see. What you are really saying, of course, is that you dislike hypocrisy, and people who can't stand by their principles. I find it so helpful,' continued Lymond, 'when some of my gentlemen have well-defined codes of conduct. It makes them more predictable. What security have I got for your loyalty?'

Redhead chanced his arm, solemnly. 'Your appraisal of me, sir.'

'Touching; but I'd prefer your appraisal of yourself. Do your principles admit an oath of fealty?'

'If you want it. I won't betray you, any of you; you can have my word on that. And I'll do anything you want,

33

within reason. I don't mind,' said Redhead recklessly, 'what crimes I commit, as long as they've got a sensible purpose. Wanton injury and destruction, of course, are just juvenile.'

'Of course,' said the Master, digesting this remarkable statement. 'Then let us be adult at all costs. Do you have a mistress? A wife? No? All, all in vain, this flors de biauté? A little quietness, if you please. We are all ready to help, you see. What else . . . Do you use broadsword or rapier? A hackbut?'

Smoothly spinning, the inexorable questions resumed, faster and faster. 'What do you know about gunpowder? Not very much, is it? How old are you? Year of birth? If you must invent, stay awake afterwards. . . . What are you like with the longbow? There's Mat's quiver: hit that tree. Passable. Now the thorn. Good. Now,' said Lymond, 'kill the man by the cooking-pot.'

Exhausted, deflated and angry, the boy directed one haughty grimace at the Master, hauled on the bowstring and sent the shot of a lifetime buzzing for the mark.

A great cheer, part shocked, part sardonic, arose. There was a blur of movement. Mat disappeared, and a swarm of curious bodies shut off the view of the target. Redhead knew, if he had never shot straight before, that he had put an arrow through blood and bone this time. He stood still.

A gentle voice rebuked him.

'Careful, careful! my slave of sin. These are Sordidi Dei. How nice,' said Lymond, 'to have simple emotions. No trouble with principles; no independence of thought; no resistance to suggestion; no nonsense about adult behaviour when it comes to one's own amour propre.'

The skin around the boy's mouth was taut. 'I'm not immune to trickery. And the Sordid Gods in this case are yours, I think; not mine.'

'Ah, no: not mine; I am godless,' said Lymond. 'Not for me to solve the enigma.

> 'When a hatter
> Will go smatter

In a philosophy
Or a pedlar
Wax a medlar
In theology . . .

'There is the waste of purpose. Whereas I always have a purpose – you were wiser than you knew, and less successful than you feared. Oyster Charlie has been giving me a little trouble. But if his wits are moribund, his hearing is sensational – a matter of compensation, I suppose. Well, Mat?'

Turkey Mat shook himself free of the crowd, grinning. 'Just a shower of blisters,' he said. 'He dodged behind the pot and got a spray of chicken bree for his pains. He's laying low now, is Oyster. He kens as well as you what that was for.'

'Excellent. The warning cock and the Devil's bath,' said Lymond, amused. 'Symbolism is coming cheap today.'

'You mean I didn't kill him?'

'No. Thus even your remorse of conscience is rooted in hallucination. Oyster is not dead; merely light boiled in the shell. I hope you will both perceive the point of the experiment.'

Lymond surveyed the grinning audience with an air of gentle discovery. 'Is there no work to be done? Or perhaps it's a holiday?'

In a moment, the spectators had vanished. Left facing the three men, the boy stood straight and with some natural dignity, although silent. Indeed, there seemed little to say. The Master evidently thought the same. He smiled warmly. 'A pleasant entertainment. Thank you. Have you thought of doing it for money? No? You should. It would go down very well on fair days at Hawick. . . . Take the young gentleman's boots off, Mat, and loose him on the hills somewhere. Preferably not within ten miles of me.'

The young gentleman turned scarlet. Of course. Having made the bear dance, turn it to the dogs. And to that, youth and hurt pride had only one answer. 'You're welcome to try,' said Redhead, and lunged.

35

Lymond got hold of the upraised arm halfway to his face. He shifted his grip, twisted, and holding the limb on the edge of agony, smiled.

'Softly, softly! Remember your superior upbringing, and your Caxton. How gentlemen shall be known from Churls. Don't be a Churl, Marigold. Full of sloth in his wars, full of boast in his manhood, full of cowardice to his enemy, full of lechery to his body, full of drinking and drunkenness. Revoking his own challenge; slaying his prisoner with his own hands; riding from his sovereign's banner in the field; telling his sovereign false tales . . .'

'You have it pat.' The boy, suddenly released, rubbed his arm.

'Naturally. My rule of thumb. We all have our religion. With Johnnie, it's Paracelsus. Mat here follows Lydgate; and your father and Ascham fit very well together. If he thunder, they quake; if he chide they fear; if he complain –'

Shocked into interrupting, Mat spoke, a broad finger directed at the redheaded boy. 'His father? He was nameless.'

'Allow me to introduce you.' Lymond, speaking mildly, was watching Bullo. 'Will Scott of Kincurd, Buccleuch's oldest son.'

The gypsy smiled back boldly. 'A prize indeed.'

Understanding and contempt filled the boy's face. 'Of course. Your diffidence is explained. But I assure you, you needn't be afraid of Buccleuch. He'll neither hound you for taking me nor pay you for ransoming me. In fact, he knows I've left to join some such as you.'

'Some such,' repeated Lymond idly. 'And didn't try to stop you?'

The young man laughed. 'He didn't much fancy seeing his son and heir exposed in the gutter. He tried. But there are two other boys in the family. He'll get used to it.'

Lymond shook his head sadly. 'There goes your day's work, Johnnie.'

Johnnie Bullo slid noiselessly to his feet, an ecstasy of white teeth. He stretched lazily, sketched an elaborate bow to Lymond, nodded to Mat, and made for his pony. On the way, he stopped and prodded the boy with a long, dirty finger. 'Home for you, laddie: home!' said he. 'You need a longer spoon than the cutlers make to sup with this one.'

'Well?' said Lymond. And Will Scott, to his secret astonishment, read an invitation in the tone.

'I haven't a spoon,' he said. 'But I had a knife I could trust.'

'This?' The Master slipped from his belt the dirk he had removed when Will, the solemn tracker, had been ambushed by his quarry. He tossed it thoughtfully once, twice, and then pitched it to its owner. Will caught it, his expression an odd compound of surprise and mistust.

With acute misgiving, Turkey Mat watched him. 'You're not taking him on, sir?'

'On the contrary,' said the Master, his eyes on Scott. 'It's the other way round.'

Matthew persevered. 'He'll wait till we're settled, oath or no oath, and then bring Buccleuch and the rest down on top of us.'

'Will he?' said Lymond. 'Will you, Marigold?'

Brilliant, youthful face confronted restless one.

A little, malicious smile crossed the Master's face.

'Oh, no, he won't,' said Lymond confidently. 'He's going to be a naughty, naughty rogue like you and me.

* * *

Much later, Lymond appeared again, still in riding dress, with a steel helmet fitted closely over his hair. A heavy white cloak marked with some kind of embroidery in red hung over one arm.

'Mat, I'm off to Annan. I leave you in charge. If that English messenger gets into trouble, Jess's Joe will report to you. Take all the men you need to free him and get him to Annan. I shall be back before dawn. Then we move to the Peel Tower.'

Turkey's hand automatically massaged his stomach.

37

'Fair enough.' He added bluntly, 'You'll not expect us to get you out of Annan if you fall into trouble?'

'My dear Mat, I can't possibly fall into trouble,' said Lymond. 'I shall be under the best protection. I'm taking Will Scott with me.'

2 · PINS AND COUNTERPINS

That evening at sunset the whaup and peewit lay quiet in Annandale and the black shadows of the Torthorwald and Mousewald hills marched east over moors prickling with movement and furtive noise.

Darkness fell, and two horsemen slipped silently around the hills and made directly for the gates of Annan, capital town of the district and newly possessed and occupied by the English army of Lord Wharton. On the last rise the riders paused to look down at the red eye in the plain, the bloody glitter of the river and the drifting thickets of white smoke. The wooden houses of Annan were on fire.

A peal of laughter shivered the silence.

> *'O wow! quo' he, were I as free*
> *As first when I saw this countrie . . .'*

The sound died away in the cold air, and there was silence again.

Will Scott, in no mood for verse, shot a look at the silver-tongued, malignant animal beside him and blurted a question. 'Why did you let me join you?'

Lymond's eyes were fixed on the burning town; his voice was entirely prosaic. 'I need someone who can read and write.'

'Oh.'

'Further. I'm anxious to meet and talk with an Englishman of the name of Crouch. Jonathan Crouch. He may be in Annan. If he isn't you shall help me find him and then, Aenobarbus, you shall have a diamond, a maiden and a couch reserved in the Turkish paradise. Meanwhile – '

'Are they expecting you,' asked Scott, 'at Annan?'

The half-seen mouth curled. 'If they are, I advise you to fly like a woodpecker, crying pleu, pleu, pleu. Lord Wharton has threatened to gut me publicly and the Earl of Lennox has a personal price of a thousand crowns on my head. No. I propose to appear in one of my twenty-two incarnations, as a messenger from the Protector, with yourself as my aid. My name is Sheriff: yours shall be – what?'

Scott had also read his poets. He quoted dryly. 'This officer but doubt is callit Deid.'

'Apt, if pessimistic. You have nothing to do,' said Lymond, 'but look beautiful, honest and English and pray that one Charlie Bannister has arrived before us to smooth our way. Our John the Baptist. A poor soul, but even if he has barely one head, much less eighteen, he will do to vouch for us. We shall converse briefly with the gullible ones at the gate, encounter Crouch – I trust – and return. An innocent and worthy programme. Si mundus vult decipi, decipiatur. Come along then, Marigold. It's warmer down there!'

And the two figures swept downhill, neck and neck, the red crosses on their cloaks bellying in their passing.

* * *

'Halt and . . .' began the Cumberland voice, and trailed off for the second time; whereat Scott found in himself an unexpected impulse to hysteria.

Above the two horses rose the gates of Annan; around them pressed an escort of the outlying guard; before them stood the gatehouse where the guard on duty was trying to extract their names and business under harassing conditions.

'Look,' Lymond was saying bitterly, 'at the dirt on your pauldrons. And your doublet.'

'. . . declare . . .'

'Your sword's filthy. And your dagger: how d'you expect a rusty blade to bite?'

'. . . declare – I can't help that!' said the guard excitedly, abandoning formalities. 'Robin! Davie! Move a step and I'll spit you!'

'Well, if you do,' said Lymond resignedly, 'for God's sake use someone else's sword.'

But when the captain came, a swarthy, middle-aged Bewcastle man, Lymond dismounted at once and introduced himself. 'You won't remember me; Sheriff's my name. One of the Bishop's men from Durham. Sorry to make a mystery of myself, but I'm supposed to tell you to your face: it's business of the red tod's cub.'

The password worked its miracle. As Lymond spoke, the captain's face changed; the guards were dismissed, and in privacy he turned to the two newcomers. 'You've a message for their lordships from the Protector?'

'On the heels of one only,' said Lymond. 'You've spoken with Charlie Bannister?'

'The Protector's man? No.'

'Damnation!' Scott shortsightedly found some amusement in Lymond's anger. After a moment he went on. 'The fool must still be on the road here – I hope nothing's come to him. I started from Leith yesterday with a message-round like the Odyssey. He was due to leave just after and come straight here. . . . It doesn't matter. I'm behind time,' said Lymond busily, 'and I've got a message for one of your men: Jonathan Crouch. That's all.'

Drinks had been brought; the captain's eyebrows rose above the rim of his cup. 'Crouch of Keswick? Then you can forget it. He was lifted in a skirmish two days ago.'

The wine went down Lymond's throat like a drain. 'One message less, thank God. Who got him?'

'Whose prisoner is he? I dunno. They're welcome,' said the captain with relish. 'Drive you funny in the head, Crouch would. Tongue like the clatterbone of a goose's arse. Are you going?'

Lymond was certainly going, and so, he hoped, was Will Scott. The captain was quite ready to speed them off . . . provided they spent ten minutes first with the joint commanders.

'A few minutes either way won't hurt you; and Wharton'll have my skin if this man Bannister doesn't arrive and I let you go too.'

Cheerfully, Lymond continued to make for the gates. 'What Wharton will do to you will be nothing to the Protector's delight if I spend half the night here. I've told you already. I left long before Bannister. We won the battle on Saturday: that's all I know.'

The captain, unmoving, blocked his way. 'Come along, man. Don't let me down. If you've nothing to say you'll be out in a trice.' There was a half-formed suspicion in his mind, and to object again was clearly unsafe. Without further demur, Lymond remounted and, with Scott, followed his guide through the main streets of Annan.

It was difficult riding. The young horses trembled in the passing glare from burnt thatch and timber. Acrid smoke rolled and hung about the narrow road and caught their throats; the streets, deserted of people, were littered with charred wood and rags and smashed pottery. Scott wondered, with an interest nearly academic, how Lymond was going to extract them from this.

Farther on, when the fires were more infrequent and stone-built houses loomed ahead, a man accosted them. The captain was wanted at the gate.

Captain Drummond was a careful man. He was about to ignore the summons when Lymond spoke, solving his problem. 'I don't suppose Lord Wharton's son Harry is anywhere about? I once knew his sister, and I'd like to meet him. He could perhaps direct us to his lordship as well.'

It was a happy suggestion. The captain, clearly relieved, spoke to the man who had waylaid them, and in a few minutes they were joined by Henry, younger son of Lord Wharton, commander of the English army on the west. Drummond explained and left with his man, and young Wharton turned to Lymond and Scott. 'Of course, I'll take you both there. It's the middle house in the square through there.' Restless, energetic, at twenty-five already a leader of horse, Henry Wharton led the way, beginning a long, newsy conversation about his family, which Lymond appeared to be sustaining surprisingly well. But Scott, some of the detachment worn off, thought: By God, he'll never make it . . .

The pend leading to the square was dim. On it lay the shifting black shadows of the tall buildings fringing the fires; the darkness was full of movement and the three horses, scared, huddled close.

As the shadows closed about them, Lymond launched himself on Wharton. There was the beginning of a cry, and then nothing but the cracking of hoofs as the other horse shied at the struggling shapes. It was then that Captain Drummond, released from his errand, cantered cheerfully up at the rear and made to join them. Then he said sharply, 'What's happening there?' and peered into the alley.

Scott saw the whistle in his hand just in time. Instinctively, the boy's hand went to his belt. He found his dagger, stood in his stirrups, and threw. The captain gave a brief cry, and fell to his horse's mane, and from there to the street.

It was suddenly very quiet. Wharton's horse stood nose to nose with Lymond's bay, snuffling gently, and there was an extra dark shadow on the road. The Master's voice said tartly, 'Dropped off to sleep?'

'Oh!' Scott dismounted in a hurry. Young Wharton was, he found, lying face down in the road, a cloth stuffed in his mouth and bent arms savagely clinched by Lymond.

'Where's Drummond?'

'I knifed him. He's lying in the road.'

'Then get him out of it, for God's sake. We don't want a public wake for him. Take two of the horses and tie them up here. Drag the captain to the wall. Is he dead?'

'I don't know,' said Scott self-consciously.

Lymond wasted no time on comment. 'Gag and bind him if he isn't, and put him on your own horse with a saddlecloth over his head.'

He was unhitching rope from his own saddle as he spoke, and expertly binding Wharton, leaving only his knees and ankles free. He then pulled the man to his feet and, wrapping the folds of his cloak about him, took the cloth from his mouth.

Wharton said, in a kind of parched croak, 'Set me free, or my men'll burn you alive!'

'If wishes were buttercakes,' said Lymond, and tossed something shining into the air, 'beggars might bite. I have a little knife which says you will take us quietly to your father.'

Scott, distrusting his ears, stared.

Wharton said dramatically, 'Never!' Lymond's elbow moved and the young man gave a convulsive jerk. 'First scene, second act,' said the Master. 'Stop play-acting, you fool, and take us in. Nobody I ever met could argue with a knife at his ribs.'

Probably, more than anything else, the supreme confidence in his voice convinced the young man. Holding his arm tight against the short incision Lymond had cut, he bit his lip, and began to move reluctantly onward. Scott, leading Lymond's horse and his own, walked after.

The events which followed were always to have for Will Scott of Kincurd the curious, narcotic quality of a bout of fever. In the course of it, he became dimly aware that they had arrived at a house; that Lymond had again produced the allusive password and, with sullen acquiescence from Wharton, demanded private audience with their lordships for himself, his colleague and a Scottish prisoner with valuable information.

It passed off without a hitch. One of the guard inquired of their lordships above; and then, clattering down, jerked a thumb. 'That's all right: up ye go!' he said. And they went.

* * *

The Provost of Annan had built according to his station; and the parlour adopted by the joint leaders of the invading English army was decently panelled in linenfold, with a particularly fine Italian desk pulled near the scarlet peat fire.

At the desk sat my Lord Wharton, knight and member

43

for Parliament, Captain of Carlisle, Sheriff of Cumberland, Warden of the West Marches and loyal and perspicacious servant of the English crown in the north. He was reading aloud passages from a paper covered with his secretary's writing, pausing for comment as he went. The Earl of Lennox, nose to nose with his own fair reflection in the dark window, was drumming his fingers on the sill and indulging in witty interjections.

Thomas, first Baron Wharton, was a tough little self-made Englishman with a whittled brown face and cold disenchanted eye. But Lord Lennox was a different matter. The Earls of Lennox reached back into the history of Scotland; this one had been reared in France and had lived blithely on his wide lands in Scotland until deciding that wealth and power lay closer to hand in the south. The title Matthew Lennox coveted was King Consort of Scotland. When Mary of Guise, the widowed Queen Dowager of Scotland, would have no truck with him, he merely turned coat, joined the forces of England and married Margaret Douglas, King Henry VIII's niece who herself had a strong claim to a crown or two.

He was, incidentally, worried about his wife Margaret. The next day's march lay through her father's lands. The Earl of Angus, head of the noble Douglas family once castigated by Buccleuch, had written to him anxiously pointing this out and hoping that his son-in-law and Lord Wharton would, if invading, remember the ties of kinship. Lord Lennox remembered them, but he doubted whether Wharton would; especially if this time Margaret's turbulent father should plump for the Scottish side and join the Queen's army against him.

Jubilation over the news from Pinkie had meantime however swept gloom from the air. Wharton was planning his exodus from Annan to the north, and Lennox was dreaming of throne rooms when the door opened.

Being well oiled, it opened quite gently, and Henry Wharton, followed closely by Lymond, was within the room before either commander looked around. By then Scott too was inside, unloading the wounded Drummond in a corner. He retired to the door and stood with his back to it just as the man at the desk turned and half rose. 'Harry! You blundering fool! What've you done?'

Unequivocably, the firelight showed the bound hands, the glitter of Lymond's knife.

His son was mute; and the hard eyes of Lord Wharton shifted to the figure behind. 'You, sir! Who are you, and what d'you want?'

Lymond laughed. He laughed again as Lennox, who had spun around, took a step forward. With his free hand, the Master pulled off his steel bonnet and tossed it neatly into the hearth. The peats clouded with smoke, then blazed around it, lighting the pallid face and the colourless hair, stained with sweat. 'Money,' he said.

Lord Lennox stared. A tide of scarlet, patched and mottled, washed up to the roots of his hair and disappeared, taking horror and disbelief with it, and leaving the face swollen with rage. 'It's Crawford of Lymond!' said the Earl of Lennox, and the pale eyes, china-hard, shot to his lordly colleague. 'Here, in Annan. In the middle of your precious guard!' He exploded into ugly language. 'Your chicken-livered rabbit of a son . . . !'

Lord Wharton spoke sharply. 'Control yourself, sir!' and his eyes, on Harry, promised payment by someone, in time, for Lord Lennox's bad temper. He addressed Lymond. 'How did you get past the gate?'

Scott had finished lashing young Wharton to a bench, and was regagging him methodically. Watching him, his knife lingering at Harry's back, Lymond replied. 'My dear sir, how to avoid it? Their hospitality was most pressing. Besides, I got the password from Bannister.'

'Bannister?'

'The Protector's messenger. He fell in with us.'

Wharton said sharply, 'You have his dispatch then?'

The fair brows were raised. 'Dear me, no! I've finished with huckstering these days. Sweet rose of virtue and of gentleness. I hope to be appreciated for my beaux yeux alone – and those of Harry, of course. Manhood but prudence is a fury blind.'

Too wise a fox to be baited, Wharton kept to the point. 'Then I take it this man Bannister is dead?'

'He was in the best of health when I left him,' said Lymond, surprised. 'In fact, I had him escorted part of the way. The roads to the north are rather busy with Scottish gentlemen.'

'In fact, you sold him to the other side, this time!' said Lennox, making his first contribution to the conversation.

Lymond looked mildly chagrined. 'Not at all. What a reputation to have! Not all of us have your lordship's gift for trusteeship.'

This was a very shrewd hit. Everyone present knew that Lennox, ostensibly acting for the Scottish Queen Dowager, had once taken delivery of a shipload of French gold and arms on her behalf; and had then shipped himself and the gold south to England.

For a moment the earl was speechless with anger. 'You have the damnable effrontery – My God, if I'd only left you lashed to your stinking oars! You were grateful enough when I clothed you and fed you and gave you money . . . more fool I. I was repaid all right! Bring a cow to the hall,' Lennox snarled, 'and she will to the byre again.'

'And foul water slockens fire,' added Lymond. His voice became noticeably mellow. 'But then I was brought up in bad company. From oar to oar, you might say.'

If his previous remark had caused an explosion, this one was greeted with a silence which could be felt. Scott, his heart thudding inexplicably, looked from Lymond's imperturbable face to Lennox, who had gone bone-white.

'And how,' pursued the Master suavely, 'is the Pearl of Pearls?'

He was talking about the Countess of Lennox, and this time the allusion was unmistakable. Scott saw in Lord Wharton's face, for an instant, the same kind of shocked surprise that he felt himself; then Lennox's sword came hissing from its scabbard and Wharton, with a curse, sprang to put a hand on his arm. 'Put up. my lord!'

The Earl of Lennox didn't even look at him. He said

46

through his teeth, 'I'll suffer insult and insolence for no man's brat!'

'Then you have me to reckon with as well, my Lord Lennox,' said Wharton furiously. 'Put up!'

There was a long pause. The knife glittered in Lymond's hand, over young Harry's spine; Wharton's fingers dug into the earl's arm. Lennox swore, and rammed home the blade with fingers that shook.

Wharton removed his hand. He said quietly, 'I remember this scum. There is no need to play his game for him.' To Lymond he continued, 'I understand you are bargaining with my son's life. Naturally, it is worth a price to me, but don't expect me to pay too much. What do you want?' Then, natural feeling breaking through for a moment, he said bluntly, 'State your business, and get you gone. The very air you breath makes me retch.'

'Courtesy,' said Lymond, 'will get you nowhere.' He fitted his shoulders comfortably into the panelled wall. 'I must say you appear to be taking your martial duties very lightly. Don't you want to know what the Protector's dispatch said? I read it, you know, before sending it on. There's been another stupendous victory at Linlithgow, and the Protector thinks you should meet him in Stirling right away to talk it over. Doesn't that excite you? Scotland conquered at last! Duke Wharton on the Privy Council; King Matthew on the throne!'

Lennox had to know. His eyes searched Lymond's face; he said, almost against his own will, 'A victory on the Stirling road . . . is that true?'

Lymond stared back. 'Why not, your Majesty? The Scottish Queen's sickly; the English King's a bastard – or so the Catholics say, don't they, Matthew? – Arran's an idiot and his son a fool . . . lo! my lords, a crown!'

Half mesmerized, four pairs of eyes watched as swiftly he leaned to the fire, seized the heart tongs and stepped back. High above his head, gripped in the metal, flamed his own helmet, red-hot from the blazing peats, bits of burning stuff falling smoking to the floor.

'A crown!' said Lymond exaltedly. 'Who will wear it? Harry, perhaps?'

This was leading the field with a vengeance. The rigor which seized them lasted less than thirty seconds. Then Lennox said, loudly and rather wildly, 'The man's mad!' and Wharton, his face rigid, reseated himself at the desk. 'Money?'

'Of course!'

'In the chest.' Wharton indicated a small coffer against one wall.

'Get it.'

All the men in the small room, wounded, bound and free, waited, in a tension which knit them together, as five leather bags were placed on the desk, and taken away by Scott.

The Master opened one of them. 'O beautiful bagcheeks. Bonnets bellissimi; ecus; ryals – Dear me, the assured ones of Dumfriesshire are going to be much the poorer for this. Wrap 'em up, my Pyrrha!'

He ripped off Harry's cloak and flung it to Scott, who made a rough bundle of the gold, and laid his hand on the door.

'And so,' said Lymond gravely, 'we see the final end of our travail. Farewell, my masters!'

But the final paraph, the flourish which in time Scott was to recognize as habitual, was still to come. As he moved from Harry, and both Wharton and Lennox started forward, Lymond let drop his arm. The helmet, dull now with black heat, fell accurately on young Wharton's brow, and the boy, his eyes staring, gave, behind the gag, an unpleasant choked scream.

'That will perhaps remind you,' said Lymond, 'not to speak to strange gentlemen in dark streets' – and in the ensuing confusion, transported himself and Scott outside the door and locked it.

Scott stumbled down the dark stairs with his bundle. He was aware of a noisy conversation going on at the bottom between Lymond and the guards, of riding gently back down the pend, fighting to keep his spurs still, and recalling with a short prayer of gratitude the thickness of that parlour door. The gate. A sharp passage, with the edge on Lymond's voice, and the sullen and abashed look on the faces of the gatemen. The creak as the timbers were drawn, miraculously, to let them through.

Outside, in the cool, flickering darkness, the free night lay waiting, and swallowed them.

* * *

It seemed to Scott, riotously crossing the moors with Lymond, that he had done pretty well. He had prevented the fellow Drummond from giving the alarm. He had successfully comported himself in the presence of English military dignitaries of the most imposing sort. If the thought of the flaming helmet stuck unpleasantly on his mind, he dismissed it. What did it matter about cross-examinations! This was man's work.

It was then that two horses appeared wraithlike in the gloom ahead, and Lymond said sharply, 'Joe! What are you doing here?' and rode forward.

Words drifted to Scott. 'Bannister, sir . . . taken by a strong party of Scots . . . yes, sir, I did . . . Turkey took all the men and went after him . . . to look out for you and tell you . . . yes . . .'

By the long-distance cramps across his shoulder blades and the worn patches inside his thighs Scott was reminded that he had been in the saddle all day; and with no great joy he felt Lymond return to his side suffused with fresh, delicate energy. 'Now, don't lose interest, my Pyrrha,' said the light voice. 'I bring, lover, I bring the news glad. Friend Bannister has got himself ambushed and now, my frivol Fortune, the ambushers are walking into the net. I'll trip upon trenchers; I'll dance upon dishes – it is now perfect day.'

And led by Jess's Joe, Lymond rode quickly onward over the dark Annandale moor, Will Scott following.

'*Lymond must wait*,' said Lord Culter; and he and Buccleuch, and the Erskines, and Andrew Hunter and Lord Fleming and every man with a horse under him and a sword in his hand had ridden to Pinkie.

Among the ten thousand dead of that day were Lord Fleming of Boghall and Tom Erskine's older brother.

Among the living, the hungry and battle-weary, with lined faces caulked with dust, were Lymond's brother Lord Culter and Tom Erskine himself, far from slight, irritating adventures with a drunken sow. With the rags of their following the two men left the battlefield together and, knowing their families to be safe with Queen Mother, baby Queen and Court in the fortress town of Stirling, they crossed Scotland from the River Forth to the River Annan in an attempt to put a block – not enough men; not enough ordnance; not enough food – between the advancing army under Lord Wharton and the treasure at Stirling.

So while the spirits of my lords Wharton and Lennox were being mortified in Annan, two parties of Scottish troops lay still in the darkness to the north: so still that Charlie Bannister, the Protector's ill-fated messenger to Wharton, walked straight into one of them. He had the presence of mind to destroy his dispatches before they caught him; but catch him they did, and took him to Lord Culter.

The man Bannister might have been weak in geography, and uncertain in his grasp of minor essentials such as avoiding the attention of large bodies of cavalry. But in one thing he excelled: he could keep his mouth shut.

Agonizingly aware of the danger to Stirling, excoriated by the need to know the Protector's and Wharton's plans, they tried every method of persuasion; for the messenger knew the gist of his message: incautious to the end, he had let that out himself.

With failure confronting them, Culter took his captain aside. The dilemma was plain. If the English Protector, now at Edinburgh, was ready to move on to attack the Queen and the Governor, he would order Wharton north to support him. Were those the orders Charlie Bannister carried? And when they didn't come, would Wharton stay a while in Annan? Long enough, for example, to let Lord Culter and Tom Erskine with their men, however few, ride back to the defence of Stirling, their two Queens, their womenfolk?

'But if you're wrong, sir,' said Lord Culter's captain, 'you unstop this hole by moving away.'

There was a short silence; then Culter took his decision. 'Get your horse and bring Erskine and the other party to me. If it is as I think, we abandon Annon and march north.'

The captain left, and still Bannister held out. Lord Culter, watching the assault, lips compressed, saw the decision he did not want to make striding toward him.

He waited unmoving as time passed. Erskine had not yet had time to join him; dawn was still a long way off. To the south, a dull red haze challenged. He watched it mechanically, then chopped a hand on the torchbearer's shoulder. 'Lights out!'

In the sudden darkness, a lookout confirmed what he had seen. 'Body of troops coming up from the south, sir!' It was Erskine, of course. He gave orders quickly. Going through the motions for defence, the same certainty lay reassuringly on the men. It was Erskine, of course.

It was not Erskine. The horses were at the edge of the wood, and the leaves shivering before they knew it; and then a growing, sphincteral circle of sound told them they were surrounded by a force much bigger. In ten minutes it was over. Pulsing inward, the incomers squeezed the Scots in a knot below the scarred trees, and held them there.

By the relit torches, the vanquished, on foot, stared at the mounted ring of their victors. The horsemen wore no emblems, and no banners were shown: the conspicuous red cross of England on the white background was nowhere to be seen. Lord Culter, weaponless and fine-drawn, stepped forward and addressed them. 'Who is your leader?'

No one offered the civility of a reply. Instead, a bald, black-bearded giant who had been fidgeting about the radius of the circle, suddenly bent from his horse. 'So there ye are, ye hell-tarnished gomerel!'

Forgotten in the bracken, the bound figure of Bannister stirred hopefully.

'It's a wae job keeping some folk out of trouble,' remarked the big man with some sourness. 'We told ye the right road, didn't we?'

Charlie Bannister, tried nearly beyond mortal man's endurance, released a heartbreaking groan. Bending over his mare's neck, the big man flicked off the ropes with his sword edge.

'On your plat feet, ye glaikit Mercury. There's a horse here ye can have, and a guide to take ye as far as Annan. I suppose you handed your papers to the bold laddies here?'

Bannister got shakily to his feet. 'I tore them up. How was I to know you directed me right?'

The big man invoked his Maker, spoiling the effect with an alarming hiccough. 'What else would we need to do to prove it: wrap you and your dispatch in a clean sark and lay you on his lordship's bed?' – with heavy sarcasm. 'Get off with you, man, before we glutted with the fair sight o' you.'

'Wait!' said Lord Culter. He defeated his own purpose. Bannister instantly discovered the use of his legs and, helped impolitely with the flat of the big man's sword, went stumbling through the bushes. Culter's instinctive move to follow was checked by the same sword.

Blackbeard grinned and swept him a bow. 'My lord Culter. Good e'en to you,' he said ceremonially. 'Now, gif you'll excuse us . . .'

'I doubt there's a decent man in Scotland will do that,' said Culter. Was it possible that they were to escape with their lives? 'Scots in English pay, I take it?'

'Maybe.' The big man was not forthcoming. More, he seemed miraculously to regard his business as complete.

Having collected their weapons and cut loose Culter's horse, he bowed again and took rein.

At that precise moment, the dark rustling spaces behind him expelled more horsemen.

'But how magnificent!' said Lord Culter's younger brother, and rode forward with unrestrained cordiality. 'Look, children: it's Richard!'

Watching curiously, Scott and all the others saw Lord Culter's face alter. Then he took a step backward, to narrow the angle between himself and the horseman, and spoke with deliberate and soul-hacking contempt. 'This rabble is yours?'

'Not rabble, Richard.' The blue gaze sorrowed. 'There's no merit in being outwitted by a rabble. Don't let your sense of superiority get the better of you. After all, I'm on the horse, like the frog in the story, and while I can stare you down, it's a little difficult for you to stare me up. You've put on weight, haven't you? And cautious! Even Nero watched, Richard, while the family became encaramelled. I hardly thought you would resist the desire to be present as well.'

Among Culter's men there was a rustle of anger, but Richard himself said nothing at all. For an infinitesimal space, the blue eyes were forced down by the grey. Then the slack lids were drawn back farther than Scott had ever seen them, and the full malice of Lymond's cornflower eyes bent on his brother.

'Talk to me, Richard. It isn't difficult. Move the teeth and agitate the tongue. Tell me news of the family. Am I superseded yet? Oh, Richard, a blush!'

'No.' Culter's voice was perfectly level. 'No. You are not superseded. You are quite safe to kill me.' And added stiffly, forcing the time to pass: 'Your services are at present with Wharton, I take it?'

Lymond's voice was absent. 'Well, he's certainly paying me. Once our friend Bannister reaches Annan, the road north is going to be a little crowded, what's more.'

Culter moved involuntarily. 'Is the Protector then in Stirling?'

'Yes, of course,' said Lymond readily. 'Take care: you asked me a question; it's the thin edge of the wedge. What's so interesting about the Protector being in Stirling? . . . Oh, Richard!' he said with an air of sudden discovery. 'You haven't packed the ladies off to Stirling for safety, have you?'

Lord Culter, guarding his eyes, was speaking mechanically. 'You should be delighted.'

'Well, it opens up a number of interesting possibilities, doesn't it?' said Lymond. 'I wonder if the Protector insists on merchetis, and his princely free access to the bedchamber, or anything novel like that. I used to know a number of women who would be all the better for a fate plus mal que morte. Which brings me rather to the point: Changeons propos, c'est trop chanté d'amours . . .' And he laid a gentle hand on his sword.

With an uneasy twist of relief, Scott recognized the climax, and drew a fortifying breath. At the same instant, Lymond said suddenly, 'Richard, my child, have you by any chance more brains than I gave you credit for?'

The words were hardly out when the rumour of noise, the furtive boot on the heather and the laboured breath resolved themselves into a torrent of crumbling sound as Erskine's incoming Scottish force flooded the wood.

In the last flare of the torches, Scott saw Lord Culter, his face alight, snatch a bow and raise it. Passion lent to the silent tongue the drama once derided by his brother. 'Your turn now, Lymond! And by God, before I let you take over my shield and my bed, I'll give you one night to remember the head of your family by!'

And as he swung his horse frantically and went crashing and bumping outward through the confusion, Scott also heard Lymond's reply.

'All right: a challenge, Richard! I'll meet you at the Popinjay in the next Stirling Wapenshaw, and we'll try then who's Master!'

He laughed, and the excitement in the laugh was the last thing Scott remembered.

2
BLINDFOLD PLAY

And hit is not fittynge ne convenable thynge
for a woman to goo to bataylle for the
fragilitie and feblenes of her. And therfore
holdeth she not the waye in her draught as the
Knyghtes doon.

In the long grass by the water's edge a man lay half buried,
with small life moving past his head and a tarnishing damp
spread into his clothing. Behind him, four miles of bog
rolled and steamed in the morning sun. Ahead, the turgid
waters of the moat sucked and plopped in a leisurely way
against the grazing meadows and scrub which lay behind
Boghall Castle.

The sun moved.

At the castle, from which Richard, Lord Culter, had
once watched the smoke of his mother's burning house,
the watch changed with weary abuse on both sides. 'If one
more old body,' said Hugh the Warden to his junior, 'asks
me to send a horseman to Pinkie to inquire after her
great-nephew Jacob, I'll skin her alive. Old quarry-faced
Wharton on the road north, and ten men and twenty-two
women to hold this castle and look after all of Biggar . . .'

But breakfast and a pint of beer must have modified his
temper, because he was patient with the next anxious
inquirer. 'Don't fret. The boys'll be back all right.'

He was reminded as he spoke that some were already
back: the barber-surgeon with his knives and ointments
had already made the double journey twice between the
castle and the thatched houses of Biggar. Hugh thought
of that: he thought of his master, the dead Lord Fleming;

55

he swore loudly and shot up to the watchtower, there to gaze earnestly and hopefully at the unstirring south.

'Oh, God! Let them come!' said he, addressing the hills. 'Oh, God! Let them come, and me and Dod Young'll make collops of them!'

The morning dragged on. At noon Simon Bogle, body-guard, got his lady's permission to fish for one hour, and left by the back postern. A dark, angular child, Sym was Stirling bred, and had for three years served the household with fierce attachment. At present, however, his mind was on fish. He passed through the bushes, untied the skiff, and shipped himself and his rod to the other side of the water. He thereupon walked twenty yards, stumbled, walked another yard, and went back to look.

A man's foot, lying in his path, proved to be attached to a body, and the body to an English cloak. He bent, gripped and rolled it over. Among a wealth of impressive detail there appeared a young man's profile, splendidly unconscious. 'Whoops, cock and the devil!' said Simon Bogle breathlessly and pounced, like divine Calypso, on his prey.

He reached the postern with his burden, dispensing pulses of excitement and bog smells as his mistress opened it from the inside; and as he explained, Christian Stewart knelt beside their captive in her garden, her dark red hair fallen forward, her blind eyes resigned.

What to Sym was an English magnifico, ripe for ransom, took, bearlike, a different shape under the hypertactile fingers – the shape of an unconscious boy, with a dirty wound, raised and sticky, in the short hair over the nape. She drew together the shirt cords thoughtfully and rose.

'Um. Well, you've hooked a twenty-pounder this time, my lad, by the feel of his clothes. . . . If I were married or promised to that young gentleman I'd sell the lead off the roof to ransom him back. Unless he's a Spaniard, do you think?'

'Not with that hair, m'lady. Maybe,' said Sym with a sort of agonized calm, 'maybe it's the Protector Somerset? Or Lord Grey?'

'Och, Sym, he's too young,' said Christian. 'Although in a way it's a pity he's not, because, Sym my lad: what are you going to do about Hugh?'

'Oh, cock!' said Sym, his excitement checked. 'Right enough. Hugh's in an awful bad temper about the English.'

'Hugh's bad temper takes practical forms,' said Christian thoughtfully. 'Ransom or no ransom, your gentleman will find himself in multiple array on the wall spikes if Hugh sets eyes on him.'

Sym devoted some thought to this. 'Of course, we can't write for ransom anyway until he wakes up and says who he is.'

'No.'

'And by that time, Hugh might be feeling more like himself.'

'I find the resemblance to himself at the present moment quite startling,' said Christian. 'But never mind. Go on.'

'So,' said Sym hurriedly, 'if we got him up the privy stairs and put him into Jamie's room, no one need know. All that wing's empty except for me, and I could look after him. Until he says who he is . . . and the window's too high to let him escape and the door could be lockit.'

Christian said slowly, 'We could, I suppose, certainly . . .'

'And if he's nobody,' said Sym fairly, 'we can just hand him over to Hugh.'

'In which event,' said Christian, 'he will certainly become nobody in record time. All right. I agree.'

* * *

To carry the prisoner within, to strip, wash and bed him, to surround him with hot bricks in socks and light a fire to heat cock-a-leeky and milk and honey sneaked from the buttery took Sym, borne on the wings of simple cupidity, less time than bedding a child.

Christian, pulled by outside necessity, set aside ten minutes to examine his handiwork and used the time to relax, hands clasped, on a chair by the bedside while Sym, a cudgel beside him, bestowed himself hopefully on the window seat.

Blessed silence, and the slow dissolving of the nagging images of the day into something near dreams. Flurried movements of the big fire, to her left. Silk, pricking her right hand as the bed curtains stirred in an eddy. A rustle from Sym's feet in the rushes. A voice far below in the courtyard, crying something she could not quite catch. A creak from the bed.

Another.

A languid stir of the bedclothes.

It was, thought Christian, fully awake and gripped with laughter, like attending a birth. Were they wrong and he was Scottish, a purebred orthodox achievement with full honours: all well?

There was a thin crackle of pillow-feather; a stifled expletive; then a voice said resignedly, 'God: my skull's split.'

It was a cultured voice, with no inflection which would have seemed out of place at any point north of the Tyne. Like the jewelled aiglettes it announced consequence, character and money. Considering it, she spoke reassuringly. 'Better not move. There's a bump on your head like the Old Man of Storr.' And to save him time and breath she added, 'I'm Christian Stewart of Boghall. My lad over there picked you up off the moor.'

There was a long pause; then he spoke, clearly with his head turned toward her. 'Bog – Bog . . . ?'

'Boghall. Yes. You were thoroughly cold and damp, and here's Sym with some broth for you.'

Unexpectedly, underneath shock and weakness there was the accent of laughter. 'Think of the Cauldron of Hell,' remarked their prisoner, 'and you have my inside arrangements. But I'll try. Like the spider, I'll try. That lightlie comes will lightlie ga . . . steady . . . That's it. I can feed myself – or can I? I'm so sorry. The counterpane is not improved by spilt broth.'

He ate, and much intrigued, Christian waited. At the

end, he spoke again. 'I was not, I hope, wearing a night-shirt when discovered?'

An artless gentleman. Christian followed the lead. 'Your clothes are drying, sir. Your weapons were impounded when we found you were English.'

'English! Lucifer, Lord of Hell!' (Here was passion.) 'Do I look like an Englishman?'

'I,' said Christian with wicked simplicity, 'am blind. How should I know?'

Used rarely and with reluctance this was, she had found, the infallible test. Braced, she waited: for remorse, embarrassment, dismay, pity, forced sympathy, naked fear.

'Oh, are you? I'm sorry. You hide it extremely well. Then what,' he asked anxiously, 'made your friends think I was English?'

Exquisitely done, my young man, thought Christian. She said aloud, 'Well, to begin with, you were wearing an English cloak. We've disposed of that for your own sake. Feeling in Boghall about the English has been running gallows high since Lord Fleming was killed. You're safe in this room with Sym and myself, but I shouldn't advise you to attract the attention of anyone else in the castle.'

'I see. Or I shall meet my fate. Without pitie, hanged to be, and waver with the wind. My beard, if I had one – Lord, I nearly have – is full young yet to make a purfle of it, even to replace the one I've stained. And why, Mistress Stewart, should you and your henchman trouble to defend me from death and horrible maims?'

'What a suspicious mind you have.' Blandly, Christian matched metre with metre. 'Why do you think? For gold, for gude; for wage or yet for wed?'

'I think no such thing: you malign me, I assure you. Every coherent sentiment escaped from the louvre at the back of my head long ago, and I am swimming in a sea of foolishness. I've already forgotten what we're discussing.'

Simon Bogle, a single-minded person, had not. 'Lady Christian and I,' he said dourly, 'were wondering what your name and style might be?'

In a feverish silence, the young man stirred restlessly.

'Lady Christian. Damnation. She has a title and I don't know it. She lives in a bog; and of this also I am ignorant. Q.E.D. I cannot be Scots. Therefore why your excessive kindness . . . Oh God! Of course. Ransom.'

'And natural virtue. For gold and for gude, in fact.' Christian, visited by an unworthy satisfaction, was magnanimous. 'But as part owner of the property, I think we should defer speech until you're more rested. You've had a sore knock there.'

'Several sore knocks,' he said, and fell silent, rousing himself only as she felt for and took away pillows. 'Don't you want my name?' And dreamily, 'This officer, but doubt, is callit Deid. . . .'

'No.' Aware of Sym's silent resistance, she spoke firmly. 'No, never mind. Not just now,' feeling exhaustion and faintness overwhelm him. Even so, he managed a gruesome chuckle.

'O lady: nor later. Deceit deceiveth and shall be deceived. It's no good and I can't prove it's no good: I shall be as much use to you as the Nibelunglied. For I can recall nothing . . . nothing . . . not the remotest damned shred of my identity.'

* * *

Christian left the situation in Sym's hands that night. Next morning, however, she woke thinking of her prisoner, and obtaining food and wine by a shameless lie in the kitchen, made her way with it up the private stair.

Inside the sickroom, she was aware of a strange step even before she shut the door; and indeed as she turned to do so, a voice said readily, 'You may want to come back later, Lady Christian. Sym is out, and I'm up and standing by the window.'

She shut the door. 'Ah, you're feeling better. My dear man, not even an attack on my virtue would drive me downstairs till I've done. I've already climbed more steps this morning than a bell ringer.'

He laughed, but did not come to help her, she noticed; and, respecting his tact, she took the tray herself to the window seat and laid it on a kist. Then, sitting by the bed, she ascertained that the fever was gone, the headache was less; that he was profoundly grateful, and remarkably well up in current events.

'So Simon has been talking to you.'

'He has seldom stopped. He tells me Lord Fleming's widow and family are all at Stirling, and thinks it uncommonly rash of you to stay behind. With which, as a special hazard myself, I must agree.'

She shrugged. 'I can do more good here at the moment than in Stirling.' And felt impelled to add, 'Naturally, I can't risk being an encumbrance, or a hostage either. If things get much worse – or much better for that matter – a friend of the family will take me to Stirling.'

'And I shall stay with captors somewhat less benign. Ah me,' he said rather ruefully. 'It may sound selfish but, as the poet said, words is but wind, but dunts is the devil.'

'Doesn't that depend who you are?' she remarked. 'If you bear a Scots name, you've nothing to fear. Or is this officer, but doubt, still callit Deid?'

There was a pause. Then he said, 'Are you quoting from me?'

'Your very words last night.'

'Oh. I must have been in dire spirits. Have you ever lost your memory? I suppose not. It's an experience. Pleasant but precarious, like the gentleman who sat under palm trees feeding fruit to a lion . . .' Pausing for breath, he added, 'I rely on you to put down any lacunae to the effects of a blow on the head. I am but ane mad man that thou hast here met – '

' – I do you pray,' she said gravely, 'cast that name from you away.'

Delighted, he took her up at once. 'Yes, of course. Call you Hector, or Oliver . . . What else? Sir Porteous – Amadas – Perdiccas – Florent . . . How common the predicament seems to be. Most of the heroes and all the poets appear to have been there before me. I am as I am, and so will I be; but how that I am, none knoweth truly . . . Disdain me not without desert! Forsake me not till I deserve, nor hate me not till I offend.' And he abandoned English plaintively.

> *'Li rosignox est mon père, qui chante sur le ramée,*
> *el plus haut boscage.*
> *La seraine, ele est ma mère, qui chante en la mer salée,*
> *el plus haut rivage . . .'*

'Your French is excellent, of course,' said Christian. 'And you disliked being called English.'

'Thank you.'

'Implying Scottish rather than English affinities – '

'I hoped you'd notice that.'

' – In which case,' said Christian reasonably, 'do you not owe it to yourself to appear in public? Someone here might even recognize you.'

'A shrewd move, decidedly,' said the prisoner with interest. 'If I disagree, I am undoubtedly lying about my loss of memory. On the other hand, it might be genuine, and my belief that I am Scots might be unfounded; in which case your friend Hugh, according to Sym, will be apt to give free play to his prejudices, and your hopes of a ransom will vanish.'

'You must think us very mistrustful,' said Christian equably. 'Why should you be lying? If you are English, you would have no motive for hiding your name. The sooner we know, the sooner we should arrange your freedom.'

'I find the Socratean method even more uncomfortable than plain sarcasm. I propose to say what you wish me to say, viz.: there are two exceptions in your category. If I were English but destitute, and if I were English and politically important, I should avoid identification like the plague.'

' – Therefore?'

'Therefore when I say, as I do, that I have no wish to appear to your friends before my memory comes back, you have no means whatever of proving the honesty of my reasons – '

'Which in fact are . . . ?'

'Funk,' he said promptly. 'Sheer terror of the dark. I don't like standing outside the door of a crowded room any more than you do, waiting to be pounced on from inside.'

Christian said, 'A priest would tell you this was pride and self-conceit.'

'If anyone so described it to you, I hope you impeached him for a pompous liar.'

'My dear man, would you have me excommunicate? It's a process of hardening one goes through. You would find me hard to shock.'

'And to deceive?'

She smiled, and threw his own quotation back at him. 'Deceit deceiveth and shall be deceived. You have an incorruptible voice and a lawyer's tongue. One thing I commend in you: you refused to add to the sins of the poets. A false pedigree is always worse than none at all.'

'Avoiding your traps, O virtuous lady, O mixt and subtle Christian. But, as you see, I am honest and good, and not ane word could lie.'

She laughed. 'I deduce that you've lived on Hymettus on honey and larks' tongues.'

'And can, I suppose, die in a bog as well as anywhere,' he said dryly.

No one likes to appear cheap. Betrayed into archness, Christian caught her temper and said evenly, 'I can't, of course, answer for what will happen to you if I leave before your memory comes back. But meanwhile, until it does, you may have grace to stay anonymous, if you wish.'

She rose, adding briskly, 'And meantime, there are many would envy you. Make the most of your freedom, my friend – you've more of it than any of us.'

'True. Only lunatics have more. I'm ungrateful to find it intolerable; and more than intolerable, of course, not to know the extent of the burden I'm putting on you.'

Christian had reached the door. She turned, and said ironically, 'No burden at all. You haven't forgotten?

63

> *"Ho, ho: say you so;*
> *Money shall make my mare to go."*

She shut the door, smiling, and left him to think it over.

* * *

This was Thursday, the 15th of September. Tom Erskine had gone south on Monday: he might very well be back for her any day now.

In the meantime, the demands on her time and her resources were continuous. All the lands of Biggar and Kilbucho, Hartree and Thankerton were in the care of the castle. In the absence of all the able men who had followed Lord Fleming to Pinkie and who had not yet returned – who might never return – the families on these lands must be succoured: given advice, news and medical help as they needed it; and plans made for their reception if the invaders broke through.

For the news from the east was pitiful. The army, ill-assorted and suspicious of itself, had crowned tactical blunder with panic: breaking up on the field, it had given way and had been hunted into extinction. While, forty miles to the north, the Court had found temporary refuge at Stirling, the English Protector, moving victorious toward Edinburgh, had put his horse into empty Leith, camped outside, and embarked on leisurely discussions about its fortification while English ships, sailing unchecked up the east coast, took and garrisoned the island of St. Colme's Inch, strategic gem in the midst of the Forth estuary north of Edinburgh.

And at any moment, they might hear of the approach from the southwest of Lord Wharton and the Earl of Lennox, and their English soldiers.

The day at Boghall wore on. The strain was bearing on them all: Christian began to feel herself drained of comfort and vitality. In midafternoon, she made time to visit the deserted wing, aware of increasing irritation with the situation. Baulked meantime of his hopes of ransom, Sym might well have tired, she thought, of acting nurse-maid-cum-jailer, and think there would be less danger and more fun if he brought Hugh into the affair. In accepting four years of Sym's unshakable loyalty, she had discovered his weaknesses. Thinking thus, she made for the private stair.

A clash of swords above her drove the blood from her heart. She stopped, and was rewarded with a crack of gasping laughter. 'Man, it's not shinty! Use yourself neatly: see, to the left; forward; *then* up and through.'

There was a further clatter as pupil evidently followed suit. She swept to the stairhead.

'You pair of fools: they can hear your swords in Biggar. Sym. Is this the way you look after a sick man? And you, whoever-you-are! You're taking our care of you very lightly.' Ignoring excuse and apology, she despatched Sym to keep guard at the top of the stair, and seized the other man by the arm. 'You deserve to hop like St. Vitus: turning fencing master with the fever hardly off you. Sit down at the stair bottom. Your head – '

' – Would serve a cat in a bowl eight days,' he said, with another gasping laugh, and set about controlling his breath.

The doorway in the turret looked onto her private garden. Overlooked by the deserted wing and surrounded by an eight-foot wall it was silent and secret. The sun was warm; the peace absolute.

Beguiled from her duty she rested too, shoulders held by the wall, face upturned to the sun. Nothing moved but great rumours of perfume swelling and fading, sforzando and diminuendo; an orchestration of woodwind in the warm air.

Silence, broken by three golden notes of a lute: her own, she remembered, left on the bottom step. She said, 'If you play, please go on. Music's my joy and my obsession.'

'What shall it be?' He ruffled the strings, and made a false start. Then a spray of notes flew into the air, modulating in descending arpeggios. He suddenly sang, neatly and gaily.

> *'En mai au douz tens nouvel*
> *Que raverdissent prael,*
> *Oi soz un arbroisel*
> *Chanter le rosignolet.*
> *Saderala don!*
> *Tant fet bon*
> *Dormir lez le buissonet.'*

He paused, and evidently accepting her smile, continued. Tentatively, Christian joined him next time:

> *'Saderala don!*
> *Tant fet bon*
> *Dormir lez le buissonet.'*

They sang the last chorus together, melody and descant, and when he stopped she said triumphantly, 'Sang School! I knew it!'

Plucking crotchets like raindrops, he responded. 'Am I a schoolmaster, think you?'

'Or a monk?' – innocently.

Laughter intensified in the voice. 'When clerics sing like little birds? – No, surely not . . .' and he swept tempestuously into a song made immortal by its far from clerical sentiments; and from there to an estampie she did not recognize.

His playing was restrained and skilled. Drifting from this to that composer, he discoursed gently about musical theory and philosophy; and she found herself stating her own views, asking questions, listening intently. With humble and rather touching delight, she entered into her own world; the world of sound, and was happy until Conscience put a hand on her shoulder. She said suddenly, 'Who is Jonathan Crouch?'

'Who?' he said lazily. 'Oh, Jonathan Crouch. He's an Englishman, at present pris –'

The hiatus, the inhalation, the shaken voice, were plain for her to hear. 'You use drastic methods, don't you?' he said.

Christian replied quickly. 'Memory's a strange thing,

taken unawares. Sym told me you spoke the name in your sleep.'

'Did I? Then it must have some personal importance, I suppose . . . but what? I'm sorry. It's vanished. Try again.'

'Then it probably isn't your own name?'

His laugh sounded genuine enough. 'God forbid! Surely I'd know it if I heard it?'

'It might strike you suddenly. Or maybe you'd rather select one? O Dermyne, O Donnall, O Dochardy droch . . .'

'No,' he said. 'Look, we could go on forever. I think I prefer being an old, nameless article to a new-minted one with a false label around my neck. Or, indeed, anything of a ropelike character. Leave me to spend my remaining wit on Jonathan Crouch, and in the meantime let there be dancing and singing and all manner of joy . . .'

The lute sang, irresistibly, and so did he.

> *'The Frogge would a wooing ride*
> *Humble-dum, humble-dum*
> *Sword and buckler by his side*
> *Tweedle, tweedle twino.*

> *'When he was upon his high horse set*
> *Humble-dum, humble-dum*
> *His boots they shone as black as jet –* '

The break was as violent as if death itself had struck. The four strings gasped, once, under clenched fingers, and there was silence.

Alone with the hammering of her heart, with infinite patience, Christian waited.

'Memory's a strange thing.' What aspect of the bold, ill-fated frog had opened the gates? Frogs – and wells. What lay at the bottom of a well? Cats; and kelpies; and curses; and cures for warts . . . and Truth, of course.

As if the thought had reached him, there was a movement beside her. The light insouciant voice showed no inclination to dive into wells.

' – Tweedle, tweedle, twino. I have a confession to

make. The first rule of prison life is to curry favour with your jailer. This I have done with some success: Sym tells me he has no desire either to hang or to impoverish me. On the contrary: this afternoon he showed me how to escape with the key of the postern and over a secret path in the bog. I promised not to use it without your permission.'

Christian said, 'I see. You seem to have been working very hard. And what is the rule when there are two jailers?'

He was silent for a moment; then said, 'Look: swear me God from top to toe in one breath if you will; but remember, I exposed myself voluntarily.'

'All right,' she said. 'Provided you have a clear idea of the situation. I take it you've recovered your senses, and your identity is not one that would be pleasing to Hugh. You are likewise unwilling to be a source of profit or revenge to Simon or myself. You are therefore asking us both, in view of past favours, to connive at your escape.'

If she had expected him to betray any further emotion, she was disappointed. 'Admirably just, and justly damning,' said the voice equably. 'Well, the remedy is in your own hands.' And he quoted mockingly:

> '*Se'l ser un si, scrivero'n rima;*
> *Se'l ser un no, amici come prima.*'

There followed a pause, during which Christian came to the annoyed conclusion that she had once more been outmanoeuvred. Possessing the key, he had flung himself on her mercy. Why? It occurred to her that when referring to the enslavement of Sym, he had refrained with the utmost tact from drawing a parallel. He had left her to do that. To betray him now would suggest the vindictiveness of a disappointed woman, and she might well, in his opinion, shrink from that.

'Amici come prima, indeed!' repeated Christian viciously to herself, and added aloud, 'I assure you that if you've persuaded Sym out of his dream of wealth through sheer weight of personality, I'm unlikely to insist on furca and fossa out of spite or low curiosity. But what I must and will have clear is that once free, you'll do us no harm.'

'I could give you my word on that, except that, like the wonders of Mandeville, my probity is problematical.'

'The thought had occurred to me,' admitted Christian. 'Therefore while accepting your promise – of course – I must make one other condition. Tell me your interest in Jonathan Crouch.'

'God!' he said; and this time she heard genuine amusement. 'Next time I'll make straight for Hugh. Rather the thumbscrews than the confessional. But I warn you, it's a poor bargain. You won't trace me through Crouch.'

'I'll risk that,' she said, and then had further words struck from her by a sudden, vast commotion, echoing among the towers. At the same moment, a familiar voice rolled down the stair. 'Good news, Christian! Are you there? Can I come down? Christian!'

She said, 'It's Tom Erskine – Outside the postern, quick. Where's Sym . . . oh, there you are. Yes, I know: he's told me. Look: go with him, take him to the cave and come back . . . it's a small cavern halfway along the path; well hidden. You can stay there till dark. I'll get a cloak and some food over to you later.'

'My sword –'

'I'll send it. Here's the postern key. Quick!'

She turned, as their running footsteps receded. 'Tom, my dear! Wait and I'll come up!'

Christian Stewart lifted her skirts and began climbing the stairs thoughtfully. 'Damm the man!' said she, as she went; and it was not at all clear which man she meant.

* * *

With Erskine were all his troops; tired, filthy and in the wildest of spirits. Biggar opened its doors to them: Bizzyberry echoed with laughter and music and at the castle, officers and garrison, suitably freshened up, shared a happy excess of food and drink in the banqueting hall.

Sitting beside Tom, smelling the white soap he used

69

and picturing him, clean, rosy and normal, Christian was moved to say, 'Tom, I'm so glad you're here!'

He said apologetically, 'I'd have been here long before if I could. You look tired to death. Idiotic of Jenny Fleming to leave you.'

She smiled. 'It's only my capacity for intelligent sympathy that's exhausted – I'm longing for simple, positive, cheerful conversation. Tell me more of your news.'

For it was not only good, but miraculous. Lords Wharton and Lennox, dug deep into Annandale, had turned tail; and pursued by himself and Lord Cutler had scampered back to England. There was a garrison still at Castlemilk – no very great danger – but the deadly thrust north had been stopped: the western arm of the nutcracker had broken.

'Why?'

'Overconfidence, we think. They spread a rumour they meant to march north, and got a shock when Culter assumed the opposite and charged in. Made a mess of poor old Annan, but nothing to what Clydesdale missed, thank God. Although I don't mind saying,' he added frankly, 'that Culter took a chance I wouldn't have touched with a billhook.'

'But it worked,' said Christian. 'And now?'

'Report to the Queen Mother. Dispatch rider ahead, of course, with details but I follow tomorrow. You'll come, won't you?'

'I think I shall, yes,' said Christian. 'If there's no threat to the castle they can dispense with me here. And I ought to take those children off Lady Fleming's hands. Is there a moon tonight?'

'No: It's got overcast,' said Tom, surprised. 'Why?'

'Oh, it doesn't matter. Sym wanted some night fishing. And I must finish packing as well,' said Christian, with the appearance of absolute truth.

* * *

The path through the bog was not easy to find. Even steered firmly by Sym, her booted feet kept gouging into wet sponges and clucking, half-dug hags. Her gown was soaked and her spirits still damper when she heard a murmur ahead.

Sym, a joyful conspirator, whispered. 'There's someone else with him in the cave, my lady.'

Christian said, 'Be quiet!' but the low voices stopped, and there was a stealthy sound to their right. She pushed Sym a little, and he stepped forward, rising surprisingly to the occasion with a bold voice. 'Stay where you are! We bring food from Boghall, but we're armed, too.'

'Doubly armed, I trust,' said the voice of their former prisoner. 'My faith, yes. Food, my sword and dagger – Sym, you're a hero. . . . Good God!' it said plaintively. 'Good God! Lady Christian. The most determined creature since Bruce. I owe you some information, don't I?'

'You do. How do you feel after your walk?'

'In good heart and excellent health. Happier than Augustus, better than Trajan. And one of my own senators, to boot, has already traced me and is about to restore me to my empire. It's the new moon. Like the elephants of Mauretania, my friends are foregathering to perform mysterious rites . . . Jonathan Crouch is an Englishman I want to speak to, that's all. I know nothing about him, except that he's a prisoner in Scotland, but I mean to trace him, if it takes me to Hell and back.'

'It needn't do that,' said Christian. 'Because I can do it for you, through Tom. He has access to all the lists at Stirling, and he'll be discreet, if I ask him. Come to this cave on Tuesday, and I'll leave word for you.'

The voice this time was brief. 'Thank you, Shahrazad, but I think not.'

She spoke bluntly. 'Crouch will be ransomed back to England long before you can find him yourself.'

'Nevertheless, no.'

Meeting the rock of his will, she had no mind to plead. 'Well, whether you want it or not, the information will be there,' said Christian. 'Ignore it if you want to. Good night.' And pulling Sym's coat, she moved.

She was stopped at three paces by long, wiry fingers

and a gust of garlic. Then: 'God damn you, Johnnie, let her go!' said the expressive, flexible voice, and the hands dropped. She moved on quickly, without waiting for more.

Halfway back to Boghall, Simon spoke. 'Who's Shahrazad?'

'A farsighted lady who kept the Shah on a leading rein by telling him stories.'

Pause. 'I don't see the connection,' said Sym.

'Oh, don't be a fool!' said Christian irritably. 'There isn't any.'

3

MORE BLINDFOLD PLAY: THE QUEEN MOVES TOO FAR

In figour suld be maid in chess a quene
A fair ladye yat galye cled suld bene
And in a chyar scho suld be set on hight,
A crowne of gold apone hir hed weile dicht. . . .
Richt sad in moving suld yir womē be
And of short space, and to no fer cūtre.

'Firearms!' said Wat Scott of Buccleuch with a powerful disgust. 'Firearms! I could do more harm with a good spit through a peashooter. . . .'

Tom Erskine located the voice without enthusiasm.

He had had a frustrating week. Stirling was his home: his father was Keeper of the castle, and in the romantic and ingenuous soul which lurked behind his round exterior, the Master of Erskine loved above all things to see between his horse's ears the Rock of Stirling, a homely Lorelei in the green meadow of the Forth.

It had taken all Friday to bring Christian Stewart and her women to Stirling. He had left them at Bogle House, which the Culter family and the Flemings shared, and had found his town like one with the plague at the door. Court, government, the tougher shreds of army command, had all recoiled on the place, and the streets were a nightmare of horsemen and wagons. More than that: inside the packed lands lived an invisible disease of fright and nerves ten times worse than the newsless, suffering strain of the country because, like proud flesh, it increased on itself. Arran the Governor, awaiting the final, destined disaster of Somerset's attack, saw Mene, Mene, Tekel, Upharsin

73

in lapidary capitals before him and was sick with nerves. The town followed his lead.

At least, Tom found, they had taken thought for the Queen. For a week, the baby had been in hiding with her mother, and Mariotta and Lady Culter, now taking the place of the new-widowed Jenny Fleming, had gone to be at their side. Later, he heard that Christian had been commanded to join them.

He could not even be her escort. He was held fast in Stirling by affairs, and by the necessities of war. On Monday night they heard that Leith was on fire and Holyrood Abbey overthrown; later, that the English Protector had struck camp and was on the move, while an English fleet was sailing farther north. No question now, of being sent to join the Queen, and Christian. Erskine stayed, and lightheaded with the despair of high crisis, the town awaited fresh news.

In the evening, it came. The English army was marching – not west, toward them, but south.

It was news that would be repeated, word for word, as long as they lived. On Monday, it was confirmed. The Protector, at Lauder, was still moving toward England. On Tuesday and Wednesday, fresh reports: the English fleet had simply fortified Broughty Castle on Tayside, and appeared to be waiting only for a wind to leave again. Thursday and today, Hume Castle had fallen to the enemy and had been garrisoned; the English army were now at Roxburgh, and apart from these outposts and the cut and dead wrack left by the storm, the pounding seas had withdrawn and the tide had flowed south.

Impossible to understand why Somerset had failed to press his brilliant advantage. The tired captains in Stirling could only surmise. The cautious pointed to the four English garrisons: two seabound on the open east coast, two within reach of the Border; but jubilation, like a truant, crept up on the town and its army.

Tom Erskine, at last free to escape, was impatient alike of wild opinions and delay, and irritated beyond reason to find Buccleuch in the company on his first visit to Stirling since Pinkie. Particularly when the company, sleek and splendid, was George Douglas, whose elder brother, the Earl of Angus, was head of the House of Douglas in Scotland and father to Lord Lennox's wife.

He walked forward nevertheless and was seized. 'Here, Erskine: you've used 'em. Hackbuts, boy! Damned dangerous things!' Fighting had left Wat Scott of Buccleuch unaltered: bonnet crammed wtih Buccleuch bees, he looked as he had done when, standing with Lord Culter on the Boghall battlements, he had watched smoke rise from the castle where his wife Janet lay with a knife in her shoulder.

And that was a theme painfully close to Erskine's mind – and Sir George's too, it appeared, for interrupting Buccleuch blandly he observed, 'Hullo, Erskine. Come to tell us about poor Will?' And so Tom had to embark, perforce, on his errand.

'I've seen your boy, Buccleuch. He's in good health.' That, at least, was true.

Circumscribed by lowered eyebrows and raised beard, Buccleuch's face did not change. '*Poor* Will?'

Sighing, Erskine discarded finesse. 'He's with Crawford of Lymond.'

The thickets of grey curls tightened. 'Lymond!' bawled Buccleuch. 'As a prisoner? A hostage?'

Tom shook his head. He told the tale quickly: of the English messenger, of Lymond's attack on his brother; of his own arrival which saved Lord Culter. At the end there was a short silence; and though Buccleuch's eyebrows were lowered, there was a pleased spark in his glare. He cleared his throat.

'The fact is, the boy came back from France with a skinful of damned, moony ideas, and I could make nothing of him – nothing at all. So he stamped out, consigning us all to the nethermost hole and the wee deils with the pitchforks. In fact' – he paused, as memory struck him – 'he said he'd probably be there before us. Which explains . . . God, Will!' growled Buccleuch, with a kind of numbed exasperation. 'You'd have a damned nerve to choose Lymond to go to hell with.'

'Oh, come.' Sir George's eyes hadn't left Buccleuch's face. 'I think we're all underestimating him. Be patient, and your Will might surprise you one day.'

Buccleuch returned the stare. 'If you're a decent body by nature, you don't sell your captain, even if he's captain of nothing but carrion.'

'But surely Will knows what Lymond is?' Tom's voice told of anxiety as well as puzzlement.

'Will is no innocent,' said Buccleuch flatly. 'He's a cocky young fool with a head too big for his bonnet, but he's not daft, and he's not twisted. If Lymond took him on, he knew what he was doing. Will won't betray him. He'll rub his own nose in the midden, to make a point of principle to his soft-heided relations, but his great new code of honour'll keep the stink from his nose while he does it. That boy,' snarled Sir Wat, 'thinks with his nether tripes – Let's have some claret, for God's sake.'

* * *

It was evening before Erskine had leave to go.

He took no escort because he knew none was permitted; but turned alone out of the gates of Stirling and rode into the sunset, which flared and died as he went.

It grew dark. Around him, the trees closed in and then fell behind: beyond them were the moors, with the hills of Menteith on his right. In a light wind, grasses hissed like spray. The path became better: he saw cottage lights and smelled wood smoke. Then he was stopped.

That was the first guard. There were two more, past the hamlet of Port, the chapel, the barns, the Law Tree. The last of the beeches moved past him: he gave his name and password and was recognized yet again; and then drew rein.

Black and unrippled at his feet spread the Lake of Menteith, one and a half miles across, island home of his brother's priory; island seat of the Earls of Menteith. Barring its texture lay like ribbons the thousand lights

76

from the two islands in its centre, and music fled across the water: organ notes from the Priory of Inchmahome, where monks sang at Compline and children slept; a consort playing a galliard from Inchtalla, where the Scottish court took its leisure in hiding.

A ferry, already signalled by its prow lantern, arrived, chuckling; and he got in.

* * *

'My dear man,' said Sybilla next day, placidly stitching before Earl John's big fire. 'Admit you've never had to live with eight children on an island, and every one with the instincts of a full-grown lemming.'

The Dowager, who had her own way of reducing tension, sat next to Tom Erskine, her aristocratic nose decorated by a pair of horn-rimmed spectacles hung around her neck on a thin gold chain, the inevitable embroidery on her lap. Christian Stewart was out, and Sybilla was free, which meant that she commandeered both Erskine and Sir Andrew Hunter, newly in with dispatches, to help her entertain Mariotta.

For the attack on Midculter had tumbled Richard's wife into a cold bath of nerves which the upheaval of the last three weeks had not helped at all. The theft of their silver had hardly touched the ledger pages of Richard's wealth: what made her flesh shiver was the thought of Lymond, and the cool, impertinent grip of the mind he had used; in five indifferent minutes pioneering where Richard's diffident courtesy had never taken him. On her husband, too, the incident had borne grossly. She realized as much during the two sleepless, congested days before he left to join the army in the east. Since then, the only news of or from Richard had been that brought by Erskine – news received without comment by the Dowager, who continued to arrange her affairs without further reference to the uncomfortable and icy springs of satire and denunciation. Mariotta turned to Sir Andrew Hunter.

He had been watching her. A distant neighbour, a near-contemporary, a gentle and distinguished landowner and courtier, Andrew Hunter was well known to the Culters, and Mariotta had learned to like him, and to enjoy his kindness, his willing attentions, and an articulate turn of speech which made her now and then sick for home. Now, on a sudden impulse, she addressed him. 'Tell me, Dandy, what do men talk about? Richard, for example?'

He was taken aback, but he answered her. 'What does Richard discuss with other men? Horses, of course. And pigs. And the state of the barley, and the new cocks, and the hawking, and what the Estates are up to, and the wrestlers, and any new shiploads he's expecting, and the rates of exchange, and taxes, and poaching, and pistols, and the price of roofing, and his deerhound litter, and Milanese armour, and the lambing.... Richard's interests,' said Sir Andrew, with a hint of defensiveness in the soft voice, 'are pretty wide.'

'But never dull. I wonder,' said Mariotta, her eyes expressionless, 'what Lymond makes of light conversation?'

Hunter sat up. 'Lymond's conversation doesn't give me a moment's alarm. It's his actions that hurt. Richard's bent on this challenge at the Wapenshaw and, my God! if he goes, it'll be suicide.'

Mariotta's eyes opened. 'But the challenge wasn't serious! Lymond at Stirling'd be under instant arrest. And besides, Richard's the finest shot in – '

She broke off. Hunter was right. What use was all that with an arrow in the back? 'God has a thousand handes to chastise,' had said Lymond, and at Annan he had nearly succeeded. Mariotta opened her mouth, but Sybilla, stabbing industriously with her needle, spoke first. 'Did you hear any word of Will Scott in town, Tom?' And added, composedly, 'We know he's with my son. Sir Andrew brought back news from Annan of his meeting with Richard.'

Saved from plunging a second time into the same diplomatic whirlpool, Erskine sat back, relieved. 'There's nothing new. Saw Buccleuch, as a matter of fact, yesterday and broke the news to him. And that fool George Douglas hovering by while I told him.'

'Where? At Stirling?' Hunter was interested. 'I thought Sir George was with his brother.'

Erskine shrugged. 'He's off to Drumlanrig by now, anyway, thank God: can't thole the man.' His mind was not on George Douglas, but on Christian, and her odd behavior last night. He had gone to the Priory first, with his report, and had been worried because the Queen Dowager kept him late, and Christian might have gone to bed. But when the ferry took him over to Inchtalla, she was waiting in the hall, pulling him by the arm before the usher led him away. 'Tom – in case we have no other chance – the name I asked about? Jonathan Crouch?'

He had told her what she wanted to know, breaking off because the Dowager materialized, carrying her embroidery and standing on his toe because she had forgotten to take off her spectacles. After that, Christian had done no more than thank him firmly for his help and indicate the matter was closed. He was slightly nettled. Despite the noble disclaimers he remembered making she might, he thought, have let him into the secret. . . .

The next day, the autumn trumpets gave tongue, the sun shone like copper, and a flaming row was taking place in the Priory cloisters. To the north the hills of Ben Dearg reared empurpled, and soft airs shuddered on the blue water. On Inchmahome, Discord beat against the ancient pillars, where five adults and a child sat or stood about the green cloisters.

The Queen Dowager of Scotland was in a state of Gallic rage. 'Will someone kindly inform me how this escapade has arrived?' Thus Mary of Guise, seated bolt upright in a carved chair.

Croaking reply from a middle-aged nurse, white as her tortured apron. 'Oh, Madame; that I dinna ken, the puir wee lassie . . .' and she broke off, shooting a basilisk glance at a younger maid, completely overcome, who was being patted my Mariotta.

The Dowager Lady Culter, who was also seated, wisely said nothing, partly out of diplomacy and partly from sheer respect for her vocal chords: a very small child with tousled red hair standing before her continued to hammer on her knee in a detached sort of way, screaming gibberish at the top of her voice.

'Hurble-purple, hurble-purple, hurble-purple!' chanted the child.

'On the rivage, in broad daylight! Murder! Kidnap!'

'She'd cuddle a milk jug, the jaud!'

'Boo-hoo – hic – hoo!'

'Elspet! You'll be ill! Be quiet, now!'

'Hurble-purple, hurble-purple, hurble-*purple!*' said the child with ascending power.

Lady Culter winced slightly, and drawing her knee away, put out a kindly but restraining arm. She spoke briskly. 'I doubt there's no need to hunt for villains, Ma'am; the lass was scatterbrained, and Mistress Kemp as bad, to let her go off alone with the child. But there was no worse intention that I can see. Just an escapade.'

'Escapade!'

Sybilla, after a daunting glance at the hysterical Elspet, returned to her task.

'Yes. The foolish girl had a tryst with one Perkin at Portend Farm, and the child wanted to visit the pleasance. There was a skiff unattended, and off they went to the shore, where Elspet apparently left Mary playing while she went up to the farm – '

'Alone and unattended,' said outraged motherhood grimly. 'And then of course my daughter is accosted, attacked! One hears her screams, the girl returns, thrusts her back into the boat and attempts to return unobserved. Oh, I grant you the girl Elspet is innocent: by returning she doubtless foiled the attempt. But how could such a thing be? Is there not a bodyguard here at Inchmahome ... attendants ... the good fathers? Are there not armed men surrounding the lake, blocking the roads? Dame Sybilla, but for my daughter's screams, where would she be now?'

'Sitting in the Pleasure Gardens, I imagine,' said Lady Culter dryly, 'although I must admit that the attractions of Perkin seem to have played ducks and drakes with our safety precautions. Suppose we ask the Queen's Grace?'

Mary of Guise, Queen Dowager, stretched an arm and called her daughter. 'Marie! Come and tell Maman what the ill-doing man did?'

'What ill-doing man?' asked the red-haired child, trailing over the grass without lifting her dress, and proffering a sticky mouth. 'Can I say my rhyme?'

Her Royal mother, ignoring this, wiped the mouth thoroughly with a clean handkerchief and said, 'The man in the Pleasure Gardens, ma p'tite. What did he say?'

Her Most Noble Majesty Mary, crowned Queen of all Scotland, found her pomander and began to play with it, with unsavory results.

'He wasn't a malfaisant. I liked him. Can I – '

'Mary, was he a monk?' said Sybilla gently, mindful of one of the unlikelier aspects of Elspet's story ('But all the monks are at Sext').

'He was a *nice* monk,' said the child, with a single inflection neatly robbing the statement of all value. She bit the pomander, spat, and relented. 'He said the rhyme, and he knew my name.'

'But . . .' said the Dowager Queen.

'But . . .' said Mariotta.

'I wonder,' said Lady Culter, recognizing defeat, 'if it could be Dean Adam back from Cambuskenneth? He went last Monday, and I suppose – Or a wandering Observant? Oh well, he did her no harm – I think her screams were annoyance when Elspet lost her head and tried to get her into the boat and back.'

'They found no one?'

'No one. Lady Christian herself had been walking there, and heard no one at all in the gardens.'

'Can I,' said the Queen's Most Noble Majesty, with urgency, 'say it now?'

81

'What . . . I suppose so,' said Maman, her brow still furrowed.

'Eh, bien,' said Mary smoothly. She recited.

> *'Hurble purple hath a red girdle*
> *A stone in his belly,*
> *A stake through his arse*
> *And yet hurble purple is never the worse.*

'What is it, what is it, what is it?' roared the Queen.

There was a shaken silence.

Then Lady Culter, in a voice preternaturally grave, said (rather unkindly), 'I think – it's a hawthornberry, is it not, chérie?'

Her Majesty's face fell.

* * *

Christian laughed outright. 'How absurd . . . "Comment le saluroye, quant point ne le congnois?" Of course I recognized who it was. Credit me with ears, at least.'

There was a moment more of the kind of constraint she remembered from their last interview in the cave, then the man beside her gave a mock sigh. 'Forgive my obtruseness. My voice again? Crying the coronoch on high. I'm sorry about the uproar. I didn't expect company, but even so, all would have gone well if that blasted girl hadn't snatched the child so suddenly. Magnificent lungs for her age.'

They sat in the short grass in the middle of the maze a previous Earl of Menteith had designed on the north shore of the lake. Dusty box hedges with an unused air shut off any view of the water: from the rear a folly in marble overhung them.

It was warm and still, as it had been at Boghall, where, as her prisoner and her patient, he had played the lute and sung to her of frogs. Christian hugged her knees. 'But how did the child find you?'

He answered ruefully, 'I fell asleep. Considerably more than doth the nightingale. And the next thing I knew she was sitting on my chest.'

'What did you say?' said Christian, fascinated.

'*She* said, "M. l'abbé" (you'll have gathered I'm dressed like a magpie) – "M. l'abbé, you 'ave greatly insufficient of tonsure." And I said, "Madame la reine d'Ecosse, you are greatly in excess of tonnage." After which exchange of pleasantries . . .'

'She got off?'

'Not at all. She bounced like a cannon ball and said that Dédé –'

'Her pony.'

'– That Dédé had long yellow teeth; and did I know –'

'That,' said Christian in chorus, 'you can tell a person's age from their teeth. That's a favourite one.'

'Oh. Well, as you say. So she opened her mouth, and I pronounced her seven years of age, and she admitted to five. (What is she – four?) Then I opened my mouth –'

'What was it, a pebble?'

'– I opened my mouth and received inside it a small fish, still resisting delivery to its Maker. After that –'

'But what did you do? With the fish?'

'I pretended to eat it,' he said simply. 'Then we played a game or two, and sang a bit, and discussed a number of subjects. Then the nursemaid, or whoever she was, arrived, and whipped off the child, crowing like the cocks of Cramond. And you know the echo, to boot.'

'I wish I'd been there,' said Christian. 'Had you been waiting long? I'd walked to the far end of the garden.'

'Not very long. But I have been, and am, all a-quiver like goose grass. My dear lady, you mustn't toss the secret of the Queen's hiding place at the feet of a complete stranger. It's not in the rules. Quite apart from perjuring yourself on my behalf just now.'

She said regretfully, 'I make some terrible mistakes. But then I'm a very hasty person. You see, they wouldn't let me bring Sym, and I'd no one to send, even if Tom Erskine had found out by Tuesday – which he hadn't. Then old Adam Peebles had to go to Inchkenneth, and I asked him to give a message to Sym so that he could go to the cave and tell you to come today. I had to make the message so garbled . . . and it was a gamble whether Tom

83

would even have reached us by now . . . but he has, so everything has turned out well. Did you have much trouble coming? And getting the robes?'

He brushed the questions aside. 'It wasn't difficult – it should have been more so: the guard is wretched. I came by the hill path, and I had your password. There again . . . I don't mind being a lame duck, but the pond you've put me into has a kingdom in it, my dear. By all means let's play guessing games. "Will you hide me, Yes, par foi! Shall I be found out? Not through me!" – and all the rest of it; but not with your life, or the child's: and think what happened to Eve, at that . . .

'Good God,' he said, coming to a stop. 'I appear to be giving you a miserable nagging for risking your life and reputation for me. Look to me as Wat did to the worm, and relieve my conscience.'

She made no attempt either to answer or to argue with him. 'Is your head quite better?'

To her relief, he accepted the change of subject. 'Quite healed, thanks to you. I fall asleep sometimes rather a lot – as demonstrated – that's all.' He hesitated; then said, 'How do you get back?'

She showed him a whistle at her girdle. 'I blow from the shore, and a boat comes. Then Lady Culter or Mariotta will meet me.' She smiled. 'We're a crowded household.'

He said, 'The Culters. Of course. Who else – Buccleuch?'

She shook her head. 'In Stirling. Tom Erskine had to tell him that – ' She stopped.

'What?'

She said, 'Oh, well. It's common gossip now. His oldest boy Will has joined forces with – '

'– The God of the Flies, the Lord of the Dunghill – I know,' he said. 'How did he take it?'

'Buccleuch? Terribly shocked, and grieved, and remorseful, I think. He felt he's driven him off in a fit of temper.'

'I expect he should have thought of that in the first

place,' he said with unexpected asperity, and she heard him get to his feet. 'My dear lady, they'll wonder what's become of you. Did Erskine really tell you about Crouch?'

She told him, rising with the help of his arm in its coarse monk's robe. 'Crouch is Sir George Douglas's prisoner.'

'Douglas has him!' There was a thoughtful silence.

'Does that help?' she said tentatively.

'Yes, of course it helps. Very much.' He appeared to be in a difficulty. 'Yes . . . I have been postponing . . . Lady Christian, when we last met you were unthinkably kind and generous – for no kind of thanks that I remember making. I swore to myself not to involve you further. Then when I got your message I was irresponsible enough to come here after all. But at least you shan't be in the dark. You shall hear – now – who I am, and if you want to call the guard, I shan't try to escape this time.'

'No!' she exclaimed. '*I don't want to know!*'

There was, for the first time, a weary distaste in his voice. 'But you require to know – you must see that. This secret – the Queen's hiding place –'

'Have you betrayed it? Will you betray it?'

'No.'

'Then leave me ignorant,' said Christian. 'What would make matters easier for your conscience might make them insupportable for mine. I prefer to be selfish. God knows I've been wrong – politically, legally, conventionally and every other way – in judgments before. But these always seemed to me the more irrelevant aspects of human decency . . . You are at least Scottish, I think?'

'Yes.'

'– And in trouble. Well, I'm human,' said Christian. 'I don't want conscience money in the form of secrets: not just now, thank you. But the day you genuinely want help, I'll be proud to have your confidence. Till then, show your thanks, if you wish to, by letting me have news of you sometimes.'

The man was silent. Then he said lightly, 'I can say naught but Hoy gee ho! – words that belong to the cart and the plough. Your confidence is fully misplaced this time, but I imagine you suspected that all along . . . Tell me: would you know again the other voice you heard in the cave?'

She nodded.

'Good,' he said. 'Yes, I shall keep in touch. Not as often as I should like, but certainly more than I ought by all the tenets you quoted.' They were almost out of the shelter of the box hedges, and he stopped and took her hand, as if examining it. 'What in God's name are you going by?' he said. 'Instinct? Intuition?'

'Common sense. Which describes your case as fortunae telum, non culpae.'

He answered, bleakly, in the same language. 'Heu! The darts which make me suffer are my own. Common sense can be a poor guide and an uncertain surgeon. Better – much better – be foolish, like me. God clip you close,' he said, and was gone.

Christian walked to the shore and there blew a nerve-racking blast on the whistle.

4

SEVERAL MOVES BY A KNIGHT

A Knyght ought to be wise, liberall, trewe,
stronge and full of mercy and pite and kepar
of the peple and of the lawe. . . . And therefore
behoveth hym to be wyse and well advysed, for
some tyme arte, craft and engyne is more worth
than strengthe or hardynes . . . for otherwhyte hit
happeth that whan the prynce of the batayll affieth
and trusteth in his hardynes and strength, And wole
not use wysedom and engyne for to renne upon his
enemyes, he is vaynquyshid and his peple slayn.

1 · MISHAP TO A QUEENING PAWN

On Sunday, the day after the affair at Lake of Menteith,
Lord Culter was also taking aquatic exercise of a kind
which all but turned his epithalamics into elegies.

Mariotta, it is certain, was not alone in finding her
husband baffling. Whatever his thoughts about being separated from his wife after three weeks of marriage, Richard
kept them to himself and applied his undeniable ability to
work.

Under his remote, laconic leadership, the Culter men
spent an enlivening week, racing through the night after
Wharton, harrying his outposts and nibbling his tail as he
recoiled on Carlisle. Then, changing with equal aplomb
to the politician's bonnet, Lord Culter set about taping
and testing the mood of the southwestern districts which
had been the theatre of Wharton's operations, and still lay
open to foray and seduction from the south.

The English had left garrisons at Castlemilk and Langholm. These, with his small force, he could not touch; neither could he do a great deal at Dumfries or Lochmaben, or with those unlucky citizens – 'assured Scots' – who lived nearest the shadow of Carlisle and had in sheer self-preservation to buy immunity with promises, and even carry them out sometimes.

But with those nineteen hundred who had promised help for England in August he had surprising success, and when he turned back north for Midculter on Friday, September 23rd, his train was slightly out of hand with high spirits and very little damaged; and he left behind him a number of impressed Johnstones, Armstrongs, Elliots and Carruthers.

Halfway home, he remembered a promise, and sending on most of his men to disperse to their homes, turned aside at Mollinburn with six horsemen to ride through the Lowthers to Morton.

On Sunday afternoon, the party he was expecting came in from Blairquhan, and he left Morton on the Sanquhar road to take the Mennock Pass north. With him rode the Baroness Herries, his six men and two women servants.

Agnes Herries was thirteen years old, inexpressibly rich, and not very pretty. In spite of two years in the Culter household acquiring, supposedly, polish and panache, she still had a loud and energetic voice, poor skin and a passion for *romans idylliques*. Even Sybilla, soul of charity and tolerance, had mentioned to the girl's grandfather that the child had regrettable taste; adding inaccurately that it came no doubt from the late Lord Herries her father, and not from her mother who had thrown over the joys of widowhood for a well-endowed marriage.

Grandfather Kennedy of Blairquhan, who was waiting with ill-concealed impatience for Agnes's two younger sisters to qualify also for Lady Culter's hospitality, had said rapidly that nevertheless she was a dear child and a pleasure about the house. He had then, mindful of his responsibilities, suggested that Lady Culter should take the girl to Court for the autumn. It wasn't to be hoped that she would ever look much better than she did then, and if the Governor expected his son to marry her (they had been affianced since infancy) the sooner they got on with it the better....

Thus Richard, escorting Lady Herries north to stay with his mother at Stirling.

It was a miserable day. Saturday's golden autumn had given way to a wet and sullen Sabbath; the rain dripped from the small feathers in Culter's cap, and showers of drops from Agnes's hood shook onto her nose.

Lest this should be misconstrued, she blew into a sodden handkerchief for the twentieth time and rode stiffly on.

Lady Herries had her own resources. Bodily, she might be damp, cold and in Lanarkshire: in spirit she was with troubadour and minnesinger in the fields of romance. There, in passages of chivalry and courtship, the heroine – thirteen, lovely and highborn – was immutable. The hero, true to legend, was apt to reassemble under pressure into different shapes. The Baroness's eyes at present were fixed on Lord Culter's prosaic back: her lips moved slightly as she rode.

'Daphne! Vision! Shining she-lamb!' Bowing, the prince removed his cap, the little feathers wet with rain. Crying, he said –

'Devil take the rain; there's someone coming. Anyone recognize the standard?' said Richard sharply. His lordship, looking slit-eyed through the downpour, was insensitive to ruined fantasy at his heels. 'Frank! Job!' The two riders in front increased speed for a bit, then wheeled. 'It's Sir Andrew Hunter, sir, and some of the Ballaggan boys.'

In a moment the two parties met. 'Dandy! Echoes from civilization at last. What's happening up north?'

Sir Andrew greeted him smiling, shoulders hunched. 'Worse than the time old Scott's patent water system broke down. I've just left your wife and mother – flourishing both – everyone's safe so far.... Look,' said Hunter. 'We'll drown if we exchange news here. Come with me

89

to Ballaggan – you could do with something hot inside you anyway. Who's the lassie?'

Lord Culter explained and introduced, and the two parties struck off in company for Hunter's house. The rain ran interminably down Agnes's nose. Covertly, she studied Sir Andrew.

Slimmer, and with better hands than Lord Culter. Lord Culter never joked. She liked dark men with a twinkle in the eye.

The prince, a slender dark man . . .

But again, they had halted. The Nith, which lay between themselves and Ballaggan, ran unusually fast and high at their feet, and an outrider who drove his horse in at the ford thudded out again, wet to the stirrups.

Culter was studying the river with some misgiving. 'I doubt the women oughtn't to try.'

For answer, Hunter dropped down the bank and himself rode into midstream. The horse staggered a little with the force, foam gathering at its hocks, but after a moment mastered its footing and stood firm. He called, 'They can't get wetter than they are already. Put a line of horse upstream to break the current. I'll come back and lead you over.'

He splashed back, and giving decorous permission, Agnes was lifted up into Lord Culter's saddle where he held her firmly, lefthanded, the reins in his right. The prince, repigmented instantly from black to brown, pressed his horse into motion while the she-lamb, cheek to chest, approved the even beats of his heart. The impartial grip redoubled; the horse entered the water, and the heiress closed her eyes.

Discomfort claimed her. The saddle poked and prodded; the powerful feet threw up snatches of spray, and she was rubbed, pricked and jagged by Culter's unaccommodating attire. He began moreover to talk to the horse. Mild resentment overtook her.

When they were halfway over, there was a sickening lurch. Culter exclaimed sharply; the pommel drove sharply into the girl's side and briefly the sky was made, blackly, of a shaking, arched mane. Then horse, rider and heiress fell, stirrups free, and in a bruising splash of colliding bodies, Agnes Herries hit the water. Wrenched from periastral dreams she became Lady Herries, just thirteen years old, and screamed and screamed with choking, soundless hysteria as the current spun her in rough fingers and shot her, buoyed up by petticoats, straight down the Nith.

Intense cold, and a weight pulling her down. Waterlogged hair, like a curtain of weed on her face, filtering air bubbles through a throat choked with water. A seething clamour in the head and a bubbling voice – her own.

A gasping voice – someone else's. Then a hand, shuddering with effort, in her armpit, and another hand ripping the cloak from her throat, wringing her hair off, exposing her face. An agony of air; an interval of bumping and pressure that hurt, and then of retching that hurt worse, her cheek pressing on mud. And then, at last, she heard a voice clearly. 'My God, we need practice at that. Shall we do it again?' said Lord Culter.

2 · A KNIGHT WINS AN EXCHANGE

They put her to bed, wrapped in woollens, and she slept, weak and full of hot milk, until the daylight had gone.

Below, in the overornate hall, Lord Cutler lay in a lugged chair, displaying collected impassivity once more, bathed and with his cuts dressed, and wearing a loose gown borrowed from Sir James Douglas, their host.

For they were in a Douglas household, instead of Hunter's elegant, exhausted estate of Ballaggan. Alone and without help, Richard had brought Agnes Herries ashore: his own men were upstream and Andrew Hunter, far ahead, had been deaf to his shouts. But afterward, warned by the commotion, he had raced to their aid, wrapped the girl in his own cloak and carried both swimmers to Drumlanrig, the cavalcade following. Ballaggan was nearly an hour's journey away and could wait. These two could not.

The house of Drumlanrig was full of Douglases, and whether sincere or not, their welcome was a suitable blend of shock and cordiality. From Lord Culter they heard simply that his horse had put his near hind in a pothole; but listening to Hunter they were left in no doubt that Richard had saved the girl's life.

Downstairs the owner of Drumlanrig had demanded the whole tale yet again for his wife's two brothers, the Earl of Angus and Sir George Douglas. Sly and splendid as a half-tamed leopard, Sir George had smiled; and the Earl, lissom Royal lover of thirty years ago lost in alcoholic fat and sparse beard, had been free if trite with his compliments.

The evening passed. Most of the household went early to bed. Sir James and Angus had gone and silence lay on the three still sitting before the big fire. In his deep chair, Culter was motionless, his face lost in shadow. Andrew Hunter glanced at him, and Sir George Douglas, alert on the second, said, 'He's asleep, I think. Did you wish to say something private?'

Sir Andrew smiled gratefully. 'Not at all. But I did want to open up a small matter of business.' He went on, with some hesitation.

'You may not know, but a cousin of mine, a great favourite of Mother's, was taken in '44, and has been in Carlisle ever since.' He paused awkwardly. 'I have a good little estate, you see, but not a very profitable one, and Jeff has no other relatives – '

'But of course,' said Sir George with fine courtesy. 'Not a word more. I shall be delighted. How much . . . ?'

Hunter flushed a deep red. 'No. I – It's true we can't pay what they ask. But if, for example, I could repay in kind . . .'

'An exchange of prisoners? Yes, I suppose that would be one way out.'

'So I went to Annan. But I was unlucky,' Hunter said, flushing again. 'And then I heard – '

'– That I have a prisoner,' said Sir George. 'Yes, I have. With a fearful stock of conversation – I've forgotten his name – Couch, or Crouch.' He thought for a bit while Sir Andrew watched, his face a little anxious.

Then Douglas said pleasantly, 'All right. I'll sell him to you for a hundred crowns. You needn't feel it's charity; and I expect it's a good deal less than they were asking for your cousin.'

'Yes . . . I'm afraid it *is* charity,' said Hunter rather ruefully. 'You could probably sell him yourself for – '

'– Very little,' said Sir George dryly, crossing a superb leg in blue silk. 'Don't worry: he's yours. Will you send for him?'

'Right away!' Sir Andrew got up with rather touching enthusiasm. 'I'll give you a bill for the money now, if I can find paper and ink. Excuse me, sir: and believe me, I'm most grateful.' He betook himself off, shuffling over the rushes a little in his borrowed shoes.

The silence lengthened. Then Sir George Douglas said, 'Why so silent, Lord Culter? Don't you approve of such transactions?'

Culter opened his eyes, and the faintest smile crossed his lips. 'Sir, when two friends discuss money, the third friend should invariably be asleep.'

Sir George laughed, and rising, clapped him on a brocade shoulder. 'Poppyhead! Get to bed, man!'

* * *

Lady Herries, arranged in antique pose at the breakfast table, laid a large and languid hand on her chest. 'Do you think,' said Agnes, gazing hopefully at her troubadour, 'do you think I ought to ride your horse today again?'

Lord Culter, who had just finished stuffing himself with baked crane and sack, said robustly, 'Not if you want to get to Stirling this week. You'll be perfectly all right in your own saddle. Anyway, don't you want to be in time to see the papingo?'

Lady Herries dropped a slice of bread, instantly lost to the dogs, and in ringing tones unsoftened by immersion, demanded data. 'Is it a real parrot?'

'Quite real,' said Sir Andrew solemnly. He put down

his tankard. 'Bright blue and yellow, with a beak like Buccleuch's.'

She said with vigour, 'My faith, I should like a papingo. I wonder how you feed them. What a waste to kill it! I suppose they'll hang it on a high pole?'

'They will. And my Lord Culter and a number of other gentlemen will shoot at it. And there'll be wrestling, and throwing, and tilting at the ring, and running, and prizes given; and then a fair all afternoon and half the night . . .'

Agnes snapped him up. 'A fair!'

Remembering something, Hunter looked across her head. 'By the way, Richard: I hope you won't be fool enough to . . . that is, your womenfolk are pretty anxious about Lymond.' He broke off, daunted by Culter's continued silence. 'Oh, well. None of my business. She'll tell you herself.'

Culter stirred and raised his eyes. They fell on Agnes, looking at him with rather a silly expression. He smiled at her. 'Child, relations are the devil. Think yourself lucky yours don't bother you. Will you come and see me shoot at this wretched bird?'

This was self-sacrifice was a vengeance. Sir Andrew threw his lordship a commiserating grin, and felt it stiffen on his lips at the look in the other man's eyes. Hot water under cold ice, then, he thought. He wasn't surprised.

* * *

'And there they go, poor dears,' said Sir George. He watched the two parties ride down the long, wet avenue and then leave the Drumlanrig policies – Hunter to the northwest; Culter and the girl for the Dalveen road.

The Earl of Angus, who hadn't bothered to get up, grunted from the fire. 'Pity the river wasn't a lot higher. That whelp Culter's done a lot of harm in the south.'

'Don't be crude.' Sir George admonished his brother, moving away from the window. 'All the same, I wish that damn fellow Lymond would get on with it. Can't we induce him to be a little more persevering?'

Sir James said, 'We can't contact him: you know that. No one can.'

'Well, one man could,' pointed out Angus. 'That brat Will Scott apparently met him in broad daylight, as plain as a fishwife on Friday.'

'Proving only that Lymond wanted to be met,' said Sir George. 'I wish to God the man would stick to one side. What I couldn't do with his intelligence system! The Protector told me – he lifted all of Wharton's campaign gold at Annan, and left your precious son-in-law Lennox black in the face.'

He looked curiously at his brother. 'What went on between Lymond and Lennox anyway? If Margaret was involved, you'd do well to hush it up.'

The Earl of Angus brushed this aside. 'No one's going to clap Margaret Douglas in the Tower these days – cousin of Edward of England; a daughter of an ex-Queen of Scotland; the wife of the Earl of Lennox, with a claim to the throne every bit as good as Arran?'

'But not as good as young Queen Mary's.'

Angus was contemptuous. 'God's Mass, George: there's bigger game than governerships and pensions. Edward's sickly. Look at him. And our Queen's four years old: well, they die like flies at that age. Arran's a fool. So's Lennox; but he's married to Margaret. And Margaret's heir to –'

'Heir to nothing,' said Sir George wearily. 'You know perfectly well Henry of England disinherited her from the succession in the midst of his uxorial fluctuations. And on top of that, she had a cracking row with him the week before he died, and he cut her out of his will. Edward, Mary Tudor, Elizabeth and then the Suffolk infants. Not a word of his own niece.'

'Yes. Well. She's highly strung.'

'Highly strung! God, Archie, that wasn't what you called her mother.'

'Oh, be quiet, George,' said the head of the Douglases. 'What do you want, anyway? The trouble with you is, you keep letting the Protector push you too far. One of these days, the Scottish Queen Dowager will see what you're up to, and then bang goes Douglas and Drumlanrig, Dalkeith, Coldingham, Tantallon and your fine neck into the bargain.'

'On the other hand,' said Sir George painstakingly, 'if the Protector feels we are insufficiently helpful, he sends in a raiding party, and bang they all go just the same.' He studied his brother's heavy, once-handsome face. He had never in his life had to worry about searching questions from Archie, and he was thankful now that it was the same old ground.

His sister's husband, Sir James, said a little petulantly, 'You're talking as if the invasion was over for good. Is the Protector really going south?'

'Oh, yes.' Sir George smiled. 'He'd only food for a month, and he didn't get the local support he'd expected – notably from the Douglases, Archie: now d'you wonder that I've been so forthcoming with him? Then a really nasty political mess flared up in London: be thankful, dear, that you have a prudent brother. The Protector's young twig of fraternity is graithing himself a nice sharp axe for Tower Green.'

He tilted the ruby on his finger, and a beam of sunlight ran over a sardonic cheekbone.

'Andrew Dudley's stuck with an English garrison at Broughty; Luttrell at St. Colme's Inch; and that senile idiot Lady Hume persuaded to give up Hume Castle. He'll fortify Roxburgh, most likely, on his way south, and supply 'em all through the winter from Berwick and Wark.' He grinned. 'An entertaining prospect, isn't it?'

Angus and Sir James looked gloomy. 'And what then?' asked his brother.

'Oh, well.' Sir George kicked a log into place in the fire. 'The Queen Dowager here, of course, will try to get some money and troops out of France. Meantime, the Protector can't do much: bad roads, difficult supply lines, winter weather and all that. He'll probably hang out until spring, and then fling in his full strength before the French come, using all these garrisons as jumping-off points.'

He looked consideringly at the Earl. 'If I were you,

Archie, I should wait until the really bad weather, and then suggest that your precious Lennox comes north with a raiding party. They'll never do it, but it'll assure the English of your good will. And then come the spring, why not ask them to send Margaret too? A joint command . . . that would stiffen Lennox's back for him!'

Sir James, in painful doubt as to whether this was meant to be humorous or not, said feebly, 'And who'll command from Berwick, I wonder?'

'Who d'you think?' said Sir George. He laughed. 'Old Grey of Wilton, recovered from swallowing a billhook, and talking, I'm told, like a featherbed with a leak in it. Do you know Lord Grey, Archie?'

Angus shook his head.

'He's been in France for years: a clammy, stiff-backed old pike. The billhook, I'll bargain, came out lichened over.' He laughed again. 'The first encounter between the old lad and Lord Wharton I shall see or die. They'll be heaving each other's guts out of the window.'

'Well,' said the Earl of Angus crossly, 'what's so funny about that? . . . You're a weird sort of devil, George,' said his brother with the flatness of long usage.

5
CASTLING

The rybauldes, players of dyce And the messangers
and corrours ought to be sette tofore the rook.
For hit apperteyneth to the rook . . . to have men
convenable for to renne here and there for
tenquyre and espie the place and cyties that
mygth be contrarye to the kynge.

1 · CAPTURE OF SOME ADVANCING PIECES

Will Scott of Kincurd was stringing his bow and singing.

> *Le douxiem' mois de l'an*
> *Que donner à ma mie?*

Life at the moment was not unbearable. He was well-fed
and warm. He had that morning shot a buck at a hundred
and seventy yards and been congratulated by Matthew.
He had a new ambition: in this penumbral region to cast
a shadow bigger, grander and more devastating than
Lymond's.

> *Douz' bons larrons*
> *Onze bons jambons*
> *Dix bons dindons*

It had not, he conceded, been easy to progress greatly
toward this goal in a month, allowing as well for the
hiatus which followed the Annan affair. His own state of
superficial injury he shared, he had discovered, with half
the troop. Dead men there were none; a telling enough
point in a retreat which had been hard-fought and narrowly won.

For Lymond had genius. When building his force, he had taken sixty heterogeneous ruffians and cut and buffed them like diamonds, each rootless creature made an artist in his own small field. Some of their stories he had already from Matthew.

Dandy-puff, of the bog-cotton hair, was their farrier, and at the horn over a small matter of a cousin's sudden death which had unluckily brought to light a series of other unexplained mishaps.

Oyster Charlie, the cook, who bore young Scott no ill will ('It's not your fault, lad: the Master's an unchancy bastard to cross.') had been dentally denuded by an infuriated husband who was also a barber and now, untimely, with Abraham.

Jess's Joe (scout) was the ex-leader of a profitable band of dock thieves; the Lang Cleg (armourer) had been racked twice, but remained an unrepentant and unskilful pickpocket. Skinner, an ex-priest, was their barber-surgeon and, at need, their confessor; Cuckoo-spit, a magician with horses, had forgotten polite usage for rheum, if he ever knew it, in five draughty years in the Tolbooth . . .

> *Neuf boefs cornus*
> *Huit moutons tondus*
> *Sept chiens courants*
> *Six lièvres aux champs*

These figures, he knew, were the grotesques in the bestiary. There were also unmarked, homeless men who for some reason had lost their farms and families, or had left them; individualists and misfits; and mercenaries like Turkey Mat, who had sold their swords over half Europe before one day falling in with Lymond and being brought here by him.

'Why is he back?' he had once asked Mat.

Matthew had grinned. 'Just to be neighbourly. Besides, there're two or three folk he wanted to see.'

'Jonathan Crouch?'

99

Turkey's gaze was direct. 'That's one. How did you know?'

'He told me. . . . Mat, you've had three years of it. How d'ye thole him?'

Mat had chuckled gently. 'Over there in Appin, a place you've never heard of, there's a bien stone house with an honest pinch of soil to it, and a doocot and an orchard and some fine dry byres. It's mine for the taking, that house, and, man, when I've cooked my own fatted calf at the Master's fire, it's me for the white beach, groaning belly and all. I'll lie on it from morning to nightfall throwing dice against myself, and whiles winning. . . . I can thole him; I can thole him.'

> *Cinq lapins trottant par terre*
> *Quatre canards volant en l'air*

He had asked Mat about Bullo.

'Johnnie? Johnnie's King of Little Egypt, and a law to his sweet sleekit self. He rules his wee pack of gypsy stoats like the Grand Turk, and keeps them happy with silk shirts and buckles forbye. You should see him work in a fair: it's a scholastic education. Johnnie,' said Mat, not without rancour, 'has all the old crafts.'

Scott said, 'I thought he worked for Lymond?' and Mat had shaken his head, rubbing rhythmically, whether of necessity or through association of ideas it was hard to tell.

'I suppose you would cry it a business partnership,' said he solemnly. 'But when their interests collide, I'm feart it's every man to his own dirk. Watch 'em together next time. Our John's sly as a snake, but he can't resist playing with Lymond, wit against wit. Man, he's welcome,' had said Mat with emphasis.

> *Trois ramiers des bois*
> *Deux tourterelles*
> *Une pertriolle . . .*

Will was ready for lapping. He picked up the waxed thread and glanced at the ruined Peel Tower, their present headquarters, which he controlled during Lymond's current absence. They moved about throughout the year, he knew: sometimes to farms; sometimes in the open or under canvas; sometimes to deserted buildings like this one.

They were extravagantly paid, all of them. In return, they suffered a grinding and despotic discipline. In Lymond's hands they were fashioned into a shining and precise instrument for advanced theft, blackmail and espionage; and faults in the instrument were dealt with instantly and with a horrid inventiveness.

For the thick-skinned, there was physical punishment. There was also a less respectable kind. Scott had seen, and would not forget, a courageous and rational man on his knees, weeping tears through his fingers as skin after skin of self-respect and human dignity peeled off him under Lymond's verbal lash.

He learned to recognize from the slurred walk and the gentle dishevelment when Lymond was no longer quite sober; and with the rest to walk softly at such times. He didn't mind. He had reached the point where he would notice nothing beyond the beauty and efficiency of superbly planned crime. One should always flee the impure. He was out of the muddle of truths and half-truths, and into the daylight. Only when – if – he were in Lymond's shoes, there were a few things he would change.

Scott finished the knots, smiling.

> *Une pertriolle*
> *Qui vole et vole et vole*
> *Une pertriolle*
> *Qui vole du bois au champ.*

* * *

The Master's party returned to the tower just before dawn, rampaging hungry and saddle-sore. They fell over and quarrelled with the litter of sleeping bodies, kicked up the cooks and battered one of the boys until he had got the tallow dips and fires going again.

Scott and Matthew, cursing, got them settled down after

a bit, and when the horses had been seen to and food was on the board, Will climbed the stairs to Lymond's room.

The yellow-headed man had lit a candle, showing his hair and clothes full of dust, and was reading what seemed to be a letter. Scott said, 'Nothing to report, sir. Did you have a good night?' with a professional woodenness, a little overdone.

Lymond hardly looked up. He finished reading, unbuckling his belt with one hand; then laid down the paper and threw scabbard and belt on the bed. 'Excellent, Marigold. One generally does, at the Ostrich.'

This was true. The Ostrich was an inn within first-posting stage on the Cumberland side of the London road, whose comforts were peculiarly comforting and whose clientele was select.

Scott said nothing. The Master, who seemed unusually happy, pulled off his boots, slung them across the room and slopped some ale from jug to cup.

'A splendid night,' said Lymond, running on. 'Of wyne and wax, of gamyn and gle. And profitable. Indeed, it's an instruction to see how human messengers-at-arms can be, when they set their minds to it, if it's minds I mean. Sic peril lies in paramours. Oh, well. And that, my Wally Gowdy, was only half the night's work.'

Scott said obediently, 'And the other half?'

'Concerned a distinguished nobleman set upon by marauders on the high road to Scotland, until bravely rescued by myself . . .'

Scott gave up. 'I didn't know you'd turned philanthropist.'

Lymond produced the sweet-rancid smile. 'I refer you to John Maxwell. He gave me to understand he was my eternal debtor for saving his life. And at that,' he said, laying down the empty cup, 'your colleagues fought each other like shrews. I thought at one time the Cleg was going to forget himself and spit me.'

Scott understood. 'This was Maxwell of Threave and Caerlaverock? You want him in your debt?'

'The Master of Maxwell,' said Lymond, 'is an important

102

personage entirely surrounded by English. D'you play chess?'

Scott, knowing him less than sober, was unstartled. He nodded.

'Then you should recognize an opening for smothered mate. Which reminds me: copy that, will you? Unless you still despise my cunning clerking?'

This had once been a sore point with Scott: now he had other things on his mind. Taking Lymond's letter, he remarked, 'I suppose you know the men are getting restless, sir?' and was lucky to get instant backing.

'God, you've hit it,' Mat, entering, yawned and eased his shoulders. 'Too much intrigue, sir, and too little rape: the boys are as unnatural nervy as water fleas. . . . And besides,' he added practically, 'we're nigh out of beer.'

The Master, leaning back, crossed his legs. 'Good God. I knew we were sprendthrifts, lechers and soaks: can we possibly be bored as well?'

This was taken at its face value by Mat. 'Well, it's three weeks since they last had a chance to spend anything, and a month since they had anything to spend.' He added reasonably, 'Anything with women and money in it.'

Lymond closed his eyes. 'Fie on their labour! Fie on their delight! Must I supply the cattle with toys? No, by God: I've affairs of my own to look after.'

There was a pause. Scott stayed dumb, but Turkey's disapproval could be seen, and even heard. The Master, less characteristically, gave a hiccough of laughter. 'Poor Mat. Sic strange, intestine, cruel strife. Alas, father, my mirth is gone. I see you think we must pander to this levity. What do you suggest?'

Turkey Mat's face broke into a relieved grin. 'Well, now; there's maybe one of the Douglas houses would repay a visit. Or Cothally Castle – Seton's away? Or a nice puckle sows from the Malinshaw –'

'Grey of Wilton's in Hume Castle,' said Scott.

'Or there's old Gledstanes, who broke his bond to us last month –'

'– If you took Grey –'

'– And Jardine of Applegarth must have got a consideration from Wharton –'

'– If you took Grey, you could set Arran and the Protector bidding against each other for him. Damn it, am I invisible?' said Scott, irritated, as Lymond's eyes remained speculatively on Mat.

Absently, Lymond shook his head. 'Fond Folie, sall I be thy Clark? And answer thee ay, with Amen?' He bent a cornflower-blue gaze on Scott. 'One: have you seen Hume since it was fortified? I thought not. Two: we should be outnumbered roughly four to one. Three: this is a diversion, not an act of war; and four: you have a hole in one elbow, and I wish to God you'd keep your boots clean.'

Scott did not bother to look down. He persevered. 'If the men will follow me, will you give me leave to try it on my own?'

The Master was flippant.

> 'And he took out his little knife
> Loot a' his duddies fa'
> And he was the brawest gentleman
> That was amang them a'. . . .'

He grinned and got up. 'Not yet, my Hinnysopps. My gentlemen are quaint cattle. You must teach them to trust you before you set up as their Rex Nemorensis. . . . Well, Mat!' He clapped Turkey on the shoulder. 'Go summon the sheep before the wolf, and we'll see.'

By the time the Master walked onto the broken dais and hitched himself on the edge of a board, the men were alerted and waiting, chewing, hugging their knees in the straw, and reasonably quiet.

Lymond collected eyes; began: 'A number of curious blunders have come to light, gentlemen, which seem to be of a piece with your general behaviour over the last week . . .' And finished ten retching minutes later with: 'I would remind you that you're here to carry out orders, not to discuss them. That's the only reason you *are* here, and not in quicklime at the crossroads. Disobey me in action *or* in spirit, gentlemen, and you'll stay alive for much longer than you want to. . . .'

Absolute silence.

'That being so,' continued the Master gently, 'I want volunteers for work tomorrow night. No one who isn't ready to exert his talents to the fullest need trouble. The rest can put up a hand. Now!'

The hands rose, slowly at first, then multiplying. Behind their chief's back, Scott and Turkey scanned the hall. Every arm was up.

The shadow of a smile crossed Lymond's face. He waited as the arms dropped, and spoke into sullen silence.

'At dusk tomorrow night a supply train of wagons is due to leave Roxburgh Castle for Hume. Among other things, it will contain the month's supply of beer for Lord Grey and the Hume garrison –'

The bang of relief and approval hit the ruined roof and brought mouldering plaster down on their regardless heads. An anonymous voice skirling through the din gave it its leitmotif. 'Now you're talking!' it shrieked. 'Now you're bloody well talking!'

Scott thought, 'Don't they realize they're sixty to one?' And answered himself wryly. 'He's the Golden Goose. They'll never touch him.'

He said to Mat, 'Your credit.'

Turkey shook his head. 'Listen. He's had it planned for days.' He sighed. 'Man, man: he can play them like a chanter.'

But Scott was listening to the Master's voice explaining the forthcoming raid; giving times, places and numbers, and making it crystal clear that anyone attempting to force Hume Castle itself had no future whatever.

Rightly or wrongly, Will Scott called that an overstatement.

To ride cross-country from Eskdale to Teviotdale is good for the liver; to do it without being seen healthier still.

The forty-five men who passed over the hills next day with Lymond and Will Scott were fortified, within and without, and sang impolite songs in discreet harmony, syncopated by beer and rough ground.

They reached the Tweed at dusk, crossed between Dryburgh and Roxburgh, and had the last of the beer and some ham and biscuits apiece, after leaving a couple of men to the north of Roxburgh. Then they lit a very small fire and settled down to a ferocious night at the dice.

The outposts came up just after midnight.

Lymond received them from a comfortable hollow in a stone outcrop, where he played a solitary game of his own with a worn pack of cards.

'They're coming, Master!' Excited in spite of himself, the Lang Cleg was peching. 'They left Roxburgh an hour back, coming the way you said. Thirty horse and five drivers; three carts and two heavy wains with oxen pulling.'

'Oxen!' Lymond looked up for the first time from his game.

The Cleg nodded. 'They took them on at Roxburgh and left some of their horses. It'll be the ordnance carts. They're ower heavy, and the castle's hard up for horses.'

Lymond said, dealing again, 'Thirty horses. How many mares?'

'Ten geldings and twenty mares, fairly fresh. They must have come up from Berwick yesterday and rested all evening.'

'All right.' Lymond gathered up the cards and stood up.

'Scott! Matthew! They're taking the route we thought and should be among the thorn scrub before the moon rises.'

He recapitulated briefly. Scott watched sardonically. ('The great leader in action.')

'We aim to disable, not to kill. We take important hostages, if any, and you, Matthew, select the beer and any other goods we need. Then we split: Scott takes as many men as he needs, parcels the rest of the prisoners, loads them into a cart with any goods we don't want, and drives them as near Melrose as he can get, joining us thereafter. Understood?'

Mat, who hadn't heard of the latest refinement, grinned. 'Melrose! Daddy Buccleuch'll be pleased!'

Scott waited for the sour smile. It duly appeared. 'Payment for goods received, let's say. Scott concurs, don't you? All right. Cry boot and saddle, my dears, and we're off.'

He turned the impervious gaze on the company. 'To horse, you drouthy maggots. Are you deaf?'

* * *

By the time the maggots were duly embedded, one mile south of Hume Castle, the English supply train was still toiling north and everybody in it was sick to death of the oxen.

The beasts straddled the causeway, two to a wainload, surging unprogressively through the night with poached and indolent eye. Behind them groaned the carts, tamped with humped canvas, and behind that, more carts, horse drawn. The mounted escort, fidgetting on all sides, was in a foul temper and raw-alert.

The night, moonless and unsympathetic, stretched around them, and visibility at thirty yards granted them a view of a quantity of stunted thorns.

The bullocks puffed gently, and a mare snickered. She was answered by one of the other horses.

Above the wheel-rumbling, someone cursed. 'Hold her nose! We don't want the whole God-damn percussion band.' But as he said it, one of the cart horses threw back its head and presented the night with a splitting neigh.

'Wait a minute!' They listened; while the speaker laid hands on the ox harness and the procession rolled to a halt.

There was silence – broken by a dim beat far out in

the night. Then the first tap was begetting others and the pattern was recognizable. Horses, in a solid body, were sweeping in on them from the moor.

A crackle of orders arose; hurried movements and sudden, heavy breathing: bows, pikes and lances readied, they made for the shelter of the carts. They barely got there before, out of the night, dim forms came flying, heaving, nudging, bouncing and kicking in a cacophony of horse language. Lost in the flailing morass, with their own mounts rearing and threshing, the supply men had a confused impression of barrel ribs, rolling eyes and merciful, saddleless backs.

'Blood an' bones!' They were hoarse with anger and relief. 'It's a damned great herd of wild ponies. Get away with you! Off! Off!' And they rose out of shelter, cursing and whipcracking at the steaming bare backs and flying manes. Hoofs sparked on the stones; horses neighed, nosed, bumped and reared.

The hill pony is a stout and independent citizen: bold, uncatchable, inquisitive and gregarious. The herd went seriously to work, exploring all these and fresh talents. The mares were going silly and even the oxen were beginning to plunge.

'Hell an' thunder!' said someone, taking a moment's breathing space to have a good look. 'That's funny!'

'What the hell's funny about it?' snapped someone else, bucketting past with heels flapping like windmills.

'Well, for instance,' said the first speaker, gasping, 'every one of these brutes is a stallion.'

But nobody heeded him, for just then the leading wain rolled in bovine panic off the road and sank two wheels up to the axle in mud.

They were attempting to drag it out, to calm the bullocks, to chase off the ponies and to control their mounts when Lymond's men descended like moths; and even then they lost seconds in realizing that these horses had riders. The infiltration was neat and unspectacular, involving close-quarter cudgel work and little injury: there were simply fewer and fewer vertical English and finally none at all. It took them longer to round up the ponies again than it had taken to capture the train.

It was a first-class haul. Matthew supervising, flour, biscuits, oats, meat, and leather powder bags with serpentine and corn powder were unloaded and put up in creels ready strapped to their own horses. One cart with hackbuts, bills, bows and arrow sheaves was unstrapped from the oxen and harnessed to a team of ponies. The rest of the ponies, without exception, carried beer.

A wooden box, heavily padlocked, yielded to maltreatment and proved, satisfyingly, to hold the end of the month's wages. It was tied to Matthew's saddlebow.

Lymond watched, moving everywhere. To Scott, roping prostrate bodies together, he intoned: 'Sawest not you my oxen, you little, pretty boy? With hemp, with howe, with hemp.... Any familiar faces? – No, of course: you wouldn't know.'

He looked over the silent row of gagged figures. 'Unfortunate. A Spanish captain, and not worth his own weight in olive stones. Take 'em all to Melrose, and the rest of the wagons too. How many do you want for escort?'

Scott said quickly, 'I have ten men: that'll do.'

'All right, Barbarossa. Allez-vous-en, allez, allez. You've a job to do before dawn.'

Scott nodded earnestly, and rode back to load up the leading cart with his prisoners.

* * *

The English lookout at Hume Castle, slumped in the empty fire pan on the roof, was doing sums gloomily in his head. Below, night hid the great sweep of the Tweed valley and the Merse. Slabbed with fortifications, packed with soldiers, and stuck on a precipice with a six-foot curtain, the place was as safe as Durham Cathedral ... and he was bored.

If the old man sent up the pay from Berwick, he was due two pounds for the month. Then he owed twelve shillings for food. That left ...

He groaned, working it out. It was a relief when he

heard the wagons approaching, and caught glimpses of activity at the gatehouse, and familiar riding dress. He made for the bell rope. 'Supply train from Berwick, ho! There's the beer, Davie-boy!' sang the lookout.

Long before the portcullis was down, word had gone from the fire pan to the allure, and the allure to the keep, where sat Sir William Grey, thirteenth Baron Grey of Wilton, Field-marshal and Captain-general of the horse, Governor of Berwick, Warden of the East Marches and General of Northern Parts on behalf of His Majesty King Edward VI of England.

Few commanders enjoy visiting outposts in enemy country: the risks of making a fool of oneself are relative to the distance from base.

Through an unlucky incident at Pinkie, Lord Grey was, as it happened, in a fair way toward doing this in any case for a little, whether he liked it or not. Sitting at his temporary desk, sleek, pink and picturesque, hair and beard a silver perfection above splendid riding clothes, he was in as petulant a mood as a gentleman of quality can be.

'I with to God,' said his lordship bitterly to his secretary, 'I with to God I wath thtuck with the Crewth again. Even Boulogne and that damn rhymthter Thurrey wath plain thailing to *thith*.'

Mr. Myles rigidly agreed.

Lord Grey gave him a sharp look; then ruffled impatiently through the papers before him. He picked one out, and slapped it down again with the same gesture.

'Fifteen labourerth dithappeared during the work at Roxthburgh: four Thpanith bombardierth and twelve pikemen climbed the wallth and gone home. If I could, I'd do it mythelf. No beer: not enough food. How can I thatff garrithonth without gold and thupplieth? And how do they think they can get thupplieth to uth when winter thetth in? Hell and perdithion!' said Lord Grey, goaded to fury by the unfair stings of Fortune. 'Ith there no word in the Englith language wanting an Eth?'

Mr. Myles was saved by the entrance of Dudley, regular

captain of the garrison, bringing the leader of the Berwick supply train to report.

'Mr. Taylor, my lord,' said Dudley; and stood back.

Mr. Taylor, a personable young man with red hair, was coolly received. 'Taylor? I was ekthpecting one of my men from Berwick.'

Taylor, in the more normal person of Will Scott, had anticipated this question. He said smartly. 'I've just arrived at Berwick, sir. I had some of your men with me, but was asked to leave the more experienced ones at Roxburgh.'

'I thee,' said Grey noncommittally. 'Well, what have you brought with you?'

He read the lists proffered without comment; handed them to Dudley with an air of private martyrdom, and turned again to Scott.

'Your men being looked after?'

'Yes, my lord.' He wasn't afraid of that. They all wore clothes stripped off the real English, and the lists were authentic. 'Ten men below, sir: I put two or three to guard the wagons until ordered to unload. Beer, my lord,' he added in explanation.

'Good. Any meth – word from London?'

Scott, standing at the door, said still briskly, 'One verbal message for yourself, sir, from his Grace. I was to deliver it for your ear only.'

Surprise registered briefly on all three faces, then the secretary, laying his papers deferentially on the edge of the desk, caught Grey's eye and left the room. Dudley raised an eyebrow and stayed.

Scott said, 'I'm sorry, sir: my orders are . . .'

Grey said, 'Thir Edward remainth,' because to his mind a general should appear to keep no secrets from a cousin of the Earl of Warwick. He hoped the boy had some discretion.

Scott, fulminating, wished his lordship had less.

At this moment of impasse the window fell in.

A second later, a crack like the Eildons parting fell on their ears, and a bouquet of flame bellied up from the courtyard.

111

Grey strode to the window and Dudley had begun to follow when, under cover of chain detonation and shouting outside, Will Scott leaped. Dudley, overcome before he realized it, gave a muffled groan and rolled over, stunned by an efficient blow on the prominent jaw.

The explosion had taken place in the middle of the newly arrived wagon train. The carts had already disappeared in smoke, and the nearest thatches were blazing merrily. Grey, staring out, saw the yard striped with shadows running haphazard about the well and courtyard. Then Woodward, Dudley's lieutenant, appeared below, and some sort of order began to materialize.

Grey opened his mouth and turned, missing in that instant a descending stick, and found himself promptly pinned from behind, with an arm across his mouth.

He bit, fruitlessly and painfully. He kicked, with better results; then, summoning his considerable reserves, embarked on a wrestling trick which most mercenaries would have recognized, but Scott did not. The boy held the older men as long as he was physically able, and then fell back for the fatal instant that was necessary for his lordship to shout, 'Help! Guard! *Athathinth*!' having little time to choose his words; and that was long enough for the guard outside to burst in, and for Dudley to erupt onto his feet.

In the brief and damaging interval which followed, the fighting was less preventative than justly punitive. By the time the interloper had been knocked to, on, and across the floor, the room was packed with avidly assisting soldiery, and the affair had taken on the look of a riot.

Dudley, at a sign from Grey, cleared them all out and gave orders to lock up all the men who were with Taylor. Two pikemen were set against the door, and then Dudley, after a brief inquiry below, joined his lordship in studying his bedraggled captive.

The ex-Mr. Taylor lay on a small carpet, bleeding copiously from the nose and with the beginnings of a glorious black eye. His shirt showed white through the tears in his jerkin, and his skin showed pink through the tears in his shirt; his red hair stood on end.

Surprisingly, he was not an object of pity. His one good eye regarded the two men with a fair assumption of calm, and he even grinned a little, ruefully, at Grey.

'The devil!' he said impertinently. 'Now we've hardly one whole set of features between us.'

Lord Grey seated himself fastidiously at his desk, first clearing a litter of papers which had whirled from desk to chair. He passed a hand over his thick, fine hair, pulled down his sleeves, and gave a jerk to the short skirt of his doublet.

'Now,' he said, putting thirteen generations of ice into his voice, 'let uth thee what we have here.' And he fixed Scott with the kind of look linked with Assizes.

'You have not, of courthe, come from Roxthburgh?'

'Find out!'

'I propothe to thend to Roxthburgh to do jutht that.' He paused. 'Do you know the penalty for arthon and attempted murder? . . . or wath it a kidnapping? In any cathe, you won't dithpothe me to leninthly thith way.'

No reply.

Grey tried again. 'I prethume you are a Thcotthman?'

His Lordship's misfortune was Scott's downfall as well. He couldn't resist it.

'Yeth!' said Scott, and got his mouth shut for him by the buckle of his own belt. He tasted blood.

Dudley swung it again, warningly. 'Keep a civil tongue, sir. What is your real name?'

'Find out.'

Again the belt. He supposed they questioned him for ten minutes, and still pumped full of excitement, he not only kept them guessing, but in a masochistic way, even enjoyed himself.

Finally Grey swung around to the desk again. 'We need to uthe thtronger perthuathion. The men below are obviouthly in colluthion too.'

Dudley said, 'They've lost their tongues as well,' and went on hurriedly. 'Woodward tells me it looks as if most

113

of the stores are missing, even allowing for what was burnt. The boneheaded fool at the gate let them in on the strength of their dress and the seals – they were authentic enough – and – of all things – because he recognized two of the horses. Of course, the train was dead on time, and he was desperate to get the beer in, into the bargain. Which reminds me – '

Lord Grey for the first time looked really disturbed. 'Not the beer?'

Dudley said, 'There's not a barrel left. Nor any ordnance to speak of, apart from what blew up. And what's more, no money.'

'What!' The two men stared at one another. This affair was serious. Water was scarce and unsafe: men had to have ale; and the horses needed hard feed to enable them to foray and keep open their communications. The need for arms and food was equally pressing.

Grey was silent for a long time, and then he got up and, walking over to the prone man, stirred him with one foot. This time, the voice was a general's voice, and the lisp was not even remotely funny. 'Where ith the retht of the train, and where are the men who thet out with it?'

The exhilaration had worn off; extreme mortification was biting at the edges of his courage. But he fought hard to keep his eyes calmly on Grey, and if the effort was visible to the soldier's practiced eye, Scott didn't know it. He said dreamily, 'Far, far away! And farther every hour!'

Dudley said sharply, 'Ah, then you had others with you who didn't come to Hume?'

They would be halfway home by now, and surprised that he hadn't joined them. Then they would find the carts had never been driven to Melrose. And tomorrow, wait in vain for himself and his party. And then, somehow, Lymond would find out: against orders, he had got into Hume . . . but hadn't the brains or the guts to get out. Scott braced himself.

'Naturally,' he said. 'I hope they keep some beer for me.'

This time he had no trouble in meeting their eyes. After

a moment Grey swung to the desk and began writing. 'Two men to Berwick for replathementth, two to Roxthburgh, to look out for thignth of ambuth, and dithcover the latht point the train got to.' He finished writing and handed both papers to Dudley. 'Right away.'

Then he stood up and came over again to Scott.

'I am thorry you've thet thuch a thmall prithe on your life. I cannot afford to feed you and your men with what food we have left. Tomorrow you can ekthpect to meet a thpy'th death. We have a prietht. If you want your relativeth to know, you had better give him your true name.'

Scott said, 'My men are mercenaries. If you pay them, they will fight for you as well as your Germans and Spanish do.'

'Pay them?' said Grey. 'With what, prithee?'

Scott was silent, in the bitter awareness that his exercise in self-expression had murdered ten men. Grey addressed the pikemen.

'Lock him up. But away from hith men . . . they might take advantage of him.'

In the revolting hole they took him to, he had only one comfort. He hadn't said who he was. If they knew he was heir to Buccleuch, he thought cynically, they wouldn't let him so much as catch cold. They'd take him to Berwick and use him as a tool to make his father do as they wanted.

For all his airy words to Lymond, he didn't think for a moment his father would stand by in public and watch him murdered. No. He'd do what the English asked him to do – again. And this time, ironically, *he* would be the cause of it. *If* he told them who he was.

He thought, lying bruised on the cold flags: This time tomorrow I shall be out of the whole damned mess. It didn't help very much.

* * *

Nor did the news that Grey's small search party had found and brought back the two remaining carts and the original English members of the supply train, found tied up and frozen where he had left them, just off the causeway.

They arrived, packed shivering among the crates, and jumped down from the wagons, shirt-tails flying, to cheer after cheer. There wasn't a man among them with a pair of hose, breeches or a jerkin on him: their teeth chattered and their feet were blue. Even the masons repairing the explosion breech dropped tools and poured over to watch as the unlucky travellers hopped into the castle. Comment was rife and on well-marked lines.

When the last of the men had gone indoors, Dudley examined the two carts and set a strong guard on them before reporting in high spirits to Grey.

'We've got some of the beer after all; and most of the heavy ordnance . . . culverin and stoneshot – '

What else he was going to say was never known.

The door burst open, the tapestries flapped, and a human tornado, enveloped in a whorl of depot-stamped canvas and trailed by protesting soldiers, erupted into the room.

The visitor brushed off his escorts, slamming the door in their faces, and strode headlong to Grey's desk.

'Madre Dios! Caballeros, su ayuda . . . su venganza! Ladrónes!' Hissing, the newcomer fixed his lordship with a burning eye, and even Lord Grey had to admit the magnificence of his rage.

'He sido mortificado, insultado – hombre – me hecho hazmerreír! – *Mirame!*' screamed the insulted one, and peeled off the canvas.

Mr. Secretary Myles, tried beyond endurance, gave a soul-destroying quack. Dudley and Grey, pinned to the petrified edge of diplomacy, gazed at the sorry remains of a ruffled shirt, pleated and trimmed with shredded bullion; hair, once black, oiled and curled, swooning from a coarse woollen cap, askew; and below, bare thighs, blue with cold, and tarred and feathered from toe to knee as a duck goes to market. A single destitute earring winked next to the highbred nose and smooth olive skin.

Lord Grey, recovering an aplomb he had hardly known for a month, rendered sympathy, concern and indignation in a mollifying buzz. By a combined effort he and Dudley got the still-detonating visitor into a chair, rewrapped in Dudley's cloak, and his feet in a pewter basin of hot water to melt off the tar. He was brought a pot of mulled wine and invited, at last, to address himself to Mr. Myles, who spoke Spanish.

The caballero was displeased. 'But,' he said with some hauteur, 'I speak the Scottish perfecto.'

'Oh,' said Dudley, taken aback. He, Grey and Myles waited.

The Spanish gentleman inspected his feet, sat back and proceeded to prove his point. He introduced himself: Don Luis Fernando de Cordoba y Avila, leader of the captured supply train, and said much about his relatives on both sides. He referred in passing without deference to His Majesty the Emperor; to the noble and adventurous life of himself and a few compatriots as masters of their own swords in London and Flanders, and drew their attention to the proverb 'Un hidalgo no debe a otro que a Dios, y al Rei nada.'

Mr. Myles was anxious to translate. Grey restrained him. 'I can gueth.'

'De veras,' said Don Luis politely. 'My Lordship has the true Spanish lisp of Castile. His Spanish sin dude is as much good as the mine.'

At this point, discretion came to Mr. Myles, and he studied the floor.

'And now,' said Don Luis. He rose splashily to his feet. 'To action, señores. Mas veen quatro ojos que no dos. If the señores will lend clothing to myself and my men, with your aid we shall follow and kill the animals who put the hand on us. By el engaño, the trick.'

The dark face flamed with renewed vitality. 'The leader, I wish to meet. The confusion with the horses, the skilful overcoming of such a man as me: there is no man mediocre. Ay, ay, dios. Y cuando ... When I meet him ...'

'You may meet him now, if you with,' said Grey calmly. 'We have him and motht of hith men locked up here.'

117

'Que pasa? How is this?' Lord Grey saw with satisfaction that the caballero was impressed at last.

'Pero – como asi?'

They explained. Don Luis, the ends of his cloak slopping in the bath, stood in astonishment. Then he swept out of the tub, imprinting the carpet with black sticky footmarks.

'This terrible Señor Huile! Lead me to him!'

'Señor . . . Wait a moment,' said Grey sharply.

Don Luis paused in the midst of a characteristic rush to the door.

Grey said, 'You don't by any chanth know how the leader wath called?'

'But of course!' said Don Luis simply. 'Do you not? It is Don Huile del Escocia.'

'Don . . .' Dudley suddenly experienced a terrible nostalgia for the King's English, unadorned. 'He can't be called that. He's a Scotsman.'

'No, no.' Don Luis was annoyed at his own stupidity. 'This I translate to remember. El nombre de pila . . .'

('Christian name,' said Mr. Myles surreptitiously.)

'. . . It is Huile, that is in Scottish. Oil. An unusual name, is it not?' said Don Luis, amused.

'Oil!' said Grey rather hollowly.

'And the patronimico,' continued Don Luis with undiminished helpfulness. 'It is del Escocia, of Scot.'

'Thcot!' said Grey. His face suddenly lightened. 'Wait a moment. Thcott! That'th Buccleuch'th name. Huile – It'th the Thpanith pronunthiathion, idiot, not the Englith. What thoundth like Huile . . . *Will! Will Thcott!* Buccleuch'th oldetht son!'

'Idiota?' said Don Luis stiffly, picking out the insult unerringly from the maze of multisyllables. His feet, a tarry mound, were ringed with pools of water from the cloak, and his eyes were narrowed at Grey. 'Idiota?'

The secretary saved the day. He took the señor's arm and murmured in his ear. Phrases floated to his lordship: 'defecto de boca . . . quere decir "ideal" . . .' Mr. Myles did his best, and only ceased when entangled with the

118

unfortunate word 'embarazar.' He flushed bright pink and released Don Luis, now regarding Lord Grey with unconcealed curiosity.

'Perhapth,' said Grey icily. 'Don Luith might be given thome help to clean hith feet and a chanth to dreth, and then we will have Mr. Thcott brought up.'

Dudley opened the door. 'Woodward! Get those men below into decent clothes, and fetch a suit for the señor.'

Woodward looked doubtful. 'We've already fixed up the men below, sir, and it's taken nearly all the spare clothing we've got. What's left woundn't be' – he hesitated – 'entirely suitable for the gentleman.'

'Then strip it off one of the prisoners,' said Dudley impatiently. 'The fellow who led them – Scott's his name – he's probably wearing the señor's own suit.'

Woodward said, 'Well, even if he is, sir, it's no good. It's in ribbons.'

There was a pause. Then the Spanish gentleman said, very distinctly, 'I do not hear aright. I trust one does not ask me to wear clothes of the common soldier with, no doubt, the louse?'

They saw with apprehension that his brow had blackened again.

Grey said, 'Dudley . . .'

'Too small, sir,' said Dudley. 'Same applies to Woodward and Myles.'

It was true enough. They were all big men, far taller than Don Luis.

Another short, pregnant silence. Dudley and the lieutenant stared into middle space. Mr. Myles thought of something.

'He's just about your own height, your lordship, if I may say so,' he said co-operatively.

Mr Woodward murmured 'Well played, sir!' under his breath and continued to look woodenly at the wall. Mr. Myles looked surprised.

Lord Grey allowed to lapse the longest possible interval consistent with civility. He then said without any sign of gratification, 'Of courth. I am afraid I require my riding clotheth, but I would be happy, naturally, to therve the theñor with my thpare dreth.'

The señor, it was apparent, was also happy. So, too, were Dudley and Woodward, but circumspectly so.

* * *

Scott was pitchforked into Grey's room an hour later.

His lordship, courtesy worn a little thin, sat again at his desk; Dudley, Woodward, Myles and some others at his side and by the window. Beside the desk lounged an elegant gentleman in tawny velvet, with combed black curls and a diamond in one ear.

'Thith,' said Lord Grey, 'ith Don Luith Fernando de Cordoba y Avila, of the forthe of Don Pedro de Gamboa, therving under the King'th Majethty in the North. I believe you had the impertinenthe to capture and unbreech him earlier tonight.' That took the smile off his majesty's face, he noted sardonically.

Scott stared.

Don Luis de Cordoba uncrossed long, exquisite legs, rose languidly from his chair, and strolled toward the prisoner. He contemplated him, face to face in silence, through half-closed eyes, blue as corn-flowers. Then, before Scott had time to dodge, he brought the percussion of his right hand with the savagery of a machine across the boy's swollen lips.

Blood from the smashed mouth welled and poured.

'We have a proverb, Señor Huile,' said Don Luis sweetly. '*Aunque manso tu sabuesso, no le muerdas en el beco*'

Scott moved bleeding lips. 'Hay un otro, Señor Luis. *Ruin señor cria ruin servidor.*'

The malicious glitter increased. 'The señor speaks Spanish? That should be cured. It is a tongue for gentlemen.'

Dudley, already on his feet, reached the Spaniard. 'Remember, Mr. Scott's a valuable hostage, Don Luis. Seat yourself, and we'll thrash the matter out.'

Mr. Scott! A sensation like the pounding of a die stamp was beginning to operate behind the boy's eyes. He parried their questions: Had his father, they asked, sent him to capture Don Luis and the supply train? How had he known the train would be there? What would his father pay to recover him?

He was jolted by a Spanish exclamation. 'Dios!' said Don Luis in vexation. 'I believe the young man faints. He is a person debil, the Scot, in spite of many words. Ay! he goes!'

For Scott, after a moment's helpless indecision, took the path thus offered. He swayed; he fell.

Woodward stooped over him. 'He's off all right. Better take him back to his cell.'

Don Luis rose. He smoothed a curl, reassured himself of his diamond, and took control of the situation. 'But no. It does not value the trouble. You have done all you wish with him now?'

Dudley shrugged and looked at Grey. 'More or less.'

'Then,' said Don Luis, 'I would prefer much to return the night to Berwick. I shall take him and his friends, and thus there is no need to waste the food. The hostage affair can also begin en seguida, and the questioning gooder organized, no?' He regarded them vivaciously.

Lord Grey became aware that he was dead tired and another hour of the brilliant señor would undoubtedly drive him crazy. He said with a sort of upheaval of a sigh, 'Well, theñor; if you and your men feel fit to go back, then it would be a great benefit to be rid of the men right away.'

Don Luis bowed. 'Bueno. If you will then write me an order for Berwick . . .'

'Of courthe.' Grey turned to the desk.

Don Luis watched him for a moment, and then murmured delicately to Dudley, 'I fear to beg also the horses from you. The ours were taken and loosed by Señor Scott, and the his will be needed for him and his men.'

Dudley looked doubtful. 'Oh. Can't you manage without? We're short of hacks just now.'

Don Luis spread his hands. 'How manage without? We

shall send more from Berwick, and meantime there are lesser mouths to feed.'

That at least was true. Dudley gave in, and had a word with the Master of Horse, who left the room.

Don Luis bowed.

Woodward bowed.

Myles bowed.

Grey bowed.

Dudley spoke to someone at the door, and two of Don Luis' men, in brave new jerkins, came in smiling and hauled off the inert figure of Scott.

Clamour from the courtyard told of Scott's men being tied to their own horses; of new horses being brought for the Spaniard's troop.

'I depart,' said Don Luis magnificently. 'For the hospitality, for the food, for the beer, for the horses, for the clothing, a million embracings. My dear lord; my dear sir; my dear gentlemen.'

Everybody bowed again.

'Adiós!' said Don Luis, and left the room.

* * *

Long after the last rider has passed the portcullis, when all at last was still and Lord Grey was preparing for bed, Dudley came, yawning, to share a last cup of wine with him.

'That damned Don!' They laughed a little, thinking of the tar and feathers. Dudley stretched.

At that moment, the wagon with the culverins blew up.

It was much later when they thought of checking the second wagon. The beer barrels were intact, but contained only brackish water, and one of them a slip of paper, which read pontifically, *No es todo oro lo que reluce*.

'All is not gold that glisters,' translated Mr. Myles, coming into his own at last.

For a long time they digested the implications in silence. Then Dudley said, rather dazedly, 'They were *all* impostors. . . . Don Luis. Who was he?'

Grey stared thoughtfully at the smoking wreck of the

opposite wall. 'I don't know. But I propothe to dithcuth thith night'th work thoon with William Thcott of Kincurd.'

They retired, but not, it is certain, to sleep.

* * *

The long string of horsemen was far away from Hume, driving westward, when the moon came up. The need for hard riding made talking impossible for the first ten miles, though a knife, tossed silver from horse to horse, let Scott and his ten men cut their lashings. Far ahead of the others, Lymond rode in tawny velvet. He had taken off the black wig, but Scott glimpsed his hair, paler than ever above the dyed skin: the nearest view he had had of him since accepting that vicious blow on the face.

He was beaten to the knees, and knew it.

Riding knee to knee with the Cleg, one of the ten whom his own recklessness had nearly killed, he had muttered some sort of apology.

The Cleg had received it with no more than his usual vacant good humour.

'Marry, man, that's just the way it goes,' he'd said. 'The Maister gave us our choice – twa-three hours in jail with you, he said, or ride bare-arsed with him an' get a new set o' clothes for it; and mindin' I catch cold easy, I chose to come wi' you. Not but what,' he said warmly, 'I never saw a loon put up wi' all what you put up wi'', for a scatterbrain scheme like yon. They must have fair bashed the brains out o' ye.'

Scott covered a burning eye with one hand. 'You mean Lymond told you I'd be asking for volunteers to go to Hume with me?' It was, of course, impossible. He had only decided yesterday to contradict Lymond's own express orders not to go to the castle.

The Cleg said, 'Ay, like I told you. He gave us all our choice, an' told us forbye you'd maybe not let on the plan to us, as you'd likely take a fair bashing.' He smiled cheerfully. 'I ken you dinna think we'd keep our mouths shut, but ye'll admit we did ye proud the day.'

'You did indeed,' said Scott, and turned his head away from the ungrudging admiration in the Cleg's eyes.

At ten miles, they overtook Mat with the pack horses, Lymond's own bunch of riding hacks, their clothes, and the remaining cart: the genuine English prisoners were already, Scott gathered, on their way, bound, to Melrose – the job ostensibly given to himself.

In the short breathing space before they set off again, Scott dismounted and, moving stiffly, walked forward to where Turkey and the Master were having a brief conversation.

'S'wounds,' said Mat. He eyed Scott's face. 'It looks to me as if someone has sat on our William.'

The Master turned, passementerie glittering. He might have changed sex, so complete was the change from the haughty, choleric Don.

'Barbarossa! We are covered with admiration. An actor manqué, my dear, to convince them so thoroughly that you expected to perish directly. You have had,' he said inquiringly, 'a little accident to the mouth?'

Busy as they were, the men around them were not deaf: the nearest, taking the remark at its face value, grinned sympathetically at Scott. It was obvious they had all known of the double plan – except him. Obvious, too, that they assumed to a man that he knew as well.

So there it was. First, corporal punishment, carefully applied. Next, spiritual chastisement – and not the obvious, open ridicule. Not with Lymond. Instead, the dreadful humiliation of accepting his own reputation, intact, from the chastising hand. That, and the corollary that Lymond found him so inconsiderable that he could cheerfully add to his stature.

What now? Reject the heroic role Lymond had prepared for him? He could explain that the Master had goaded him into a private attempt to take Grey: had made an opportunity for him to do it; had foreseen that he would bungle it; and had in fact based his entire plan on that certainty . . . and on the genuineness of the apprehension that he, Scott, would betray inside Hume. He could easily say all that, and earn himself the biggest guffaw since Cuckoo-spit hooked his own ears at the salmon.

Young Scott heaved a long sigh, and meeting the sardonic blue eye, said flatly, 'Not an actor, an apprentice ... but I hope to learn. And one day to be able to play without the gift of a pawn.'

The glittering eyes appraised him. 'Certainly. But next time take care, or you may be receiving the Bishop, with appropriate rites. Any questions?'

One puzzle still nagged. 'How,' asked Scott, 'did you know that the leader of the supplies would be Spanish?'

The Master raised weary eyebrows. 'He wasn't.'

That was all the conversation he ever had on the subject; and soon they were safely back at their tower. Drinking went on for two days after the barrels were broached; and Will Scott made a point of surfacing into sobriety as little as possible.

Amid the brawling, dancing, chorusing and squabbling, he was aware of Lymond, totally and grossly drunk, with the tawny velvet creased and stained with beer and food. He appeared to be in amatory mood, and was singing long Spanish love songs to his own accompaniment on the guitar.

6
FORCED MOVE FOR A MINOR PIECE

> Efter also yis pownis first moving
> Frome poynt to poynt ye course furth sall bring,
> And never pass to poynts angular
> But sa it be to sla his adversar
> The quhilk is lyk, be his passing yan,
> In anguler wyss, to spulze sum pur man.

As news will, news of the hoax at Hume got out.

By breakfast time on the second day, a kind of collective snigger, moving downwind from the castle to Edinburgh and points west, betrayed the progress of the story: the discovery of the entire English troop bound and frozen outside Melrose Abbey swelled the snigger to a belly laugh.

Sir George Douglas, breakfasting in his castle of Dalkeith seven miles south of Edinburgh, got word of it with his quails and became unusually thoughtful.

Thoughtfully, he allowed himself to be dressed and barbered, his beard trimmed, his lounging robe slipped over discreet Swiss shirt. Thoughtfully, he opened the tower door which led out of his bed-chamber and climbed twenty steps to his private study, where a dishevelled-looking person was waiting. He shut the door. 'Forgive the delay. I cannot always receive the Lord Protector's messages as freely as I should wish.'

The rain was driving against the exposed tower window: the man's outer clothes were sodden. He pushed back his hood, revealing a close cap fitting from eyebrows to ears, and said courteously, 'I am sure his Grace would be unhappy to think otherwise, Sir George.'

This was a trifle near the mark for a messenger, but Douglas had his mind on other things. He said briefly, 'I must confess, as matters now stand between myself, Lord Grey and the Protector, I had not expected to hear from London yet.'

'How providential,' said the hatted one comfortably, 'that you didn't on that account have me stopped at the gate. So fickle are statesmen. Today the palace, tomorrow the oubliette and the elegiac distich.'

This time, Sir George turned his full attention on the stranger. 'If you have a dispatch, sir, I should be glad to see it.'

'In a way I have,' said the other cheerfully. 'Je suis oiseau: voyez mes ailes. And then again, in a way I haven't. Je suis souris; vivent les rats. What I have is worth hearing, though. Shall I read it to you?' And he pulled from his coat a creased bundle of papers. 'Here we are. Rather long, but I'll spare you the clay and disinter the lotus. For example –' And picking out a page, he read quickly aloud.

' "Sir George Douglas, the laird of Ormiston, and two of the Humes have been here, Douglas coming as a Borderer to serve the King. . . . I reminded him of his benefits from the late King, and threatened him if he revolted again, I should pursue him and his friends to the death. He answered he would advance the marriage, and promised to draw his brother and the rest clean from the Governor . . . and to do his utmost to put the Queen in our hands, if requited in England for his lands – which I have guaranteed with my own lands. I have resolved to prove him, and if he does not keep his promise, the very next day Coldingham shall down, and himself smart for it . . ."

'Postscript – Oh,' said the stranger disingenuously, turning over the last page. 'I remember. I left the postscript with my friends, although that was rather interesting too. What do you make of it all?'

What Sir George thought was soon forthcoming. With undisturbed calm, he drew his gown about him, and seating himself negligently near the door, remarked, 'I should guess this to be a somewhat naïve effort at blackmail. I assume that unless I pay you a large sum of money, and release you unharmed, your friends will send the original to the Scottish court.'

'Well, at least you seem to know what it's all about,' said the reader, refolding the papers. 'The extract is, of course, copied from a dispatch from Lord Grey to the Protector, and I am sure you are about to take the wind from my sails by telling me that the Queen Dowager knows all about it.'

If alarmed by this perspicacity, Sir George gave no sign. 'She does, of course.'

'Quite. But even if I believed that – which I don't – I still think you might be interested in seeing that postscript. It does exist, you know. So does the copy. I'm King of the Fidlers and swear 'tis a truth. You can have them all for a nominal price.'

'And the nominal price?'

'You have an English prisoner called Jonathan Crouch,' remarked the blackmailer, affably, and was interrupted by Sir George himself, showing the first signs of animation.

'Dear me!' he said. 'You seem to be a remarkably subterranean young man. I took such a prisoner, yes; although it is not generally known.'

'Let me see him and you may have a report.'

There was a short pause. The offer was nicely put. No one, however reinforced by his sovereign's complicity, could be expected to resist the lure of a postscript devoted to his own affairs in an English dispatch. That the postscript existed he felt sure: the fellow was too damnably pat with the rest. Ergo, by falling in with the suggestion, he was admitting to no more than natural curiosity: a subtle and far from fortuitous point.

There was a further consideration. He did not particularly care that this dispatch should reach the Queen. And there might be others which he would care about even less. At this point in his meditations Sir George cleared his throat. 'You appear to take monumental measures for a very simple end. A man of your resource would prefer, I should have thought, to use his powers of . . . interception for a more rewarding cause.' He slipped the cabuchon ruby off his thumb and tossed it on the table between them.

'Fools make news, and wise men carry it. You could become a rich man.'

'I *am* a rich man,' said his visitor. He fixed a cool eye on the Douglas, disregarding the ring. 'As you, I am sure, are a busy one. If therefore our bargain is concluded, perhaps Mr. Crouch might be bought here.'

There was nothing else for it. Sir George said regretfully, 'I am afraid I cannot keep my side of the bargain. A matter of some disappointment to me. The gentleman you mention was sold to a friend of mine some time ago.' He added kindly, 'If it will serve, I can direct you to him and even enable you to enter the house, if you wish.'

A pause developed, and prolonged itself to uncomfortable lengths. Then, unexpectedly, the other laughed. 'Oh Douglas, oh Douglas, Tender and true . . . I am moved to respect. Very well. The bargain stands. Tell me the name of your friend, and you shall have your documents.'

Sir George rose, crossed to his desk, and tossed a paper from it into the other's hands. On the one side was a signed note from Sir Andrew Hunter, promising payment of one hundred crowns for the person of Mr. Jonathan Crouch; on the other was a scrawled note in Hunter's handwriting. It said, *For our friendship, send me word if there is an attempt to trace Crouch. I would not lose him to enemies before I can exchange him for my cousin.*

His visitor read both sides and smiled. 'You weigh your scales generously. Thank you.'

Sir George said, retrieving the paper, 'Of course, I cannot as a gentleman ignore the note. I propose to send one of my secretaries to Ballaggan, with a fairly large escort, to warn Sir Andrew that a stranger has indeed inquired about Crouch. Hunter keeps a well-guarded house, but it is not always possible to make sure that, in the confusion of entering, a party such as mine might not become larger than it should be . . . a common risk, I fear, in these times.'

'Yes. Oh, indeed, I am quite aware of the risk,' said the other, and a long, slow smile pleated the skin around his mouth.

Sir George found himself for some reason smiling back. For an instant he was overcome with an extraordinary feeling of kinship for this odd sharp-witted person. Borne on the tide of this sensation, he said, 'Then to seal our bargain, will you drink with me? I have a very fine claret to hand . . .'

His visitor assented politely, adding, as Sir George crossed to the armory, 'Although I trust you have nothing against beer?'

'On the contrary,' said Sir George, pouring with an anticipatory hand.

'Because – your health – ' said the other, 'I took the liberty of leaving a hogshead for you with your Chamberlain below. A little stirred up, I'm afraid; but it should settle.' And, understanding each other very well, the eyes of the two men met; Sir George's alight with evocative delight.

Left alone after bidding his anonymous friend goodbye, Douglas returned to the study and stood for a moment, playing absently with the ruby where it lay on the table. 'Well, I shan't make *that* mistake again.'

He slipped it back on his finger and gazed at it for a moment. 'But if he doesn't fancy bullion, what sort of bait *is* he going to take, this wild cormorant, this acidulous osprey of ours? Something. There must be something he wants. And whatever it is, by God, I'll find it and make a collar and chain of it with "Douglas" in fine Gothic letters on the neck.'

* * *

The spirit of Ballaggan Keep, imperious, impervious, implacable, brooding over its fastness like a tribal mascot, was Dame Catherine, Sir Andrew's mother.

Catherine Hunter was rising seventy, and crippled in

her lower limbs to a degree which condemned her to bed or chair for life. This, together with the loss of her husband at Flodden and the death shortly afterward of a brilliant older son, had turned the wines of her palmy days – already rather a variable commodity – into a corked and vinegary brew.

The keep, tall, gauche and of no particular charm for the passer-by, was stuffed inside with the prizes of Lady Hunter's epicurean eye. No rushes covered the floors; these were set with Spanish azulejos and covered with rugs from Turkey and the Levant. The beds were wrought and gilded, and hung with heavy taffetas; the chests and tables in marble and scented woods wore tapestry cloths and carried a pellicle of Aldine folios. Other specimens of her library shared bedside honours with her Maltese terrier Cavall.

The accretion of all these aids to graceful living would have taxed a larger estate than Ballaggan. Lamentably aware that – even if gold mines sprang beneath his feet, like Olwen's trefoils – his mother's fancy would still outpace him, Sir Andrew was sometimes reduced to a state of nervous irritation very close to rebellion. That he invariably spared her either complaint or reproach labelled him a soft mark among his fellow knights and earned him a solid revenue of womanly sympathy.

It also brought him the admiration of Mr. Jonathan Crouch, whose temporary career as a prisoner of war, or a sort of promissary note on two legs, had brought him finally to lodge with Sir Andrew.

With Mr. Crouch came his tongue, his teeth, his lips, his hard and soft palate, his maxillary muscles, larynx, epiglottis and lungs: all the apparatus which enabled him, ne plus ultra, to talk. Like the enchanted garden of Jannes, tenanted by daemons, the keep of Ballaggan encased the ceaseless drone of Mr. Crouch's voice. He droned through September until it and his captors were exhausted; then pounced on October with undimmed vigour and worried the blameless days for a fortnight.

By the middle Saturday of the month, atrophy had set

in, reaching its nadir in the dead time between two and four, when Sir Andrew, whatever business was pressing, visited his mother's room to sit with her. Lady Hunter, strutted upright with pillows, was brushing the terrier rhythmically as it lay cushioned across her knees. Her face, bewigged and topped by a hooped pearl cap, had the skin of an invalid and her mouth, lightly whiskered, was hatched, above and below, with the spidery wrinkles forced by powerful lips. Her black eyes were fixed unwinkingly on her son, who in turn was directing his aquiline profile, with an air of polite attention, toward Mr. Crouch.

Mr. Crouch, wittily obese like a middle-aged titmouse, sat enthroned on his stomach, giving tongue. Incidents of his boyhood surged to cataclysmic peaks of pointlessness. Episodes from his career in the Princess Mary's household explored tedium to its petrified core.

'Never,' said Mr. Crouch, pulling himself out of a frenzy of adjectives, 'never shall I weary of describing it, if I live to be a hundred. *That* I won't.'

Something like a strong shudder passed over his host. Almost involuntarily Sir Andrew said, 'By the way, are you married, Crouch?'

If the titmouse was surprised, it was also pleased. It beamed. 'Why, yes sir, I am; and what's more, God and my Ellen have blessed me with six lovely children; every one a girl, but the Lord will provide. I've had my share of adversity, sir; but as I always say, the way I met my Ellen goes to show that Providence is on our side; as you'll agree when you hear the full story which, since you so kindly ask, I shall have great pleasure in relating to you in due course.' There was a brief pause, during which Sir Andrew shut his eyes; then Mr. Crouch – his intention duly filed and registered – picked up the limp threads of his monologue. 'And then – '

'Andrew!'

'Yes, Mother?' said Sir Andrew. He shot an apologetic look at the soloist, who broke off politely but providently took a fresh breath.

'The people with whom you have contracted to buy fish

have been cheating you for five weeks,' said Lady Hunter, brushing steadily at the terrier's coat. 'The fish served to me while you were away on whatever business you discovered was not only bad, but often putrid. Putrid!' she repeated, with horrid inflection. 'Yet it seems a relatively simple matter to arrange.'

Mr. Crouch, a kindhearted person, shut his mouth and fiddled with his points. Sir Andrew said, 'Mother, you should have mentioned it before. I'd no idea, of course. I'll have it put right.'

'You were hardly visible long enough to listen,' remarked Lady Hunter, brushing. 'You must forgive me for imagining you were much too busy. The wool coming in for spinning, incidentally, has *not* improved in quality. Whatever steps you took about *that* seem to have been baulked by another agency. You must tell me if you are finding things a little difficult, Andrew,' pursued the lady. 'After all, no mother expects *both* her sons to be alike. Dear Andrew,' she said, fixing her black stare on Crouch and brushing still, 'is going to be a great help to me in my old age.'

'I'm sure, Mistress,' said the titmouse, glancing uncomfortably at his host's submissive head. And from his good-natured soul he added, 'And he did you honour in the fighting last month, I'll be bound.'

The black eyes travelled slowly over Sir Andrew's body, and rose to his face. 'My son is always remarkably fortunate in battle,' she said. 'He has never yet received a mark of any kind.'

'And damn it,' Mr. Crouch was to say much later to his wife, his face reddening again at the thought, 'the old sow said it as if she'd have liked him better mincemeat.'

As it was, the occasion was awkward enough to make Hunter flush and force a change of subject. Shortly afterward he set Biblical phrases buzzing in Mr. Crouch's head, by producing from his purse a small wrapped bundle which he laid on his mother's bed. 'I thought this might interest you: I came across it the other day.'

The paralyzed woman looked neither at him nor at the

packet; she allowed it to lie until she finished grooming the lapdog, replaced the brushes, and with a sudden ill-tempered smack sent the stertorous creature bundling to the floor. Then she smoothed the counterpane, pulled away a long, tawny hair caught in one of her rings, and opened the parcel.

A vast, hexagonal brooch set in ebony and diamonds shouted into the sunshine in a cacophony of light.

The thing was enormous. Crouch, sitting within yards of the bed, could see the centrepiece was a heart set with pointed diamonds: around the heart and attached to it by foliated gilt wire were crystal plaques, each bearing an angel's head, bewinged and carved in onyx: the plaque below the point of the heart was joined to it by a scroll, and on the scroll in diamonds were the initial letters H and D, entwined.

It was the most expensive-looking jewel Mr. Crouch had ever seen in his life. He looked, suffused with pleasurable excitement, at Sir Andrew. Hunter, his expression at once eager, deprecating and defensive, watched his mother.

'H for Henri, D for Diane de Poitiers!' cried Mr. Crouch. 'My dear sir, seldom if ever have I seen such an exquisite piece. A tour de force. A veritable masterpiece. I am surprised,' said Mr. Crouch, taking thought, 'I must own, that the French King's – er – lady should have allowed it out of her hands. A piece of – '

For the second time he was interrupted by his hostess. She raised her black eyes from the gift to her son, and the expression in them deepened at the expectancy in his face. She threw the covering back across the jewel.

'A remarkable piece of vulgarity,' she said. 'I fear, Andrew, that a stronger woman might have been able to do more than I to educate your taste a little. It is a great grief to me that I cannot help you more. However, there is no need for you to waste your purchase. I am sure there is some good burgess's daughter whom you have a kindness for, who would be perfectly satisfied with it. I believe,' she continued without a pause, 'that I saw some new arrivals cross the courtyard a few moments ago. I don't wish to appear to remind you continually, Andrew; but as master here you really must not appear discourteous. I am sure Mr. Crouch will excuse you.'

Mr. Crouch hastily did. Sir Andrew, with an apology, left the room, and Lady Hunter tossed the rejected gift on to her bedside table. Mr. Crouch ventured a remark.

'That'll likely have cost Sir Andrew a small fortune, now,' he said. 'Nor it won't be easy to resell, I wager.'

The crippled woman directed her unwinking stare at him. He wriggled. 'The price of aesthetic education, Mr. Crouch,' she said, 'is never small.'

Mr. Crouch (for once) did not feel competent to answer.

Belowstairs, even among the crowded majolica ware, the air was freer, and the need to welcome visitors a blessed distraction. Sir Andrew knew and liked Sym Penango, Sir George Douglas's secretary: he made him welcome and received his message over a cup of wine, while his men were accommodated in the buttery.

An inquiry about Mr. Crouch? Oh. Did Sir George say from whom?

But Penango had no further information, and supposed Sir George had none either. Presently he excused himself: he and his men were expected at Douglas. In due course the stragglers were collected, wiping mouths on padded sleeves, and the troop rode off into the dusk.

Sir Andrew went thoughtfully upstairs, stopping to relight a torch which had gone out on the landing. Inside his mother's room it was becoming dark. In the failing light from the windows he could see her, upright in bed, her head turned toward him.

Something struck him vaguely as odd, then he placed it: the miraculous silence. Crouch wasn't talking.

A closer look showed the prohibition to be quite involuntary. Mr Crouch was sitting on the floor beside his chair, tied and gagged.

As Sir Andrew took this in, the door behind him banged, locked, and a knee like the hammer of God took him, hard, in the kidneys and hurled him to the floor. His

135

chin hit the blue tiles like a pharmacist's pestle; he tried, swimmily, to roll over and found himself pinned by a relentless matrix of bones. He heaved, unsuccessfully, felt his assailant groping for purchase to wrench back his arms, resisted, and finally did manage to roll over.

For a moment, the two men breathed the same sweating air. Hunter saw a pitiless mouth, two intent eyes behind a black mask, and a head covered with some sort of woollen cap. The mouth twisted; so did the deadly trained body, and pain leapt from a lock on his knee. Black-mask gave a sudden, triumphant laugh. 'The Common Thick-knee,' he said breathlessly, 'is a bird . . . capable of running at great speed.' He increased his leverage, grinning. 'Now here, Dandy mine, we have a specimen of the *Un*common – '

How he broke the lock, Hunter never knew, but he afterward wondered if the strength which surged up in him would have done so but for the anger at the stupid jibe. He jerked, broke the hold on his legs and threw the other man half on his side, driving off at the same time the predatory fingers feeling for his throat. Then he flung himself on his opponent. The clenched figures rolled over completely, then again; a fine stool splintered, its prowling leopards bifurcated, and a row of medicine bottles fell from the bedside table with a tympanitic crash. Catherine Hunter, her eyes like charcoal over her bound mouth, stared without expression at her son. Crouch, pink with emotion, watched, squirming in his bonds.

Hunter was on top. He wanted to shout, but all the power of his lungs was occupied in driving his body; the sound of both men's breathing was like tearing cloth. Feeling the black eyes on him, Hunter set his teeth and grinned; then, listening to his muscles speaking, exerted all his force to flatten the other's body and approach the twisting throat with his thumbs. The masked figure writhed desperately; its arms threshed; it began to go limp. Sir Andrew, his fingers finding and burying themselves at last in the flesh over the great vessels, threw caution to the winds and, raising himself, exerted all his power in

136

pressing on the neck below him. He had an instant's vision of eyes screwed, not in pain, but a kind of barbarous hilarity, and then booted feet curled themselves neatly and smashed into his unguarded and exposed groin; one of the searching hands, now armed with iron from the hearth, cracked open his face and beat him back as he knelt, retching; then Black-mask, rising, threw away his andiron and bent over him.

Hunter, racked with the torments of the damned, heard him say through the throbbing in his brain, 'Come along, Dandy . . . observe the modus operandi . . . How can thou float . . . without feather or fin.' He was gripped by wanton arms, balanced a moment, helplessly convulsed, and then with a sickening wrench sent hurtling across the room. Chairs, candlesticks, books, fell. The world vanished in a bloody mist, reappeared inspissate with pain, disappeared. Playful, inhuman fingers rested on his collar, hooked below it, and methodically began to flay his head against the high gloss of the tiles.

The voice said, erratically, 'Who . . . falls upon rushes, falls soft; beware of . . . vain pride in terrestrial treasure, Sir Andrew. And . . . doused lights . . . and fireirons . . . and wrestling in slippers.' He was released, and lay, three parts unconscious, looking up at his tormentor.

'And of tempting me further,' said Black-mask, smiling. 'I have come to see your little English friend, Sir Andrew; but I'll break you a limb in the Turkish style as often as you like. . . .'

Hunter, drowning in tides of nausea, closed his eyes, and shut out the mask, and the black, unwinking eyes in the bed.

137

7
A VARIETY OF MATING REPLIES

For suth ye Rok in to his first moving . . .
He may nocht pass, nor of his steid to steire,
Quhill knycht or powne is standard hī so nere,
And in mydfield, gif he be stedit still,
To four poyntis he passis at his will . . .
Two rokis may a king allone put downe,
And him depryve of his lyf and his crowne.

1 · PLAY WITH A ROOK PROVES
DANGEROUS

The shop of Patey Liddell, goldsmith, was on the south
side of the Middle Raw in Stirling, handy for the Burgh
Yett, and only a short walk from St. John Street. It was a
tall thin building, with a coloured timber arcade, and outside steps to the first floor where Patey stored his stock,
and Lady Culter was sitting having her miniature painted.

From time to time Patey peered down, Cyclops-fashion,
to the shop proper through a neat hole in the floor boards,
partly to watch for customers, and partly to howl threats
at his apprentices, known caustically as the Seven Little
Masters, who dwelt among mystic coloured fires at the
back of the shop.

Mr. Liddell was lively as a frog, his small face niellated
with gold dust, and his white hair trained over his ears,
which were missing. Patey readily explained how this happened, and the numerous versions, in toto, lent substance
to Sybilla's private belief that the man was a rogue. He

was also a brilliant goldsmith; and the source to Lady Culter of much simple entertainment.

Why she had made this appointment for today, the morning of the Wapenshaw, was beyond her to recall. Why indeed the plans for the Wapenshaw had been allowed to stand so soon after Pinkie was another matter, but the Dowager could guess. She thought, with unusual depression, that it was probably just as well, under the circumstances, to have a count of arms: that had begun in the morning and would be over by now. And if the Queen thought that outdoor exercise would keep the lieges from one another's throats until the meeting was safely convened, she was probably, in a French way, right. This brought her mind on to her son.

'Patey!' said the Dowager at the top of her voice. 'It isn't a tapestry! Haven't you done yet?'

Patey Liddell raised a denunciatory finger. 'You moved!'

'I can't help moving,' said Sybilla, in a nicely controlled shriek. 'Your wretched cushion's come adrift from the stool: it's like trying to steer hurley-hackit. Are you going to be long?'

The old man beamed, nodding vaguely. 'A wee thing to the right.'

Lady Culter turned obediently. 'Are-you-going-to-be-much-longer?'

Patey worked away, his tongue silently tracking the strokes of his brush. 'As to that,' he said piously, 'the gude Lord alone kens. You've changed your hair, tae.'

'I've washed it,' said Lady Culter tartly. 'If you think I'm going to remain unchanged and unwashed for sixteen months while you immortalize me, you're wrong. If you could pin up the sun permanently in the top left corner of your ceiling, you would.'

'Ah, the bonny lad,' said Patey, working phonetically through the last sentence. 'Only the other day I said to him, says I: wi' the separations o' war, says I, whitna better than a bonny picter o' the wee lassie tae carry neist the heart.'

'What did he say?' shouted Sybilla with interest.

'He said,' said Patey, a shade reluctantly, 'that he'd think about it when he kent whit I was charging for this yin. Acourse, I told him, it's all in the frame. Says I, gin ye choose gold now, that'd be a wee thing costlier than your dear mother's: on the other hand, tin's dirt cheap, and if the lassie puts up wi' the insult, who'm I tae – ' He raised an astonished eye from the floor. "S breid! There's a customer!' And before Sybilla could murmur, he skipped to the stairs and vanished.

The Dowager instantly got off her seat and picked up the miniature. The likeness was, she thought, fairly good. Appraising her face at one remove, she was glad to find that sixty harassing years had left it, on the whole, quite presentable. The eyes and bones, of course, had always been good.

'But I must have it today!' A familiar voice, laboriously distinct, rose through the peephole, and the Dowager, entranced, prepared to listen.

Patey's voice said, 'Well, it's no done yet, Sir Andra.'

'Then when will it be ready?' Hunter sounded impatient, and Sybilla sympathized. There was another exchange, then silence as Patey disappeared to the back of the shop. Then a new voice:

'Hullo, Sir Andrew! Man, what's happened to your face?'

The Dowager had no special interest in Sir George Douglas, but her wandering attention was jerked by Sir Andrew's reply.

'My face?' said Sir Andrew, and laughed ruefully. 'God; like the beggar, I'm all face. It was that damned Crouch man, the prisoner of war.'

'Good Lord!' Sir George sounded startled. 'I must say, he'd none of the air of a man-eater.'

'Dammit, it wasn't Crouch that did the damage,' said Hunter. 'It was some murderous brute with a black mask who smashed the house open, tied up Mother like a boiling fowl and thumped me – I must confess – to a pulp. It wasn't too funny at the time.'

'No, of course not. . . . What about Crouch?'

'Departed, protesting, with the rescuer. God knows what the man wanted; my impression is he hardly knew himself. All I got out of it were a couple of English names they bandied about; if I had any contacts over the Border I'd follow them up for the devil of it, to see if I couldn't track down my agile friend. I don't suppose they mean, anything at all to you? Gideon Somerville and Samuel Harvey?'

Sir George admitted they didn't and his commiserations were halted by the arrival of Patey, grousing, with Sir Andrew's finished brooch. Sybilla had seen it being altered. She admired it again, listening still; but the conversation had drifted to less interesting channels.

'. . . And what duplicity!' said the Dowager much later, describing all this over pheasant at Bogle House to Christian Stewart and her son Richard. 'After telling the rest of us the bruises came from a fall from his horse. But of course Dandy is shrinkingly sensitive about money; heaven knows how he manages to shower his mother with diamonds. It must have been someone he was hoping to ransom, poor man.'

'No,' said Richard. 'He was going to exchange him for a cousin of his own held prisoner in England.'

The Dowager eyed her son with such gentle surprise that he explained. 'Overheard him discuss it at Drumlanrig. He bought the fellow from George Douglas there.'

'Well, *I* never heard that he had a cousin in England,' said Sybilla; 'and even if he has, I don't see why poor Dandy should have to redeem him. What that man wants is to marry an heiress, although heaven knows I shouldn't ask Medusa to share her castle with Catherine.'

Richard, she thought, was looking tired. The weeks she and Mariotta had passed at Menteith had been spent by him in harassing activity. He had visited them once at Inchtalla: that apart, it occurred to the Dowager, he had hardly spent a complete day in his wife's company since the battle.

She had been extremely cross to find him at Bogle House when she arrived there, late, from Patey's; to learn that he had been released from those activities she had circuitously arranged for him at the castle, and that Tom Erskine, arriving in his absence, had taken Mariotta and Agnes to the games, leaving (perforce) Christian, who insisted on waiting for herself.

She was considering the next move when fate forestalled her: a roaring separated itself from the excitements of the street, wound up the stairs in increasing volume, and debouched into the room at the tail of a disorganized servant.

'Hey!' said Buccleuch, hauling off his hat and nodding perfunctorily at the ladies. 'I've been looking everywhere for you! You've missed the best of the wrestling!'

'Sir Wat!' said Lady Culter.

'And the jumping's over!' said Buccleuch, unheeding. 'And the running! Where've you been? There's only tilting at the glove, and the ring, and then the Papingo. The butt shooting's nearly finished, too, and these damned Kerrs are having it too much their own way.' He made for the door. 'Come on. Where's your bonnet?'

'In his room,' said Sybilla, outstaring her son's sharp glance. 'And there it stays. Wat Scott, I knew you had no manners out of your first two wives, but I thought Janet Beaton had taught you how to address a lady.'

'But I'm not here to address a lady,' Buccleuch pointed out unwisely. 'I want Richard to – '

'But since you've called, and I'm hostess, I'm afraid you can't avoid it,' explained Sybilla. She agitated her hand bell. 'Malmsey or Canary?'

Buccleuch cast an agonized glance at Richard, got no help and tried Sybilla again. 'We're going to miss the Popinjay,' he pleaded.

'*I'm* not!' remarked the Dowager. 'I never liked birds, and still less when they talk – Canary, please, John.'

It all but succeeded; by the third cup Sir Wat well launched on a detailed theory about hard snaffles and would have been there yet had not Hunter's face appeared around the door, anxiously addressing Buccleuch and Lord Culter, after a quick bow to the ladies.

'I've to bring you both quickly. They're getting to the Popinjay.'

The look which passed between Sir Andrew and Buccleuch was the briefest possible, but Sir Wat jumped guiltily to his feet, his eye wandering agitatedly toward Lady Culter.

Sybilla sighed. 'Don't say a word. I can guess. The news of Lymond's challenge is being shrieked from the chimney tops.'

Sir Andrew had the grace to look uncomfortable. 'I'm sorry, Lady Culter. But the crowd have got to know that your sons are to compete – '

'Stuff and nonsense,' said the Dowager irritably. 'How can they, with one of them at the horn?'

'They know that,' said Christian from the fireplace. 'It's not a shooting match they're expecting. It's an assassination.'

'It's no use, my dear,' said Sybilla. 'We are face to face, like poor Janet Beaton, with a severe case of Moral Philosophy, and there is nothing we can do about it.'

Lord Culter crossed to the settle and bending down, kissed his mother on the hand and on the cheek. 'It'll be over in an hour,' he said. 'Don't be afraid. I'll come back, if only to teach you the proper meaning of Moral Philosophy.'

The door closed behind them all.

* * *

'Well, I must say,' said Lady Herries definitely, and loudly enough to turn several interested heads, 'if I were married to Lady Culter, I shouldn't let her spend the whole afternoon at the games alone.'

'Thank you very much,' said Tom Erskine, grinning at Mariotta, who sat on his other side.

She smiled politely back, and Mr. Erskine's soul moaned within him. Reduced, singlehanded, to coping with so much potential gunpowder, he felt himself, like the bird which cleans crocodiles' teeth, assailed by hideous doubts.

Privately, he agreed with the brat. He couldn't blame the Dowager for taking her own measures to keep Richard away, but then, she didn't know how public the thing had become. Neither did the two girls beside him; and the Herries child, ignorant of the challenge as well, insisted on fretting at the subject like a bitch at the spit. Exiled from his own group of friends by his female company and unwilling, in any case, to listen to his neighbours sharpening their wits at Richard's expense, he wished heartily he were elsewhere. A Lindsay won the butt shooting and his annoyance increased.

Had he but known it, Mariotta too was battling with an acid frustration. The girl was pretty, rich and wearing new clothes. Today, sitting under streaming banners, with peers and pageantry around her, the green grass in front and the castle soaring above, was her first public appearance in Stirling since her wedding. And it was Tom Erskine, not Richard, who sat beside her and supplied the endless introductions. It was all exactly as she had insisted and devastatingly flat.

It was flat when the procession of contestants wound down the hill, flags and livery mincing in the sun, musicians playing apoplectically against the wind. When the Queen and the Governor had made a brief appearance among the royal benches. When the tilting was at its best, with deal splinters flying among the spectators; when one of the wrestlers broke an arm.

Then they were pulling arrows out of straw and targets, and clearing the way for a vociferous, red and white centipede, which turned out to be the 120-foot pole and its rigging for the last of the contests: the Papingo Shoot.

'Come along,' said Tom, getting to his feet. 'This is where we move back.'

'Why?' said Agnes. 'Oh no, Mr. Erskine: we must see the Papingo first.'

'Back,' said Tom firmly. 'Unless you want a hatful of arrows. Sixty yards' clearance for spectators: that's the rule. Look! There's the parrot in a wicker cage: see it?

They'll take it out and tie it to a crossbar on top of the pole before they hoist it.'

At this precise moment, to Tom Erskine's heartfelt delight, reinforcing troops arrived in the person of Sir Andrew Hunter, looking not unlike an uncommonly ruffled parrot himself after a stormy passage through the crowd.

He exchanged greetings. 'Papingo shoots! If you haven't the slashed style to begin with, you're certainly wearing it by the end, and be damned to the Continental rules – I thought you might want to compete,' he explained to Erskine. 'I don't – no bow with me, anyway. Oh' – in good-humoured answer to Lady Herries – 'I can manage all right at the butts, but I'm a fool at perch shooting. Tom knows.'

'Tom certainly does,' said Erskine, grinning. 'The Kilwinning baillies used to hand down their suits of armour like chains of office for when Dandy was perch shooting at the steeple.'

Sir Andrew aimed a friendly cuff at him. 'Watch your own step. The old man won't be pleased if you break one of his windows.'

Since the Keeper's quarters were not only several hundred feet up the castle rock but invisible, this seemed unlikely. However, Tom replied, 'You're safe, as it happens – I'm not competing either. But if you'd do squire for me, Dandy, I'd be grateful. There's something I must do in town.'

He received Hunter's cheerful acquiescence, took leave of the ladies, and burrowed away, to a chorus of exasperated groans.

The field, having encouraged the perilous rearing of the perch, settled down into its new stance. Well back from the danger area there was an air of comfortable expectancy.

Looking around, in the bright, sparkling air, Mariotta found that, like tesserae in a mosaic, her warring emotions had merged, peaceably, into untrammelled pleasure. She was sorry for the papingo, winking blue and yellow in the

145

sun on his high pole; but admired the sunlit castle rock behind him, the wide grass arena, with its elderly, occupied officials which spread on its three exposed sides; and even found something to please her in the crowd, of which she was one, which impinged on three sides of the grass behind the barriers, filling all the space between the arena and the bright rows of pavilions behind.

Protocol, having much the same separatist requirements as a good, fancy jelly, produced much the same results. The layer of peers, in wind-blown furs and large flat hats, was naturally in the best position, next the barrier; then came the clergy, almost indistinguishable except for their plainer headgear; then the merchants and their wives, obviously full of good dinners and dressed at cost, in much better cloth on the whole than the nobles; then the less prominent burgesses and the more reserved professionals, nonclerical lawyers and teachers and Household and other people with minor positions at Court; then all the people one saw in the street, whom one's steward dealt with, and, occasionally, one visited. The fleshers and brewers and smiths and weavers and skinners and saddlers and salters and cappers and masons and cutlers and fletchers and plasterers and armourers and porters and water carriers, and the one-eyed man who had called at Bogle House selling fumigating pans. And country people on holiday, and beggars, and pickpockets (no doubt) and sorners and the wandering unemployed.

The sun shone. Trumpets blared; and drew every nose to the field as one of the heralds, his tabard looking a trifle end-of-season and tarnished, made an announcement, inaudible. More trumpets. Then a temporary barrier was removed and the competitors, fifty noblemen and fifty commoners, filed self-consciously onto the field and around its margin.

One recognized one's friends at once from the banners. The pages were obviously enjoying the parade much more than their masters, who were smiling in a resolute sort of way at their friends in the crowd, indicating that they only did this kind of thing to entertain the tenants. One looked for the warmth and hilarity which halfway through, by unexplained custom, would suddenly enliven and vulgarize the proceedings.

Nevertheless, and not to be carping, the long file of athletic and purposeful bowmen looked very splendid, though not as splendid as if one's own husband were there. The wind blew the standards straight toward the castle rock.

Blue and silver. She liked her own standard. The St. Andrew's Cross; the crest (argent, a phoenix azure), and the highly ambiguous motto, chosen (of course) by the First Baron, which always eluded her, Contra Vita – whatever it was.

As the thought crossed her mind, the motto itself appeared, almost within touching distance: CONTRA VITA RECTI MORIAMUR. The Culter slughorn, carried by Richard's servant. And walking behind it, looking neither to left nor to right, but perfectly self-possessed, unaffected and blasé, Lord Culter himself. Mariotta was aware of a dismayed flutter in the stomach.

'My God!' said a voice behind her. 'There's old man Culter decided to make a pincushion of himself after all: now we should see some fun. All the same' – generously – 'rather him than me.'

* * *

Fighting his way uphill to the top of St. John Street, past the corner of St. Michael's, the almshouse, and then the uneven row of buildings of which Bogle House was one, Tom Erskine found no difficulty at all in stifling his better feelings, which told him he had bequeathed to Sir Andrew a thoroughly unnerving afternoon.

The death of Lord Fleming had naturally made a good deal of difference to his household. Having buried her husband at Biggar, Lady Jenny had rejoined the court with her children, and the halflife she had always had, as the little Queen's governess, was now her whole career. Of the older children, Margaret had moved like an uncertain ghost between her late husband's home at Mugdock, her married sisters', and Lady Culter's friendly, undemanding hearth; and the duties Lady Fleming had discarded at Boghall had fallen on her blind goddaughter's shoulders. And Christian, though now staying with the Dowager at Bogle House, would very shortly be leaving for Boghall to take them up. Which argued a need for haste.

Tom Erskine therefore hopped in and out of the crowds down St. John Street, got himself admitted to Bogle House and bolted up the stairs fired with missionary zeal, to find himself nose to nose with his loved one on the middle landing.

'Who is it? What's happened? Have you news?' said Christian.

He was startled. 'What about? It's me. Not particularly.'

Relief showed on her face. 'Oh, Tom. That's all right. Come along in, then.' And she added in sufficient explanation as they walked toward the parlour door, 'Richard's gone to the Papingo Shoot, you see.'

Erskine was not, at bottom, a selfish man. He said, 'Oh, damn,' and paused irresolutely. 'I didn't know. I'd better get back. Left Dandy with the ladies – he didn't say; must have thought we knew – and there'll be the devil to pay if . . .'

Christian took his arm. 'Believe me, if anything's going to happen, nothing you can do will stop it. Anyway, I want you here.'

'You do?' He was delighted.

'Yes. How long will the shoot last? An hour? Two hours?'

'A hundred men – two shots each: Oh, over two hours, if they all shoot, but of course it will end if someone hits the papingo.'

Christian said, 'Then will you take Lady Culter and myself around the Fair, Tom? Until the shoot is over?'

This was hardly the programme he would have chosen, but it was understandable enough. He said, 'She's worried, is she?'

'Well, she's not exactly tolling the passing bell yet, but she oughtn't to go out alone, and you won't get her to go out with you and leave me. I know it's early and there won't be much happening yet, but at least we can try and forget that God-bereft bird.'

Tom looked at her in some astonishment. 'I believe you're as much on edge as Sybilla.'

This time she snapped. 'If you would tear your mind sometimes from backgammon and horses, you'd see something in the Crawfords that'd make your rattlepated friends look pretty thin. If I remembered my own mother, I don't suppose I'd value her half as much as I do the Dowager. And Mariotta may not be what you fancy, but there's breeding and spirit there too, if you're minded to look for it – ' She broke off, her brow cleared; and with one of those competent mood changes that was one of her chief characteristics, gave him a friendly push. 'Go on. Tell Sybilla we're all off for a jolly day a-fairing. And *don't* let her sidetrack you either.'

* * *

'I don't suppose – ' said Sybilla.

'*No!*' rejoined Tom Erskine and Christian Stewart in unison.

'No. I see not. Our hands are rather full, I'm afraid. But Agnes adores gingerbread – I wonder,' said the Dowager doubtfully, 'if it would sit in my hood.'

The progress of Sybilla though a market was the progress of worker bee through a bower of intently propagating blossoms.

Everything stuck.

From the toy stall she bought two ivory dolls, a hen whistle, a rattle and a charming set of miniature bells for a child's skirts: all were heroically received and borne by Tom, henceforth marked by a faint, distracted jingling.

From the spice booth, set with delicious traps for the fat purse, she took cinnamon, figs, cumin seed and saffron, ginger, flower of gilly-flower and crocus and – an afterthought – some brazil for dyeing her new wool. These were distributed between Christian and Tom.

They listened to a balladmonger, paid him for all the

verses of 'When Tay's Bank,' and bought a lengthy scroll containing a brand-new ballad which Tom Erskine read briefly and then discreetly lost. 'No matter,' said the Dowager cheerfully, when told. 'Dangerous quantity, music. Because it spouts sweet venom in their ears and makes their minds all effeminate, you know. We can't have that.' He was never very sure whether she was laughing at him, but rather thought not. They pursued their course purposefully, and the Dowager bought a new set of playing cards, some thread, a boxful of ox feet, a quantity of silver lace and a pair of scissors. She was dissuaded from buying a channel stone, which Tom, no curling enthusiast, refused utterly to carry, and got a toothpick in its case instead. They watched acrobats, invested sixpence for an unconvincing mermaid and finally stumbled, flattened and hot, into a tavern, where Tom forcibly commandeered a private space for the two women and brought them refreshments.

'Dear, dear,' said Lady Culter, seating herself among the mute sea of her parcels, like Arion among his fishes. 'I'm afraid I've forgotten which are the squashy ones. Never mind. If we spread them out, they can't take much hurt. I should think. Unless the ox feet ... Oh. What a pity, Tom. But I'm sure it will clean off.'

They sipped their wine and chatted. The sun, doing its best for an October day, threw the crow-stepped shadow of the Town House on the quantities of gay little booths, the bunting and the coloured wares; and the drone of professional singers made comic counterpoint with the chorus of street cries and exhortations, the gypsies' pipes and tambours. It was bright, airy, innocent and gay.

'Ribs o'beef!'

'Fine, skinned hides!'

'Crusty pies, hot as hell!'

'Rushes green!'

'Fine broken geldings, stark and stout!'

'Hoods for my lady!'

'Guts for your playing, six shillings the dozen!'

'A rare pretty parrot in a cage ...'

'Well. Ce n'est pas tout de boire; it faut sortir d'ici,' said the Dowager. 'There's a cloud over the sun, and if the saffron gets wet, Tom, you'll be *or* as well as *gules*, and very likely rampant as well. Come along.'

They left the tavern.

Almost immediately, Christian, pulled along by Erskine's hand-clasp, felt a tug at her gown. A voice, very close to her, said in a sort of whine, 'Tell your fortune, my bonny mistress!'

'Wait!' she screamed above the din to Tom, and felt the strain on her arm slacken as he stopped.

'What is it?' asked the Dowager over his shoulder. 'Oh, a fortune-teller, how delightful. Of course. Wait a moment,' she said, cocking her head in its blue velvet hood to one side. 'I've seen you before, haven't I? Of course! It's the gypsies who were in Culter last August. Aren't you?' she ended in triumph.

The would-be fortune teller flashed beautiful teeth at her. 'Of course, my lady; and had the pleasure of performing for you as well.'

'Of course,' said Sybilla. 'And what are you doing? Fortune-telling – '

'Tumbling, dancing, singing . . .' The gypsy waved an airy hand. From a scatter of bright mats behind him, a group of black-eyed young people were watching their leader. 'Every kind of entertainment.'

The inevitable thought struck the Dowager. 'Tom! Christian! Why shouldn't they come to Bogle House tonight? Buccleuch's never seen them, nor Richard, nor Agnes. We'll get Dandy Hunter in, and the older Fleming children . . .'

Polite argument was futile, and any other kind unthinkable. For an enormous fee, to cover their temporary absence from pitch, the troop undertook to perform that night at Bogle House.

The Dowager was enchanted. 'So good of them. Have you any money, Tom dear? I seem to have spent all I had with me.'

It took their concerted efforts, hindered considerably by

the leaking of ox feet, to get at Tom's pouch and extract from it the necessary number of angels. 'Now, *straight home*,' said the Dowager, a suspicion of tiredness making itself heard in her voice at last; and they made for the end of the Square, arm in arm, and started down Bow Street.

Dandy Hunter met them at the bottom. They saw him from some distance away, boring weevil-like through the thickening crowd, and waving.

'Just as well he's as flat as a turbot,' said Tom Erskine judicially, watching him. 'That's twice he's breenged through his betters today.'

But by that time they were close enough to see his face.

'Something's happened,' said the Dowager in a voice notable for its unsurprised grimness, and led the way quickly toward him, clutching all her parcels as if these, at all costs, she would preserve.

* * *

Owing simply to Lord Culter's presence, the October Papingo Shoot moved through its stately preliminaries to the beating of a fierce expectancy. Mortal challenge was not only piquant but eerie when the challenger was also wanted for treason.

Tension brought the automatic reaction. Ten thousand heads, capped, hooded, bonneted and bare, bobbed and jerked as the betting surged from point to point, fed by rumour: he isn't among the competitors; they've got guards all around the field; Culter's shooting twentieth.

The odds rose.

'The brother's game-shy, man: a shirker. Never finished a contest in his life.'

The odds rose higher.

Andrew Hunter, standing between Richard's wife and Lady Herries, cursed Tom Erskine continuously under his breath. Mariotta would not go home. Staring in a hypnotized way at the side view which was all she could see of her husband, she seemed unaware, he was thankful to note, of what else was going on around her.

Agnes Herries, however, was both aware and equipped

152

with opinions on the subject, which palled only as the drawing of lots came to an end. Listening with half an ear, Hunter noticed she was now complaining of the viewpoint she had been given. This, since he could do nothing to improve it, he ignored.

'It strikes me,' said Lady Herries, reminded suddenly of a sore subject, 'that a Ward of the Crown might as well be a by-blow for all the difference it makes. A *girl* Ward, that is. Who wants to marry John Hamilton? Not me. I've never *seen* the man, even.'

A more unsuitable place in which to air her opinions about her contracted fiancé could hardly be found. With the speed of a watchful mother, Sir Andrew said, 'Look: there's Buccleuch.'

He failed, as better men had done before him. 'Yes. But if I'd been a boy,' pursued Lady Herries, intent on her theme, 'I'd never have been contracted to John Hamilton.'

This penetrated even Mariotta's preoccupation. She turned, diverted against her will. 'Well, *that's* true enough.'

'What I mean is,' said the Ward of the Crown, frowning, 'that people have no business to settle other people's future for them when they're five years old. It's a typical man's scheme,' said Agnes ruthlessly. 'It's not for our own good; it's no use saying it is. It's to add to their rotten lands, or because they need to carry on the family name, or because it'll bring them enough money or tenants or rights of lineage to stop a war, or start a war, or carry out their own uninteresting masculine affairs.'

There was a short, respectful silence. 'Well,' said Mariotta soothingly, '*I* wasn't contracted when I was five.'

'Yes,' said Lady Herries with devastating frankness. 'That's just what I mean. Trust a man to take advantage. Brood mares and – '

Whether her own undeniably single-track brain or Sir Andrew called a halt first, it would be hard to say; but in the net result the Baroness shut her mouth rather suddenly and Hunter said, 'Look: the shooting has started.'

On the field, an orderly pattern, pleasing in itself to the eye, had fallen into place. Far out to one side stood the

Master and officials of the games, dressed in Arran's red and white livery; and beside them a group of arrow boys, minute fungi under cartwheel rush hats. Beside that again, in a long line against the painted barriers, the competitors waited; a trifle uneasy; a trifle tense now the moment had come.

The first bowman, flexing his shoulders, took his place in the centre of the field below the high, painted pole, and footed the mark. The parrot, brilliant in the eye of the sun, struggled and screamed against the backdrop of the castle rock, scarlet with bracken and the autumn glory of beech and sycamore; above the rock, the Palace windows gave back the sun in stabs of flame behind their cage grilles. A voice shouted 'Fast!'; the archer raised his longbow smoothly to the sky, nocked his arrow, drew, held and released; replaced his second shaft, aimed, held and released again.

The papingo squawked bad-temperedly and swore with an Aberdeen accent; the arrow arched and fell harmlessly, six yards to the left. To a roar of sardonic cheering the tension broke, and Sir Andrew suddenly moved.

'There's only one place Lymond can shoot from,' he said, almost to himself. 'And that's from the shelter of the rock.'

Mariotta heard him. She raised her eyes as he had done and studied the broken face of the crag. 'Shooting against both the sun and the wind?'

'That's the difficulty, of course,' he acknowledged. 'But look. The rest of the field is hedged in by the crowd: a man couldn't raise his arms in it, never mind aim six feet of a longbow.' He hesitated, and then said, 'Lady Culter, if you'd give me leave, I'll climb up and look through some of that scrub there.'

But Mariotta, unimpressed by the suggestion that he should safeguard Richard's life at the risk of his own, refused and would not be persuaded. He argued uneasily, found her adamant, and dropped the proposal. In silence they watched.

The wind, violent and skittish, was making better sport

of it than the competitors were. Buccleuch, shooting third, nicked the post with his first shaft and overshot with his second, retiring bellowing amid a chorus of witticisms. The next two were wide; the fifth caused a mild sensation by breaking his bow and nearly amputating himself with the shards; the sixth lost his thread and bungled both draws; and the seventh squirted off like a firecracker.

The eighth nearly got it.

'Oh!' said Agnes, sparkling. 'It's very exciting, isn't it?' And she added, a little wistfully, 'A woman would enjoy being married to a wonderful archer.'

In the midst of their anxiety, the eyes of the other two met, and laughter sprang into Hunter's. 'My dear girl,' he said, 'your mind's running a great deal on marriage today, surely?'

Lady Herries looked surprised. 'Not specially. But I'll have to get married this year, I expect; and if I've *got* to be sold like a packet of wool – '

'Agnes!'

'Well. I mean, having children and doing embroidery may not be fun, but it'd be more so if at least they fought battles for you and pretended they liked it. Courts of Love, and sonnets, and scarves in their helmets. That's what I think. Otherwise,' pursued Agnes, 'there's not much point in it all, is there?'

'Well, I'm afraid Johnnie Hamilton won't write any odes to your eyelashes,' said Sir Andrew cheerfully. 'Besides, that's a limiting form of courtship, isn't it? You'd be much more comfortable with a husband who worked up a connection at Court, or developed his lands, or exercised his money in trade so that you had diamond bracelets by the gross and a house in each county.'

'But I've got all the diamonds I want,' said Agnes succinctly. 'Like Mariotta. And the little Queen. So *I* don't see there's any point in marrying, unless it's to get something you haven't got already. And nine times out of ten, you needn't marry for that, either,' she added as an afterthought.

Watching the twelfth bowman loose off, Sir Andrew

155

said unhappily, 'How much land have you got, Lady Herries? And how many able-bodied tenants?'

She looked at him with vague distaste. 'You sound like Grandfather Blairquhan.'

'Never mind. How many, and where are they all?'

She said rather sulkily, 'You *know*. I share them with Cathie and Jean. Terregles, Kirkgunzeon, Moffatdale, Lockerbie, Ecclefechan .... next to the Maxwell lands on the Border.'

'H'm,' said Hunter. 'On the Border. You don't say how many tenants, but I imagine it'll run to a few thousand. And who do you imagine is going to look after all that for you and protect it from the English? And, if you'll forgive me for being practical, who's going to lead them into the field in wartime? You can't dodge your national obligations, even if you think you can dodge your moral ones.'

'I *knew* you were going to sound like Grandfather Blairquhan,' said Agnes pettishly. 'Anyway, we've all got men kinsfolk who'd do that for us, surely, without having to marry them first. The point is, whether it's kinsfolk or husbands, they'd do it just because it suits them, no matter whether we were fifty and fat and had bowlegs, and that,' she ended with dignity, 'simply isn't romance as I see it.'

Mariotta suddenly intervened. 'Don't be silly: what do you want? An altruistic uncle for security and a boudoir full of lovers for pleasure?'

'I should like,' pronounced Lady Herries with a stately air, 'a husband who put me before business or politics.'

'They don't exist.'

'Oh, yes, they do,' said Hunter unexpectedly. (Fifteen.) He glanced down, his lips twitching. 'You're being a bit hard, you know; both of you. It's pretty well a full-time job, these days, keeping a family housed and clothed and warm and protected. Doesn't leave much time for poetry under the apple trees. But chivalry hasn't gone: don't think it. You'll even find it paramount still with some people, but a trifle the worse for wear, because it's not the best protection against an aggressive and materialistic world. . . .' He smiled again, rather ruefully. 'And don't

156

forget: a man has other claims and duties too – to relatives; and old folk; and his friends. He's not always free, as you seem to think, to slap down the money and carry off the bride of his choice.'

Mariotta said, instantly repentant, 'We know that, of course. Agnes only means, I think, that often in arranged marriages there's a good deal of unhappiness on both sides.'

'– And it's a pity to go through with it for the sake of posterity if posterity is simply going to repeat the process. Yes. I see that,' said Sir Andrew. 'But look around you. I think you'll find that marital bliss sometimes fights its way to the surface in the end. And then, you see, there are so many other things involved as well – the continuance of a great house, for example – family loyalty's a powerful thing, and that's as it should be. Even sometimes the continued existence of a nation – that's the price royalty pays. And that's got a romance of its own, of course; not quite the kind you mean, but one that lies perhaps a little deeper.'

'As far as I'm concerned,' retorted her ladyship, 'it can bury itself. They won't get me to marry anyone I don't want to, contract or no contract. Oh, look: there's Menteith shooting.'

They were already looking, for young Menteith, Mariotta's host from Inchmahome, was the nineteenth archer, and the crowd was now perfectly quiet.

He took position, aimed and loosed. His first arrow struck the crossbar on which the parrot was bound. The bar jerked, and held; the arrow twisted and plummeted as the second flew, ruffling the bird's plumage. Two good shots. A subdued shout went up, followed by a crawling hum of anticipation. The arrow boys, one of them with a goose feather waving in his hatbrim, ran forward briefly into the field; the perch, chipped and scratched, threw a thin wavering shadow toward the castle rock; the autumn leaves, lit by the dipping sun, turned from tawny to crimson.

Richard Crawford, holding himself uncommonly

straight, walked steadily across the field and paused at the foot of the perch, looking down momentarily at the big yew in his tabbed hand, then up at the crossbar. He took his stand, and Mariotta, reaching out panic-stricken, found Sir Andrew had gone.

The silence was absolute; the stillness profound. But for the ruffling of the trees and the gentle singing of the perch stays, a man might have thought himself deaf. He nocked, raising his arm with the poetic, compact motion of the master bowman; the thin, echoing official voice called 'Fast!'; he drew, held lovingly, and loosed.

His arrow leapt; but another was already airborne. Slender, deadly, red as hot steel in the sun, a shaft came hissing from the farthest suburbs of the crowd. There was never an instant's doubt of its destination. It drove into the crossbar, slicing off the crude ties with a razor barb, freeing the papingo in the instant that Culter's arrow flew toward it.

From the audience, a sea of upturned faces, rose a breathy gasp. Weak and stiff from its bonds, the bird jerked grotesquely, fell, wavered, flapped; and with a sudden strong upbeat, recovered itself.

As if over its corporate soul the crowd, mesmerized, yearned over the bright wings. At its back Andrew Hunter, his face set in anger, had already reached the higher ground, racing; thrusting; running free like a madman.

They hardly noticed him. For as the parrot, gaining height, swooped wildly away from the field, a second arrow breathed by and feathered into its mark. The papingo, transfixed in its blundering flight, stopped, tilted, and dropped like a stricken star to the ground. A yellow feather, wanton and unseemly, danced it way after.

Then, on the wave of a roaring uprush, the crowd was moved to action: too late, for the third arrow was already launched.

It arched in the air, a gleaming parabola, the feathers susurrant with curses, and found this time its designed, human mark.

Culter, standing white, taut and watchful at the base of

the perch, flung out an arm blindly, held himself a moment upright against the pole, then slowly folded against it and thence to the ground.

2 · CHECK AND CROSS CHECK

That evening, bright in the dusk, a great fire glowed in the parlour at Bogle House, bestowing light, warmth and comfort on its occupants. It flickered on the faces about it: the Dowager, Mariotta, Buccleuch, Hunter, Agnes Herries, Christian and Tom Erskine. It glittered on the table beside it, on which lay three arrows, two of them dark with blood, a longbow and a leather embroidered shooting glove. It flared, lastly, on the calm face of Lord Culter, lying stiffly bandaged on a long settle before it.

For the arrow which struck Richard came from a great distance and had to fly over many heads to an almost invisible mark. Unlike the first two, it was not faultless. It had dropped, losing power, and had torn its way across cheek and ear to bury itself beside the collarbone. And so, again charmed, again flouted by tragedy, Lord Culter was able, studying the exhibits on the table, to hold a post-mortem on a parrot.

'An English bow: that'll be part of the booty from Annan, I expect. And three arrows from the same source, fully barbed . . . very naughty, in a perch contest. And a glove.'

He picked it up and sniffed at it. It was a right-hand glove in white buckskin, its newness betrayed by the absence of rubbing on the first three fingers.

'Discreetly perfumed,' observed Lord Culter, turning it over. 'Beautifully stitched, and some jewellers' work on the back, to boot. A nice toy, if you can afford it – and since friend Lymond presumably paid for it with my money, he can. God!' he said. 'I'd give my chance of heaven, nearly, to match against him, perch or clout.'

Tom Erskine observed critically, 'Wind behind him,

of course; and he had a bit of elevation too, hadn't he, Dandy?'

Sir Andrew nodded. 'He shot from behind one of the dressing tents, just where the ground rose to the wood. I was just too late getting there. Found the stuff where he dropped it. . . .' He groaned. 'We all underrated him. I worked out that he couldn't possibly shoot from among the crowd. It didn't cross my mind that a first-class marksman might just do it from the ground behind.'

'Well, you gave us a shaking-up all right, Culter,' said Buccleuch. 'Thought you were away with the papingo, my lad!'

The Dowager, who had been, for her, unusually silent, remarked at once, 'Well, it wasn't very reassuring, I admit, coming back to find Richard laid out all bloody in one bed and Mariotta fainting in the next, but then Wapenshaws are notorious, aren't they? Did anyone remember to ask who got the prize?'

Tom said, 'Well I suppose, strictly speaking, they ought to give it to Lymond, but I should put it past even his impudence to claim it.'

'I don't know.' Mariotta's voice was detached. 'He seems able to do almost anything he wants.'

Agnes, her eyes fixed on Culter, heaved a sigh. 'I thought I was going to *die*.'

'Well, you behaved very sensibly, darling,' said the Dowager. 'And now we shall enjoy the gypsies all the more.'

'*Gypsies!*'

'Yes, of course. From the fair: had you forgotten? And here they are,' said Sybilla.

It was a truimphant example, in the outcome, of her own brand of humane genius. Under the spell of the entertainment, even Mariotta's taut nerves slackened, and colour came back into her face. Christian Stewart, listening gravely to Erskine's commentary, sat with her hand on Agnes's shoulder, thus regulating (but not eliminating) her interruptions, aided by a tactful Sir Andrew. Culter himself lay quietly, his eyes heavy, under the watchful gaze of the Dowager, who was having a long and intermittent discussion at the same time with the leading gypsy.

Toward the end of the performance, and during a phase which involved something noisy with a tambourine and much stamping, she caught Buccleuch's rather distracted eye, and slipped out of the room, followed by Sir Wat.

Sybilla shut the door on the noise.

'Dod!' Sir Wat, breathing the cold air on the deserted landing, wiped his forehead. 'Clever rascals, Sybilla, but not just my meat, y'know.'

'I thought you stood it very well,' commented the Dowager. 'And really it's a great comfort to have you, for I mustn't bother Richard, and Sir Andrew and Tom are dear boys but a little occupied; and they have their own troubles anyway.'

'Sir Wat looked apprehensive, not without reason.

'About the bloodhounds,' said Sybilla.

'Bloodhound yourself,' said Buccleuch, jerked, in his alarm, out of even the nominal form of courtesy he usually practiced. 'How did you know – '

'Oh, I know Richard,' said Sybilla. 'I always could interpret these silences, you know, more easily than half an hour of his brother's chatter. He was performing very prettily in there, and I'm sure all the girls felt better for it, but I didn't. What did he ask you to do?'

Buccleuch shrugged, and gave up. 'Track down Lymond, of course. There's the glove, and – you're right – I still have the dogs at Branxholm.' He looked down at her, an unaccustomed diffidence struggling among the appalling burst-whinbush whiskers.

'He's been made a fool of – twice, you know,' he said. 'Feels like a sulky fat goose in a barrel, being shot at by gutter boys. Can't stomach it – won't stand for it. Wouldn't try to stop him, either.'

'I shall,' said Sybilla.

'Why? Discredits you all – sorry, m'dear – as it is. The boy's no good to himself or anyone else till it's settled.'

'Yes,' said the Dowager. 'But *I* shall settle it, not Richard. Anyway, aren't you supposed to be ill? You *are* a fool,

Wat,' she added, with a kind of affectionate resignation. 'You know perfectly well word'll reach England inside forty-eight hours that you're playing games at Stirling when you're supposed to be too ill to go and speak nicely to old Grey at Norham.'

Sir Wat accepted the stricture with surprising meekness. 'Well, as to that – ' He scowled at the landing arras. 'That's what makes it unco knotty, if you want the truth, to do what Richard asked.'

'Which was?'

'Well, to let go everything else and hoe up the country till we find Lymond. We could do it – but – '

'– But in Richard's present mood, in bringing Lymond to face his deserts, he's also liable to bring Will Scott to face his,' said the Dowager concisely.

Buccleuch wriggled. His face got red, then the spaces under his hair; finally he burst into speech which lost no violence through being compressed into undertones.

'Dod, Sybilla: if you want to know, I'm in the hell of a jawboxy mess. Seymour's Lord High Suleyman the Magnificent Grey at Norham's been sending me polite notes ever since Will snipped his nose for him at Hume, asking when I'm coming to parley and assure them of help. It's damned awkward. They know it was Will – how, I can't understand, for at my last taste of him he was too blasted whaup-nosed to claim his own mother. But there it is, and if I refuse to help, they'll burn me to the ground on the next raid. I've put it around that I'm ill, but short of following it up that I'm dead, I don't know what to do next.'

The broad, capable Scott hands, with their spatulate fingers and white scar seams, gripped the balustrade and blanched, as he leaned his uneasy weight on them. 'I'll have to disown Will publicly, and hope they'll believe I had nothing to do with Hume. I doubt they won't, though; it looks too damned neat, right to the cartload of cutty sarks on my land at Melrose.'

He stared disconsolately at Lady Culter. 'And here's the joke. I'm not a praying man, Sybilla, but I've had these

162

baw-heids at the chapel on their knees ever since he went, hoping that Will'd see he'd been a damned stupid fool, and come back. Now, if he does, I'm made to look an accomplice to the fiasco at Hume, and Grey'll see I suffer accordingly. Whereas if he doesn't, and I'm forced to disown him to Grey – and if word of it gets to the Queen – and if he's captured with Lymond –'

'He'll get the same treatment as Lymond. But not if *I* catch him,' said Sybilla.

Buccleuch eyed her. 'Then, by God, I wouldn't care to be in Lymond's shoes.'

'How my sons turn out is rather my affair,' said the Dowager coolly. 'And involves rather less risk, on the whole, to Richard. If you'll co-operate.'

'By not co-operating?' Sir Wat gave a relieved bark. 'It'll give Culter a poor opinion of me, but I don't mind. No. My dogs'll be sick; and I'll be sicker than the lot put together. Listen – someone's coming.' He broke off hurriedly as light and warmth streamed in on them.'

'And so,' said Sybilla placidly, 'I had a long talk with him – Johnnie Bullo, his name is; a real gypsy king – and he tells me he knows how to make it.'

'Make what, Lady Culter?' It was Christian who had opened the parlour door on sounds of imminent departure from within. 'The gypsies are just going.'

'Make the Philosopher's Stone, dear,' said the Dowager, driving haphazard but triumphant into her subject. 'You know, the thing that turns tin into gold, and makes frisky old gentlemen *senex bis puer*, and mends broken legs and all sorts of practical things.'

'It's what we need at Branxholm,' said Sir Wat gloomily. 'Janet broke another vase last week.'

For some reason this tickled both Sybilla and Christian. The Dowager was the first to recover.

'Just you wait,' she said. 'I have it all from Bullo, and it all sounds remarkably well authenticated, considering. Anyway, he's coming again to Midculter to explain it to me.'

'Good God!' said Buccleuch, to whom the Dowager

was the source and fount of all astonishments. 'You don't mean you believe all that rubbish! I've enough of it at home with Janet; and the Lee penny never out the house.'

'All what rubbish?' said Sybilla. 'You see, you don't know yourself what you're talking about, and neither shall I,' she added as an afterthought, 'until Master Bullo has been and explained it again.'

'Well, I don't know what you want the Philosopher's Stone for,' said Christian. 'It seems to me that as a family you're quite indecently rich already.'

'Oh, you never know,' said the Dowager mysteriously. 'Healing charms – elixirs of life – love potions – '

'What I came to ask,' said Christian, her face rather red, 'was whether we might all go to the Fair – Agnes, Mariotta and myself, I mean. The trouble is – '

'The trouble is, Master Bullo won't read our fortunes here: he hasn't got his crystal, he says, and he won't go and bring it back.' Agnes, squeezing through the door, provided the explanations, fortisimo. 'But he says we can call at his tent, and Tom'll go with us – '

The Dowager spoke quietly. 'What about Richard?'

'It's all right.' Christian was quick in defence of the absent Mariotta. 'As a matter of fact, he's asleep, and . . .' And it won't do him any harm to be spared a performance of wifely reproach, her hesitation added.

The Dowager made no objection. So the gypsies left, and a little later, wrapped in heavy cloaks and hoods, the three girls walked out with Tom Erskine, and an unobtrusive following of Erskine's men. Sir Andrew and Buccleuch left. In the snug parlour the big fire hissed and murmured in the silence, glimmering on mother and son. Sitting beside Richard's quiet couch, Sybilla put on her spectacles and threaded a needle. Then she put it down and sat quite still for a long time, staring owlishly into space.

And it was into space that at last she spoke. 'Oh, my darling!' said Sybilla. 'I do hope I've done the best thing.'

* * *

'Are you all right?' asked Tom Erskine. And again, later on, 'What's wrong? Are you feeling all right?'

'Of course. It's the cold,' said Christian rather snappishly, and relaxing her grip on his arm, tried furiously to still the uncalled-for and humiliating frisson set up by her nerves.

It was not cold, as she well knew. It was the crowded strain of the day; the blaring darkness; the devils' orchestra of uncouth music; the coarse chatter, the catcalls and the mindless, ganting laughter. The Fair had become by night a bloated Saturnalia, sodden, sottish and leering of voice. She was buffeted by blundering bodies and twitched by grasping hands. Smells assailed her: beer smells, food smells and leather smells; the stink of human bodies and once, as two struggling shapes crashed into her, the reek of blood, forcing on the mind the warm fire and the reeking arrows of an hour before – Culter's voice: 'If that's what a life of depravity does for your archery'; Mariotta's: 'He seems to be able to do almost anything he wants'; the Dowager, bandaging with cool hands, refusing to panic . . .

'But a rare pippin!' said a voice in her ear. 'A fine rosy pippin for a fine rosy lass – '

'A chain of gold for that bonny dress, now! Five crowns and a kiss for yourself, my bonny may!'

'Hatpins, sweeting: a thousand and a half for sixteen pence – '

'A puppet for your sister!'

'Mackerel!'

'Hot pies!' – And grease brushing her cheek as the pastry was thrust upward. The shaking became uncontrollable.

'Tell your fortune, lassies!' in the sly, garlic-laden voice.

It was some kind of a booth. First Agnes went in; then Mariotta; and they were both quite remarkably reticent when they came out. Tom, waiting with Christian, was bored. 'It sounds poor stuff to me. Let's go home.'

Agnes objected. 'Christian hasn't been in yet.'

'Fortune, lady?' said Bullo's voice again, at Christian's elbow. 'One other lady?'

'I'll come with you –'

'Oh, no you won't.' Christian eluded Tom deftly. 'If I'm going to have the secrets of my boudoir revealed, you're staying outside. Master Bullo will take me.'

Silently the gypsy caught her sleeve, and they moved forward. Something brushed her hood, and from the deadening of noise, she guessed the tent flap had closed behind her. Underfoot, the street cobbles were spread with fabric; the darkness was stuffy and cold, smelling vaguely of cheap incense. She walked a few paces, and then was aware of a new aperture. The grip on her elbow disappeared; Bullo's soft steps could be heard receding; then these in turn were cut off. This time, there was absolute silence.

Her face forced into lines of composure, her betraying hands tightheld behind her back, Christian stood quite still and waited in the cold and the dark.

Mothlike in its lightness and rapid insistency, the so-familiar voice spoke. 'This, of course, is the chamber of devils, who sit in hexagon babbling like herring gulls about the ruin of charity and the disorderly rupture of souls . . . The aforesaid malignants have provided a chair, a little to your left: that's it. Before you lie four feet of carpet; then a box upon which I am rudely – but I hope reassuringly-seated. Nothing else is worth noting except a bundle of effects belonging to Johnnie Bullo – you'll have discovered his name. He was, of course, my friend of the cave. A long time ago. Is that better?' he asked. 'I wonder what frightened you?'

Astonishing that a voice should carry such power to soothe and disarm. She said, seated, clasping her hands, 'It's been a bad sort of day – I'm sorry – and the Fair on top was a little too much.'

'A day remarkable, certainly, for a wholesale slaughter of the innocents,' he said. 'I wonder how the parrot enjoyed its brief second of freedom. And the victim of the less schismatic shaft, how's he?'

She told him, and he received it with a hint of mockery, adding: 'Don't, for your own sake, begin weaving fantasies of evil around me as well. I haven't tried to kill anybody today, I give you my word.'

'Well, if you had, I think you probably would have succeeded,' said Christian. 'Do you shoot?'

'Yes. Very well, as it happens: one of my vanities, you see. It's handsome to watch, and satisfying to perform; it's convivial and competitive and artistic and absorbing. Poets love it: they rush home to unpick all their quills and write odes with them.'

'Others don't,' she said quickly. 'Others kill.'

There was a little silence. Then he said, 'And that's what you're afraid of, isn't it? Violence?'

It was true, and she acknowledged it. 'Except that it isn't trained and purposeful violence that terrifies me: it's the negligent, casual kind. All these people today . . . They were taking wagers, you know, on Culter's chances of life. And violence of a nasty, inconsequent kind, tonight at the Fair. Or the kind that amuses itself by stuffing women and children into a cave and smoking them to death. In slaughtering livestock and burning a harvest for fun. Or after Pinkie, when the army broke; and the Durham and York and Newcastle boys, and the landknechts and Italians and Spaniards sat on their beautiful horses and flew along the Leith sands, and the Holyrood road, and the Dalkeith road, hawking men with their swords like butterflies . . .'

'Violence in nature is one thing,' said Christian, 'but among civilized mankind, what excuse is there?'

His voice was cheerful. 'Nothing more civilizing than a good crack of thunder. One hot unsettled summer and whole countrysides end up like St. James with their knees hard as camels . . . No. I take your point. But what in God's name had that poor, enthusiastic, politically imbecile troop of Englishmen last month got to do with civilization? And what's going to stop them? Religion? With their music, their churches, their prayers, in a rag bag at home;

His Most Christian Majesty of France egging on the Turks to scimitar the head off His Most Catholic Majesty King Charles; the Bishop of Rome seducing the Lutherans in Germans to secure his posterity . . .'

Christian said, 'What kind of excuse would you make then for a private assassin?'

He was silent for a moment, then said, 'Let's get one thing clear. I'm not excusing anything. I'm no theologian, only a pedagogue in rhetoric, with whatever shreds of humanity the universities have left me with.'

'Well, as an apologist for human nature, then. What of private murder?'

'What of it? This afternoon's, if you mean to particularize, was neither very private nor very successful, by all accounts. It shouldn't be difficult to classify. Not high-spirited; not casual; an act of instructed force, like Somerset's: a matter of policy, in fact.

'And brilliantly carried off – by the Old Man of the Mountains himself, obviously, the Sheikh-al-jebal, twanging his hemp instead of eating it. Motives: greed, hate, envy – I don't know. Excuses: there don't seem to be many. He might, of course, be a saintly old sheikh, whose doctrines Culter was denying; or a lascivious old sheikh, whose mistress Culter had alienated . . . except that Culter, Jerome bless his childlike head, is such a remarkably dull and blameless creature himself.'

'For a humanist,' she said, 'you're very scathing on the subject of virtue. For one thing, you shouldn't confuse stolidity and self-control.'

'You admire self-control?' he asked, and she took her chance.

'I admire candour.'

He retorted instantly. 'Oh, nothing better – in the right place. "It's only right you should know" – I wonder how many that classic bêtise has driven to the river and the dagger and the pillow in a quiet corner. Truth's nothing but falsehood with the edges sharpened up, and illtempered at that: no repair, no retraction, no possible going back once it's out. If I told you I'd murdered my own sister you'd register appropriate feelings of hate and revulsion; and if you found later I hadn't, I'd be sure of your interest and sympathy in twice the depth of your hate. Whereas, if you simply found proof positive that I *had* killed her . . .'

'. . . I might loathe you, but I'd respect your courage,' she said candidly. 'Besides, that sort of truth wouldn't hurt me, would it? It might affect you, but then you'd deserve it.'

She had surprised him into laughter. 'Oh, God! Generously abstaining from the sword in order to macerate with a cudgel. Pax! Leave me some pride. Pretend at least that you wouldn't collapse in a delirium of joy as I dance a vuelta on the widdy. In any case, I stick to my point. Not ninety-nine women out of a hundred really prefer that kind of honesty; and even if you are the hundredth, I'm the last to help you prove it to yourself. No. Si vis pingere, pinge sonum, as Echo rudely remarked. If you want a full study of me, then paint my voice. It's all there is on display at present.'

'To be sure,' said Christian serenely. 'And painting with breath is my stock-in-trade – you'd forgotten that, hadn't you? I'm an architect in lexicography; I can build you a palace of adverbs and a hermitage of personal pronouns . . . and I can give you information about Crouch.'

For the first time, she felt him at a loss. She went on serenely. 'Jonathan Crouch. The man you asked about. George Douglas sold him to Sir Andrew Hunter, who wanted to exchange him for a cousin, or something. Then Crouch escaped with someone – Hunter doesn't know who, but he's violently angry about it all, and swearing death to whoever released him.'

'I see – wait,' he said. 'How do you know all this?'

'Because,' said Christian, rising, 'he was overheard giving George Douglas two English names mentioned by Crouch, and he more or less asked Douglas to help track them down in the hope they'd lead to the man who freed his prisoner. I thought you'd be interested . . . and now I must go. Oh!' She sat down again, smiling. 'Hadn't you better tell my fortune first?'

To her glee, he sounded taken aback. 'Oh, Johnnie looks after all that, although under certain circumstances I tell him what to say. Do you really want it done?'

She laughed. 'Not really. It'd be more to the point, I think, if I could read yours.'

'Yes. Well, you'd qualify for M. Rabelais's next Almanac if you could do that,' he said dryly. 'But if you're anxious, I'll tell you something that'll satisfy our misdoubting Tom. Your loof, lady. I'm sorry, a bit closer. The only candle is guttering like a drunk man's fancy. Now.'

Firmly, her wrist was taken, and the fingers spread out. 'A fine, capable hand. Line of life – hullo! You appear to have died at the age of seven.'

'The embalmers are exceedingly skilful nowadays,' she said gravely.

'But I will say this . . . You'll get the most out of life, never fear; and meet the sort of man you want, that too; and get your heart's desire, I think, in the end – if you believe the results of Johnnie's teaching. But what are we, after all? Charlatans, faiseurs d'horoscope . . .'

She did not know quite what to say. 'It sounds like an exemplary future?'

'If you bring your own candle next time, I might do better. Equipment rather limited, imagination in free supply. Are you leaving Stirling soon?'

'On Tuesday. If Lord Culter can travel. All the Crawfords and Agnes are going back to Midculter: I shall go with them, and then on to Boghall until Christmas.' She hesitated. 'There's still nothing I can do? We seem to waste all our meetings talking nonsense, and all the time I feel . . .'

'. . . The sands are running out? Well, if they are, it's only from one end of a great silly pot to the other. Someone'll come and stand us on our heads, and the sand'll run back again – same sand – same span of time, all the grains saying excitedly to one another: Hullo! It's

170

you again! Met you in '47 in a fortuneteller's booth in Stirling!'

'I'm not sure,' said Christian carefully, 'but I think that's cheap theology.'

'Well it's a poor apologue, I agree,' he said, 'and a sorry kind of note to leave on. All right. Cancel the sand.

> *'Li jalous*
> *Envious*
> *de cor rous*
> *morra*
> *et li dous*
> *savourous*
> *amourous*
> *m'aura . . .*

'No, dammit,' he said, dissatisfied. 'Too fleshy a note altogether . . .'

'Goodbye!' she said, feeling behind her for the curtain.

'My measures are all mad. They prick, they prance, as princes that were woud . . . Goodbye,' he said, part-returning from sunny contemplation among the iambics. 'There's Johnnie coming now: he'll see you out.' He clasped her hand briefly. 'I may not see you for a while, but perhaps I shall write.'

'*Write!*'

'Yes. It's all right. I mean that – I haven't forgotten: wait and see,' he said rapidly. 'Till then!'

There came a firm grasp on her elbow from behind, and Bullo led her to the outer tent. For half a dozen paces she could still hear his voice, soulfully declaiming, half to himself, she thought:

> *'And evermore the Cukkow, as he fley*
> *He seyde Farewell, Farewell, papinjay!'*

* * *

Johnnie Bullo, his eyes speculative, watched the party go from the doorway of the tent. Then he returned inside, lit another candle, and opened the inner flap.

The man inside, deftly booting one supple limb, looked up.

'Have they gone?' said Lymond. 'Thank you, Johnnie. Your performance with the first two filled me with respect. For chastely phrased double-entendres you have no master.' He adjusted his straps. 'Three well-endowed kitties.'

'Well, two of them were well enough,' admitted the gypsy. 'The wee one had a face like a pound of candles on a hot day.'

'The devil she has.' Lymond put one spurred foot on the floor and reached for the second boot. 'The wee one, as you call her, has a face informed with beauty, wisdom and wit. In other words, my Johnnie, she's thirteen, free and stinking rich.'

'Oh. Then you've had a good day of it, I suppose.'

'Then you suppose wrong,' said Lymond shortly. 'I've had a damned carking afternoon. A Moslem would blame my Ifrit, a Buddhist explain the papingo was really my own great-grandmother, and a Christian, no doubt, call it the vengeance of the Lord. As a plain, inoffensive heathen, I call it bloody annoying.'

He stood up. 'Where's my cloak? Oh, there. I'm off, Johnnie. A small memento on the table.;

Bullo saw him to the doorway. 'You're off south tonight?'

'I am. There's a gentleman I have to meet on the Carlisle road on Friday.' The Master glanced once, with calculation, around the tent; and then brushed past the gypsy. Without further leave-taking, he had gone.

'And not to the gentleman's profit, either,' said Johnnie to himself with a grin, watching the nondescript figure merge into the dark crowd. The grin became wider, became a laugh, became a convulsion of secret mirth.

Johnnie Bullo, hugging himself, went back into the tent.

PART II
The Play for Gideon Somerville

1

SMOTHERED MATE

The sixthe pawne . . . resembleth the
Taverners, hostelers and sellars of
vitaylle . . . Many paryls and adventures may
happen on the wayes and passages to hem
that ben herberowed within their Innes.

1 · REMOVAL OF A BLOCKING KNIGHT

Lord Culter, gently examining the tapestries in the big
hall at Branxholm, was talking in a soft and savourless
voice which his host found peculiarly uncomfortable.

Branxholm, great throne of the Buccleuchs, lay twelve
miles from the English border. The present house, less
than twenty years old, was built from the crusts of the
Branxholms which had already been fired, and fired again,
by the enthusiasms of its neighbours. Branxholm was a
bald edifice of vile architecture and no blandishments of
moss or ivy. Inside, it was the tilting ground and battlefield
of the Buccleuch young.

Babies bounced and abounded in the Scott household:
babies with mouths round and adhesive as lampreys;
babies like Pandean pipes, of diminishing size and res-
onant voice; babies rendering torture and catalysis among
the animate, the inanimate and the comatose. The Buccleuchs themselves were totally immune. While their young-
lings fought, and nurses and tutors swooped and called
like starlings, Sir Wat and Dame Janet pursued their own
highly individual courses, and talked to each other about
whatever came into their heads.

Today, a morose and pallid Friday in November, the

subject was Lymond. In a childless oasis at the end of the big hall Sir Wat glowered uneasily in his big chair, feet in furred boots stuck out before him in the rushes, a woollen nightshirt peeping through the folds of his ample damask nightgown, and a variety of dogs heaped panting about his legs. Dame Janet, her gown napped with tufts and trails of wool, was spinning and swearing indiscriminately when the thread broke and when her husband roused her temper.

From the wall behind them both, his eyes still on the battered hangings, Lord Culter said, 'I've already gathered you have no intention of helping me, I wondered if, perhaps, you meant actively to hinder me instead?'

Sir Wat irritably shoved from one knee a heavy jowl which confidingly and automatically replaced itself, chumbling. 'Man, have I to go yap, yap all day with the same tale? I've told you. I'm sick.'

Dame Janet gave a bark of laughter. 'Sick to the tune of two flounders, a pike, a cod, a quart of claret and a quince pie. Hah! You'll do yourself a hurt, Wat; forcing the nourishment down at all costs, and you a sick man.'

Buccleuch snapped, justifiably riled, 'It's the English I'm supposed to be ailing for – or am I to live on sops in wine in case Grey of Wilton's sitting up the kitchen lum? I've told you all till I'm tired. Grey wants me. I'll have to promise something. I've asked the Queen and Arran to let me give the Protector some sort of lip service: until I have proper permission I'm ill, and I stay ill. Dod, Culter: have you seen what Seymour and his wee friends from the Lothians did to Cranston Riddell in September? And the Wharton brats and the Langholm garrison popping in and out like hen harriers – three weeks ago they were raiding Kirkcudbright and Lamington. It'll be Branxholm next, and you'll wish you'd listened to me when you're frying like eggs on the saddle roof.'

Lord Culter left the tapestry. He strolled to the fire, turned, and looked down on Buccleuch. 'Then stay at home and give me your men and your dogs.'

There was a harried silence. Then Buccleuch said bitterly, 'The implication being that I enjoy sitting here on my behind while there's danger in the wind. Were you at the last Council meeting? Arran's off to lay siege to the English garrison on the Tay, the Ambassadors are off to ask men and money from Denmark and France. And meantime it's all the clack that a sort of unofficial hint has gone from Paris to London promising neutrality if the English'll get out of Boulogne. A fine lookout, isn't it? And winter here, and no excess of food, and precious few ships getting through the blockade, and half the able men shot to the devil at Pinkie. Be damned to your brother!' said Buccleuch heatedly. 'I've got my own worries.'

Culter watched him quietly, one hand pattering on the chimney piece. 'I'm sure you have. I thought perhaps you might consider me less dangerous to Will than Lymond will be. Or to be less parochial – that you might agree that obstruction of royal messengers and leakage of state information ought to be stopped by responsible people.'

'Responsible! That's nearly a bad word to a Buccleuch,' said Dame Janet, pouncing as she spoke on a snatch of down. She missed it: it became incandescent and whisked up the chimney. 'And there's Will's immortal soul for you,' said Lady Buccleuch, seizing her moral with evangelical skill from her own hearthstone. 'And here's his father, worried yellow in case the poor creature scandalizes the nation and promotes an international incident anent the Buccleuch family.'

'International incident my -!' said her husband rudely, going red in the face. 'Let the Council put the chains on Will, and he'll be lucky to escape with his silly neck. You wouldn't be so rarin' keen to haul him into the light of grace if he were a son of your own, Janet Beaton. And why the sour mouth, pray?' pursued Buccleuch, who on a celebrated occasion had pulled an even sourer. 'What unnatural sort of corruption is Will to meet at Lymond's that's new in the French court? Credit the boy with more strength of mind that a new-gutted lamp-wick. Or are you maybe not so much worried about Will as anxious to put a bit rope round that yellow-headed cacodemon's neck? I

177

told you at the time, if you kept your mouth shut, you wouldn't have got a hole in your shoulder . . . Dod!' – as a storm of juvenile complaint exploded in the rafters – 'Woman, can you not keep those brats quiet! Some folk,' said Buccleuch to Lord Culter with heavy sarcasm, 'have woodworm and weevils. Branxholm has weans.'

Lady Buccleuch was tart. 'And whose fault is that?'

'Oh, mine; mine; mine, I suppose,' bawled Sir Wat. 'I'm a fair oddity: I can raise my weans in an annual crop like barley all on my own, and I'd think a wife just a plain interference in the business.'

'I wouldn't just say you were wrong,' said Dame Janet cruelly. 'At least you were getting some fine yields, by all accounts, before ever a priest said a marriage service over you.'

'Oh, is it sermons now? You'll make a bonny figure in a surplice, my lady: Sister Berchta with the long, iron nose and the ae big foot; and it forever slap in someone else's business . . .'

The Buccleuch's, foaming pleasurably, pranced into battle. Richard stood still, his eyes on Sir Wat's profile: a cheek more than usually red proved that Buccleuch was aware of it. The exchange continued. The argument became corybantic and public; it blared; it stopped. A commotion at the door, a magnetic tumescence of children, a bright voice and a beaming servant announced the unlooked-for arrival of Lord Culter's mother.

'Sybilla!' Buccleuch, in a spray of cushions and offended dogs, got up and went forward. Janet, her tongue arrested in blistering flight, rose likewise from her coiling threads and hugged the small, self-contained figure. 'Come and sit down.'

'Well, Richard!' The Dowager, relinquishing her furs, approached the fire and offered a cheek to her son. He was courteous, but with a wariness in his manner which did not escape Lady Buccleuch. They all sat, Sybilla capturing the nearest child, drying its thumb and setting it firmly on her lap. 'I want sanctuary from the Herries child.

178

You're looking very well, Wat. Being in a decline suits you.'

Janet said quickly, 'What's wrong with young Agnes?'

'We have had a visit,' said the Dowager gloomily, 'from the prospective bridegroom. Arran's son. He was not well received.'

'What about it?' said Buccleuch. 'She's a ward of the Crown. Arran can dispose of her as he wants, and if he wants the Herries lands for his son, who's to stop him?'

'His son,' said the Dowager prosaically.

'Good lord.' Buccleuch stared. 'There's nothing wrong with that lassie's face her dowry won't correct.'

'I don't think even her dowry can drown her voice,' said the Dowager. 'When exercised with intent. Besides, she's waiting for a thin man with a romantic smile named Jack: palmistry can be so embarrassing. Which reminds me. Janet, you're bid to Midculter tomorrow week. We are to have a dissertation on the Philosopher's Stone.'

'The Phil . . . ?'

'I knew Wat would forget to tell you.' In greatest detail, Sybilla explained. She outlined the properties of the talisman and the subtleties of its manufacture. From there she launched into a technical description of the cure for a tertiary.

Thus drummed out of the conversational stakes, her son rose. The Dowager declined his escort home, gracefully accepted an invitation to stay the night, and watched as, impeded by remarkably little pressure on all sides, Richard prepared to go home.

Lady Buccleuch, walking with her guest to the yard, was in no carefree mood either. 'Wat has a tongue on him like an anteater, and he doesn't much care what he does with it. Damn it, I *like* Will. He's as much to me as any child of my own.'

'Buccleuch understands that, of course,' said Richard. 'All he's concerned with is protecting the boy, after his fashion. But the brutal fact is that there is no protection. I tell you, Lymond has taken three months to kill all the years of my childhood. He'll destroy Will Scott in a week.'

Not the statement but the expression of it moved her. She valued him sufficiently not to show it, but said flatly instead, 'You don't need to convince me. I'll go further and say I'd stop at nothing – nothing at all – to part Will from the Master.'

Richard was silent. Lady Buccleuch waited, then trapped an arm, and with it, his eyes. 'God – if your conscience is as tender as that, *I'll* say it. I know what's good for Buccleuch. One of these days he's going to catch up with Will, and when he does, he'll take good care that you don't get to hear of it. But there's nothing to stop *me* from telling you – Wait, now! Wait and hear me. Lymond dead means Will captured and facing his deserts. Buccleuch's afraid of just that thing; but surely nothing could make it clearer to England that Will has been acting without sanction? And no one, surely, on the Scottish side is going to hurt Buccleuch's oldest son – the more so since his venture at Hume. That's common sense; and being so, I haven't the slightest compunction in going behind Wat's silly back. Do you agree with me?'

There was another pause. Finally Richard said, 'I do, of course. But – I'm sorry – I can't see myself entering into a kind of conspiracy against Wat. Not when his own views are quite clear. Persuade Buccleuch of all you've just said, Janet, and then I'll be glad to get all the help I can from both of you.' He mounted, and eyed her from the saddle. 'Janet Beaton: go in and manage your man. Then I'll discuss it with you.'

Lady Buccleuch's face split into its disarming grin. 'Och, I've finished discussing it,' she said. And smacking the rump of his horse, she waved him goodbye.

2 · IRREGULAR PARTIE BETWEEN TWO MASTERS

Three days later, the land was choked with fog, consuming the sight from the eye and the air from the nostrils of Scot and Englishman alike. In the two estuary forts the militia were hagridden in the white gloom by the creak of marauding rowlocks; Hume and Roxburgh went red-eyed to bed, and the Borderers lay sleepless at night with their swords and dirks warm about them. The Peel used by Lymond's men was likewise lost and cradled in fog. In the ruinous hall of it, the heir of Branxholm was playing cards with every mark of professional ease and skill.

'Play the eight,' advised Mr. Crouch intelligently. 'Then Matthew can put down his ten.'

Turkey Mat, flinging down his cards, dragged a horny palm over his bald head and breathed like a sailing skiff, lee rail under. 'Fancy now: I had the queerest notion there that you were out of this game.'

Mr. Crouch was unperturbed. 'I am. You told me yourself to keep off, or you'd play the next with my chitterlings.'

Turkey, grunting, unbuckled a leather purse at his belt, reversed it, then let it fall with an eloquent flop on the table. 'And you needna skin your nose looking for the reason,' said he. 'It's the ones with the smooth pansy faces that turn out to be the know-alls at cards. Three months' wages off me in as many minutes, and my very breath pledged before it comes out between my teeth. Englishmen? Sharks! And the cooing voice on them like a bishop piping for his red bunnet.'

'Your mistake.' Will Scott, sprawled elegantly over a chair, had in two months found a certain style, and was enlarging on it. 'Next time look at its teeth before you fleece it.'

'You can talk.' Turkey eyed the pile of money in front of the boy. 'I'll swear Crouch has been giving you lessons. You were safe for twenty crowns any day when you first came, and now you've a nose for pips like a peccary hog.'

'Mr. Scott has a quick mind.' Since his enforced residence at, and his lightning departure from, Ballaggan, Mr. Crouch has been short of an audience, and he was not the man to loose a chance. He said, a trifle wistfully, 'The best man I ever saw at the tables was Buskin Palmer –'

'Him King Harry hanged for taking too much off him at cards?'

'Him. He,' said Mr. Crouch, a stickler for accuracy. 'The great master, that was. I owe any little touch I might have at cards to that man and his brother. When I was in the Princess Mary's household –'

'And when would that be, now?' inquired a new voice.

The trio turned. With some forethought, table and stakes had been set up at a distance from the other activity in the crowded room, and the authority of Mat had so far kept their bailiwick exclusive. When Turkey turned, it was with a snarl which changed to a mild roar. 'Johnnie Bullo! Man, I wish you'd take to wearing clappers on your breeches; you're desperate sore on the arteries. And that last damned powder you gave me would have done Jimmie of Fynnart a twelve-month and pointed up the whole of Linlithgow if you laid it on with a trowel. Will ye bring to mind it's my inner workings you're repairing, not the Toll Brig o' Dumfries.'

Johnnie Bullo, gently oblivious, drew up a barrel, sat on it, and again addressed the Englishman. 'So you were in the Princess Mary's household, were you? When? Was it the year of Solway Moss?'

Jonathan Crouch looked blank.

Johnnie expounded. 'The year the Scots King James died, and the small Queen was born. The year Wharton broke up the Scottish army on the Solway and took half of it prisoner to London, including Lymond. The year Lymond's pastime was first discovered in Scotland, and the English gave him a fine manor for his pains. Fifteen forty-two.'

Mr. Crouch said, 'Well now . . . Yes. I'd be with the Princess about that time. Five years ago, near enough.'

'I thought so,' said Johnnie. Mr. Crouch looked confused, Matthew seemed vaguely annoyed and Will Scott, removing Turkey's purse from the board and laying down a fresh card, said, 'Well, go on. We can't bear the suspense.'

The gypsy settled on his barrel and flashed the white teeth. 'Why,' he asked Mr. Crouch, 'did Lymond release you from Ballaggan?'

'You may well ask,' said Jonathan strongly. 'To send me home: that's what he said. And what does he do? Lock me up to catch my death in an upended quarry I wouldn't dignify by the name of a house, with robbers and cutthroats for companions – present company excepted; no intellectual resources – present company excepted; and no clothes but the one clean shirt on my back.'

'You're away ahead of present company there,' said Johnnie. 'Why?'

'Why? How should I know?' exclaimed Mr. Crouch with exasperation. 'The man hasn't spoken two words to me since I came here.'

'Matthew knows why,' said Johnnie, and smiled to himself.

The Englishman presented Turkey with a face of indignant inquiry, and Matthew sighed. 'The Master has notions about being discussed behind his back. But it's not all that private. The fact is that since the money began coming in fairly easy we've been filling in our time looking for a gentleman, and Lymond thought you were maybe him.'

'And it's a fine thing for you that you're not.' Bullo's white teeth shone. 'For – at a guess – the man the Master is looking for is the man who betrayed all those treasonable games of his to the Scottish Government five years ago. Am I right, Mat?'

Mr. Crouch got up so quickly he upset the cards. 'Is that true? Because – '

'It's right enough. What of it?'

'Because,' said Mr. Crouch with agitation, 'I gave him the names of the two other officers of the household of my own rank in those days. Somerville and Harvey. I told him the names in all good faith. And now, from what you say – '

'You've dispatched at least one of them to a very fancy death,' said Johnnie Bullo cheerfully; and watched Mr. Crouch, making little ejaculations to himself, shoot in the direction of the door.

Will Scott reached it just before him. 'Where are you off to?'

'I demand,' said Mr. Crouch, 'to see the Master of Culter, or whatever he calls himself. I find his whole treatment of me intolerable, and I intend to tell him so.'

'Lymond isn't here,' said Will. With dreamlike punctiliousness the door beside them opened and white fog swam and curdled about them. A shadow, beaded and plateresque, spoke. 'Ring the bells backwards: on his cue, he is here. Who wants me?'

Mr. Crouch peered and was rewarded with a study, sfumato, of unmistakable hands ungloving themselves deftly. Then the door closed and Lymond became wholly visible, embracing Scott and Crouch in the heavy, unpleasant regard. 'Well?'

For a moment the Englishman's heart failed him. Then he said stoutly, 'I demand some satisfaction from you, sir. Four weeks have passed since I left Ballaggan in your company, and no effort has been made to restore me to my home. Had I stayed with Sir Andrew I could expect to be ransomed and back with my Ellen a month before this.'

'I doubt it,' said the Master. He threw the gloves on a chair and took an alepot from a tray hurriedly brought him. 'I am disappointed in you, Mr. Crouch. Here you are in our Paestum, warm, fed and rent free, and with a face like cheese rennet. Are your companions dull? Surely you can educate them? Are they poor conversationalists? Then edify them: they should make princely listeners. Do they have little skill at cards? Then ruin them: you have my permission. It is really time,' said Lymond, 'that you were developing some sense of social responsibility.' And he walked to the fire and seated himself, his eyes sliding over Matthew and Johnnie and the scattered cards. Will Scott sat down near him. Mr. Crouch, affronted and unhappy, stood stiff-legged before the fire. He began: 'If I had stayed at Ballaggan – '

The Master, stretching in a leisurely way, looked up at his prisoner. 'The ass with the voice of Stentor,' he remarked. 'That was all you were to Sir Andrew, I regret to tell you. The cheese in the mousetrap, Mr. Crouch.'

Will Scott suddenly found his tongue. 'A trap to catch you, sir?'

Lymond clicked down his tankard on the table beside him as a fresh one approached. 'Who at Annan knew we were asking about our friend here?'

'The captain at the gate, I suppose, who let us in?' said Scott, remembering.

'Who let us in and suffered accordingly. When the English got out of Annan and my dear brother got in, the captain was left to breathe his last. He did so, I fancy, into Sir Andrew Hunter's ear.'

'– And guessing you had an interest in Crouch, Sir Andrew set about getting hold of him in order to take you . . . but,' said Scott, working out the problem with some care, 'why keep it to himself in that case?'

'It's not difficult to imagine,' said Lymond dryly. 'First, Sir Andrew is a young man living considerably above his means; second, I have a price of a thousand crowns on my head; and third – ' He paused, and Scott saw his eyes were cold. 'The third reason,' said Lymond slowly, 'is still open to conjecture. In any case: the ensuing flight of fancy has cost friend Hunter a broken head and Mr. Crouch – I see – a cold in the head and an unhappy lapse in good manners.'

'Now look here,' said Mr. Crouch, too riled to be afraid. 'I've had about enough of this. I was taken a prisoner of war, all right and proper, and I've got the right to be exchanged or ransomed back, as soon as may be, according to the law on both sides. You talk,' said Jonathan heatedly, 'as if it were a privilege to be shut in a damned, filthy – '

'But it is.' Lymond uncurled and rose; with a long index finger he pressed the titmouse into his own seat and closed his protesting fingers around the second mug of beer. 'But it is. Such a study you will never meet again. Here we are, our beards smugly shaven, prolixt, corrupt and perpetuall. You have come until the grisly land of mirknes, and

185

with reasonable luck you may leave it yet. And that, Mr. Crouch, is the greatest privilege of all.'

Mr. Crouch, pot in hand, make to speak. Lymond forestalled him. 'No. You spend your speech and waste your brain. Accept our gifts and be grateful. Either Gideon Somerville or Samuel Harvey is a douce and God-fearing man and has nothing but legitimate shock to expect from me. Whatever happens to the other he will probably deserve and would have happened most likely whether you helped or not. But I don't want my birds flushed, Mr. Crouch. When I've spoken to both, you can go home.'

The prisoner was not reassured. 'I want to go now,' he said starkly.

'You can,' said Lymond gently. 'Oh, you can. Whenever you wish. Fragment by fragment. Drink your wine and learn gratitude. Quoi! Ce n'est pas encore beaucoup d'avoir de mon gosier retiré votre cou?'

Mr. Crouch, succumbing to force majeure, drank his wine: the Master, turning his back on him, rambled to the card table and idly fingered the scattered suits. 'Blind Fortune, stumbling chance, spittle luck, false dealing – take to cards if you will, Marigold, but must you stare at me like a kitten with its dam? . . . Johnnie, are your gypsies all here?'

'A mile away. I smell wind later on.'

'Good. Away thou dully night. Scott, into what impurities has Turkey led you, other than the giddy vaults of gambling?'

'Impurities!' exclaimed Mat, indignant on principle.

'Moral irregularities,' said Lymond. 'Diversions.'

'Oh, diversions,' said Mat, with the air of a man who understood all. God: we've been that damned hard at it, we havena had a diversion since the last night at the Ostrich.'

Scott, his face still crimson, said belligerently, 'I've never been to the Ostrich.'

The familiar, chatoyant glint was in Lymond's eyes. 'The Ostrich is in the hands of a common woman, that dwells there to receive men to folly. The question is, do we seek such madness? The answer is, we do.'

He looked from one to other of the three men, his eyes flickering. 'Let us go to Paradise, where every man shall have fourscore wives, all maidens. Let us go tonight, and speir at the Monks of Bamirrinoch gif lecherie be sin . . . Scott?'

Will's eyes were bright. He nodded.

'Matthew? Yes, I'm sure. And Johnnie, who is going in any case.'

Johnnie Bullo smiled, and hissed between his teeth. 'Just so.'

Scott, caught watching Lymond again, blushed scarlet. The Master addressed him thoughtfully. 'Are you anxious to go? These serpents slay men, and they eat them weeping.'

Sophisticated at all costs, Scott quoted Rabelais. 'But the ravens, the popinjays, the starlings, they make into poets.'

'No,' said Lymnond. 'The popinjays they dismember.'

*　*　*

The four men and the gypsies reached the Ostrich Inn at nightfall in thick fog.

During the long ride, Will Scott stayed with Bullo. In the first moments, the Master's sorrel disappeared among the hoary beasts of the gypsy troop and stayed there: burst of muffled laughter and occasional snatches of song excoriated the ears of the other three. Turkey Mat, flesh with the flesh of his horse, rode solitary: long tail, fluid back and supine, sentient wrist. Bullo, at Scott's side, sat as an owl might sit, listening for the folding of long grasses. Once, with the uncanny thought-sense Scott had noticed before, he said, 'He's wild tonight,' and the boy hardly realized another had spoken.

To the new Scott, the core and engrossment of his days was their central figure. Nothing of the warm vulgarities of Branxholm or the artifice of the Louvre or the ambitious, emotional expediencies of Holyrood had prepared him for the inhumanities of Lymond. To the men exposed to his rule Lymond never appeared ill: he was never tired; he was never worried, or pained, or disappointed, or passionately angry. If he rested, he did so alone; if he slept, he took good care to sleep apart. ' – I sometimes doubt if he's human,' said Will, speaking his thought aloud. 'It's probably all done with wheels.'

A scintilla in the fog was the gypsy's smile. 'He proved very human in September. I seem to recall you had a sore head as well, after the skirmish with Culter and Erskine?'

Scott's horse halted. He swore, kicked it on again, and said, 'I was on my back for four days: d'you mean Lymond was hit?'

'Very humanly. By a stone. And led us the devil's own dance bringing him back, Mat and I. We had to leave him under cover – Culter and the rest came about us like bedbugs in an almshouse dorter – and when it was safe to go back, the infallible Lymond had found himself a horse and vanished. We found him, of course.'

'Where?'

'It would be a shade indiscreet to say. Particularly with the two most interested parties at our elbow. You perhaps noticed that when we came back there was no mention of our passing faiblesse. Lymond, you see, is omnipotent, as you were saying.'

The white teeth flashed again. 'Ask me again. I'm going to Edinburgh this Saturday, but when I come back, we might meet over it. The story'll charm you. You'll maybe want to write a poem about it, if you're that way inclined: how Lymond passed the days after Annan. It's a bonny tale.'

Scott listened, and hearing in Bullo's voice an acid counterpoint to the high, sudden cackle of gypsy laughter behind, grinned sedately to himself and rode on.

They had kept to the high ground, where the fog was thinner and the ground less rotten. At some point the heather roots and tarnished bracken of Scotland became the heather roots and bracken of England. They crossed the Border like a fixed and hidden constellation and passed silently over lost grass behind the dim, leading form of Johnnie. The whiteness turned to black; the day withdrew, and they breasted the last incline.

Before them, vast golden parhelions blistered the fog. They approached. The colour changed and sharpened, became windows lit by lanterns and candles; and an open door, and faint music and voices, and a warm, stinging fragrance of roast meat curiously laced with musk. Became a courtyard with running ostler-wraiths, appearing and evaporating with the horses and, finally, an enormous shadow in the wide doorway: a monstrous, eighteen-stone shadow of a woman with a fresh, childlike face, who stretched powdered arms, calling, to Lymond. 'It's yourself . . . and Johnnie! Back at last . . . Lord! We thought we were abandoned.'

'Why else,' said Lymond, 'are we here?' The eyes were sea-blue and the expression one of celestial affability. 'This, Marigold, is the Ostrich Inn. So hop Willieken, hop Willieken: England is thine and mine . . .' and moving swiftly to the threshold, he scooped up the tremendous form of his hostess, accepted a hearty kiss and a dimpled arm along his shoulders, and disappeared indoors.

Scott found Johnnie Bullo looking at him with an ironic glint in the brown eyes. 'Come along,' said Johnnie. 'We're allowed in as well.'

* * *

Men keeping vigil at the dawn of battle spoke of the square common room of the Ostrich. It rose two silken stories high, and whole oxen confessed to the fires at each end and reached sizzling Judgment on the crowded tables, alongside pies and puddings and heaped fragrant trenchers and jars of bland, too-warm wines.

All the pleasures of unfilled time belonged to the Ostrich. For those who were shy about sleeping in public, a wooden arcade around three sides of the room supported a gallery at first-story level, off which opened the private rooms. Wax lights blazed. The gypsies, flooding the centre floor with music and violent colour, danced in the footsteps

189

of tumblers and harpists and magicians and monkeys; of bears and minstrels and dogs and play actors and mimics; and the painted walls and brilliant hangings kept a sense of them. Combers of talk and laughter rolled aggrandizing from pillar to pillar with the beat of drum and guitar; the air bounced with fat enjoyment and gourmandise, and bright ministering women like chaffinches flew and darted between the dark arcades.

Will Scott, at one of the fires, found his fogged eyes swimming with the blaze of marching lights and his senses drugged with fleshly smells and mulled wine and the heat of the fat-spitting fire. Lymond had vanished; Johnnie Bullo was plying his trade with his gypsies, and Mat, after an encounter half glimpsed in the pillars, had disappeared too. A gigantic and violent nostalgia for venison seized Scott: in its very midst he saw on the table before him a perfumed and steaming haunch, laid by the white, ringed hands of the she-monster.

She smiled at him. She was beautiful. The round, rose-petal face was clear and young and yet maternal in its look; her hair was shining and clean, her great bulging torso massy with velvets and ermines cut to show the great snowy shelf of her breast, on which rubies lay, calm, beaming testimony to her serenity.

He rose uncertainly. She put down wine and two tank-ards, bread, sweetmeats, cheese and knives and salt; then swung off her tray with one hand and pressed him back into his seat with the other. 'You don't get Molly serving you every day ... but then, you travel in very special company.' Her fine eyes with their dyed lashes appraised him. 'Nice manners! You're strong, but you're kind: that means gentle birth and a pitying heart ... What's your name, my dear?'

Her sweetness was irresistible, and her bulk meant nothing. He smiled back. 'I'm called Will.'

'Will! That's better!' The lovely eyes and mouth melted; she ruffled his hair gently, as his mother might have done. 'Make a good meal, my dear, and your golden-haired friend will be with you shortly. Oh, God!' said Molly, and raised heavenly blue eyes to the rafters. 'That hair! He was born to wreck us, body and soul, that one. Look at this!'

She lifted a white arm and fished below the rubies. A thin chain came into view, and at its end a ring with a single, magnificent square diamond. 'I suppose I've had more jewels in my life than most, but this is the one I wear; the one I got from him.' She laughed, and let it slip back. 'Don't look scared! Diamond rings are proper currency for such as him, but you won't need to pay for your dinner at the silversmiths. Never mind my babbling. Go on, eat up, and drink, and forget your troubles, whatever they are. That's what the Ostrich is for.'

She went quickly, gentle-footed, and he saw her go with a pang, and with a sudden, pleased resolve to do with diamonds. Then he turned to the table and forgot her. The venison was rich and savoury and cooked to tender perfection. The wine was warmly fumed and superb. The candies were strange and sweet; the cheeses firm and flavoured.

Life was glorious.

With a soft elegance Lymond slid into the seat opposite, and drew wine and plate toward him. He had changed into fine, fresh clothes: studying him, Scott was made conscious of his own splashed jacket and breeches. Slicing the venison, the Master remarked, apropos, 'Molly doesn't clothe giants, unhappily, my Pyrrha. You've met her?'

Will nodded.

'Molly married an innkeeper,' said Lymond. He poured wine and drank it, his eyes studying the other tables. 'And the innkeeper was never seen again. He married Molly, and brought her to the Ostrich – and next month, there was just Molly. Molly and her girls.'

Will said, 'She's a great admirer of yours.'

'She likes my money,' said Lymond, and catching the look in Scott's eye, grinned nastily. 'Which ring did she show you? The diamond or the seed pearl?'

Resentment on Molly's behalf faltered. 'She showed me a diamond ring,' said Scott defensively.

191

Lymond grinned again. 'If you're fool enough to wear a valuable stone in your bonnet, you must expect to be sized up accordingly.' He laughed outright. 'Never mind, my innocence: everyone falls in love with Molly. But not, of course, uniquely with Molly.' The pensive blue gaze continued to travel. 'The dark wench by the other fire is Sal; the redhead by the kitchen door is Elizabeth, and the one at the next table Joan.'

Will looked at Joan. She was pink and brown; her eyes sparkled like tourmalines and she had sharp ankles and red-heeled shoes. 'I've seen worse,' he remarked, and raised his tankard with an air. Lymond refilled it, and his own; and when Scott had finished his, filled it again. 'Multa bibens . . .' Then he looked around, signalled, and returned the gentle, appraising stare to Will's face. 'And now,' said the Master, 'suppose we fulfil our glad destiny?'

A cloud of musk approached and Molly in it, a cherub in its nest. 'You're ready, dear?'

'We are. And the room?' asked Lymond.

'Waiting for you. Number four, dear.' A key changed hands. 'You remember the stairs?'

She laughed, and Lymond said, 'They haven't left any great impression, but I recall they exist. We'll find them. Come, Marigold.'

Where there is no custom of reticence in childhood, there is no vice of which a well-brought-up young man need be ignorant – even a young man who three months before has cherished the purest ideals. When Will Scott got to his feet, his heartbeats were behaving oddly, but he was not slow in following the Master across the jammed, leg-strewn room, up a dark stairway leading from arcade to gallery, and along a long, stifling passage railed off on one side from the room they had just left. Wooden doors on the other side of the corridor were numbered. Lymond unlocked the fourth and went in, with Scott at his heels. The Master turned, and kicked the door shut.

The room held an uncurtained bed, a mirror, an armory, a table, two candlesticks and a youngish man, sitting on a low, cushioned bench. As Scott approached, the man jumped to his feet, frowning. He was tall, with long, fine hair and pale, opalesque eyes set shallowly in a triangular face. He said, 'I am expecting a gentleman. Are you . . .?'

'I am Lymond.' The Master moved into the candlelight, and recognition and relief showed in the other's eyes. 'And this is my lieutenant, Mr. Scott. Will – the Master of Maxwell.'

Three months of Lymond's company had taught Will Scott presence of mind. He bowed, and out of the wreckage of his emotions salvaged the necessary recollection: of the Master staging a rescue on the Carlisle road on a dark, October night, and of his voice saying afterward, 'The Master of Maxwell is an important personage almost entirely surrounded by English . . . Consider this an opening for smothered mate.' Scott, directing a private grimace at Lymond's unresponsive back, seated himself fatalistically on the edge of the bed; the Master of Maxwell was also reseated. Lymond, bringing a jug and cups from the armory, said, 'You're making for Carlisle, Mr. Maxwell?'

'If it's any affair of yours, I am, sir.' Yellow tiercel eyes notched with black stared at the Master; Lymond, impervious, poured wine. Scott, his interest suddenly commanded, thought, A show of muscle, by God! Have we found one gentleman who hasn't yet succumbed to the legend?

In silence, Lymond offered Maxwell wine; in silence, he took it. Then the Master hitched himself smoothly on the edge of the table, glanced at Scott, who had buried his nose in a cup, and said, 'I chose the Ostrich as our rendezvous, Mr. Maxwell, because of its uncommon properties. This is the sounding board of the North. No whisper is too low for the Ostrich. No movement too faint for its eyes. Consider, for example, who passed north recently. Ireland, for one – your brother's priest from London. He'll be waiting for you at Threave, anxious to have your views on Lord Maxwell's offer to surrender Lochmaben to the English. Who else? A surveyor from Calais, on his way to Wharton. The Scots garrisons at Crawford and

Langholm are worrying his lordship: Mr. Petit is to advise on the best ways of fortifying Dumfries, and Kirkcudbright, and Lochwood, and Milk, and Cockpool Tower, and Lochmaben – when they have it.

'Then Mr. Thomson, Lord Wharton's deputy, came north. That was in order to meet your uncle, Drumlanrig. Sir James failed, I'm afraid, to persuade him that between men of integrity hostages are irrelevant. And, of course, a number of gentlemen from the West Marches passed through to Carlisle to sign the celebrated oath. To serve the King of England, renounce the Bishop of Rome, do all in their power to advance the King's marriage with the Queen of Scotland; take part with all who serve him against their enemies, and obey the commands of the Lord Protector, lords lieutenant and wardens ... And most recently, one of Wharton's men came south with an indiscreet letter from your brother-in-law the Earl of Angus to someone else, which is going to interest the English considerably.'

Even to Scott, most of this was news. If it were true – and Maxwell would certainly know – it was a show of strength that even he could not afford to ignore. John Maxwell stretched his long legs, put down his cup, and lay back, the yellow eyes fixed on Lymond. 'Do you own the Ostrich? Or only a capacity for pleasing Molly?'

The blue eyes smiled. 'A distinction without a difference.'

Maxwell said, 'Mr. Crawford, there is no need to show me the hood. I respond quite well to the lure. Our last talk intrigued me a good deal.'

'Sufficiently?'

'Sufficiently for your purpose.' The luminous eyes, apparently satisfied with their diet, released their grip. Maxwell rose, refilled his cup and sat down, continuing in his dry, brisk voice. 'I have the information you wanted. Samuel Harvey, who is a bachelor, lives in London and is there at present on duty and unlikely to come north. Gideon Somerville is a wealthy man, now retired from court, with a manor called Flaw Valleys on Tyneside near

Hexham. He is married and has a ten-year-old daughter. I made these inquiries privately when last in Carlisle: there is nothing to connect them with your name.'

'I'm obliged for your care. As it turns out, it hardly matters.'

'You've no interest in these men?'

'I intend to meet them both. But one of your brothers-in-law is aware of it, and either he or Grey will almost certainly prepare the ground for me. No matter. Of Cat, nor Fall, nor Trap, I haif nae Dreid.'

'Your self-confidence is incredible, sir,' said Maxwell dryly.

'Subject to intelligence,' said Lymond, 'nothing is incalculable. Your marriage, for instance.'

Scott, fascinated, thought he saw John Maxwell's eyes narrow. There was the briefest pause, then the tall man said, 'I have considered your suggestion. On my present standing with the Queen Dowager, neither she nor the Governor would conceivably agree, even if the plan worked.'

'Your standing might be improved.'

'My brother, Lord Maxwell, is still a prisoner in London. And there are hostages at Carlisle for my good behaviour.'

'It might be improved without overt harm to your reputation in England. It's now mid-November. In two or three weeks' time, the Earl of Lennox is due at Carlisle, and if affairs are favourable, he'll try another experimental march into southern Scotland.'

'And so . . . ?'

'And so, by pure chance and natural greed, Lennox's men might bungle the raid. The real nature of the chance being known only to the Scottish Government, acting on your advice. Lennox blames his men for the failure: the Queen knows it is due to the Master of Maxwell.'

Silence. Maxwell moved. 'Is this possible?'

'You shall hear. I'll describe it to you now; and in greater detail later when we know Lennox's exact movements. And the credit shall be yours.'

195

The Master of Maxwell said, 'I am trying to persuade myself that all this is not a matter of great disadvantage to yourself?'

Lymond smiled gently. 'The road Lennox will take passes the road to Hexham,' he said. 'I told you there would be a trap. And the English will spring it for me.'

They rose at midnight, Maxwell lifting his cloak and hat, gloves and whip. He nodded to Scott and stooping, turned in the doorway to Lymond. 'And curb your mad, antic mind, I beg you. I've no heart to spend myself sustaining what you are creating for me.'

'Have no qualms,' said Lymond gravely. 'We are well matched.' Maxwell, astonishingly, laughed and went out.

Lymond shut the door. 'And that,' he said to Scott, 'is how mulberry trees grow into silk shirts.'

'Yesh,' replied Will Scott.

Lymond tilted the wine jar toward him. Then, with a sardonic flash toward the faintly squinting Scott, he opened the door, crossed the passage and shouted over the gallery rail. 'You keep a damned dry house, Molly.'

She was sitting under the blazing lights at a crooning, besotted table of guests: she raised two jewelled arms to Lymond. 'Come down, my duck. We're a poor, sleepy company down here.'

The Master grinned, surveying the spent and torpid room. Men snored; drinkers drooped and murmured about the slow fires; and snatches of wavering harmony smoothed themselves in the reeking, smoke-hazed air. In a corner, the gypsies slept in a limp heap like gillyflowers. Mat had reappared and lay stomach down on a bench, his bald head rosy in the firelight.

'Have I to teach your your business?' asked Lymond.

'Give us excitement!' demanded Molly. 'Come down! Have you lost your storms? Come and enliven us, Lucifer!'

Lymond withdrew an arm, found his tankard, and spun it accurately at Matthew, who awoke and fell off his bench with a crash.

'It's a terrible thing,' said the Master, 'to lose consciousness at the very start of a party. Molly has a hogshead of claret in her wine store, Matthew. Bring it out for her, and we shall part the Red Sea again. Then, Molly, my sweet honey-mountain, my day's darling, we shall want both fires made up, and fresh candles and more of them, and music.'

'And you, my love,' said Molly. 'But there's devil a note of music in it. The players are as drunk as sows.'

The yellow-haired man straightened, and his laughter brought Scott wavering into the passage. 'There are nine devilish notes not two yards away. Have you forgotten, my sweeting, who is in room number one?'

'Hell!' said Molly, and added a word which even the wives of innkeepers seldom pronounce. 'Did I not shut the door?'

Lymond shook his head.

'No!' screamed Molly. She clapped her white hands over her ears and the rubies flared. 'No!' A sleepy voice from a private room raised itself in complaint, and one or two sombolent drinkers, roused by the shout, made querulous inquiry. 'But yes!' said the Master, and disappeared.

The vast room, swimming in heat and hazy light, and heavy with dreaming murmurs and drunken croonings, sank into torpor. Will, propping his elbows on the rail, stared below and saw that Molly, her fists still over her ears, had doubled over the table in mild hysteria. Her eyes were tight shut.

Then several things happened at once.

A dim thunder outside the arcades heralded Matthew with the hogshead; the fires flared with fresh coal and peats, and a white dazzle searched the floor as candles were renewed.

A little silence fell; the silence, fateful and perspiring, of the imminent storm.

Then a desolate, mammoth, mourning Troll inflated its lungs and uttered. Through the shocked air tore a stern, snoring shriek followed by another. It became a united bray; the bray a wobble; the wobble a tune. High above the gallery balustrade swam a human head, inhumanly antennaed; the cheeks plimmed, the eyes closed, the fingers leaped, and all audible hell released itself. Tammas Ban Campbell, piper to Argyll, ransomed prisoner of Pinkie now travelling north and home, stalked around the three-sided gallery of the Ostrich and gave them *Baile Ioneraora* so that beam roared at beam and door at door; so that glasses smashed and windows rattled and hams vibrated and fell; so that sleepers snorted and leaped awake with their dirks in their fists, sots opened bloodshot, maddened eyes, and the sober dissolved according to temperament into shocked laughter or oaths.

There was a man in the corner who went down on his knees and prayed, but the rest of the Ostrich rose and roared, like a summer herd of caaing whales, to the foot of the stairs to the gallery.

Lymond met them at the top, sword in hand and his eyes like jewels. He had peeled off his doublet and had locked every door in the passage, as thunderous hammerings testified. Will, dazed but willing, hesitated behind him and Mat, summoned not an instant too soon, was at his side.

Faced with three sword blades in the narrow stair, the tidal wave stopped. Lymond looked down on the carpet of crimson, jostling faces and pitched his voice against the bellow of the pipes, which had switched to *Gillie Calum*. 'What about it, my dormice! D'you mislike my lullaby?'

A tall well-built man in a green fustian coat screamed, 'Listen, my friend: put your walking mandrake on Ben Nevis and myself on the Cheviot, and it's still too close for my liking. Do you stop him, or do we make the two of you digest the drones for your supper? There's honest folk trying to sleep down here.'

A chorus of assent bore them two steps up; a flash of the sword drove them three down again. 'Such nice, fine, miniken fingering,' said Lymond. 'You should skip like Alexander. Where are your ears? The best piper in Scotland: eight warblers between the bars, and eleven if you give him a whisky between the second and third variation. Sleep! Whoever slept at the Ostrich between midnight and

198

five in the morning? You're a trashy, glum company for men of music. Are you awake yet? Then bring the blood out of your feet and up to your fingers. My companion and I will give you a match.'

'Oh, God!' said Molly. 'I knew it! It knew it! Stop it, you mad poet, will you?'

'A match?' repeated Green-fustian, out of continuing cries of rage and distress. 'Give us the piper, that's all we ask. Or the pipes. But unhabble the one from the other, for God's sake. Blood! There's not a drop of mine moved from one vein to the next since that belly-prophet of a Scotchman corked his mouth with the chanter.'

'All right,' said Lymond. 'We have the piper, and you have the women; and here's the proposal. If you've a wrestler among you able to throw Matthew here or myself, he gets free access to Tammas and the pipes. If we throw one of you, we earn the kitty that's with you. Shoulders once to the floor mean a throw, and no bodily harm to come to the piper. How's that for a wager?'

The man in green fustian, who appeared to be spokesman for the crowd, grinned and looked around. 'I'm for it: fair enough. What about it, dormice? Are you ready to fight for your rights, or d'you like being miscalled by a towheaded daisy with a private banshee?'

There was a roar of response. Scott, watching through the vague fumes of alcohol, saw that the faces were mostly good-humoured: the fancy had fired loose imaginations and the guests, now fully awake, appeared ready for anything. The man in green turned back; above the variations to *Spaidsearachd Cloinn Mhic Rath* he shouted, 'It's a match. You and your friend to wrestle any of us, turn about for a single fall. If either of you is thrown, the winner gets to silence the piper. If any of us is thrown, we give up any lass we have with us. We'll play it on the floor, and I'll stand guarantee for all of us down here.'

Lymond waved assent. The party flowed back down and into the common room in tumult and laughter and a filling of tankards, while a centre space was cleared for the fighters. Lymond held the hilt of his sword to Scott. 'Your job is to guard the stairs for the winner.'

Scott eyed the blade. 'Up here?'

'Up here. God, I thought you were musical?' Scott closed his eyes and took the sword. Tammas, reaching the third wall, turned and paced steadily back, and Will shuddered and leaned to look over the balustrade.

The transformation was memorable. Lit like a stage, with a tester of candlelight, the improvised wrestling ground was ringed by the audience, hotly vociferous, the girls squealing in flattered excitement. In the centre, white shirts rebuffing the light, Lymond and the tall spokesman stalked each other, arms hanging, on soft stockinged feet. Green-fustian leapt; the two figures hurtled, rolled, separated, joined and clasped. There was a gasping cry, a crash, and Lymond, laughing, stood over a prone figure.

The throw was agreed a fair one. Sally, giggling, wiped her leman's scratched face, saw him escorted off, shaking his head, and ran upstairs to hang over the gallery with Will. Beside them Tammas, turning smartly, took a deep breath and started, with a nice appreciation, on *Cath fuathasach, Pheairt*.

Mat took on a stout blacksmith with thews like tubers and threw him in five minutes. Joan came upstairs.

Lymond threw for the fun of it a young clerk and a Dutch pioneer, neither of which had a girl to give up, and retired for Mat who, in conquering a shoemaker from Chester with an agile wrist, inadvertently broke his arm and, all solicitude, splinted and bound it and shared a pot of ale with the victim before the play was resumed.

He found it a little difficult after that to find a challenger, the more so as the audience by now was making more noise than the piper; but he heaved a lawyer through a window, and the Master followed up by winning Elizabeth from a lithe packman, who put up a cracking fight for twelve minutes. This he topped by two easy successes, each of which was greeted by storms of applause.

There was a brief caesura.

Molly herself brought fresh wine to Lymond and he

took it, grinning, in one hand while blotting the sweat from his eyes with the other. 'Drink, you wildcat: did I ask for this? I must have been mad. Give over, now, before the whole house is in shivers and shards. Stop that damned piper and let's have some music.'

Lymond raised his eyebrows. 'You'll have to throw me first.'

'That I will!' said Molly purposefully.

Scott, deaf and enchanted in the gallery, and the whole row of pretty heads at his side saw the concerted rush on Lymond: his assailants downed him without malice and eighteen stones of Molly planted themselves on his chest. 'A throw!' said Molly, and Lymond, half buried, gave a choked whoop of laughter and raised a defeated hand in signal to Tammas.

Silence, like a supernatural thunderbolt, burst upon the Ostrich.

It lasted perhaps two seconds. Then a shout of responsive laughter hit the roof, the guitars and fiddles of the gypsies started up, and life flowed across the common room. Lymond, released, flung his head back and, viewing his winnings, gave them solemn dispensation to descend for the space of the dance. He asked for and obtained some chalk, and set to marking his and Mat's property where the cross was most obvious and the whim most appreciated. Then he swept Molly off her feet and into the dance, and the room rocked with beating feet and whirling bodies, and the candle flames bent like comets in the wind of passing skirts.

Scott, laying down his sword and with Joan's hand in his, ran downstairs and into the rollicking hall and danced blisters into his shoes; he drank; he danced; he had something else to eat, and he danced again. Then, as muscles and musicians tired, the trestles and benches were drawn to the fires and song after song went around until the choruses became rounds, and the rounds trios, and the trios duets, and finally one solitary, happy, wavering voice made itself heard.

Scott's eyes closed. Joan and the other woman had

disappeared, and Lymond was missing. Thick murmurs vying with the snores finally ceded to them. His head, brighter than the fire, jerked, drooped, and laid itself at last on the table. The Ostrich slept.

At five o'clock Lymond, dressed again in his riding clothes, came to Scott and took the alepot out of his lax hand. 'Dronken, dronken, y-dronken. A wilted and forfoughten Marigold,' he said caustically. 'Upright, sluggard. The fog's lifted, and I propose to be gone before daylight.'

Will didn't remember getting up. From nowhere, it seemed, a sweet, blowing air touched the sweat on his face, and he saw that he was in the courtyard of the Ostrich, in the flinching light from the broken window; that his horse was beside him, ready saddled; and that Matthew, mounted, was waiting at the gate. Lymond threw him up, then mounted himself and raised his head.

Under a pale, fresh moon, trees and bracken sighed and gentle cloud washed over the sky.

'Th'erratic starres heark'ning harmony. Look up,' said the Master. 'And see them. The teaching stars, beyond worship and commonplace tongues. The infinite eyes of innocence.'

But Scott was too drunk to look up.

3 · CROSS MOVES BY A KING'S KNIGHT

Lord Grey of Wilton, general of the northern parts for His Majesty King Edward of England, had swallowed a sour autumn and was encompassing an acid winter since the unlucky affair at Hume Castle.

On the Eastern Marches the River Tweed, with Berwick at its mouth, divided England and Scotland. Like the ancient pike Sir George Douglas had once called him, Lord Grey bitterly patrolled his forces on this boundary throughout October and November. On a slipstream of orders, reports, demands, inquiries, case papers, he stalked from fortress to fortress on its brawling banks and now, on the last Tuesday in November, swam back to Norham with the complaints and entreaties of Luttrell, Dudley and Bullmer pursuing him like hagfish. To the keep of Norham Castle, he summoned Gideon Somerville.

The court office which had crowned the painstaking career of Jonathan Crouch had led Gideon Somerville to the inner chambers of the Palace, the favour of King Henry, and the friendship of any with that commodity still to spare. On Henry's death, Gideon had brought his wealth and his young family north to Hexham, had settled there, and was little seen unless for summons of war.

Or but for the importunities of Lord Grey. Gideon was sufficiently well-born to please the Lord Lieutenant, and good-humoured enough to suffer him. So he waited now in a room at Norham, listening to his lordship – not a young man, except in resilience and a certain honest hardihood of mind: a man with clear eyes and a pink skin, and hair thickly grey like a badger's.

'I suppose,' said Lord Grey, coming at last to the point, 'I suppose you've heard of the occurrence at Hume?'

Gideon, a compassionate man, shook his head.

'Oh. Well. That fellow Sir George Douglas has offered to give me access to one of the Scotts – Buccleuch's heir, in fact. He's roving the Borders in bad company, and one of his associates has a vendetta with someone in London. Douglas suggests we trap young Scott through this man.'

'Someone in London . . . ?' sought Gideon.

'Samuel Harvey's the man this bandit – whoever he is – wants, but the bandit himself doesn't know it yet,' said Grey. 'He thinks it might be you.'

'I assure you, I haven't a vendetta with anyone,' said Somerville. 'Particularly a Scottish desperado. I didn't know Sam Harvey had, either.'

'Well, I haven't communicated with Harvey, so I don't know what it's about,' said Grey impatiently. 'But that doesn't matter. The point is, this associate of Scott's is going to try and get in touch with one of you, and as Flaw Valley's near the Border, it's likely to be you first.'

'How pleasant,' said Somerville. He looked a little taken aback. 'And who is this spadassin who is about to visit me, and what do I do with him when he comes?'

'He's got to trace you, so it may be some time before you meet him. Who he is doesn't matter – Douglas was vague about his identity and I haven't inquired. All you have to do is act as messenger for us, Gideon. When the man comes, give him this letter from Douglas. It's all in order – I saw it before it was sealed. Here's a copy for you to see.'

Somerville read the letter in silence. At the end he said, 'And the only way of reaching him is through me?'

'The only way we know.'

Gideon pushed back the paper and getting up, walked about the room. 'You're thinking of Kate,' said Grey. 'But you needn't worry. I'll give you as many men as you want for extra guard. All I ask is that you let the man in when he comes, and hand him that letter.'

Somerville said, 'Forgive the egotism, but I'm thinking of myself as well as of Kate. I can't quite see myself convincing an irate mercenary that I am actually his best friend. In any case, may he not even bring the man you want – Scott, is it? – with him?'

'All the men I shall give you will be capable of recognizing Scott, if he comes,' said Lord Grey; and for some reason his skin darkened. 'Scott and another man, a Spaniard I'm anxious to catch. Yes. If Scott comes, they'll take him. And you can tear up the letter.'

'Hum. And what if I'm away from home? If I'm called to Carlisle for Wharton's next sally – '

'You have leave to refuse in my name,' said Lord Grey, with a certain satisfaction. 'This time you can serve the King better by staying at home.'

'I can see,' said Gideon, 'I'm going to be popular everywhere. Willie, I'm a peaceable man with a happy family life trying to mind my own business. What on earth am I involving myself in this for?'

'Because,' said Lord Grey, 'you're a fair and loyal friend to your country.'

The clear eyes viewed him. 'Have it your own way,' said Gideon Somerville resignedly. 'As usual.'

2
DISCOVERED CHECK

The third pawne . . . ought to be figured as a clerk . . .
yf they wryte otherwyse than they ought to doe
may ensewe moche harme and damage to the comyn.
Therefore ought they to take good heede that
they chaüge not ne corrumpe in no wyse the
content of the sentence. For than ben they first
forsworn. And ben bounden to make amendes to
them that by theyr tricherye they have endomaged.

1 · DIAGONAL MATING BEGINS

If the Richard Crawford who went to Branxholm was a
troubled and reticent man, the Richard Crawford who
returned was, as his wife ruefully put it, as sociable as a
Trappist monk.

From this aspect, it was a pity his wounds were no
worse. The tender bonds of love and service which Mariotta would cheerfully have wrapped about a helpless and
stationary invalid were stretched instead, frayed and snapping, to the heels of an absent, overactive, uncompromising gentleman, up before he should have been out of bed
and out before he should have been up.

Lady Buccleuch, approached by Mariotta, had proved
an unhelpful confidante. 'That's his job,' she pointed out.
'You don't, I suppose, want to flit here and yon tied to
the man's collar like Agrippa's dog with the devil.'

'But are you telling me the two circles never meet?'
cried Mariotta in exasperation. 'Are we to spend the young
days of our lives with never a shared doubt, or pleasure,
or worry but what falls crash at our feet the one rare
Sunday in five we're together?'

'God,' had said Janet. 'I'm not likely to buy doubts off Buccleuch. I've enough myself for the two of us, and I'll fight to the death to keep Wat's great blundering thumbs out of them . . .'

That was at the start of November. Very soon afterward, the first parcel of jewellery arrived.

Mariotta found it, wrapped and anonymous, in her solar: discreet inquiry could not discover how it came there. Inside was a handsome ring-brooch, disingenuously inscribed *Nostre et toutdits a vostre desir*. There was nothing else to betray its origin, and from that fact, and the arrogance of the message, she thought she guessed the sender.

Lady Culter passed an uneasy afternoon, considering what to do. Tell Richard? She might be wrong. There might be a letter on its way with a perfectly innocent explanation. Or another less innocent. But Richard in his anger had already exposed himself too rashly to his brother: to repress further injury was something the Dowager, at least, would approve. She decided to wait.

No letter came, but a week later, a second packet. This was a bracelet, demanding boldly, *Is thy heart as my heart?* with an insolence which was almost its undoing. Mariotta roamed her room, arguing and counterarguing, dogged by a recollection of blue eyes and a blurred, inebriated voice.

It was monstrous, of course, even to compare the two men. A well-balanced, mature woman of nineteen would unpin the ring-brooch from inside her bodice and put it and the bracelet in Richard's hands saying meekly, 'Your brother is paying court to me. What do I do?'

Mariotta didn't ask what to do. She wore the bracelet and waited for Richard to comment first, and Richard failed to notice it. She wore the diamond brooch when it came as well; with the same results. The Dowager, on her return from Branxholm several days later, admired it, taking it for an Irish piece of Mariotta's own. Committed, the girl did not contradict her. Then Lady Buccleuch had arrived, as invited, on the nineteenth, had remarked cheerfully on the pale, glittering gold, and had added: 'Sybilla, that reminds me. Did Richard ever do anything about that glove of Lymond's that he dropped at the Papingo?'

The Dowager shook her white head. All three women were in Sybilla's own room, and the firelight, rosy in the November mirk, fluttered over bed and desk and gave odd, frenetic life to the wall hangings.

'The glove's still in that French cabinet of mine in the Stirling house. Of course, we came south as soon as Richard was up, and he's been so busy since . . . Oh, here we are,' said the Dowager placidly as the door opened. 'Come along in, Master Bullo. We are all agog to hear about the Philosopher's Stone.'

* * *

When Lymond left the Ostrich, Johnnie Bullo had stayed on, moving only to go to Midculter the following Saturday. His troop, as guilelessly advertised to both Lymond and Scott, had gone – without him – to Edinburgh.

Shown now into the small, warm room, his bright eyes flickered over the Dowager and Mariotta, and rested a little longer on Lady Buccleuch. Janet dabbled in alchemy and medicine herself, and he was not altogether pleased to see her.

But he took, without diffidence, the stool offered him at a proper distance; and plunged, as arranged at Stirling with the Dowager, into the strange and fabulous history of the Philosopher's Stone.

Time passed. The small panes of the Dowager's window became grey, and then ultramarine, and the hot, scented air fondled and set about itself strange words. Sulphur, mercury and salt. The essential unity of matter. Meteors, perfect and imperfect compounds and the flesh of the Universe: Saturn and lead, Jupiter and tin, iron and Mars. The twelve processes of multiplication and projection. Cauda Pavonis. Ferrum Philosophorus. Dragon's Blood.

Johnnie Bullo, judging his moment, stopped when the room was quite dark. There was a heavy silence. Then Janet Beaton said reflectively, 'Lapis philosophorum. The basic idea is simple enough. In man, perfect proportion of the elements means health; in metals, it means gold. Equate the two produce a system capable of creating such an elemental fusion and you have a means on the one hand of creating health – long life, power, vigour – and on the other, of creating – '

'Gold,' said the gypsy softly. He watched their faces: Mariotta's afraid and fascinated, Lady Buccleuch's intent and practical, the Dowager's vividly interested. 'I have the secret. But I need the means of practising it.'

'And having made the Stone?' said Sybilla.

'I can transmute plain ore into gold, in any quantity you may want.'

Lady Buccleuch said practically, 'We should, of course, have to reach a proper commercial agreement about that,' and Mariotta exclaimed, a shade wildly, 'Dragon's Blood!'

'It's just a name for the residue, dear,' said Sybilla thoughtfully. She looked up with decision. 'Glassware – I can get that: Janet, you'll advise me. Ore . . . What sort? Lead? I can send to Edinburgh. Furnace . . . We'd have to rebuild one of the disused bakehouse ovens at the back of the courtyard . . . Yes. Master Bullo,' said the Dowager, 'I understand if we supply all this equipment, you're willing to work here on creating the Stone, and to give us the benefit of it when it's done?'

'If you do that,' said Johnnie sincerely, 'you'll be making an unique contribution to the great science of alchemy and the sum total of human wisdom . . .'

Much later, when he had gone, Christian and Agnes Herries joined them and heard the tale.

The Baroness's eyes were wide as platters. 'The Philosopher's Stone! We'll all live to be ninety, and have everything gold!'

'Remember Midas, dear,' said Sybilla mildly. 'Did you enjoy visiting Boghall?' And while the unsparing account unfolded itself, found and absently flourished a letter. 'It came for you while you were away.'

209

Agnes stopped dead. Letters in this expensive and empty young life were rare birds: her mother never wrote; her grandfather seldom. She seized and bore it away without a word.

A moment later, she was back. 'Can anyone,' asked Agnes in a voice oddly muted, 'can anyone besides Christian translate Spanish?'

'No.'

The Dowager glanced over. 'You seem to have a remarkably erudite correspondent, surely? But tell Christian if you want to. We shan't listen.'

Agnes said, after a moment, 'It doesn't matter. It's a poem.'

'A poem!' exclaimed Lady Buccleuch. 'That girl's got a love letter, or you can call me Ananias.'

The Dowager's voice was gently amused. 'I think you'd better put us out of our misery, Agnes. Who is it from?' And the Baroness, in a voice in which surprise, pride and a kind of simple gratitude could be heard, answered, 'The Master of Maxwell.'

She read the letter aloud, in the end, with no persuasion at all.

I fear to write. The great Pan is dead: there is no magic to bring you the likeness of my heart. My physical likeness you can have; but that will show you only a camelopard – no hero of romance; no prince of myths and sagas. My face will never do duty for my heart; my voice can never scale the barriers of your youth, your wealth, your hand promised – they say – to another.

But birds of paradise feed on dew and rare vapours and men on Pytan live by the smell of wild apples: so perhaps may the sound of words nourish us both. From here where all is night, I see a foolish-fire, and stretch my hands towards it and hope for miracles.

I cannot come to your nectary. I can only boom like a bittern on my marshes and say, Have pity now, O bright, blissful goddess. Once, I wished to marry you. Now you are betrothed and I must not wish it . . . but in writing these words I have attained all my object; I have achieved what, with your help, has been all I desired.

210

Read and remember sometimes the writer. You may see here no more than Mercury's finger, but its office is no less sincere ...

And it ended in Spanish:

> *Rose das rosas, et fror das frores*
> *Dona das donas, sennor das sennores ...*

A whole verse of it followed; then the signature: JOHN MAXWELL.

There was a stunned silence. Christian, staring where she knew Mariotta to be, scowled like a heathen, daring her to laugh. Lady Buccleuch, greatly taken, said, 'Well, for thirteen years old I call that a prodigious compliment: hardly a word under four syllables.'

The Dowager was reflective. 'Mercury's finger. How odd. The Spanish, Christian – is it difficult to translate?' She had to repeat herself.

'The Spanish?' said the blind girl. 'Oh, I know it. In fact I recently – It's very well known,' she ended rather lamely.

'You recently translated it? Did you?' asked the Dowager.

'I was going to say, I recently heard someone sing it,' said Christian truthfully. She gave them the gist, her mind elsewhere. *I cannot come ... In writing these words I have attained all my object ... I have achieved what, with your help, has been all I desired.* The mischievous, overdecorated tongue was the tongue – surely – of her nameless prisoner of Boghall and Inchmahome and Stirling. The song was his. The artifice was his. But the letter was from the Master of Maxwell: the seal was authentic and the messenger had been from Threave. Finally, it was addressed to Agnes, and not to her.

But he had promised, odd as it had seemed, to write; and he knew that of the household, only she could speak Spanish, and would be shown such a letter. And in it, embedded in sly absurdities, was the news she wanted. Christian became aware that Agnes, in the same tentative

211

voice, was saying, 'Then you think I should answer?' and Sybilla was replying, 'I think you certainly should. Of course, it's ridiculously sudden, and you can never tell a man from his letters, and I certainly shouldn't mention it in the hearing of a Hamilton; but a flirtation by correspondence never did anyone any harm.'

Pause. Then said Agnes, 'I can't write Spanish and I've fogotten all my Latin.'

Sybilla answered the panic too, in her calm way. 'Then perhaps Christian would help you, dear. Write it together, and see how you get on.'

This was dangerously apt, and Christian felt herself go scarlet. Yet she could certainly help Agnes. And it might be possible – and could do no harm – to slip in some sort of ambiguity of her own. She got up. 'Come on,' she said. 'We'll go to your room and compose an answer straight away.'

* * *

The letter had been finished, a meal had been served, and Richard had joined them when Wat Scott of Buccleuch arrived to collect his wife.

The Dowager, who had excellent control of her facial muscles, dispatched servants for food and wine, and drew Buccleuch in a cloud of disarming inquiry to the fire.

Sir Wat sat, throwing an uneasy glance at his host, who said politely, 'Your illness taken a turn for the better, I see, Wat?'

Buccleuch shifted in his chair, casting an inimical look at his wife. 'No, no. I'm not out of the wood yet, but Dod, I can hardly hold house all winter like a moulting hen. I'm taking a wee trip here and there betimes but incognito, you understand; without my pennants.'

Richard, continuing with unruffled persistence, said, 'What a pity. Then you won't be with us at the cattle raid?'

'This suggestion of Maxwell's? Now, there's a queer thing if you like,' said Buccleuch. 'Here's a man who's been at Carlisle so often . . .'

'– Or will you?' said Richard like the crack of a whip.

Sir Wat halted. He said, 'Well, as to that ...' and stopped again.

'Will you listen to this?' demanded Dame Janet of the ceiling. 'The man's lost his tongue and found a cricket's hind legs. Wat Scott, will you say plain out what you mean?'

She turned to Lord Culter. 'The Queen's agreed to Wat parleying with the English, provided he gives enough anonymous proof of his good intentions in other directions. So he'll have to go to the raid, willy-nilly, if we have to put his head in a box to keep it quiet from those sharp-eyed ferrets at Carlisle.'

An echo from Buccleuch's own words arrested the conversation.

'A suggestion,' demanded Anges Herries, 'of the *Master* of Maxwell?'

'That's right,' Buccleuch, offered an escape route, was concerned only with disappearing along it. 'The idea was John Maxwell's, though whether we can trust it is another story. But the man's offered to send us time and place for Wharton's next invasion across the Border, and at the very least to hold his own men from interfering. It sounds fair enough when you think of it: he's dead anxious to keep in with the Queen.'

'The fellow's fairly running himself to a shadow,' said his wife. 'We've been busy at it all afternoon reading correspondence from the same Master of Maxwell. Tell Buccleuch your news, Agnes.'

Agnes conveyed, with a certain nonchalance, the gist of Maxwell's letter. The eyes of the two men met, this time in irresistible speculation. Buccleuch said thoughtfully, 'I see. Well, it'll do no harm. She's to reply, Sybilla?'

'She has already,' said the Dowager placidly. 'I thought it might be best.'

Lady Buccleuch said, 'What about it, Wat? Is he safe to deal with?'

Buccleuch took a deep breath. 'He might be. The Protector's got him by the short hairs, of course; his brother's in London, and Maxwell himself was due to report to

Wharton just about now. Add to that the fact that all his lands are two hours out of Carlisle and the Earl of Angus is married to his only sister, and you've got the pattern of a harassed man. Harassed, but not stupid,' added Buccleuch. 'It's just possible he may be capable of juggling them all: we'll have to wait and see.'

When, finally, the Branxholm party rose to go, Dame Janet dropped behind with Lord Culter. 'I'm remembering what we spoke of at Branxholm, Richard. Wat's heard nothing from the boy up to now.'

Culter said briefly, 'You know what I think about that.'

'Well, you heard him,' said Janet. 'He's not likely to change. It's for you to decide how badly you want Lymond.'

He offered no reply and, looking at him, she spoke under her breath. 'And if you'd a different look on your face, my dear, I'd give you some damned good advice about your wife as well.'

2 · AN EXCHANGE OF PAWNS IS SUGGESTED

For the gentlemen, officers and heads on the west parts of Scotland entered to the King's service said the notice. Read aloud by a staid, cultivated voice, it proceeded to expect the English gentlemen thus addressed to muster their horsemen at Dumfries on the following Sunday night, when the Earl of Lennox and Lord Wharton's son Henry would command them in an attack on the Scots.

'Goodness me,' said Kate Somerville, peering at and then watering a rather dilapidated flower in a pot. 'What it is to be on holiday when the rest of the school's at work. How would you spend your vacation, Philippa, if you were Father?'

Philippa, a serious ten-year-old with long straight hair, thought. 'Go hunting?'

'In this weather? No, darling. Father doesn't like wearing his tarry shirt unless he has to.'

'Play backgammon?'

'Father disapproves of gambling with people who play better than he does.'

'Make us a new song?'

'Now *that*,' said Kate, 'is a harmless, genteel and civilized occupation for an unemployed gentleman. Certainly, he might make us a song.'

Gideon Somerville laid down Wharton's notice and gazed at his wife and daughter. 'I may be old and unemployed, but I am not yet reduced to being administered totally from above, like a worthy but derelict sundial. Not yet. I am not going to compose a song for you. Or if I am, the idea will strike me of its own accord.'

'Today,' said his wife, 'Father is in a tetchy mood. Give him food, listen to what he has to say, but ask no questions, even intelligent ones.' And she grinned at her husband.

Kate Somerville in her twenties was a neat brown creature with melting brown eyes and the temperament of a mature and witty old lady. All her life, and not least by Gideon, Kate had heard herself summed up as 'sensible'; and no one, not even Gideon, guessed how she disliked it. An unusual blind spot, for Somerville was of all things perceptive: in his wife's present smile he saw at once the reflection of his own uneasiness, and got tragically to his feet.

'All right. I know my place. To the music room!' he observed, and had the satisfaction of seeing his wife and daughter laugh and make with one accord for the door. Soon Lord Wharton's summons and the importunities of the Lord Lieutenant alike had vanished from his head, and as the winter rain fell on Flaw Valleys and its gardens and yards, on the stout, skeletal barrier trees and the Tyne, distantly hissing, and on the brown, patched hills and moors beyond, the Somervilles wrote and read and made music like bells in a campanile, and ignored the summons to Lord Wharton's attack.

But no English family within striking distance of the Scots Border ever sold its ears completely to pleasure. Kate, listening to the concert from her adjoining bedroom, heard voices outside, and against the sound of Gideon's voice warbling happily ('Sir, what say ye? Sing on, let us see') she distinguished one of his men below, calling. ('Now will it be, This or another day?') She nodded encouragingly, shut the window, and returning to the next room, interrupted Gideon ruthlessly.

'Come on, Chanticleer. There's a crisis in the farmyard.'

He followed her down.

An agitated crowd of men broke the news. 'It's the horses, sir! Someone's got into the stables and taken the lot. There's not a beast in sight, sir!'

Gideon questioned them sharply. They had seen no one. The groom in charge had been felled from behind and could tell nothing. They had heard the drumming of hoofs and had run after, to see a pack of scared horses sweeping down on the gatehouse. There, the guards had rashly run out and had been engulfed; in spite of them the gates were opened and the herd disappeared down the road.

'And what about –' began Gideon, and stopped. 'You – and you – and you!' he said sharply. 'Shouldn't you be elsewhere?'

As he spoke, a tumbling figure appeared, calling. Kate, standing quietly in the background, clicked her tongue. 'I thought so. Your sly old nags have been decoys for your cattle, Gideon. Someone's emptied the byres while all our sleuthhounds were sniffing after hoofprints.'

She was right. Someone had not only emptied the byres, but stripped the farm of its livestock. Every sheep, every cow, every heifer on Flaw Valleys had gone.

The men of the household were seldom berated, but not because Gideon Somerville was incapable of straight talking when he felt like it. They listened, and then ran like hares under his voice to beg and borrow every horse his neighbours could muster and to collect food and weapons for the long chase that might be ahead.

Gideon turned to his wife. 'I'm sorry, lass. Employment for the unemployed gentleman after all.'

'Oh, well. Everyone else has suave, cosmopolitan sheep: why not us? The Millers at Hepple have a ewe that's been to Kelso three times, and they've never been farther than Ford in their lives.' Kate peered absently into the farm pond, and clucked again. 'Thoughtless creatures. They've forgotten the fish.'

'I'll come back as soon as I can,' said Gideon, undeceived. 'Those damned guards at least will be on their toes now.'

'All right,' said his wife philosophically. 'Double the guard; put the fowling pieces under the bed and call in the chickens. If this is a trick, it'll have to be a good one to catch a Somerville sleeping, again.'

Gideon bent and kissed her, and shortly afterward, armed and mounted on borrowed horseflesh, led his men out of the yard and north after the raiders.

* * *

The raid on Flaw Valleys was the most easterly of a series of robberies which swept the south side of the Border that day and were guided and controlled by Crawford of Lymond.

While, like some fissured lodestone, Lord Wharton presided at Carlisle and drew toward him the reluctant hearties of Cumberland and Westmorland, the unmanned farms of both counties were neatly stripped also of their tenants on the hoof, and a stream of hide and wool toiled docilely to the Border, bleat and bellow mingling with soprano from the outraged hearths.

Will Scott, working fast from herd to herd, showed the marks of his three months' apprenticeship. Meeting him in the press, Johnnie Bullo grinned. 'Man, for a minute I thought it was your chief, except it's a different sort of sneer.'

At Carlisle the Lord Warden, totally unaware, marshalled his force, conferred with his colleague the Earl of Lennox and consulted the sky, which told him that something unpleasant was probably on the way and made him very glad indeed, in the small and unkempt civilian corner

217

of his soul, that the Earl of Lennox and not himself was going on this expedition.

In Scotland at the same time, the Queen's forces made somewhat confused rendezvous at Lamington, as directed by John Maxwell, and prepared to march south, Lord Culter and Wat Scott of Buccleuch among them.

By nightfall, the hail was already whipping down in gusts and the raids on livestock in Northern England were coming to a systematic close. Trickles of animals met and joined, tributary met tributary and river engulfed river. By the time the Earl of Lennox left Carlisle the united four-footed Sabaoth was already ahead of him and steering at a tangent for his line of march. Beyond them to the north the Scottish army was bedded down on their line of march, the ice making faint and Aeolian music about their steel helmets.

Between England and Scotland here lay river and marsh: on the west the smooth, treacherous skins of the Solway estuary; on the east the high, wild Roman hills. As the English army under Lennox marched through that night the lightly covered ground opened polyp mouths to their hoofs and made thick mud-slides of every bank. They foundered and staggered and trotted and cursed, and Lennox the commander spat with fury when his scouts reported out of the dark that there was a cattle blockage in the narrow road ahead.

There was nothing unusual in the wilder Border clans taking a dark night to steal some cattle on the Scottish side and drive them south. The Elliots in charge of the herd were apologetic about it and no doubt did their best to clear the road. But when Lennox and his men arrived they met nose to nose with what seemed like every beast in Scotland with four feet to it.

Lennox looked about. Deep, quaking marsh lay on his left and right; the road ahead of him was banked above it and exceedingly narrow. Fifty yards off on his right a small hill thrust up from the bog and overhung the road on its eastern edge. Between this escarpment and the western marsh the dim white of the causeway was hidden by

218

packed and ponderous bodies. 'What's the road like beyond that hill?' snapped the Earl of Lennox.

'Wide and flat, sir,' said the Elliot. 'You'll have no trouble there.'

'You mean *you'll* have no trouble,' said Lennox viciously. 'We're going to turn your herd and drive it back through the defile, my man; and then I shall ride through them. If you think I'm staying here to be nudged into the marsh by a baron of beef, you're mistaken.' And, rising in the saddle, Lennox's men with whoops and cracking of whips cantered down the road toward the hill; and the herd, after much eye-rolling and heavy breathing and ponderous caracole, heaved itself around and trotted back the way it had – supposedly – come. The citizens of Cumberland gambolled after it.

Who can tell by what signs, on a dark, stormy night far from home, a farmer can recognize his own? Lennox's army was just moving under the lee of the hill when the first shout rent the night. 'Hey! Wait a bit! I could swear . . . God damn it, there's three of my cattle over there!' It was joined by another. 'Here – those are Gilsland sheep!' And an anguished recital began. 'Hey! Wait! Stop! Turn them!'

Lennox, riding irritably in front, had his bridle seized by a sweaty hand. 'There's been a mistake, sir. These aren't Scottish cattle, they're our own; and sheep and hacks too. We'll have to turn them.' And the speaker, releasing himself, shot past him and was followed by half the army.

Lennox stood in his stirrups and shouted himself hoarse, but no one replied. He was alone with a handful of men on the southern fringe of an inextricable mess of animals and men, and the latter were exclusively engaged in finding and rounding up their possessions. The Earl of Lennox sank back in the saddle, and at that moment, there was a hissing of wet, grey feathers and the arrows began.

They fell from the heights of the small hill to the east, and from the Scottish end of the road to the north, and as the English, abandoning their livestock, faced about –

from the south as well, from over a small group of cattle which, appearing from nowhere, blocked the only way out.

Lennox's men, pulling out bow and quiver with numbed fingers among the nudging rumps and dripping muzzles, found themselves handicapped players in an unpleasant and one-sided game. They dismounted very quickly indeed, and dodging bent among the heaving flanks, began to make hopeless dashes like mice in a cornfield. The arrows fell faster.

On the slope overlooking the trap, Scott of Buccleuch was enjoying himself hugely. 'One for Tam Scott, and one for Bob Scott, and one for Jocky Scott, and one for ... Christ, they'll make off down that Carlisle road if we're not careful.'

'It's all right.' One of his officers reassured him, peering through the dark. 'Someone's driven a small herd across the south end of the road as well, and they're fighting across it.'

'Dod, are they? Someone's got brains,' said Sir Wat admiringly. 'Well, come on then. Let's help him.' And he swept over the hill, passing the men fighting at the top – strangers and Maxwells, he supposed. At this point he also saw something else. A shadow. An easy, competent-looking shadow, with wide shoulders and an adroit way with a horse.

Buccleuch waved on the rest of his men and let them pass him, his eyes glued to the solitary horseman. Then the figure opened its mouth to give some advice to a heifer and Sir Wat roared 'Will!' in a voice unmistakable over six counties. His son wheeled.

Against an infernal fresco of heaving cattle Scott saw his father's Red Jimmy beak and two sparks for his eyes; Buccleuch saw a hard elegance of outline and suspected an unaccustomed set to the mouth. He said, and had to clear his throat first, 'Boy – will ye come back with me? Now? They won't miss you in the dark' – speaking fast because men were coming toward them.

He thought the boy jerked, but Will only said in a low

voice, 'No. It's too late ... I must go,' and gathered his reins. The others were nearly on them.

'Will ... meet me then. Just to talk. I won't keep you, I swear, unless you want it. Send me word, and I'll come anywhere. Will you do it?'

They were Lamington men coming toward him; Buccleuch watched them in a ferment of fury. Then his son nodded. 'Very well. I'll send word when I can come.' The boy lingered a moment with a look odd, and almost avid; then he wheeled and drove his horse down the road.

After that, the rout was complete. Broken between panicking animals and remorseless archery, provisions lost, weapons lost, nerve shattered, Lennox's troops escaped into the moss and out of it as best they could, and a good many did not escape at all. The Scots had begun to withdraw when Lord Culter noticed that the group of cattle blocking the Carlisle end of the trap had disappeared. It was trotting instead across the faint, crooked path which led to the hills in the east with men all around it, driving it on. And at the head of the circle, knotting it tight and glittering in the sudden, faint moonlight, was a bright yellow head.

Lord Culter dismounted, running, and pulled the bow from his saddle as his horse passed. He fitted an arrow and flung up his arm.

All his vision was filled by a broad, carapace back, leading a troop of men unerringly along the path of his bowshot. It was Buccleuch, bellowing as he went. 'A Scott! A Scott!'

Warned, the golden head turned. Culter saw a white blur; then a curtain of arrows fell between Buccleuch's men and Lymond. The men hesitated, drew up and turned back as the raiders, in that moment's grace, vanished.

Standing where he had dismounted, Lord Culter, the enigmatical, the impersonal, the impervious, raised a stiff right arm and smashed an expensive yew bow like a whip on the rocks. Sir Wat, slightly discomposed, was trotting back.

'Dod, did you see who that was?'

Lord Culter said dispassionately, 'How your son debases himself is no concern of mine. You might however recall that to protect a murderer and a traitor is a capital offence.'

Buccleuch, braced for rebuke, had not quite expected this. He took a whistling lungful of Border air, swallowed it down with offence and resentment, and said simply, 'Man, you're obsessed. Come on. Everyone's waiting.'

'Just a moment. Understand me,' said Lord Culter, and his eyes for a moment were as foreign as Lymond's. 'Next time, regardless of what is in the way, *I shoot*.'

But Buccleuch's patience, a slim and frangible thing, could carry no more pressure that night. With a brief, unforgiveable click, it snapped. 'I had rather,' said Sir Wat through his beard, 'have a son tried and hanged for being driven into bad company, Richard Crawford, than be known in company, honourable or otherwise, by a name fit to spit on.' And wheeling, he drove his horse into the night, leaving Culter motionless, unseeing, at his back.

In the small hours of Sunday morning the sky cleared, the temperature dropped, and the stars described a country silted and sparkling with white. Trampled mud grew a coating of thin, icy paint and the marshes spawned their own sluggish and gelid roe. The earth became very still. In all Cumberland nothing stirred but a round, black herd of beasts, running swiftly east within a circle of horsemen.

* * *

In the valley of the Tyne, the manor of Flaw Valleys waited with vacant stable and empty byre for Gideon's return; and in the yard and in the garden Grey's men crammed themselves into impossible corners out of the wind and rasped together glazed palms.

The sound of hoofbeats alerted them. Kate heard it too, and opened a window, her shadow languishing, dimly sparkling, on the grass. She called, 'Are they coming?' and someone above her replied, 'Yes, ma'am, I see them –

Allan! Get the gate open! – And good work too, ma'am. Looks to me as if he's got the whole herd back.'

Kate's face sparkled like a new penny. She ran for Philippa. Together they hung, fascinated, out of the window and watched the seething backs filling the yard below. Above the din they could hear men on horseback shouting, and the crack of whips combing the excited beasts back to their quarters. 'Don't they look tired?' said Kate sympathetically, of a huddle of sodden and glass-eyed ewes. 'I don't see Father, Philippa, do you?'

But Pippa's brown eyes shone, and she turned away from the window, plaits swinging. 'I know where he is! Listen!' said the child, and opened the door.

Along the corridors of Flaw Valleys poured the notes of a harpsichord, played triumphantly and fast. Kate seized her daughter's hand, and pranced along the passage. 'Do you suppose sheep can play Morales? No? Then it's Father with four hands,' she said, and flung open the music room door.

It was not Gideon. 'Lord: the tame assassin!' said Kate, and popped Philippa outside the door.

'There are some rough men of mine in every passage out there,' said a cool voice from the harpsichord. 'You will both be safer with me. Shut the door.'

Kate brought Philippa in and closed it.

'And sit down.'

Firmly tightening the belt of her oldest wrap, Kate took her daughter and sat. In her orderly brain, the situation was clear. This was the man of whom Lord Grey had warned Gideon. It was her task to convince him that Gideon was not the man he was after, and without frightening Philippa. She longed to know if her husband was in the house.

Mrs. Somerville ran her tongue round her lips and spoke weakly. 'I hope you won't find us tiresome, sitting here looking at you.'

He could certainly play. He continued to do so, paying not the slightest attention.

'I don't suppose,' said Kate sociably, 'you get much time for practice. Are you here for a long stay?'

'I am afraid,' said the cool voice, 'you must have patience until your husband comes back. He's been following me carefully: he won't be long.'

'Following you . . . Did *you* steal the animals?' exclaimed Kate, surprised into an unpremeditated question.

'And brought them back.'

'Oh!' She hid her face. 'These mighty marksmen of Lord Grey's . . . Of course. And they opened the gates for you, thinking it was Gideon. Oh, shame on you. Is there no God who looks after *little* brains?'

Silence. So she was on her own, Kate thought, and instilled all the friendly helpfulness she could into her next question. 'Excuse me, but are you the bad company young Mr. Scott has got into?'

In one gentle movement, the yellow-haired man lifted both hands from the keyboard, rested one on the instrument, and swivelled to face mother and daughter. Kate, her arm around Philippa, met wide eyes like a kitten's; then he said without stress, 'A humourist, I see. Why did you mention Scott's name?'

'If you're the person who's in company with Buccleuch's son, we have a letter for you,' said Kate. 'But you'll have to get it yourself, if you've got feet under there. I'm all against heroism in women.'

He found it without trouble as she directed, and then crossing to the door with the same, noiseless, lingering tread, held it open. 'Your company enthralls me,' he said. 'But I believe I can dispense with it. Get out, please.'

It meant he wanted to read the letter by himself, and probably see Gideon alone, which wasn't at all what Kate intended. She got up slowly, taking Philippa's hand. 'We are adjudged suitable company for the rough men outside – ' and broke off. 'Oh, *Gideon*!'

Gideon Somerville, marched along his own passage by strangers and deposited outside the door of his own music room, gazed in a perplexed way at his wife and child, and then at the silent man who held the door open. His fresh skin lost colour, and a very real consternation came into his eyes. Then Kate propelled Philippa firmly back into the room, reseated herself, and addressed her husband as he walked slowly past the other and into the room.

'That's right,' said Kate. 'Behold the fruits of Willie Grey's little scheme. He came in with the cattle, that also be fair beasts and well smelling. He's got the letter.'

Back to the shut door, the intruder watched them, the unopened letter tapping against his leg. With characteristic hesitation, Gideon said, 'You have put – put us all to a great deal of trouble for nothing, my friend. I was told to expect you, and to help you when you came. If you'll read the letter, it will tell you I am not the man you want.'

The other man continued to study him. Then he walked slowly to the far end of the room and, turning by the desk where he could keep them all under view, he broke Sir George Douglas's seal and read. When he had finished he smiled, the long lashes fluttering. 'That proves nothing,' he said.

Kate could feel the weariness and anger in Gideon, but he kept his voice level. 'Then ask me anything you want. I can assure you that till the ridiculous performance tonight I've had no enmity for you, and have never, to my knowledge, done you an injury. I don't even know your name.'

'My name is Lymond.'

It was unknown to them. 'Well, Mr. Lymond –'

'Lymond is a territorial name. My family name is Crawford.'

'Then, Mr. Crawford –' said Gideon patiently, and broke off, for the yellow-haired man was looking beyond him.'

'Philippa!' said Lymond.

Crouched at Kate's knee, the girl made no movement. Kate said, 'This child needs her beauty sleep. Off you go, pet. If the gentleman wants to speak to you, he can catch you tomorrow with your eyes open.'

Lymond opened his hand, on which lay the key of the door. He said, 'What the letter says and what you say are

225

unsupported evidence. You claim you are not the man I want. All right. Let the girl prove it.'

Kate's brown eyes were blazing. 'My dear Mr. Crawford, you're not thinking. This child's been a Messalina from birth.'

The blue, feminine gaze moved to Gideon. 'Send her here.'

'Not unless she wants to.' Gideon was quite unarmed.

Philippa got up, the plaits swaying and her short dressing gown dragged away from the white nightdress. She said, her lips trembling, 'Don't worry, Father: I won't tell him anything.'

Her parents' eyes met. Then Gideon said, with an effort, 'It's all right, chick. You can tell him anything he wants to know. He can't hurt us.'

The child said again, 'Don't worry. He shan't make me speak. Don't worry.'

With one raging glance ahead, Kate slid to her knees, pulling the child's head to her breast, her mouth in its hair. 'Pippa. Pippa, we're awful fools. What Father means is that truly nothing we have ever done can harm us, and Mr. Crawford has mixed us up with someone else. But you know what unstable-looking parents you have. He doesn't believe us, but he says he'll believe you. It's not very flattering,' said Kate, looking at her daughter with bright eyes, 'but you seem to be the one in the family with an honest sort of face, and your father and I must just be thankful for it. Go over to him, darling. I'll be behind you. And just speak,' she said with an edge like a razor. 'Just speak as you would to the dog.'

There were tears on the child's cheeks, but she was not crying. She got up and walked down the room, stopping just out of Lymond's reach. 'I'm not a liar,' she said. 'Ask anything you want to.'

Gideon jerked. 'I can't stand this –' and was gripped by Kate's fingers. 'No. Let her be. It's the only safe way. Damn and blast Willie Grey,' said his wife passionately under her breath.

The ugly business began. The man Lymond, his back

226

half-turned, bent stiffly over the desk, his weight on both hands, seeking inspiration perhaps from the polished wood between them. He asked, 'How old were you when you left London, Philippa?'

She thought, and replied steadily.

'Do you remember the oldest English princess? The Princess Mary? Did your father work for her? Do you remember when you lived at Hatfield? What time of year was that? Were you playing in the garden? Then when did you leave?'

She did not always remember: sometimes he led her to answer by deduction; sometimes Kate helped a little, without actually prompting. At length, the questions seemed exhausted. There fell an odd little silence during which Kate thought, He has exquisite wrists and hands. What an unspeakably foul thing to do to a child. Out of the mouths . . . What had she really told him? Enough to clear Gideon? Or worse, something damning . . . some childish error; a confusion of dates . . .

Rage boiling inside her, she said, 'Well, Mr. Crawford. Are you satisfied, or would you like to try all over again with a divining rod?'

The fellow raised his head and turned to Gideon. 'I am satisfied that you were not present at the time my unknown friend became adventurous with my reputation. Therefore the unknown friend must be Samuel Harvey. You might think there are easier ways of discovering that simple fact, but I assure you that if there were, I should have spared myself a long and unexciting evening.'

'I hope,' said Gideon shortly, 'by that definition never to experience an eventful one. May we hope to be rid of you now?'

'Probably.' The roving gaze fell on Philippa's white face: her brown eyes fixed on his looked out of bruised circles, as if the orbits had been minutely pummelled.

Lymond dropped to one knee. With the musician's hands he transferred from his doubled to her night robe a pin with, in its centre, a spreading, flowerlike sapphire the colour of his eyes. The girl shuddered as he touched

227

her, but bore it passively: when he drew away she looked down and touched the brooch, fumbling with the unfamiliar catch. Then, before anyone could stop her, the brooch was out, and on the floor, and being smashed, and smashed again by Philippa's stout wooden heel. Then she ran.

Holding the child sobbing in her arms, Kate looked at Lymond with calm eyes. 'And that,' she said, 'settles, I think, any matter of insult by apology.'

For a moment he stood, the fair face quite still; then he walked softly to the door and opened it. 'If it seems any recompense, your animals have performed in the night a feat of multiplication which I believe, genetically speaking, to be quite fabulous,' said Lymond. 'Good night.' And the door closed.

* * *

Collecting his men unmolested, the Master left Flaw Valleys, picked up Scott and the rest of his force and camped at daybreak in a sheltered and uninhabited valley where fires would be unnoticed, and where a stunted belt of firs gave dry fuel and protection.

During the ride there, Lymond made no secret of his mood. His eyes were savage and his voice, freezingly hostile, rang out again and again as the men riding silently with him came under the lash. The Lang Cleg had suffered a passing fancy to go into the cattle business for himself. Pitilessly exposed, the whole tale was soon complete, and Lymond did what he rarely troubled to do: personally flayed the man, tied wrist and ankle to a tree, with his great riding whip.

Scott watched until the Cleg slumped bloody from his ropes, and turned away sick.

Then it was over, and they lay close-wrapped about the big open fires as a frosty dawn bleached the hilltops and the watch, turn and turn about, paced on the heights.

And now, when the longed-for sleep was on him, Scott could not rest. In a dark corner of the trees, remote from interfering light he lay and listened to the incessant whisper of Lymond's footsteps. Then the familiar voice, directly above him, said, 'Sit up. I want to speak to you.'

His face in shadow, Lymond leaned against the next tree and looked down on him. 'You had a long talk with Johnnie Bullo today, didn't you?' he said. 'You adhere for three months, and now we are sundered. We are no longer articulated. We are no longer articulate. What did Bullo tell you?'

Scott had seen a man flogged that night, but he was in no mood for finesse. He said uncompromisingly, 'We were discussing your aberration after your visit to Annan in August.'

'I see. And Johnnie told you – '

'How you arranged for a blind girl to save your life without giving away to her who you are. How you induced her to spy for you. How you arranged to meet her, secretly, after you shot your brother in Stirling.'

There was a pregnant pause. 'I thought it was that,' observed the Master. 'You object, do you?'

But Will was no longer an easy subject: a reflection of Lymond's own irony gleamed in his eyes. 'Why should I? You've made no secret of your habits.'

'And those very habits are feeding and clothing you, so why indeed?' The Master dropped neatly to the ground, and resting his back against the tree, looked up into the dark branches. 'And yet you do object, my sullen one. In that fine, unreasoning, Pharos-like brain which works so hard at reflecting other people's emotions, some minor luminary is sitting intoning disticha: it's damned unchivalrous to employ women agents; and infamous to employ them without their knowledge; and indecent to employ them when they are physically defective. And such an offender will never enter the Kingdom of Hawick. So here you are, complaining thus in black and white and grey, and armed with a moral code like an ogee.'

It was clear that Lymond was out for trouble. Scott said, 'Does it matter?'

'That's what Buridan's Ass kept saying. It matters to this extent. If you are going to develop a pure and unspot-

229

ted psyche you'll need a freer air than this to develop it in. Did Bullo tell you the name of the girl?'

'Yes. Christian Stewart. I played with her when we were children,' replied Scott quietly. 'I swore to do all you asked of me and I have. I haven't changed. But I can't match your tone over this episode, that's all.'

'You'll allow me pogrom and heresy, but not Christian Stewart. Why?'

Scott replied crisply, 'I don't mind hitting anyone who has a reasonable chance of hitting back. The girl thought she was helping someone in need. Instead, she's spying for a condemned man, which means that if she's found out, she'll hang.'

The Master's manner continued to suggest that he thought he was having a companionable chat. Will said with sudden violence, 'I'd cut off my right hand rather than do that to a girl.'

'No doubt you would,' said Lymond, twirling a dry sprig. 'And sacrifice everyone else for your principles as usual. But bend that stern eye on the other side of the picture. We know the disadvantages to the lady: what price the advantages? Is she happier for my coming? Modesty is clearly out of place. She is, in the purest sense, ravished. Is her life more exciting, more filled with achievement, pride and natural enjoyment in a charming and docile member of the opposite sex? Yes. Finally – if she is found out, will she suffer shame and discomfort? She will not. She will be revered as the delicate subject of outrage, and the odium will fall on my always inaccessible head. Three formidable weights on my side of the scales. And I haven't troubled to list the advantages to myself, which are enormous.'

To separate truth from sophistry was almost beyond Scott's tired brain. He flung off the wraps and got to his feet. With his back to Lymond, fidgetting among the leaves, he said, 'I can't understand how you could do it,' and the voice was the voice of an upset boy.

Lymond also rose, suddenly. 'You can't understand how *I* could do it? By God, what pit of feminine logic have we tumbled across now? What are we discussing, a test case in casuistry or my personal complexity of habits? If you have a saint in your soul, I'm willing to bait him for you, but I'm damned if I'm going to meet you stumbling about with a candle inside my *pia mater*. For one thing, you would find it harsh on the nerves.' Lymond stretched out an arm, and digging in long fingers, twirled Will painfully to face him. 'Don't you believe me? I can prove it. If you were truly conducting an analysis, my dear one, you would want to have this as evidence.'

Will Scott took the paper Lymond held out to him, noting the broken seal. The familiar knot twisted his stomach again. The letter was headed simply, *To the Master*, and went on:

> I am leaving this in the hope that one day you will call at Flaw Valleys. You will already have discovered that in other respects your visit is in vain. The gentleman you wish to interview is Mr. Samuel Harvey, and he is not only in England but quite inaccessible to you.
>
> He is not inaccessible to Lord Grey. The proposal he has made to me is that Samuel Harvey will be brought north, and an interview arranged between you and him, if in exchange you provide Lord Grey with the person of Will Scott of Kincurd, Buccleuch's heir, who is at present under your disposal. The arrangements have been left for me to conclude; and for this purpose I am prepared to make myself available to you at any time on any day at one of my castles. My movements are doubtless well known to you.
>
> To obtain access, you need only mention that you bear a message about Mr. Harvey.

The letter was signed, GEORGE DOUGLAS.

Scott felt as if he were being suffocated. He knew his face was white, and his eyes were almost too heavy to keep open. He pulled himself together and said, with a trace of his original irony, 'I see. Have I been sitting another test? It hasn't escaped me, of course, that Grey wants me because of Hume. And that it was you who arranged for me to be prominent at Hume.'

'Partly,' said the Master. 'You did some of it yourself . . .' And struck, perhaps, by the confusion in Scott's face, Lymond suddenly began to laugh. For a moment, so amused and so tired was he, the laughter was less than controlled and Scott, shocked, recognized in the other for the first time since he had known him, the outward signs of extreme fatigue.

Then Lymond said, 'And now where are we? It's difficult, isn't it, to know whom to trust? Fide et diffide, in fact: and that is the moral of this little story. Be mistrustful, and you will live happy and die hated and be much more useful to me in between.

'Sit down,' said Lymond, and waited while Scott dropped again to his blankets. He took the letter from the boy's hand and straightened. 'I showed you this, my would-be catharist, because I don't need you as a barter. I've got something George Douglas wants much more – information. And if that fails, I have a feeling I can acquire a hostage of my own worth two – forgive me – of Buccleuch's expanding nursery. In that, indeed as in all else,' he added with exaggerated courtesy, 'I shall want your help.'

Scott lay back on his rugs. He said cravenly, 'I understand. If that's so . . . I'll help all I can.' Sleep swam in his head, his lids closing with it.

'Of course,' said the Master politely, and tossed a blanket over the boy. 'For my boy Willie . . .

My bird Willie, my boy Willie, my dear Willie, he said;
How can ye strive against the stream? For I shall be obeyed.'

3

FRENCH DEFENCE

The seconde pawne that standeth tofore the Knyght
hath the forme and figure of a man . . . By this is
signefied all maner of werkman, as goldsmithes.

1 · TOUCHING AND MOVING

In the two weeks after the cattle raid, several moves followed each other in apparently random sequence.

Christian Stewart, adroitly missed an encounter with
Tom Erskine, left Lanarkshire and went north to Stirling
to await the coming of the Culters and Lady Herries to
spend Christmas at Bogle House. Shortly after, Buccleuch
and Janet left also for the Scott house in Stirling, moving
slowly to accommodate Walter, David, Grisel, Janet and
seven ninths (as Buccleuch crudely put it) of Margaret.

The Culters stayed at home until the third Sunday in
December; then, leaving Richard to his inevitable business, the Dowager seized a break in the weather to transport herself, Mariotta and Agnes to visit Sir Andrew Hunter's mother.

Before the gates of Ballaggan, and after they had
crossed the Nith safely and dry-shod on its upper reaches,
the Dowager rallied her party. 'Hear me, children,' said
Sybilla. 'This is a naughty old woman, but she's too old
to change, and too feeble to be lectured. So speak up,
keep your tempers, and remember you'll be naughty old
women yourselves, one of these days.' So they went in
and, Sir Andrew being temporarily absent, were taken
straight upstairs.

Lady Hunter's room was as warm as a byre and as forbidding as a lying-in-state. Cocked on her pillows, the paraplegic greeted and seated the three visitors. Then the puckered mouth, fiercely active, said: 'Mariotta. Come and let me see you.'

She studied the girl. Mariotta, hanging grimly to her temper, gazed back. 'I have good news of you,' remarked Lady Hunter. 'You haven't the bones for it, but that can't be helped. None of the Crawfords would make more than a hen-sparrow. When will it be?'

Mariotta's face was pink with controlled emotion. She said politely, 'In the spring.'

'Hum. Richard pleased?'

'Yes. Of course.'

'He will be. Hah! Sybilla. That's two lives between Lymond and the money. You'll be happy now, I dare say.'

Mariotta, supposing herself dismissed, returned to her seat with an expressive glance at the Dowager who said mildly, 'We were all perfectly merry before, so far as I know. I can't say I ever considered the matter in a racial light, but it will be nice to have babies about again. You ought to prod Dandy a little: it's high time he got married. It would do you good to nurse something other than that smelly terrier of yours.'

Lady Hunter's brittle fingers played with her rings. 'In these days of opportunism, Andrew has little to commend him to an heiress, either in fortune or appearance. Unlike his brother.'

Forgetful, Mariotta contradicted. 'Oh, surely not? He has everything to recommend him ... There must be pretty girls by the score who'd give the nails off their fingers for him.'

'Oh, yes. Plenty of those. Ballaggan can't afford that kind, however,' said Lady Hunter. 'Pretty girls with no dowry are for the hedgerow, not the altar. We are not all as fortunate as Richard.'

'Dear Catherine: yes,' said the Dowager. 'How lucky that we are all rich *and* beautiful. Otherwise we should be so affronted. Do you drink everything in those bottles?'

And the conversation was safely transferred to physics, and from there to herbs, on which the old lady was expert and, in her own acid way, entertaining.

Mariotta listened, more interested than she had hoped to be; Agnes, within reach of a lethargic Cavall, amused herself by parting its fur idly with her slippers; and neither did more than give fair ballast to the conversation until the Dowager, gauging swiftly the amount of time to be filled before Sir Andrew might come, got to her feet saying something bantering about vaults.

The bite returned to Lady Hunter's voice. 'If you were bedridden as I am, Sybilla, you wouldn't care for all the affairs of the household to lie about for servants to read. As I've told you before, these recipes are worth money: there is no call to be careless with them. The keys are behind you.'

The Dowager disappeared, and after a sizable interval returned in time to disentangle Mariotta from an appalling inquisition into the state of the linen at Midculter. With her she brought the promised book of recipes, which lasted safely until Sir Andrew came in.

Mariotta, watching him, found her defences rising on his behalf. She knew him already as a kind and ready confidant. No one, looking at the fine hands and good carriage, could say he was uncomely; no one listening to the warmth of his voice could find him displeasing ... Poor Dandy.

The evening passed and then, as the invalid slept early, they went their separate ways. But not before Mariotta contrived to have a word with Dandy alone.

In his private study, he installed her gently in front of the fire. 'Two minutes; and then I'm going to pack you off to bed. So you finally broke the news to Richard?'

'About the baby? Yes, Dandy. With magnificent results. For a week now, no air is pure enough and no whim too foolish for the mother of Culter.'

'And the presents are still coming?'

Mariotta nodded, and touched a small and very fine string of pearls around her neck. 'They just appear in my

235

room.' A nervous giggle overtook her. 'Lymond can't know yet about the baby. What an I supposed to do? I've no way of returning them.'

Sir Andrew got up and, crossing to the fire, kicked the logs with his boot. 'Mariotta, my heartfelt advice is to tell Richard about it. I'm willing to help all I can, but you must know how he'd feel if he thought you felt driven to confide in someone outside the family, no matter how well-intentioned we both are. And this business of Lymond is serious.' He turned and said soberly, 'Tell him, my dear. It need cost you nothing: you have, surely, all the jewels that you want and you of all people, have had a chance of judging exactly what the Master is.'

Waiting, Sir Andrew of a sudden looked sharply at the girl's face. Then she said, playing with the pearls, 'He isn't unattractive, Dandy. If he hadn't been forced into outlawry by a single mistake, all those years ago . . .'

'A single mistake! Do you know how many died and how many were taken prisoner at the battle of Solway Moss?' exclaimed Hunter with sudden savagery. 'Do you know how many years he had been spying for England before that? That when the secret leaked out they got him safely to London and Calais to save him from hanging? That when the French caught him and he was freed by Lennox he served Wharton and Lennox for years until they found he was cheating them too, and he had to turn mercenary abroad? Tell Richard, tell him quickly, and let him look after Lymond. All we both want is to see you safe and happy.'

For a moment Mariotta continued to twist the necklace. Then she got up, with a sudden impatience that made Hunter step back. 'Surely there's some way out of it other than setting them at each other's throats? . . . Oh, never mind! But I doubt very much who's going to be safer and happier if Richard finds out about all this . . .' said Mariotta.

2 · A QUEEN'S KNIGHT FAILS SIGNALLY TO ADJUST

A letter lay on the round, cypress table in the parlour at Bogle House.

Christian knew it was there. Passing and repassing, she was aware of it; it sat among her innocent and mundane thoughts like a tiger among peahens. In all Stirling, none was gladder or more relieved than Christian when at nightfall on the 23rd the yard exploded into life and Lord and Lady Culter, the Dowager, Agnes Herries and all their formidable train arrived.

Agnes pounced. 'Another letter! From Jack?'

'Jack?' said the Dowager, turning.

'Jack Maxwell. I wrote him we'd be in Stirling for Christmas.' And she broke the seal and read it, standing. 'Christian! he says will I answer him as usual, but he may be with me before I get a reply . . . he means to come to Stirling!'

'Does he say so in English?' inquired Christian warily.

'Yes, as plain as can be. Listen!' said Agnes.

Christian heard her read, thanking heaven for the child's verse-infested mind which saw nothing strange in the outrageous metaphor in which her messages were wrapped. He had managed, she gathered, to eliminate one of the two men he must see, and was in train of seeing the other. A suitable moment, obviously, to break off the correspondence; to snap the whole tenuous link; for Johnnie Bullo, former ally and messenger, seemed now to avoid her.

So a curious, painful episode in one's life bid fair to end. But she had to admit that, whatever it purpose, the dignities of happiness had transformed Lady Herries.

* * *

That night, snow fell on the Lowlands, and Stirling woke to its Christmas Eve bowered in white above the grey river and eye-aching plain. Against tender blue the distant hills gave eye for candid eye with the sun, and above castle and Palace the griffins sat, capped and chaliced in snow.

Warmed by the snow and melted by the season, Mari-otta sought early for her husband and found he had left the house, no one knew why. While sharing her bafflement with the Dowager, the thought struck Mariotta. She marched to Sybilla's inlaid French cabinet and flung it open.

The top drawer was empty.

'It's gone!' said Richard's wife, spinning around, her violet eyes black. 'The glove we found at the Papingo has gone. Richard's taken it – on Christmas Eve, on his own, without a word to any of us – our fine, cold, brass-blooded hero has taken it to try and trace Lymond.'

* * *

Culter had indeed taken the glove, but had not carried it far.

The bullion with which it was decorated must have been supplied by a goldsmith; and since some time today he must call at Patey Liddell's for the completed miniature of his mother, he took the glove with him to Patey's, and left very early so as to be back before Mariotta missed him.

Patey was not yet up. After an interminable amount of banging, a moplike head thrust itself from a top-story lattice and Patey's voice yapped, 'Chap away: I'm as deif as a board – oh! It's yourself, my lord. Wait you, and I'll be down.'

Below in the shop, a purple robe over his nightgown, Patey handed over the miniature, not without an involved search, and after pocketing the outrageous cost of it, bent over the glove Richard produced. He held it at arms length and smirked at it.

'The bonny piece! The bonny, bonny stonework!' He tapped the twinkling cuff with a treadlike finger. 'You wouldna get finer gin you took an elephant down Spittall Street and got off at Colombo. Man! They went at a bargain, too: I could have got twicet for them.'

The glove, flicked from his surprised grasp, arrested his

attention. 'Have you seen this before?' demanded Culter in a controlled shout.

Patey was astonished, but ready to oblige. 'No, no. I havena seen the work before, of course not; it isn't mine. But I supplied the bullion and the gems. I'm maybe not an Admiral on the side like Chandler of London, or so handy with a knife as yon Italian fellow, but I've got jewels like peevers and I ken them like weans . . .'

His client was talking again. Patey listened hard. 'Who ordered it? Now, hold you there and I'll tell you.' The great ledger came out, and Patey after a methodical search for his spectacles, pored over it. The index finger trailed down page after page and then stopped. 'There you are!' He reversed the book for Lord Culter to see. 'Ordered by Waugh, the St. Johnstone glover, on October the second.'

'Where do I find this Waugh?'

Patey's crusty eyes opened. 'Are ye for going there? Well . . .' He tipped a packet of sand on the counter, drew a map with a sable and furnished its landmarks with jewels. 'There.'

Richard thanked him and left. As he remounted, Patey climbed the stairs back to bed, tittering under his breath. 'And a right merry Christmas to ye,' said Patey to the air.

* * *

The city of Perth, or St. Johnstone's, is only thirty-three miles to the northeast of Stirling; but not a pleasant ride when the moors are humped with new snow and your adored and incalculable wife is looking to you to attend her at her first Christmas at Court.

Lord Culter, riding alone and fast, reached Perth before midday. Once through the heavily guarded main gate, he dropped his pace to a walk, and steered the mare through a bustling and nervously armed High Street, past Cross and pillory, chapels and churches, Kirkgate and tenements and expensive houses with neglected gardens dating from the years when capital and Parliament were both in the city. But when he reached Glovers' Yard, the booth was

239

quite obviously closed and the windows shuttered above it.

Richard Crawford had not stopped for a meal on his way north; he was disturbed, cold and hungry. He hitched his mare to an iron hook and, taking his riding whip, began on the left side of the yard and beat methodically on every door until he finished on the right.

At the end of this operation, several bonneted, capped, tufted and indignant heads stuck in echolon, like heads from a dovecote from the three sides, and voided venomous complaints on his head. He stepped back and addressed the most responsible-looking, a blotched and stubbled gnome who listened, spat accurately on the cobbles and grinned, displayed horrid yellow teeth. 'Jamie Waugh's no in. You'll not catch Jamie Waugh wasting his time inside on a holiday.'

'Where is he then?' asked Richard, to the interest of a swelling audience.

The yellow teeth displayed their stalwart abundance again. 'I wouldna just trust myself to say,' said the aged one eggily. 'Forbye, it wouldna be the least bit use to ye. Jamie Waugh never works on a holiday.'

'I don't want him to work!' shouted Richard, trying to throw his voice two storeys up and no father. 'I only want to talk to the man.'

'D'you tell me? Well, I'm glad for ye that you've saved your time,' said Yellow-teeth serenely. 'For you'd have just wasted you temper looking for him. Ye canna expect to speak to Jamie Waugh on a feast-day: he's aye deid drunk on a feast-day, is Jamie.'

'I can sober him,' said Richard grimly. 'Just tell me where I can reach him.'

'Sober him!' As if the words had touched off a hydraulic, Alexandrine weight the projecting heads gave a unified jerk and set themselves nodding. The ancient one looked sadly at his lordship. 'Sober! You'll not see him sober till Twelfth Night, nearabouts. Jamie's the sturdy boy for the drink.'

There was a short silence. Richard was thinking, and

the aged one was weighing him up with a rheumatic eye, setting the obvious urgency of his quest against the cut of his lordships clothes. When he spoke again, his voice had a croon in it.

'Mind you, I'm not saying he couldna be sobered. I'm just saying it's never been tried. And while I doot there's a soul in the Yard could tell you rightly where to find Jamie – Jamie being incapacitated to clients at Christmas, ye understand – I would be willing to stretch a point for a gentleman. You look,' said Yellow-teeth, with a certain facility, 'like a sporting gentleman to me, and that's a grand wee dirk at your belt. Forbye you claim you can sober Jamie. Aweel, I'll gie you his location at the price of a wager. I'll lay you a pair of gloves against your dirk that you canna bring him back to this yard by St. Stephen's Day normal – or as near normal as God made him. Now. There's a fair proposition before witnesses, and a wee frolic to tell the wife about, and anyway,' he ended practically, 'there isn't a soul else can direct you to Jamie.'

Richard folded his arms and stared at the artless one. A glance at the Yard had shown him he could expect little help from there. The proposition was ludicrous: at any other time he would have dealt with it promptly and sharply. But time was against him. He swore under his breath, and then said curtly, 'All right. I accept your wager. Where is he?'

He had to wait until the aged one, disappearing and re-emerging at a lower door, took fond and personal custody of his knife ('just a formality') before he received his answer. Horny hands picking and stroking at the jewelled hilt, the old man said, 'Aye, aye. I kent ye were a gentleman. You bring Jamie Waugh back sober, and I'll have dirk and gloves set out for you. He's at his sisters house in the Skinnergate,' said Yellow-teeth, retreating strategically within his doorway. 'The fifth on the right going down. Merton's the name. Merton.'

Richard, unwilling amusement in the grey eyes, put a foot in the stirrup and swung himself on the mare again.

'Merton of the Skinnergate. Thank you. And your own name, sir?'

'Me?' The teeth yawed. 'You're easy named a stranger: every St. Johnstone's man kens Malcolm – Chuckie-moued Malcolm, that's what they cry me. Malcolm Waugh at your service, sir; faither o' Jamie of that ilk, and an honest, sober man to be cursed with yon loose black glover. Good luck to ye, sir! I'll keep the dirk safe! Trust me, sir!'

Richard turned his horse out and suddenly laughed aloud, as windows popped shut the peace of Christmas Eve descended again on Glovers' Yard

Snow had fresh-laundered the Skinnergate; had put new bonnets on its thatched roofs and dressed the stakes in the yards. But the hands and feet of the Skinnergate children had returned the narrow land to it pristine state of mud and offal, and cold weather or no, the ripe animal smell of the trade hung resonantly about the doors.

The fifth house was easy to find: the Mertons were holding festival, and the rest of adult Skinnergate and most of its children were choked into the single room above the yard, with the overflow jamming the stairs. Jamie Waugh was easy to find also: he was sitting in the fireplace with smoke slowly rising from his skin breeches, singing acceptably through a large earthenware jug upside down on his shoulders. The corners of the room were piled with undressed sheep and calfskins of bold personality, and a young heifer couched in the middle was giving warm seating to four or five men. Beer was in free circulation, and a fat cheerful women in an apron, whom Richard took to be Mistress Merton, was dispensing winkles from a pot of boiling water and pins from a wooden box.

She had offered Lord Culter a spoonful before the implications of his dress struck her: she blushed, put down the ladle and wiped her hands. 'Were you wanting Jock, sir?' He's not in the Yard today, but if you'd call tomorrow of the next day . . .'

She seemed a bright, honest person. He told her what he wanted, but not of the bargain perpetrated by Waugh, senior. Her reaction was much the same as that of Glovers' Yard. 'Jamie! Oh, Jamie'll not be sober till Candlemas, nearly.'

'With your permission,' said Richard, 'I was proposing to sober him now.'

She gave him a doubtful smile. 'Well, sir, you're welcome to try,' and bending over the happy Mr. Waugh, she pulled the jug off his shoulders. A plump, almond face revealed itself, remarkably like the old man's, with a retroussé and rosy nose and ruffled black hair.

'Jamie, there's a gentleman come to see you,' said Mrs. Merton. The suffused eye wandered distractedly from Lord Culter to his sister and back again; with a lurch and a jerk, Jamie Waugh got to his feet. 'T'horse!' he exclaimed and bending dangerously from the waist, gave Richard a view of the lower hemispheres of two mottled corneas. Then he folded backward in a quick graceful arch, straightened a little, and declaimed:

> *Tohorsh, tohorsh, maroyaleesh;*
> *Your faesh shtand on the Shtrand.*
> *Full Twenny-thoushand glitt'ring Shpearsh*
> *The King of Norshcommandsh.*

Seeing that her brother had reached, if not the end of his repertoire, at least the end of his breath, Mrs. Merton laid a hand on his shoulder, at which he gently folded up and sat on the hearth again. 'Jamie. It's someone wants to see you.'

Jamie's eyes were fixed on the ashes.

'Here maun I lie, here maun I die,' said Mr. Waugh, who seemed to favour verse in heroic form. 'By Treachery's flash guilesh,' and laid his cheek morosely on one knee. A tall, thin man pushed through the crowd, and Mrs. Merton went to him. 'Oh, Jock! Here's a gentleman wanting to speak urgently with Jamie, and he's just at his very last wink.'

Mr. Merton eyed Richard, who told an edited version of the story yet again. 'Oh, if ye want to trace a sale, Jamie's the only one that can do it. Think ye can sober

243

him?' said the skinner doubtfully. 'I've been merrit twenty year and I've never known him able to speak this side o' Twelfth Night, but maybe coming to it from a fresh airt, as it were, might make all the difference. What were you thinking of?'

'A swim,' said Richard. 'And I'll need some rope.'

The skinner's face webbed itself with leathery wrinkles. 'Man, I never knew Jamie in water for twenty year either,' he said with callous delight. 'God: it's a great day for the Waughs.'

They took the drunk man downstairs between them, and the inhabitants of Skinnergate, winkles and alepot in hand, poured down after. They rollicked down the stair; they lurched singing into the lane in black and merry procession, and they stood on the brink of the swift and icy River Tay as Richard solemnly addressed his victim.

'Mr. Waugh, what I'm about to do is as much for your own good as mine. I hope, when sober, you'll appreciate it.' Then, receiving from the ready Mr. Merton a coil of light hemp, he noosed it, slipped and tightened the loop around the glover's waist and to ringing cheers picked Jamie Waugh up in his arms and threw him plump in the middle of the river.

There was a splash, a yell, and a crunching of gravel; then two knees and a head appeared: Mr. Waugh was reclining on the river bed. Richard pulled gently on the rope. Mr. Waugh rolled over, leaned on his hands, and could be heard swearing vigorously into the waves. Richard pulled again.

Mr. Waugh stood up. 'What the – are you – 's doing?' he bawled.

His brother-in-law called in reply, 'Come on, Jamie. We've got you roped. You can walk to us, nearly.'

Mr. Waugh's reply to this cast even his previous remark in the shade; indeed, he seemed ready to stand practicing vowel sounds in the middle of the Tay till night fell. Mr. Merton, with less patience then Richard, leaned over. He gave a mighty tug at the rope, and the vociferating figure at the end disappeared in a flurry of spume and vituperation. His sister, tears of merriment streaming down her comfortable cheeks, said brokenly, 'He'll catch his daith! Better pull him in now, sir. Oh, Jamie!'

They pulled him in. He arrived not only sober but fighting mad, and Mr. Merton, who seemed to be an expert, took him over. The flailing arms were imprisoned in someone else's coat; he was swept back to the house, towelled, reclothed and plied with hot milk. Then Mr. Merton came to the door and nodded to Richard, who came in and sat on the stool before the limp, riled and distrait swimmer. 'If you want to blame anyone, blame me,' he said pleasantly. 'I'm the one who threw you in.'

Mr. Waugh rose, bent-kneed, to his feet and was sternly pressed down again by well-wishers. Richard continued. 'I'm sorry about it, but I need some information from you, in a hurry, and you won't be out of pocket over it.' He threw a small bag, chinking, on the glover's lap. 'You can pay the damage to your sobriety pretty quickly with that, and have some left to spend at Pasche, perhaps.'

Jamie Waugh opened the bag, and the whole almond face altered. 'Man, if it comes up your back again just send word to Jamie, and I'll spend Lent in a stickleback's front parlour. What did you want to know?'

'Something very simple.' He threw Lymond's glove on top of the money. 'Can you tell me who ordered that?'

The glover's broad, brown fingers fondled the work. 'I'll have to look up the books in my shop, sir. But it's my work, right enough. I remember it fine. I got the gold for it off Patey Liddell in Stirling.'

Richard got up. 'Can we go to your shop now?'

'Surely, surely.' The other laid down his mug, picked up money and glove and made for the door, slapping his sister in passing. 'I'm off to the Yard for a minute, Jess: be a fine lass and put on the ham for when I'm back; my insides are clapping together and my mou tastes like a haddock's spit-oot.' He eyed Richard diffidently. 'You'd no care to come back and have a bit with us, sir? It's ham, just; but, man, I tickled her backside day in, day out when she was fattening, and there's not a wrong bit in her.'

Lord Culter put a hand on the wiry shoulder. 'Jamie Waugh, you can count that ham half gone already.'

* * *

The early dark began to fall as Richard, with Waugh, returned to Glovers' Yard, and candles in the thick, misted windows patterned the dirty snow below.

Jamie was not one to stand on ceremony. He no sooner set foot on the cobbles, walking smartly by Richard's stirrups, than he flung back his wet head and roared, 'Faither!'

Propelled by curiosity, the windows of the court shot up. After a pause, Malcolm Waugh's front window glimmered with an approaching taper; the casement opened, and the erratic parent looked out. 'Jamie!'

'Aye: Jamie. I want in to the shop, Faither.'

The bristled jowl quivered. Mr. Waugh, senior, leaned farther out of the window. 'Jamie! Are you sober, lad?'

The glover, who was sitting a little tired of the continuing stress on his condition, frowned. He said tartly, 'A damned sight too sober to stomach the sicht o' the wagglin' chops on ye muckle longer. Will ye come down?'

But Faither only hung farther out. 'Jamie! Tell me! Ye havena had an encounter with a sleekit-spoken chiel . . .'

Richard, leaning on his pommel, looked up.

'Oh, it's yourself!' said the old man hurriedly. A yellow grin, hastily summoned, jerked into place. 'Man, you're a great case. From the Mull tae Dunnet Heid there isna another body could have brought Jamie Waugh to his faither as stone-sober and ill-tempered as the day he was weaned.' He ducked smartly as a stone, flung by his impatient son, cracked on the woodwork. 'Just wait; wait now. I'll be down.'

He let them in and watched as Jamie, having lit a candle, opened his ledger and conned it. Richard, looking around the perfumed and flickering gloom, saw something wink on a table, and strolling across, picked up his dagger. Slipping it back in his belt, he grinned into a lugubrious bloodshot eye. 'I'll excuse you the gloves I've won, Mr. Waugh. It's been worth the experience to know you.'

The loose mouth wobbled. 'Man, I can just say the same: there's many an alehouse would keep you in drink for life for a loan o' your talents.' He melted unobtrusively into the gloom as his son came forward slowly, the big book spread in his hands. There was a pause, then the man Jamie gave an exclamation, laid down the book and held the glove over to the light. 'The deil!' he said. 'He's used it as a shooting glove!'

With some grimness Richard replied. 'He certainly has.'

'Well, it's no meant for a shooting glove!' said Jamie Waugh in righteous indignation. 'It's a fancy glove that – one of a pair, and far too much decoration on it for shooting with. I mind it fine, and the chap that bought it.'

Richard found a seat and dropped very gently into it. 'Do you? Tell me what happened.'

'Well; in comes this fellow ordering gloves, and as fussy as a flea in a bathtub over the pattern, and that Patey has to do the gold, and – '

'What did he look like?'

The glover thought. 'Kind of fancy-looking – no offence, sir, if he's any relation. Yellow hair, and an awful tongue in his head.'

'In aurum coruscante et crispante capillo,' said Richard unexpectedly, and gave a kind of a smile as Waugh stared at him. 'Have you ever seen him before, Mr. Waugh?'

'Never. Nor since. He's not a native of these parts.'

'No. Go on.'

'Well, when it comes to the bit, he hadn't the price of a full pair on him, and we had a bit of an argument. However – as you'll understand, sir – he's not the sort of person it's just easy to cross. He paid a bit – just some silver, and left his address, and said he'd accommodate me by taking one glove and collecting the other when he sent the money. I knew it was a tale,' said Mr. Waugh with some reminiscent anger, 'but he had such a manner on him – '

'I know,' said Richard. 'And has he ever sent the money?'

Jamie Waugh went and rummaged in a cupboard, returning with the twin of the embroidered glove. 'No. There it is. No one's come for it.'

'Would you permit a man of mine to watch the back of your shop till this man arrives? I'll pay you of course.'

Surprise showed on Jamie's face. He hesitated, then shrugged. 'Just as you like, sir,' and was about to shut the book when Richard stopped him. 'Just a moment. What address did you yellow-haired man give?'

Waugh peered along the crabbed entry. 'It'll be a false one, belike ... Address ... Address – oh. Here we are. Aye, it's false, I'm afraid. "Castle of Midculter, County of Lanark," it says.'

Richard got up suddenly. 'And the name?'

'Well, now. He didn't give his own name, just the name of the man he was to send to pay for the gloves. Devil, where is it? Oh, here. "Richard Crawford, third Baron Culter." How's that for impudence? A lord, no less. Man, you can't trust a soul nowadays. When did you say your man would be here?'

Whatever bitter self-mockery lay behind the impassive face, Lord Culter showed none of it. He said coolly. 'I shan't require now to send anyone ... I have made the mistake of underrating my friend,' and, laying a gold piece on the table, added, 'No one will come for the gloves now. Keep them both, and look on the sale as discharged. Now: there was some talk of ham ... ?'

But with all that, the man was only human. He didn't return to Stirling that night, but buried anger and disappointment in the Skinnergate, under rashers and eggs and ale and good company; and Jock Merton said, sotto voce, that gentleman or no, he was damned if the fellow wasn't good value at a party and could hold his liquor like a fisherman: a statement of Mariotta, and perhaps even the Dowager, would have been astonished to hear.

It was late when he left. They were loth to let him go, and he might have been overpersuaded to stay but for

248

Jamie, who had spent the evening making up for lost ground and achieved the full cycle, as Culter mounted his horse, by descending the stairs in one airborne step. Richard waited only to make sure the glover was unhurt, then waved and set off.

He had no notion of arriving at any of the houses known to him at Perth with a thick head in the middle of Christmas. After a little thought, he directed the mare to the castle where he could command a bed for a few hours and set out for Stirling at the crack of dawn next day.

It was no fault of his that the English army at Broughty Fort also set out that night, with malicious intent, on a punishing raid of the neighbourhood. He was wakened at five in the morning by a crash of emergency and, driven by duty, set out to pass the day not at Stirling but by the side of the Provost and Constable of Perth at Balmerino.

He rode to the fighting in no cheerful mood. 'I thought,' said Richard wearily, 'there was only one man playing hell with my life. But by God! Ruthven, it's become a national pastime.'

* * *

At midday – and with still no sign of Richard – Sybilla exercised her native wit and, putting on furs and boots refusing escort, plodded down the street to Patey Liddell's.

'Well, now – your ladyship's all wet – This is a pleasure, but – Come away over to the furnace – You know Lord Culter went off with the picture – That's a comfortable chair, now: sit you down ... He's not here,' said Patey, who under the forcible blue eye seemed a little upset.

'I guessed that,' said Sybilla. 'Where did he take the glove, Patey?'

The goldsmith eyed her and decided evidently that only truth would serve. 'To Perth,' he said simply.

'Oh, *Richard!*' exclaimed Sybilla in extreme exasperation. She turned the blue eyes on Patey again. 'Is that where the glove was made?'

He nodded, hesitated, then volunteered, 'No one'll lay a finger on him, your ladyship: I warrant you that. Jamie

Waugh's a terrible man, but there's not a drop of harm in him, and he'll treat his lordship as kind as a maid with her rich new joe . . . You'll take some spirits?' added Patey, at a speed suggesting a desire to efface his own conjecture.

'No, I must go back,' Rising, Lady Culter bent to look at a small nugget lying on the smith's bench in a drift of sparkling dust. She lifted it to examine it more closely. 'It was a pretty glove. That pale yellow gold is from Crawford-muir, isn't it? You use a lot of it, Patey.'

'What?' said Liddell. He grinned vaguely. 'It's a bonny wee nugget, that. Gold.'

'I wasn't talking about the nugget,' said Sybilla, 'particularly. What's the tax on Scottish-mined gold these days, Patey? Farily high? And isn't it all supposed to go straight to the Mint?'

'Scottish gold?' said the smith, and shook his white head. 'It's well enough; well enough; but a wee thing soft, and there's them that prefers a good brosy yellow to yon pale stuff. No. Whatever it is you're wanting, you come to me and I'll show you gold that'd make crowns for angels.'

'Well, that'd be a change,' said the Dowager sourly, 'from making crowns for Patey Liddell. You're a perverse, deaf old man, and I don't know why I come to you.'

'Do you not?' said Patey, exerting to the full his highly selective aural powers. 'Then I'll tell you: it's to get a good bargain; and you can be sure of this: whatever Patey Liddell's got a hand in'll never hurt a Crawford.'

'Then I suggest,' said Sybilla, making for the door, 'you steer clear of my daughter-in-law; or something Patey Liddel had a hand in this day is going to be a sore affliction to Patey Liddell.' And she went home.

* * *

So Christmas, unappalled at Lord Culter's absence, came cantily to Stirling.

It was a French Christmas; a debonair Christmas full of frolic and folly; a spry, Gallic unctuous Christmas. Henry of France, at last roused to boldness and the cunning exercise of spite, had sent a small fleet to Scotland,

and in it money for the Queen Dowager, and French military experts for her guidance and the better security of her fortresses. The military experts, tricked out in scent and white satin, danced like well-mannered clouds and talked in the Council Chamber of chests of money and major landings of troops waiting to come with better weather. The Government blew a sigh of relief, eyed the cut of the white satin and, flinging its armour out of the window, bawled for its valet.

The Court danced. The Court played rough games and watched masques. Cardboard cumuli, joggling cautiously from ceiling to floor emitted Spirits of Love, giggling, with siren voices half a tone sharp with nerves. Forty-two different kinds of main dishes were offered at one sitting, and even the puddings burst asunder and became sweating cherubs released from cardboard confinement and prone to emergency and fits of tears.

Sybilla, animatedly and comfortably at home, found time to watch her small flock. She observed Agnes Herries, graced with a new diffidence and dancing, under the Governor's orders, with the Govenor's son. Christian, who did not care to dance in public, had been strategically waylaid by Tom Erskine. Mariotta, who should not have been dancing, was doing so, incessantly. The Dowager breathed a faint prayer for the well-being of the future heir of the Culters and returned her gaze to Lady Herries.

So she saw a tall, stooping figure appear in the distance; saw Agnes Herries hesitate, and then saw her disappear up the turnpike stair which gave access to the wall-walk on the roof. The tall figure followed her.

The Dowager walked over to Christian and sat down. 'Hold my hand and talk to me,' she demanded. 'Something interesting is happening on the tower stairs and I feel nervous and grandmotherly.'

Christian turned on the older woman her affectionate grin. 'Nothing like practice,' said she.

* * *

The tall man was dressed in blue silk. Agnes, watching

251

him emerge from the tower, noted the deliberate, light walk and the brome-grass hair ruffling in the night wind. He came nearer, and she saw yellow peregrine eyes with black, buried pupils.

'Lady Herries?' he asked; and when she nodded, he smiled suddenly.

'You're so small. I have something for you, my lady – but it's like Abbey Craig speaking to Dumyat. Perhaps, if you'll allow me, we should settle our differences first.' And before she could object, he put both hands around her waist and swung her easily to the broad parapet. She arrived with a bump, had a fleeting thought about the state of the ledge, then arranged her skirts and turned again to the gentleman's eyes. They were still very yellow, but kind. He took her hand and put something into it. 'From Threave,' he said.

Agnes looked down. Between her fingers, dark with melted snow but warm and perfect, was a sturdy red rose. She said 'Oh!' in a surprised delight, and repeated it as his words penetrated. 'From Threave?'

'From Jack Maxwell. With his respectful love. Well, Lady Herries: are you disappointed?' asked the Master of Maxwell.

She shook her head. 'I think,' said Agnes, with a young and tender naïveté, 'you are as handsome as your letters, sir.'

* * *

Long after the parapet was empty, a clatter of hoofs foretold a latecomer approaching the Castle Wynd, riding alone on a stumbling horse. The captain of the guard admitted him instantly and, soaked and battered with mud, Lord Culter dismouted and walked into the yard.

Richard had come straight from Perth, and brought with him from the Provost of Perth an account of the raid on Balmerino Abbey in which he was notably concerned. This he gave to one of the Queen's officers, being hardly presentable enough to ask for audience himself. On the same grounds, he asked that his wife should be brought to the Palace to speak to him.

Crossing the flying bridge from Hall to Palace, Mariotta was aware of a very creditable sense of relief. At least the bloodhound had taken no actual harm this time; although his behaviour remained erratic, antisocial and evasive. Mariotta marched into the Palace with reconciliation to sell, at a price; Richard rose to welcome her with an expression which the Dowager would have recognized as discomfort and guilt. In the net result, Mariotta looked angry and Richard looked wooden, and the opening round was not one to inspire confidence.

This was because Richard made the mistake of blaming his absence on the fighting outside Perth. Mariotta heard him in silence, and then inquired stonily about the tracing of the glove. Richard's account of this was lamentable. Told in the cold light of reason, the sobering of Jamie Waugh sounded remarkably like a drunken brawl: the exact points of difference were hard to define. He was brought to admitting, austerely, that the entire trip had been a wild-goose chase expressly fabricated by Lymond; he then apologized again for his absence and indicated that, if she would allow him, he would leave for Bogle House and change his clothes.

Mariotta listened to it all, sitting judicially in a whirl of velvet with all the Culter jewels and the emerald necklace for moral support. She said thoughtfully, 'I wonder you didn't tell us where you were going? Were you afraid we should refuse to let you leave?'

Richard looked at her quickly, then studied the floor. 'I knew you might be worried. As I said, I expected to be back quite soon.'

'We were very worried. You don't think,' said Mariotta carefully, 'that it might even have been helpful to talk it over beforehand?'

'Oh?' said Richard. 'Who with?'

Lady Culter got up and stalked to the door. 'The Great Chan of China,' said she with awful an unaccustomed sarcasm, and swept out.

At that precise moment, the Dowager Queen sent for him. So he had after all to cross to the Hall in his travel-stained dress, and had a brief interview with Mary of Guise, magnificent on her dais with laughter and French wit for canopy. She had some shrewd questions to ask; then she abandoned business and introduced him to her compatriots and chaffed him on his pretty wife. Richard who, when clean, was a presentable as well as a solid person, responded adequately and at length was allowed to go. He got as far as the first door, and was arrested by a vigilant figure which whisked him out of sight around the standpost.

'Stay there while I speak to you. If Wat sees you, he'll burst,' said Lady Buccleuch. 'What's come over you? You'll be a fat old bigot like Buccleuch if you keep on at this rate. Never mind. Here's the point – Wat's made a rendezvous with the boy.'

For a moment, she thought the man looked at her as if she was talking Hebrew; then his face changed and he sat down, a trifle heavily. 'By God, has he? How did he get in touch? Will Lymond be there?'

Will sent a message – they met at the cattle raid affair, I think. I don't know if Lymond is involved – officially, I don't know anything: Sybilla is the one in Wat's confidence at the moment. But I got a wee glisk a the note when it came, and it said –'

'Wait a bit.' Richard rubbed two fingers and a thumb over his brow, transferring to it a long smear of harness dye. 'Before you say any more. Buccleuch and I had words recently. We're not on good terms, and we've got different opinions about how this business of Lymond should be treated. You know all that. The last thing Buccleuch wants is to have this piece of information in my hands.'

'What Buccleuch wants and what he gets,' said Dame Janet serenely, 'don't always coincide in my experience. Don't be a fool, man. You may whinny at the method, but you can't deny we've got motive and provocation enough to defend it to the Pope, if need be. With or without Lymond, Will's engaged to meet Buccleuch in the beech wood at the foot of the Crumhaugh – the hill between Branxholm and Slitrig Water – at dusk on the first Sunday in February.' She rose laboriously. 'There you are. Do what you like about it.'

Richard looked past her into the Hall. A new dance had begun and the Queen – the youngest Queen, aged five – was leading it, cheeks like fruit below a fiercely combed and shining head, one arm erect as a flag in her partner's grasp. The lines of long, slow sleeves marched and swayed with the music; coloured limbs were pleached and latticed in pattern. The music, piping, thudding, nasal, escorted the murmur of voices. Somewhere in one of the ranks Mariotta was dancing, and behind her, Agnes Herries with the Master of Maxwell.

Richard looked down at his own muddy clothes and rubbed his face again. 'Yes.' He added abruptly, 'You understand, I'm not interested in Will. I want to take my brother.'

'Do that, and the boy will come back of his own accord,' said Janet. 'Look, there's Wat hunting for me. Goodbye. If you've a grain of sense you'll go straight home to bed.'

'Good night – and thank you. I'll take care Buccleuch doesn't hear where my information came from,' said Culter.

'Och, I'll tell him myself,' said Dame Janet. 'Just so soon as it's all over. He'll be all the better of a good row after mincing away with Kincurd and his morals. Wicked Wat of Buccleuch! Saints preserve us.' She turned back into the Hall, and Richard went home.

3 · ANOTHER ROYAL LADY ENTERS THE GAME

To Lord Grey of Wilton, the Protector's Lord Lieutenant of the North, Gideon Somerville reported in full the incident of the cattle raid and of the assault on his home and the taking of Sir George Douglas's letter. He was frank and even pointedly detailed with one exception: he held beck the name of the interloper. Gideon had no intention of being asked to reopen negotiations with him, should he be known to Lord Grey.

The interview took place in the Castle of Warkworth on the bright, bracing coast of Northumberland.

For domestic reasons, the English Protector urgently needed a splendid success at something, and his first instinct was to put a stop to the squabbling inaction in the north. This he did, characteristically, by ordering his Lords Warden to meet and devise an instant plan for, first devastating the House of Buccleuch; second, pulverizing the House of Douglas; and third, joining the power of the three Border Marches and burning Scotland up to the eyebrows. The object of this last, as ever, was to wrest the child Queen from these antique and wiry arms and rear her, unequivocably, as the bride of the King of England. The Lords Warden, answering faintly, undertook to excel themselves and arrange to meet on this last Friday in January at the Castle of Warkworth. The Lords Warden detested each other, but they distrusted the Protector more.

Gideon was present at the historic meeting, and with him was Lord Wharton, who had spent a night at Flaw Valleys on his way. The fourth member was Sir Thomas Bowes, a large and silent man who was Warden of the Middle Marches.

As senior commander, Lord Grey chose to open the meeting with a striking list of his activities on the east of Scotland. In the front of his mind was a courteous desire to complete the military picture for his fellow officers. In the back of it marched a procession of letters from the Lord Protector, making concise reference to some aspect of Lord Wharton's energy and initiative on the west. He went on.

'Now, what we have to do most urgently is to break this mood of optimism. This French arrival had done a lot of damage: men and money pouring into Scotland from the French king, and the promise of more – we can't ignore that. And your friend Lennox crawling into Dumfries and home again like a half-drowned kitten, Wharton, hardly had the appearance of a military tour de force.'

'The Earl of Lennox, like the baker of Ferrara, thinks he is made of butter,' said Wharton dryly. 'I am in no position to disabuse him of the idea.'

'Well, he's no tactician: that's obvious,' said Grey. 'Figureheads are dangerous. Would never touch 'em. And if I had to, I should go with them and make damn sure they didn't get into mischief.'

'I bow to expert opinion, of course. But the gentleman is married to the King's cousin. The effect is to make him touchy about bear-leading.'

'Tact!' said Lord Grey.

'It is a little difficult,' said Lord Wharton, 'to convey acceptably to a noble gentleman that he is an interfering fool.' And he let a pause develop just sufficiently before going on. 'If I might suggest it, we should be better employed in considering just how Lord Lennox might be used — since inescapably he must be used — in the next combined raid. And how he can help us against the Douglases ...'

They had got exactly so far when Margaret Douglas, Countess of Lennox, was announced.

* * *

Meg Douglas in girlhood had possessed the gorgeous, leonine sort of beauty that her uncle Henry VIII had frittered away, and of which her father, the Earl of Angus, was the vestigial affidavit. In sixteen years' residence in England, careening at Henry's whim from near-throne to near-block, Margaret kept her splendour.

Her mother, Margaret Tudor of England, had been married to King James of Scotland nearly fifty years before; and had stayed in Scotland to become Angus's wife when her first husband lost his life at Flodden.

Now Henry was dead; his sister was dead; Angus had married again and Margaret Douglas had become the good-conduct prize which persuaded the Earl of Lennox to abandon his singlehanded bid for the Scottish throne, and throw in his lot with England. She was not an unwilling bride. Once, when Henry was in the throes of illegitimizing his children, the Lady Margaret had been heiress to the throne of England. The royal blood which she and Lennox shared and which ran in their children was a powerful claim to both the English and Scottish thrones. Lennox might be a bad tactician, but his wife was not.

Her entry into the solar at Warkworth was consciously magnificent. Gideon, effacing himself, studied her. Her hair was a dark, lichen-blonde and the features strongly marked in a pale skin, the mouth warm and decided, the chin cleft, the eyes observant. His impression was one of natural graces overlaid by years of merciless experience.

She was speaking with perfect composure. 'I'm afraid my family have been troubling you greatly. It's never easy for an Englishman to understand all the pressures Scots are subject to.'

No one had any illusions that this was a social call. Lord Wharton was blunt. 'Saving your presence, Lady Lennox, I have made no secret of my views about the Douglases. I know the difficulties they are under. But until they show themselves friends, we must treat them as enemies. I have raided Angus's land and Drumlanrig's land on instructions from the Lord Protector, and I regret if Lord Grey feels that his friendship with Sir George and his private promises of immunity are endangered, but further than that I cannot go.'

The Lord Lieutenant was taut with temper and the need to preserve the social decencies. 'I dislike, as any gentleman would, the appearance of breaking my pledged word,' he said. 'The damage done, however, I agree that the Douglases have taken unwarrantable revenge and, as you know perfectly, I have pledged my word to punish them.'

'We'll be lucky if we get the chance,' said Wharton bluntly. 'But in case we do, I've asked everyone who is able, to report to me for service as soon as they can. If you will carry out your second raid on Buccleuch, Lord

Lieutenant, I shall put all the force I can to shake the Douglases out of their bushes.'

'Wait a moment.' Lady Lennox spoke, and both Grey and Wharton, intent as circling dogs in their antagonism, showed their surprise. 'The Protector told me this intention was that you should enter Scotland again, Lord Grey and, form a new centre of operations at Haddington, just south of Edinburgh. Is that right?'

'The Protector wanted all three armies to invade at once, but that is impossible because of the weather and the ground, Lady Lennox. Quite impossible. In a month's time, I might be in a position to march to Haddington. In the meantime, we are to attack Buccleuch.'

'I understand.' She looked at her wine. 'In that case, it seems a pity for Lord Wharton to draw on himself the undivided attention of the west. Would it not be better to wait a week or two for better weather, and then to synchronize your raids?'

Bowes ventured. 'But time is against us, Lady Lennox. The French –'

'The same wind blows in the Channel as on the Solway,' she said. 'No fleet will put out in this weather.'

Gideon interposed briefly. 'The Protector is asking for action quickly against the Douglases, Lady Lennox.'

'And that he shall have,' said the woman serenely. 'If you will allow me to make a suggestion.' She looked up at four, noncommittal faces and smiled. 'There was a time when I was a Douglas, and then I became more Tudor than Douglas. Now I am more Stewart then either. Listen.'

And she outlined a plan which was bold, practical and, unintentionally, quite formidable in its ultimate effect. In which she showed herself to be, after all, more Tudor and Douglas then Stewart.

* * *

With Will Scott at his side, Lymond met John Maxwell briefly by appointment in a bothy of mud and thatch in the hills near Thornhill.

Sitting watching by the bright, whining fire, Scott saw

that Maxwell was now handling the other men carefully. He made one flattering reference to the conduct of December's cattle raid, but did not repeat the mistake. He referred also to his meeting with Agnes Herries ... 'That goes very well. You were right about the letters. She had already created the mould, and I stepped into it. Not a bad thing. I shall try not to disappoint her.'

'What did you make of her?' Lymond asked.

'Your reading was perfectly accurate. She will make an excellent wife – if that were the main issue. And if her marriage were a matter of free choice, I should be Lord Herries tomorrow. But of course, it's not. I'm afraid it will take more than one cattle raid to shake off Arran. He's determined to have her for his son, and he has a promise on paper.'

'The Queen Dowager is not unsympathetic,' remarked Lymond.

'But Arran is Governor.'

'And as such is accountable to the French for the fervent persecution of the enemy.'

'Arran won't attack: he has neither the stomach nor the power.'

'He won't attack; but he'll have to defend, shortly. There's another combined attack from Carlisle and Berwick coming next month.'

The pupils in the golden eyes narrowed and expanded. 'How do you know that?'

'Spies. I have no direct contact with Carlisle,' said Lymond laconically. 'If you want my opinion to reinforce your own, then that's your bargain. Throw the Maxwells openly this time against Wharton, and you have the Dowager on your side. She likes the girl, and she's being pushed for results by her relatives in France as well as by the French Ambassador. Let her persuade Arran for you.'

There was a long silence. Then the Master of Maxwell said, 'The real deterrent lies with my hostages at Carlisle. If I turn, they may hang. But, as you no doubt will tell me, life is cheap.'

Lymond raised fair brows. 'It is another disease that

grieveth me. What I will say is that sentimentality is expensive. Let them hang: it is still a good bargain.'

Maxwell said, 'I am not so ruthless.'

'We might differ about that ... But save the Carlisle chickens, and you let the Stirling stables burn.'

'Some might feel one hen of a sort was worth twenty horses,' said Maxwell.

'And yet you won't get far without horses, be your poultry never so prolific.'

Lymond was clearly mocking, and the other switched subjects curtly. 'Do you wish to continue the letters to Agnes Herries? We agreed that you should had this channel for messages.'

Lymond said, 'Let it lapse. I can find other means now, if need be.' He rose. 'I am grateful for your co-operation. We may still meet, of course. Next month, for example. In spite of your fondness for the chicken run.'

Maxwell also got up. He hesitated, stooping a litte under the low roof, his half-armour fogged with condensation. 'There is one piece of news you might find of interest,' he said. 'It's not the kind I should pass on to Edinburgh, as the woman is, I suppose, a niece by marriage ...'

Lymond's face and voice were his first weapons, and he used them consciously with the same control that in his brother kept expression away.

But this time, something new filled the blue eyes; and Scott, sitting forgotten, saw it, and his breathing stopped. Then it was over, and Maxwell, unobserving, was still talking.

'Lennox and Wharton are trying a new gambit this time. The Countess of Lennox is being sent north to Drumlanrig to try and splint together all those burst Douglas loyalties before the army invades.'

Lymond said in his accustomed voice, 'The Lady Margaret Douglas? Angus's daughter? When is she coming?'

Maxwell shook his head and took up his hat. 'I have no other details. But I expect she'll arrive shortly before they march, and wait for her husband. I thought you might be interested.'

He turned in the doorway, one hand on the lintel. 'Good day to you both. I fancy these meetings will not be our loss.'

'I fancy not,' said Lymond dryly; and Maxwell, mounted, leaned down. 'You have a nice touch with the Latin tag, but I found the French a little indelicate, here and there.' And, one of his infrequent smiles lighting the solemn face, the Master of Maxwell rode off.

Scott, straightening from dousing the fire, found Lymond waiting with both horses at the door, his expression angelical. 'O rubicund blossom and star of humility! O famous bud, full of benignity! O beautiful Master of Maxwell!'

Scott came out and took his horse. 'What's happened, sir?'

'Ce n'est rien: c'est une femme qui se noie,' said Lymond, and laughed. 'Love Mr. Maxwell, my cherub: he had brought your old age with him today. We require a hostage to exchange for Samuel Harvey. And behold, we have a hostage. My brilliant devil, my imitation queen; my past, my future, my hope of heaven and my knowledge of hell . . . Margaret, Countess of Lennox.'

PART III
The Play for Samuel Harvey

1

BITTER EXCHANGE

This knycht he aw his folk for to defend . . .
Off gret corage he is that has no dreid
And dowtis nocht his fais multitud
Bot starkly fechtis for his querell gud.

1. OFFER OF A PAWN IS DISCUSSED

Meg Douglas, the boy Scott was thinking, his hands slack
on the reins. Margaret Douglas, Countess of Lennox.
What could have forged a link between the refulgent, self-
contained Lymond and this woman?

The meeting with Maxwell lay behind them. Riding
north with the Master, Scott had time to dwell on these
and other matters, other women. He remembered the cold
dawn camp after the cattle raid. Lymond was unique:
perhaps he was entitled to a unique relationship with the
Stewart girl. Perhaps. It was none of his business.

But because of it – every man has his private affairs –
he had said nothing to the Master of his promise to meet
Buccleuch.

His motives were wholly chaste: he meant to toy a little
with the old man, giving his father the chance of a good
look at him. He wanted to inspect the banners of the
angels so near to the merry ranks of Mahoun, and make
self-satisfied comparisons.

But he said nothing of that to Lymond. The devyll, they
say, is dede; the devyll is dede. But Kincurd, renegade,
would revive him fast enough, thought Will Scott, and
kept quiet as they moved toward their new winter quarters.

Affairs around the Peel Tower were becoming a little

too busy; and Lymond had decided to move. Tomorrow, Scott was to leave for the old Tower to supervise its final dismantling. Tonight he would spend at the new Tower, at Crawfordmuir.

The gold mines at Crawfordmuir were not very old. For thirty years, Dutch and Germans and Scots had been mining there, and the Queen Dowager Mary of Guise had also brought French miners from Lorraine. Since James V died, the Dowager Queen had not renewed the contract.

So the mines lay derelict, the ruins of workmen's huts and storehouses littering the broken moorland, with rotting spades and wheelbarrows and crumbling dams and shallow, timbered pits.

The rock yielded no fabulous artery of yellow ore, but pebbles and scourings grained and gritted with gold dust and, rarely, an attenuated nugget. Mining was furtive and unlicenced. Week in, week out, the earth brought down by the spring rains was cherished and riddled, and the sparkling fragments folded in twists and rags and taken to a friendly goldsmith who might choose to forget that a tenth of all lawful takings on Crawfordmuir belonged to the Crown.

This was the land to which the Master brought Scott: up through bog and heather and packed moss and harsh root to two thousand feet above sea level where they stopped, and the boy looked about him. Here were four rivers, Lymond had told him, and Eldorado between them as the ancients thought it lay between the four rivers of Paradise. There were other graces. In this harness of high, safe hills they were surrounded by escape routes.

Lymond pointed. Below and to the left, a burn wandered into the hills with heaps like molehills about it and the figures of men moving. ' – Your colleagues looking diligently for alluvial gold. It amuses them and helps fill the treasury. It also explains our presence and gives us warning of anyone using the valley . . .' And led the way to their destination, an excellent stone tower, thick-walled and small-windowed, built in a grassy socket of the hill.

There, in Lymond's new winter quarters, Scott passed

the night and next morning, pleased at the prospect of a little autonomy, left for the Peel Tower. A little later the Master also rode out and, turning sharp east, began the journey to Tantallon Castle.

* * *

'It grieves me deeply to break up your manège,' said Sir George, 'but I can't accept the alternative. If you want me to trace Harvey for you, you must sell me Will Scott.'

Lymond spoke idly. 'It sounds as if you *have* been endearing yourself to the opposition. Can't you repair your relations in some other way? I have several keen bargains in political information: or is Grey no longer interested in our life, our lust, our Governor, our Queen?' His face expressed only mild enquiry.

Both men were in a stoutly furnished room in the East Tower of Tantallon. Beyond the window the North Sea crawled and roared at the bottom of hundred-foot cliffs; far out, the Bass Rock stood in a nest of white floss, with gannets plummetting like so many celestial lead lines into the jumping sea. Douglas turned impatiently from the sight.

'If I could conduct this transaction simply by buying information from you, I would. As it is, I am ready to take on my own account anything you may have to sell. For that reason, as you probably noticed, I avoided addressing my letter to you by name. Nor have I given your name to Lord Grey although – let us be as open as we can, Mr. Crawford – I had very little trouble guessing your identity. . . . I hope you were less severe on Mr. Somerville than you were with Sir Andrew.' He paused. 'You're swimming in very deep waters, aren't you, Crawford?'

'But life in an aquatic kettle can be quite entertaining,' suggested Lymond. 'And what keeps out water will also keep out steel between the shoulder blades. Gideon Somerville, if you are interested, is in pristine health, and Jonathan Crouch is at home. That leaves Samuel Harvey and his purchase.'

Sir George was broadly reasonable. 'Why hesitate? Get

yourself another disciple, man, and be done with it.' Sir George badly needed Scott to bolster his tattered prestige with Lord Grey.

'But Scott is extremely useful to me,' said Lymond. 'Besides, he gives me excellent cover from Buccleuch.'

'Once we have him, Buccleuch won't trouble anyone any more.'

'He won't trouble you: he'll use up all his surplus energy looking for me. And another thing. If I gave you Scott I should want absolute possession of the man Harvey. Would Grey agree to that? I imagine Harvey, for one thing, would object quite violently.'

'There's no reason why Harvey should know,' said Douglas after a moment's quick thought. 'I tell you, Grey wants Scott badly enough for anything. If this unfortunate man is your price, I think I can promise he will pay it.'

'In the siècles de foi you would be irresistible,' said Lymond generously. 'But I have arrived in the age of reason. You'll need to provide some pretty imaginative security before I believe that.'

'And if I do so?'

Lymond smiled again, and Douglas's hands, in spite of himself, opened and closed. 'If you do so,' said the Master, 'of course I shall give you the person of Will Scott.'

Before Lymond left, Sir George repeated his own private bid for his services. It met with bland refusal. 'My offer was to exchange information for Harvey; not to plunge into general commerce.'

'If you can afford to say that, you're a fortunate man. I wish I knew your source of revenue. I notice incidentally,' said Sir George, understandably irritated, 'that in your somewhat frenzied quest for Mr. Harvey your other project has fallen from sight.'

'Everyone credits me with projects. I sometimes feel like a latter-day Hercules. Which one?'

'The one concerned with preserving your brother from

the ills of old age. I imagine Lady Culter's pregnancy has complicated your problem?'

It was news to Lymond. The fractional pause told Sir George that, and he was irritably thankful, in passing, that he could still read a man to some degree at least. Then the Master said with amusement, 'Are you suggesting that I should add to my tally?'

Sir George's answer was ready. 'If Lord Grey and I are happily reconciled, and if his lordship's plans for this country are successful, we shall remember our friends. As to the granting – or reinstating – of baronies, for example.'

There was a respectful pause, broken mildly by Lymond. 'Setting aside anarchy and murder and returning to simple conveyancing – how soon could Samuel Harvey be brought north?'

The essential bargain, after all, had been made; so Douglas's exasperation was well-hidden. A common posting station, a hovel they both knew, was agreed as a means of communication, and the pact was sealed. At the door, Sir George turned and smiled. 'I can't imagine a Scott resigned to authority and bars. What will your callow colt make of the snare?'

'Scott is trained to authority already,' said Lymond. 'The bars are a trite enough sequel.'

He reached the Peel Tower on Sunday the fifth of February, finding it already unrecognizable in the torments of chaotic removal. He walked from room to room, dispensing criticism and looking for Will Scott.

In this he was unsuccessful. Will had left the Peel early that afternoon for an unknown destination, and had not come back.

2 · BRIEF RETURN TO HOME SQUARES

The meeting between Will Scott and his father was due to take place at dusk. After banging violently about the castle all day Buccleuch left, rather too early, for his supposedly secret encounter, and his family was overjoyed to see the last of him.

Wat Scott of Buccleuch was a man crammed with sentiment, which accounted for the peculiar harmlessness of half his explosions. The sight of his heir at the cattle raid had produced an unwonted tremor among his principles, and he was shy of repeating the experience.

Of all his brood, Will was least like himself. His oldest and illegitimate son, Walter, was a stuffy and powerful lad, and he was setting him up as befitted his first-born; but Will had a head on his shoulders, if a fat one, and Buccleuch was not the man to underrate that. The boy's scruples he put down, with some justice, to the company of flutemouths and dishwashing writers in books; and he rode out therefore alone to meet him at Crumhaugh with a fine determination this time to stand for no stupidity.

It was still light when he reached the hill and pressed into the copse on its side. At first, peering through the trees, he thought the little clearing was empty. It was a place in the wood, known to Will and himself, where larch and oak and juniper gave way to a quincunx of soaring beeches so old that the aisles between were cushioned with a permanent autumn of red leaves. Then he heard a hoof strike, and the clunk of bit on teeth, and the next moment saw his son's horse with its reins loosely tied to a bush, and Will himself standing just beyond.

The boy was quite different. His thick neck was strapped with muscle; he had eyes like sea pebbles, and his red hair roared like a lion. Buccleuch got rid of his surprise and dismounted. 'So you came!'

His son regarded him austerely. 'I said I would.'

There was a slight pause, a bellow as Buccleuch cleared his throat, then Sir Wat waded in. 'Ye might like to know that your Englishy friends have burned me out of Newark. Missed Janet and myself and the weans by half a day, just.'

Will was distressingly calm. 'Well, you seem to have survived.'

'No thanks to you!'

'Why blame me? If you chose to move all the cannon to Branxholm, it was no fault of mine.'

This error of judgment was no sweeter for being Buccleuch's own. He remembered just in time what he was supposed to be doing, and wiped his mouth with a large hand.

'Will. We've had words in the past, and I don't mind saying you were damned disrespectful. And wrong, forbye. But you won't get any righter by burying your carcass to the neb and over in Lymond's muck heap. As far as I'm concerned you can stop making an exhibition of yourself and come on back home. Unless you're so damned keen you've begun to reform the bastard yourself.'

His son's mouth twitched. 'I haven't, cross my heart. But don't flatter yourself that I'm suffering so that I can read you a homily on crime. I'm with Lymond because I like it.'

Buccleuch's face expressed disbelief and disapproval. 'Dammit, I believe George Douglas was right. You're planning a coup. Don't deny it! You're going to embroil Lymond as deep as he can get, and then lead the Queen's men to him. Is that it?'

Scott didn't trouble to deny it. He said, 'That, I am quite sure, is what George Douglas would do,' in a voice of energetic scorn, and added after a contemptuous interval, 'I'm staying with the Master. Why not? We're a well-regulated, efficient society. We've got health and companionship and excitement and money, a common aim and a common justice. We are our own masters, afraid of nobody but the one man, and he's worth fearing. Show me its like, and I'll join you.'

'I can show you its like,' said Buccleuch. 'In the jungle. What you're living by is four-footed law, and what you're living off is the blood and marrow of the rest of us. You've money, you say. Money from where? From spying and stealing and so-called protection – the money of folk who're poor because they've had the stupidity to fight two wars for their country. That's where your ideal community comes from – from corruption and treachery. And by God, it takes a thick hide to snuffle and drool after your own dirty pleasures while bairns starve in Teviotdale for want of meal. Dod, you'll fairly have a stitch in your side watching Branxholm burn the same way Midculter did.'

'I'd nothing to do with that.' The words were nearly cold enough to belie the passionate resentment in Scott's eyes.

Buccleuch was shouting. 'You're doing a hell of a lot to stop it. Dod, I'd better warn the wife. We're to live alfresco this winter, if I don't get my throat slit the way Culter got his shoulder and Janet her arm.'

The same frigid voice said, 'If the English intend to burn you, how do you possibly imagine I can stop it?'

'You can stop bleating your name to Grey of Wilton for a start!' bawled Buccleuch. 'So that every rotten device you practice on him doesn't get traced home to me! If you'd done that a bit earlier, there'd be some folk at Newark who'd be much obliged to you.'

'Oh, God!' said Scott, and let go. 'A minute ago I was being overfriendly with the English: you're not very consistent, are you? And if you're supposed to be luring me back to the herd, I must say you're making a damned bad job of it. If you really want to convince, you should at least get your facts straight. And argue them with some sort of logic. And keep your head while you're doing it. In the first place, I wasn't responsible for Grey discovering my identity. In the second place, Lymond is doing no more, openly, than half Scotland is doing underhand. In the third place, he is considerably less popular with the English than you are yourself. In the fourth place, you would fare a damned sight worse under the attention of my colleagues if a person like Lymond weren't there to control them; and lastly, I prefer company where inflated prejudice and intellectual tedium get the place they deserve – among the granddads and dummies and the drink-fuddled half-wits in a fifth-rate common alehouse.'

A diatribe worthy, Scott felt, of its inspiring genius. The response was the kind he often felt like making to Lymond, and had once made. Buccleuch's knotted fist came out like a joiner's mallet and drove at his son's head.

With a beautiful, cool-breathing ease, Scott slipped under it, closed his own fist, and released a blow which sent Buccleuch travelling like a cannon ball across the clearing and down with a skid into the beech leaves.

There was a moment's stupefied silence. Buccleuch lay, temporarily winded and making repulsive noises, and his son stood looking at him, with the excitement shrinking out of his face.

It was a standing joke that Sir Wat was incapable of reasoned argument. There was no victory and less virtue in first provoking him to violence and then hitting a man twice his own age. He could imagine what Lymond would say. Scott stood for perhaps two seconds, then took the clearing in two strides and dropping on one knee, heaved his father to a sitting position, one arm around his great shoulder. 'Father – '

Wat's scarred, knotted hand shuffled tenderly over his jaw, and his small bright eyes turned to his son. 'By God!' He sat up fully, and resting an elbow on his knee, moved his lower mandible gently from side to side. 'Where the hell did you learn that?' demanded Buccleuch.

Scott gave a half-laugh and releasing him, sat back on his heels. 'Lymond.'

'Well, he's taught you one thing worth knowing. But there was no need to practise it on me.' He got to his feet with the help of one hand on Will's shoulder and stood for a moment, holding the boy in front of him. 'He's taught you quite a few things, hasn't he? A fairly cavalier way with opposition, for one thing.'

'I notice,' said his son, and grinned, 'that you weren't exactly relying on rhetoric yourself. But I didn't mean to hurt you.'

'Just to knock the head off me,' said Sir Wat, raising his hand to feel his jaw again. Scott, disappearing for a moment, returned with his handkerchief folded into a soaking pad, which he proffered Buccleuch. 'Was it true about Newark?' he said.

Applying his back to a root, Sir Wat nodded. 'They didn't get into the house, but they burned the village and nearly stripped me of beasts, Will. Grey's doing.' He shot a keen glance at his son's face. The boy had seated himself on a broken trunk and was studying his hands.

'So they have the better of you both ways,' said Scott thoughtfully. 'Grey for my misdeeds, and the Dowager if you dissociate yourself with them.'

'That's how it fell out.' Buccleuch, watching him quietly, held the pad to his bleeding face. 'It's been fairly damnable all round – no less for you, of course. You're no match for a clever sycophant like yon. Whatever his purpose, he's managed to stick my neck in a cang; and he looks like making a fine scapegoat out of you, if you let him.'

The boy was silent. Then he said, 'I'm supposed to be beyond redemption, am I?'

Like a sea urchin calling in its needles, Buccleuch's whiskers withdrew. 'There would be some explaining to do. But damn it, I count for something yet in this country. If we went back quietly now, just the two of us, I'd see no one harms you. And you can have the satisfaction of fighting in the open, by the side of your family. You can surely see the way it is. In my position some kind of double-dealing can't be avoided, and I won't pretend my hands are clear of it yet. But no one can tell me I'm not a Scotsman as well as a Scott, and the one as much as the other. So what d'you say?'

Sitting against a tree, one hand clapped to his face and an expression of limpid encouragement on the rosso-antico face, Buccleuch was more persuasive even than he knew. His son got to his feet without grace. 'I've sworn to follow Lymond.'

'He's excommunicated. You know that?'

'Yes. But –'

'You have not only the power but the duty to break any pledge to him. D'you know why the Church expelled him?'

Scott had heard so many possible reasons that he kept quiet.

'Five years ago, when you were in France, his spying came suddenly to light. Before that, he was taken on trust, the same as Culter, and nobody thought of suspecting where the leakage was coming from. It came to light because a dispatch of his was found – a dispatch referring to other reports he had already made, and enclosing information that led Wharton to find and put an end to us at Solway Moss. But by the time it was found Lymond had already got himself to London, and was sitting safe with King Harry heaping land and money on him.'

'I know that.' Scott shifted uncomfortably.

'Yes. But did you also know this? In its last page that report described the locality of a damned great gunpowder dump of ours; a store that had been left in or near a convent. Described it fine: Dod, it was graphic enough to put a chorus to. It was so bloody ingenious that a raiding party was sent from Carlisle which blew up the nunnery, killing every last woman in it.'

'But Lymond – ' began Scott.

'Lymond planned it. God, I saw the letter and the signature, and every stroke of the pen was as much his as that damned doll's hair. Ask Sybilla. Ask Culter. Ask anyone. Even his own mother didn't pretend it was a forgery – it wasn't.'

The colour had run out beneath Scott's fair, unpigmented skin. His father said aggressively, 'You didn't know that? Or the other thing about it?'

'What?' said Scott. 'What other thing?'

But Buccleuch had scrambled to his feet, the pad dropped from his grip, his face changed. Scott turned.

With a rustle and a squirm, Johnnie Bullo emerged from the juniper and trotted across the clearing, an agile silhouette which made Sir Wat, unrecognizing, put a quick hand on his sword.

But Will spoke first, all his anxieties turned to acid on his tongue. 'What are you doing here! Spying for Lymond?'

'No.' Johnnie Bullo, keeping a tree between himself and Buccleuch, was unperturbed, though breathing faster than

275

usual. 'Just a call from a friend. I thought you'd like to know you're in a small trap. The wood's encircled by armed men.'

Buccleuch overheard, as he was meant to, and the hand on his sword moved with a rattle and a hiss. Scott said instantly, 'Lymond!'

'No, no. Lymond's busy. It's Scottish troops: fine fellows on big horses with dirks all over them like hobnails. Friends of your pa, here, no doubt.'

Scott's breath whistled between his teeth. 'Hardly friends of my father. After all, we undertook to keep this meeting secret, didn't we? And as good, honest churchmen our word is inviolate.'

'I did keep it quiet.' Suddenly alive to his danger, Buccleuch rushed to reassure. 'There wasn't a soul . . . Who are they? Hey, you!' roared Wat to the shadowy figure of Johnnie. 'Who are these men?'

'Don't you know?' asked Scott. 'What a pity you couldn't tell them things were going surprisingly well and their services wouldn't be needed. They could have disappeared quietly and I should never have known.'

Buccleuch was choking with frustration. 'Don't be a fool, man. They're there by no wish of mine. I didn't – I haven't – Listen, will you?' as the young man turned away.

'I rather think I've listened enough, don't you?' said Scott over his shoulder. ' "Come back quietly, just the two of us"! By God, I admire that for a piece of chicanery!'

'Will!' Buccleuch, regardless of a possible audience, fairly roared in his anguish. 'What's happened I don't know, but believe me, I'd cheerfully flay them alive, whoever they are. You must believe me! They're not mine . . . I don't know how they got there. Dammit!' he bellowed. 'They must be Lymond's.'

'They're not.' The gypsy's brown eyes, dancing with enjoyment, rested on Scott. 'Well. They're waiting for you. Are you going with them or with me?'

'Is there a choice?' snarled the boy. 'We're both trapped, aren't we?'

Bullo snickered. 'You are. I'm not. I have a pony just

outside. If I mount and draw them off to the left, can you ride for the gap?'

'I can,' said Scott grimly. He strode to Buccleuch's horse and threw the reins to Bullo. 'There's another decoy for you. Send the brute ahead. He'll split them still more.'

The gypsy caught the bridle and began to move, his smile flashing. 'So you're for Lymond after all.'

Scott's grim face as he flung himself on his horse was reply enough. Buccleuch caught the bridle. 'Will! Man, you're that bedazzled your thick head's nothing but heliotrope. Listen. These are not my men! I'll swear to it on anything you like! Wait for just a moment – give me a chance to identify them – if they're Queen's troops I'll send them about their business!'

'No doubt. And their business will be Will Scott.' The boy whipped the reins free. 'No thank you. I've had enough of decency. I'm too weak in the stomach for it.'

'Will–' It was too late. A distant thudding and a burst of noise told that the gypsy had drawn the pursuit after him; with a rustle and a whirl of cold air Scott cantered across the clearing without looking round and put his horse fast through the thickest part of the wood.

Sir Wat, horseless and breathing heavily, stood still. He heard the uproar a moment later when his son was spotted; he heard the shouting as the riders following the two decoys were recalled. He heard the chase recede around the base of the hill and falter, and finally, the sounds of riders returning, disconcerted. He drew his sword and walked steadily to the nearest group. The trees thinned, the voices became louder and he saw the colour of the livery: blue and silver.

Wat Scott of Buccleuch shot his sword home in the scabbard with a noise like a pistol and stalked forward. The horsemen wheeling at the sound faltered. 'Buccleuch!'

'Aye, Buccleuch,' said that person. 'Did ye find what ye were looking for?'

They fidgetted. 'No, Sir Wat.'

'Have you a horse you can give me, then?' They had.

277

It was brought forward eagerly and Buccleuch mounted, his eyes sweeping the wood. 'Where's your master?'

The nearest man stammered. 'He'll be back, sir. We was to meet here if . . .'

'I am here,' said an unemotional voice; and Buccleuch turned. Lord Culter, armed, with a long scratch across one cheek from his scrambling chase after Scott, was sitting still on his horse at the edge of the trees.

Amid deathly silence, Buccleuch rode over to him. Within touching distance he halted and, leaning across, gripped Culter's reins close to the bit, so that the other could not move. 'So I see. You're having a bonny revenge for the cattle raid?'

Culter shook his head. 'I only want Lymond.'

'You only want Lymond,' repeated Buccleuch, and flung the reins from him so that Culter's horse jumped and reared, neighing. 'You only want Lymond, and you're ready to sacrifice everyone and everything for it. Your mother – your wife – the folk who used to be friends. How many friends have you got now? Tell me that.'

'Enough.'

'Enough to yap at your heels while you trample busily back and forth over the rest of us in this panic-stricken, muddleheaded harrying you're launched on! The Queen wanted you at Stirling, and where are you? Riding down my son in the name of your mim-faced honour! And why? Sybilla doesn't want it, and she's twice the cause you have. You'll achieve nothing, as we all know, unless it's to make the fellow kill himself laughing. Why go on with it? No one cares. And there's some saying freely that it's not a matter of justice at that, but plain, green, roaring jealousy that's got into you.'

Richard said violently, 'Hold your tongue, Scott!' and then restrained himself, the plates of his jack flashing with his breathing. 'I won't debate it with you.'

Buccleuch muted his voice. 'Oh, I've nearly done. I've just got to say this: as well as Lymond, you've got me against you now. I loathe the man as you do, but I'm going to get Will safely away from him. And until I do, there's no plan you can make against Lymond that won't find me there before you. I wish no ill to you, or to your wife, or to your mother, but you can hinder me at the risk of death or maiming: I'll have no care for you.' And turning, he galloped his borrowed horse out of Crumhaugh wood.

* * *

Johnnie Bullo got back to the Peel ahead of Scott.

When the boy arrived, he found most of the men gone, and all the animals except a few horses. The building, always derelict, had a sullen air, as if in the emptying the last, lingering kindness had been wrung from the stones.

Lymond sat in the broken hall, and by him stood Johnnie Bullo. From the brilliance of the gypsy's smile it was palpable that the story of Crumhaugh had been told to the Master. Will Scott stalked forward prepared to get full value from the wrath boiling in his veins, and met the wall of Lymond at his worst.

'My dear! I hear the bosom of your father produced a clatter like the Archbishop's conscience, and you have returned to cast yourself on mine.'

'I was a fool to expect anything else.' Scott glared at Johnnie Bullo and shifted his eyes back to the Master. 'You were perfectly right. I'm damned if I trust anyone, from now on.'

'The encounter seems to have had its share of bathos,' rejoined Lymond blandly. 'How were you able to warn him, Johnnie?'

'Oh, I picked up a hint in one of the houses I was playing at. It made me think there might be a trap afoot.'

'So you sprang it.' The Master, rising, strolled to the door. 'On the whole, this business of manumission is a little trying. I doubt if I have the nervous stamina to sustain it much longer.' Johnnie, having withstood the blue eye for as long as self-respect demanded, shrugged, rose and sauntered outside. Lymond shut the door and came back.

'Johnnie – ' began Scott furiously.

'Johnnie makes mischief as cows make milk. You know that as well as I do. But at least he does it with his brain, and not his stomach, or wherever you keep your unique emotions.' He had deployed himself against the mantelpiece, tapping the stone softly with one hand, and Scott realized suddenly he had better collect his wits.

'You kept your appointment secret,' said Lymond. 'Why?'

'Because it was none of your business.' Scott was still angry.

Lymond said gently, 'Let us bathe in moral philosophy, as in a living river. Double-dealing is my business.'

'I know. But it isn't mine,' said Scott rudely; and Lymond smiled. 'I don't believe you.'

There was an unsettled silence. The boy, still aggressive, broke it. 'I simply wanted to talk to my father. There's nothing to get alarmed about in that.'

'Nothing. Except that you kept it secret.'

'You don't catechize Cuckoo-spit everytime he disappears with his women!'

'Cuckoo's women don't have a pack of bloodhounds and two thousand men-at-arms behind them – not the most willing of them. You are the only person here who might discover he has something to gain by selling out. You are the only person who, whatever he does, is sure of a warm, moneyed niche waiting for him on the right side of the law. You are the only person with a shaky interest in ethics and the emotional stability of a quince seed in a cup of lukewarm water. Either you keep the oath you so dashingly pronounced last year, or I deal with you accordingly. I don't propose to sit here like a pelican in her piety, wondering what you're doing next.'

Scott, shaking with temper, replied, 'Oh, I'll tell you, if you want to know. I'll tell you if I sneeze. I'll tell you if I part my hair. But I still don't see that it was any of your damned–'

'Lord Culter was there,' said Lymond softly. 'Wasn't he? And I might have relished meeting Buccleuch.'

'I daresay. But I didn't know Culter would be there. And oath or no oath, you can hardly expect me to sell my father quite yet.'

'A nicety he hardly seems to appreciate.'

'I've already said I made a mistake.'

'So, obviously, have we.'

'Why? I'm here, am I not?' blared Scott. 'I didn't break my word. It was Buccleuch who –'

'After he allowed you to knock him down. I heard about it.'

'Allowed!'

'Buccleuch doesn't think with his stomach either. Didn't it occur to you that I could damage your precious family rather more thoroughly than Lord Grey?'

'I –'

'And if you leave us, I certainly shall.'

'But –'

'So that, Marigold, if you are going to be forsworn, you must be thoroughly forsworn. You must give us all up as well. That's what your father was counting on.'

Silence.

'Well?' asked Lymond.

'You needn't be afraid,' said Scott frigidly. 'It won't happen again.'

The Master stared at him. 'There are times when your utterances are refreshing, and times when they are flower-like beyond belief. I am not afraid. I can tell you now that it will not happen again. I am waiting for an apology.'

Scott's reply was inaudible, and Lymond walked straight up to the boy. His riding clothes, swiftly tended since he had come from Tantallon, were sartorial perfection, his hair shone like glass and his voice glittered to match. He was impeccably, unpleasantly sober.

'You have my warmest good wishes for any urgent need you may discover to injure me, personally. Just try it. But I will not have you endanger sixty men through maudlin sentiment and a watery school-boy defiance. Whatever you meant to do, you drew about yourself and nearly about us a major armed ambush – whether it was of your father's devising or not is of no importance. Intentions, yours or anyone else's, don't matter; they never matter and never excuse: get that into your head. If I allowed any one of

281

your dear old friends now on Crawfordmuir to hear this they would decorticate you like an onion, and you'd deserve it. Next time I shall inform them myself. Is that clear?'

It was damned unfair. Seizing the first weapon to hand, Scott said furiously, 'It sounds well, coming from you. Why should I trouble about them? It wouldn't hinder you from selling any one of us if it paid you. Unless you restrict yourself to wiping out women in holy orders.'

There was an appalling silence. Then Lymond said carefully, 'Ill-advised, Scott. Don't bluster. And particularly don't bluster in that direction. You may now get out of my sight.'

There was nothing to add. Scott left the room, mounted and rode off to Crawfordmuir hardly realizing that of all the checkered exchanges between them this was the first in which he had, after a fashion, held his own.

As Scott rode west, his father travelled north.

It was some time before Buccleuch, jogging bitterly home from Crumhaugh, thought to wonder how Culter had heard of his appointment with Will. He had told Sybilla, but she was as anxious to keep Culter away from Will and Lymond as he was. Who else?

He thought. Only one person could have seen the note and was likely to act on it in just that way: Janet. Sir Wat's hands cramped on the reins. Janet! By God, thought Buccleuch, I'll teach that long-nebbit braying bitch of a woman to keep her nose from now on out of my business. . . . And he put his horse into a canter for Branxholm and lifted his head to scan the night sky.

There was something wrong with the light in the south-east – an underglow of crimson flushing the low cloud. He stared at it for a long moment doubting his eyes; then wheeled and galloped toward the fire with curses fothering the cleft air at his back.

Lord Grey had been as good as his word. Setting out with foot and mounted hackbutters from Jedworth and Roxburgh, Sir Oswald Wylstropp and Sir Ralph Bullmer marched west with orderly authority, reducing everything in their way to ashes. They took thirty prisoners, all the sheep and goats they could manage, and reduced Hawick to a series of ovens in which the resisters were cooked in their skins like new lobsters.

Buccleuch, flying to the scene through paths choked with women and children and the pitiful domestic debris of flight, found his Branxholm men ahead of him under his own captain, and deploying them, took what vengeance he could, since it was too late to save. In the exploding, light-torn darkness, with all the power still left in the district they snapped and tore at Wylstropp's heels as he left, and killed some of his men and saved some of the animals. It was a poor enough salvage, and a poor enough revenge. After it, turning back with the west wind sick in their lungs, they scattered through the stricken, smoking district, and gave what help they could.

At dawn, Buccleuch rode back to Branxholm with an ache in his back and red eyes and a great fury inside him. In the hall, he remembered something else and strode to his wife's room with a streaming candle. 'Janet Beaton!'

The woman in the bed stirred and opened her eyes; and the big-nosed, generous face split into a sleepy grin. 'Well, stick me if it isn't Wat,' remarked Lady Buccleuch. 'Late as usual.'

'I want to have words with you, my lady.'

'Oh, you do? What about?'

'About the heir to this castle, madam. My oldest son Will.'

'Oldest legitimate son,' corrected Janet. 'Did ye miss him?'

'I missed him all right,' said her husband grimly.

Janet appeared remarkably spry with it. 'Och well, never mind,' said she. 'You know what they say. Ye havena lost a son but ye get a daughter.'

Buccleuch stared from under the eagle-owl eyebrows and Janet stared back. From beyond the bed a wavering and disenchanted wail rose, intensified and died. Janet's beam developed overtones of beatitude. 'The newest Buccleuch,' said his wife. 'Unpick that damned basilisk stare and go and glower at your new lassie for a change.'

Sir Wat slowly went red in the face. A raffish smile struggled up from the depths of his beard and he covered it with one hand, but the eyes bent on his wife were as soft as a spaniel's.

'Oh, well enough,' he said. 'Well enough. We'll say no more. It's over and done with. But – ye needna expect to put me off this way every time, woman!'

'Och, Dod! Don't worry!' said Janet, from the muddy embrace. 'I'd sooner the scolding!'

*　*　*

In such a way ended Sunday, the fifth of February.

Shortly afterward, Sir George Douglas wrote Lord Grey that he hoped before long to appear before the Lord Protector in London, the accredited Ambassador of Her Majesty of Scotland, to arrange the royal marriage.

The Lord Protector wrote to Grey. 'You have spent,' he pointed out, 'sixteen thousand pounds in nine months, and have only the Buccleuch raid to show for it. . . .'

Lord Grey sent a laconic message to Lord Wharton. 'I set out on Monday week to invade Scotland almost to Edinburgh's gates. I expect you and the Earl of Lennox to time your entry with mine.'

And then, above the complicated board, freezing the pieces in their busy tracks, hovered a speculative finger which no one could outplay.

The child Queen Mary, the very knot and core of all their plans, fell mortally ill.

2
THE QUEEN'S PROGRESS BECOMES CRITICAL

> The pawōn that is sette tofore the quene
> signefyeth the phisicyen, spicer and
> Apotyquaire ... The cyrurgyens ought also
> to be debonayr, amyable and to have pytye
> of their pacyents.

1 · A NEW PAWN IS TAKEN

They feared the English more than her disease. The sick baby Queen was taken to Dumbarton, rocky fortress on the Clyde, and Lady Culter and Christian Stewart were among those summoned to care for her.

The message was brought to Boghall by Tom Erskine. He found the girl standing at the window of Jamie's empty room, her hands laid loosely on the sill. Simon announced her visitor, allowed Erskine in, and banged the door as adequate comment as she turned.

Left alone with his destiny, Tom Erskine embarked headlong on his message: he had come to take her as far as Midculter before going off himself to the fighting. The conclusion of the gabble may have sounded more petulant than heroic, but Christian didn't notice. She said sharply, 'What fighting?'

'There's another armed push on the way. From Berwick on the east and Carlisle on the west. The Carlisle inroad is my affair.'

'Who else is going? Lord Culter? John Maxwell?'

'Culter's going, yes. What Maxwell will do is anybody's guess.'

It was their chief anxiety. Rowelled by French heels, Governor Arran had at last been brought to an ultimatum. Agnes Herries was destined for his son. But the Master of Maxwell had made it delicately clear that the Herries bride and the Herries estates were the price of his continuing interest in things Scottish; and Maxwell's interest in the coming invasion was likely to be vital. So with affronted howls on one side from Lord John, and mute reproof from his treasury on the other, Arran let it be known at Threave that appropriate help would receive appropriate reward, and hardly knew what to wish as a result.

Christian was not impressed by these half measures. 'Good God: Maxwell either for us or against us will be the turning point of the whole thing. Fortunately she likes him, poor lassie; but whether she did or not I should take her to Threave by the scruff of her neck and beg John Maxwell on my knees, if I were Arran, to come to our side.'

Tom said philosophically, 'Well, if you don't know what he'll do, then neither does Wharton. . . .' Memory of his real errand had come to him. He coughed disastrously.

'Christian, listen. We've seen a lot of each other in the last six months. . .'

His voice died away, but Christian's face betrayed only sympathetic amusement. 'Dear Tom, there isn't a verb in the dictionary that wouldn't float like a benison on your innocent breath; but I've a devil of a lot to pack. If you're intent on launching a review of your winter relationships. . .'

He was not put off, but simply accelerated. Without finesse, Tom Erskine shot forward and seized one idle hand. 'Christian! Do you like me? Could you put up with me? . . . Will you marry me, Chris?'

To keep the normal, comforting directness in her voice, she squandered all her training. 'To have your love is a wonderful thing, Tom, but you're wasting it on an obstinate woman.'

In his eagerness he mistook her meaning. 'There's no

one to cross you in Stirling, my dear; and my God, I'd like to see anyone try elsewhere.'

In spite of herself she smiled. 'Build a hedge around the cuckoo? I don't think perpetual summer would be very good for me, somehow. In the same way – in the same way that I don't think marriage would be good.'

His bewilderment reached her, even though she couldn't see. Releasing her hand he said slowly, 'You're afraid of marriage? Or is it of me?'

Christian said quickly, 'Not afraid: no. My reservations are of another kind. And not any dislike of you: of course not.'

'Then there's someone else?' he said.

It had not occurred to her that he might think that. With an effort, she applied her mind. 'Under the circumstances, that's rather flattering of you. But no – there's no one else. It's simply that –'

That what? It was not simple at all. Love was no pre-requisite, whatever Agnes Herries might think. He must indeed be wondering why she hesitated; wondering perhaps if she was after bigger game than himself. She had money and her birth was higher than his own. She had no need to be diffident about her handicap, but it was the only excuse she had. So she went on. 'It's just that, my dear, a blind wife is no asset to a future Lord Erskine.'

'Rubbish!' It was a mistake: the boisterous relief in his voice told her that. 'My dear lass, I'm the best judge of that. D'you imagine I'd give two thoughts to it? Are you afraid of leaving the places you know? We'll build us a house in Stirling, and I'll teach you every timber and brick of it as it rises so that each one is a friend to you. I'll give you a family of eyes: more eyes than Argus; in all Stirling there'll be no woman with younger or purer sight than you shall have. I shall –'

'Tom!' She cried out, desperate to stop him. 'Tom, if it were that alone, I shouldn't hesitate. Or if there were any single good reason I'd tell you at once. The trouble is I have a hundred reasons, none of them good. The war; Lord Fleming's death; the need to set Boghall in order;

my own liking for freedom and my friends and the old days – a mixen of wretched, feminine evasions.'

His silence lasted so long that she bit her lip, raging at her lack of sight; but he was only thinking over, very seriously, what she had said. At length he spoke. 'Yes, I see, Christian. I think I understand. You mightn't want to marry me now. But later, perhaps? When the invasion is over, and the Queen is better, and Lady Jenny is free. . . ?'

He didn't say, as he might have done, 'And if I come back.' She had to be merciful, but how?

In the end, she took the easier way. 'I can offer nothing, Tom; and it would be unfair to let you think I might. But if you still feel as you do, sometime in the future – '

'When? Next month?'

Christian, who had been thinking weakly in terms of six months or a year, suddenly decided. She said, 'Next month if you like, Tom: a month from today, on one condition, if you'll allow me the presumption of making it. That you abide by my answer then, whatever it is.'

He said rather pathetically, 'Do you think by then . . .?' but she groped for his hand, found and tucked her own firmly into it and walked him to the door. 'I haven't the faintest idea, but I can say this, my dear. If I were going to marry anyone – anyone at all – it would be Tom Erskine.'

* * *

Three miles away at Midculter, Sybilla was also preparing to leave for Dumbarton. Richard, looking for her before setting off south with his troops, found her coming out of the courtyard, her manner a little distrait and an unaccountable smell of sulphur lingering in her hair.

They conferred briefly, discussing the guarding of the castle and the safety of Mariotta, who was to stay; and had almost parted when Sybilla remembered something. 'Oh, Richard. Dandy Hunter brought one of his mother's appalling herbal concoctions under oath to make you take it on your next campaign, but I haven't the heart to inflict it on you. I gather it would save you from Podagra and

288

the Protector and every evil in Grimoire. You don't want it, do you?'

Richard smiled faintly. 'Not really. But I'll take it if it'll please her.'

'Oh, my dear, Catherine has made enough martyrs without adding more. I shall tell Dandy you drained every drop and left in a condition of enteric rapture: only remember to fib when you see him.' And she smiled and nodded, and disappeared again.

He had now only to take leave of Mariotta. He went to her room quickly, kissed her, and gave her a brief recital of his plans. Sitting before her mirror, she listened with perfect composure, arranging a lace scarf carefully about her shoulders. Still listening, she picked up and clasped the scarf with a magnificent brooch: a diamond-set heart surrounded by angels' heads.

Recently Mariotta had been very quiet. Richard had said nothing to her of his encounter with Buccleuch at Crumhaugh, and was not to know that she had heard it in detail from Sir Wat and Sybilla. Now she waited until he had finished, and then said soberly, 'Richard . . . The country districts are in a fairly bad way. How many of these raids can they stand? Assuming you repel this one, that is?'

There was a little pause: he was evidently surprised and rather relieved. He said, readily enough, 'It's all a matter of who tires first. We may damage the English so much this time they can't afford to try again.'

'With all their resources? With all their mercenaries from Spain and Germany?'

'They cost money, you know.' He smoothed a corner of crumpled lace on her shoulder, the fine threads catching on the roughness of his fingers. 'And meantime we shall be getting troops of our own from France.'

'For nothing?' said Mariotta. She was watching him in the mirror. 'But isn't it sometimes more expensive to accept favours than it is to buy them?'

He smiled. 'You're in a very inquiring frame of mind today, surely?'

289

'Yes, I am,' said Mariotta briefly. 'Don't people who dispense favours quite often expect a return for their trouble? Such as an alliance, or a marriage? Or special favours in trading? And if so, might there not be very little difference between an alliance with England and an alliance with France? And wouldn't a truce with England now have the advantage of saving thousands of lives before spring?'

She was ready for the first sign of ridicule: all the more ready because the ideas were less her own than the Dowager's.

But he was still patient. 'France, of course, is the ancient ally, tied to us by history and temperament and blood and religion. But there's sense as well as sentiment in it. By supporting us with troops, France forces England to divert men and money from Europe. Besides, France has never tried to conquer us by force as England has. Three English kings have claimed to own Scotland, and have done their best to hack their names on the door . . . What sort of a people would we be if we tolerated that?'

'You would rather have France as your master?'

'There is no question of either,' said Richard quietly. 'Whatever price we have to pay to France, you may be sure we shall keep our sovereignty.'

'Which is more,' said Mariotta, 'than one can count on at home.' And her eyes met his in the mirror.

She might have meant anything; but his face emptied of expression. After a moment, she went on.

'You talked of disliking overlordship, and I suppose all it implies – an indifferent superior, a denial of free choice and policy and the rest.' She had rested her elbows on the table, covering her face with her fingers so that nothing but her tired voice could betray her. 'I hate it, too. I don't know if I can go on with it, Richard.'

So there it was. He found a chair and sat heavily. 'Mariotta . . . I'm no good at this sort of thing. You know you can spend what you want – order what you want – go where you please – '

She was determined not to be childish. She was determined not to refer to the child, to his pride in his livestock, to any of the hurtful things that ran daily through her mind. She said instead, 'I can go where I please. To the Three Esates?'

'No, of course. Women aren't – '

'To state conferences at Boghall?'

'You can't expect – '

'To any gathering, meeting or convention that is going to shape the whole course and fabric of my life, and even possibly the manner of my death? No. Yet Arran, whom I've heard called a weakling and an idiot, not only goes but directs our policy. Lennox went, and proved a self-seeker and a traitor . . .'

Richard said gently, 'Men have no absolute monopoly of foolishness, Mariotta. The burdens of land, home, children and service to one's country are heavy enough for two people without asking both to do the same job.'

Mariotta dropped her hands. 'I'm not, heaven forbid, suggesting I should take my sewing to Parliament any more than I'm belittling the importance of your children. But I could fill a fifteen-year-old as full of moral precepts as a sponge, and I doubt if he'd keep them long in the sort of world you've made for him. Shouldn't I have some say in that, through you? Shouldn't you have something to tell your children, through me? Our work mayn't over-lap; but shouldn't your job and mine at least touch?'

Her voice died away. Richard, bringing his clasped hands up to his face, tried to think clearly through the millrace of pressing business in his brain. 'I don't know how to satisfy you – I'm going to be at home of course so little. But if it would help, I could ask Gilbert to let you know each week what happens in Council. Would that do?'

Three unfortunate words. That his wife was begging him to think differently about his whole relationship with her; that she might wish to share his personal life and his personal decisions – to shoot at the Wapenshaw – to ride alone to Perth – to interfere at Crumhaugh – to deal with his brother – never entered his head.

Mariotta said in quite a different voice, 'It might, except that I don't recollect marrying Gilbert. And while securing your fabulous, much-hacked front door you might have remembered, my dear, the wicket gate at the back.' She got up suddenly and faced him, gripping the edge of the table. 'The unlatched postern, Richard. You've convinced yourself that the killing of one man is more important than your marriage, and it's taken you into strange country. Which has its own irony. You should have looked nearer home.'

She had never before watched the blood drain from a man's face. The flat planes of Culter's skin became glistening pale and his eyes, shrewd and grey, turned disconcertingly blank. He rose to his feet and she was frightened: nervous enough to back to the window and stand there, watching him move uncertainly toward her. He stopped and said, 'Say it again. What are you saying? Tell me.'

Her anger, and her courage, came back. 'There's nothing to tell,' she said. 'Only that I like to be entertained. And Lymond is more perceptive than you are.'

The effort of self-control was so great that he was literally shaking on his feet: one hand shot up and gripped the wall to one side of her; the other, following more slowly, held the other side, locking her in the deep embrasure. 'Lymond has been here?' He didn't touch her.

With the remembered warmth of his nearness, her temper flared again. 'The man has been paying court to me for months. You might admire his enterprise, at least.' Beneath her anger was a rising excitement. Where was the stolid face now? At last – at last she was laying him bare; he was speaking to her direct, without a hedge of competitive thoughts, and listening to her – straining to hear her words.

He said blindly, 'Paying court to you? My brother? While I was away . . . for *months*?' The blank eyes rested on Mariotta, not seeing her, but seeing, she thought, a gallery of grotesque pictures filled with laughter and a dallying, gilded head. His voice, when he spoke, was extremely queer. 'Lymond is your lover?'

His right arm shook suddenly as his wife brushed under it and into the room. He did not follow her but waited, looking at the dark glass of the window where her figure was reflected, pulling things out of a drawer. He saw an emerald necklace; then pearls, some rings, brooches and collars, buttons and combs followed until the table shivered and sparkled in front of her. Lastly, she pulled off the splendid brooch at her breast and flung it on the heap. The violet eyes, turned full on him, were as bright as the jewels. 'No!' said Mariotta with contempt. 'But he might have been.'

She had meant to hurt him, and she had meant to force him outside his defences. Even yet, she did not recognize what she had actually done. In the long silence that followed, he put on a stiffer armour than she had ever been allowed to see.

Without looking at her, he picked up a piece, read the inscription on it, and flung it back on the heap. 'How long has this been going on?'

'For three months. They come anonymously to the house.'

'Bidding appears to have been commendably brisk. It's friendly of you,' said Richard, ' to allow me to compete. What would you like next?'

If she had never been able to shake him when he chose to be wooden, she was paralyzed by this behaviour. She said, shocked into stammering. 'I've t-told you the truth because he was making such a f-because people are drawing comparisons. I've never made any move to meet him – '

'I'm sorry,' said Richard. 'But on the whole I'd rather appear a fool than a cuckold. As a result of your efforts I now seem to be both. I should have looked less ridiculous, perhaps, if you had chosen to tell me about this when it first began?'

Cornered, she snapped. 'I might have done, if you hadn't been missing three weeks out of four. I was miserable, and idle, and not very well, and it happened. I might have agreed to tell you earlier – but as it is, I've told you now. Does it matter? Is it so hard to believe?'

The slip escaped her notice, but not Richard's. 'He said, '*Agreed* to tell me? Agreed with whom, for God's sake! Lymond?'

'No! No.'

'Then who? One of the girls? Buccleuch? Tom Erskine? Rothesay Herald? You didn't manage to tell me, but I'm sure you made certain we should both be the clack of the shopkeepers. Who was it?'

Mariotta said furiously, 'I needed advice, and he noticed . . . Anyway, he's been a good friend to me. To you as well. It was Dandy Hunter.'

'So he advised you how to conduct this very comic marriage of ours. How friendly. And was it only advice he gave you? Or has Dandy, like Lymond, been showering you with expensive and unsolicited gifts? It was your maxim, I remember: it's often more expensive to accept favours than to buy them. What did Dandy exact for his services?'

'Nothing! Stop it, Richard!' said Mariotta. 'I'm sorry. I was a fool not to tell you; I was mad to tall Dandy first; I shouldn't have told you now in the way I did. But I *have* told you . . . I didn't need to. You would never have found out.'

Richard said, staring at her, 'No, I don't suppose I should. I should have been one of those odd stock characters, the ludicrous deceived husband, which would have afforded Lymond endless innocent pleasure . . .'

'No!' She tried to catch hold of him, but he moved away, pacing the room.

'Lymond . . . Dandy . . . Who else? Who else, now?' He stopped dead, a square, monumental, derisive figure. 'You must think. After all, we've got to give this damned child an identity.'

Mariotta sat down, 'It isn't true.'

'Can you prove it?'

This time, steel met steel. 'No!' said Mariotta, and dropping her arms, she turned to her table. Watched by this venomous new foe she lifted her jewellery piece by piece and put it on: the emeralds around her pretty neck; the bracelets and rings, the long earrings and the combs, drifting sparkling in her dark hair. She turned to him covered in light, in a blaze of many-eyed, expensive vulgarity, with her voice doubly, diamond hard.

'No!' she repeated. 'No, I can't prove it. Why should I? What do I care for you or your brother? You're both Crawfords and you're both Scots, the one alien to me as the other, except that one of you has a way with women and the other has not. Believe what you like.'

She saw him, with a belated fragment of clear vision, standing against the door, his clothes engrailed with the flash of her jewels; and his eyes were not blank. He spoke slowly.

'I will bring him to you,' said Richard. 'I will bring him to you on his knees, and weeping, and begging aloud to be killed.' And he went.

It was over.

Mariotta waited until the Dowager, with Christian beside her, had left for Dumbarton, and until Tom Erskine, joining arms with her husband, had ridden out of the gateway and turned south. Then she locked the door and began to pack all she owned.

* * *

The Queen was feverish, the fat wrists pounding and the red, sore limbs thrashing restlessly; the tangled red hair gummed to the pillow, to her brow and eyes.

The doctors had chosen a high, deep-walled room in Dumbarton Castle for her sickroom, with its roots in the rock and the stormy grey tides of the Clyde Estuary slapping at its base. There the child lay in a formidable four-poster nursed by her ladies, by Lady Cutler and by Christian. The bedclothes were tumbled night and day, and the satin pillowcase patched and stained from the crusted lips and swollen, broken face.

On the invisible filament of this one life, the two English armies moved in to attack, one on the east coast of Scotland and one on the west. First, Lord Wharton and the Earl of Lennox left Carlisle on Sunday, the nineteenth of February, and in two days had reached Dumfries.

On that same Tuesday, Lord Grey of Wilton led an English army into Scotland from Berwick and camped for the night at Cockburnspath. By nightfall next day he had established himself and his army in the town of Haddington, less than twenty miles from Edinburgh, and was proceeding to dig himself in.

At the same time, Lord Culter's Scottish force, driving south, discovered the route taken by Wharton and Lennox and veered to come at their flank, thus missing a spearhead of horse sent ahead by Lord Wharton under his son Harry.

Harry was tough and confident. His orders were to bypass the house of Frumlanrig, to destroy the town of Durisdeer, and to give fight only if the Douglases did.

He expected little trouble from the Douglases. Report said most of them had already fled from his way: their head, the Earl of Angus himself, was at Drumlanrig and with him, whispering in his ear and stiffening his gouty resolution, was his daughter, Margaret Lennox.

The disaster exploded in Lord Wharton's face: Wharton, the most experienced of them all, plodding north with his foot soldiers in his son's wake.

He was eight miles north of Dumfries when one survivor brought the news. The Douglases had not fled. They had joined up with John Maxwell in orderly ambush, and falling on Harry's advancing horse, had smashed them to pieces. In this they were helped by the Earl of Angus and Drumlanrig himself, whose house Wharton had spared and where Margaret, ignorant of her appalling failure, must be waiting.

And further aided by one half of young Wharton's own force of Border English and forsworn Scots who, peeling off the red cross of England, had abandoned him with a ferocious joy at the first onslaught and had joined the Douglases.

There was no time for mourning: in an hour the Scottish army might be upon him. Wharton turned from the messenger and found Lennox beside him, the fair, unreliable face whiter than his own. 'Margaret!'

He had his horse gathered to go when Wharton took rough hold of his bridle. 'No! I'm sorry, sir, I can't risk your being taken hostage. The whole Scottish army lies between here and Drumlanrig. Even if you got there, your wife'd be worse off in your company than she is now in Angus's. For God's sake – '

He waited only to see the resolution fade from the earl's face, and began to issue orders. It was then that he heard, unbelieving, that fighting had already taken place on his right wing. Culter, always gifted with a special intelligence in the field, had found Wharton's outposts and advanced to strike his flank.

Maxwell's men, pouring over the hills half an hour later, found the English troops streaming south with Culter at their heels; in minutes they had closed the gap and themselves caught the skirts of Wharton's army. It staggered in its tracks, turned uncertainly, and willy-nilly, came to grips with the combined Scottish troops, renegades and all.

This time they fought side by side, the Maxwells and Douglases, Buccleuch and Culter, and if they were irrestible, it was partly because they despised each other and partly because they dared not lose. Wharton, even in his despairing rage, could make nothing of them. He recoiled, and recoiled again, leaving his dead and wounded where they lay, and within an hour it was nearly over, and a rider was off, wearing his exhausted horse to the hocks, to tell Carlisle of the annihilation of the whole of Lord Wharton's army.

Tom Wharton, the Warden's older son at Carlisle, sent the news to Lord Grey at Haddington. It told of the total overthrow of the entire company led by Lord Wharton and the Earl of Lennox, including the loss of his father and his brother Harry, and it was the death knell of the combined plan. Lord Grey dared not hesitate. Leaving a garrison to fortify the town of Haddington, he marched straight home to Berwick.

There he learned with a shrill and incredulous fury that Harry Wharton was alive; that escaping with some men from Durisdeer he had been able to rescue his father from his later sad straits and that, although much diminished both in numbers and in confidence, Lord Wharton, the Earl of Lennox, Harry and a large proportion of their troops were all happily safe at Carlisle.

What he did not learn, and what the Earl of Angus, much mystified, could have told him, was that when the Douglas returned to Drumlanrig after the fighting, his daughter Margaret Lennox had totally disappeared.

Sybilla took the news to the Queen, hesitating outside the sickroom where Mary of Guise had remained now all day. Then she gently opened the door.

The priests and the doctors had gone. Alone in the room, the Queen Mother knelt by the bedside, her cheek on the smooth coverlet. For a moment Sybilla paused; then she walked steadily to the bedside and looked.

The child had turned, and was sleeping quietly under the fresh sheets, one hand under her cheek, her breath stirring peacefully in a deep and feverless sleep.

Sybilla blew her nose with muffled energy, and touched the Queen Dowager on the shoulder.

2 · BUT PROVES TO BE COVERED

By sheer chance, Lord Culter's irreverent cadet was less than fifty yards away from him when he swept down the Durisdeer road in murderous pursuit of Wharton. Lymond let him go. Except for an episode which he made memorable both for John Maxwell and Lord Wharton's son, he took no part in the fighting, his concern at the time being solely to supervise an extramural activity on the part of Turkey Mat.

Will Scott, sitting under orders in his room, the Buke of the Howlat open on his knee, heard the party leave

Crawfordmuir for Durisdeer. They came back much later, and Turkey's voice was audible, first on the floor below him; then travelling up the stairs which passed Lymond's room, off which his own opened. The jostling of several feet came next; they passed Lymond's door and ascended to the third and top story, where they halted. The lock of a door clicked, and a woman's voice said icily, 'Assuming that you now feel safe, will you be good enough to unbind my eyes?' Then a door banged, the lock turned again, and the tramp of feet repassed the door and disappeared below.

In the racket from the first floor he nearly missed the soft opening and closing of the stairway door into Lymond's room. Then the fire-lit walls in the adjoining room bloomed yellow in new-lit candlelight and his own door swung open. 'Bored?' asked Lymond.

Scott dropped the book he had not been reading. 'I heard Mat and a woman. Was that the Countess?'

'That was Margaret Douglas.' The mobile face was virginal. Lymond said, 'The sweet woman doesn't know yet who has her: I thought it would be nice to let her speculate for an hour or so. When she's brought to me you will stay here and listen. In the dark with the door two-thirds shut. God knows why it should be left to me to educate you, but I feel in all fairness you ought to be equipped for life.' At the door he added mildly, 'Enjoy yourself,' and went out.

Scott tried to read. Except for the muffled voices from the lower stair, the tower was silent; the hills and half-mined valleys outside lay quiet in the dripping darkness. Next door, there was no movement either, although he could hear the fire crack and see the resulting flare through his own near-shut door. He had no idea what Lymond was doing. He remembered suddenly a revealing expression used at Annan, and wondered if it had been reported to Lady Lennox; and what a well-born majestically reared young woman would make of this wildcat eccentric.

When he thought the time was nearly up, he snuffed

his own candles and found a place from which he could comfortably see without being seen. As an afterthought, he took off his boots. Then he settled to watch.

Matthew's knock on the staircase door, when it came, was thunderous and his voice when it opened rolled like Pluto welcoming one of the damned. 'The Countess of Lennox,' he said, and retreated, closing the door behind him.

Margaret Douglas, standing just inside the room, was cloaked to the chin and very frightened indeed. The quality of her startled Scott: the near-leonine vigour, the firm chin and big, shapely hands. Then the unexpected black eyes took on fire from the reflected light, her lips parted and she unclenched and dropped her hands. 'Francis!' Few people, except perhaps those with Scott's opportunities, could have told that the recognition had preceded the fright. 'Francis!'

'Yes. Come in,' said Lymond pleasantly, coming into view. He was dressed, as Scott had hardly ever seen him, in white shirt and hose, sleek white and gold in the firelight: the effect was damascened and deliberate.

Momentarily bemused, the Countess of Lennox moved forward, her blue robe brushing the new wood of the floor, until she shared the firelight. Her hair was wet with rain; its fairness darkened. 'Was I brought here by your orders? I wish you had told me. I was very frightened.'

Lymond drew out a chair for her, and waited while she sat. 'You should perhaps allow yourself to be frightened now. It would be very suitable and maidenly.'

The intelligent black eyes were without guile. 'It probably would. But I have a husband.'

'A rather indifferent one.' The silverpoint voice was equally bland.

'A very partial one ... At least I trust him to protect my good name,' said Margaret. So she was not ignorant of what happened at Annan. She added reflectively. 'And he saved your life, once.'

'True,' said Lymond. 'But then, I spared his at Annan.

I've regretted it since. I think that, like the dolphin, he would be prettier dying.'

Margaret exclaimed gently. 'Dear me: now, what have we here? Revenge or jealousy? You want me as a weapon against my husband?'

'What else should I want you for?'

Her eyes sparkled, but her voice was calm. 'To insult me, perhaps?'

'No. What a low opinion of me you have,' said Lymond tenderly. 'I haven't captured you to exchange for Lennox. Not at all. I was proposing to offer you to your husband in return for your small son.'

At last, the Attic tableau exploded. 'Harry!' She was on her feet. 'Not my baby: no! Francis, please! That's being vindictive beyond all sense and sanity. Even you can't be callous enough to ask a small child to suffer for . . . Matthew won't send him!'

'Of course he will. He can always have more.'

'Unless you fail to send me back.'

'Unless I keep you both.' He was irradiated with a soft cheerfulness. 'But I hardly ever indulge in acts of retribution: they're usually bad for trade. I propose to offer the child for sale to the Scottish Government, whether alive (which they might find awkward) or dead, which might be more convenient, diplomatically speaking. As a Catholic, you see, his existence threatens the Scottish throne rather more than the English one. I do hope you are *not* pulling all your simple faith in the Protector, because I think that would be most unwise.'

The dulcet voice floated out to Scott, sitting wrathfully in hiding. So that was the scheme. And if Margaret Douglas was sent back to England, who was Lymond proposing to offer to Grey in exchange for Harvey? He felt a surge of sympathy for the Countess of Lennox.

She was saying in a numb kind of voice, 'I'll pay as much as . . . I'll pay more than the Scottish Government to save the boy,' and the Master promptly agreed.

'I could get the money that way, of course; but without quite the same moral effect. It would be rather refreshing to upset the Earl of Lennox and enter the good office of the Earl of Arran at the same stroke. Frankly, I doubt if I could resist it.'

There was a short, tortured silence.

Lady Lennox made a limp gesture with her hands, and suddenly the tears were there, blurring her picture of him before the fire, his hands loose at his sides, his head a little bent. 'These things we've heard about you – how can this have happened in five years?'

'Cinders dressed up are still cinders. Like Petroneus, perhaps, I take pleasure in committing suicide at leisure.'

She shook her head, the tears streaking her cheek. 'When you know the art of living, you don't look for death, or half-death; you don't hide in a hole like a chub. One accident; one reverse! You had only to force your way through it, and what mightn't you have been?'

He shrugged, one arm along the mantelpiece. 'Who can tell? One enjoys being the most debauched chub in the kingdom.'

Loosened by the headshake, her thick woven hair was falling loose across her shoulders; she had forgotten both it and her shift, glancing white through the blue cloak. Stung by his tone she said, 'You blame me. You blame me for what happened.'

'Why should I? I've escaped the grand mal and the petit mal and even the Duke of Exeter's daughter . . .'

Her hands were gripping each other hard. 'We had to send you to France for your own security. You must remember. Your friends would have killed you. We had to get you away from London. I didn't even know you were being taken – it was the King who – '

'Who arranged my convalescence in the English fortress at Calais whence, by stupefying bad luck, I fell into French hands. And none of it would have happened but for that very ill-timed dispatch.'

Margaret bit her lip. 'I heard about it. The one the Scots found, that our man left by mistake. After the convent was destroyed.'

302

The blue eyes, unveiled, were directly on hers. 'By mistake?'

'But – yes! The destroying party took your letter to follow your instructions, and when the leader was killed it was found by his body . . . What else could have happened? What else did you think? There was no double-dealing on our part, I would swear to it.'

'Could you swear to your uncle's share?'

'The King?' She looked startled. 'Surely not. He could be violent, but not – '

'But not what? Was there anything he was not?' said Lymond. 'Henry of England had all the virtues and all the faults, and solved the contradiction by making scapegoats and sin-eaters of half his entourage. If it suited him to discredit me between breakfast and dinner he would, like a shot from Buxted.'

He stopped as she laid impulsive hands on his arms, crushing the thick silk. 'How can we know what happened, so long afterward? We can't drag young tragedies forever through our lives, or carry our years like enemies, as you are doing.'

Extravagantly, the fair brows lifted. 'Alas, my sweet nonage. But five years of these vigorous times would remove the bloom from Lord Lennox himself.'

'And bitterness is a new thing.'

'Not at all. My natural habit, like the squirting cucumber. Any further traces of rot?'

Her gaze holding his, she let her fingers slip down his arms until, touching his hands, she felt and turned them palm upward. They lay lax in her own. Then Margaret Lennox looked down.

Scott did not hear the sound she made as, clenching her fists over the two curled hands, she carried them to her breast. 'The galleys? The galleys, Francis? Your beautiful hands!'

'And my beautiful back!' he said caustically, and she released him instantly and turned away.

'You're right, of course. Whatever you're going to do, you have every right. We let you fall into the hands of the

303

French – we betrayed your loyalty even if we did it by accident – '

'And if it wasn't an accident?' said Lymond mildly.

She turned and faced him. 'Then if the King was responsible, I am his niece. Take what revenge you want.'

Moving with exquisite care Lymond came close to Margaret Douglas for the first time of his own accord. With two pensive fingers, he released the clasp of her cloak, and it dropped, a slither of blue, to the ground. The white of her dress, lit by the fire, flowed like summer snow into the eyes. 'And what about Matthew?' he said. 'The very partial husband?'

Her eyes were wide. 'What's Matthew? One step to a double – perhaps a triple throne.'

'Is that all?'

'Yes. All.'

She was as pale as the silk. Scott saw Lymond's gaze rest on her, delicately practised, just before he moved. Then he touched her, and the woman's eyes closed. Folded with infinite care on the sweet edge between agony and delight she suffered a kiss of an expert passion which made itself lord of all the senses, of thought, and the dead fields of time. The fire blazed on Lymond's shoulder and arm and his bent head, and Scott saw something regal in the still, white and gold figures melted into one, pliant as a painting in honey and wax.

Then Lymond raised his head, releasing her mouth, and taking the woman's hand, drew her to the long settle by the fire. Margaret slipped to his feet.

'Come away.' Words were choking her. 'Come away with me. Work for us again. The Protector will give you all you lost – your manor – your money – more than you can ever have here. This wandering exile is slow death for a man of your sort . . . Come back with me!'

He drew a slow finger across her cheek. 'With the game so nearly won? I'm heir to Midcutler, Margaret. If things go well, my rooftree will be more impressive than any the Protector is likely to offer.'

'More impressive than Temple Newsam?' said Margaret; and the two pairs of eyes locked.

The fine, scarred fingers which had killed the papingo and set fire to his mother's house played gently with the thick, beautiful hair. 'You would take me to your home?' said Lymond softly. 'But even Lennox – '

' – daren't gainsay the Protector. And if you proved yourself valuable to Somerset, as you could – Francis, with your mind, your imagination, your leadership – '

' – And my savoury reputation. It's hopeless, Margaret. If my character in Scotland were intact, I could make Somerset uncle to an emperor; as an outlaw, my practical value is nil. Unless a good name can be created for me. Or restored.'

He didn't go on, and there was a silence. The woman had laid her cheek on his knee, her long hair fallen on the shining firelit swaths of her robe, spread about the hearth. A log dropped, turning the man's hair a brighter gold. Without moving, Margaret repeated, 'Restored?'

Lymond's soft voice was reflective. 'Mightn't some story be concocted that the authorities would believe? Of forgery – strategic betrayal – something with witnesses, convincing enough to clear me?'

At bay before every weapon of his mind and body, Margaret answered him unwillingly. 'It's no use, Francis. It does no good to pretend. Nothing can restore the past: how could it? The man who left the dispatch is dead. I could teach speeches and confessions to any number in his place, but do you think they would withstand the boot or the rack? Arran would make very sure this time he was not being deceived again. You can't remake a reputation out of nothing.'

'I can't, perhaps; but you generally manage to get what you want. Even me, for a consideration. I've told you my price.'

This time, the pause was a long one. The woman gasped suddenly. '*I* make no conditions.'

'And I make only one,' said Lymond, and with smooth

305

strength pulled her up momentarily, his mouth on hers. 'Do you want me, Margaret . . . at Temple Newsam?'

'Yes.'

'Then will you pay my fee?'

'I'll pay you . . . I'll pay you anything,' she said, 'if you'll come away with me tonight.'

'Tonight?' asked Lymond, and thoughtfully lifted the hair from her neck. 'What will you pay me?'

She kissed his roving hands. 'I'll find a man – someone to swear your dispatch was a forgery.'

'What man?'

'Anyone. A prisoner, perhaps. Or a condemned man. I could get him to do it for the price of his life, couldn't I? I promise. I'll make it convincing. Will you come? Oh! my love, will you come?'

Scott had the second's warning Margaret lacked; saw the face above the felicitous hands; glimpsed the relentless eyes. Margaret Lennox said, 'Oh! my love, will you come?' and Lymond slipped from her like a fish, leaving her kneeling, empty-handed, addressing half-mouthed endearments to an empty settle.

'Shall I come? *God; no, darling. I like my sluts honest.*'

There was a single sound, dragged on the intaken breath; then the woman sank on her heels and Scott saw the blood on her lip where her teeth had snapped shut on it. 'Well?' said Lymond, grinning, from across the room, and she flung to her feet, spitting Tudor venom and Tudor fluency into the fair, insolent face.

'Conceited peasant! Gross, degenerate weakling, reeking of ditch philosophy and decay – Do you imagine I'd let you touch me if there was an alternative? I offered you freedom and security – '

'You got me in purgatory, and you are offering me hell,' exclaimed Lymond. 'Poor Thomas Howard. Did you offer him life and liberty too?'

'Have you the effrontery to reproach me with lovers? What of your own?'

'Mine all have whole necks and go to bed with me for

306

joy, not for lions on their quarterings and galloon on their underwear.'

'I would have you roasted alive.'

'You would repent it. Who else can give you this brand of excitement? Not our marrowless Matthew, anyway.'

'He doesn't suffer from – from satyriasis, if that's what you mean.'

'I can't help that,' said Lymond brutally. 'Take your petty claws out of the prey, my sweet. I want your infant, not you.'

There was silence. Tiger being revealed to tiger, the roaring died and was replaced by a brooding watchfulness. Then Margaret Douglas said, 'You will never get my son.'

'I shall, you know.' Lymond was the image of despotic calm. 'Unless you get the proofs I ask for. I admire ingenuity, but not quite so much of it. My capture by the French was no accident. King Henry's decision to make a scapegoat of me was no accident.'

'Very well,' said Margaret. 'It was no accident. And because of it, your beggarly deceits were made public property. What can I do about it? What false proofs and pseudo-confessions would convince when the world knows them to be extorted by threat? No, my dear Francis, you've closed that door yourself. Your life as a man ended five years ago: your life as a cur depends on how long you please your numerous masters – '

'Or mistresses.'

There were tears of rage in the black eyes. 'Can I never forget?'

'No. Why should you? I think of it often, with a certain aged melancholy. Chargé d'ans et pleurant son antique prouesse . . . Must I send for the boy?'

Margaret Lennox stirred. Walking away from the fire, she lifted her cloak and threw it over her arm with a certain detached grace. 'Your antique prouesse was a little better than this. Preserve me from naïveté.'

His eyes were guarded but his voice was blithe. 'It's the simple life. An atavistic return to primitive barter. An instinct to buy things and people with shells, like the French.'

She smiled. 'I have no intention of giving you what you want. My son is quite safe.'

Lymond's expression conveyed qualified warmth. 'You want to stay here and mend my shirts. But as I've already said, the positions are all filled.'

'On the contrary. You will send me away yourself. Because,' said Lady Lennox, 'we have your brother's wife.'

For a long time, no one spoke. The silence stretched on until Scott's whole listening body tingled with it; then at length Lymond's eyes dropped. The cord of his shirt had loosened, and with one hand, still looking down, he drew it together. 'How do you know of this?'

'By letter.' Smiling, she produced from her cloak and held out a longish letter which Lymond read, one hand still arranging his shirt. She watched him. 'Can you make out the writing? She was captured by young Wharton during the march north on Wednesday, and should be with my husband now at Annan. He wanted me to join him quickly and chaperone her. Then he was going to hold her to ransom.'

She relinquished the letter, still watching him cynically. 'And that, my dear Francis, makes me an awkward possession. When Lennox hears I am missing, he has one simple remedy – to offer the life of the young Lady Culter in exchange for mine. And that means that the whole weight and power of your brother and his friends will be bent toward finding me.'

'I am distraught at the prospect.' Lymond spoke readily enough, though his hands were white at the knuckles. 'He's exceedingly unlikely to do so. And what makes you think that Mariotta's future – or lack of it – has any interest for me?'

'My dear Francis,' said Margaret blandly. 'Of course it interests you. Her death brings you one step nearer Midculter, doesn't it?'

His unemotional face seemed to stir a curious animation in her. She went on swiftly. 'Send me back to England

308

and the Scots have lost their counterhostage. Send me back, and I promise to see that your sister-in-law lives for thirty years apart from her husband – and that her child fails to survive.'

'I have a better idea,' said Lymond, and finished lacing his shirt with both hands, his eyes resting on her. 'Suppose we have an accident with you. Her death will naturally follow.'

'But then your brother would be free to remarry.'

'True.' He had crossed the room to a writing table, and was inscribing a long message on the back of the letter she had given him. Her voice sharpened a little, and she moved toward him. 'What are you doing?'

He didn't look up, but continued to write quickly and fluently. 'I prefer to be my own butcher.'

He finished, opened the door, and called Turkey Mat. When the big man appeared, red with the climb and with open curiosity in his eyes, Lymond gave him the letter. 'This is a message to the Earl of Lennox offering to exchange his wife for the young Lady Culter, whom he holds prisoner. He was known to have her at Annan, but he may be in Carlisle by now. This gives a time and place for the exchange, and also asks for a safe-conduct for our escort. I want someone to deliver it now, and a reply brought back as soon as possible. Can you arrange that?'

'Easily enough.' Mat opened his mouth to say something else, caught the Master's eye and thought better of it. He clattered down the stairs while Lymond stayed by the door, holding it open for Lady Lennox to pass through. 'Let me speed you to your slumbers,' he said sardonically. 'It has been a fascinating evening.'

Triumph glowed in her face. 'You concede me my victory?'

'Out, alas! Now goeth away my prisoners and all my prey. If you mean do I agree that you've saved your off-spring at the expense of Lady Culter's, the answer is yes.'

For a moment the black eyes lingered. 'You would have been wiser to come with me.'

'I prefer to be unwise and safe.'

Margaret moved slowly to the door. 'And Lady Culter? Are you reserving for her one of those filled positions you were speaking of?'

'What – Mariotta too, do you think?' asked Lymond. 'Good God, is there no peace? Is there no privacy, even in my present squalid estate? Shall I send you each an eye on a thorny stick like St. Triduana to preserve my chastity?'

Standing close beside him, her face was as hard as his. 'How you hate women! They succumb too easily. They give you no contest for power. They don't understand the ironies and the obscure literary jokes. You make love with your nerve ends and all the time the brain under that yellow hair is scheming, planning, preparing, analyzing . . . Worn machinery may rattle on for a time, my dear; but there comes a day when the axle chafes and grinds, the rod breaks and the engine is nothing but scobs and lumber fit for the madhouse . . . Go on driving yourself. Drive your men. Conceive more and subtler ways of getting the better of a sniggering world. Take out the spigot of your spleen and let it choke your masters. But when you're brought to infest my door with your begging, expect nothing; for I should sooner pity Apollyon himself.'

'For our next meeting I must put my own phrases to fatten,' said Lymond. 'In the meantime – good night.'

There was a flame in the black eyes. 'That hurt, did it? Is it possible? Krishna among the milkmaids gored by a cow?'

He warned, impassively. 'Make an end, Margaret. My patience can outlast your dignity.'

The reminder brought her to herself. The wildness faded from her eyes; the full lips twisted in a grimacing smile. 'By all means, let us remember our manners. It would be rude not to take leave of our audience as well.'

The smile broadened, and before Lymond could move, she turned on her heel and crossed the room. Scott, caught half rising from the floor, blinked in the rush of light as the intervening door was flung open and the Countess of Lennox confronted him, bright contempt on her face.

'What! Only me!' she said. 'How rash of you, Francis!'

And, to the boy: 'I hope your cramps won't trouble you. Your master is too verbose.'

Wretchedly angry and embarrassed, Scott could find nothing to say, and saw that she knew it and was laughing at him. She held out the cloak on her arm – 'The stairs are so draughty' – and waited while he clumsily put it around her. Then without thanking him she turned and swept back to the staircase where impassively Lymond waited. He, too, let her pass; and spoke when she was already on the steps. 'Go up and lock her in.'

Scott carried out the order soberly and quickly. He would not have crossed the Master then for all the breeding gold in the nurseries of these dark hills.

* * *

Later, it was different. Later, his sensibilities muffled with beer, Will Scott wandered upstairs and tried to get into his room. The outer door to Lymond's through which he had to pass was locked. He tried the handle twice before he realized this; and ran downstairs. Matthew grinned when he saw him, and hiccoughed lightly. 'No entry?'

Scott shook his head. 'God: he's been in there for hours . . . He hasn't come down?'

'Always excepting he's raxed himself scaling the window, no.'

'Well, I'm damned if I'm going to sleep on the floor because his lordship has gone to bed with the door locked. I'm going up to wake him.'

Matthew continued placidly to hammer nails into his boots, a process that seemed to disturb his neighbours' sleep not at all. 'I shouldna bother, if I were you. You can have my bed down here.'

Scott stared. 'Dammit, why should I take you bed? I've got one of my own. What's up with him now?'

Bang. Mat took another nail from his strong teeth and set it in the big sole. 'Nothing that three days of concentration won't cure. He likely couldna come down if he wanted to.'

311

Scott, leaning over, whipped the remaining nails from between the broken teeth. 'Why can't he come down?'

A hairy elbow was wagged.

'For three days?'

'It's the usual.'

'And what,' said Scott, outraged, 'if the Queen's troops come looking for the Countess of Lennox? Good God, we're sitting on explosive, and he knows it better than anyone. Doesn't anyone stop him when this happens?'

'There's no right reason,' said Turkey, investing in another crop of nails, 'why no one should. We just prefer not to, that's all. There's nothing to stop you, if you're keen.'

'I'm not keen. But I don't see why he should be allowed to drown his inadequacies at the cost of our safety. Why,' said Scott, who had drunk quite a bit himself, 'are you scared to go up?'

Matthew looked at him indulgently. 'Scared? Not the least bit of it. We just like to give a man leave to enjoy himself . . . God: are ye going?' For Scott had risen and was making for the stair.

Matthew's beard split and all the nails fell out of his mouth.

'Jesus, you're the brave fellow,' he said. 'Here, laddie: take a lend o' my hammer.'

* * *

Through the door, Lymond's voice was perfectly clear and composed. 'Who is it?'

'Will Scott.' He stopped banging. 'I want to come in!'

'Well, you can't come in,' said the voice pleasantly. 'The door's locked.'

'I know that.' Scott, already irritated, began to get angry. 'Let me in!'

There was a silence. 'Why?' said the Master.

'I want to speak to you.'

'You are speaking to me.'

'I want to go to bed.'

'Go to bed downstairs.'

'I want to go to bed in my own –' Scott, finding the ring of this a little undignified, revised it. 'Open the door. Or' – with a rush of spirits to the head – 'or I'll open it for you with a hatchet.'

This worked. There were no footsteps, but the key suddenly turned and the door opened on a drawn sword. Lymond, slender and gently dishevelled, regarded his lieutenant with a reflective blue stare.

Scott was suddenly very prudent indeed. Lymond sober was someone distinctly to be reckoned with: Lymond sodden was a child of danger. 'I wanted to speak to you,' said the boy. 'But not over a sword.'

'Through it, then.' The silk shirt was crumpled and sweat-stained, the hair tawdry, but the point of the sword was unwavering.

More than a little hampered by his public downstairs, Scott prevaricated. 'I came to suggest that you had some food. There's a lot to plan for. Your brother might already have traced the Countess . . . and there's Lady Culter to be looked after when she comes.'

The sword gave a small, evil flash. 'Don't fuss, my sackless father-lasher: everything is being taken care of. I don't want a meal. I prefer you to sleep below tonight. I don't wish to continue this conversation. Good night.'

Unfortunately, a Buccleuch was incapable of leaving well alone. Scott said truculently, 'You can drink yourself into a jelly any other time. This is an emergency.'

Above the blade were merciless eyes. 'Emergency? But what emergency could be outwith your ineffable talents? Or Matthew's?'

This exposed the root of the trouble. Scott said sharply, 'You know they'll obey no one but you when there are women about. You can't mean to expose Lady Culter to that rabble downstairs!'

'Why not?' asked the obliging, slurred voice. 'I've every confidence in the rabble downstairs. None of them, for example, has so far tried to teach me my job.'

Restraint was impossible. 'It might be a good thing if they had,' said Scott, and flung himself to one side as the

313

steel drove at his throat. He hit the doorpost, ducked, and with a speed and accuracy that Lymond himself had taught him, pulled the Master's doublet from a doorside chair and with muffled hand snatched and twisted the attacking blade.

The sword fell instantly to the floor. Scott slammed the door and picked it up, but slowly; for it came to him that the Master was a good deal less drunk and a good deal more dangerous than he had thought. Lymond, watching him, said, 'Look after it. If you let me touch it a second time, I shall kill ... You're admirably pretty emerging from your pupa robe a chevalier des dames; but I've a dislike of interference amounting to morbidity ... And I fight only with women.'

Scott, with his next remark cut from under his feet, floundered. Then he said baldly, 'What are you going to do with your sister-in-law?'

'Sit on my sacrum and sneer at her,' said Lymond. He walked to the window and turned, supporting himself on the sill. 'All right. Strangle your inchoate chivalry and take yourself off. I'm being indecently reasonable, but my control doesn't last long in this state.'

It was too much.

Already weakened, the steel over Scott's eyes jerked and broke through, and he stared at the other man with the eyes of an enemy. Th blue eyes narrowed in response: Lymond was no fool. 'Well?' he said, and this time his voice had no slur.

For answer, Will Scott raised one arm and sent the Master's sword spinning from him across the floor. 'Take it,' he said. 'And befuddle yourself under the table if you want to. It's no affair of mine.'

'Ah,' said Lymond. 'You're going downstairs to assume command?'

'If they'd accept me, I'd do it.' Scott's hair flamed above his excited, light eyes; he stood by the door, tall, wide-shouldered and pale. 'As it is, I'd be glad if you'd treat me from now on as one of the rest. I'll keep faith with you as far as I'm able. But I want no part in your mudrak-

314

ing personal habits and your dealings with women.' And, maddened by the sheer, lax boredom in Lymond's face, Scott burst out. 'What wanton notoriety is left for you to dabble in? What devilry inspires you to gut the nerves of every man and woman trying to befriend you . . . ?'

'For God's sake!' The exclamation was so quick and so savage that Scott froze. 'For God's sake!' said Lymond. 'Isn't one bitch with a rage for dramatics enough for one day? Spare me your mimicking morals and spring-tailed sensibilities for tonight, at least! What do you know of any of the women you presume to defend? You look, and puke, and scuttle away like a duck that's laid an egg in a geyser . . . Do you consider yourself better equipped in all your purity to lead this troop than I am?'

All fear had left Scott. 'Yes, I do,' he said quietly. 'But as I have said, they would follow no one but you.'

'Unless, perhaps, I instructed them to look to you as their leader?'

Scott's face was set. 'I'm no hanger-on waiting for a madman's shoes.'

'I am as sane now as I shall ever be,' said Lymond grimly. 'I'm offering you a chance to take command now, if you want it. Complete control. Of the men, and all the destinies of my female friends. Will you take it?'

This was – wasn't it – what he had prayed for; what he had dreamed about and, more recently, what he had longed for to sting Lymond into shame. But –

'What,' he asked hoarsely, 'do I have to do? Fight you for it?'

' "I am thi master: wilt thou fight?" No. I am too much your master there, my sweet one. There's another way.' He held out his mug.

'Drink with me. I have some hours' start on you which is, shall we say, a just handicap. Match me cup for cup for as long as the beer lasts; and it'll last longer, I promise you, than either of us. The man insensible first is the loser: the man with the staying power to open that door thereafter, walk down the stairs and show himself to Matthew has control of us all in future.'

Scott, making no move to take the beer, eyed the other with something like fright in his eyes. 'God, but . . . to wager so much on a drinking bout!'

'Don't you want the chance?'

'Why, yes – but – At least make the contest a real one!'

'Don't you want the chance?' said Lymond again.

'Yes!'

'Then take it. It's the only one you'll get. The first qualification for leading a band of hard-drinking cut-throats is the faculty of drinking harder and cutting deeper than any of them. You needn't be squeamish,' he added contemptuously. 'I'm not too drunk to know what I'm doing, and I shall abide by the result. I have an excellent reason as a rule for everything I do, except perhaps recruiting red-headed predicants from the more notoriously pig-headed of our families.'

'And if I win,' said Scott, ' – if I win, can I do what I wish about Lady Lennox and Lady Culter?'

'You can set up a seraglio with them if you want to,' said Lymond. 'Agreed?'

'Agreed,' said Will Scott, and raised the first cup to his mouth.

* * *

High on the hilltops, among the wet scrub by the burn, a blackbird was singing. The notes, round as syrup, melted into the raw air of dawn and coaxed the cold, reddened sun to its day.

In the new tower, thick walls enclosed a warm, snoring darkness: men and dogs rustling together like the carved and stubby images of Asiatic deities in the straw of the common room. Then, far up the twisting staircase, a door opened above.

Matthew, supine on a straw paliasse, hands folded on his belly, snorted, belched and turned laboriously on one side, where he continued to snore. But now he faced the dark square at the foot of the stairs.

Silence. Then, distantly, the same door shut; there was a pause; then footsteps fell, descending with infinite care.

316

They came nearer. Matthew lay still: lay and snored while a dark figure appeared in the low entrance, took two unsteady steps and halted, outflung against a wall, snatching security in a grave and preposterous game with imbalance. Throbbing with birdsong, the grey light of morning searched and pricked along the plaster, illumining a flattened hand, a silk sleeve and a wry, colourless profile.

Behind the Assyrian beard and half-shut eyes, Matthew was grinning. 'Well, well. And fu' as a puggie . . .' He got up quickly and followed as Crawford of Lymond, pushing himself at last from the doorway, propelled his way from wall to wall and out of the door.

Mat reached the Master as he was taking his head out of the water barrel, his hair dark and streaming and his skin involuntarily trembling in the sharp air. Lymond expressed no surprise, but buried his head in the towel Mat held out, saying after a moment in a voice still stifled by the cloth, 'The message from Lennox. Has it come back yet?'

'Half an hour ago,' said Mat, and met the other man's eyes emerging from the towel. 'They agree to exchange the Countess of Lennox for Lady Culter and have appointed a time and a place for tomorrow. And a safe-conduct.'

'Good.' Lymond dropped the towel, supporting himself on the edge of the water butt. 'You know what to do.'

Although he had not thought it necessary to tell Scott, Matthew had received the fullest instructions about Mariotta. So, though his eyes on the Master was thoughtful, he simply said, 'Yes, I know,' and picking up the cloth, waited patiently.

Lymond moved to the staircase and dropping on the bottom step, head in hands, said nothing for a while. Presently, he looked up. 'I'm going away. I don't want to disturb the others. Get my horse, Mat, will you? And my bow and a blanket and some clothes.'

It didn't take long. Once in the saddle, Lymond looked rather better. 'There's some food in the bag,' said Turkey aggressively. 'And a cloak.'

'Thanks . . . I don't expect to be off long.'

'And – ' Matt was not prone to ask questions, but the event was too much for him. 'And young Will?'

'Upstairs. A jewel in its setting,' said the blurred voice, with a trace of its normal caustic assurance. Then Lymond turned the horse out of the yard and a moment later put it to the trot down the hill.

Matthew went in. No one had moved, although as the light grew, strange and welcome noises could be heard in the kitchens. Turning into the narrow staircase he walked up to the first floor and opened the door of Lymond's room.

One solitary candle was burning still. The room reeked of tallow and spilled drink, and last night's fire was a mess of charred wood and ash in the grate. Across the hearth, his head in the cold rubbish and his hand still clutching a pewter tankard which had emptied itself about him as he fell, lay Will Scott, snoring ferociously in an alcoholic stupor. Someone had loosened his clothing at the neck, put a cushion under his head, and laid a towel and a basin neatly and squarely on his stomach.

Matthew absorbed the spectacle; grinned; and still grinning, walked to the door and shut it gently behind him.

* * *

From Crawfordmuir, the Master made his way slowly across country to Corstorphine.

It took five days to arrange a rendezvous with Sir George Douglas, for Lord Grey, learning wisdom at last, was keeping Sir George fast by the shirt-tails at Berwick while awaiting the arrival of Douglas's elder son, the expected pledge of the Douglas good will. But by the beginning of March, Sir George was back at Dalkeith and free to arrange with Mr. Crawford of Lymond the more precise details of the exchange of Samuel Harvey for the life and person of Will Scott.

It was shortly after this that one of the Queen's surgeons arrived late at the baby's bedside at Dumbarton. He had more than elixirs to offer; he had astonishing news: of a

318

tale of blindfold seduction. Of how he had been forced to care for a young woman in premature childbirth, in a tower solely frequented by men. Of how the child was stillborn, and he had stayed, perforce, a day or two after, until a woman arrived to relieve him of his task. Released, he had no idea of the tower's location; but he had thought to ask the sick girl her name. She had told him: Mariotta, Lady Culter.

He had asked who brought her there, and she replied, her husband's brother, Crawford of Lymond. He said, very conscious of the sensation he was causing, that the girl would recover.

3
MATE FOR THE MASTER

A Quheyne movand scho shuld kepe colour aye,
In hir first moving may scho diverse waye,
First to ye poynt before ye mediciner,
Syne to two poynts verraye anguler,
To ye poynt void befor ye notair.

1 · A BEREFT KNIGHT IS CHECKED BY HIS OWN SIDE

After seventeen days in the field, Richard rode back to Midculter, intending to apologize to his wife.

She was not there. She had left some time ago, with a small escort, and it was assumed that she had joined Sybilla at Dumbarton. So he turned his weary horse and rode there too.

They came to the small Queen's bedroom to tell Sybilla he had arrived. She glanced up, seeing the change in her own heart reflected in Christian's blind face; the looked down and tucked the two flaying hands under the sheets for a second time. 'Tomorrow,' she said.

The Queen made a hideous face. 'Now.'

'Tomorrow you shall get up,' said the Dowager firmly. 'And 'put on the yellow dress. And go and see Sym's cuddies in a jug. *If* you are a reasonable child today.'

Melting eye and embouchure veered from Sybilla to Lady Fleming, just beyond. 'When I am ill you must do as I want.'

The Dowager saw the trap before Aunt Jenny did. Aunt Jenny, despite a dig in the arm, said brightly, 'But you're not ill any longer,' and Mary pounced. 'Then in that case – '

'You're convalescent,' finished Sybilla swiftly.

'What's – '

'It means going to be well provided you do what you're told.'

A thwarted silence. 'Then I had rather,' said the Queen sulkily, 'be ill.'

'In many ways, things were easier,' agreed Sybilla. She bent over the little girl, curled tight as a leaf bud in the bedclothes, kissed her and handed over her vigil thankfully to Jenny Fleming.

Outside, she took Christian by the arm. 'Richard has come – you heard. Will you go with me to see him?'

The blind girl hesitated, but only for a moment. If Sybilla was willing to sacrifice Richard's pride, it was for a very good reason. And in the coming encounter she had a queer feeling that the Dowager would be more vulnerable than her son.

In Sybilla's parlour, Richard began as they came in, with no preamble at all. 'They tell me Mariotta isn't here. She isn't at Midculter either. Where has she gone?' And – 'Is she dead?' added Richard, in the same incisive voice, looking straight at his mother.

Sybilla sat down suddenly. Hearing the little scrape of the chair, Christian found one for herself and dropped quietly into it. Then the Dowager said, 'No, she isn't dead. I know where she is. But I wish to say something to you first. If you're alarmed, it's because you deserve to be, you know.'

He walked impatiently to the fireplace and back to the window. 'She has been comparing my romantic attentions unfavourably with – with others?' He shied at the name only at the last moment.

'With Lymond,' said Sybilla composedly. 'No. She might have done, but I haven't heard her. It was about Lymond that I wanted to talk.' Her eyes, blue and compassionate, achieved a critical stare. 'You've had a free hand so far, Richard. We haven't discussed the raid on the castle, or the attack at Stirling, or the presents Mariotta has been receiving – oh, yes!' as he made a startled movement. 'In some things I'm less blind than you are.'

Richard said nothing; after a moment the Dowager continued quietly. 'But we are going to discuss them now. For I think you have come to the point where you must choose. Which do you want most, Richard – Mariotta or Lymond?'

He stared back at her. 'You can hardly expect me to answer that kind of question. Or to chatter about my wife's . . . affairs. There has been a misunderstanding. It can be repaired easily when I meet her. It will vanish altogether when my brother comes to heel.'

'What I am telling you,' said Sybilla evenly, 'is that if you insist on destroying Lymond personally, you may lose Mariotta altogether.'

His voice sharpened. 'Lymond will take her life? Or she will take her own?'

'I mean that unreasonable hatred of Lymond now will convict Mariotta publicly of deceit. I mean that if he has become important in her eyes, you'll win her back by being magnanimous, and not by destroying the monster and fighting the myth to your dying day. I mean that Lymond is with Mariotta now; that he has not touched her; but that she should be taken out of his influence as soon as possible. And if you will abandon this madness, I shall find her and bring her back to Midculter.'

He was on his feet before Sybilla had half finished. Christian heard him, her own hands crushing the arms of her chair, her mind invisibly protesting. No! . . . Dear God! thought Christian drearily. How could Sybilla, so clever, so acute with others, read her own son so badly?

In a queer, weightless voice, Richard was speaking. 'Where are they? How long have they been together?'

Sybilla answered quickly. 'I don't know. It doesn't matter. She was very ill when she came to him, Richard – she has been dangerously, terribly ill.'

Utter silence. Then Lord Culter said, 'The child?' And there was a long interval while he read his answer in his mother's face.

At length he spoke quite steadily. 'So the child is dead. What would it have been? A girl?'

'A boy.' And Christian, with compassion, told him the surgeon's story.

When she had finished, he laughed. At the tone of it, Sybilla cried out, and he rounded on her. 'But this is genius! My irrepressible little brother ... the infallible Lymond, with success at the end of each of his pretty fingers ... You say you know where to reach them?'

By now Sybilla must have known what was coming, but she spoke steadily. 'I said that if you would give up your hunt for him, I should probably manage to trace Mariotta for you.'

'And what possible use,' said Lord Culter, 'would Mariotta be to me?'

'For God's sake, you foolish man!' said Christian, and jumped to her feet. 'Give the situation at least the amount of unprejudiced thought you'd give to one of your damned pigs in farrow. What possible misdemeanour can be expected from a woman at death's door through childbirth? And why blame your brother? You ought to be damned glad that surgeon was called. If Lymond's all you say he is, he'd have gone about it like Hephaestus with a hatchet.'

'Mariotta is Lymond's mistress,' said Richard shortly. 'She as good as told me so before she left. Where are they?'

'She was lying to spite you,' said Christian.

'Or telling the truth to spite me. Where are they?'

There was nothing more Christian could do. As the question was flung at the Dowager for the third time she heard Sybilla say, 'I've told you. I don't know the exact location. I won't tell you what I do know unless you promise – '

Richard laughed again. 'With this story around the whole of Scotland? I admit very few things would make me look sillier than I do now, but the idea of making Lymond a gift of my complaisance is one of them. Why shouldn't she prefer him? All my women did. Nothing was every mine that didn't instantly become his – even your dearest hopes and first-born love – '

Sybilla's hands suddenly clasped themselves. 'Richard!'

'It's true, isn't it? Isn't that why you are trying to save him now? Because you love this one son: not my father; not me; not even your own daughter – my sister – *his* sister – the girl he murdered?'

'Richard!' This time Christian was on her feet, stumbling across to the Dowager's chair. She knelt, her arms tight about the older woman's shoulders, as a voice bawled Culter's name in the corridor outside.

The Dowager sat like a little ivorine, her blue eyes wide and dark. Richard himself stood by the fireplace, drawn to his greatest height and tension, as if his body were a metal mesh without bone or tissue. The door banged. 'Lord Culter!'

The Dowager stirred, and Christian rose slowly, staying by her chair. A scared face appeared in the room. 'Lord Culter? The Queen Dowager's been waiting for you this last half hour, my lord. We couldna find – '

'Then she can continue to wait,' said Richard.

'My lord!' This time it was a new voice, a second page. 'You're wanted to come right away – '

Unstirring, Richard flung words at his mother. 'I may be mistaken. It is for you to prove it. I ask you to tell me how to reach him.' The two pages shuffled.

For a long moment Sybilla looked Richard straight in the eyes, and neither pair flinched. Then, still mute, she shook her head.

'Very well,' he said. 'I shall not ask you to outrage your feelings.' And, spinning on his heel, he was out of the room before they knew it. The two pages started, looking at each other, and made for the door. 'Lord Culter! You're wanted. . . .'

Inside the room, Christian slipped to the floor and laid her cheek on the Dowager's warm, velvet lap. After a moment she felt Sybilla move, and the thin, pretty fingers began gently to caress her hair.

* * *

Much later, Sybilla left the room quietly. She was on her way downstairs when Buccleuch rounded a corner and pulled up tiptoe on the landing, nose to nose. 'Sybilla, dammit!' He gave a kind of choking whoop, then stopped and eyed her closely. 'Have ye been ailing?'

'No,' said Sybilla, and returned the compliment. 'And what's happened to you? You look as if you'd been boiled in a pot with a Pasque flower.'

Sir Wat's beard lurched sideways, a sure sign of embarrassment, and he crowed again. A glimmer of amusement shone in the Dowager's wan face. 'Come on, Wat. Something to do with my family?'

Guilt and a sort of nervous self-satisfaction struggled on Buccleuch's face. 'You'll want to kick my bottom through my merrythought,' he warned. 'And Dod, I'm telling you: you'll have an a priori case for it.'

'What have you done?'

'I've had that lunatic Culter stotted into a punishment cell under close arrest!'

'What!'

'It's a fact,' said Buccleuch with undisguised pleasure. 'You've no idea, Sybilla! He's been flouting orders right and left – he shouldn't have left the Queen to go to Crumhaugh in the first place; and since he came in today –'

'He kept the Queen waiting: I know.'

'Dod, yes: pages running on their shinbones and he ups and flits; but that was the least of it. When he did come in he began by snapping the faces off the lot of us, and then stalked through and told her Majesty that he wasn't just ready to do what she wanted.'

'Which was?'

'Oh, to ride through to Edinburgh and help the Governor who's in a stoory panic because he's expecting Lord Grey and the English to march in again on the hour like the bell for Prime. You know Arran. So does everyone else, but no one's going to tell the Queen that he's a jelly-footed puddock with his wits in his wame.'

'Good God!' said Sybilla. 'Did Richard?'

'Not just in so many words,' allowed Sir Wat. 'But he was damned rude. He couldna see the need to go; he didn't have the time for it; he wouldna go; he wouldna say why: Peely-whatsit on Ossy-whatsit until the de Guise, who has a strippit tongue in her head herself, snapped that she supposed the affairs of his womenfolk were claiming all his attention.'

'Oh, good Lord!' said Sybilla weakly. 'Did he knock her down and jump on her?'

'Well, hardly,' said Buccleuch, eying the Dowager with a touch of curiosity. 'But he sucked in his cheeks, looked her up and down, and said that she could think what she pleased, but he had done his share of work for the King of France and wasn't doing any more. And then – well, Dod,' said Sir Wat defiantly, '*someone* had to take a hand –'

'So you exercised your usual tact.'

'Well. I said that likely enough Lord Culter was anxious to lay hands on that brother of his, which would be doing a public service –'

'Quite. You're an unprincipled ruffian, Wat,' said Sybilla. 'And of course, seeing that Richard had already disobeyed her because of a private family feud –'

'She told him what she thought of him and his loyalty, and he answered back. Man, I havena heard him speak so many words at the ae time since I taught him all the verses of Sir Guy – and the upshot was, he was clappit below.'

'At Buccleuch's suggestion.'

'I wasna exactly holding them off,' admitted Sir Wat. 'Are ye mad at me?'

Sybilla looked at him a little sadly. 'On the contrary,' she said. 'I wish I had thought of it first.'

From Sir Wat, she went straight to her own room. Before nightfall, with the Queen's permission, and Sym, borrowed from Christian, riding at her back, the Dowager had left Dumbarton and was travelling quickly south.

Deep in the rock of the castle, the room Richard now occupied was not unpleasant. It was barred, and there was not overmuch furniture; but it was possible to sit and read in relative comfort, and his jailers served him respectfully and well.

Later, they left him alone. Sounds of the world faded early outside, and the cool night air, flowing through the clenched bars, whispered peacefully.

> *O row my lady in satin silk*
> *And wash my son in the morning milk.*

* * *

'Slippers?' asked Kate Somerville.

'Yes.'

'Razor?'

'Yes.'

'The blue doublet?'

'Y –'

'I knew it!' said Kate triumphantly, and whipped open the case. Artfully concealed beneath the top layer of clothing was an antique and greasy garment which, shaken out, assumed the shape of a shambling and corpulent Gideon, unlike and yet hideously familiar. 'This year,' said Kate, 'the maids will have blue dusters. It's snowing again. Don't you wish you were staying at home?'

Gideon, introduced to fresh misery, groaned. He glanced at the shopping list his wife had tossed to him, and groaned again. 'Why you should believe that the shops in London will be any better than the shops in Newcastle . . .'

'I don't suppose they are,' said Kate frankly. 'But if I go to Newcastle I pay for it; whereas if you buy it in London, you do. . . .'

Gideon Somerville had no desire to go to London with Lord Grey. Since the curious December episode of the cattle raid, the winter at Flaw Valleys had passed in snow and relative peace. He set out now because he would not ignore a summons from the Lord Lieutenant, who was uneasy about his command, and who would not rest until he had laid his troubles before the Protector himself.

While he and Lord Grey were on their way south, the Protector issued a proclamation in the boy King's name to the gentlemen in his main recruiting shires.

> Our rebels the Scots, relying on foreign succours, pre-pare to attempt the recovery of the forts which we have won and built in that Kingdom, and to annoy those who have submitted to us and our subjects on the frontiers. We have already gained such advantages over them as may make them remember our tender years, and wishing still to defend our country, we require matters to be taken to this end in your shire...

The Protector also sent for the Earl and Countess of Lennox.

*   *   *

As all Scotland now knew, Mariotta was brought to Lymond's headquarters, and laid in the Tower. The sur-geon came; her son was lost; the surgeon left. Alone of all the people involved, Lymond himself knew nothing of these things. A week before Richard's arrival at Dumbar-ton, Lymond left Dalkeith at last and rode through the snowy goldfields to the Tower.

He heard the news from Turkey, almost in silence; then climbed the stairs slowly to his room.

Sitting before the fire, a sweet and ample vision of pink and gold, was Molly. Divorced from the glittering background of the Ostrich, the shining hair and limpid eyes were emblems of innocence: she looked as if she had been attending decumbitures all her life.

As Lymond came in she pulled herself out of her chair and, holding him in her warm embrace, kissed him lightly and drew him to the fire. Then, signing for silence, she moved quietly to the intervening door into Will's room, and shut it. 'The girl is in there,' she said, and came back and seated herself beside him.

'How is she?'

'Fair enough. You heard we got a doctor?'

'So I heard.'

'Yes. Well, it was that boy of yours, Scott, who insisted. Incidentally – '

'Yes?'

She hesitated. 'It was the same boy who came to fetch me from the Ostrich. Did you know he also had business with Dandy Hunter?'

The preoccupied blue eyes came up, fast. 'Tell me.'

Molly shrugged. 'Nothing much to tell. Hunter spent nearly a week with us, for no very good reason, and seemed to have a lot of questions to ask on some curious subjects. Joan saw Scott speaking to him the night he came for me.'

'Did she hear?'

Molly smiled. The Ostrich's entrails were drumskins and sounding boards, as they both knew. She gave him a verbatim account of the talk between Scott and Hunter, and he listened without comment. At the end she said, 'Take care. Hunter is a lot wiser than the child. It could mean trouble.'

The fair face did not change. 'It means trouble, of course: what else? Without trouble, how could we live? There the thorne is thikkest to buylden and brede.'

'Yes; well . . . Watch that the thorns don't get too thick. . . . This is damned awkward for you, isn't it?' she asked, suddenly. 'The brat's dead, and there's an inheritance in the wind, and the girl talks of nothing but Crawford of Lymond.'

There was a brief silence, then he said, 'Does she? I hope you preserved the myth: I shall enjoy being worshipped. In any case, it was good of you to come, my orchard of jewels. Can you stay for a little yet?'

'For you, I will,' said Molly comfortable. 'I never bring you trouble, do I?'

'No,' he said thoughtfully. 'No. And by God, I think

you're the only living person who doesn't. Come along, my hinny, and I'll take you below to a worthy supper.'

He held open the door and Molly, her eyes as bright as her diamonds, sailed downstairs like a whole cloudy sunset stooping to the sea.

* * *

Mariotta had heard his voice. But it was nearly a week before, sitting wrapped in a chair by the window, she heard his footsteps cross the inner room and knew that at last he was coming to seek her.

For some days now, the pain had gone; and the feverish dreams. Coming out of the racking darkness she had no idea at first where she was; then the fat, soft-voiced woman with the jewels had told her, and her empty body and numbed mind became inhabited with only one idea: to bathe her hurt pride and rejected love in the warm tides of Lymond's admiration.

The child was dead. It had never been anything to her but the final proof of Richard's marital philosophy, and she found a bitter pleasure in thinking that in this, at least, she had thwarted him. When she needed help, it was Lymond who had come, and not Richard. Lymond . . .

And on the thought, he knocked, and opened her door. 'I've been waiting for you,' she said.

He was meticulously dressed: not at all as she had first seen him; his hair crisp and neat, his linen immaculate. But the half-hidden eyes and flying mouth were the same.

'I am generally tidy when sober,' he said, answering her eyes instead of her voice. He walked over and leaned on the wall beside her. 'I'm not a very good doctor, I'm afraid. I'm sorry about the child. But I hear you are better.'

She was perplexed, then her brow cleared. 'But didn't you know I had left Richard?'

For an instant his surprise showed. '*Left* Richard? Why?'

'We quarrelled,' she said. 'He's obsessed with the idea of hunting . . . of . . .' Her fumbling fingrs touched the brooch of her night robe, and she ended incoherently.

330

'And I told him about the jewels. They took them at Annan. I'm sorry. This is all I have left.'

Lymond's eyes were on the diamonds. He said slowly, 'I see. When you were captured, were you trying to find me?'

'Not quite – but – but I thought Dandy Hunter might look after me until you – if you found out where I was, or sent me any more –' She stopped, exhausted by the difficulty of gracefully shaping a surprisingly awkward situation. Then she added more firmly, 'I don't at all want any more jewels. You must understand that. I would have made you take them all back in any case. But I thought –' Again she stopped.

'What did you think?'

'That you are so much cleverer than Richard, and I could talk to you. I used to talk to Dandy,' she went on, her eyes overbright, 'but he wasn't at Ballaggan, and I was wondering what to do when the English came, and then your men came for me, and the pain came on – I'm sorry,' said Mariotta painfully, bright colour in either cheek. 'Perhaps you didn't know about the baby.'

The younger Crawford turned his head away. Without answering, he walked to the mantelpiece, planted his elbows on it and sealed his eyes slantwise with his hands. Then he said, 'Let's clear away the ground rubble first. What exactly did you and Richard quarrel about?'

Her face drooped. 'It's too complicated,' she said peevishly.

'Never mind. Tell me exactly what it was.' He released his hands and, turning, sat down not far from her chair. 'Now. You said you wanted to talk.'

So she told him. As she related the desertions and the disappointments, the disagreements and the follies which had stripped her of contentment and driven her to revolt, Lymond studied the floor. She told of her first emotions about his presents; of her decision not to tell about them; of the ultimate quarrel where Richard had instantly believed the worst of her. She ended with the same superb naïveté. 'So you see, I could hardly stay, after that.'

He was on his feet, in a silent, characteristic movement, pacing to the other end of the room and back; looking down on her black hair and upraised lashes. Her eyes were full of tears.

'Don't you think,' said Lymond, 'that I seem to be the disruptive serpent of the Ophites and not Richard? The exciting prospect of punishing me seems to have been the mainspring of all the poor man's peccadilloes.'

The violent eyes were solemn. 'He'd give you no chance,' said Mariotta. 'He hates you because you're different. . . . That's unjust; and I despise him for that the worst of all.'

The blue eyes, supremely adult, were seraphic. 'What, for lack of family feeling? If you'll forgive my reminding you, the boy is only a beginnner.'

It was true: she had forgotten the burning of Mudculter. But she retorted, 'You didn't know what you were doing.'

'All I ask in this world,' said Lymond a shade grimly, 'is half an hour when I don't know what I'm doing; but no one has granted me the privilege yet.'

'I could help you.' She leaned over suddenly and caught one of his hands; he surrendered it with perfect indifference, saying, 'You have an entrancing and hagioscopic view of my character that is entirely your own. Do I understand that you are proposing to join the Portugese Men of War? Because if so, I shall have to tell Molly.'

'Molly?'

'The woman who is looking after you. She keeps a bawdyhouse in England, and while I'm extremely flattered, I can't have my dearest friendships upset just to irk Richard.'

She smiled shakily. 'You're trying to frighten me for my own good.'

Lymond spoke happily. 'On the contrary. It's most important that you should stay here until you're quite well. After all, I've gone to a good deal of trouble to get you – unlike Richard, I hold my women in fondest esteem.'

He withdrew the hand she was holding and stretched it thoughtfully before him, its beauty of shape, the long

332

fingers and fine bones totally cancelled by the weals on the palm. 'It's a pity, isn't it? I was a galley-slave for two years after they found out about Solway Moss, and we had two very calm summers. I used to think a good deal then about our modest yeoman enjoying his lordship at Midculter.'

Mariotta recoiled in her chair. 'You're still trying to frighten me. I don't believe you; but please will you stop?'

'It's the air of nasty reality that frightens you,' explained her brother-in-law with abandon. 'Corrupt, ill-smelling and five days old. I don't give a damn whether you're frightened or not, because in a month's time you won't be here anyway. If you had a brain rather larger than a chick-pea, sweetheart, that would have occurred to you. I should hardly trouble to rid Culter of his heir without making sure he had grounds for divorce also. The peripetia will be so tidy. If he were a little more sprightly by nature he might even oblige by removing himself; but I doubt he'll have to be encouraged. Prior exiit, prior intravit, as the good old saying goes.'

'My jewellery,' said Mariotta in a whisper.

'My angel, I had to prise you away somehow, although I had no idea Richard would throw you out so fast. I wish I'd been present. Richard displaying emotion! It must have been magnificent: Atlas in labour, no less.'

She said dully, 'Why do you hate each other? What does it matter – a paltry title – can't you forget?'

'Forget! With Richard tapping on my funny bone like a yaffle on a pear tree?'

'You're brothers!'

'Well: I am his brother as much as he is mine,' said Lymond with perfect clarity. 'One gets a little tired of too much Suivez François and Fan Fan feyne. It's Richard's turn, dammit, to call off the hounds.'

In her weakness and misery Mariotta was crying, the tears washing unchecked over her thin face. 'Why shouldn't he hurt you? You tried to kill him at Stirling!'

Lymond looked shocked. 'Mariotta, my Sarmatian poppy! Such a violent volte-face! I thought you loved me as the marabou loves its one-legged mother. I though we should be shikk to shikk, indivisible, like Richard and his piglets. And now!'

But drowned in dreary, heartbroken tears, Mariotta was beyond retort, or argument or complaint; beyond speech and beyond the lash of his mockery. She did not even hear the door slam as he left.

Lymond received Molly's scolding that night without comment, only remarking that if the girl needed company she had better tell her sorrows to Will Scott for a change, and they could moan together.

The fine, sharp eyes had already noted the redheaded boy, so high in favour at the Ostrich. Because he was like the son of one of her girls and she was sorry for him, and because in the long run she usually did as Lymond asked, Molly did send Will upstairs to sit with the invalid. It was the last time anyone did so.

Next morning Mariotta had vanished. Lashed by the Master's furious tongue they hunted for her all that day, but of his sick and errant sister-in-law there was no trace.

* * *

It was a chance meeting with a drunken piper of Argyll's which led Sir Andrew Hunter to haunt the Ostrich Inn where, eventually, he met and spoke to Will Scott. From there, he went straight to Branxholm.

Buccleuch listened to Hunter's account of the meeting in relative silence. At the end, he spoke sharply. 'Lymond's selling my son, you say?'

'Will isn't sure. But I've told him what I know. Lord Grey is being pushed by the Protector, and he's even more anxious to lay hands on Will than before. And Lymond's been seen twice in the neighbourhood of George Douglas's house. The boy won't leave Lymond. He won't say anything about his life, or the Master's plans – '

'Or about young Lady Culter?'

Janet, listening, interjected. 'Dandy didn't know that Lymond had Mariotta, and Will never mentioned her although – '

'Although he looked ill, Wat,' said Hunter soberly. 'I made him promise to tell me if ever he thinks the Master is about to get rid of him. It was all I could do. And if that happens, of course I shall send you word instantly.

'Instantly,' he repeated; and the slightest rough edge was audible in the kindly, courteous voice.

* * *

Prinked and painted and stencilled with spring sunlight, the city of Edinburgh celebrated the wedding of the Lady Herries and John, Master of Maxwell, and the sound of its bells ploughed the fields of Linlithgow nearly deep enough for the barley, and made the coals quake underground at Tranent.

Inside the palace of Holyrood, the scene seized the eye with light and flowers, cloth of gold and bunting, and sparkling multitude, their rents and pensions glittering on their sturdy backs. Agnes Herries had a smile – a blinding smile full of teeth – for everybody; and an unaccustomed vivacity in John Maxwell was also noted. 'And wha wouldna leer like a sprung joist,' said the cynics, 'that's just merrit the hale chump-end of Scotland?'

Once, during the evening, bride and groom slipped away to keep a private appointment. In a remote room of the Palace, John Maxwell introduced his wife to a stranger: a cool, fair-haired figure with an easy, disturbing voice.

'Agnes, this is someone without whom we might never have been able to marry. He – made it possible in many ways; and not least in helping me escape young Wharton's sword last month at Durisdeer.'

She was instantly thrilled. 'You didn't tell me. He saved your life? But how can we thank him?'

'No need for thanks. I have all the reward I need.' Both Jack and the stranger seemed to be affected with an uncommon sonority. 'I was merely the Baptist, the Bean King: the helical star before the sun. My anonymity you must forgive – I am no longer master of my own identity. Nevertheless' as sympathy and delight shot into her eyes – 'nevertheless, if nameless, I am not empty-handed. In remembrance of an experience – a rewarding, if tantalizing experience – will you accept this?'

It was a crystal and onyx brooch, set with diamonds and angels' heads, and worth more than her total parure put together.

Maxwell's eyes met the other's, their curiosity undisguised. 'There was absolutely no need . . .' he said.

'Not at all. My pleasure. Although I must, as you'll understand, ask your forbearance in not revealing where it came from.'

They promised, and took a warm and even tender farewell of him.

* * *

Christian also received a summons on this, the day on which she had promised her answer to Tom Erskine. It took her along the same corridor and into the same empty room, where she waited, steeling herself for Tom's cheerful presence.

She filled in the time by pacing out the room. It seemed small, with a side table, three chairs, and a fireplace giving off a good deal of smoke. Not the ideal place for a proposal, she thought drearily; but what on earth do you expect, woman? Some seedy cavalier to sing beneath your window?

She sat down determinedly in the nearest chair and turned her mind to counting up sheets and bedcovers. Acute though her ears were, she missed the footsteps in the passage and heard nothing until the door opened and closed with the softest of clicks.

'Good God!' said someone gently. 'The Pythia in a lemon fog. Do you like smoke? Cheer up: it's spring outside.'

A window opened, and fresh, grass-scented air flowed into the room, and the song of thrushes. Christian felt the blood spinning to the ends of her fingers. 'It's not – I was expecting – Is it you?' she asked, out of bodily and spiritual chaos.

'Unless like the elephant I have two hearts, or like Janus

336

two heads, or the boa two skins, it is I, indeed. I have stopped writing double letters under a pen name, and am re-registering my interest with you in person. You've lost weight.'

She was, by now, herself again. She said tartly, 'It doesn't help to find oneself bedevilled with persons making Eulenspiegel-like appearances and disappearances. I live for the day when we can be formally introduced. Don't you think it would be better than coming to me like –'

'A thief in the night is the phrase. Have I upset you? But I did offer once to tell you my name, and you refused. I'm sorry. I should infinitely prefer to call on you with sixteen pearly elephants and a litter of jade, with silver trumpets and sarcanet and schorl and satinwood, spring water and roses from Shiraz . . . would you receive me?'

'Provided you gave me time to array my dusky charms. "And who is this? Great Alexander? Charlie le Maigne?"'

'Royster-Doister, visiting the Castle of Perseverence. Have good day: I goo to helle.'

'I think you manage to carry it about with you,' said Christian.

'Perhaps. I have been gifted with a surfeit of Satanity and the need to live up to it. Frère Estienne, do we not make excellent fiends?'

'Far too well. It seems devilish, for example, for anyone with such a passion for secrecy to contrive not only to enter a royal palace, but to deal in appointments and summons therein.'

'I have friends at Court.'

'Oh. At which Court?' she quoted, and he broke in on her words.

'I won't put up with Skelton as well as Stewart. At this Court, lady.'

'I had no idea you were so powerful. Do *they* know who you are?'

'Whose temper are you trying to lose?' the pleasant voice said. 'Your own, or mine? I have behaved atrociously, I freely admit, but my object is exemplary: to convey gratitude and keep you at all costs out of my ruinous affairs.'

'Don't you think that if you didn't clutch them to your evil chest like Epaminondas and his javelin, your affairs might be less ruinous?'

'No.'

'I see,' said Christian. 'Then either you don't think much of my discretion, or you think I couldn't stomach your conduct. Either way, it casts a certain shade over your continued visits, doesn't it?' This was risky. Once, to accept his confidence was to lose him. She was secure now from that; but he might still rebuff her for asking.

When he did speak, however, it was with a shade of resignation in his voice. 'So I've got to spin you some sort of tale, have I?'

'I should prefer you to measure me the truth.'

'– But it all depends on what kind of worm I am. I see. I'm not sure, you know. My kind of story would go down better with Agnes Herries.'

'Then pretend I'm Lady Herries,' said Christian.

'God forbid. The fact is, that like many another gentleman in trouble, I was misunderstood in my youth. A situation which I thought could be retrieved by one person. Unfortunately I didn't know this fellow's name; only his station, and this left the field open for three people – '

'Jonathan Crouch, Gideon Somerville and Samuel Harvey.'

'Yes. You see, it all fits in rather cunningly with what you know already. Crouch was ruled out; Somerville was ruled out; and that leaves Mr. Harvey.'

'And how,' she asked, 'are you going to find Mr. Harvey?'

'I have found him. At least, through a distressingly commercial transaction which would only bore you, I hope to have him soon.'

She pursued: 'This transaction: do you act directly with England? Or do you need an intermediary?'

'I have an intermediary ready-made. An embarrassingly eager one.'

'Of course. George Douglas,' said Christian lightheartedly. 'You needn't tell me. But it seems fairly inevitable, after your transaction with Crouch . . . Do you think Harvey can help you?'

'I have no idea,' he said. 'He might. On the other hand, it's always easy to undermine a statement – even a true statement – made under duress, and he mightn't be believed. And even if he is believed –'

'Yes?' she demanded as he came to a stop. He laughed. 'I don't know. I have money. I may find I have the habit of lying on my face even when turned, like George Faustus.'

'I don't think, if I were Agnes Herries, I should believe that,' said Christian.

'No. That was an off-stage observation. We end, in fact, with a long piece about the evils of absolute monarchy and unreliable women, with a graceful aside exculpating the fair audience. I should make a wonderful epopee, don't you think?'

'You could make anything,' said Christian, 'including a perfect farce of your epics; but I shan't worry you. It was a magnificently economical performance.'

'I dislike being candid in public. Christian – this may or may not succeed. If it doesn't, this will be our last meeting.'

'And if it does?'

'Then it would be rather pleasant. I should be all on the right side like a halibut, and someone may formally introduce us. But whatever happens, you have from these fossorial depths my unstinted gratitude and fondest applause. Whatever you touch will return warmth to you and whoever you share it with will be twelve feet tall like St Christopher.' He hesitated. 'You know that if you hadn't been blind, these meetings would never have been possible?'

She nodded.

'I'm not being thick-skinned. But I want you to remember that – if you've been entertained, or diverted, or found some enjoyment in this adventure – it was one small thing brought you by your lack of sight.'

A bitter pill, that: for the long tolerance was over, and she had begun to live with her blindness in rage. But she managed a smile, and heard him approach and take her hand.

He kissed it, and then, unexpected, her cheek. 'A woman,' he said, 'with a familiar spirit. I won't promise any grand transformations for your lame duck, but at least it will bear your crutches proudly. Goodbye, my dear girl.'

'Goodbye,' said Christian, and sat still as the door closed.

* * *

While she was away, Tom Erskine had been looking for her. Sybilla told her as much, and added, her manner a little odd, 'Also . . . You know Richard is here?'

'*Richard!*' Christian, her mind recalled from miles away, cried out. 'But isn't he still . . . ?'

'In prison? No. I've just been told the Queen has pardoned and released him so that he can attend the celebrations. He should be here soon.'

'Oh, Sybilla!'

'Yes, I know,' said the Dowager. 'I think I must be getting old. Do you know, I'm rather frightened. My sons sometimes seem so much stronger than I am.'

'Very soon afterward, Tom Erskine found her, and in five minutes, during which her heart in its cold cage took wearily to itself a new, lifelong burden of protective and fond understanding, Christian Stewart became his affianced wife.

* * *

The third Baron Culter had the sort of pride that makes a man walk straight back to the place where he has been publicly undressed and dare the universe to look down on him. He entered the crowded ballroom at Holyrood with the flourish of an emperor, and reaped the reward of it in the first minutes of an encounter with Sir Andrew Hunter.

Dandy of all people knew how to handle such a situation. Ignoring the interested, the friendly, the speculative glances thrown at them; ignoring Culter's own impassive, bleak face he spoke naturally of the wedding, and of the news that Lord Grey had gone to London and was expected to stay until the end of March – 'a respite till Easter, at least.' Then he said, Richard: tell me. Are you sick of Buccleuch and his outrages? Or could you stomach a rapprochement if I arranged it?'

Culter stared at him with acid humour. 'The millennium has come. Is this a Scott wanting to apologize?'

Hunter answered bluntly. 'I've had a message from Will Scott. Lymond's selling him to the English through George Douglas. The boy has discovered how it's to be done, and wants our help. Will you join us?'

The look on Lord Culter's face was answer enough.

In a private room, Scott of Buccleuch was waiting for them. Richard moved forward.

'You're getting to be a damned slippery acquaintance, Wat. Are you on the doormat this time because you need me or because you want to be?'

Buccleuch hesitated; then chin and cheeks parted and he produced a rumbling chuckle. 'Things have changed. If you're for taking Lymond, so am I.'

'So I hear.' A shadow of a smile crossed Richard's face. 'I suppose if Will hadn't written to Andrew, I'd still be in jail.'

Sir Wat blew out his cheeks. 'Some of you laddies talk as if I were Michael Scott the wizard and not just an old, done man. Sit down, sit down!' he added irritably. 'You'll solve nothing planted there like a couple of bauchly tenors at a glee.'

Hunter laughed and sat down, and after a moment Richard did likewise. It was an odd sort of olive branch, but all he was likely to get. Then Sir Andrew pushed over to him the letter from Will.

The difficulties were clear enough. Scott had not given

away Lymond's headquarters, presumably not to implicate the rest of the band. What was known was that Lymond proposed to ride east to secure from Sir George Douglas and Lord Grey the price of his bargain – a man called Harvey; and that having got Harvey, Lymond intended to send for Scott on some pretext and deliver him on the spot to Lord Grey.

What the boy proposed was that on receiving this summons from Lymond he should send word of it instantly to Buccleuch, who could then ride with all his men to the appointed rendezvous with the fair certainty of taking not only Lymond but Douglas and Lord Grey as well.

The three men sat for a long time drawing up plans. 'And afterward, I suppose,' said Culter finally, leaning back, 'the boy will find his own way home to you?'

'Aye. That's the idea,' said Buccleuch. He fumbled for a moment in his purse. 'You heard what happened to the poor devils that Maxwell and the rest left as hostages in Carlisle? Wharton came straight back from Durisdeer and executed half of them. Here!'

He produced a paper and flung it on the table in front of Culter. 'That's what the black-gutted murderer had put out on the day they all died.'

... Professing [it ran] that they and their friends should set forth the godly marriage and peace between His Majesty our Sovereign Lord of England and the Queen's Grace of Scotland, and for their untruth and perjury against such most godly marriage and peace, and not regarding their faith, being therefore themselves and their blood the occasioners, this their death is thus appointed. ...

Buccleuch's sharp eyes surveyed them. 'There in front of you is the price of the marriage we witnessed today. And no less the price of the marriage we avoided when we turned back after Durisdeer. We're all paying for the same thing – these men here, and the fellows who fell at Pinkie and Ancrum and Annan and Hawick; and you with your brother and me with my son as well. We're seeing times,' said Buccleuch, 'that crack the very marrowbone of tragedy, and compared with it, neither your trouble not mine counts as much as two tallow dips in the circles of Hell.'

Richard's eyes were on the table, and he said nothing. Buccleuch waited; then with a scream of wood scraped his chair back and shoved himself to his feet.

'All right. If that's all, let's get back,' he grunted, and led the way from the room.

Coming back, the first person Richard saw was his mother.

Alone, waiting for him outside the ballroom, she met the visible hardening of his face with a frontal attack of her own.

'I know: I'm Mère-Sotte, and you'll use all I say to make outrageous theories with. Fortunately it doesn't matter. Mariotta isn't with your brother any more. She escaped – Will Scott helped her – she's now in the convent at Culter, very frightened and rather ill. Lymond has not been kind. He got her by sheer chance – she was caught by the English running away from you and they offered her to him. He hasn't been kind, as I say, but he did no harm to her or the child. You ought to know that, I think.'

Richard heard her, leaning against the door: an uncomfortable shadow of Lymond at Midculter. 'A noteworthy salvage effort. I applaud your resolution in sacrificing Lymond in order to patch up my marriage. But it's a little too late for repentance – anybody's repentance. When we catch Lymond, we'll perhaps get at the truth.'

Blue eyes met grey. 'When . . . ? Will it be soon?'

'Very soon. And this time, there's no fear of escape.'

'And what,' said the Dowager flatly, 'shall I tell Mariotta?'

'There's no message,' said Richard. 'I don't want her back. You could, of course, congratulate her on the birth of her son.'

343

'*You* don't want her back,' repeated the Dowager, a rare anger lighting her face. 'Did you think she would come? Your wife, my dear, has no wish to set eyes on you again.'

4

CONCERTED ATTACK

There is no thynge so strong and ferme
but that sometyme a feble thinge
casteth down and overthrowe hi. How
well that the lyon be the strongest
beste . . . Yet sometyme a lityll birde
eteth hym.

1 · THE FOUR KNIGHTS' GAME

The duet between Lord Grey and the Privy Council in London went on intermittently for a fortnight, during which Gideon Somerville had himself rowed up and down the river, landing at familiar green steps and unearthing old friends. Playing cards with Palmer, Grey's new engineering adviser and an erstwhile ally, Gideon sat cheerfully blinded by gold-wire dentistry and absorbed the latest rumours.

London had French fever again. After the sad fiasco of February, nobody was looking forward to reopening the Scottish campaign. It was know that the child Queen was recovering from an illness: it was said that there was no public move yet to marry her into France, and that the Scots Governor was fighting overt tooth and subterranean nail to keep her for his own son.

Palmer, with a glitter of ox bone, thought it unlikely that Denmark would risk offending Spain by sending ships to help Scotland, and that France's promise of further aid was a myth to distract attention from Boulogne.

Gideon listened to it all, and passed on to Lord Grey as much as he thought fit. Two days before their final orders came through, Gideon went with Palmer to the Tower to complain about a bad consignment of arms and, returning, met the Countess of Lennox who knew Palmer well, and remembered Gideon from Warkworth and remoter days when they were both in the suite of the Princess Mary.

Knowing of her shattering failure to persuade her father to support the English at Durisdeer, and of the curious episode which had lost them a hostage when she found herself trapped by unnamed Scottish outlaws, Gideon was surprised when she mentioned George Douglas herself.

He observed with some restraint that he and Grey were to meet Sir George when they got back north. Douglas had promised them a hostage, a boy Lord Grey had wanted for a long time. Buccleuch's heir, in fact.

Margaret Lennox said, 'My father told me that Buccleuch's son was working with . . . a band of broken men on the Borders.'

'That's right,' said Gideon. 'It's not a very savoury story. Apparently it's his own leader who's selling him out. Not but what, having met the gentleman, I should be surprised at his selling his mother for cat's meat.'

She was avid for a description of the man; for more details. 'And what is he selling the boy for? Money?'

There was a pause made hideous for Somerville by a sudden recollection. Tom Palmer, listening with mild interest at the lady's other side, was a cousin of Samuel Harvey, whose life was to be exchanged for Scott's. He cleared his throat. 'As a matter of fact, the thing is a little delicate at the moment. Not quite settled.'

She smiled understanding. 'I suppose your Lord Grey wants the boy Scott because of what happened at Hume? I'd have thought to see him much more anxious to find the Spaniard who double-tricked him.'

'I expect he was anxious enough,' said Gideon, sorry for Grey's sake that the story seemed to have reached the metropolis. 'Only he never found out who the man was. And of course his value as a hostage wasn't as great as Will Scott's.'

346

'Fair hair,' she said aloud to herself. 'And blue eyes, perhaps?'

'Who?' said Gideon. 'Not the Spaniard. The man Scott eventually joined had.'

'Of course he had. I know him. Or I knew him once, in Scotland. Blond, blue-eyed, rapacious and polyglot.'

There was a startled pause. 'He might speak Spanish?'

'He does speak Spanish.'

And there were always black wigs. . . . 'That means,' said Gideon thoughtfully, 'that our Spaniard and Scott's leader may be one and the – Perhaps,' he said, 'you should mention this to Lord Grey or the Protector.'

'Oh, I shall,' said Margaret Lennox. 'Tonight.'

* * *

Two days later, the Protector made his mind known.

Lord Grey was to return to Scotland, and not merely to enthuse from the poop. He was to march into Scotland on the 21st of April to meet his loyal Scots at Cocksburnspath, and go from there to Haddington, tidemark of his former advance. There, he was to fortify and garrison the town to make of it a fortress, a warehouse, a steppingstone and a threat to the whole of Scotland.

Gideon with him, the Lord Lieutenant left London. With him also went the memory of certain acid quips of the Protector's, and a vindictive wrath against a glib and Spanish outlaw who was huckstering with the might of the English crown.

* * *

When the convent on the estate of Lymond was blown up by the English on information received from its former landlord, the remaining nuns found shelter in a large nunnery near Midculter. In this convent Mariotta had now been resting in collected misery for six weeks, visited regularly by Sybilla.

The Dowager, taking Lady Buccleuch with her for the first time, was subjected to some pointed questioning en route.

347

'What I can't understand,' said Janet, 'is how Will suddenly discovered his finer instincts and whisked her away from friend Lymond. I thought he was dedicated with the rest to murder and nasty-minded rituals at the full moon.'

'He was sorry for himself, I think,' said Sybilla wisely. 'And that breeds so much fellow feeling. Anyway, he talked with her just after Lymond had been abominable, and they wept metaphorically all down their shirts and shifts, and he promised to get her away secretly next day, and did.'

'And *how* extraordinary,' said Janet for the sixth time, 'that they should meet you like that.'

'Yes, wasn't it?' said Sybilla.

'And be able to hand Mariotta over to your care.'

'Yes.'

'And go back without being suspected so that he could help his father to trap Lymond.'

'Yes. Here we are,' said Sybilla cheerfully, and entered the convent. Where the first person they saw was Will Scott, talking to Mariotta.

It was hard to know who was most taken aback: Will himself, his stepmother or Sybilla. Janet, the first to find her tongue, said, 'God Almighty!' and showed all her teeth in an enormous grin. 'Look what we've got! Orpheus wriggling rump first out of Hades with his chivalry ashine like a ten-thread twill.'

What Scott mumbled was hardly heard, because Sybilla said quickly, 'I think perhaps he's waiting to see me: he knows I come on Mondays. Will you excuse us a moment?'

Unhappily, Will was flustered, as well as being unaccustomed to the Dowager's little ways. He said, 'It isn't private, Lady Culter – just a letter I wanted you to pass to Andrew Hunter for me.' And he thrust a paper into Sybilla's unresisting hand.

'*Andrew?*' said Janet, gazing fondly at her stepson. 'What's the point, Will? He's already left with the rest.' He looked puzzled, and she repeated. 'You know. Left with Wat and Culter when they got your message.'

'My message?'

'Your second message telling them where Lymond and

Lord Grey were going to be.' She gave an apologetic glance at the Dowager. 'I didn't tell you, Sybilla. But Will's message came through just before we left. Wat and the others should be well on their way to the east coast by now.'

Sybilla sat down abruptly beside Mariotta. Scott said, 'But I haven't sent any messages!'

'Eh!'

'No! This is the first I've ever sent anyone since I joined Lymond except – except about Crumhaugh, of course. This is just to ask Sir Andrew to keep his promise to stand by me if – in case – when I leave the Master.'

This time it was Janet who sat down. 'You haven't sent Dandy any messages before?'

'No.'

'Nor any more to Buccleuch?'

'No.'

'Then who,' said Janet, with a tremor in her strong voice, 'wrote in your name to all of us today telling us to go immediately to the old manor garden at Heriot where Lymond, Sir George Douglas and Lord Grey of Wilton could be had for the taking?'

There was an appalled silence.

'Lymond,' said Mariotta, and laughed hysterically.

* * *

Mariotta was quite right. Having galvanized both his brother and Buccleuch into five weeks of expectant planning, Lymond arrived at Cocksburnspath with Jonnie Bullo in attendance two days before Lord Grey was due to make his next march into Scotland. Under cover of his safe conduct, he and Johnnie were taken direct to Sir George Douglas.

The advance army waiting at the ravine for Lord Grey was under canvas, and Sir George shared a tent with the commander, Sir Robert Bowes, Warden of the East and Middle Marches. He was however alone when Lymond was ushered in, the gypsy waiting outside.

Sir George greeted him, his face a dim, shadowless

beige under the sunlit canvas. He was about to lose the most promising ally of years, and he hated the prospect. He said without preamble, 'I've just come from Lord Grey. You ought to understand that I've kept my part of the bargain: I obtained his lordship's promise to produce this man Harvey for you. But – '

'Ah!' said Lymond, airy and stylish in dark blue. 'There's a but. Like Glaucus, we have a but, but no honey in it. Lord Grey has changed his mind?'

'The Protector changed it for him. Harvey is still in London; he isn't coming north.'

'– And?'

Douglas said curtly, 'And Sir Robert Bowes has orders to see that you send for the boy Scott regardless. You'll be paid in money, not in kind.'

'And if I don't?' asked Lymond.

'Your life is not in danger. Only your good health.'

Sir George's angry glance met Lymond's sardonic one, and there was an uncomfortable silence. At length the Master stirred. 'So. Not the honey barrel, but the tilly-seeds of torture, so that I disgorge the secrets of my bed and board.'

Douglas was flushed. 'All that is wanted is a message in your writing which will bring the boy here. Your gypsy friend can take it . . . but you will not, of course, be allowed to tell him the conditions under which it is being sent.'

'I see. You expect this to give you, personally, some security?' said Lymond suddenly.

Douglas's voice was sharp. 'If there were any alternative, be sure I should take it – ' And broke off as the Commander came in.

Sir Robert Bowes straightened, nodded, and surveyed the Master at leisure from fustic head to silver spurs. He smiled. 'Is this the fellow?'

'– But even a gib-cat has claws,' said Lymond, returning the smile and answering the thought. 'Where is Samuel Harvey?'

'In London,' said Bowes comfortably. 'Are you going to send this message to Scott for us?'

Lymond surveyed him with mild distaste. 'Why should I?'

'Thumbscrews,' said Bowes picturesquely. 'The iron glove – hot lead – pincers – knives. And the whip.'

The Master's eyes were hilarious. 'What, all in your baggage? There's the English army for you. My God, do you have to whip them from behind as well?'

But it was bravado. He told them almost immediately all they wanted to know, and inscribed a letter to Will Scott with which Bullo uncomplainingly set off.

Arriving with the rest of the army on Monday, Lord Grey was charmed with the news. 'This afternoon, at the pond belonging to that old house at Heriot,' said Bowes. 'He'd already made a verbal arrangement with the boy, to be confirmed with his letter, and we thought it best not to change it.'

'Splendid. Good work. Thought all he had to do was collect Harvey, send the message and leave, hey? That'll show him!' said the Lord Lieutenant. And on learning that a party, including Lymond and Sir George Douglas, had already left for the fateful appointment with Will Scott, Lord Grey collected Gideon and trotted off on the same path to enjoy the denouement.

* * *

Sir George Douglas was extremely uncomfortable.

To begin with, his elegant length was curled frondwise round the base of a holly tree whose bulk was a perfect screen, and whose eavesdrip was agony. And secondly, thus fixed and transfixed, he was being pricked, railed at, attacked and generally sacrificed to the playful god Momus.

The patch of ground at Heriot chosen by Lymond for the vigil for Will Scott had once been the kitchen garden of a large, fortified house, long since burned and bombarded and reduced to a masons' boutique.

Among the twisted remains of medlar and apple trees, kale and gooseberries, thyme, catmint and pennyroyal, bramble, blaeberry and camomile and a bower of nettles, a select squad of Bowes' own men lay in approximate concealment, watching the moors to the west. In the open, beside the green mud of an ancient fishpond, sat Lymond, on a block of hewn stone, with his ankles and wrists inconspicuously lashed to each other and to the block.

Although tethered like a billy goat, he had no impediment to speech. Thus suited Lymond, happily aware that for an hour or two he had never been safer. Despite almost tearful threats from Bowes, he sat amber-headed in the April sunlight, melting as the tears of the Heliades, and tore them to shreds. After a while he got quite carried away himself.

> '. . . He and the King of Naverne
> Were fair feared in the fern
> Their headēs for to hide –

'– The other extremity, I see, is harder to conceal, the merry merry holly. It might, of coure, help to stand up: why not stand up? No? Well, yours are the marybones: I am perfectly comfortable and capable of reciting verse until the thyme withers and the pennyroyal is debased. Give me death, but not dumbness. Let Parrot, I pray you, have lyberte to prate. And a captive audience; an attentive audience – an increasing audience. Your noble commander, no less, and – who else? Art thou Heywood, with the mad, merry wit? Good lord, no. It's Flaw Valleys, in person.'

Lord Grey of Wilton, stalking into the clearing with a fine scorn of concealment and Gideon at his heels, had his eyes fixed on its soliloquizing centre.

The hair was different, the clothes were different, but the voice with its rapidity, with its lowering excess of mental agility, were the same. 'The Spaniard; we were right; it's the same man. You've got him!' pealed Lord Grey, and came to a halt.

Lymond looked over his shoulder and back. 'Spaniard? Behold,' he quoted sadly, 'my countenance and my colour. It's only Sweet Cicely awaiting the bees, and blushing in young modesty like a seraphim; two wings over the eyes and the other four pinned with some damnably hard knots: God save Flamens and keep all the knotless from high winds and short memories.'

Paying not the slightest heed, Lord Grey pursued his idea. 'The Spaniard who stole my horses and supplies at Hume Castle. Deny if you can that you're the fellow.'

A delighted smile spread over Lymond's attentive face, and then faded in consternation. 'You want your tawny velvet, and I gave it away.'

'You insolent blackguard!'

'Muy illustrissimo y excellentissimo señor,' responded Lymond politely. 'How did you find out, I wonder?'

Lord Grey said frigidly, 'You made two obvious mistakes. One was to show yourself to Somerville here, and the other was parading your miserable polyglot talents before the Countess of Lennox.'

'Ah!' said Lymond; and a moment later continued. 'Manerly Margery, Mylk, and Ale. Por vos suis en prison mis; Por vos, amie! I wondered at the Protector's sudden tenderness for poor Mr. Harvey.'

'And you may as well know,' said Lord Grey, high colour in his cheeks, 'that you'll have plenty of time to reflect on the folly of your tricks. Plenty of time. I mean to have you hanged – '

'– Higher than Haman and the ramparts of Hume – '

'– And burned – '

'– More successfully than Polycarp. And ripped, salted and stuffed with myrrh and cassia and set up painted to remind all low people, all boasters and braggers and bargainers, that villainy is mortal. And what about Douglas? Does he suffer the same if Will Scott doesn't appear? He's present, as a matter of fact, though you might not think it – somewhere.' He looked wildly around. 'But where? My joy, cry peip! where ever thou be!'

Lord Grey also looked around. Part at least of Sir George must have been visible because the Lord Lieutenant said irritably, 'Get up, man: are you broody? No need for that yet. The boy will be hours yet by all accounts.'

A derisive groan broke from the bound man. 'Nay, not so. I am too brittle; I may not endure. . . .'

'Hold your tongue!'

The prisoner smiled and settled himself as luxuriously as he could against the cold stone while Lord Grey and Douglas conferred.

Gideon, watching the relaxed profile with its veiled eyes and lightly contemptuous mouth, was gifted by remembered anger with an extra insight.

The man was coiled like a spring, waiting. Waiting for what? With the whole might of the English army lying behind them at Cockburnspath, Gideon couldn't imagine. But this was no broken Colossus, waiting to be whisked off for old metal: it was a clever man, and an expert actor.

Gideon left Grey's side and strolled unobtrusively over to the pond, where Lymond greeted him without expression. 'Any friend of Meg Douglas has my respect.'

Gideon looked down, hands clasped loosely behind his back. 'As it ha-happens, I don't greatly care for her. What are you waiting for?'

The impudent mouth widened. 'Rescue,' said Lymond. 'Why not?'

Somerville gave him back the same smile. 'Not while I'm here.'

'You probably won't be. Lord Grey is leaving.'

Looking round, Gideon saw that this was true. Satisfied at having identified Lymond and unready to abase himself behind prickly evergreens, the Lord Lieutenant was preparing to go back to camp.

Gideon crossed to him quickly, and in a brief exchange, got permission to say behind, having pleaded in vain for more men to stay with him. On a billow of diminishing comments, Lord Grey disappeared. Gideon manfully selected a gorse bush which happened to be the nearest cover to Lymond, and the little clearing settled down to comparative silence.

* * *

Since Johnnie Bullo took the summons to Branxholm

instead of to Will Scott; since he delivered it verbally through a dear friend who was unknown to Buccleuch; and since he represented it as coming from Scott and not from Lymond, Sir Wat and Lord Culter set out forthwith with all their men to Heriot under the natural impression that they were about to lay Lymond and his allies by the heels in the act of bargaining over Buccleuch's son.

Johnnie had been generous with his information, both about the site and its hazards. As they rode, Sir Wat and Richard laid their plans, which were simple: by riding north around the bluff on which the house ruins stood, Lord Culter would silently infiltrate behind the Englishmen; Buccleuch with his men would appear in full panoply along the wide, exposed moors to the west and south, and dash the would-be ambush back into Richard's arms.

The prospect was intoxicating. In a state of near euphoria the Scotts and the Crawfords drove at the hills lying between Branxholm and Heriot and the hills vanished, as small fish into the gape of a whale. Then the blue and silver wheeled and passed to the northeast, while Buccleuch slackened his pace, and prepared to time his attack.

They appeared to Gideon, to Bowes and to Douglas as a sparkling comber on the horizon, which unrolled as they watched, and crystallized into helmet, steel plate, spearhead and sword. Scots, and in superior numbers, armed, on horseback, and making straight for them with instructed assurance.

The kitchen garden disintegrated. The holly and laurels ran for their horses, but the gorse bush alone lingered. As Bowes' men pushed past him and curses flew and horses stamped and shuffled, Gideon ducked and ran across to Lymond. He had an impression of a bright eye and some breathless laughter; then he slashed the cord at the Master's feet and flung him up at sword point before him in the saddle of his own horse. With the ground vibrating under his feet with oncoming hoofs, he set the gelding, doubly laden, galloping after Bowes and the other men.

Richard saw them coming from beyond the small hill,

and sent his men streeling like floats on a salmon net over the coastal road. The approaching horses veered, racing parallel with the Scottish horse in a rhythm of flashing forearms and outflung, muscular necks, and the heather clods thudded like meteorites.

They engaged as they galloped. Richard, his grey eyes half-closed, his riding faultless and his right arm invincible, defended himself and scanned every face. He saw the Douglas colours and ignored them; he saw a heavily built rider, presumably Bowes, try to rally the men, lost him, and was involved in a thumping clash of steel and horseflesh and labouring bodies, through which he got a glimpse of a yellow head.

He was going through the battling parties indiscriminately, like a flame through wax, when the thunder of horses about him checked as if the gates of the atmosphere had shut in their faces.

Lord Grey had thought twice about Gideon's warning, and had detailed a company of horse to watch the situation at Heriot. Straight from Cockburnspath, red crosses glittering, fresh and rosy as apples, the new horsemen fell joyfully on Culter's men and on the Scotts sweeping up to their rear; surprised them, engaged them and devastated them until, broken and bitterly enraged they turned, outnumbered, and fled back over the moors.

Gideon Somerville, caught in the middle of the early fighting, hacked grimly with one hand and controlled his horse and his prisoner with the other. He had almost cleared a road for himself when he was taken by surprise in the rear. He experienced a shattering blow on the back of his head; realized with surprise and fury that he was falling, and knew nothing more.

* * *

Mr. Somerville opened his eyes to a circle of queasily ambulating trees, shut them again, and tried to move. He found this impossible because his hands and ankles were tied. He opened his eyes again quickly and looked.

It was a small wood. Two battered horses were grazing

356

quietly under the trees, and Crawford of Lymond was sitting placidly quite near, with his hands clasped about his knees.

'Oh!' said Gideon.

'Quite,' said Lymond cheerfully. 'Your horse was killed, so I rolled you like Sisyphus's stone to the nearest shelter. Everyone was much too busy high up to notice what was happening in the long grass. You had it wrong, you know. It was to be an evisceration party, not a rescue.'

His cords? wondered Gideon vaguely. Cut them on his, Gideon's, sword, probably: it was missing. Damn. Aloud, he said, 'I suppose we have young Scott to thank for all this. I might have done more to warn Lord Grey, except that I found it hard to believe you would put yourself within reach of your own countrymen.'

'Don't blame Scott. I sent for Buccleuch and Lord Culter,' said Lymond. 'Which is only just, since Lord Grey didn't bring my Mr. Harvey. In other words, we have all been energetically cheating. Although I should have sent the message in any case.'

'Inviting the evisceration party? That seems a bit odd,' said Gideon dryly.

'It nearly turned out to be very odd indeed. But then, I didn't expect to be among the welcoming party – or if I had been, I expected to be enjoying the society of Mr. Harvey, which would have altered things a trifle. However, as it happened – '

'As it happened, it seems to me you were abnormally lucky to escape from your own cross fire.'

Lymond agreed dreamily. 'Nemesis nodded. I know.'

'And now?'

'And now you shall come with me to my home for a change . . .

> 'Now in dry, now in wete,
> Now in snow, now in slete,
> When my shone freys to my fete –
> It is not, Mr. Somerville, all easy.'

357

* * *

The horses Lymond had captured were tired, and the journey to Crawfordmuir took the two men rather longer than it need have done.

About halfway there, they came across the redheaded boy.

He was a formidable and well-grown young man, on the horse almost as weary as their own, and beside him a small swarthy gentleman on a long-faced brown pony. Lymond reined instantly before the boy's drawn sword, and effervesced into gnatlike mockery.

'Will Scott! With chin driven into his chest as if he's been thumped on the head with a fact. Facts and Mr. Scott never meet: they collide. What's wrong now?'

Scott! Gideon's eyebrows shot up; the black-haired man grinned; and the young man exclaimed with an unhappy, controlled violence, 'What have you done with my father?'

'Exercised him and sent him home. Johnnie, you shouldn't frighten the child.'

The dark person smiled, showing beautiful, sharp teeth. 'I didn't. He got the story elsewhere and was wearing himself out trying to track you all down. I thought it would be handier to help him find you.'

Scott ignored it, his whole mind set on Lymond. 'I thought I was the person wrapped ready for sale; but no. I was nothing – the grease around the candle, the keyhole for the key. You sold my father and your own brother to the English, but by God, you've still got a reckoning to face for it! Get down.'

'Make me?' invited Lymond, and unfurled himself with terrifying suddenness. There was an explosion of movement. Scott, swordless, was ripped from his horse and stood gaping, while Lymond addressed Gideon.

'We're not always so uncouth. I'm sorry. You were at Heriot. Would you say that the Scots who surprised you were falling into a trap?'

Gideon, fascinated, spoke the truth. 'Oh the contrary.

358

Scott of Buccleuch and his friends had prepared a very efficient trap of their own.'

'I told him,' said Johnnie virtuously. 'I gave all the help I could to Buccleuch.'

Scott's hands were doubled. 'But you completed the bargain somehow. You've got Harvey.'

Prompted by the eye of his impresario Gideon responded, amused, to the cue. 'My name is Somerville,' he said quietly. 'I'm afraid Lord Grey steered rather an erratic course as well. He didn't keep his promise to bring Harvey north.' And out of charity, he added, 'Your father took no harm in the fighting. They didn't get any prisoners through a chance intervention of mine, but both Buccleuch and Lord Culter got away quite safely.'

Scott's eyes never shifted from Lymond. 'I seem to have made a fool of myself again?'

'You put yourself in a damned silly position to begin with. But you can put half the blame, if you like, on the universal habit of pattering off to Dandy Hunter with one's troubles. Is that a fair comment?'

The red-haired boy flushed, and then went pale. 'I suppose so, yes. All right. I suppose I should apologize again. Or would one omnibus grovel cover all past and future failings?'

'Anything,' said Lymond, 'that will prevent you from leaping like a chamois to unutterable conclusions. Seen all you want to, Johnnie?'

The white teeth flashed. 'I like watching acrobatics. If you want me again –?'

'– I shall consult the viscera of a fish louse. Goodbye!'

Gideon found himself looking into a pair of snapping brown eyes. 'He pays well,' murmured Johnnie; and nipping his pony between his knees, darted off. The Master's gaze, unusually wide, followed him.

It had been folly to lose his temper, however briefly, and both he and Gideon knew it.

* * *

Unlike his predecessor Mr. Crouch, Gideon Somerville

had within him considerable resources of scholarship and wit. Life at Shortcleugh he found full of a freakish interest; and after two days he had a thoroughgoing admiration for the assurance with which the dominus quod-libetarius did his job.

On the second day he was brought down from the top floor to Lymond's room, and began himself, briskly, on entering. 'Your plan now, I take it, is to exchange me for Samuel Harvey.'

Lymond considered this, tapping his teeth. 'Do you think the Protector would give Harvey up?'

'I like to think he won't,' said Gideon.

The Master threw the pen he was holding on the desk and got up. 'I doubt if Lady Lennox can persuade him a second time. But in any case, you're a friend of Lord Grey's. He'll bring Harvey north if the Protector doesn't.'

'He may,' said Gideon. 'But it won't make any difference. I've no intention of buying my freedom at the price of someone else's life. Money, yes: you have a right to ransom me if you wish. But you'll neither find me nor make me a party to any other arrangements, alive or – or dead.'

Lymond moved restlessly. 'Honest men are notoriously hard to do business with. . . . Harvey's life will be quite safe with me.'

Gideon said, 'I'm afraid I cannot take the risk.'

'Your wife wouldn't see it as a risk.'

'My wife would agree with me,' said Gideon in a final tone, and waited again.

Lymond prowled across and reseated himself. 'You can't stop me, of course,' he said flatly. 'I've only to send your signet ring and a message to Grey, and keep you stuffed full of drugs till the exchange is effected.'

'I recognize that, of course,' said Gideon. 'But I'll make it as diff-difficult as I can.'

'Then I'll offer you another bargain,' said Lymond, and looked up suddenly. 'Since honesty is your surest asset, let us gamble with that. There is your sword, your knife and the key to your room. There is a horse waiting for

360

you downstairs. You are perfectly free to go home provided you will take it on your conscience to arrange for me to meet Harvey without any danger to my life, and with any measures you like to safeguard his.'

The word 'free' startled Gideon into movement; then he put the tips of his clean fingers together and surveyed them calmly.

What was the flaw? Not a threat to his health: he had to be kept alive for the purpose of the exchange. But as soon as he left his prison, he was out of Lymond's control. He could go home and do nothing further: this time he would set a guard, he promised himself grimly, that wouldn't admit a one-legged mouse. Or he could go home and make the desired arrangements, and then capture Lymond in turn when he came. Either way, the Master was putting himself entirely at his, Gideon's, mercy.

As if answering his thoughts, Lymond's voice said, 'There isn't any trick, though you can take time to hunt for one if you like. Whatever you do, the power and the initiative are with you, and not with me.'

'Why?' asked Gideon bluntly.

'An Easter present.' And as Gideon continued to frown at him, Lymond said coolly, 'I owe your family an act of sensibility. Remember?'

Somerville stirred. 'If you don't want Harvey's life, what do you want him for?'

'For his ethological small talk,' said Lymond. 'You must decide on the data you have.'

'I have decided,' said Gideon unexpectedly. 'I'm not going to do what you want, I tell you frankly, for no better reason than that you want it.'

'I was afraid of that.' Lymond's voice was surprisingly mild. 'You may set fire to churches and cribble empires through your bloody fingers, but the one irretrievable mistake is to misjudge a fellow being.'

'Or force a child to judge its parents.'

'Oh, quite. Nemesis has wakened up again. My hoofs, it appears, weigh more than your halo. It's a most damnably one-sided balance, but that's not your fault. Put on

361

your sword and go and get your gear; Matthew'll put you on the Redesdale road.'

The sword drooped in Gideon's amazed hand. 'I haven't given you any undertakings.'

'I know. You haven't given me anything except rather incoherent arguments, and I already have a fruitful source of those under my roof.'

Gideon was still at a loss. 'I warn you, Flaw Valleys will be totally impregnable from the time I get back.'

'You can have ten bowmen to a brick for all I care,' said Lymond with sudden exasperation. He strode to the door and shouted. 'Matthew!'

Gideon moved as quickly. Standing at the other man's shoulder, he said, 'Why do you want Samuel Harvey? Is the reason so squalid?'

Matthew came. 'The horse for Mr. Somerville,' Lymond said, and turned back into the room, leaving Gideon by the door. 'Not squalid, my friend: ludicrous.'

'In my scale of values,' said Gideon, 'a matter of dignity is always on the trivial side of the reckoning.'

'I can't help that,' said Lymond. 'Pride is a congenital disease in my family, and I'm damned if I'll put five years' hard labour into the trivial side of anything. This is on the other scale, along with the hoofs and the haloes.'

Madness took possession of Somerville. He said brusquely, 'If I arrange a meeting, it will be in my own time, at a spot chosen by me and surrounded by my men. The interview will take place in my presence, and you will arrive unarmed. If you attempt to injure Mr. Harvey, or threaten him, or in any way molest him, I shall reserve the right to hand you immediately to Lord Grey. Do you agree to these conditions?'

A trace of colour had risen under the thin skin. 'Of course,' said Lymond evenly. 'Without reserve. But there is one risk you ought to consider: that Lord Grey might discover I had visited you. I don't think Harvey will want to tell him; but if need be you may hold me until you know that you can safely let me go. I'm going to disband my men first, in any case.'

Gideon said curiously, 'You set great store by this meeting, surely, if you're going to abandon your livelihood for it. I doubt if I could face the situation so calmly.'

'I pay my price,' said Lymond, and smiled suddenly. 'But if I'm going to hear from you, I shall stay sober.'

In less than an hour, Gideon was on his way home, wondering if, like Evagrius, he would receive the receipt for these pious outgoings in his coffin.

* * *

It was a soft spring that year, with spotted eggs where the winter cattle walked, spindle-legged; with fawn in wood and cub in hole and white lambs under the whin. With the sun came green shoots and flat water and a fresh courage erumpent which depressed Lord Grey into a welter of gloom at Haddington.

He had marched there from Cockburnspath and found a wind egg which had to become a monolithic fortress. In the shallow bowl of the Tyne, overlooked on both sides, he was threatened hourly by the nearness of Edinburgh, of Arran's three thousand five hundred, and by five thousand Frenchmen, delicately scenting the infested terrain.

On the other hand, once done, he had a classic tourniquet on the Lothians, on the routes north and south and on the crop-growing farmlands. He took all the rest of April and May to it, and had his men boring like gimlets and building like corals to render him his defensible fortress.

By the last week in May, Lord Grey had over five thousand horse and foot in and around Haddington, and stores for them all. By then also, Sir George Douglas's honeymoon with England, already badly damaged by the muddle at Heriot, began to slither to an end.

'The captain of Haddington,' wrote the Protector, 'is to train as many hackbutters as he can, to do all he can to get Sir George in his hands, and having him, keep him. And notwithstanding any treaty, to destroy the country as he may.'

Lord Grey took the necessary steps. He did more. Without consulting Somerset or Palmer or his own staff, he sent for Samuel Harvey.

2 · THE PINNING MOVE

It was Sybilla who, mistrusting the apathetic security of the convent, installed her daughter-in-law, in Richard's permanent absence, at Midculter.

There, she found herself in the embarrassing position of the social suicide who wakes up after the laudanum: the skies had fallen and had done nothing but add to the general obscurity. The Dowager, wishing strongly that Christian Stewart was with her instead of staying with the Maxwells, did her best to amuse; but all that could stir Mariotta to the mildest interest was the alchemy experiment.

In recent months, the laboratory which Sybilla had equipped for Johnnie Bullo had glowed with strange lights of an evening, and bad smells infiltrated lovingly into the fabric of the house. Johnnie explained, frequently, what he was doing, but so far little was visible save a sticky and unsavoury residue in blackened retorts.

On a mild, sunny afternoon at the end of May, however, encouraged perhaps by the presence of Janet Buccleuch as well as the two Lady Culters, he had gone further. Standing by the odorous furnace and tapping a dirty copper he intoned.

'Calcination, dissolution, separation, conjunction, putrefaction, congelation, cibation, sublimation, fermentation, exaltation, multiplication and projection,' chanted Johnnie, his dark face ferociously solemn. 'These and none others are the twelve processes.'

There was a respectful silence. 'Twelve processes of what?' demanded Janet, who liked to have things straight.

The bright, mystagogue's eyes appealed for sympathy to the intellectual Culters. He explained. At the end –

'Yes. I see all that,' said Janet. 'Go on to the bit about the Paradisiacal fruit.'

'Yes. Well,' said Johnnie, who was not overfond of being quoted. 'The fruit has ripened. If it's dry, you add mercury until silver Luna rises. In time, that yields to the Sun. Then the phial is sealed and put in the furnace: mine went in a month ago as I showed you – white fumes with a black residue as I showed you also – perfect putrefaction of the seed.' His eyes shone.

'Now I shall increase the heat, and you shall see the glorious colour changes – green to white – the White Tincture. If we troubled with it, we should find it transmutes metal to silver.'

'Aren't we going to trouble with it?' asked Mariotta.

He shook his black head. 'We wait until the furnace becomes hotter still – yellow, orange – citron – and finally, blood red.' He paused weightily. 'And that day, Lady Culter, will be very soon now.'

'And what,' asked Sybilla, the blue eyes shining, 'happens then, Mr. Bullo?'

His expression altered from the grave to the bonzelike. 'Cooled and powdered, what is left has become heavier than gold, dissolvable in any liquid, a panacea for all diseases, and a transmuter of lead into gold.'

A breathless silence, fraught with fat visions, stretched on and was broken by Janet. 'There is someone,' said Lady Buccleuch in annoyance, 'at the door.'

It was a travel-stained man from Ballaggan with a letter for the Dowager.

The reek of the furnace and the dirty crucibles rolled out into the courtyard as she read it; Johnnie's words vanished; the litter and alembics became commonplace. 'What is it?' exclaimed Janet.

Sybilla spoke to the messenger, her voice flat. 'Tell Sir Andrew that Lord Culter is not here; but Sir Wat will come as soon as we can reach him. And tell him we suggest he takes his prisoner to Threave. That will save troubling Lady Hunter while they wait for Buccleuch.'

'Prisoner?' said Mariotta. 'What prisoner?'

The wide, cornflower eyes were brilliant. 'Oh, Lymond; Lymond!' said Sybilla. 'Who else? What else? He's driven that ridiculous boy half out of his mind, and this is the result.'

Mariotta's face, too, was white. 'They have him?'

'Tomorrow,' said Sybilla. 'Lymond goes to England tomorrow, alone, Dandy says. They know where; they know how – the Scott boy has told them. Before Lymond crosses the Border, Hunter will have him.'

Janet spoke uneasily. 'They want Buccleuch's help?'

'They wanted Richard,' said the Dowager with a great weariness. 'But failing him, Buccleuch, to take over Lymond from Sir Andrew and bring him north. But Richard's away, thank God. Thank God,' she repeated, her voice brittle. 'Because the young fool plans to trap Lymond at the convent. The ruined convent where five years ago his sister was killed.'

They did not see Johnnie Bullo slip out. To do him justice, he set out south at full gallop.

It was not his fault that he was too late.

PART IV
The End Game

1

TWICE TAKEN

And what is a Knyght worth, wyth oute
horse and armes?
Certaynly nothynge more than on
of the peple,
Or lasse, pāventure.

1 · FORCED PLAY AGAINST TIME

Since its untimely dissolution, the convent at Lymond had
invented new graces. Its tongueless bell slept unharried
among the cuckoo flowers and behind painted robe and
beaded halo its broken beams, leafed like an artichoke,
fed a thousand mouths. Of human life there was none
nearer than the adjacent hilltops, where armed men waited
and watched.

Lymond, with Scott and Turkey Mat, left Crawfordmuir
before dawn, in a mild, vaporous rain that soaked them
all. Scott rode mute, his breath unsteady in his lungs.

It was Oyster Charlie who had first hinted that the band
was to be broken up. Will had howled at the idea. 'The
Master abdicate? Not while he can act like Cyrus King of
the World and be paid for it.'

But the rumour got stronger. He had tackled Turkey
Mat and Turkey had pulled a yellow face, his hand on his
stomach. 'It's maybe likely. He's off to England soon to
meet this fellow Harvey and be made a lord, like enough.
There's no cause to keep the force on.'

Why had he imagined the company to be perpetual?
It had been created at Lymond's whim, and was being

disbanded by the same lordly hand.... Scott took to watching for the return of the weekly messenger to the Ostrich, and he knew before anyone when the word finally came summoning Lymond to the Castle of Wark on the second of June for his portentous meeting with Samuel Harvey.

The Master announced the disbandment the same day in the hall, over the uproar of sixty furious employees. The Long Cleg had the loudest voice. 'We dinna want to go. There's no need. We're doing fine. We want to go on.'

'By all means. But without me.'

'No! You're to stay!'

'And who will make me?'

The thunder increased. 'We're sixty to one!' And Turkey had turned from his comfortable seat in the front. 'Two, man: two. And I'm the only other one that kens where your pay is.'

Lymond snatched the ensuing decrescendo in which to be heard. 'If you want to be paid, I'm afraid you must accept it. And even if you don't, you really can't make me stay, can you?'

And, of course, they couldn't. Sardonic to the last, he had surveyed them. 'All right. Get out. Think for yourselves for a change. You've been pedlars: go and be merchants. You've been mercenaries: go and find something of your own to defend. You've finished teething and there's the world: crack it open if you can. It's a damned sight pricklier than I am. In any case, whatever you do, keep well clear of me....'

They were paid, and took their leave, clattering out in twos and threes: Oyster Charlie, the Long Cleg, Dandypuff, Jess's Joe. Turkey and he were last, as Scott knew they would be, because they had special claims. The money for them was in French gold and was in Scott's own custody. But not in the tower.

Dreading a homily, Scott was relieved to find that Lymond himself, travelling light, was packing quickly for his journey to Wark and made no effort to see him alone.

When the matter of the gold cropped up, the boy said nothing about a convent. He said casually, 'The store's on your road, as a matter of fact. If you like, I'll take a pack horse and ride with you so far.'

Lymond had been indifferent, but Turkey was not. He thought bluntly that a fellow fetching a double salary of gold ought to have company on the way back as well. He attached himself firmly to Scott, who attempted to argue and only succeeded in making him obstinate.

Thus in the long run, Turkey Mat as well as Scott took the Wark road along with the Master. The golden dales of Crawfordmuir fell behind them, broken, gouged and abandoned, and whether the four rivers they left were of Hell, or the Pischon, Dichon, Chiddikel and Perath of Paradise might have been hard for any one of them to say.

That was this morning. The question now was how far the tiger would enter the cage.

Lymond was riding very fast, taking no risks, although he had plenty of time to reach the north of England by next day, when Harvey's convoy would pass through Wark. Turkey Mat, knee to knee with him, was talking more than usual, and it was a little time before either realized that Scott had halted.

Waiting, the boy saw the Master turn, and then bring his chestnut in a fine arc back to him; saw Lymond's eyes flicker to the splintered, obelisk elms on his left and then alter. When he came abreast, however, he merely inspected Scott's green face and groaned. 'Oh God: sermons and symbolism; I can't stand it. Don't bother to tell me. You've put the gold in the convent.'

Scott said heavily, 'It seemed a good place to me. The basement is quite intact, you know.'

Unexpectedly, Lymond failed to rage. 'Then go and get your money. Half for you; half for Mat, and for God's sake jump off the pendulum next time before it gets my length. . . . Mat! This is where I leave you both.'

Mat had heard, cantering up. 'Already? What about your share of the gold?'

Scott let him talk. He had thought of this possibility too: he had thought of everything. He moved restively behind the two men and made his unobtrusive signal and then rejoined them, a little sulky and very young, his brow round and flecked with the sun. Mat was still arguing, but only seconds elapsed before they all heard the drumming of hoofs from behind the hill they had just passed.

Lymond's head came up instantly, listening; weighing up the quality of the sound. It was a large body of cavalry not yet in sight: Scots or otherwise hardly mattered; both were a danger to him, and a danger at this special and delicate crisis in his affairs.

He turned quickly. There was only one source of cover, and it had to be reached before the first riders came into sight. After the merest hint of a pause he collected the chestnut, jerked his head, and followed by Turkey and Scott, raced for the convent.

They got there, as he intended, before the first horses came into sight. They jumped the broken wall, dismounting, tying their horses out of sight in the roofless, rubble-filled building and flinging themselves among the toadflax as the grey light flickered like St. Elmo's fire on the pikes and drawn swords of galloping horsemen rounding the hill.

Turkey, his beard full of burs, his clothing soaked with the light rain, spared breath for an ironic cheer as the troop streamed frieze-like along the road: they galloped to the exact point the three men had just left, and then forsaking the road entirely, bore like a grey and shining harrow through the wet grass, making straight for the convent.

Mat's mouth fell slightly open. 'It's the second sight. It must be: I'm damned if they saw us.'

Brittle as exploding glass, Lymond said, 'They didn't see us. They expected to find us here. They're Ballaggan men.'

'The horses –'

'Too late. You heard Scott: there's a basement,' said Lymond, and twisting like a dorcus led them full tilt through the shattered rooms, Scott beside him and Mat at his heels. The stairs plunged downward, broken and shallow. At the head of them the Master took a quick step, wrenched Scott's sword screaming from its sheath and flung the boy weaponless down the stairs with such force that he landed knee and shoulder at the first bend. The look in the blue eyes chilled even Turkey. 'You lead. Another trick and I'll kill you.'

Then they were running downstairs, Lymond with a sword in each hand. Mat said, 'The boy . . . ?'

'Of course: who else? But he may not know there's a passage out of that cellar. Unless it's full of Hunter and his friends, waiting for us.'

It wasn't. At the next bend there was a light: a sickly glint from a wall taper exposing the sunk treads and check-ered green walls. Then they were in the basement.

The floor was littered with rubbish from the groined roof, and dust covered everything. In a corner stood a heavy leather chest, securely locked: their useless gold. They sought instead what their lives depended on: the low and obscure door to the nuns' underground passage. It was there. They saw the lintel. The rest was blocked, triumphantly and symbolically indeed, with stacked cases of gunpowder.

It was suddenly very quiet.

Overhead, they could hear the jangle of harness and men's voices but no steps descending, although Mat moved instinctively to the narrow stair and put his sword across it. Scott was standing motionless between the gold and the gunpowder, the tallow dip in his hand, light and shadow racing in freshets over the stone between leader and accolyte.

Softly Lymond said, 'You put the cost of your pride at three lives?'

'Three!'

Lymond answered Mat without turning his head. 'Why do you fancy he's holding the torch?'

373

It was quick, of course, admirable; but quick thinking would hardly rescue him now. Scott raised the flare, beside red ear and thick jaw and tousled, marigold hair. He said, 'Just a precaution. You have ten minutes to walk upstairs and give yourselves up; otherwise they fire stoneshot, and then Greek fire, and there'll be an explosion like Muspelheim. By waiting, of course, you'll take me with you; but that's a dull prospect compared with setting a score of young lassies to fry . . .'

'You bloody little traitor, shut your mouth!' It was Matthew, not Lymond.

The direct assault on the memory was intentional: a revenge indeed for every doubt and indignity and misery that Scott had suffered. He had perhaps reckoned without Lymond's peculiar strength.

No trace of the ordeal was visible to Scott. The raw light shuddered on the Master's face but Lymond himself was quite still. He said, 'You evidently want to be taken seriously. I am now doing so. You are prepared to take responsibility for Matthew's death?'

Buccleuch had hinted, and Sir Andrew had confirmed. You don't make concessions to a man who has killed his own sister. 'Matthew's safe,' said Scott. 'We're all safe, for ten minutes. She was called Eloise, wasn't she? Why did she die?'

'Because in this age only the intolerable have survived. Matthew, quickly.'

Scott reached the gunpowder before them, the tallow spluttering in his hand, smiling. 'Touch one box and I'll explode it.'

The dreadful, fragile little situation was too much for Mat. He raised his heavy sword, inhaling stale air with a roar. 'Explode it then, you bloody little rat: you don't have the guts!' and stumbled, arrested by Lymond, iron-armed.

'You're dealing with hysteria, not guts or lack of them. Scott: if I were alone I'd say throw and be damned. Burn us into red and white rose trees. Make sweet cinders of our bloody gold. Exercise this pitiful, feckless piety you've discovered and reap your own trashy reward. Why the

374

melodrama, I don't know. If you were determined to trap me, it seems a fairly simple thing to do without the busking. If you want the satisfaction of a discussion, you won't get it. Make your decisions, such as they are: you're in command. I have nothing to say to you.'

'Hell, but I have!' said Mat. 'Jump him! Start on the boxes. He won't throw.'

'He will,' said Lymond calmly. 'Big bangs and primary colours appeal to the young.'

'What then?'

'Up to the realms of this universal patron.'

'Dandy Hunter? Give ourselves up?'

'Unless like Hanno you wish to sail by steams of fire. Unbuckle your sword. The suicide impulse is very strong in the air.'

Lymond was already, left-handed, unfastening his own sword belt. He pulled it off complete with scabbard and dropped it on the rubble behind him. Mat's followed. In his right hand Lymond continued to hold Scott's sword. 'The ten minutes are nearly up. You were saying?' he said to the boy.

It was the steadiness of the voice that shook Scott. He exclaimed, 'For God's sake: this is where she died. Doesn't that mean anything?'

'If I killed her, why should it? If I didn't, I'm not likely to be goaded into triple suttee, even to enable you to expire in a spray of madder-fed milk.'

'You are willing,' said Scott harshly, 'to give yourselves up?'

'We are waiting with, I hope, well concealed impatience to do so.'

'In that case, I'll take back my sword.'

Knowing Lymond, Scott was well prepared. He expected a thrust or a cut, or even the heavy blade hurled in his face. Instead Lymond said briefly, 'I'm damned if I'll give it to you. This one wrote a betrayal. It can stay and sign it.' And he hurled it away from himself, far across the dark cellar where it spun with a little tongue from the torch flame, carrying the boy's gaze instinctively with it.

In that one small blind instant, like the tiger of Scott's own fantasy, Lymond jumped.

Too late to avoid him, Scott had all the time in the world to do what he wanted. The heavy torch, flung with all the boy's strength, left his hand and soared high over the gunpowder boxes, jettisoning sparks. The shadows pounced after it; the new, rough wood of the boxes bloomed under its high star; then it fell.

Halfway to the powder it collided with the clogged, sodden wool of Lymond's cloak, simultaneously thrown. Torch and cloak fell together; the wrap, batlike and sluggish, rolled over the lower boxes like a carpet and the tallow dip, upright, hit the topmost box, hesitated, bowed, and then halting in the surge of its own fire, toppled slowly forward and into the cloak. There was a flare of light, writhing over ceiling and uneven, web-clotted walls. Then Matthew leaped forward and Scott, borne to the floor by Lymond's hard strength, twisted vainly to stop him. There was a shrinking of light; a stink of tallow; a hiss; and the shock of utter darkness seized them all.

There was no light; there was no air. Scott heard Matthew blundering about, seeking them. He could hear Lymond's quick breathing, close to his face and his own raucous panting. He could feel cool fingers bending and turning, the weight of the lean, clever body and the steady leverage on his own limbs. . . . Kill girls! He could kill girls; but he wasn't going to stop Will Scott.

He broke that hold, and the next. He knew some of Lymond's tricks, but not all. The pressure on his ribs had gone. Now he needed only to get his right hand free. He twisted.

Matthew stumbled on them and laid hands on something. Lymond's voice, breathless, told him curtly to keep away. There were men's voices in the convent above, and someone shouted something, but the blood roaring in his ears deafened Scott. He crashed again on his side, bruising his hip agonizingly against fallen stone, gritted his teeth, and shifted his own grip again.

It was bitter delight: to feel Lymond, the cool, unassailable Lymond, wince beneath his grip. He pressed with all his weight, and felt the other man jerk. Then, brutally as Dandy Hunter had done, Scott felt a surge through their locked limbs; cramp gripped his legs, and he was raised in the air and smashed on the rubble.

His own grip weakened. 'God . . . !'

The powerful muscles opened again; again he fell, and this time struck his head, his senses spinning with the pain. He had rolled halfway across the Master's legs; he had no sort of hold at all; Lymond could do as he pleased . . . but he wasn't going to. Scott's right hand was free. Thank God, to be reminded in time. His right hand was free; his jerkin was torn apart; and beneath it, strapped to his body, was the small, sharp knife he had put there long before.

It came to his hand like a child. He balanced it a moment in the dark, cherishing it; and then with a grim and godly triumph, drove it up to the hilt into Lymond's hard flesh.

The blow delivered, energy, initiative and even normal sensation left Scott. Lying flaccid on the dark stones he was aware of noise and vibration; aware dimly that the roof was shaking and men's voices, shouting, were calling his name. There was a crash, and plaster and stone rattled about him, sifting lax into eyes and hair. He laid a hand over his face.

Matthew was shouting, and now he knew. Of course. Stoneshot first, then Greek fire. He ought to get up and stop them; after a moment he did get up. In the dark, there was no movement beside him.

Painfully blundering, he found the stairway and began climbing just as Matthew, working obstinately in the darkness from wall to wall, found and fell on his knees beside Lymond.

Covered with dust and mould, with blood on his hands from the sharp stones, Scott waited in the open air with the rest while Sir Andrew Hunter and a few others went down with lights. He had resented the sardonic cheer they gave when he appeared.

Presently, Sir Andrew also returned to the daylight. Collected as always, he walked over to Scott and took from the boy's hand the bridle of Lymond's riderless horse. 'Wake up! It's a fine June day now.'

Scott changed colour. 'Can we go?'

'When your friend has mounted,' said Sir Andrew calmly. 'What did you think you had done to him? He has a bad shoulder, that's all.' And Scott, the colour driven out of his face, looked where he nodded.

In the centre of Hunter's men, Lymond was waiting equably, handkerchief to shoulder, while they prepared to truss and mount first Turkey, then himself. He was as dirty as Scott, the stained white shirt gaping between broken points and his face white with shock and masked with stone dust. But there had been, clearly, no lethal, no maiming wound.

Sir Andrew Hunter's gaze was critical. 'The fabulous Lymond, trapped like a rat in a cellar.'

'Like cats to catmint. Everyone finds you so irresistible, Dandy: are you surprised?' Lymond had heard him.

He was unhelpful, but they put him firmly on horseback, and in a moment they were moving, with the Master riding between Hunter and Scott, and Turkey well back in the cavalcade.

The rain had gone, leaving a haze of sunshine. Hearts-ease quailed under their hoofs and honeysuckle dispensed bees and a yearning of scent; the elms passed like weeping seneschals. Behind them, dwindling into a green silence, lay the convent, denying its fractured bones to a tranquil grave; ravished and inviolate; wearing the nimbus of its injuries like a coronal.

But neither Francis Crawford nor the boy Will Scott looked back.

* * *

Twenty miles from Threave, Lymond's silence became intolerable to Hunter as well as to Scott, already pierced between the shoulder blades by Matthew's gaze. Then Sir Andrew said something at last which aroused the man between them. Lymond looked at him suddenly, and the flexible mouth curled. 'Other than apologizing for not being Asmodeus, what can I do?'

Scott's classical knowledge fell short of the reference, but he saw Hunter change from red to white. Lymond went on. 'Do you usually bolt your rats with other people's terriers?'

'Your young friend came to me of his own free will.'

'Initium sapientiae,' said Lymond absently, 'est timor Domini. You may look in vain for the sapientia, but the timor, I promise you, will be very much in evidence.'

'I don't think he'll have much to fear. There's another saying. Wha sits maist high shall find the seat maist slidder.'

There was a spark in Lymond's eyes. 'Or – Like to die mends not the kirk yard: how does that one suit you? And how is Mariotta?'

Sir Andrew answered repressively. 'Lady Culter is alive. No thanks to your monstrous efforts.'

'Sadder, but also subtler. The intellect and its cultivation, as someone once said, bring a higher form of fertility and a nobler pregnancy into human life.' Having delivered this sentence with perfect aplomb, Lymond addressed Scott. 'Cheer up. Better luck next time.'

Scott snapped without dignity, 'You would have done the same to me!' and Lymond was about to answer when his gaze went beyond Scott. Stark-free of frivolity, his voice rang out. 'My God,' said Lymond furiously. 'No! You fool.'

For behind them, the column had burst asunder.

Scott, holding the Master's reins fast with his own, saw that Matthew, the wily campaigner, had seized his moment. While the men around him, grinning, listened to the entertainment ahead, Mat had kicked his horse out from the others and riding at full gallop, disappeared through the trees.

It was easy to follow, and they did, strung out through

the wood while Turkey crashed with unnecessary violence through scrub and undergrowth, his hands freed with the practice of a dozen similar embarrassments. Unluckily the wood wasn't big. As the trunks thinned out, they caught sight of him, and Sir Andrew gave an order. A shower of goose feathers hissed through the air.

Turkey continued riding for perhaps a minute after; then he lurched forward, his bald pink head bewigged among the tangled grey mane of his horse.

Scott, his sword out and his hand tight on Lymond's reins, worked both horses around and cantered through to the others. There he dismounted, and after a moment's hesitation, untied the Master and let him get down.

Turkey Mat, pulled from his horse, was lying flat on his back under the trees, with Sir Andrew bent over him. As Scott and Lymond came up, Dandy straightened. He was rubbing a handful of grass between his palms, and they saw the skin stained green and red. 'I'm sorry, Scott,' he said. 'Whatever possessed the fool to do that?'

Scott, knowing very well, said nothing, but Lymond dropped like a shadow beside the heavy, scuffed body. 'Mat,' he said quickly.

The tough, scarred face was twitching with pain, but Turkey opened his eyes and grinned into Lymond's blue ones. The grin disappeared. 'Did yon greetin' wean stop ye?'

'No. I didn't go. Mat, you damned senseless fool!'

The prone man opened blue lips. 'It's nae loss: I'd have been sweir tae see ye leave, and me with nothing but my big wame on my mind from morning to night. Tell Johnnie I got there one step ahead of his mixtures.'

'I will.'

'And tell the boy he's a – '

'No,' said Lymond. 'It was my bloody fault.'

'Aweel. I'm not for arguing,' said Turkey, and his voice suddenly was hardly audible. 'If you get a chance at the gold, my bit's yours. And the croft. Appin's a nice place,' he said with a faint wistfulness. 'But it's damned cold in winter.'

And his eyes, moving aimlessly among the trees behind Lymond's head, suddenly halted there with a pleased look, as if a sunny beach and a flat board and a pair of celestial dice had manifested themselves among the leaves.

* * *

Violence was the odour of Threave. As the rose and the rat and the whale and the beaver yield their essence, so the glands of Threave answered love, warmth and terror with dispassionate violence.

It was two hundred years old. Under the Black Douglases, the River Dee which islanded it had cherished blood as its native weed. Under the Maxwells it gathered to itself a robust bride; it cast its suggestive shadow on John Maxwell's exchanges with England, and it let fall its mailed fist at random to flex its power the while.

When Hunter's long train, with his disreputable prisoner, swept through Causewayend, forded the Dee and clattered into the courtyard at Threave, the reception, fremescent to a degree, gave fierce delight to Scott and allowed him temporarily to forget the raw episode of Turkey Mat's end.

About Lymond's sinful head, publicly exposed for the first time, blew the rages, the jeers, the curses and the gibes which had five years' ripening to them. He sailed through them as white and insouciant as swansdown but, thought, Scott, his emotions for once must be a little irregular – have I touched some pulse? Or will this sudden exposure do it for me?

John Maxwell was away, to Scott's overwhelming relief. Until Buccleuch came for Lymond, Dandy and he would be passionate jailers. Not that Maxwell, whatever his past relations with the Master, would have risked an inch of his new security to help him; but one would savour the situation more expansively away from that remembering yellow eye.

Threave, pockmarked and exigent, hung above them. While a temporary prison was being made, Lymond, fingered impiously off his horse, was lashed to one of the four

381

drum towers of the wall. He was now very white; his fingers unobtrusively linked in the tethering ring behind held him firmly erect. Scott, talking to a fleshy man with a thick yellow eye and jovial smile, the captain of Threave, looked away as the crowd surged around the drum tower; and then was driven to look back as, mysteriously, the quality of noise changed.

They reached the wall none too soon. Lymond, out of what looked like sheer boredom, had begun answering back. Scott could hear the sound of his voice, followed by a roar; then someone else speaking, then Lymond and another roar. The response was not threatening, it was appreciative. In a minute, Scott recognized with fury, it would become laughter, and laughter like Cupid is a notorious locksmith.

For their essay in comedy the crowd had launched a mock trial. Pressing thickly about the prisoner's negligent person they clamoured accusations and he replied instantly with the kind of double and even triple entendre commonly fished for at the bottom of an alepot and commonly never caught. The captain roared with laughter; he was wildly amused and even joined in; he saw, to Scott's annoyance, no possible harm in it. The castle had emptied itself; so had the kitchens and the buttery and the brewery and the bakehouse and the stables and the byres.

The little performance lasted ten minutes, and then Lymond suddenly stopped. They slung their ripostes at him and this time he shrugged his shoulders impatiently. They shrieked and he was silent; they went on shouting and he ignored them. Perhaps he had tired of the game; perhaps under its besetting pressures, invention had failed. At any rate, there was no mistaking the hubbub now. These were threats, and these, clattering off the tower wall, were stones.

The captain forced his way through. 'None of that, now: we want the fellow alive. What's happened to you? Answer them, can't you, when you're civilly spoken to?'

Lymond said nothing, but his stare was an insult.

Or so the captain thought. 'Ho!' he said. 'Jesus, you're

particular, aren't you? Canna trouble to reply to the likes of me. Man: you're going to stand there and sing like a linnet before we shift you a step. So cheep, my laddie, give us your tongue. . . . '

Nothing.

The captain raised his voice. Scott could see he was a popular man. 'Oh, fine then. We know how to sort this kind. There's a legal punishment for refusing to plead. Alec: have we got any weights? Well, chains, then. Plenty of chains. Davie: there's two high rings. Cut him off and stick his hands on these. Now. That's a fine bit of chain, man. A shade rusty but no harm to it: we wouldna want to dirty a nice clean one. We'll put the first one around his neck.'

The Peine Forte et Dure was a perfectly valid punishment for silence: it used weights to achieve a gradual pressing to death. Scott said, 'Wait a moment. We're supposed to deliver the man alive. The courts won't exactly thank you for doing their job for them.'

The captain was engineering the laying of the first chain like a Roman with his first viaduct; he didn't even bother to look around. 'Never heed. We'll have him talking that fast he'll wear his tongue thin.'

And they would, of course. Lymond might be capriciously vain, but he wasn't foolish. Like some mountainous and ironic chain of office the cable bedecked him; he had braced himself against its weight so that there was no needless drag on his arms, spread-eagled above. His face was set like iron. Never before had Scott seen so clearly the force of his will.

The captain was bringing forward another chain, ostentatiously, to cheers. Lymond took the strain in silence, with an odd mixture of impatience and resignation, and Scott, bemused by the sickly luxury of the event, almost missed the flickering lashes as Lymond looked fleetingly up and beyond the crowd. Scott turned unobtrusively.

At an open window on the first floor of the castle stood Christian Stewart. He saw her, saw the blowing red hair and listening face and then no more, for with an uproar greater than all Threave could offer, his father and his father's train appeared. The sharp Buccleuch eyes swept over the throng; over the grotesque, taut figure by the tower over the captain, whom he jerked to his side, and over his son's red face.

'Chains. That's a new idea. Thank God ye didna have them at Crumhaugh. . . . Are you the captain? Just so. The Master of Culter may be anathema to you, as he is to the rest of us, but that doesna alter the fact that . . .'

The window was empty. Christian had gone, thought Scott, mercifully missing the name. Then he saw a billow in the crowd: a red head and two stout elbows made remorseless passage and Christian Stewart, agonized and dishevelled, arrived among them like an arrow, Sym flying at her side.

'Buccleuch? They're killing a man here. Your snivelling whelp and that ape – '

'Hey!' said the captain resentfully.

Buccleuch, with plenty on his mind, looked both annoyed and alarmed. 'Are you staying here? Well away back in: Hunters there; I've seen him. Nobody's being killed, and this is no place for lassies.' But she was off, Sym pulling her, and paid not the slightest attention.

Cleated with iron, his wrist tendons stark and his yellow head poised like a tassel, Lymond watched her like a cat, chilling even Sym's red-faced grin into blankness. Within a yard of him, the blind girl said, 'Mr. Crawford.'

The way it was said caught Scott by the throat. His father's breath hissed through his teeth; there was a surge of intrigued whispering and Lymond turned his full regard for the first time, wide-eyed, on Scott. The boy jumped forward, and put a hand on her arm.

He raised his voice. 'It's Lymond, Culter's young brother, they've got,' he said. 'Let me take you indoors. We'll look after him: don't worry.'

'I know who it is, you fool: I heard your father,' said Christian. 'Are those improbable, schoolboy chains still on him? Sym, take them off. Francis Crawford: you're another fool, playing Macarius with the lockjaw. I told you

384

sound was my stock-in-trade. I've known your voice since I was twelve. You intended, I suppose, to sink like a pressed duck into a vertical grave.' There were tears of fright in her eyes.

Sym's sturdy arms raised the last garland of cable, its manifold prints embedded below in pulped cloth. Lymond, obsessed and unheeding, opened tight lips at last and hurled words at her. 'There are two hundred people listening to you. Buccleuch, damn you: get her out of here.'

'I don't care,' snapped Christian, 'if there are two thousand. I'm not accustomed to denying my friends in public.'

'Lady Christian knows the prisoner?' The captain, no less than his audience, was fascinated by this glimpse of frailty in high places. Scott rushed to her aid. 'The Master imposed on the lady's kindness without telling her who he was.'

That touched off the explosion. Ignoring Buccleuch's hand on her elbow, Christian rounded on his son. 'I knew who he was. To know isn't necessarily to inform, as with some people.'

'But he believed you didn't know, didn't he? Hence the pantomime.'

The captain was impressed. 'Jesus, that's crafty. He wouldna pipe up in case the lassie linked his name with his voice, and let on that the two of them . . .'

'I told you!' said Scott angrily. 'He got her to shield him. You've no right to assume . . .' But his voice was lost in the deluge of ribald laughter and comment.

The row lessened as Buccleuch let out a roar, but it didn't stop. He gripped Christian's arm afresh and she shook him off. 'I don't move until he's safely out of this yard.' Her face creamy white within the masking red hair, she was quite unflinching. 'It's more than time some things were said and done in the open, instead of underground like a nation of moles. This time, I'm going to stop a man from knitting his own noose. Mr. Crawford – '

Lymond's voice, carrying its full power, cut across her words. For his own sake, clearly he must silence her. He did it in his own way, raising his voice in a mockery which insolently denied pain, or strain, or any experience of ignominy.

'There goes my epic moment again!' he said. 'Pantomime! I'd have held the Rose of Hamborough in twenty fathoms on a gravel bottom in a southeast gale, and all for nothing and less than nothing: my illusions destroyed, my deceptions dragged into the light of day and my speech miscarried and scattered to the hyenas. I do not complain. You may have your frolic. But on one thing I insist. I will not have my name coupled with a redheaded woman. Red-ribboned mares kick. Red-horned cattle gore. Rowans poison, and so do red-heads, given the chance. . . . Is that clear?'

Sym had drawn back. The blue eyes pursued him coldly. 'Well? What more? You heard her. She won't move until I'm freed.'

He had lost any good will left to him. Sym, in a nod from the captain, moved forward doubtfully to unlock Lymond's wrists. The captain cleared his throat uneasily. Inside the castle his temporary prison was ready, and there was an escort of soldiers waiting; the sooner the fellow was locked up now the better.

He glanced sideways. In spite of what they'd just heard the girl showed no signs of anger with the jackanapes. And she had high-up friends, he knew. As the shackles were unfastened, he addressed her. 'It's a fine, dry cellar, my lady, and he'll come to no harm. Forbye, we hardly laid a finger on him.'

'Ye leid, ye leid, ye filthy nurse,' said the prisoner pleasantly. 'One hand free. God. Manus loquacissimae – its pantomime all right. And the second free. Competently done. Restored without loss to the parent trunk: ulna, radius, humerus . . .'

There was a long pause. 'Not very,' said Lymond rapidly. 'Not at all, in fact.'

He had lowered his arms very slowly. Ceasing to speak, he cupped his face momentarily, grimacing; then with a gesture of half-comic resignation slid like a trout through Sym's grasp to the ground.

And the odd thing was, as Scott bending sardonically over him discovered, that he really had fainted.

* * *

They had Maxwell's permission to use the castle for one night, leaving for the capital next morning.

In the privacy of Threave, once the prisoner had been battened down under triple guard, the chief actors expended their nervous excitement on each other. Christian, frustrated in her efforts to visit Lymond and irritated by Buccleuch's wholesale damning of that gentleman's anonymous ways, finally lost her temper completely and went off to bed. Scott fared little better.

The question was one of naming his former colleagues. Accused of standing with one foot in each camp; of leaving the countryside at the mercy of leaderless cutthroats, of lack of responsibility and of owning a head full of pulp and pips like a Spanish orange, Scott replied in kind without a trace of exhaustion, and he and his father were still going at the subject hammer and tongs long after Hunter had collected his men and departed. Finally Buccleuch roared. 'It's a pity, since you're so keen on them, ye didn't stay with your precious friends!'

Will, already on his feet, snatched up his cloak. 'All right; I will!'

'Ye kale-heided coddroch! They'll cut ye in triangles if ye show your neb there after what you've done!'

'Then I'll go somewhere else!'

'You'll go somewhere else all right,' snarled Buccleuch, and rang the handbell as though he were twisting a cockerel's neck. 'You'll spend the night where you can't do any harm and where you'll have every chance of comparing your dear old friends with your new ones – Fetch the captain.'

Scott jumped to his feet, but Buccleuch's heavy hand was on his sword arm. When the captain came, Wat alarmed him by continuing to shout. 'Here's another prisoner for you. I want him under lock and key for a night to clear the mud off his brain.'

The captain was anxious to please, but unprepared. 'I havena a fast room, Sir Wat. The dungeon's blocked, and there's only the cellar . . .'

'That's what I mean,' said Buccleuch vindictively. 'Put him in the cellar.'

The captain hesitated. 'But the Master of Culter's in the cellar.'

'I know that, you fool!' said Buccleuch. 'Put him with Lymond for a night, and let's see if he's hare, hound or rabbit, the fool.'

Will Scott fought every plank of the way to the kitchen; he fought while they unbolted the heavy trap door in the floor, and he bit and kicked while they shoved him through it and halfway down the wooden steps which led to the cellar. Then the trap thudded shut above his head, the bolts clattered, and he was left alone with initium sapientiae and the Master of Culter.

* * *

There is nothing very jolly about being locked in a cellar with a man whom, in every possible sense, you have just stabbed in the back. As Will Scott crashed into the stair rail and heard the trap thud above him, his very thews melted with apprehension.

The cellar had been used as a storeroom. Opposite, two barred windows near the ceiling imprisoned the night sky. There was a well in the shadows on his right, and a quantity of sacks, barrels and boxes. On two of these Lymond lay stretched at ease, a solitary candle at his side.

Within the light, shapes and colours were sudden and strong: the butter-yellow head, impeccably neat, with a bag of meal under it; the fresh Hessian bandaging; the silver spark of burst points and the blue of the light cloth at shoulder and raised knee; at neck and cuff, the half inch of cambric glinting white. All that was unsightly had been removed from Lymond's appearance.

Looking for traces of the day's humiliations or the languor of bodily weakness, Scott found neither. With the face of a Della Robbia angel, Lymond spoke. 'In a day of gimcrack cannibalism and snivelling atrocities, we have now touched rock bottom. God send,' pursued the voice as Scott, descending, made his way to a trestle by the well, 'God send that somebody else is about to flay the gristle from your inestimable backbone.'

Scott sat down. He had already had enough of physical violence. The other kind hung in the air, a raw miasma, sapping his robust and righteous anger. He said curtly, 'You challenged me yourself.'

'To attack me. Not to engineer a cheap death for Turkey Mat.'

'It was his own fault. Father would have looked after him.'

'Father would have had his work cut out, after your Jove-like pyrotechnic at the convent. Don't fancy yourself the neo-Christ of Branxholm, by the way. You weren't saving anybody. I'm used to being taken for a cross between Gilles de Rais and a sort of international exchange in young mammals, but I draw the line somewhere.'

All the tormented emotion, the anger and fear and vexed and mauled spirit of the unfortunate Scott sprang affronted from his lips.

'I can guess the kind of names you'd like to call me,' he said with cold fury. 'I betrayed you to Andrew Hunter; I tricked you into hiding in the convent; I used a knife on you – badly; my God, how ineptly – but at least I made you wince in some sort, once, however briefly. When my father delivers you to the law, I'll have paid the debts of the cheated dead and the warped living and the wrecked lives of four women. . . . Can you deny it? Am I not right?'

'Right?' said Lymond. 'You pathetic, maladroit nincompoop, you're never right; but this time you can squat in your misconceptions like duck's meat in a ditch, and let them choke you.'

Scott, viciously, was on his feet. 'Go on. Explain my own motives to me. Or if you won't explain yourself, shall I try? Someone once said you hated women, and you do, don't you? You despise everyone – even yourself – but above all you hold women cheap . . .'

He got no further. 'You bloody, insalubrious little fool,' said Lymond, and uncoiled like a whip, forcing Scott to retreat. 'I'm not calling you names, my dear: I'm telling you facts. Today you murdered a friend of mine. You treat that very lightly. I hope his tolerance and his honesty and his infirmities break their way into your imagination and sphacelate in your insufferable vanity. That and another thing. To hell with your piddling vendetta: the bits you were bragging about never mattered, and the things that do matter you know nothing about. But what the *hell*,' said Lymond with fury, 'what the *hell* do you mean by subjecting that girl to a public ordeal?'

Scott was stunned. 'It was you who – ' but Lymond swept on. 'If I could keep my mouth shut, surely you could take the trifling trouble to keep her out of the courtyard? You don't care whom you sacrifice, do you, as long as you imagine it will damage me?'

'I didn't deceive her!'

'Do you think I did her any harm!' exclaimed the Master. 'But for your meddling she was perfectly secure!'

'I remember,' said Scott. 'You don't like red hair.'

The untamed face stared into his. 'She was one of your four women, was she? Then it certainly seems that she lost security, reputation and peace of mind through one of us today. Who else?'

'The Countess of Lennox.'

'Lady Margaret was responsible for the fiasco at Heriot which nearly cost your father his life. Who else?'

'Your brother's wife.'

'You know the truth of that as well as I do.'

'Do I?' said Scott. 'I was stinking drunk on the floor of your room at the time, as I remember.'

'All right. I leave you to work out why, having seduced my sister-in-law and slaughtered my nephew, I should keep coy silence while you shuffle downstairs at three in the morning with that bantling-brained romantic done up in an oatsack?'

For one dumb moment, Scott sympathized with the man who disgorged a sponge into water and found his throat cut. He recovered. 'Because you wanted rid of her, I expect. As with your young sister.'

'As with my young sister,' agreed Lymond. Like the sun in eclipse, the candle at his back rimmed his unregenerate head; he held himself lightly and easily, the poised Roc pitying the elephant. 'I should have warned you. I can wrestle with one arm as well as with two.'

The light in Scott's pale eyes was contemptuous. 'It won't be necessary. I know enough about you. I don't want to know any more.'

Lymond said delicately, 'What are you afraid of?'

'Me? Nothing!' exclaimed Scott. 'If you want to fight, I'll fight.'

'But not with ideas? You're beating drums and brass kettles, Scott. Thick skin and prejudice won't keep the dragons away.'

'I'm tired of a landscape with dragons,' said Scott violently.

'What, then? Retreat underground into hebetude: retreat under water like a swallow: retreat into a shell like a mollusc: retreat into the firmament like some erroneous dew. . . .'

'I don't retreat.'

'You don't progress much, either.'

'I scotch the dragons.'

'And how,' said Lymond precisely, 'do you know a dragon when you see it?'

Despite every endeavour, Scott was trembling. He said, 'Because I'm a human being, not a toy, a familiar, a piece of unconsecrated wax to malign your enemies with. I know you. I didn't mean Turkey to die. I wouldn't intentionally have hurt the girl, but it's done, and if it had to be done again it would be worth it. You know all about the law of talion: you've hunted Harvey, poor devil, like a thing from beyond the grave. You're a master – my God, don't I know it – of the art of apposite punishment. I made damned sure you'd get a taste of both before you got out of my reach. You won't get over the Border to kill Harvey now.'

'Teaching you to speechify is another thing I should have my throat cut for,' said Lymond. 'My appointment is broken; I may be said vaguely to be aware of that. Your intentions were majestic. To teach me to sing re, my fa, sol, and when I fail, to bob me on the noll. Only the field is now littered with other bobbed and blameless nolls and I am left, as it happens, singing ut to Johannes, which should delight you indeed. Why are you here?'

There was a pause. Scott said nothing, and the blue eyes suddenly narrowed. 'Is this, by any chance, a modest silence? Good God!' Lymond sat down. 'Have you been protecting your former colleagues?'

'I had no quarrel with them.'

Continuing to stare at him, the Master gave a hoot of derisive laughter and sat back, nursing his injured arm. 'My only success, and I was too damned preoccupied to watch it coming to the boil. Who locked you up here? Oh, your father, of course.'

And, stretching like a cat, Lymond lay down. Mysteriously, the chill of animal danger had gone; mysteriously, there was an unwilling amusement about his mouth. 'I have licked you like the cow Audhumbla from the salt of your atrocious upbringing, and am watching the outcome with a fearful joy. . . . Your father, as you no doubt realize, will have to argue himself into fits to get you accepted at Court again: you should tell him that the dispatches which you copied for me so resentfully in your own inimitable hand will do precisely that for you, mentioned in the right quarters. They are all in Arran's possession. They got there, by the way, through a very wily gentleman called Patey Liddell, who should not be involved. He would in any case be deaf to questions – you've no idea how deaf.'

There was a startled silence. Scott said, 'Is that true?' And, quickly: 'It's a trick of some sort.'

'It's blackmail. I want something in return.'

'What?'

'Undo some of the feckless damage you did today,' said

Lymond, and held his eyes. 'Pull the girl clear. Drive it home to every gossiping fool that whatever Christian says, she didn't know what she was doing when she gave me refuge. Conjure up Shamanism and the Black Mass if you like. Anything. But get it about that she was not responsible for her actions. Understand?'

'I should do it in any case. It won't help you,' said Scott.

'Nothing ever does. That's why I help myself so frequently.'

There was another pause. 'Those letters,' said the boy. 'Much good they'll do me when they find out we've been selling copies to England as well. In my writing.'

'In that case it's lucky for you that we haven't.'

'Haven't traded with England? For God's sake, I copied them myself!'

'And for God's sake, I tore them up.'

'What!' Scott was halfway across to the other trestle when Lymond snapped at him. 'Go back and lie down. I don't want your coddled features singing Kassidas over me. What the hell does it matter? You've done your job.'

Scott walked back. He sat on the edge of the boards and repeated: 'You tore them up. If you tore them up, why did we trouble to capture them?'

'For sixty avid reasons. Mercenaries are exceedingly mercenary, you know. And suspicious. Also, curiosity on my part.'

'But you tore them up. Why?'

'Because I'm on your side, you damned fool,' said Lymond.

The cellar was very quiet. The Master's face, closed, offered nothing to Scott's strained scrutiny. After a moment the boy collected his own limbs and stretched back slowly on the bed. 'That would be your story in Edinburgh, of course,' he said eventually. 'Can you prove it?'

There was a brief pause. 'From here?' asked Lymond sardonically. 'No, Mr. Scott. I have no proof now, nor am I likely to have.'

Out of the dark and disastrous muddle, a fragment of

pattern asserted itself. Scott swallowed. 'Harvey? Harvey had something to do with it?'

'I rather think so. Perhaps not. In any case, it's too late now, isn't it? Look at the stars.' Lymond's eyes were on the high windows. 'I offered them to you once before, on a celebrated occasion. Forth quenching go the starris, one by one; and now is left but Lucifer alone . . . And what can Lucifer do, with a bolt and a bar and over a hundred horseless miles between him and his illusions? – It's a sad world, and the candle is going; so unless like Al-Mokanna you can cause moons to issue from our well, we are destined to sorry together in the dark. Good night. You're a damned nuisance and a public danger, but so is your father. It's a thrawnness in the vitals of the body politic which will either kill it or save it yet.'

The voice was resigned, but not unfriendly. The light from the candle, a weak conspirator, searched the face of Scott's celebrated prisoner, touching for a moment on its secretive ironies; and then went out.

* * *

Will Scott had been right in thinking that the Master of Maxwell would move not an inch to help a man of the notoriety of Lymond. Maxwell and his wife were at one of their lodges, hunting, when Hunter's message arrived. Maxwell sent a congratulatory reply making Sir Andrew and Buccleuch free of his castle and its prisons until the following morning, and continued to hunt. He did, however, dispatch his wife home, as was fitting, to see that his guests, voluntary and involuntary, were comfortably housed.

At eleven o'clock that night, Agnes Herries stalked into the hall at Threave, making a dozing Buccleuch jump like a rabbit over a somnolent game of prime; and demanded to know whether he was out of his senses, locking up his son with a desperate man like the Master.

As was his due to his hostess, he explained his reasons, succinctly. She questioned them. He explained, more fully. She contradicted him. At midnight Buccleuch, grousing, unbolted the trap door in the light of the torch held by Agnes Herries and called down. 'Will! Are ye all right?'

'Of course!' replied his son's voice, rudely.

'Then ye might as well come up,' said Sir Wat ungraciously, and abandoning the trap to Lady Herries, stumped off without waiting for the sight of his heir.

Will Scott crossed the cellar stiffly. Lymond's buried head did not stir. For a moment the boy stopped, looking down at him; then he turned and ran quickly up the wooden staircase.

At the top, the trap door was held open by Agnes Herries. Beyond her, he saw that three men still stood guard in the kitchen and passage, but that the guard had changed, and none of them was a Scott. He hesitated.

'Gracious!' said Lady Herries. 'After all the trouble I've taken to get you out, can you not walk a little quicker than that? I want to go to bed.' Her eyes under the heavy brows met his with a vigorous impatience, and as the young man set foot on the kitchen floor she dropped the trap with a thud that shook the pans on their shelves, and the bolts rattled. She straightened. 'Well?'

'All right,' said Scott, making up his mind, rather to his own surprise. 'I'm half asleep, that's all. I'm sorry. Lead on. It was very good of you to . . .'

And in ten minutes he was in bed, although it was a long time before he fell asleep.

*　*　*

Long before he woke, Christian Stewart left the castle with her retinue, riding as fast as Sym would allow her. It had taken her a good part of the night to accept the fact that she must leave; and Buccleuch, who had no liking for playing the jailer or the spy, was relieved to see her go.

At six o'clock, a fist crashed on Scott's door, and a roar summoned him to fling on a robe and meet his father in the hall. He did so, and found a room full of cowed servitors, his hostess in a state of fluent resignation, and his father in a temper.

'Ho!' said Buccleuch, when his son appeared. 'Ho! So it's come to it that ye canny even snib a bolt behind ye, now. Or didn't ye mean to snib it?'

With his new arts, Will Scott kept surmise and recollection out of his face. 'What bolt?'

'What bolt!' snarled Sir Wat. 'The wee snib on the back yett to the kennels. The trap door in the kitchen, ye gomerel. They found it this morning, as free as Hosea's wife, and yon three stookies littered in the passages with their heads dunted.'

Scott's mouth opened. 'Then Lymond's gone?'

His sire was sarcastic. 'Well, he didna pop out of the hole, bash three fellows on the head and pop back in again, just for the devil of it. Of course he's gone! There's half Threave out hunting him, but deil knows the start he's got. And it's your fault, ye damned fool!'

This was a surprise. Scott said indignantly, 'How?'

Agnes Herries said severely, 'I told you to bolt that trap properly. How you could be so careless!'

Scott stared at her. 'You told me . . . ?'

She stared back. 'Sleepy you may have been, but not too sleepy to forget that, I hope. Even my three men remember it quite distinctly. So if the trap wasn't properly fastened, you have only yourself to blame.'

It was no use protesting. Having turned the other cheek, Will Scott submitted, with as much tranquillity as he could muster, to having it slapped. He mounted with his father and spent the rest of the daylight hours scouring the countryside for the escaped man, without any success whatsoever.

* * *

At Midculter, Sybilla occupied herself that Friday and Saturday in turning out cupboards and making long and superfluous lists of her gold plate. Mariotta, who had been straying restlessly from room to room ever since Janet

Buccleuch left, burst into ill-considered speech. 'How can you sit there and do that?'

They had heard nothing since the news that Lymond was to be trapped: nothing of Will; nothing of Hunter; nothing of Sir Wat. Listening to Mariotta's hand-wringing tirade Sybilla, who was rather pale, sat back on her heels and reached a decision. 'Look,' she said incisively. 'I try not to interfere, but we may as well be honest with one another. Whom are you afraid for? You've cast off Richard, and you find my other son detestable.'

Mariotta said indistinguishably, 'I don't want any harm to come to him.'

'Who?' said the Dowager sharply. 'Incidentally, if it interests you, my guess is that Lymond hardly knows you exist.'

'I meant Richard,' said the girl.

'I see. Well, Richard for all his flummery, worships his wife. Unhappily, neither of you knows what the other is dreaming about half the time.'

She said defensively, 'He's not easy to understand.'

'And yet you rather expected Richard to read your mind, didn't you? You thought he pictured you encysted forever with pots and pans – A woman is a worthy thing; they do the wash and do the wring. And so on. Whereas – '

'Of course I did. No other thought crossed his mind.'

'Heaven forbid,' said the Dowager crossly, 'that I should tattle over other folks' errors like an unemployed midwife; but look. Wat Scott is like that. With Wat it's sew Tibet, knit Annot and spin Margerie and no nonsense. He'd think it a downright insult to his manhood to clatter of his affairs in the house.'

Mariotta sat down, prepared to argue in spite of herself. 'But Janet seems to me to know everything that's going on.'

'Exactly. What's more, in her wrangling way, she makes sure that Wat knows her opinion on everything that matters. In other words, she uses her own methods of informing herself on everything Wat's interested in, and half the time he's acting exactly as Janet is making him act.

397

'You want Richard to be interested in the minutiae of your day: it works both ways. Do you ever wonder what Richard is doing with these building experiments of his? Did you ever get him to tell you of the time he carried off all the prizes at Kilwinning? Did you know, for example, that he's probably the best swordsman in the country, and that he sometimes teaches, for Arran, when some of the nobler scions turn out to need a little polish?'

'If you mean,' said Mariotta, red-faced, 'that I should copy Janet, I hardly think – '

'I don't mean anything of the sort. I'm only doing a little dissecting work on adjacent marriages; you can draw your own conclusions. Look at the Maxwells, for instance.'

'Agnes?'

'If you like. While thinking she was choosing, she was being chosen. While electing this man as hero of one of her appalling romances, she was marrying a hardheaded intelligent person who will be clever enough – and kind enough – to preserve the fantasy, or at least let her down pretty lightly.'

'And Richard?'

The Dowager put a wandering hand to her white hair. 'Richard. I can't tell you the path to take there. You'll have to find it for yourself. But I can tell you two things about him. One is that the most serious thing in his life is his country. The other is this. The only thing that could kill Richard is a lack of stability.'

Mariotta's face darkened. 'You mean inconstancy.'

'I mean,' said Sybilla gently, 'the folly of allowing oneself to be attracted always by superficial glitter. I mean a craving for change and excitement – even the nasty excitement of waiting to be found out about those jewels.'

Mariotta was silent. Then, unexpectedly, a tear appeared and made its way down one cheek. 'But,' said Mariotta miserably, 'how can I change now?'

Sybilla rose and with an odd compound of a sigh and a smile, sat down in her own carved chair. 'Time will do it for you, my infant, and much too quickly. Your tragedy was that the man you became involved with was the very person who created the flaw in Richard's maturing. And if that was anyone's fault, it was probably mine. . . . How prosy we are; drunk with the dear indulgences of synthesis and self-pity and criticizing other people's love affairs. Do you feel better or worse?'

'Better,' said Mariotta; and crossing to sit on the arm of the Dowager's chair, bent to kiss one flawless cheek.

Tom Erskine was with them when, much later, Christian arrived from Threave. She was aching and dirty, with more than weariness in her eyes. Sybilla, watching the blind face, seated her quickly, and the girl wasted no time. Turning the fine eyes on the Dowager, she said simply, 'They have Francis.'

The reaction was curious. 'Who?' demanded Erskine. And '*Who?*' said Sybilla in a tone so different that the blind girl gave a quick, rueful smile. Sybilla possessed herself of one of Christian's hands. 'So,' she said. 'We are coming into the open. Tell us.' And she did so.

At the end, the Dowager spoke. 'Richard knows nothing of this? Good. Tom – you're not to tell him, either. The longer we can keep them apart . . . I wonder . . .'

'Stop wondering,' said the girl. 'It's my turn now.'

'Go on,' said Sybilla gently.

'I made a mess of things at Threave,' said Christian bluntly. 'There was some pretty dangerous horseplay going on, and by the time it was stopped they knew I wasn't quite – disinterested. After that I was guarded; Sym as well. But the point is this. He had great hopes, apparently, of an encounter with a man called Samuel Harvey: he was on his way to meet him at Wark when he was taken – I got that much out of Buccleuch's idiot son. Well, he's missed that meeting now. But maybe another could be arranged – for us. At any rate, George Douglas is mixed up in the business somehow, and I'm going to see him. If persuasion or threats can do anything, I'm going to make him help.'

'Help? Help who?' demanded Tom Erskine, bemused.

There was a moment's silence. 'My younger son,' said Sybilla quietly. 'We are a tenacious family, and you have a very kindhearted fiancée. Helping Lymond has been rather a concern of ours – am I right, Christian? – for some months now.'

Christian opened her hands in mock despair. 'How did you guess?'

'Nobody ever,' said the Dowager sorrowfully, 'credits me with normal thought processes. When a mysterious man creates a royal scandal on the banks of the Lake of Menteith with the keenest ears in Scotland strolling utterly oblivious – by her own account – in the locality, I begin to wonder. I also wonder when a delicately reared child sends a court into fits with a riddle which I invented myself. And when Andrew Hunter and Richard both mention a name I have heard you repeat, and the name is connected with Lymond . . .'

'And then you probably noticed the gypsy.'

'I noticed, certainly, that the gypsies who put in such a timely appearance before I lost all my silver were the same ones you were so anxious to speak to in Stirling – yes.'

'Was that why you kept Johnnie Bullo beside you?'

'To begin with. I'm disappointed in Johnnie,' said the Dowager with some severity. She opened a workbag, took out her embroidery, and put the horn-rimmed spectacles on her nose. 'Johnnie turned out to be rather much of an individualist. It would serve him right if someone taught him a lesson.'

'Bullo . . . ?' said Mariotta. 'But that's the man who . . . I don't understand,' she said despairingly.

'We're congratulating each other on how clever we've been,' said Sybilla. 'Quite without reason. For there is the dear man in prison at Threave, and here we are, doing very little about it.'

'*You've been helping Lymond?*' said Mariotta, and stood up.

Sybilla looked up. She put down her needle, drew off her spectacles and gave Mariotta all her attention. 'I'm sorry, my dear,' she said. 'Sit down. We're rushing a little ahead of you in our worries, that's all. You see, my son Lymond is not quite the drunken renegade of the legend.'

'He didn't entice me to Crawfordmuir?' said Mariotta. 'He didn't kill my baby? Insult me? Try to burn you out? Corrupt Will – kill Richard – take advantage of Christian? A moment ago you yourself called him superficial and glittering.'

Gently, the Dowager replied. 'I told you what attracted you to him. I didn't say there was no more to discover. He's caused no intentional harm to me or to you: you can't, I think, seriously accuse him of destroying your child; and I think he had his reasons for what happened afterward. He has a great deal, naturally, still to account for, but – '

'Don't let's be misled,' said Tom Erskine suddenly. 'You want to think the best of him, of course. But his aim all along has been to obliterate Richard. I can't presume to tell anyone to choose between their own children, but it seems to me that the danger to other people is something to take into account. Christian, I didn't know you even met this fellow.'

For a moment, the girl was silent. Then she said, 'I met him in September, but it would hardly have been fair to ask you, or anyone else, Tom, to share that particular secret.'

Erskine said with a sudden anger, 'But you might have been killed!'

'Perhaps,' she said. 'But I don't think so. In any case, I'm safe now, amn't I? And the truth can do none of us any harm. Sybilla, I'm calling at Boghall, and then going straight on to Dalkeith. I'll let you know what happens. Tom . . .'

He said heavily, 'You're determined to go on with your championship of this – this – '

'Outlaw? I want to finish what I've started, Tom. Is that a bad thing? If I'm right, then I'll have prevented an injustice. If I'm wrong, then the popular point of view – and yours – is vindicated. In any case, you are the man I

401

am contracted to marry. You don't suppose I have forgotten that?'

He had no words to meet that kind of attack.

Afterward, when Christian had gone, he came back and sat for a long time, sunk in thought, before the Dowager's parlour fire. Eventually he looked up, drawing Sybilla's kindly eye. 'She isn't the sort of person to be easily deluded.'

'No.'

'Or stupidly bedazzled.'

'No.'

'And yet, beyond rhyme and reason . . . why?' demanded Tom of the air.

'Because she thinks one of her lame ducks is about to turn into a swan,' said Sybilla. Her lenses flashed in the glare like scarlet lamps.

Searching, questioning, his eyes moved from Sybilla to her daughter-in-law. 'The man's a saint?'

'No,' said Sybilla. 'Not a saint. An artist in the vivesection of the soul. But only because he has known the knife now for five years.'

'It's damned nice of him,' said Erskine, 'to make sure we all suffer too.'

'I told you he wasn't a saint,' said the Dowager. 'And there's a limit to everyone's endurance. I only hope – ' Unexpectedly, she halted.

'What?' said Mariotta.

'That if he's going to break under it, he doesn't break too soon. He's probably the only person in the world now who can restore Richard to any sort of terms with his own future. If not indeed,' said Sybilla, taking off her spectacles, 'the only person who can send him back to you.'

* * *

On Sunday, the third of June, the day after this discussion, Francis Crawford of Lymond was sitting on the crumbling wall of a sheep fank on the Scottish side of the River Tweed, throwing pebbles idly into the reaming waters.

It was a restful, a delicious scene. Plump clouds like

amoretti hung in a blue sky; shining rooks cawed from among shining leaves and an otter with a half-eaten fish shivered the bog orchis with his shoulder as he passed. Lymond watched him go, and tossed another pebble into the water.

Across the river, the green edge of England lurched upward into an uneven ridge and plunged behind into the hollow where lay the village of Wark. On top of the ridge, toe to toe with its own deliquescent outline, reared the English Border fortress of Wark, on whose tower walk stood Gideon Somerville, both hands shading his eyes.

'There, sir,' said the soldier beside him.

'I see.' Gideon scrutinized the seated figure, far across the water. The bent head was unmistakable. 'He hasn't tried to cross the river?' There was a ford of sorts at that point.

'No, sir. But the river's a bit high.'

'I see that. All right. Send a boat across for him and bring him to my room.'

Downstairs, waiting at his desk, it seemed to Gideon a long time before the door opened. Someone said, 'The Master of Culter, sir,' and shut it again, and Gideon looked up.

It was the familiar, elegant presence, but quieter, less dynamic than he remembered. Lymond came only a few paces into the room; not far enough to catch the dying light from the windows, and Gideon saw only the pale gleam of his head, with indistinguishable, two-dimensional features, as if face and hands had blown like flock to their appointed places in the shadows. Lymond's voice was pleasant, unchanged. 'Armageddon,' he said.

'Hardly,' answered Gideon dryly. 'You got my message?'

'Admirably delivered. Yes. Mr. Harvey came?'

'And went. We waited for you all day yesterday.'

'Then,' said Lymond dispassionately, 'I'm too late.'

Gideon was annoyed. He said brusquely, 'Mr. Harvey was in charge of a convoy urgently wanted at Haddington. I could hardly keep him indefinitely to suit your convenience. Our arrangement was quite clear.'

'I know. My fault. I was detained,' said Lymond. 'The little squirrel, full of business. It was good of you to make the appointment at all.'

'I set some store by keeping my word. The matter was not, it seems, of very great moment to you after all.'

There was a pause. Then Lymond, rather helplessly, began to laugh. 'Strike on, strike on, Glasgèrion. Prophète de malheur, babillarde . . .' And as once before, was betrayed by the uncertain, wanton luxuriance of voice. 'You're drunk,' said Gideon, disgusted to the soul, and slammed back his chair.

'*Drunk?*' The voice was alight with self-mockery. 'O my God . . . Of Paradise ne can I not speak properly, for I am not there . . . Damnably, damnably sober, Mr. Somerville,' said the Master unsteadily.

Gideon crossed the room in three steps. Faultlessly erect, his clothing a bloody pulp, his eyes brilliant, Lymond spoke quietly. '—But sicker than Rudel. Don't be alarmed. It's merely the effects of insufficient transport over damnable country in inclement weather. I was locked up in Threave until yesterday morning.'

Gideon said incredulously. 'You came here on foot?'

'Most of the way. Running like a dog. And aquatics, too: hence the mess. I was sorry to give your boatman the trouble of fetching me, but nothing short of Buccleuch's bloodhounds would make me swim any more.'

'I'm damned sorry.' Gideon was uncomfortably shocked.

'It might have been worse. But it would be a courtesy,' said Lymond with care, 'if I could make myself presentable before we talk.'

In ten minutes of Gideon at his most practical, the prisoner of Threave found himself, unresisting, in bed at Wark.

* * *

At his own request, Lymond came back to the study at nightfall, clean, bandaged, freshly dressed and anointed, as he pointed out, with delicate things of sweet smell. He seemed, if not exactly full of energy, at least perfectly composed.

'I warned you about Scott,' said Gideon, who had opened by demanding an explanation of the Master's delay.

'It was my own fault for being so intent on the unfortunate Harvey. As to that –'

'You say,' said Gideon, interrupting calmly, 'that you have disbanded your men?'

'Cryand with many a piteous peep – by God, they hated it. Yes.'

'And are now therefore entirely at my disposal?'

'The Scot, the Frencheman, the Pope and heresie, overcommed by Trothe have had a fall. Again yes.'

'I wish to God,' said Gideon with mild exasperation, 'that you'd talk – just once – in prose like other people.'

'All right,' said Lymond, and quoted with malice. 'And as for Scottishe men and Englishe men be not enemyes by nature but by custome; not by our good wyll, but by theyre own follye: whiche shoulde take more honour in being coupled to Englande than we shulde take profite in being joyned to Scotlande . . . One God, one faythe, one compasse of the see, one lande and countrie, one tungue in speakynge, one maner and trade in lyvynge, lyke courage and stomake in war, lyke quicknesse of witte to learning, hath made Englande and Scotlande bothe one.'

'Do you believe that?' asked Gideon.

The blue eyes were level. 'What do you want to find out? Whether I profess the "damnable opinions of the great heretic Luther"?'

'You quoted Ascham. I wondered why.'

'I also quote the late King James the Fifth. I echo like a mynah, that's why. Sticking to birds: if I were a wren, I shouldn't want a crocodile's egg in my nest.'

'Even to protect you from other crocodiles?'

'On the contrary. We are remarkably pest-free in our part of the world. It's England, I think, that needs this alliance.'

'Well, of course,' said Gideon impatiently. 'Look at the

mess at Boulogne. Between the Protector and the Emperor and the King of France, Europe's become a crocodile's convention. I don't want to become part of the Holy Roman Empire, and it wouldn't do Scotland any good either. You're a threat to three million people out of all proportion to your size. You can't expect us to leave you alone, to watch you siphon up the dregs of Europe and inject them into our backside. Your Government agreed to this miserable marriage, and then broke its word. It announces that it can't abide anti-Papists and it can't let down its dear old ally France. But your man Panter has been in Paris all the same, soliciting for a separate peace on behalf of Scotland with the Emperor.'

'Chess,' remarked Lymond. He spoke on equal terms, concisely, with little trace of the dilettante manner. 'And France has been to London soliciting for a separate peace with England. All moves in the game. And sometimes the feint turns into genuine play; sometimes not. France may sell us for Boulogne: I don't think so, but she may. Or she might simply use us as a temporary blind for her real attack. The Lutherans among us think so, and so does the noble faction in need of English money. Religion and cupidity are on your side.

'Against that, you haven't seen what your late king managed in the way of practical persuasion, with Somerset following. You haven't seen abbeys brought to the ground, villages annihilated by the hundred, a nobility decimated, a country brought to poverty which thirty years ago was graced above any other in Europe with the arts of living. That has bred hate, and hate is a factor like any other.'

'If hate can be learned, it can be forgotten,' Gideon said. 'I know all about chess: I would rather have an honest emotion – even hatred. The Emperor presses us to help his Flemish subjects recover the money you owe them, since the poorer you are, the more easily you will fall to us, and the worse off the French will be. Nothing emotional about that. Or about the Scots Commissioners trying to reopen negotiations for the royal marriage at every threat of danger, while the Queen Dowager perfects her plans to bring the French in and keeps Arran quiet with a promise to marry the Queen to his son.'

He sat forward in his chair.

'What if she succeeds? Where's your inde-independence then? You'll be a province of France, under an implacably Catholic King, with French in your key positions and your fortresses. I know all about Henry's claim to be King of Scotland. I know all about the broken promises on both sides – the reprisals, the sinkings, the Border raids and the rest of it. But will you be any better off under the French? Because you will be under the French. Mary of Guise will marry that child to the King of France if she possibly can. What has France ever done for Scotland? Look at Flodden.'

'Look at Haddington,' said Lymond. 'Now you are conjuring up crocodiles. France has too many commitments to spare enough troops to rule Scotland. Good lord, if England can't do it, then France isn't likely to. That leaves Scotland under a regent in the Queen's absence – and if I were the Scottish Government, the Queen would become absent, damned quickly, from now on.

'Where are they worse off than they are now? And in the future, they can expect the Queen's children to rule France and Scotland between them. Another royal line will put in an appearance and the two countries will probably fall apart again with little harm done. That's French diplomacy.

'The alternative is English force: reprisals and raids and counterraids and broken promises, as you say. Of course you must try to secure this alliance. You might have achieved it in the last reign but for Henry. It was he who fostered the cult of the honest emotion, and you're still paying for the mistake.'

He paused, his hand straying unconsciously to his bandaged shoulder. 'Chess can be just about as brutalizing; I grant you that. You know about the Border raids last year, back and forth: you burn me and I'll dismember you. The one the Scots made in March, for instance – Lord Wharton made two reports on it, one for the Protector, and one with all the damage exaggerated to be passed to the King of France. The purpose was to justify your invasion in September. Were you at the battle of Pinkie?'

'No.'

'I was. It was as precise an exhibition of honest emotion as you're likely to see. It won't be the last. I told you religion was on your side, and that's the bloodiest emotion I know. If this develops into a religious war, then God help us.'

Gideon, intensely interested, noticed that his own affairs had no place in Lymond's mind, and that he had dropped entirely most of his irritating mannerisms. The Englishman scratched his chin with his clasped thumbs. 'What's your solution? Why not let the children marry?'

Lymond said slowly, 'I haven't got a solution. But I'll give you a few objections, if you like. The Queen's five and the King's nine. If Mary's brought up in London, as Somerset is stipulating, she'll either lose or be accused of losing interest in Scotland long before she gets to marrying age. And that small excuse is enough to touch off a religious and baronial war up here that might make the Protector's efforts look silly. It only needs some fool to crown himself, and the whole process of expostulation and invasion begins again.'

'But,' said Gideon, 'if she goes to France, won't the same thing happen?'

'Not quite. There'd be less religious friction. And Mary of Guise would have the power and the standing to keep the throne warm for a little time, at least.'

Gideon said thoughtfully, 'The alternative, I suppose, is to let you keep the Queen peacefully until she's of marriageable age. And then – '

'– To arrange a marriage with Edward as a good conduct prize on both sides. That's the unemotional solution. France would hate it; so would the Douglases. Would Somerset agree to such a wait?'

Their eyes met.

Gideon shook his head slowly and wryly. 'It isn't any use getting intelligent about it. His Grace's own position is damned shaky. He needs action, and success, right away. There's always the Princess Mary, you see. He's bound to try and get hold of your Queen.'

'In fact, stalemate.'

Gideon studied him, over the rime of his hands. 'Why aren't you at Edinburgh with your people?'

'They threw me out,' said Lymond calmly.

'Why?'

'Youth, women and bad company. Nothing sentimental about that either. Or rather, not women. One woman.'

Gideon said suddenly, 'Could I make a guess? Someone connected with Samuel Harvey and the Princess Mary's household? Someone like Margaret Lennox?'

Lymond replied, 'Very like,' and didn't add to it.

After a moment, Gideon probed. 'You wouldn't care to . . . ?'

'No.'

Somerville got up. Looking at his feet, he walked to the door and back again, aware that the barrier of nationality had fallen between them, and the shutters closed again. He resumed his seat behind the desk. 'About Harvey.'

Lymond crossed his legs. 'You're under no obligation in that respect. Similarly, I am in your power of disposal, even though the meeting was never held. That was the arrangement.'

'I have given this some thought,' said Gideon, rolling his pen between pink, clean fingers. 'The convoy which passed through here to Haddington will be returning in a week or two's time. It might be possible for a second interview with Mr. Harvey to be arranged. Unfortunately – '

'I knew it,' said Lymond with equanimity. 'The sliding joy, the gladness short; the feigned love, the false comfort. Unfortunately – '

'Unfortunately,' pursued Somerville, laying the pen down. 'I've got to go and meet Lord Grey on his return at Berwick. I could guarantee you a certain degree of safety here under my presence, but without me I'm afraid you would end fairly quickly at Carlisle.'

'And so it might be quicker to take me to Carlisle in the first place.'

'What!' said Gideon dryly. 'Put such a singer in the soup? No. I hope to be back before Harvey returns. Until then, I am taking you to Flaw Valleys.'

There was a pause. 'To your house? I see. But will your wife, almighty Mohammet, whose laws tenderly I have to fulfil?'

Gideon rose. 'You'll find nothing particularly pleasant about your stay. You will be under lock and key, and a regime as strict as my wife cares to make it. I shall return for you when I can.'

Hand on door, Lymond had stopped, his face expressive of conflicting emotions. 'I should dearly like to know why,' he said.

But that was something Gideon did not even know clearly himself.

2 · SHAH MAT

Sybilla heard nothing of her son's escape from Threave until the Wednesday of that week.

Arriving at the castle in a flurry of women, armed men and boxes, she heard the story piecemeal from Will Scott, who was monosyllabic, and Agnes, who was jubilant, and drew her own conclusions.

She was not, indeed, as impressed by the feat as Agnes expected, but asked sharply, 'Have you looked for him?' Scott replied respressively that his father's men has scoured the countryside with dogs since Saturday without finding a trace. He filled an awkward pause by adding, 'How is Mariotta?'

Sybilla, though dressed with her usual éclat, was less fantastic in her manner than usual, and a good deal more pointed. 'Very well. Christian told us of Francis's capture, but she didn't know, naturally, of his escape. Did you hear,' added the Dowager abruptly, 'about the raid on Dalkeith?'

Will Scott, not at all sure what the Dowager thought of all this, followed her with some bewilderment. 'Dalkeith? No!'

'It only happend on Sunday night,' said Sybilla, seating herself. 'Lord Grey sent out troops from Haddington. Some of them burned up the country all round Edinburgh, and the rest attacked Dalkeith. George Douglas escaped, I hear, but his wife and all the rest of the household had to give themselves up.

'I thought Sir George and Grey were on good terms,' said Scott.

'Did you? Agnes, my dear,' said the Dowager. 'Bonnie has some new satin for you, if you can find the right box. Just the shade for your turquoises. Will and I shall be quite all right here.'

Scott watched the girl go with a sinking feeling. He said, 'I suppose you know my father isn't altogether pleased with me. I don't know what he expected. After what happened to Mariotta, no man could stand by and–'

'Rubbish,' said Sybilla. 'Mariotta is a silly child, who deserved a lesson, though not quite the one she got. At least you haven't told your father about Wark.'

Scott flushed. 'I don't believe Lymond went there. He was too late.'

Sybilla smoothed her dress. 'Did you know why he had to get there?'

'No.' Scott hesitated under the blue gaze. 'Not really.'

'He didn't tell you – even when you were locked in together afterward?'

'It was some information he wanted,' said Scott sulkily. 'Something he expected to put him in a good light with the authorities. I didn't know. But I don't see that it could have done him any good now. Not after all he's done.'

The Dowager made no reply, and the boy found himself overcome with exasperation. 'Are you *sorry* I captured him? I can tell you his brother won't be.'

'Sorry? Yes. Aren't you?' said the Dowager mildly.

Scott met her eyes squarely. 'I don't know. I don't know what to believe. In any case, what could I do about it?'

411

'You could try and find him,' said Sybilla. 'You know where he might be. And you could try and trace Harvey. Then at least – don't you think? – we might get the truth.'

'The truth?' said Scott harshly. 'What good will the truth do to anybody? What good has it done Christian Stewart? The only thing that will help her now is a piece of good, solid lying.' The memory of a promise came back to him. 'And I've got the job of doing it . . . I suppose. she's back at Boghall?'

'No,' said Sybilla. 'She takes her friendships a little more seriously than that. The last time I saw her, she was on her way to visit Sir George Douglas at Dalkeith in an effort to neutralize the effects of your little plot here.'

Scott shot to his feet. 'Dalkeith!'

'Yes,' said Sybilla pleasantly. 'The place the English raided on Sunday. Not a very clever thing to do under the circumstances, was it?'

* * *

In delivering Lymond at Flaw Valleys and then returning himself to Berwick, Gideon faced a round trip of something like a hundred and forty miles. It was a measure of his interest that he took it without hesitation, and a measure of his speed that he and his retinue arrived, with the outlaw, in the early afternoon of Monday.

The inevitable skirmish took place as he was changing into fresh clothes, under the amazed brown eyes of his wife. 'And where,' said Kate Somerville expansively, 'did you say you had put him?'

Her husband's expression, already wary, became turgid. 'In the bedroom at the end of the top passage. Under lock and–'

'Tut!' said Kate. 'What are you thinking of! No silk sheets! No goose-feather mattress! And two stairs and a nasty muddy yard to cross before he can even round up the livestock, unless he starts with the mice.'

'Kate – '

'And then food. Is he choosy? We could manage stavesacre and dwale, with a little fool's parsley and half a thorn apple, stewed, with toadstools.'

'*Kate!*'

'I think you're suffering from necrosis of the brain,' said Kate, a little less passionately. 'Have you told Philippa?'

Gideon nodded. 'I told her he was here to be punished.'

'Oh. In that case she's probably in the room at the end of the passage with a chabouk. Or is it locked?'

Gideon held out a key. 'I must eat and go, sweet. Some of my men will take in his food and look after the room—'

'And here was I, preparing to recede into a gentle old age like Philemon and Baucis. Don't you think you should retire again? The first retiral seems to have got mislaid. No? Well, I shall have to look after your nasty friend, but don't blame me if he isn't quite the same person when you get back,' said Kate Somerville.

* * *

She put off no time. With Philippa out of the way and Gideon eating, Kate set off along the top passage and, leaving her bodyguard militantly outside, unlocked the end bedroom and went in.

The room seemed empty. Nobody at the window, or on the window seat: no one in the bed; nobody before the empty grate. That left the Legacy, a chair inherited from Gideon's family and carved by a failed student in zoomorphics. Snarling with oaken tooth and paw, the Legacy was drawn before the window, its back to the door. Kate walked firmly round it and found him.

Slack by the palsied Behemoths, hands open, head thrown back, Lymond slept. It was an uncommonly sound sleep. Stretching one finger, Kate drew aside the stained jerkin without rousing him. It was enough to tell her what she wanted to know.

Below, she confronted her husband. 'Why, Gideon?'

He was obtuse. 'Why what?'

'Invoke the maternal instinct precisely now. I should rather be rancorous too.'

413

Somerville wiped his mouth. 'Scourge away. That's what he's here for.'

'Whatever he's here for, he's bleeding over Grandpa Gideon's oak chair like a Martinmas pig,' said Kate bluntly.

There was a faint smile in Gideon's eyes. 'Not my doing. But I admit to setting a fast pace this morning. He didn't complain.'

'Then allow me to make up for it,' said Kate. 'The air is filling in a familiar way with hideous subtleties. All right. Instinct it shall be. After all, everybody always brings the old broken-down things for me to patch up: there's nothing actually new about it. When will you be back?'

'Soon, I hope.' Gideon rose, and presently took leave of his wife, running lightly downstairs to the courtyard. Kate watched him go, observing with misgiving the bland assurance on the kind face.

The procession next time along the top corridor was formidable: a kind of barmecide feast of invalid diet as well as jugs, bowls, bandages and clothes, towels, ointment and a small wooden bathtub bound in brass. Walking through the assembled equipment, Kate unlocked the end door this time without ceremony, and went in.

He was not to be caught a second time unawares. Lounging in the window, Lymond viewed her acolytes with a faintly etched interest. 'Coals of fire. No. I observe that's the only thing lacking: such a warm day. Was it you who came in just now?'

'It was,' said Kate grimly. 'And I had a good look at you, so you might as well sit down.'

The blue eyes were cool. 'Why? Are you going to bathe me?'

'Hold your tongue,' said Kate. 'Charles will do that. And then, for no gratification that it will afford me, I'll dress your shoulder. Who performed the public service of perforating it?'

'Oh . . . a worm that turned,' said Crawford of Lymond.

'A bait which refused to be hooked. A brandling which snatched itself from the burning. I am quite capable of washing and repairing myself, if your people will leave the wherewithal.'

Kate paid no attention, but mustered her materials and ushered in Gideon's servant. 'Charles. I'll be back in half an hour,' she said, and shut the door.

The noise of hammering brought her back before then. She found the man Charles, streaming with soapy water and pounding on the outside of the captive's room, which was ludicrously locked from inside. Kate pushed him aside and vibrated the handle. 'What do you think you're doing? Let me in!'

Through the thickness of the door, his voice came, slow and flippant. 'Mistress Somerville! The proprieties!' said Lymond; and though they banged and rattled and threatened, nothing more could they get out of him that day.

* * *

A week after this event, Lord Grey of Wilton crossed the Border back into England and put up at Berwick Castle, leaving behind his newly fortified Haddington under a captain. On arrival Lord Grey, who had had a very hard month, was told that the Countess of Lennox was waiting to see him.

He exploded to Gideon, there to smooth his lordship's first hours. 'Margaret Lennox: what next? She got herself into a fine mess in February; and all her father did was laugh in her face and march over to the Scots. Well! I've taught that family a lesson!'

'I heard about the Dalkeith raid,' said Gideon. 'How did it go?'

Grey looked pleased. 'Splendidly, splendidly. I hope everyone heard about it. I hope all friend Douglas's allies and sycophants noticed it and took a lesson from it. Sent Bowes and Gamboa out on Sunday night, and they burned around Edinburgh while Wilford and Wyndham went for Dalkeith. We undermined from the base-court and the white sheets were hanging out of the windows before we'd blunted a pick. Got the whole garrison – Douglas's wife, second son, lairds and Douglases in dozens, and cartloads of furnishings – I tell you, Gideon,' said Lord Grey, flushed with recollection, 'we came back from that day's work richer by three thousand pounds *and* two thousand head of cattle, *and* three thousand sheep, not to mention as notable a bunch of prisoners as you'd wish to get compensation for.'

'But Sir George himself got away?'

Pleased reminiscence faded. 'Damned coward,' said Lord Grey. 'Slipped out of a postern and fled to Edinburgh, leaving his own wife to be taken. Well, he's got little enough reward for it. I shouldn't be surprised if he's back on his knees by the end of the week. His wife thinks so. I sent her back to him.'

'Sent Lady Douglas back?'

'Yes. She thought she could persuade him to be honest with us at last. But it doesn't matter,' said Grey expansively. 'We've got half his relations in custody here, including his two sons. And an odd creature – nice-looking, too – a blind girl called Stewart. Ward of the Fleming family and well thought of at Court. She'll be worth quite a bit. You'll see her in a moment – I've sent for her.'

He bent down heavily for his shoes. 'I could do with six months out to grass. I've got all this damned coming and going to Haddington – convoys three times weekly; serpentine pouches, hackbuts, iron, matches, sickles, scythes, pickaxes, what have you. And the horses are being used too much. And the French fleet is here.'

Gideon, whose attention had slackened, sat up sharply. 'Are you sure?'

'Saw them myself,' said his commander gloomily. 'They're lying off Dunbar. A hundred and twenty sail, I should judge. A damned great navy.'

Gideon said, 'What about our fleet?' and saw Grey's lip curl. 'What about it? Fitting out in the south. It's been fitting out since it was launched, and it'll be fitting out at Christmas, I shouldn't wonder. . . .'

He was still talking when Christian Stewart was ushered in. After her came Grey's secretary Myles.

During the introductions, Gideon observed the blind girl curiously. She was sturdily built, by his standards, with good features and shining, dark red hair framing a surprisingly calm face. While Myles kept Grey's attention, Gideon spoke.

'Have we met before, I wonder? You seemed to recognize my name.'

She had a splendid smile. 'I've heard of you. Through a friend.'

Gideon made the commonplace answer. 'Nothing too bad, I hope,' and the girl smiled again.

'Quite the reverse. He – we thought at one time you had had an injudicious past, but now we know better.'

'Good,' said Gideon, but the reply was mechanical. 'But now we know better.' Was it possible she was referring to . . . ?

He looked up, saw that Grey was still engaged, and took a chance. 'Or perhaps . . . not so good for Mr. Harvey?' he said.

There was a little silence. The the colour came back into the girl's fair skin. 'Do you know him?' she said quietly.

'Who? Harvey?' He was disingenuous.

'No.'

A friend of Lymond's. Well, well, thought Gideon. 'I've met him,' he said circumspectly, aloud.

She was uncertain, obviously, of his standing; and doubtful also of being overheard. She made a small pause and then said, 'As an antagonist?' Which made Gideon himself stop to think.

'At first; yes,' he said. 'Things are a little different now. Do you know him well?'

'Know who?' said Lord Grey, piling the last paper on Myles' outstretched arms. 'Harvey? She probably met him at Haddington.' He looked up accusingly. 'You asked me about that man before. I told you. He's got this wound in the leg and he can't get back to Berwick yet – maybe not for weeks. It's damned awkward. I only put him into that convoy as an excuse for bringing him here, and now he isn't here, and that Lymond fellow has disappeared into smoke.'

Neither Gideon nor the girl said anything.

'Anyway,' said Lord Grey, calming down. 'I've got a job for you, Gideon. Have to tear you away from our fair company here. Which reminds me.' He pinched a lip, staring with vague approval at the blind face. 'I must get a proper chaperone for you. Wish my wife were here. Or – by God, that's it!' he exclaimed, struck by a brilliant idea. 'The Countess of Lennox! Get the damned woman away from under our feet!'

There was no change in the girl's serene face. Gideon said without thinking too much. 'But – Willie, I don't think that very suitable.'

'Why not?'

Gideon couldn't think why not. He repeated, emphatically, 'I don't think Lady Christian and Meg Douglas would have anything in common. Lady Lennox's dealings with her countrymen – some of them – haven't been particularly savoury,' he said distinctly, and saw the girl's intelligent face turn questioningly toward him.

She said tentatively, 'You mean the Countess might try to harm my friends through me?' and Gideon knew that although Grey might and did think it nonsense, the girl understood.

He gave her a friendly farewell a little later, and went off, in high good humour for no evident reason.

* * *

The interview between Lord Grey and Margaret, Countess of Lennox, was everything he was afraid it might be. It began with the lady's cool voice saying, 'I'm afraid I have to convey to you the Lord Protector's displeasure, Lord Grey,' and included some plain questions.

'And am I supposed to believe that of all the officers in London this person Harvey was the only one capable of leading a convoy to Haddington?'

'Harvey,' said Lord Grey with an effort, 'is a very able man. I'm sorry, since you take such a interest in him, that you can't meet him. A slight wound made it necessary for him to stay at Haddington.'

The black eyes were sparkling. 'I do take an interest in him, as it happens. I came here expressly to make sure that he returned to London directly. I believe Mr. Palmer leaves you today?'

Lord Grey agreed that Harvey's cousin was due to leave Berwick for London.

'Then I hope he can take to His Grace the assurance that Mr. Harvey will follow directly he can travel?'

Lord Grey, with private reservations, agreed again.

'I am glad to hear it. I shall remain and see that he does,' said the Countess and ruthlessly delivered the coup de grâce. 'You will have heard that your friend Lymond has been caught.'

'Caught! By Wharton?'

'No. By the Scots. When,' said Margaret, having applied the black draught, 'do you think Harvey will be able to travel?'

The Lord Lieutenant rested vague eyes on her. 'What? Oh. I've no idea. I'll ask the girl.'

Margaret stopped arranging her dress. 'What girl?'

'There was a girl among the prisoners from George Douglas's who took an interest in him at Haddington. They were all kept there for a spell before coming here.'

'Took an interest in *Harvey!*' exclaimed the Countess. 'Who is she?'

Grey told her what he knew, and felt much better. 'Lymond and she seem quite friendly,' he concluded, and raking in his desk, found a letter. 'We took that from Lady Douglas just before we released her. It's a letter to Sir George from the Stewart girl, written for her by her servant lad. She's blind, you see. See what it says.'

'Blind!' Her face fixed in astonishment, Margaret Lennox read the paper once, then a second time. 'Signed, Christian Stewart.'

She looked up. 'This assumes that the Master of Culter

will be in touch with Sir George . . . "or someone on his behalf." He is to be told that all is well, and he need pursue his objective no longer, because she has done all that is necessary. What does that mean?'

Lord Grey shook his head. 'I had the girl in today asking her about it, but she'd say nothing.'

'Did Lady Douglas know what was in the letter? No? I should like to see this girl,' said Lady Lennox with a ringing and unanswerable finality.

* * *

Since the shock and physical buffeting of her capture at Dalkeith, Christian Stewart had stumbled unwillingly to Haddington, and then in a kind of stupor of relief and anxiety here to Berwick.

Miraculously, the key to the whole strange problem lay now in her hands. But to use it, she must be free. And whether Francis Crawford had been helped to escape, or whether he was still in prison, she must prevent him from appearing on trial, or from risking his liberty again before she could find him.

Her letter to Sir George – a hopeless attempt to do just that – had failed. She had no other means of sending a message. She had tried to persuade them to release Sym, without success. She had even contemplated approaching the man Somerville, who had seemed friendly, and might perhaps be trusted. But he had left the castle, she had been told.

What next? All day she walked up and down, thinking: of Boghall; of Inchmahome; of Stirling; of Edinburgh. '*If I told you I'd murdered my sister you'd feel hate and revulsion.*' '*I haven't tried to kill anyone today, I give you my word.*' '*A thief in the night is the phrase.*' And the bleak '*The darts which make me suffer are my own.*'

She smashed her fists in sudden anger on the sill of her window. Oh, to get out! To get out of here!

To the Countess of Lennox, paying a regal prison visit,

Christian was an astonishing, a calm, and impenetrable steel wall.

The name was soon spoken: Francis Crawford of Lymond. 'I don't suppose you know him. It isn't thought patriotic to know him these days,' said Margaret ruefully. 'But we were once very good friends.'

The blind girl answered serenely. 'As a matter of fact, I do know him,' and Margaret was softly eager. 'You do? Is he the same? Where is he, these days?'

'In prison,' said Christian prosaically. 'I suppose he's the same. He talks a great deal.'

'In prison!' echoed Margaret, her voice sharpening just too much. 'In Scotland? But that means he'll hang! Is that true?'

'I believe so.'

Lady Lennox said agitatedly, 'But can't something be done? Is anyone helping him?'

'Who could help him?'

Margaret said, 'You're his friend. I'm sure you are. If you were free, couldn't you do something?'

If she were free . . .

A crease appeared between the large, direct eyes. 'I don't see what. I've done him a small service – I got him the home address of a man he wanted to see for some reason. But that won't be any good to him now, naturally.'

So simple an explanation. Margaret, comforted, gave a sigh. 'So sad. All that talent – but people, I suppose, make their own ruin, however much their friends try to help. Now,' said the Countess cheerfully, 'Is there anything I can bring that you would like?'

After she had gone, Christian sat alone for a long time in her own black world, conquering the rage which would have alarmed her visitor. Then, dismissing the incident with an effort, she spared a moment to thank the well-intentioned spirit of Gideon Somerville before resuming the furious pacing of her prison.

Gideon's errand for Grey took him to Norham, and he

was forced to stay overnight. Making casual inquiries on his return he found that the prisoners taken at Dalkeith had been dispatched that day to the Archbishop of York; and that, before she left, the blind girl had asked once or twice after himself.

He might, left to himself, have pursued the party; but Lord Grey had other ideas. With his best men scattered like caraway seeds over the countryside from Roxburgh to Broughty, he needed an able officer at his side.

Gideon tolerated it, his desire to return home tempered by the discovery that Margaret Lennox was still at Berwick, and meant to stay there until the man Harvey was well enough to return. If the Countess could play a waiting game, then so could he, thought Gideon, and caught himself with a surprised grimace. One would think it was his affair.

The following Monday, he was ordered to Newcastle to discuss finance with the Treasurer. 'By the time that's over, I shall probably be in Newcastle myself,' said Lord Grey. 'Probably see you there. You ought to be off, anyway, by the morning. Oh – you were interested in Sam Harvey?'

'Yes!' said Gideon, suddenly alert.

'That Stewart girl said he was slightly injured. Well, he isn't. He's got a ball in the thigh and it's damned dangerous. They're not sure if he'll live.'

Gideon said quickly, 'When did you hear?'

'Just now. Bad luck on the fellow. I feel a shade guilty,' said Lord Grey peevishly. 'I shouldn't have brought him up at all if I'd known that Lymond fellow was out of action.'

'Yes. Bad luck,' said Gideon. 'Willie – d'you mind if I leave now instead of tomorrow? I could call in on Kate on my way.'

'On your way?' said Grey indulgently. 'Twenty miles out of it, I should have thought. But never mind. That's husbands for you: I've done the same myself. All right. Give her my love.'

'Yes, I will,' said Gideon, and slipped out, calling for

his man. He was on the road in less than an hour; and by next day, Tuesday, the nineteenth of June, he was home at Flaw Valleys.

2

THE ULTIMATE CHECK

The corrouers and berars of lettres ought
hastily and spedily do her viage that
comanded hem with oute taryenge. For
their taryenge might noye and greve them
that sende hem forth, or ellis them to
whom they ben sent too. And torne hem
to ryght grete domage or villonye.

1 · THE FAST MOVES

Lymond recovered from his wound with characteristic
rapidity; from the beginning, in fact, he acted as if it did
not exist, and Kate was perfectly willing to do the same.

A frangible and archaic courtesy reigned at Flaw Valleys. Katherine forbade none of its offices to her guest:
he was under permanent escort, but free to wander where
he chose. At her request, he shared her table and occasionally her parlour. His unspoken resistance to the situation
delighted her, as did the way he dealt with it.

He set the tenor for the encounters the first morning
after the incident with Charles. He unlocked his door,
made some necessary apologies and conformed to the
reigning atmosphere of frigid politeness.

Kate, however, was only choosing her weapons. By sup-
pertime on Friday, and after four days of shrewd observation, she opened fire. 'I notice,' she said, passing the
salt, 'that you were outside today. Did you meet Philippa?'

Lymond accepted the condiment, but not the challenge.
'We had a few words,' he said. 'She is a – striking young
person already.'

Kate helped herself. 'We think so. What did she say to you?'

'Her remarks were few and deflatory,' he said. This was an understatement, as Kate knew very well. She observed, 'I'm afraid she's being rather unresponsive. We've been trying to teach her to feel sorry for you. I do dislike personal hatreds in a child.'

This time, after a moment, he called her bluff. 'Perhaps Philippa and I should be thrown together a little more. She might become attached to me if she knew me better.'

Kate, brightening visibly, ignored the gleam in his eye. 'That would make her sorry for you?'

'It might. The object of any sort of clinical study deserves compassion, don't you think?'

'Snakes don't,' said Katherine inconsequently. 'I hate snakes.'

'And yet you feed them on honey cakes and forbid them to defend themselves.'

'Defencelessness is not a noted characteristic of serpents. Anyhow, I can't have them lying rattling about the house. It gets on the nerves.'

'It does if you handle it by rattling back. I've no objection, you know, to practicing the social arts.'

Kate viewed him suspiciously. 'I don't see why I should abandon my entertainment because of your conscience.'

'It isn't quite conscience so much as horrified admiration,' said Lymond. 'From cuticle to corium in four days.'

'You have to be quick with them. They grow another skin. I thought it mightn't be conscience,' said Kate, collecting platters.

He was gazing down at the table. 'I really can't go on apologizing. It would be too monotonous.'

Kate, taking a dish from the cupboard, halted beside him. 'You don't owe me anything, except a little amusement. Why not bite back?'

'Because,' said Lymond, lifting his eyes suddenly, 'I'm a constant practitioner of the art and you are not.'

'I don't mind,' said Kate wistfully. 'Won't you bite?'

'Like a shark. It's a habit. And habits are hell's own

425

substitute for good intentions. Habits are the ruin of ambition, of initiative, of imagination. They're the curse of marriage and the after-bane of death.'

Katherine surveyed the indifferent face critically. 'For an advocate of chaos, you're quite convincing. There is such a thing, you know, as habitual disorder – as of course you know: few have had such a permanently unsettled regime as you have. Suppose you had a chance to lead a normal life?'

'Let's leave my sordid affairs out of this, shall we?' he said. 'You've missed a point. There's a nice difference between rootless excitement and careful variety.'

'If I can't be personal, I don't want to argue,' said his hostess categorically. 'I may be missing your points, but you're much too busy dodging mine.'

'Yours aren't points, they're probangs. I don't see why I should help.'

'I do. Because Gideon would help cook his father if the cannibal quoted poetry at him,' said Kate.

'And I have drunk of Castalia as well as bathed in it.'

'It was Charles who bathed in it, as I recall. I forgot,' said Kate sardonically. 'You like your privacy. My apologies for scrabbling round the edges in an undignified way. Pay no attention. Grimalkin goes quavering back to the chimney piece.'

The long, slender fingers tightened about the salt cellar. 'Leave it, can't you?' said Lymond softly.

There was flat challenge in Kate's rigid spine. 'Is there any reason why I should? I want – '

He interrupted her, pushing away the heavy silver vessel so that it slid precisely, like a curling stone, into the centre of the board between them.

'What you want is very clear. You want my confidence. If you can't have that, you want to goad me into making admissions about myself. If you can't have that, you use moral pressure. I'm quite conscious of my obligations and misdemeanours toward the members of your family. I disagree abut the mode of compensation, that's all.'

Her cheeks were scarlet. 'Mr. Crawford, I really doubt if you're in a postion to agree or disagree about anything.'

The impatient, ruthless gaze lifted to hers. 'Nor do I need to be reminded. You may expose me; you may baulk me. I've no remedy.'

'If you prize reticence more than your life,' said Kate dryly, 'then you're certainly beyond remedy.'

'Reticence? No,' he said. 'But I prize freedom of the mind above freedom of the body. I claim the right to make my own mistakes and keep quiet about them. You have all the licence in the world to protect your husband. My life is at your disposal, but not my thoughts.'

'Dear me,' said Kate, rising. 'I doubt if I could stomach your thoughts. It was just a few basic facts I was thinking of, such as whether you were one of these people who can eat goose eggs. The creatures keep laying them: an appalling habit, but we can't break it.'

Untenable positions were not for Kate. His mouth relaxed, and he rose smoothly and opened the door for her, laughter lines gathering at the corners of the veiled eyes. 'I thought the conversation was cutting an ovoid track. I wouldn't for the world deprive you of the last bite.'

'Thank you,' said Kate. 'If we're referring to snakes. Not if you're talking about fish.'

'Pythonissa,' retorted Lymond, and unexpectedly smiled.

* * *

She conceded him his victory.

In the days that followed, she did no more probing; partly because she now saw that these ferretings had no relation to the level on which his mind worked; and partly because his wits were too sharp. She could tire him; she could anger him. Four days had taught her that she could nearly shake his self-control and that he was himself shaken and dismayed by his weakening grip of himself. But she could never override him, and she stopped attempting it.

He had tried, she knew, to come to terms with Philippa,

427

but without success. On the last occasion he had entered the music room, roving as he often did to the window; and after a moment, idly picked up Philippa's lute which lay there.

He had forgotten, obviously, that Kate's room opened from this one. She had been resting; and although during these last ten days she had found him civilized and undemanding company, she stayed where she was to avoid embarrassing them both. Thus she was able to hear the sweet, preoccupied roulades of the lute, and the crash of Philippa's eruption into the room. The child stopped just inside the door, as her mother, opening her own door a judicious half inch, was able to see.

'That's mine!' said Philippa. 'That's my lute you're playing!'

Lymond laid the instrument gently down, and sat himself before Gideon's harpsichord. 'Lute *and* harpsichord?' he said. 'That's pretty erudite of you.'

The child pushed back her long hair. It was uncombed, and the hem of her gown, Kate was sorry to see, was grey with dust. Philippa said belligerently, 'I can play the rebec as well.'

'Oh?'

'And the recorder.'

Philippa! Philippa! said Kate to herself, grinning. Lymond turned to the harpsichord. 'Then you're the person I want to see. Which d'you like playing best?'

'The lute.' The voice of ownership.

'Then,' said Lymond, rousing the keyboard to delicate life, 'tell me how this finishes. I never could find out.'

It was only *L'homme armé;* a tune Philippa had certainly heard in her cradle and was bound to know every note of. She sauntered across the room.

'It's *L'homme armé.*'

'I know. But how does it go on?'

She sidled past. 'I don't know.'

The harpsichord rang with jubilation. 'Try.'

Kate could see the pull of the music in her daughter's eyes; she could imagine the fascination of those magic fingers. Philippa's arm shot out. She trapped the lute like an insect-eater trapping a fly, and flew to the door, panting.

'That's my father's instrument,' she shouted. 'You're not to touch it! Leave my father and my mother alone. Nobody wants you here!'

Kate was afraid for her. Her hand tightened on the door, but the music didn't stop, although it fell to a murmur. Lymond's voice said quietly. 'Don't you want me to play?' *There sall be mirth,* said the harpsichord. *There sall be mirth at our meeting.*

Philippa looked at him with her mother's eyes. 'No!' she cried. 'I hate you!' And clutching her lute, she did indeed run from the room.

The music stopped, and there was a long silence. After a time, Kate slipped through the door.

He was still there, looking unseeing downward, his head on one hand. Then, politely rueful, he saw her. 'You see! I'm out of practice, I know; but the effect must be worse than I thought.'

She sat down, her eyes on him. 'Who taught you?'

'My mother, first. My father thought that not only did music make men mad, but that only madmen indulged in it in the first place.'

'Then you inherit your military talents from him, perhaps?' said Kate idly. 'Not many musicians contrive to be the toast of the Wapenshaws as well.'

'Some do: witness Jamie's drummer who whipped the English off the butts. I never achieved anything spectacular of that sort; I never cared for it.' He ran one hand down the keyboard. 'My brother is the athlete.'

'He's an archer?'

'Sword or bow. He excels at both.'

So there was a brother. 'There is such a thing as a born eye for athletics,' observed Kate. 'Two of a kind in one family would be a bit trying. It's probably just as well for the sake of peace that you were differently gifted.'

He agreed with her amiably, returning to his playing. Watching him, Kate found herself thinking of something Gideon had said after his short stay at Crawfordmuir. 'It isn't all done with words either; he makes damned sure of that. He can outshoot them and outfight them and outplay them: he's got a co-ordination that a hunting tiger would give its hind legs for.'

She drew a little breath and Lymond looked up. After a moment he observed, still playing, 'Versatility is one of the few human traits which are universally intolerable. You may be good at Greek and good at painting and be popular. You may be good at Greek and good at sport, and be wildly popular. But try all three and you're a mountebank. Nothing arouses suspicion quicker than genuine, all-round proficiency.'

Kate thought. 'It needs an extra gift for human relationships, of course; but that can be developed. It's got to be, because stultified talent is surely the ultimate crime against mankind. Tell your paragons to develop it: with all those gifts it's only right they should have one hurdle to cross.'

'But that kind of thing needs co-operation from the other side,' said Lymond pleasantly. 'No. Like Paris, they have three choices.' And he struck a gently derisive chord between each. 'To be accomplished but ingratiating. To be accomplished but resented. Or to hide behind the more outré of their pursuits and be considered erratic but harmless.'

'As you did,' said Kate shrewdly. 'Committing the ultimate crime.'

'No,' said Francis Crawford, watching his own fingers slipping down the keys. 'Man's ultimate crimes are always against his brother. Mine, in my competence, my versatility and my self-important, self-imposed embargoes, was against my sister. . . . For God's sake,' said Lymond, 'don't speak.'

In the sudden silence she did as he wished, sitting still in her low chair. Then he swore aloud and she looked up, heartened by these expressions of honest rage.

Standing by the window, Lymond regarded her crookedly. 'Your fault,' he said. 'These were some of the things you wanted to know, weren't they? And as soon as the pressure was lifted, I started talking about them . . . I don't

430

as a rule inflict my more tawdry reminiscences on people, you must believe me. I'm sorry. It's one of the penalties of being incommunicado for five years, but I can usually control it better than that.'

She stood up also. 'You think a lot of your self-possession, don't you?'

'I did, when I had any. One can't, obviously, control other people unless—'

'And you want to control other people?'

He grinned. 'I take your point. I have none now to control. But all the same – '

'You would want it in normal life. Are you ever,' said Kate, driven by her own feelings into asking one of the dangerous questions, 'are you ever likely to *have* a normal life?'

Lymond grinned again, slightly, walking to the door. 'That depends on Samuel Harvey. There is, of course, another thing. I might be able to gull the law. But as soon as I appear in public, my brother is likely to get himself hanged for killing me ... We're devils for complications on our side of the Border.'

Kate accompanied him to the door. She said bluntly, 'How much more of it can you stand?'

'Don't worry,' he said, answering what he took to be her anxiety. 'If it's going to happen, it won't happen here.'

* * *

Gideon arrived next day, and had Crawford brought to the parlour, where he was standing with Kate. After greeting his prisoner he said without preamble, 'The man Harvey is in Haddington; he's seriously wounded and it's possible he won't survive. I came here to tell you.'

'Oh,' said Lymond. After a moment he added, 'Then that appears to dispose of my problem.'

Gideon had had a talk with his wife. He said abruptly, 'I can't help you to get into Haddington.'

'I know that, of course.'

'But,' said Gideon, 'if you think there is any possibility

431

of doing so yourself and coming out alive, I'm willing to lend you a horse to try.'

There was a pause. Lymond drew a steady breath. 'I see you mean it,' he said. 'I shan't sicken you with protestations of gratitude. But it means a great deal.'

'I know. What will you do?' asked Gideon.

'Go to George Douglas,' said Lymond slowly. 'I can influence him a little, I think . . . And try and get Harvey out. Or if that fails, to get in myself.'

'But –' said Kate involuntarily, and Lymond's eyes moved quickly to hers.

'There really is no other choice,' he said, and she was silent.

Gideon had opened the door. 'Come then,' he said, 'I came as fast as I could, but there's no saying how long he'll live. You'll need all the speed you can make. Quickly. Kate –'

She was already through the door. 'I'll collect what he needs.'

In a very short time he was mounted, and they watched him canter down the avenue, turning with raised hand at the gates. 'The fools!' Gideon said. 'Those damned fools at Edinburgh! What a waste of a man.'

And they turned and went about their business while Gideon's stallion, stretched flat with extended rein and curbless mouth, printed with sharp cloisonné the baked green sides of the hills and glens leading to Scotland.

* * *

While Lymond was in Northumberland, Will Scott was scouring the Lowlands for him. He stayed in the vicinity of Wark Castle until he was sure the Master was no longer near the original rendezvous. He visited the farmyard where he had first joined the troop, and the lairs he had learned to know since.

Only twice did he come across any of the men he had fought with for nine months. The Long Cleg, horse-coping placidly with a string of broken-winded hacks, waved a friendly arm and asked mildly if it was right that he and the Master had had a fight over the money and he'd broken Lymond's head for him. Scott muttered something and got away as soon as possible. The other encounter took the form of a narrowly averted arrow which met him at one of the biggins where they used to keep fodder. He never found out who it was: he didn't want to know.

Fourteen days after his uncomfortable meeting with Sybilla at Threave, Scott returned to Branxholm empty-handed and full of misgivings, and Lord Culter, calling that day on Buccleuch, found him there, alone in the hall.

'Will Scott!'

The boy looked up. The square, powerful figure, the direct grey eyes, the flat hair, were like phantasmagoria from the bolting, glittering winter: a wood on the way to Annan, and Lymond's voice saying, 'Richard! A challenge!'

He got up slowly, and was unprepared for Richard's hand chipping masterfully and painfully on his shoulder. 'You damned puppy; *where is he?*'

He reacted as he had been taught: with one smooth violent movement he was out of the other's grasp and viewing him from a useful distance. 'I didn't come home to be handled,' said Will Scott pleasantly. 'My father is outside, I believe.'

'You've learned manners to fit your morals, I see. Have you brought your master with you or not?'

'What, again?' said Scott insolently. 'I've already brought him to Threave at the beginning of the month – did nobody tell you? How often am I supposed to repeat the service?'

Lord Culter wouldn't show excitement again. 'I've already asked you. Where is he?'

Scott shrugged. 'Who knows? Linlithgow? London? Midculter? He escaped.'

'From *Threave!*' said Richard.

'Aye, from Threave,' blared a new voice. Buccleuch, sweating, came into the room in his shirt sleeves, sneezed in the cooler air, and bawled for something to drink. 'Lifted the latch and walked out. You'd think the damned place was a sieve. Ye see Will's back?' said Sir Wat unnecessarily. 'It was Will got your lassie away from Lymond, you know.'

'A Herculean task, I feel sure,' said Lord Culter. It struck Sir Wat too late that it was no use trying to ingratiate with his lordship any man who had witnessed his wife and his brother together. He dropped the attempt and said, 'You've come for me? Sit down; sit down. I'm ready packit. I've got to take this damned fool anyway to Edinburgh to get a formal pardon for him. What's happening?'

The answer was brief. 'We're to muster on Monday to attack the English garrison at Haddington.'

Sir Wat put down his beer, and the seamed skin about his eyes puckered alarmingly. 'Wait a minute. Have the French promised to attack?'

'On the obvious conditions. You'll hear them tomorrow. They want the main forts, of course – Dunbar, Edinburgh, Stirling. They have Dumbarton already.'

'By kind permission of her French Majesty. Uh-huh. Well, they might get Dunbar, but I'm damned if I'd let them sniff the threshold of the other two. What else do they want?'

'What they've always wanted,' said Lord Culter. 'But I think that's a matter for discussion elsewhere.'

So absorbed was Buccleuch in his calculations that he missed the implication. His son didn't. Rising, Will said flatly, 'Naturally. Any associate of Lymond's is suspect. I'll go.'

The door banged, as Buccleuch rounded on his neighbour with a bellow. 'There was no need for that! Dod, are ye wandered! It was the laddie who led us to capture Lymond in the first place!'

Richard's expression did not vary. 'I'm not trying to offend you, Wat. But this is one secret nobody dare take risks with. There's a good chance the country is going to agree to France's main stipulation, which is – '

'– To send the young Queen to France.'

'Yes. To be brought up at the French court, and to be married in due course as her mother and the French King

434

decide. If we and Parliament agree. Otherwise the French fleet lifts anchor and sails back home without a fight.'

He studied the wayward eyebrows, the falcate nose and the stubborn chin. 'Would you agree, Wat? Which side are you for?'

Buccleuch, slapping a hand on the table, heaved himself up. 'The same as yourself: what's the alternative? The Protector's black face bobbing up the Canongate and France in a huff and making dainty wee steps in the direction of the Emperor? No. We're stuck like a toggle in a bite, and we've got to put up with it . . . Are ye in lodgings in town?'

'I've taken a house,' said Richard. 'In the High Street.'

'And Sybilla?' demanded Sir Wat, with a brilliant lack of tact.

'I've no idea what my mother's movements are,' said Richard. 'I haven't seen her for some time.'

'She's got your wife back at Midculter,' offered Buccleuch, and pursed his cracked lips so that the whiskers leaped. He said, 'Have ye ever thought that your brother might be driving a wedge deliberately between you and your family? Because if so, he's finding you easy meat.'

'I must ask him when I find him,' said Lord Culter.

'Dod,' said Buccleuch caustically, 'I'm glad to hear he'll survive long enough to listen to ye.'

'Oh . . . he'll survive,' said Richard. 'For a long time, after he's caught. I'm in no hurry. None at all.'

'Poor devil,' said Buccleuch perfunctorily, and finished his beer.

* * *

Next day, behind closed doors in Edinburgh, it was agreed that the young Queen Mary should be sent to France as soon and as secretly as possible.

The plan was both simple and brilliant. In eight days' time, four galleys would lift anchor in the Forth and sail not south, but around the north coast of Scotland, stopping at Dumbarton on the west, where the Queen would embark. So, while Lord Grey and the English fleet rubbed

435

and fretted at an empty mousehole, the galleys of France would be sailing safely home.

The meeting broke up quietly. Lord Culter, leaving Holyrood with Buccleuch, crossed first to Tom Erskine and, making a rare gesture, put a hand on his shoulder. 'Any news yet about Christian?'

Tom's eyes flickered from Culter to Buccleuch and back. 'She's at Berwick,' he said slowly.

'Safe? Dod, you're a lucky man,' said Sir Wat bracingly. 'It'll drain your purse to buy her, maybe, but a least ye'll have her back before ye get that meagre that ye slip down the town stank.'

There was no answering smile. Erskine said wearily, 'We've just had a message from Lord Grey. They won't ransom her. They want an exchange.'

'What?' barked Buccleuch. 'An exchange? Who? Who? We haven't taken any captives that matter since they came north.'

'They think we have,' said Erskine dryly. 'They want Lymond.'

*　*　*

Sir George Douglas's lodging was in the Lawnmarket. He walked back there from Holyrood in a pleased frame of mind. In his treasury was a large sum of French money which was the price D'Essé had paid for his and Angus's continuing interest. In his purse was a safe-conduct allowing a messenger to pass freely to England, in order to convey to the Earl of Lennox and to his niece, the Countess, his anguished request for the kindly treatment and quick return of his younger son. He swung into his house, and found there waiting the Master of Culter.

Lymond was very tired. It was clear in his face, and in the steel undisguised through the velvet of his voice. He wanted Samuel Harvey. He made it perfectly understood that it was a matter of blackmail, and that he had no services but only silence to sell in return.

The Douglas brain moved smoothly behind the statesman's brow. Sir George walked to a cupboard, and as he

436

had done once before, poured two glasses of wine and moved one across. 'You look as if you've ridden a long way, and to no purpose. I'm afraid neither you nor I nor anyone else will have the privilege of speaking to Samuel Harvey in this world, Mr. Crawford. Harvey is dead.'

The other man did not touch his drink; but neither did his precious control fail him. After a pause, Lymond raised his glass in a steady hand. 'Can you prove it?' he asked.

It so happened that Douglas could, and the proof was convincing because, rare among Sir George's fantasies, the story was true. At the end, when the last servant had left and the man had come to light the tapers, Sir George addressed the Master's cogitating back. 'What will you do?'

Lymond replied without emotion. 'Eat, sleep and spend money, I expect. What else does anyone do?'

There was a little silence. Then Douglas, tilting his glass so that the wine caught the light, said gently, 'You know Grey is bartering the Stewart girl's life for yours?'

The reaction this time was instant. Lymond spun around, stopped himself, and put his empty glass on the table. 'No. I hadn't heard.' He stood waiting, his eyes open and unwavering on Sir George while the Douglas, gazing back, extended to these fresh fields his style of gentle apology.

'. . . Ironic, in a way, Mr. Crawford. If you hadn't been quite so clever at Heriot, Dalkeith would never have been attacked.'

Lymond heard him without interruption. Sir George, who was enjoying a malicious sense of power, ended. 'Perhaps a life imprisonment in England is the best thing that could happen to her . . . I assume you have no romantic urge to offer yourself at Holyrood so that they can send you in her place.'

Lymond's face was quite blank. 'If it suits me, I shall approach the Court, however uneasy it makes you.'

'And make a killer of your brother and a life prisoner of your benefactress? Not a very economical programme,' said Douglas blandly. 'Suppose we are practical. Are you going to surrender to Lord Grey?'

'Why? Do you want the privilege of sending me?'

For once in his life, Sir George was completely frank. 'Yes. I do. I need Grey's favour, and I have the perfect arrangement ready. A messenger of mine leaves at dawn for Berwick with letters from me to my niece and nephew. I can arrange it so that his safe-conduct allows for one accompanying soldier-at-arms.' He knew the type, knew the gesture would be irresistible; and was disconcerted to find in Lymond's gaze the mocking reflection of his thought.

'The war horse's answer to death by old age and pink-eye. How can I refuse?' said Lymond.

Sir George got up with some deliberation. 'You'll go? You'll go to Berwick tomorrow with my man and exchange yourself for this girl?'

'Do-to the book; quench the candle; ring the bell. Of course I shall go. Why else was I born?' said Lymond with bitter finality.

2 · THE TRAGIC MOVES

Next morning Lymond, swordless, left Edinburgh's Bristo Port with a courier carrying Sir George's letters and Sir George's safe-conduct.

The day was breathless with promise; the cobbles shining like milk glass in the quiet; the gables asleep in blanket rolls of mist. In the streets there was no sign of the grumbling, scraped-up army of men who were preparing to face battle in the warm summer weather.

As the first sun fed on the early haze there was a stirring in the houses. Smoke rose from new fires, and a man with water plodded along the High Street alongside a creaking cart, leaving a trail of splashes like silver shillings on the cobbles. Then he leaped to his horse as a small company in Erskine colours plunged past him and drew rein outside

Lord Culter's door. Tom Erskine, in its lead, dismounted and hammered on the knocker until it opened.

He was inside for less than ten minutes. Richard, half out of his tumbled bed, listened to the beginning of the story, and jumped for his clothes.

The Palace had found a spy, cleverly concealed: a man who had heard not only the Council in session but all the subsequent orders for the Queen's escape to France. They had uncovered him, and chased him, and lost him; then captured him finally after rousing half the town in the middle of the night.

Erskine rattled on, pacing the room. 'The hell of it is, he'd already passed on what he heard. They know that. They're still trying to get him to say whom he told.'

'And if the information has left Edinburgh?' Standing up, Richard stamped himself into his boots, fastening the buckle of his sword belt.

'It's our job to trace it. Quickly . . .' And followed by Lord Culter, Erskine made for the door.

At the Castle, their methods of persuasion were not subtle. By the time Tom Erskine and Culter got there, the spy had confessed. All the plans discussed the previous night had been committed to paper and had been sent to Lord Grey that morning by a special messenger – by a messenger who happened to be going to England under safe-conduct with letters from Sir George Douglas.

'Douglas!' said Culter at this point, and got a nervously irritable glance from the Governor, grey and sleepless in wrinkled day clothes.

'Purely fortuitous, so I'm told. We'll see. Meantime, Erskine – Culter – it's your job to catch that man. He's an hour at least ahead of you. By the Bristo Port. You know what it means if these papers get to Grey.'

'They won't,' said Tom Erskine briefly.

* * *

Adam Acheson, driving his neat, fast mare as quickly as he dared along the Berwick road with Sir George's letters in his pocket, was a man with no ties and no home. But he had drinking cronies in every inn between Aberdeen and Hull, and he kept them and himself in luxuries by ceaseless industry, a willingness to ride twelve hours at a stretch if need be, and a reticence like a warden oyster.

If he had been surprised to be saddled at the last moment with a companion, he had no special objection. He pronounced at the outset: 'I've orders to deliver as fast as possible, and to Lord Grey personally. If he's not at Berwick, we ride on until we get him. I hope you're ready for a hard trip.'

The fellow made no difficulty. 'Ride as fast or as far as you like. I'll stay with you.' And side by side Adam Acheson and Lymond cantered in silence under the hot sun.

* * *

The same sun, grilling the steel jackets of Erskine's troop, added sting and exasperation to the anxious morning as, without pennants or insignia, Culter and Erskine with a dozen men at their heels galloped south.

The porters at Bristo had given them their first inkling that they were chasing two men: 'a black, brosy yin on a nice bay, and a swack, smert yin on a chestnut.' The first answered the colouring of the man they knew to carry the papers.

At Linton Brig they stopped again and were lucky enough to find someone who had been up early with a calving. 'Aye, sir: a good while ago, and riding like the hammers . . .'

At Dunbar they ate on horseback and refilled their flasks, and from a packman, got one more detail. 'It stuck in my heid; they were that different: corbie and doo on the ane twig.'

Richard remounted rather quickly and started off; Erskine looked at him sharply but followed, saying nothing.

At Innerwick the description was confirmed; at Cockburnspath the description was specific. Tom Erskine, listening, watched his companion's face for a moment and then glanced away. Beneath the cold sweat Lord Culter was white, and in his eyes and the set of his mouth lay an exultant and frightened savagery. Smiling, he raised his right arm, and smiling, brought the whip precisely across the heaving rump of his horse.

'I thought so,' he said. 'The man on the chestnut is my brother.'

* * *

As the two hunted men raced south, followed by their pursuers, a third retinue set out, this time from Berwick: a leisurely caravan, jewelled with flags and fringes. Margaret Lennox was travelling south, and taking the Stewart girl with her.

Since yesterday, and a stormy interview with Lord Grey, Lady Lennox had known that Harvey was dead. And further, that Lady Christian Stewart, now back in Berick awaiting her ransom, had spent much more time with Samuel Harvey than she had allowed to appear. It was then that, with Grey's reluctant permission, Margaret decided to take Christian Stewart to her own home of Temple Newsam.

So it happened that while Lymond and his brother neared the Border, Christian, moving away from them, arrived at Warkworth Castle on the first stage of her weary journey south. There, high above the looped and shining Croquet she lay safely behind dusty curtains, listening to the dandling of moored boats and breathing the savour of the sea – and wondering if she had given anything away under the ceaseless questioning of the day.

She had told of her encounter with Lymond at Boghall, accounting thus for her interest in securing Harvey's address for him. She had shown mild alarm when told of the dissipations of her protégé. She had even, with a bitter effort, hidden her rage and fear when Margaret told her than Francis Crawford was being demanded as the price of her own freedom.

Had he escaped from Threave? If he had, these people knew nothing of it. If he hadn't, then the Queen Dowager, spurred by Erskine and Lady Fleming, would certainly

441

agree to the exchange and Lymond, for nothing, would throw away his life.

Or worse, if he escaped and heard of her plight, he would come of his own accord. She was realist enough to recognize that his code of conduct would demand it, and that he would do no less for Will Scott, or for Johnnie Bullo, or for any dependent of his in the same position.

Next day they reached Newcastle in the late afternoon, and the first voice she heard in her new quarters was that of Gideon Somerville.

* * *

In Berwickshire by the same evening the hounds were very nearly up with the hares when the scent ran suddenly cold, and, casting about, Tom Erskine and Culter found traces of a considerable company of horse recently passed through to the north.

It was Richard who turned about in the tracks of the convoy and, cutting off the first straggler he could find, made him talk. At dusk he rejoined Tom Erskine, his face ridged with weariness. 'It was a convoy for Haddington. Their scouts took in the two men we're after – Wylstropp honoured the safe-conduct and let them go – but they haven't gone to Berwick.'

'They haven't!'

'No. Grey is at Newcastle, and he's leaving there for Hexham to pick up reinforcements from Lord Wharton. Our men are making cross-country for Hexham. One other thing.'

'What?' said Tom Erskine with the flatness of apprehension. They should have caught these men before they reached Berwickshire. Now they were adrift on the Lammermoors, with the reel of their journey suddenly doubled in length.

'They know we're behind them. Wylstropp's forward scouts had already spotted us and decided not to interfere.'

Erskine said sharply, 'Well, what of it? They'll expect us to make for Berwick, not for Hexham.'

Lord Culter spoke savagely. 'You don't know my

brother. He's no fool. In all Britain, Grey couldn't have picked a better man to help him.' And whipped up his tired horse.

* * *

Arriving at Newcastle that same Friday, Gideon Somerville discovered that Lord Grey had gone to Hexham and was expecting him there. At the same time he found that the Countess of Lennox was in town with the girl Stewart in her train. Gideon, who had mentally made every plan to avoid her ladyship, changed his mind.

He had five minutes alone with Christian Stewart: no more, but enough to learn of the bargain made for her life.

She had trusted him; he could do no less in his turn. 'Lymond is free,' said Gideon briefly. 'He went to George Douglas to try and get access to Harvey.'

She arrested a sudden movement. 'But Harvey is dead. He's been dead since Tuesday.'

He understood her dismay. 'Crawford left to go to Douglas on Tuesday. I suppose there's no doubt Sir George will know of Lord Grey's demand and will tell him. It's damnable . . . but it seems to be your life or his, you know.'

'Do you think they'd dare touch me?' said Christian with contemptuous rage. 'And even if they did, that it would matter? He must be stopped,' she said. 'He must be stopped. But *how*?'

'But how?' was still unanswered next morning, when he found with mixed feelings that he was to have company to Hexham. Grey's meeting with Wharton was to be graced with the presence of the Earl of Lennox, and the Countess, on hearing that only twenty miles separated her from her husband, decided to join him instead of going direct to her home. Lady Christian, her women, her men-at-arms – and Gideon – went with her.

Without any very high hopes Somerville had spent part of the night making his own limited dispositions. He had posted a man north of Newcastle in case Lymond tried to trace the girl so far, and sent a small party of his own household in a belated effort to watch the other hill routes which a man crossing from Scotland to Hexham might take.

It was more of a gesture than a plan. It seemed likelier that Lymond would make straight for Berwick and there be captured, voluntarily or involuntarily. As his party rode out west through the green water meadows of the Tyne that morning Gideon, sunk in thought, rode in the rear and left Margaret Lennox and Christian to their own devices in front: a small lapse, but one that afterward he found hard to forgive himself.

On the night before Lady Lennox and her party left Newcastle, two parties of men slept in exhaustion on the Redesdale hills, closer than they knew, until, sensing the coming dawn, the most hardened of them all raised himself on his elbow.

Acheson was furiously regretting his errand. He had bargained neither for pursuit nor for a difficult cross-country ride. Not only that, but he had been forced to put off hours, so close was the pursuit, in covering his tracks and dodging about these damned, dry hills, so that the message he expected to deliver on Thursday night was still in his pocket.

That brought him to something he had been considering all the previous day. Making sure that the man at his side was sleeping, he drew out a third letter – the letter he had to deliver personally to Lord Grey – and broke the seal.

Shortly afterward he roused his companion and, collecting their tired horses, the two men resumed the last lap of their journey. It was Saturday, the twenty-third of June, and a glorious day.

In less than an hour. Mr. Acheson's odyssey of frustration had come to a surprising end. They were waylaid.

Acheson had his sword half drawn to deal with the strangers when his silent colleague stopped him, his eyes

444

on their badge. 'Wait!' said Lymond. 'Were you looking for me?' They were Somerville men.

Acheson let them talk. The man Lymond might look inconsiderable, but he had proved a master of ingenuity in a tight corner. Besides, they had made ground that morning, and he was thirsty. He dismounted, fanning himself with a dock leaf, and was unprepared for the sheer cutting quality of the man who turned back to him.

'What a pity. It seems I'm not coming with you after all,' said Lymond.

Acheson put a hand on his sword, then took it off quickly. It was none of his affair, but he liked to keep on the right side of his employers. 'What about this exchange business?'

'Later,' said Lymond airily. 'First of all, we are making a small detour by the house of a friend.'

'Then,' said Acheson sensibly. 'I'll go on alone.'

'And tell the others I'm in the neighbourhood? I'm afraid we can't have that either,' said Lymond pleasantly, and closed in. The black-haired one snarled and lunged, but a crack on the knuckles and another on the head cooled his ardour, if not his rage.

He was blindfolded, disarmed, mounted, and led at a smart trot over the remaining moors to Flaw Valleys.

* * *

Christian had noticed a moroseness about Simon Bogle very soon after her retinue set out for Hexham. He rode in silence, her long reins in his hands, and didn't even bid her good morning until she had addressed him twice. The deficiency was made up by the Countess of Lennox, who unrolled mellow conversation through the small dales like a Turkey carpet.

By the afternoon, some little sharpness and corners began to show through. The conversation took an unexpected turn toward Christian's fiancé.

'So different in appearance, of course: poor Tom; I shan't disillusion you. After all, you are affianced to him,' said Lady Lennox. 'Although you must have a soft spot for our naughty friend to do what you did for him at Haddington.'

'I like to think,' said Christian steadily, 'that I'd do as much for anyone in trouble.'

Margaret laughed. 'What an extraordinary person you are! To spend days by the bedside of a dying man, just to ask his address!'

Christian was silent.

'Or was it just his address?' asked Lady Lennox, and the black eyes were sparkling. 'Sym didn't think so, last night. I like your young bodyguard, my dear; but he hasn't a strong head, has he?'

'Sym!' said Christian sharply. 'Damn it . . . !'

The boy's voice wailed in her ear. 'I was drunk. I didna know what I was saying!'

'He was certainly drunk,' said Margaret's cool voice.

Christian said again, 'Sym –' and checked herself. He was gabbling. 'I couldna help it. Ye ken I canna hud up under beer . . .'

She made an effort. 'It doesn't matter. Lady Lennox: I depend on Sym for a great many things. There's nothing to stop you from associating with my servants if you want to, but I'd prefer not to have the younger ones reduced to a state of crapulence for your purposes.'

Irresistible but impolitic. Margaret said blandly, 'Am I worrying you? I'm sorry. But there's nothing wrong in listening to a dying man's confession; or even in getting it recorded and signed by a priest and thereafter hiding it – where have you hidden it, I wonder? Never mind. There'll be plenty of time to look, at Hexham.'

There was a little silence. Then the blind girl said slowly, 'You're quite safe, you know. Harvey confessed to a lot of things, but they had nothing to do with me. If he signed anything, it's probably on its way to his relatives in the south. Why on earth should I want it? If you don't believe me, I'm quite willing to be searched.'

'That's very sensible of you,' said Margaret Douglas cheerfully. 'Because I don't believe you, and although I'm

446

sure you've been most ingenious, I was proposing to search you very thoroughly indeed.'

Sym, coming out of a cloud of misery, suddenly took her up. 'Search her! Just try and touch her, ye bitch! Try and touch either of us!'

'You misunderstand me,' said Lady Lennox. 'I wouldn't soil my fingers. On you or your complaisant little mistress.'

Sym cried out. 'What have I done? She means ye harm: what have I done? I didna mean – it was just the drink – and she asked me – '

'Never mind, Sym,' said Christian. 'I'm afraid it was a mistake. She's no friend of ours – or of our friends.'

She could hear him swallow. He said in a low voice, 'The Master of Culter? She wants to hurt you and the Master of Culter?'

'Yes.'

'Then she willna!' said Sym, and hurled himself at Christian's horse.

The impact of his body jarred her forward, breathless. She felt him settle behind her, the brush of the reins as he gathered them tight; the firm clasp of his arm around her waist. The horse drew himself in, quivered, and answering Sym's heels swerved, spun, and drove like an arrow through the cavalcade.

Burst asunder, rearing, scattered, speechless, they looked after the flying horse; then, streaming up from the green Tyneside meadows, scrambling and pecking and hullooing over the little hills, they followed in full cry.

Christian had no breath. Crushed in the boy's grip, thought was driven from her by the speed of the animal; her hair buffeted and flew about her face, and her skirts tugged and twisted. The clasp at her waist shifted, and she managed a gasp. 'Sym, you fool, go back! We'll be overtaken and it'll be – all the worse for us both.'

For answer Sym drove his spurs again. 'I started the trouble, and I'll get you out of it, if it's only to find a place for those papers . . . could ye get them ready, now?'

She couldn't. Samuel Harvey's statement – the paper she had denied to Margaret Douglas – was sewn very

447

thoroughly in her saddlecloth. Nor were they likely, doubly burdened, to make enough ground to retrieve and hide it unseen. She said forcibly, 'Simon: stop this horse and turn around. It's no good!'

He didn't answer her. Instead, above the thud and jangle and creak of the galloping horse there came an odd, rustling noise. It stopped suddenly with a bump, and Sym gave a little grunt. The arms about her slackened and the pressure at her back shifted. Christian cried once, 'Simon!' and then with a clatter the whole body behind her shook itself loose and, rolling over the gelding's haunches, thudded on the heather.

The horse, already overexcited, entered a glory of self-induced fright and, the reins swaying against its knees, took the bit between its teeth.

The lifeless weight had nearly pulled the girl off too. But, barely realizing what had happened, Christian closed her knees instinctively and gripped the uncut mane with one hand, groping for the fallen reins. They eluded her: the horse was galloping wildly, shoulders and haunches lurching on the uneven ground; scrambling up slopes and down them, reaching higher and higher ground. Bushes clawed at her and once, a whipping branch stung her cheek.

She was holding now with both hands deep in the coarse hair. What kind of country? Not the homely paths between Boghall and Culter, or Stirling, or Dumbarton, or the High Street in Edinburgh with Simon, or Tom, or Jenny Fleming chatting placidly, describing the way to her.

A foreign land. Enemy country, where the earth existed to foster her ill-wishers, and trees to shelter them, and bushes to hide them. She who already carried in her eyes her own enemy.

Pursuit sounded now far distant. Ahead, the soft air of her passing pressed freely against her and the sound of birdsong came from great distances, as if spread sparkling through the warm air: a singing dust. Singing sand . . . Would she ever visit the islands again? Or be with the children? Or Sybilla. Or Wicket Wat. Or the man for whom she was now flying blind, on an uncontrolled horse through the small hills of Redesdale?

Behind, swooning on the air, rose a great shout. It rolled, remote and hollow, over the moor, and sank whispering among the flags.

Her pursuers saw, as she did not, the stalking, gem-cut line of the Wall ahead; the clustering gorse bushes and the debris of fifteen centuries which hid the brink of its twenty-foot ditch. Long before that warning cry faded, Christian's horse had taken those deceptive bushes in its stride; had hurtled into the fossa beyond, trundling, rolling and threshing its broken limbs in agony as the girl, a flash of white arms and dusty skirts and dark red hair, tumbled with him.

Margaret Douglas stood and watched Gideon's gentle, bloody hands lift Christian Stewart, the red hair drifting in his face. Then Lady Lennox stooped in turn by the dead horse and with nimble fingers and a sharp knife ripped open first the girl's pack, and then the trappings.

The cloth gave up its secret immediately. She pulled out a small bundle of papers, separated them, glanced on both sides, and made a curious sound, so close to a laugh that Gideon turned sharply on her. She was refolding the same papers and stuffing them back into the lining where they had been hidden. She did it quite carefully and then stood up, dusting her hands.

One of Gideon's own men had already helped him lift the quiet figure into the saddle in front of him: there was hardly any pulse. Margaret looked curiously at the unconscious face. 'Is there a house nearby where you can take her?'

Kate wouldn't have recognized the look in Gideon's eyes. He said levelly, 'My home isn't far away. She may as well die among friends.'

The black eyes raged at him: Margaret also had had a shock. 'It's hardly my fault if my bowman tries to stop a prisoner from escaping. That's what he's paid for.' She kicked the saddle and its furniture. 'You'd better take that, too. Her family might want it.'

'Is that all you have to say?' said Gideon.

'She was blind. It's too great a handicap. She's better out of it,' said Margaret in a staccato voice, and mounted her horse.

'Was that her sin?' said Gideon, watching the cavalcade move off. 'I had come to fancy it might be something quite different.'

3 · THE LAST MOVE

When Lymond set foot for the third time in Flaw Valleys, Gideon went downstairs to greet him slowly, and found his upturned face abounding with an electric vigour which quite overlaid the marks of his journey.

'I'm sorry,' he remarked ebulliently when his host was halfway down. 'Adhesive as St. Anthony's pig. Qu'on lui ferme la porte au nez, il reviendra par les fenêtres. Thank you for your messages: your name will fly tetragrammaton round the world, and this fair blind Fortune will be made immortal. I've asked your henchmen to lock up an indignant gentleman who was leading me to Lord Grey and here I am. Where is she? How can we free her? – and what, my God what, did she learn from Samuel Harvey?'

It was worse than Somerville expected: it was frankly damnable. After just too long a space, as Lymond's face already began to alter, Gideon said bluntly, 'She's freed herself. There's nothing to do. I wish to God you'd never got my message.' And nodded, regaining proper hold of his tongue, 'There's been an accident.'

As he expected, Lymond took the news undemonstratively, in answer to his training; however much the flesh might shrink and melt, the sarcophagus was decently void of temperament. 'Where is she?'

'Kate is with her upstairs. She hasn't much time. I'll take you to her.'

'Thank you.' An automatic reply, and an automatic climbing of the stairs. As they went, Gideon told his story, shooting curious side glances at the younger man. The

450

blond face was lightly sheened with perspiration, but it was a warm day; there was no tremor of sentiment in it.

The music room was filled with sunlight and the smells of warmed wood and fruity earth from Kate's pot plants. They passed the lute and rebec and the fiddle and harpsichord sealed in silent jubilee, and crossed to the inner room.

Kate had also heard the story, attacking the situation with her mind and squashing emotion and surmise with a prompt if temporary thumb.

She did what was necessary out of the bounty which suffering naturally commanded, and out of a sharp reaction to the courage of the injured girl. Conjecture firmly dismissed, she sat down beside her own bed, when every service of comfort had been performed, and took quiet and efficient note of the quiet and efficient messages enumerated from the pillows.

Christian's mind was perfectly clear. Her chief anguish, clearly, was the death of the boy Simon. Beyond that she wasted no time on regrets or self-pity, except perhaps when she had said all that was vital to say, and after lying silent for a moment observed: 'You know, life has so many ridiculous hazards when one is blind – and yet I never expected somehow to die so far from home, without anyone of my own.' She smiled quite successfully and added, 'I don't suppose it matters. We're all pretty solitary anyhow, aren't we? Is someone else coming in?'

Kate hadn't heard Lymond enter. Across the bed she saw him tweak a strand of dark red hair gently between finger and thumb, and then slip into a chair beside the pillow. 'Don't be so superior. Someone of your own is here,' he said.

The girl's control was weaker than his. Her brow creased and tears sprang into her opened eyes. She shut them and said shakily, 'It's witchcraft. You are about to babble like magpies and herring gulls.'

'But not about the ruin of charity: in Flaw Valleys it

451

multiplies like rhubarb. . . . What in God's name must you think of me after all the drivel I had to talk at Threave?'

There was an undeniable smile on the white face. 'That you expected to be hanged. And didn't want me to be pointed out solely as the girl with a strong attachment for her dependents. It was all right. I understood.'

'It wasn't all right,' said Lymond flatly. 'It's been all of a piece. I've been a joyless jeweller up to the last, exquisite drop from the crucible.'

'There aren't any dregs in my cup,' said Christian. 'You're the only person who could make me swallow them. I'd do what I did over again. I never cared for old age, or the idea of outliving my friends and being a chattel to my relatives. I mourned a little because nobody would ever point to a page of history and say, "The stream turned there to the right, or to the left, because of Christian Stewart." You could make that come true for me, if you think you owe me anything. And you could promise me not to retreat to a wine barrel and reduce what we've both done to a few artificial bubbles of regrets and self-blame. You prophesied yourself that I should have all I wanted from life, did you not? And I think I have,' she said.

He answered her like the lash of a whip. 'There seems no doubt I've been reserved for great things –

'Io son fatta da Dio, sua merce, tale . . .
I am the chosen of God. He will see
That your suffering does me no harm
That the flames of this fire never touch me.'

The impact of the words was almost physical. Kate flinched and the girl in the bed cried out, 'No!'

He broke off of his own accord. 'No,' he agreed after a moment. 'God knows why you think it's worth it, but I wouldn't have the puny effrontery to waste what you've done. When I think of my brilliant pose of anonymity . . .'

A smile twitched her lips again. 'I knew you'd be much too high-minded to come back if you suspected I knew. That's why I stopped you at Inchmahome.'

452

Lymond's face was as white as the girl he was talking to, but his voice hardly varied.

'I am grovelling. I also owe you one or two stinging innuendoes for those letters. If Agnes Herries ever stumbles on a glossa inter-linearis there will be civil war.'

'Erskine made her burn them. . . . Is that your hand? It's colder than mine. I told you not to worry.'

Christian blinked suddenly and roused herself. 'My mind's wandering. Listen: I have something for you. It's sewn in my saddlecloth. Mr. Somerville will show you. Hurry!' Her face, framed in the strewn hair, was as matronly as a nurse commanding a treat for a child.

For the first time, Lymond's eyes met Kate's. He rose slowly and walked to the door. Kate heard her husband speak in the corridor, and then both men's footsteps receding. After no more than a few minutes, Lymond returned.

This time, his eyes never left the girl in the bed. Sitting beside her, he raised her hand and put under it a crumpled fold of small papers bloodstained – as Kate saw – in one corner.

Christian's face was alight. 'You've read them? They're all there?'

'I've read them. But how . . . ?' Lymond was saying in a kind of lunatic daze. 'How the devil – how the *devil* could you do it? To have it in black and white at the eleventh hour . . . Did you threaten him? Cut off his ears and souse them in vinegar? Propose to confine him in a locked room with Lord Grey for six months?'

The girl gave the ghost of a laugh. 'It was on his conscience. He dictated the whole story and signed it. The priest was there too – that's the second signature. Is it what you'd hoped?'

There was the fraction of a pause. Then Lymond picked up Christian's hand and carried it to his lips, holding it afterward folded in both his own. 'More than I ever dreamed of,' he said – and like the serpent she had once called him, snarled voicelessly into Kate's eyes as she looked up, horror-struck, from what the girl's lifted hand had left revealed.

For the sheets of creased paper which Christian had brought with such pains from Haddington, which Margaret had found not worth her attention, and which Lymond had at last received, were quite blank.

Kate gave nothing away. Christian, it appeared, wanted her company. Since she couldn't go, she was forced to sit and watch, listening to the murmur of their voices. They were talking of things and people Kate knew nothing about, but she knew contentment when she saw it, and didn't interrupt even when the girl's voice began to lapse and the air to falter at last in her lungs.

Christian did what was necessary herself, turning her head painfully toward Kate. 'I was never much good at waiting,' she said. 'It's a sign of immaturity, or something. I wonder if maybe music would be soothing? If someone would play . . . Not you,' she added quickly, as Kate rose. 'If you don't mind. It's comforting to have you sitting so close.'

'Of course I'll stay,' said Kate, her mind racing. 'Would you like Mr. Crawford to play for you? The music room is only through a door by your bed.'

She had, obviously, guessed right. The smile this time was one of relief. 'He still has to finish a song he played for me once. Do you remember?'

'The unfortunate frog. Of course,' said Lymond, straightening. Kate met his eyes and nodded: she thought he looked almost at the end of his endurance, but he could be relied on to make no mistakes. He bent quickly and taking both Christian's hands, kissed her on the brow. 'The frog was a pretty poor creature. This time you shall have music to sound in a high tower – '

'– So merrily that it was a joy for to hear, and no man should see the craft thereof. . . . You give me such pleasure,' said Christian.

A moment later the music began, and Kate shrank beneath the onslaught of its message: the fury of hope and joy that towered in the notes, outburning the sunlight and outpouring the volumes of the sea. All that was bold and noble and happy in created sound burst from the metempirical quills, and it was a blasphemy not to rejoice.

Christian died in its midst, purposeful and successful; the last struggle unseen by anyone but Kate, and laying no bridle on the living. Kate drew the bright curtains around the bed.

> *Jouissance vous donneray*
> *Mon amy, et vous méneray*
> *Là où prétend*
> *Votre espérance*
> *Vivante ne vous laisseray*
> *Encores quand morte seray*
> *L'esprit en aura souvenance.*

Her eyes were closed with tears: strangers – foreigners – what were they to her? The man was playing still, his eyes resting on the windows as they had done all along. Through the glass she saw that a column of mounted men had come over the moor and up to her lodge gates: like squirrels their faces were pricked at her windows; like Ulysses perhaps their ears were tingling with the music of the sirens. She dried her cheeks and walked forward a little, and Lymond, seeing her reflection in the panes, raised his hands.

The horseman in the lead was bending down, addressing someone very young or very small. Kate saw the white flash of a face, and one bare arm waving toward the house. She was infinitely more afraid of the immobile man at the keyboard. She rested her hands, as in prayer, on the instrument. 'It happened peacefully.'

'Did it?' said Lymond.

The entire file had moved forward to the gatehouse. There seemed to be a moment of confusion, then the doors opened and the horsemen came through, rather fast.

'I believe she meant what she said,' said Kate. 'About being contented.'

She wasn't sure if he heard her. After a moment he stirred, and lifting a hand to the keys again, picked out some slow chords. 'It was the Frogge on the wall, Humble-dum; humble-dum.'

'You didn't finish it for her, after all,' said Kate.

The house was alive with noise. He said nothing and did nothing; and at length even Kate's resolution gave way. 'Who are they? What do they want? Who is it?'

He had watched the long file of horesemen sweep over the moor: while he loosed his fierce elegies he had watched them sense the music on the wind and point to him like hounds. He had promised Christian music for her minion and outrider, and he kept his promise.

'What is it?' cried Kate, and Lymond turned with grim finality from the keys. 'What is it? The end of the song. Where Dickie our Drake, Mrs. Somerville, takes the Frog.'

And on the last word, the stark and pitiful peace of his anthems had gone. With a crash of bruised post and split panels and an assault which sent gut and sounding board screaming, the door of the music room opened.

'– Richard, my brother,' ended Lymond.

It was Culter, his search over.

Broad, powerful, shivering within the frame of smashed wood, he was a primitive figure, of pantheistic and dreadful force. Standing still, all his mind and his passions embraced the two silent people by the window, allowing the texture, the luxury, the exquisite savour of the prize to drive him to ecstasy. A little sound, involuntary and wordless, broke from him.

For a moment, she thought it was going to strike an answer from Lymond. Another person might have screamed at him, or at the intruders; but Kate did neither: she literally held her breath, watching pressures she could only guess at being licked by this vengeful fire. She obeyed an instinct to keep quiet, and by lending Lymond the support of her calmness, to avert the thing that would destroy them all.

He succeeded. In the teeth of unleashed hatred and on the heels of tragedy he shackled human reaction and, rising smoothly and quickly, addressed his brother as men poured into the room.

'I know. Aha, Oho, and every other bloody ejaculation. Let's take it as read. You're delirious at the idea of man-handling me and can't wait to start. I in turn may say I find your arrival offensive and your presence blasphemous, thus concluding the exchange of civilities and letting us get out of here. If there's anything novel or extra you want to add, you can think of it on the way home.'

The words struck and fell dead to the ground. Richard made not the slightest movement, his grey eyes wetly shining; the fat veins visible on his temple and neck. 'He's in a hurry, isn't he? It's a love nest, as I live. Who's the wench?'

'The wench is a lady, and mistress of this house,' said Lymond in the same controlled and insulting voice. 'Erskine: take him downstairs. Something's happened.'

Lord Culter grinned lecherously. 'I'm sure it has.'

'Later, Richard. You can have all the sport you want. Erskine –'

Tom Erskine said, 'Come on, Richard. We've got him: there's no point in wasting time.'

Lord Culter ignored him. He was wandering around the room, touching things and still smiling. Kate moving quickly before him shut the door to her bedroom and returned to Lymond's side. 'There has been –'

'Be quiet,' said Richard pleasantly. 'And you, little brother. How would five years of this sort of thing appeal to you, Tom? Where's the bed, I wonder? Behind the door they're not looking at? With another wench in it, maybe?'

He had an unlooked-for agility. He reached the bed-room door a second before Lymond and got it open. The Master's hard shoulder crashed into him and he hurtled back with the shuddering wood, but already half-braced and with a purchase on his brother's arm which brought Lymond stumbling with him. Then there was a rush to help, and the Master went down under six others.

They pulled him to his feet as Richard, rising, was confronted by the young woman who had first shut the

457

door. 'Get out of this room and listen to me, you uncivilized lout!' said Kate.

Richard struck her to her knees with the hardened flat of his hand, the first blow he had ever aimed at a woman, and wrenched back the yellow silk curtains.

Over their tawdrinesses grieved the benign detachment of death.

At Richard's blanched rigidity, Lymond fell silent, unstruggling, by the door; Kate rose and found her way obstinately to a chair, one hand to her face; and Tom Erskine, struck by the silence, moved from the doorway. Lymond's long fingers shot out and halted him.

'There's bad news. We tried to tell you. It's Christian.' Erskine broke from his grasp without a sound.

Presently, Lord Culter moved from the bedside, leaving Tom where he knelt. Back in the music room where his men waited, silent and uneasy, he picked out one with a glance. 'Send for the man – Somerville, is it? I want him here.' Then he turned to his brother, his face as hard as the bones of the earth. 'I'd neither foul a cage by capturing you nor offend justice by taking you to Court. Covet the sunshine: you are dying.'

'No!' exclaimed Kate Somerville from the doorway. She had dropped her hand from her bruised face. 'No, you're wrong. The girl met with her accident while travelling in English company to Hexham. When Mr. Crawford arrived she was already dying. He did all he could for her.'

'Concluding with jigs and hornpipes over her deathbed. I know. My God, we heard him!'

'What my wife says is true.' Gideon had arrived in the doorway.

Richard didn't turn his head. 'Exposing her to public obloquy at Threave – that's another fact. Cheating her about his identity. Making this blind girl an accomplice traitor, and accomplice murderer, adulterer . . .'

Lymond's voice cut sharply across. 'We've all had as much as we can stand, Culter. You know perfectly well you can't kill me here unless I resist capture: it needs one busybody to pipe up in Parliament and you'll be arrested yourself. Let the fools argue it out in Edinburgh: I'll go quietly. Come along. Half the English army's at Hexham. I don't want to meet Grey, even if you do. And for God's sake get Erskine out of that room for a start.'

Lord Culter paid not the slightest attention. He was issuing quiet, concise orders to his men, and to Somerville, who listened tight-lipped. When he had quite finished, he turned back to Lymond.

'I don't murder anybody. I'm offering you a proper trial – trial by combat. Observing all the rules. You may even think you have a chance of killing me. If you do, you are free, of course.'

Gideon's eyes met his wife's. He said quietly, 'Take him to Edinburgh as he asks. He's quite right – Grey and Wharton are at Hexham. If anyone calls, you haven't a chance. And,' added Gideon with some bluntness, 'you haven't seen his swordplay.'

A heretical insolence had found its way back to Lymond. 'Why worry, children? I'm not going to fight.'

'I thought we'd have that,' said Richard calmly. Somerville, after hesitating, left, pushed by two soldiers. 'You'd prefer to be skewered like a sheep?'

'I'd prefer to take a nice, quiet journey to Edinburgh and stand my trial. Think how deliciously prolonged it would all be.'

The flat grey eyes were unmoved. 'You'll fight,' said Richard without emotion, and jerked his head. Preceded by Lymond and the rest of his men, he left the room.

Kate saw them go, her brown face stiff with trouble, and then turned back into her bedroom. For a moment she watched the kneeling man, and then bending over him, touched his shoulder. 'Mr. Erskine. Please come away.'

For a moment nothing happened. Then he raised a face curiously blurred, as if the subcutaneous fat had melted and recongealed in his grief. He said thickly, 'It's all right. . . . How did it happen?'

She pulled a chair toward him and he sat, while she told her story. At the end there was a pause, and then he said with difficulty, 'I wondered . . . I couldn't quite understand why she did it.'

Kate said with care, 'She would help anybody, I think: wasn't that so? And then – you've all condemned him pretty thoroughly as a blackguard, haven't you?'

'What else is he?'

'Well,' said Kate. 'I'm not one of the simple kind who spend a jolly time romping on Olympus with the object of becoming a little, leering star at the end. I never met the girl before today: I don't know what their past relations have been. But I can say that he spoke of your Lady Christian with nothing but respect. By her desire I was with them both till she died, and I should be ashamed to think of guilt or offence in anything they said. And more than that. It was you I was to tell of her regrets, and to you I was to give her love.'

He got up slowly, a man not incapable of a moment of insight. But he said only, 'Thank you. I'm glad you were with her,' and walked out, without looking back.

Kate smoothed the crumpled sheets with gentle fingers, and spoke aloud. 'He was very nearly good enough for you, that one,' she said; and drawing the yellow curtains, shut out the sun.

* * *

Since he was quite a young man, Gideon Somerville had grown used to the role of bystander. Other men – less intelligent, shallower men – plunged into a tidal race of action, conflict, argument and sinewy bravado. But within Gideon something shrank from pressing his intangible opinions, his doubt-ridden intellect and humane heart on the destinies of others as helpless as himself. He knew the ache of indecision too well.

Today, brought to disturbing acquaintance with new minds, he weighed them up, watching with his clear eyes, and tacitly stepped aside. There was no tangle here that he or any stranger could undo. Flaw Valleys was no prison. His staff could break out if he incited them: he could send a man to Hexham for help if he tried; but he had no wish to try. He asked quietly that his wife shouldn't be asked to be present; he made sure that Philippa wasn't left unwatched or frightened; and he brought to Lord Culter a pair of matched rapiers and two daggers.

As the weapons arrived, Tom Erskine came into the hall and took charge.

The fact that he did so sobered them all. In a year he had become used to command: his father, after all, was within the most intimate circle of the Court; his grandfather was Archibald, second Duke of Argyll; his grandmother and his sister had borne sons to two kings. He came now into the room, collected everyone's attention and said quietly, 'Richard: this is a warning. This man is a prisoner of the Crown and has to answer to the Crown for his crimes. To do what you mean to do demands strong cause. Do you have it?'

'*You* ask me that? Yes. Of course I have.'

'To kill this man in a private house for a private quarrel in foreign territory may lead you to be charged with his murder. Could you refute that?'

'Yes,' said Richard. 'As you very well know. At this moment he's carrying papers that'd mean the end of us as a nation and very likely the death of the Queen if they reached Hexham.'

Lymond, who had been staring out of one of the tall windows and drumming with his finger tips on the shutter, came to life and spun around. 'That isn't true!'

Erskine kicked something at his feet. 'Is that your baggage roll?'

'Yes.'

'And this, which was in it, is your letter?'

Without speaking, Lymond accepted the papers Erskine held out – papers which, as Erskine and Culter both knew, gave in detail the plans for the Queen's escape to France.

He took a long time over the pages, his eyes staying a moment, unseeing at the foot; then he returned them. 'Well?' said Erskine.

'The man with me: Acheson. Have you questioned him about these?' asked Lymond. 'He's locked up belowstairs.'

'Yes,' said Erskine. 'We've seen him. He was carrying two letters from George Douglas about the safety of his sons. That's all he's got, and that's all he knows about.'

'I see,' said Lymond slowly. 'The obvious answer, of course. The classic escape from this kind of situation, as you know, is for each party to blame the other. In which case, I assume for safety's sake that you'll take him back home with you? I should strongly advise you not to let him out of your sight.'

'He put the papers in your baggage?' said Richard helpfully.

'Something like that. But let's put it at its lowest. He knows the contents of the papers. So for God's sake don't admit him to your social circle just because you're happy he's given you a hold over me.'

'And has he?' asked Erskine – and misinterpreting the ensuing pause added, 'Well?'

'Well enough for everybody's purpose,' said Lymond without passion. 'One crime more or less isn't going to deter Richard now.'

It was treated as an admission; there was a murmur of abuse and contempt, irresistibly, and someone spat. Erskine turned his back on the younger man and addressed Richard again. 'That being so, you have a public reason for bringing this man to trial here and now. You also have private reasons?'

'Yes.'

'What are they?'

Richard was silent, his jaw doggedly set.

'State them,' said Erskine sharply. 'If this is to be trial by combat, the defendant has a right to hear your complaint.'

Lord Culter said, speaking very fast in a low voice, 'He has degraded our family name ... committed theft and arson and attacked a guest beneath my roof. He has tried to take my life repeatedly.'

Lymond made a sudden movement, apparently involuntarily, and the gesture restored Richard's voice. He said quite clearly, 'He has dishonoured my wife and killed my only son.'

Nobody spoke. Between man and man the sunlight hesitated, sparkling, and sank to the floor with the languishing dust. Gideon bit his lip. 'What have you to reply?' asked Erskine.

Lymond's voice was undramatic and his face unreadable. 'Your choice is between executing me here or in Edinburgh. I will not fight.'

Erskine had begun to say, 'Do you admit, then . . .' when Richard interrupted. 'Wait a moment. Let us all have it clear. If one of us fails to fight, it means he admits he has no honour to defend?'

'That is the usual interpretation.'

'In other words, that he admits the truth of the charges against him. Do you freely admit to treason, brother? To murder and rape? Fratricide as near as may be?'

'I admit none of it.'

'Yet you won't fight. You admit your – connection with my wife?'

'No!'

'And yet you won't fight. You admit that you deceived that girl upstairs into becoming your blind and complaisant mistress, and then killed her when you tired of it?'

Erskine's voice clashed harshly with Lymond's. The Master's prevailed through sheer bite. 'You uncivilized maniac: that's a damnable lever to use.'

'If you won't defend your story, we must assume it's true.'

'You can assume,' said Lymond, stirred at last into straight speaking, 'that I'm trying to prevent you from getting your bloody throat cut; that's all.'

'You imagine,' said Richard, his voice rocketing between prayerful hope and excitement, 'that you could fight me and survive?'

'I could see you drop dead this minute from paralysis of the brain cells and burst into uninhibited applause. I had nothing to do with Christian Stewart's death, nor did I touch her when she was alive. I'll defend that, damn you, against anybody. Set up your tin-foil trial and try and prove otherwise if you can.'

Richard, flexing the fingers of his right hand, raised his eyebrows at Tom Erskine. 'You heard? He's going to fight,' he said gently.

Set below the music room, the hall at Flaw Valleys was lit by the same pattern of tall windows along one of its long sides; on the other, double doors at its centre made the only entrance. The shining wood floor had been cleared of furniture and the spectators stood behind rope at either end: Gideon to the right, with six of his own men, and Erskine and Culter's men to the left. Within the arena, Lymond had resumed his stance by one of the window seats. Both Culter and Tom Erskine were missing.

Conversation was low. Gideon wondered what his wife was doing. He thought of the music he had heard that afternoon, and of his conversations with Lymond, and of something Lymond had said to Kate. 'If it's going to happen, it won't happen here.' But how much, indeed, could flesh and blood stand?

A table was put in the centre of the room. On it, Gideon could see the four weapons, four slots of blue; and beside them a heavy book: a volume of the Four Gospels impressed with tarnished gold leaf, which had belonged to Kate's mother. Culter came in and stood by it; then Erskine, and the doors were shut.

Erskine stood just in front of the carved oak. He was still without colour, but composed and firmly in authority. He looked at his audience to the right and left extremities of the room, to Lymond by the window and to Richard in front of him and said quietly, 'You know the purpose of this gathering. We are about to hold trial by combat between these two men here before you, and I take to myself the authority to regulate and to take oath as if this were done in Scotland, in champ clos. Will you both abide by that?' He waited for their assent, and then in a grave, clear voice began to administer the oath.

'You, Richard, third Baron Crawford of Culter, laying your right hand upon this Book, must swear the truth of your complaint in all its points, from the first to the last charge in it, and that it is your intent to prove the contents to be true, so aid you God.'

'So aid me God.'

Culter's voice was steady. Erskine proffered the book again. 'Richard Crawford, third Baron Culter, laying your hand on the Book this second time, you must swear that you stand no otherwise appointed than by me, with a rapier and a dagger; that you have not any other pointed instrument or engine, small or great; no stone or herb of virtue, no charm, experiment or other enchantment by whose power you believe you may overcome your adversary who here shall oppose you in his defence; and that you trust not in anything more than in God, your body, and the merits of your quarrel; so God you help.'

Richard's voice, quietly taking the oath, and the pad of his stockinged feet as he stepped back broke the silence. There was a tightening of the figure by the window and Erskine's even voice, slightly raised.

'Francis Crawford of Lymond, Master of Culter.' After the briefest hesitation, the man came to him. 'Laying your right hand on this Book . . .'

Erskine's eyes this time were intent. He read the oath still with his voice a little raised, like a challenge. At the words, 'So aid me God,' repeated without emphasis, a ripple of comment made itself heard in the quiet room. Erskine ignored it. 'Lord Culter. Please come forward.'

Richard moved this time after a distinct pause and took his place before Erskine at his brother's side. Erskine captured his eyes and held them. 'Take ye each other by the right hand, laying the left on the Book.'

'He won't. Damned if I blame him,' said the man next to Gideon. Richard was grinning. 'I have no right hand, Mr. Erskine.'

His temporary Constable neither argued or pleaded. He simply observed, 'I have the power to make that true, as you should know. Face your opponent and take him by the right hand.'

It was Lymond who made the move. Richard touched

465

the proffered hand with the tips of his fingers, his left hand on the book between them so that their joined arms made the required cross, and his eyes were anarchists in the community of his hands. 'I charge you,' began Erskine solemnly:

'I charge you by your faith and your right hand, which is enclosed in the hand of your adversary, that you use your power and make use of all advantages to make good your appeal, to force him to a rendering of himself unto your hands, or with your own hand to kill him before you part from this room, and so God you help.'

They swore, and the blades were lifted from the table: the thin tempered rapiers with steel quillons and counter-guard; the daggers with their thick, double-edged blades, twelve inches long. Richard received his weapons: sword for the right hand and dagger for the left; and then Lymond. The Gospel was removed; the table taken away. Erskine, his eyes travelling over every face, Scots and English, gave the familiar address.

'We charge and command every man that he approach not nor that he speak, make any noise, give any sign nor by his countenance or otherwise direct either of these parties to take any advantages the one upon the other, upon pain of life and members.'

He paused, looking up at the brilliant windows and Kate's bright chestnuts beyond. A goose, frowning, marched across the grass. Inside, the sun prinked and patterned the floor, aureoled the two white-shirted men, standing widely separated, and fell upon itself, reflected in the steel, with redoubled kisses.

'The day is far passed,' said Erskine, making the herald's formal pronouncement. 'Let them go, let them go, to do their endeavour.'

To do his endeavour, Lymond waited in the hall of Flaw Valleys, a slender, feral figure, limbs relaxed, eyes wide awake and steel in either scarred hand; and watched his brother advance. 'Quicker, Richard. We're meant to explode into action.' The voice was ribald.

Face to face with him, Lord Culter answered softly.

'There's no hurry.' And there was a flicker of movement and a click, as Lymond parried, sliding sideways to miss the twinkle of the short blade. Richard waited. He was indeed in no hurry.

'Since we are here,' said Lymond conversationally, 'why not pronounce something appropriate? "Eh bien, dansez maintenant"? Or, "We came both out of one womb: so shall we lie both in one pit"? And there's "Brother, whi art thou so to me in ire?" – the killing of Abel, my dear: a mine of suitable commentary . . . Come along,' said the playful, savage voice. 'Let us fight with sugar in our mouths like the litigating tailors of V – ' And he ducked.

'Oh, no. No, no, no,' said Lymond. 'Nature works in the . . . shortest way possible. If you really want to reach my guts . . .'

The sun was on his face. 'I do,' said Richard. 'But not immediately.' And this time he thrust, traversed and lunged again, the dagger poised and intent, waiting for Lymond to duck out of the sunlight.

He did exactly that. Richard, smiling faintly, whipped up his left arm and halted, blinded in the act by the light from his brother's blade. '. . . trying lunging in a straight line,' ended Lymond, serene and safe. 'Useful thing, sunlight. Play up, master swordman. You're rolling about like a pear in a pottle.' They drifted apart again.

His intention was obvious. Gideon was not inspired to laugh, but some of his men were, and he saw that Culter was aware of it. Lymond was of course behaving atrociously: he seemed prepared to make any sort of fool of himself rather than allow his brother near. Culter, by no means playing seriously himself as yet, was testing the other man's strength, or trying to. The Master eddied around the floor, talking.

If Richard had meant to make his power felt gradually, he was forced to drop the idea. Unless he was to be a laughingstock, he must force Lymond to fight; and his brother, as well as Erskine and Gideon and the waiting men, read the sudden purpose in his face. But Lymond got in first.

'Bloodthirsty, Richard?' he asked. 'Husband your humours. Think of the fair ones at home. His heart was light as leaf on tree, when that he thought on his – '

It was one quotation he never did finish. There was a growl from Richard, an unconscious yelp from the spectators, and the fighting had begun in earnest.

In all the length of the bare room, no one spoke. The long blades exploded together, cracked, chimed and clattered; the stockinged feet slid and shuffled and the two men breathed in gasps, quickly, traversing and gyrating, slipping in and out of sword-length, each in a cocoon of whirring light. A blizzard of suns on walls and ceiling enclosed them.

Culter was a master, worth seeing on any terms: worth seeing even when wrought up with anger. His brain directed; his eyes and feet, shoulders and wrists answered, and the result was sure and powerful swordplay. Lymond said once, in a breathless voice curiously close to laughter, 'He's *twice* the size of common men, wi' thewes and sinewes strong,' and then retired to silence. The daggers, sparkling over and under the swords, darted like serpents.

Within the first three minutes Richard's sword touched his brother's shoulder. Gideon, with the rest, said, 'Oh!' and then smiled. There was no harm done: the shoulder was already protected by the old bandage of Scott's thrust. The lids veiled Lymond's eyes as they disengaged. 'Reaping the eddish. Try the other side next time.'

There was no next time. They fought themselves across, to and against the ropes on the Master's side, the watching men pressing back against the wall; and then slowly moved back to the centre. Culter was attacking fast and brutally and his brother was displaying, one after the other, every trick at his command in a prodigious effort to defend himself.

He succeeded at the cost of being whipped forward and then back again across the floor, his parrying arm taking again and again the jar of the meeting blades. He showed surprising mastery with the dagger hand, and his excellence with that was something Richard clearly had to allow

468

for consistently: again and again it baulked his follow-through and his feint.

The cost to both men was a growing tiredness, magnified by the long chase and by the emotional battle upstairs. After his first violence Richard's speed dropped, but he fought like a textbook, missing nothing and giving nothing away. Lymond, his shirt soaked with perspiration, recoiled incessantly.

Ten minutes later, they were still fighting, and the watching room was quite silent. At Gideon's elbow, Tom Erskine said suddenly, 'I tell you: no man has ever stood against Culter's sword for so long.'

There was trouble in Somerville's eyes. 'I could have warned him,' he said.

Erskine's breath hissed. 'If one of them isn't fighting. I shall stop it.'

'It won't be necessary,' said Gideon quietly. 'I think Lord Culter has realized.'

It was true. Fighting against a sword so weak as to be incapable of riposte or counterthrust or attack of any sort, he had still failed to penetrate Lymond's guard. With grim fortitude, Richard put a monstrous theory to the test. In the middle of an imbroccata he dropped his left hand, exposing his whole flank momentarily to Lymond's right blade.

Lymond parried and withdrew, the blue eyes quite impersonal.

Lord Culter disengaged. He did more: he drew back his arm and hurled his sword quivering on the floor, his eyes bitter as squill. 'Damn you to hell. You're not fighting?'

A man's voice called through the silence of the room. 'He's escaped!' Lymond, breathing quickly, stood without speaking.

'I'm to be your buffoon here, as everywhere else. . . .'

The shouting voice was nearer. It said, 'Mr Erskine, sir! The black fellow: he's got a horse and escaped!'

Richard didn't even pause. 'You bloody-minded little vampire – how in God's name can I hurt you enough?'

469

Lymond said briefly, 'Don't underrate yourself. . . . Erskine: if Acheson has got loose, he'll go to Hexham. Do you know it?'

'No, but don't worry,' said Erskine grimly. 'We'll get him before he arrives there. Richard –'

'Do what you like. I've business to finish here,' said Culter.

'Oh, for God's sake, Richard,' said Lymond harshly. 'Erskine: I can take you straight to where the man is going. How the hell do you expect to stop him otherwise, if you don't know the road? Give me a horse and all the escort you like but be quick about it. I don't give a damn who you think carried the dispatch, but Acheson knows its contents.'

Calmly Richard, picking up his sword, moved between his brother and the door. 'You won't wriggle out of it that way.'

'Richard –'

'Don't be a fool. He'll lead you straight to Lord Grey.'

'Then it's a risk we must take,' said Erskine steadily. 'He's right, Culter. Let him go.'

'Not until we have finished this.'

Erskine was trying desperately hard to keep his temper. 'Listen. If that message gets through . . .'

Richard rounded on him. 'Are you relying on *Lymond* to stop it? Then you're a simpleton. Go if you want to. I'm not holding you back. But you're not taking him: I'll kill the first man who comes near him.' And he turned, his eyes sparkling in his white face, to his brother.

'You were too superior to attack? Then you can damned well attack now.' His sword was in his hand, a fine instrument of latent death, sparkling largo to larghetto with his dagger. 'The way to that door is through me. Take it brother, if you can.'

There was a pause. Erskine said sharply, 'Hob, Jamie: take your horses and try and pick up the tracks. We'll follow as soon as we can.'

Lymond stirred. Sleek, cold, finely polished as his own steel, there was an air about him now that none of them had ever seen. 'Very well,' said the voice that sixty outlaws had known. 'Since you offer, I'll take it.'

And he moved in straight to the attack.

It was as if some flawed and clouded screen had slid from the air, leaving it thin and bright; informing the white figures and pale heads, fair and brown, with an engraver's beauty of exact and flexible outline, and lending a weightlessness and authority to their art.

For the brothers were natural swordsmen. The slipping and tapping of the fine blades, the unfurling movements growing smokelike one within the other, showed no trace of the grim and gritty striving of a moment before. It was classic swordplay, precious as a jewel, beyond any sort of price to the men watching, and concealing in its graces an exquisite and esoteric death.

They had always known Richard for a master. They now saw Crawford of Lymond grow before their eyes, the tutored power entering behind the elegance, the shoulders straight, the wrists of the temper which had withstood all the force of Richard's long aggression and which now adventured, strong and pliant, with every trained sinew of his body.

To the two men, existence was in the end the flicker of the other man's steel; his brown arms and wrists; a blur of white shirt and white face and the live, directing brain betraying itself through grey eyes or blue. The men watching, unable to breathe, heard the click and clash and slither of contes, froissées, beating and binding: saw first one man and then the other bring his art to the pitch of freeing his blade for the ultimate perfection, only to bow before the other's defence.

Lymond fought consistently within measure, intensely fast, with an attacking dagger: Erskine, his heart frozen by his eyes, saw him beating constantly on Richard's blade, moving it out of his way; out of line; pressing it down and opening the way for a lunge.

Tap, tap went the compound riposte, the soft feet slith-

471

éred – and then Richard's blade moved, Lymond's right arm whipped stiff, and the flat of his blade adhered to the flat of his opponent's. There was a glottal whine. The point, glittering, slithered down and down to Culter's counterguard until Richard, with all his compact strength, wrenched it free, slipping and flicking aside the automatic flight of his brother's dagger. He moved forward himself, and attacked.

He was possessed by one instinct: to wipe out the insult of the last twenty minutes. In this soil there flowered a strength which lapsed sometimes, but never seriously, and which gained leisure, more and more often, to answer the astonishments of Lymond's attack. For here, perhaps for the first time in his life, Lymond also was stretched to the limit, his breathing raucous, his concentration a tangible and frightening thing.

Very soon after Richard, he made his error. He was at the end of a thrust, his right arm rigid and his bright point nearly level, when Culter caught the blade flat with his own, pressing on the steel and then dropping his own point.

Circling his brother's blade, Richard's sword adhered to it gratingly, the forte of his foil acting on the foible of Lymond's; and the intent blue eyes narrowed. This was the first step toward disarming and the Master knew it. His attention was   for a second wholly concentrated on disengaging from the danger point and Richard with a single movement, took his slender chance.

He gave way suddenly with his right hand, moved quickly with his left and then with his supporting rapier; and trapping Lymond's dagger, whipped it from his hand to the floor.

With an answering, animal-like twist the Master leaped back out of close range, the sweat running down his face and into the hollow above the collarbone, and covered himself with his single blade against the unleashed power of Richard's following attack.

The force of it drove Lymond the full length of the room; that, and the need to keep out of measure, out of the range of Richard's left hand. Corps à corps fighting was death to the Master now. Richard knew it and rose to his full, triumphant stature as a swordsman, the blades in his hands swooping like the many scythes of Chronos, driving the other diagonally back, into the rope and into the corner of the rectangle.

There was, throughout the room, the soft hiss of an intaken breath. Somerville, unconsciously looking away, found the palms of his hands were wet. Lymond, his back to the rope, allowed himself one fleeting glance to his side. As the skilled, tempted blade rushed toward him he dropped like a stone, left palm to the ground in a perfect stop thrust. Richard overshot, stumbled and whipped around: Lymond was already rising, his recovered dagger in his hand.

Lord Culter was shaken. Like his brother, he was breathing in retching gasps, his hair soaked, his wrists numb with the vibration of the blows. There was, for the first time, a moment of loose play. The men about them sighed, as if in an hour's suffocation they had purchased a little precious air, and Richard's eyes kept for a moment their look of bewilderment and appraisal. Then his head came up; beneath the thin shirt his muscles spoke a fresh conviction, and he turned on the fair, fastidious presence of his brother with a mighty and flagellant hand.

Lymond had recovered no such resurgence of energy. He was tired, the shadow of it dragging at his brilliance; but he fought like a fiend when Culter sought to drive him again across the length of the room. Somerville, watching, saw that he was fully aware of the ropes behind; of the small traps devised for him. But what he should fear and did not was the long wall of windows with their hard girdle of seats, and below them, the rough opened pack from which Erskine had taken the damning letter betraying the Queen.

Richard was aware of it; had had it burning behind the grey eyes for five long minutes; was beyond now considering the laws of the sword and the shallow lessons of courtesy and fair play. He drove Lymond like wind whipped by rain from the ropes, back across the room, back to the windows, and finally back across the soft, shadowed litter of the pack.

Lymond stepped back into the trap. The cloth caught him; he stumbled, and Richard, with all the power of his shoulder, brought three feet of accurate death to cleave the fair, unsettled head.

It fell on a crucifix of steel.

Fully aware, stumbling with precision to the exact place he must occupy, Lymond had already launched his two blades on high. Fiery with light, they caught Lord Culter's sword between their crossed hilts and wrenched it from his grasp. There was one, sweet, invisible turn, an impact on the fine bones of Richard's dagger wrist, and the short blade in its turn jerked free, dropped, and followed the longer to the ground.

In a matter of seconds, astonishing to him as anything that had ever happened in his life, Lord Culter was disarmed.

To stop was almost to faint, such was the strain. They stood very close, face to face, the breath shaking their ribs; and the rapier flared in one of Lymond's hands, the dagger in the other.

He raised them slightly, the blue eyes haggard and wanton.

'My victory, brother Richard. My chance. My choice, to sheath either or both in fat, brotherly flesh.' The long fingers whitened on the two hilts as he held them out. 'Handy Dandy prickly prandy, Richard ... Which hand will you have?'

No one spoke. Culter's gaze, at this ultimate moment, was steady and unafraid.

Lymond laughed. And laughing, hurled the rapier to the floor and leaped to the window seat, the baggage roll scooped in his arms. For a moment he was poised there, collected, elegant and fleetingly analytical. Then – 'If you won't lead, try following!' said the Master; and in a storm of contemptuous glass swept the pack through the window and followed it himself. They heard, as they ran forward, the thud, the pause, and the quick recovery as he rolled on the soft grass below. From there, as they knew, it was a step to the horses.

And so they had to follow.

Gideon found Kate in the music room, her eyes on the road south. He put two hands on her shoulders. 'How good an Englishwoman are you?'

He felt her shiver. 'I don't know. Not very good, I'm afraid. It was Philippa who told them.'

'I know.'

There was a long silence. 'Did they fight?' asked Kate at length.

'Quite brilliantly,' said Gideon. And he took her below where the air blew soft through the tall panes, and where the fallen rapier, like the Master's discarded victory, lay unmarred among the glass on the floor.

They were riding into the yellow, grit-blasted socket of the sun, following the wisp of dust which was Lymond.

Somewhere ahead, presumably, was the man Acheson. Somewhere ahead, certainly, was the English army. A little down the road the two men Erskine had sent ahead joined them at a tangent from the moors, with no news except of a baked and unprinted crust of hills, and it became certain that their only hope, as well as their greatest danger, lay in following the incalculable figure ahead.

Lymond flew before them like a honey guide seducing a vespiary, sparing them nothing: they jumped ditches and peat pits, scrambled up banks and old diggings and crossed streams where the shallow mud embraced pastern and coffin bone and left some horse shoeless. The dust of whin and seeding grass, of baked earth and broken pollen attacked and burned them until the freshest of their horses stumbled. The gilded head in front never dropped from their sight.

Richard was sitting heavily in the saddle. Erskine,

watching him drop back from the lead, recognized that Culter was worn out, riding on will power alone, much as the man in front must be. It struck him that today's disastrous encounter between the two had done nothing so much as reveal how brilliantly alike the brothers were. It further struck him that if they did approach any closer to Lymond, his job was to prevent Osiris from being destroyed by brother Set. Until, at least, he had shown them the way to Acheson. He singled out Stokes, his best man, and edged him out of Culter's hearing as they galloped.

'If Lymond gets to Hexham first, I'm going alone after him: one man might just bluff his way through. The rest of you will have to wait for me. Give me an hour or two, and then make your own way home. . . . And Stokes.'

'Yes, sir?'

'Stop Lord Culter from following me.'

The other man met his eye. 'Yes, sir.'

They were riding uphill, over high ground: a cavalcade of asses after a bizarre and amorphous carrot. Then the rider ahead slipped out of sight down the other side of the hill. Erskine swept up after him and drew rein.

They were on the verge of a long and stony escarpment which ran as far west as he could see. Below the cliff, a track led through flat meadows to the broad and tranquil banks of the Tyne, crossed it by a humped bridge and after traversing a narrower strip, shot precipitously into the Alpine bosom of Hexham.

The town smoked morosely on its hill. Tom could see the Abbey tower, the prison, the tall houses of the church offices and the solid town gates, halfway up the hill. The streets seemed to be crammed with people. He dropped his eyes, and witnessed a small drama nearer at hand: a man, spurring his horse without mercy, was approaching the bridge from this, the north side. As he reached it, another rider galloped toward him across the turf, calling something: the sun glinted on fair hair, and Erskine held his breath.

He saw the man at the bridge look around for a second

and even hesitate; then, he raised his arm and with a slap of his hand, sent the rowelled horse bounding over the river. Erskine saw Lymond's horse leap forward also, and then race flat out for the bridge; but there were two hundred yards between the two men, and Lymond was not closing it. Erskine swore under his breath.

Behind him, his men were arriving on the crest and halting, arrested by his arm. Culter was nearly last. He rode to Erskine's side, his eyes, reddened and painful with dust, searching the new landscape; and suddenly pointed. 'There they are!'

'Yes. I'm going after them,' said Erskine. 'Stokes!'

'Then I'm coming . . .'

'You're staying here,' said Erskine sharply. 'So are the men. Stokes: there was a building of some kind back there; a burned-out one. See what shelter you can get there for yourselves and the horses. Not more than two hours.' And he put his horse down the cliff.

The last thing he saw, as he held the mare's neck high and felt her haunches slither among the scree of rough sandstone, was Stokes' hand on Richard's rein, and Richard trying to fight off three of his men. It came to Tom, wryly, that the round, blackened building he had seen was a dovecote.

* * *

Adam Acheson, arriving at last at his destination, found the whole of Hexham in the street and in the market at the top of it, bent on commercial prey, and squeezing a quick fortune from Wharton's men-at-arms.

While taking no risks in open country, Acheson had no political reason for distrusting Lymond. On the contrary, his relationships vis à vis his own countrymen and the English were from Acheson's point of view perfectly satisfactory. The attempt to delay him was Acheson's main grievance, and he was willing to overlook it if the fellow, abandoning this irrelevance, had arrived at Hexham after all.

So, when the porter at the gate looked at his safe-conduct and read laboriously, 'And bodyguard?' Acheson jerked his head down the road, and waited while the porter, after argument, found an escort for him to the Abbey. Acheson was ready to grant that Lymond's presence was conclusive guarantee of his good faith. Still, there was the matter of the opened dispatch he had slipped into the other man's baggage. He wanted the credit of delivering the fellow, but without undue personal risk.

But the Master, it seemed, bore him no ill-will. He rode up as Acheson, dismounted, was chatting with the three men of his guard. He looked a little wild-eyed, perhaps, but with nothing threatening in his face.

Admitted through the gate, he guided his horse toward Acheson, smiling, and drawing abreast, bent down to address him.

Only one of the four men standing around them saw the twelve inches of steel in Lymond's hand, and he shouted too late. Acheson took the stab full in the chest, propelled backward with the force of the blow; then the blank amazement in his face gave place to vindictive fury. He straightened. The dagger, falling from the rent cloth over his breast, betrayed the sparkle of chain mail beneath. Acheson was unhurt, and five men leaped at Lymond.

There was one weapon left to him. Driving his feet hard into the mare's flanks, Lymond dragged her soft mouth back and guided her plunging hoofs. Acheson, isolated under the iron soffit of the rearing horse, screamed once, the blood leaping from a great cut on the temple, before he was kicked to the ground.

There was just time for Lymond to see as much before he, too, was overpowered.

Erskine heard the story five minutes later when he in turn arrived at the gate. Affairs at the wicket were in some disorder, but he made hectoring play with the vacant cover of Acheson's dispatch, and was admitted immediately and directed to Lord Grey.

Having asked as many questions as he dared, Erskine

478

hesitated. Both Acheson and his assailant, he now knew, had been taken to the Abbey, where the commanders were in conference. No one knew how seriously the messenger was hurt. But if the two men possessing this secret were in the Abbey, then there, clearly, he must go.

He pressed his horse slowly through the crowds and up the steep hill. His chances of coming down it again were something, he thought fleetingly, he wouldn't care to wager money on. And the decisive factor was whether he had to assassinate one man, or two.

Through several centuries, predecessors of Tom Erskine had found a morbid attraction in the fat cows and silver plate of Hexham, with damaging results to the fabric. It cost Erskine some bluffing, some skin off his knuckles and a bruised shin, but he got inside, unseen and unmolested, and was violently relieved to find his end of the church plunged in gloom.

He was in the west nave; and while cleaving to the White Canons, he gave a passing nod to the Augustinian sense of proportion, material and intangible. About thirty yards ahead there were lights, of a sort, and the murmur of voices: the meeting, or gathering, or conference seemed to be taking place in one of the transepts. As his eyes grew used to the dark, he looked about him.

On his right, a flight of steps rose into the wall, presumably leading to the west offices of the cloister and therefore of no immediate use. But above his head, a row of lancets ran along the south wall of the nave, supporting the upper part of the wall, and with their feet firmly planted on a ledge a full yard wide.

Where staging went, a man could go. Erskine made a silent dash for the stairs, and after two twists debouched through an open door onto a dark and dizzy ledge high above the nave. Moving silently from group to group of its pillars he slipped toward the heart of the church, flattening himself against the wall as the candlelight grew stronger.

Another doorway appeared ahead. Through it, he found

the wall turned at right angles. The ledge continued, and the supporting pillars, but instead of looking down into the church, the open side was sealed. Before him instead was a long, narrow tunnel, completely dark, with a glimmering light at the end. Then he realized what was happening: the wall here turned to run along the west wall of the south transept, and the space between the columns had been hung with tapestries.

He edged his way a little along, feeling the cold stone on his right and touching the hangings on his other side with the tips of his left hand. The dim light at the end came from a stairway which spiralled both up and down. Investigating, he found that a short descent led to the corner of a broad gallery filling the end of the transept. A flight of wide, shallow steps led from the gallery to the floor of the church. He retreated up the staircase and halfway back along his ledge.

His best hiding place was here, and here probably his best view of the transept. Judging his distance, he halted and with careful fingers made a gap in the tapestried wall of his tunnel. Candlelight fell on his fingers, and animated conversation sprang to his ears with a paralyzing vigour.

Then a known voice, Lymond's voice, beating home some fragment of rhetoric, said startlingly, 'I can give you one name that you can't give me: cuckold, Lord Lennox!'

* * *

Within the Abbey, this singular and unlooked-for capture slipped like a midsummer halcyon upon the sour and surly waters of incompatibility.

Lord Wharton, exhausted with the effort of being civil to Grey, irritated by Lennox and stricken at the prospect of parting with a company of excellent horsemen whom he would probably never see again, was sunk in highly secular gloom at one end of the long, polished table.

The Earl of Lennox, bored and more than a little put out by a cool reception from his wife, fiddled with the inventories and bills lying in front of him, and crossed his

480

long legs under the table in such a way that neither Grey nor Margaret could sit in comfort.

Lord Grey, missing Gideon and worried as well as annoyed by this tale of Margaret Douglas's, was unfolding a long and complicated saga of his Treasurer's short-comings and Lady Lennox, who was pale, was sitting upright in an uncomfortable chair and frowning abstract-edly at the floor.

Then Mr. Myles came in and whispered; an officer from the gate came in and made a statement; and the guard helped to carry in and deposit the recumbent and unconscious form of Mr. Acheson on a convenient tomb, while two other pleased-looking stalwarts filed in and closed the door. Between them was Lymond. At the unli-keliest moment, the fish had swallowed the hook.

He wore no jacket and no boots; he was dishevelled, as might be expected, and looked tired and disreputable. He also looked, thought Lord Grey with a pang of fury, roughly as humble as Shishman, Emperor of the Slavs: Brahma finding pest in the henhouse might have worn such a look. 'Did you do that?' snapped the Lord Lieuten-ant, and jerked a finger toward Acheson's prostrate body.

Lymond turned his head. 'Gushing Hippocrenes at every joint. No. Strictly speaking the blame belongs to a strawberry roan. The gentleman carries two letters for the Lennoxes, and I have come with him in answer to your ultimatum. If you are wondering, Margaret, whether I know that the ultimatum is void and why; I do. Mr. Ache-son was rash enough to tell me just inside the gates.'

A severe and brilliant triumph illuminated Meg Douglas's face. She didn't ask how Acheson knew. 'Your little redheaded friend was unintelligent but persevering. She forgot there are rules in war as well as in love ... Kill him, Matthew.'

'In your experience they are the same rules, aren't they? Slay those who are great in heart for they are blind. Mat-thew can't in decency kill me, Margaret, until Lord Grey has spoken, and by then I shall have said a great deal myself.'

481

'Will you? I doubt it. By God,' said Lord Grey, 'there isn't a man here, I should think, who wouldn't be happy to slit – '

'I should certainly like – as a major sufferer – to lay claim to the body,' said Lord Wharton. 'What happened at Annan is very freshly in my mind, and so is the disruption of my courier service and your several and inventive actions when under my command.'

'As I observed,' said Lord Grey impatiently, 'this miserable man is evilly disposed to us all. I have not forgotten Hume and Heriot nor has Lennox, I imagine dismissed the events at Dumbarton. We are not, I suppose, going to terminate this remarkable history by squabbling over the manner of his death. No. We are pressed for time. This is war, and this man is of the rubbish thrust to the surface by war. Let the guards take him to the market place and hang him for a treacherous Scot.'

Four voices broke upon his ears with exclamatory advice; and were in turn defeated by the single, carrying voice of the prisoner.

'One at a time,' said Lymond. 'Remember your English unity, for God's sake, or we are all lost. Think hard; don't let the principle escape you. What are you? A great and godly nation speaking with the voices of corporate right: one brain, one heart; a thousand members drawing life from each. A nation of loving lambs dutiful to the bell-wether: chickens of the world-egg following the hen-figure gladly into the eye of the cannon. Unity, solidarity and brotherhood. *Brotherhood!* My God.'

Grey shut the ledger before him with a snap. 'At least this is a nation with a religion, a head, a status, a policy. Not a damned Noah's Ark: a chicken here, a lamb there, a family of wolves in the next field. I suppose you are proud of your French Queen, playing dice with Scots knucklebones for the greater glory of her native land? Of Arran, the fool, bending like a springal toward the weightiest pocket? Of your Douglases and your – '

'Lennoxes?' Smoothly, unhurriedly, the Master was playing for time. 'They serve their turn: why not? A

Lennox pressed is a Dead Sea apple, held by London instead of by Paris; and for the richest, not the fairest. Fairness has nothing whatever to do with the Douglases.'

'I think,' said the Earl of Lennox, white with emotion, 'that my wife and I have heard enough insults. And I can dispense with a dissertation about our national characteristics. Knock him down! Hang him!'

Lymond turned suddenly. ' "Our" characteristics? Whose? Whose are yours? Brought up in France; fêted in Scotland; would-be bridegroom of Mary of Guise; would-be ruler; would-be conspirator; full of terestrial appetites and an eagerness to feed your kindred flesh to all the feared and threatening raptors at your heels . . .

'What are you? A citizen of Europe or of the life of the shore: a thief, a renegade, a liar and a coward, as you have named me? But I can give you one name you can't give me: cuckold, Lord Lennox!'

The Earl had risen slowly to his feet. As Lymond flung the word at him Lennox's voice rang out, high-pitched as a bird's. 'My God, you stopped me once, Wharton, but not this time. Not again! Clear the way – move aside – '

His path to Lymond was unexpectedly blocked. 'Who the devil are you?' said Lennox hysterically. 'Get out of my way!'

Henry, Lord Wharton's son, shut the door behind him and blinked at the white and angry face. His gaze, mildly surprised, sought his father at the table and then, roving, fell on the Master of Culter. 'Him!'

Ignoring Lennox totally, Henry Wharton flung his arms in a wide gesture of exultation, divesting himself with a twist of bow, quiver, helmet and pack. They fell on the table with a crash. 'Lymond! You've got him?'

Repressively, Lymond himself answered. 'I dislike being discussed as if I were a disease. Nobody "got" me,' he said. 'And where have you been, my billy: to the devil and back to have your beard combed?'

Before Grey's astonished gaze, the scene of a moment before began to repeat itself. They had to hold the young man, struggling, away from the Master. Grey shoved him into his father's grasp and said sharply, '*You* control him. What's so inflammatory about . . . ?'

Wharton answered curtly. 'Made a fool of himself at Durisdeer in February. Milked like a cow tree.'

'How?'

Lymond, irrepressible, answered. 'It was a wonderful beard he had, a magnificent pelt. He was bearded like a Dammar pine, of the fashion of prophets and pards, one hair sitting here, another there . . . But was it fitting? Was it well-considered? I asked myself: peach or nectarine, clingstone or freestone, bald or – forgive me – downy . . . which?'

'What,' said Lord Grey impatiently, 'did he do to Henry?'

'Shaved and cropped him with his own knife,' replied Lord Wharton shortly, and the angry faces around the table, with the furious exception of Harry's, broke into ill-repressed smiles.

'A picture,' observed Lymond. 'It isn't considered proper to shout in church. Besides, Lord Lennox is talking.'

He had courage, or a singular rashness. Tom Erskine, his hands gripping the tapestry, wondered also, jaw set, if Lymond had observed what he himself had just seen: the smallest stirring in the inert body of the messenger Acheson, lying stunned on the marble face of a tomb.

It forced Erskine himself to a decision. With infinite care he edged along the narrow passage behind the tapestry, reached the spiral stair, and slipping down it, stepped out on the wide, stone-flagged balcony which overhung the south transept where Lymond stood. Bending low, Erskine crossed the flags and lying still beneath the stone balustrade, raised his head cautiously and peered below.

From his low and castellated rampart he caught a glimpse of a yellow head. He raised himself higher. At the same moment Lymond stepped back two paces before Lennox, who was shouting abuse: this brought him half-

484

way along the table with his right side to the balcony and the catafalque with Acheson on his left.

He was, then, keeping the messenger under his eye. A moment later the Master turned his head to speak to the Countess of Lennox and raised his eyes a fraction, searching the stilted lancets and then, briefly, the wide Midnight Stairs and the gallery at their head. Erskine was by then almost certain the quick blue glance had identified him.

Someone was saying vehemently, 'That's a lie!'

Lymond seemed undisturbed. 'Don't be simple. Didn't you know that Margaret spent her sojourn in Scotland with me?'

The woman raised her brows. 'Haven't we had enough of this? When I was captured, I was taken to Lanark. Matthew knows that. The offer of exchange came from Lanark, not from you.'

Lymond replied gently. 'I naturally covered my mediator by giving him good credentials, but he did not, I'm afraid, come from Lanark. How deceitful of you not to have told your spouse. I wrote my offer of exchange, I remember, on the back of a letter from Lord Lennox to his wife which in itself was a thing of joy. I recall, for example . . .'

Lord Lennox shot a pale glance at his wife. 'There is no need to go on with this nonsense.'

'. . . I recall, for example, a good many things, but don't excite yourselves. I shan't embarrass the dynasty. Didn't you know she was using the war as a fulcrum for her fishing line with myself as the prey? I was to be driven into the nets since, unlike the beaver, my self-defence stops short of unserviceable gestures. Do you find that objectionable? Pitiful? Even a little ludicrous, perhaps? A self-interest so insanely exclusive that it includes even murder?'

Now Margaret as well was on her feet, her eyes burning. Lennox was pale; around the table the others looked angry and uncomfortable, as if mesmerized into allowing the intolerable scene to go on.

The man Acheson stirred again.

485

'Murder?' repeated Lord Grey. 'Oh: the Stewart girl? She was killed riding.'

'She was killed riding, by an arrow. She was threatened, pursued, her young guide killed, and done to death herself as surely as if the arrow had been directed at her.

'If your eyes burned from their sockets now you would be lost and terrified and appalled as she was – and you are men. You're not in enemy country, in the hands of a cruel and bitter woman; or galloping blind on a frightened horse over unknown fields with a dead body behind you and a pack of the hounds who killed him baying at your heels. That isn't only murder: it's murder of a very special and damning kind, and there is a name for those who engage in it . . .'

The admirable voice was stripped, as was Lymond's whole bearing, of his normal pleasant negligence. He went on.

'I have no very gratifying memories of Crawfordmuir. I offered myself for sale, as I remember, in exchange for the truth. Your wife was eager to buy, Lord Lennox; but she also deals in adulterated coinage. She told me something was unprovable which I knew could be proved, and she told me a man had been killed whom I knew to be alive – so I withdrew my offer. But to save Christian Stewart from these attentions, believe me, I should have honoured it at any cost.'

There was a grandeur in Margaret Douglas's fury. 'Stop your foul tongue! You paltry, conceited liar!'

'Did Christian Stewart die? How did she die?'

Lady Lennox stepped before him, shaken with rage. 'She died of a fall from her horse. It was no fault of mine. She's better off than she ever was as a mistress of yours! Only you won't blacken my name from revenge in front of these people!'

The answer was implacably hard. 'Look at your husband's face. Look at Lord Grey. *Blacken your name*! Are you known, do you imagine, as Zenobia?'

She whirled on Grey. 'Take him away! Can't you stop this?'

'And al was conscience and tendre herte,' said the clear, forbidding voice. Grey cleared his throat. Wharton's eyes were fixed on the roof corbels and their coats of arms; his son, standing sulkily by Grey, was biting his lip. The Earl of Lennox looked hard at his wife, his eyes glancing white like pale, sea-washed pebbles. Lymond addressed him, not looking anywhere near Acheson; not allowing anyone's attention to stray to the white marble and the uneasily stirring body.

'Oh, you haven't been cheated. You are one with Black Douglas and Royal Tudor, and through her with any man from the highest to the most humble whom she wants to dominate. *Any* man. The rotten apple, Lennox, hangs lowest. There's more ambition in one of those tears of fury than in the whole of your Godforsaken career. You must let her push you; you can't rest any more; you can't fail her or she'll destroy you. Won't you, Margaret?'

Acheson groaned.

With sharp distaste Lord Grey said to Lymond's guards, 'Take him away!' but Margaret was already advancing on her tormentor. With all her considerable strength she struck at his mouth with the back-driving flat of her hand and Erskine, his heart in his teeth, saw the Master call smoothly on his reserves.

The woman's wrist was caught and pulled to him. Then, behind the shield of her body, he side-stepped and snatched. With young Wharton's bow and quiver in his free hand he backed to the stairs, dragging Margaret, wildly struggling with him.

He held her, one-handed, until he reached the foot of the steps; then hurling her from him an instant before she fought quite free he turned and raced up the wide, shallow treads.

Erskine was ready. As Lymond crashed breathless beside him in the shelter of the balustrade his sword was out, ready to cut back the expected rush; but the other man was already on his feet again with the bow strung. There was only one arrow. He said under his breath,

'Keep down, damn you!' and as Erskine knelt, Lymond took aim below.

Wharton and his son, halfway up the stairs, halted.

'Get back!' said the Master.

There was a long pause. Lennox, at the foot of the steps, was bent over his wife. Grey, still at the head of the table, hadn't moved; the two guards stood helplessly beside him.

Against a bow and a fine marksman, their swords might be unbarrelled shooks. The Whartons recoiled down the stairs and the tilt of the bow followed them. Behind, the gallery was empty, a half-open door leading to the deserted monks' dormitory, the day stairs, the cloisters, the refectory, the storehouses: a thousand hiding places and a thousand exits.

They held the hour in their fingers, like a day lily. They had merely to destroy Acheson and go.

The bow in his hands, Lymond stood motionless. Erskine was turning on him, riven with urgency, when he saw the movement above his head. On the narrow ledge to the right, the twin of his own former stance, a man stood with a hackbut.

From that ledge there was no turnpike down to the gallery, but the arquebusier had no need to come closer to Lymond to have him fully in range. Erskine turned, frantic exhortations in his mouth, and saw, at last, why Lymond had made no effort to shoot.

For Acheson had moved. Sitting up, hands on marble, he was attempting weakly to stand. Until he did so, he was totally screened by the parapet. And there was only one arrow.

The loading of an arquebus is a protracted affair. Hidden under the low wall, Erskine had a terrible leisure to watch this man's quick fingers. He saw the glimmer of the manipulated barrel and knew from the tightening of Lymond's fingers on the bow that he also had seen.

The Master gave it no other attention. He was talking, the limpid, carrying voice penetrating the transept below as Acheson, disgruntled and bloody, rubbed his black head and muttered.

'Keep your voices down,' said Lymond. 'Don't move. Don't shout for help. I can kill any one of you from here.' His eyes were tranquil, of a clearheaded strength: there was no hint in them of the day's exhaustions and disasters. Talking, he moved slowly along the wall, trying to uncover Acheson. The hackbutter, in his haste, dropped something with a small bump and picked it up again.

'. . . teach you a lesson with some *ex cathedra* observations,' Lymond was continuing. 'You may feel a little foolish; you don't appear so to me. Wharton is a master of his profession: it's a profession where one cannot stay detached, and he has paid that penalty. But he knows very well that corrective pressure and armed coercion are two of the longest, least successful and most offensive ways of waging a war.'

He paused, his eyes flickering to the obscured figure of Acheson and back to the upraised, angry faces. 'Every war has the man on the balcony, the man in the tree, the man in the doorway. He stings; he frightens; he causes loss of face; but he is always caught in the end. Turn aside to hunt for him if you must, Lord Grey; but don't ever unleash your vanity on his track. Today . . .'

In the heavy eyes, new life suddenly blazed. 'Today,' said Lymond, 'such an error has cost you a war.'

'Lord Grey?' said an uncertain voice: Acheson's voice. 'Take me to Lord Grey? I've a dispatch . . . about the Scottish Queen.'

Grey said 'What?' as the glimmer of a slow match swept through the dark transept like a firefly. The black mouth of the hackbut, steady as a wand, inexorable as Melpomene, turned like a dark flower to its killing, and Erskine cried softly, 'Oh, God!'

Adam Acheson repeated dizzily, 'It's about the Queen'; and walked out into the centre of the floor.

The fine bow drifted in Lymond's hands like the frail, side-slipping glide of a heron; the steel tip steadied, sparkling, and his knuckles whitened. In the darkness opposite, the hackbutter's arm jerked. Lymond smiled once, with a kind of surprised pleasure, and releasing the deadly, unerring arrow, shot Acheson through the heart.

The explosion of the hackbut drowned Margaret's scream. Aiming for Lymond's body, given the brilliant, unmoving target of his white shirt, the marksman made no mistake. He was defter, indeed, than he meant to be; because the shot, raking the stone coping of the balcony, acquired missiles and satellites of its own and struck home not once but several times.

Lymond flung up his head, turned half around with the force of the explosion. The bow fell. For one second – two – he held fast to the broken coping, defying the heralds of agony and an easy darkness. Below, Erskine caught a glimpse of the circle of white, upturned faces about the fallen body of Acheson.

Then the riven flesh and burst vessels made their protest, the freed blood springing liberal and scarlet through the fragments of Lymond's shirt. Erskine saw the long hands loosen, the sudden, uncontrolled sway; but was not prepared for the drowned, revealing blue gaze meeting his like a blow.

'And died stinkingly martyred,' said Lymond, with painful derision; and losing hold bit by bit, slipped into Erskine's gentle grasp.

3
KNIGHT ADVERSARY

And also hit behoveth . . . that they first have the cure
of themself, and they ought to purge themself fro
alle apostumes and alle vices . . . and that they
shewe hem hole and pure and redy for to hele other.

1 · STRANGE REFUGE

The bell of Hexham Abbey opening it lips to the pagan
moon, sent its voice across the river: *Vice mea viva depello
cuncta novica*; and the men waiting across the water in a
blackened and doorless dovecote heard it; and heard also
the rattle of approaching hoofs.

Somebody – a hospital, a manor, a priory – had once
owned five hundred fat pigeons here, and had housed
them fittingly with fourteen tiers of holes and ledges, a
bathing tub filled by a spring, a stone table and a tall and
creaking potence, its revolving arms scanning the circles
of tiered nests so that the two men on its wheeling perches
could pocket the warm squabs.

Now the broken doorway admitted rats. But rock doves
had found a way through the glover to the safest, topmost
nests; and when Erskine's men went in, birds arose with
the sudden rattle of an emptied topsail. Waiting for Tom
to return, they could see shocked golden eyes darting from
the lantern edge high above.

The sudden inaction, agitating to Erskine's men, was
dreadful for Richard, bereft of his prey and of any part in
the climax of this hideous marathon. He would have been
at the gates of Hexham fifty times if Stokes had let him.
If Erskine could get in, then why not himself? If Erskine

failed, wasn't it his duty to replace him? And who gave Erskine the right to annex another man's quarrel?

Stokes, luckily, was gifted with patience. As the light faded he returned his decent, sensible answers, without pointing out that but for Lord Culter himself, they would all have been safely on the Edinburgh road hours since. Eventually, even Richard relapsed into silence, and occupied himself with an explosive pacing of the dusty floor.

The hoofbeats, like harried spirits, followed the tolling of the bell. Stokes, signalling silence, went himself to the miniature door and then fell back, the grin on his face red-lit by the low fire. It was Tom Erskine.

He was barely inside when Richard's hands seized his shoulders. 'Well, damn you: well?'

Erskine, looking queerly, jerked free. 'We've stopped the message being delivered. Acheson was carrying it in his head.'

'And Lymond?'

Nothing else and no one else mattered. Erskine's own gaze, newly fierce, newly level, beat down Richard's to the floor before he answered curtly. 'They loathed and feared Lymond. If you believed he was England's secret insurrectionist, you're wrong. He killed Acheson himself.'

There was no real change in the fanatical grey eyes. Richard said, 'Where is he?'

Someone had already unloaded Erskine's horse. The heavy roll lay near the fire: bending, Erskine turned back the blankets.

Devoid of mischief or anger; silent; defenceless; Richard's brother lay at his feet. Erskine knelt by the plastic body, clothed and clotted with blood, and touched Lymond's hand.

'Is he dead?' They stared, like men mesmerized. Erskine said abruptly, 'Stokes: collect the horses and get the men out. The job's done. We can't risk staying any longer. Quickly.'

The exodus began against Lord Culter's unmoving figure. He repeated himself, without raising his voice. 'Is he dead?'

Erskine's face was as hard as his own. 'He won't survive an hour on horseback. We must leave him.'

Richard swore coldly. 'Damn it, how can we? He knows all Acheson knew.'

'Then he can tell it to the pigeons,' said Erskine, harshly, and flung wide the rugs. 'How long d'you think he'll live like that?'

'Someone might find him.'

'All right. Someone might find him. That's your concern: he's your brother. That's why I brought him back. This is one decision I'm not making. I saw him risk his life to kill that fellow today.'

There was no softening in Richard's face. 'He had to choose between Grey and you, and he plumped for the likelier prospect, that's all. . . . Justifiably: you rescued him, didn't you?' His fingers slid up and down the quillons of his sword. There was a pause; then he pulled them away. 'No. I'm damned if I do. I want him killed publicly and lawfully and painfully and fully conscious, at least. Take your men and get on the road. I'll stay and get him home later.'

They were alone; they could hear the trampling as the horses were brought up outside. Erskine said, 'You've fought him once already: isn't that enough?'

The firelight glinted in Richard's eyes. 'Do you think he's innocent? I'm willing to save his life: what's wrong about that? And if he's guiltless he'll have a chance to prove it: what's fairer?'

Someone called to them through the doorway. Erskine stepped outside and returning, threw at Richard's feet his baggage roll and cloak. 'You'll need these.'

He added abruptly, 'Come with us, Richard. Let him alone. You can't seal him alive in the larder like a bloody wasp with a fly.'

There was no answer.

Erskine had to go. But in the dovecote doorway he glanced back, once. Richard had stooped over his brother and, with excited face, was scanning the engrossing tally of his wounds.

Long after, Richard himself stood in the doorway, gazing out at the quiet night. Then, moving noiselessly, he collected the wood he needed and stacked it inside.

It was late. The fire, rebuilt under the overhung ledges, glimmered on his brother's face: the artless, sleeping face of his childhood.

But Lymond was now in the cold sleep close to death. Experienced soldier and countryman, Lord Culter had faced the spilled blood, the spoiled muscle, the split bone with no qualms; and he washed, cleaned and bandaged with steady hands, missing nothing: the scarred hands, the old whippings; the last degradation of the brand.

There was no more he could do now. The door cloth secure, he stretched at length by the fire, his saddle for pillow, and waited side by side with the silenced tongue which had mocked him so long. The cushats had long since returned sidling to their roosts. As stillness fell, they settled too, with frilled feathers and the rasp of dry feet. Then it was quiet, and the only sound in all the warm June night was Lymond's faint, gasping breath.

Through the darkest hours of the short night Richard slept, wrenched by sheer exhaustion from his vigil; and woke stupid, forgetting.

Then his bemused eyes picked out the pale, dawn-lit arches of the lantern above him and the wintry skeleton of the potence, and the dark, enclosing walls with their hundred upon hundred of empty sockets, black and salaciously flickering with the dying glimmer of the fire. And the wide, fathomless eyes of his brother, resting on him.

In that crude second, neither spoke. Culter rose, and stooping to the fire, rebuilt it with unhurried care. In its spreading light, pale hair gleamed beside him, and whitened cheekbones and white lips, all tinged to health by the flames. Roseate and sardonic in extremis, Lymond spoke with the least possible expense of sound.

'You still snore like a frog. Did Tom Erskine get me out?'

Richard was building a cathedral of boughs. 'Who else? He brought you here and then took his men home. We're just outside Hexham.'

There was a difficult pause. Then Lymond said clearly, 'If you're waiting to preach in articulo mortis, don't put it off for my sake.'

The oblique inquiry gave Richard the metal he needed. He said with a grim pleasure, 'I don't mind waiting.'

Something – hardly laughter – glimmered in the heavy eyes. 'Neither do I. But the fenestration seems fairly extensive.'

Richard had hung a can of water over the new fire, and his fresh bandages were waiting. 'Not if you have a good surgeon.'

The careful voice was resigned. 'Two chapters of Anatomia Porci and they think they're Avicenna. Don't trouble. No wriggling and no recantations from this quarter.'

'You're surprised?' Richard tested the water with a broad finger. 'What did you expect? That I'd curse you, kill you and drop you in the Billy Mire?'

'Yes. You tell me why not: I can't help you. Overtures of friendship from me would sound damned silly at this point . . . I can't drink any more.'

Richard took away the flask. 'You said no recantations.'

'That doesn't rule out the plain, freestanding explanation.'

'Make it later,' said Richard equably, unwinding bits of torn sheet. 'You'll have plenty of time.' He knelt, and the incalculable eyes dropped.

It was not a pretty business: a grim, forbidding task even had there been proper gear and the skilled treatment of the doctor he was not. The bowls of water became scarlet and the makeshift wads reeked. . . .

Explanations. What explained the killing of one's son? The seduction of one's wife? And these were the hands that Mariotta knew better than he did: this the mouth; this the marked body. . . .

Lymond took too long to recover when the dressing was done. But in the end his eyes opened, and after a time he spoke. 'All right. I love sadism too,' he said. 'But try too often, Master Haly Abbas Cat, and you won't have a mouse left to play with. . . . Your move.'

Richard was careful. 'Not yet,' he said. 'When I make it, I want your undivided attention. All you have to do is get well.'

* * *

That day Lord Culter spent some time looking for a fresh harbour for his patient: one that would give some shelter, and be sufficiently remote from both houses and paths.

Late in the afternoon, on his last sally, his arms full of moss for dressings, he found the ideal spot. A small stream running through sandstone had created a toy gorge within which for perhaps twenty yards the bottom widened on each side of the water into a secluded and grassy meadow. There was room there, and in other and more distant bays, to graze his horse, and better still, a place where the rocky sides of the banks steeply overhung and enclosed the grass, forming a shallow cave within. There he could safely light fires, and there too they would be dry in bad weather.

He explored it thoroughly, and it was later than it should have been when he returned.

Lymond watched him pack with bright eyes. 'Hullo! Are we setting up house elsewhere? Far away?'

'A short ride. I'll strap you to Bryony.'

There was a pause. Then, detached, the Master observed, 'Richard. You can't seriously picture me pursuing a healthy career as a sieve. Time isn't on your side either. Stop toying with the prey and let's get this thing over with. Say what you have to say to me.'

'We didn't,' observed Richard, 'take long to get to the wriggling.'

'No. I'm only trying to find a knee-high viewpoint that'll interest you. Before one of us bores the other to death I have to talk to you about Mariotta.'

Lord Culter straightened, the two packs under his arms. 'Not to me.'

496

'To you, here and now. After which you can make your own conversation in whatever damned draughty hole you've picked for yourself, and put your own bloody feet over your bottom like the Romans when it rains. Mariotta—'

'You're not dying,' said Richard. 'Keep your pitiful confessions for someone else.'

'Whose guts are they?' demanded Lymond, offended. His hair was dark with sweat and his fingers cramped, resisting the oncoming tides. 'I'm going to tell you what happened, brother mine. You'll have to execute me, leave me, or listen to me.'

'Or remove your tongue.'

'Happy are the cicadas' lives. Go ahead. But then you'll never know the truth.'

'I know all I need to know.'

'What do you know? How to match, but not how to marry. How to choose, but not how to husband. Grand Amour should be received royally, Richard, as a harsh and noble art. You idiot. . . . You nearly lost her. But not to me.'

The sword was in Culter's hand. The thoughtful eyes of his brother and even the shadowed walls of the dovecote disappeared. With the last rags of self-possession, Richard drove himself out of the door.

And bathe my son in morning milk, said the doves. And other voices, too, hammered in his ears. Here, reeking and blubbering over the green fields, were the resurrected deaths he had died because of Lymond. 'You haven't packed the ladies off to Stirling, have you?' – An arrow, tearing ignominiously into one's shoulder, before a shouting crowd – a drunken glover and a frozen ride – the prison at Dumbarton and the walk across the ballroom floor – the failure at Heriot; the trickery with Scott; and monstrously, Mariotta, Mariotta, Mariotta, blazing with jewels.

'Believe, if you like, that the child is Lymond's.' . . . *'He is with Mariotta now.'* . . . *'It would have been a boy.'*

The grass at his feet, the blue sky, the short purple

shadows of the trees, came into focus again. He unbuckled his dagger, and laying it together with his sword within the doorway, walked back and seated himself on the edge of the stone table. 'Go on. We have five minutes to spare. Discourse on the seductive arts. I want to quote you to Mariotta.'

'I,' said Lymond plaintively, 'am the octogenarian who planted. In my marrows are my monument; and your wife, thank God, is no marrow of mine. I was gallant at Midculter, God save me, through being most damnably drunk: but never again.'

'You didn't approach her, or she you?'

'My dear ass, I ran like a corncrake. You can ask leading questions till you're cross-eyed as Strabo: that's what happened. Unfortunately, becoming tired of home life, she ran too; and got herself taken by the English. I had her redeemed, like a fool, and my poor morons brought her to me when she fell ill on the road instead of running like hell when at least she'd have arrived at Midculter unsullied, if dead.'

Richard said quietly, 'I hope she thanked you for the trinkets, since she had the chance.'

'She did. It was a little embarrassing,' said Lymond. 'Because I didn't send them.'

'Oh. You haven't any idea who did, I suppose? Buccleuch, for example?'

He bent suddenly to enclose Lymond's wrist, his eyes intent, as the Master's weakened voice said, 'I don't see why I should spoil another man's fun. . . . Although he must have been damned annoyed to find me getting the credit for it all. . . . If you're curious, you could try asking Mother.'

Richard laid down the scarred hand. 'I don't mean to exact retribution from all my wife's lovers. Just those actually related to me. Although you'll be glad to hear that Sybilla is still your infatuated devotee.'

His brother's gaze was unexpectedly severe, with a marked line between the brows. He said, 'But Mariotta is not. She made it quite clear before she left that she thought my existence unnecessary, and that the third baron was her only patron. What you did when she got back God knows, but it didn't sound very intelligent in the fourth-hand version I got, and if she agrees in the end to come back to you it'll be a miracle of constant vapidity over assiduous obstinacy. . . .' Prone on the spread rug, he studied Richard's expression of harsh amusement. 'Not very convincing?'

'No.'

'No, I suppose not. I could enact you Phoenissae-like tragedies and you'd believe them, but the truth, as I once said to someone –'

'What?'

'Is a queer thing to meddle with,' said Lymond rapidly. 'Must we go? Accord me a niche. I don't mind being calx in a columbarium: the doves will feed me and I shall rise and found Nineveh. . . . Hic turtur gemit, drowning the groans of the Britons. . . . Must we go? An elephant's head riding on a rat – the symbol of prudence, Richard. Are you listening?'

Richard was already kneeling, hands gripped as if physical force could hammer back the shutters closing on life and consciousness. 'You aren't going to die. Not until I'm ready for you.'

'Don't be silly, Richard,' said Lymond, coming from a great distance. For a moment his quick mind cleared; he squinted at the darkening cupola with clouded eyes, and then closed them with a wisp of a grin. 'God, I forgot. You don't like glovers.'

He fought for Lymond's life for two days: thorough, methodical, intelligent; mending with dedicated skill like a man cleaning and mending an engine of war. He longed for his brother, desperately ill as he was, to know what was being done for him, and to savour this devoted nursing at his hands.

On the second night in their new home, sitting in the mellow darkness with the stream bubbling companionably beside him and the odours of warm, fresh turf and flowers and quenched mosses breathing into the withered air, he thought of that coming moment with pleasure.

Lymond was steadier; the pulse a fraction stronger; the sound of his breathing more settled. Assume he survived. Assume a convalescence of weeks – two or three, perhaps, before they could move north . . .

This was a man who prized his self-control. This was the contaminating mind whose presence in daily life was insupportable. Three weeks – or even two – should be enough.

* * *

> *'Is this fraternall charitie*
> *Or furious folie, quhat say he?'*

Since Lymond was alone, the question was pointlessly rhetorical. After a moment he removed a grave blue stare from the clouds and closed his eyes again.

Two days of fever: two of infantile helplessness. The stream, a strip of grass, the rug, the makeshift pillow, and immobility under the hot sun. He stirred in a difficult, indistinct way, the light beating on his closed lids, and then lay painfully silent.

A pebble dropped.

Richard, approaching downstream with a bouquet of fish, watched the effect of it, smiling. Lymond, instantly awake, gave no answering smile as his brother strolled up to him.

Richard's skin, amenable to the sun, was smooth and brown, and his hair bleached from umber to something near straw colour where it stood ruffled around his head. After five days of foraging, neither his shirt nor his hose were particularly respectable: he wore light shoes from his baggage which were already much the worse for wear, and his brother was wearing his only spare shirt.

These sartorial deficiencies were clearly not weighing on him. He cast down the fish, bestowed an effervescent twinkle on the Master and said, 'Comfortable?'

'Acutely so.'

'You don't *look* very comfortable,' said Richard, arrested.

'How odd of me. More delightful little fish. Where are you hatching them?'

There was an uncomfortable pause. 'I'm doing my best,' said Richard gently. 'I haven't your touch for killing birds.' He walked around, and grasping the edges of his brother's makeshift pallet, pulled it two or three yards into the shade. 'Has Patey Liddell ever been publicly whipped before?'

The change brought such physical relief that Lymond closed his eyes. He opened them again and said, 'He only does what he's told. I thought you'd enjoy a trip to Perth. Good for the olefactory senses.'

Culter shook his head over the fish. 'Crawfordmuir gold and Liddell: how dull of us not to connect the two.'

'How dull of some of you. What a delicious smell. You nurse; you cook. Do you sew?'

'I reap. Who was the exception? Mother?'

'And getting quicker, too,' said Lymond's light voice admiringly. 'The country must miss you on the frequent occasions when you are absent. How long were you in prison for?'

Richard rubbed the palm of his hand on his seat, and then held it up, square, clean and unmarked, for Lymond to see. 'I was lucky. No one could tell, could they?'

'The point is registered. Pannage, my dear brother. You're a butterfly as much as I am. You failed Arran, you defaulted at Dumbarton, you walked out on your wife and mother, you engaged Janet Beaton in a charming little conspiracy behind her husband's back and displayed a remarkable incapacity on the rare occasions when you did set foot on a battlefield. If you contrived to nip the enthusiasms of young Harry a bit quicker at Durisdeer, to mention only one, you might have had Lords Wharton and Lennox behind bars for the asking.'

'And stopped your income?' asked Richard, laying the cleaned fish neatly on his baking stone. 'Not when you

501

must have needed every penny to cajole your rabble of thieves into obedience. Or does one simply glut them with women and drugs?'

'One uses force of character. Wo worth your tedyus synne of lechery. That's a damned silly way to bake fish.'

'It works. You know,' said Richard, rubbing his fingers on a handful of grass, 'considering who you are, you choose intriguing subjects for invective. Are you still quite comfortable?'

'In this line of country,' said Lymond, 'I have a phenomenal staying power. Probe on, if you want to.'

'Thank you. I thought an exchange of civilized opinion might help pass the time. Until you can travel.'

There was a pause. 'All right,' said the Master at length. 'That was quite artistically done. Behold me in a state of suitably agitated inquiry. What then?'

'Guess,' said Richard amicably.

'Oh, try somebody else's sudorific. This really is too damned childish.' Lymond's eyes were black with fatigue. Richard observed it, as he observed everything about him, eagerly and with a clinical thoroughness.

'Nothing childish about having a respect for the law,' said Culter cheerfully. 'Once up on your feet; once up on your horse; and it's Edinburgh for you. Prison and chains and a series of unpleasant questions. You're going to stand trial before Parliament as indicted, brother mine.'

No recoil, but a temper as taut as a fishing line. 'There's nothing juvenile either about having a care for one's family. You know what kind of sensation this will make.'

'Beautiful,' said Richard. 'You'll enjoy it. You know how you like extravagant gestures. Have some fish.'

His brother ignored the outstretched hand. 'Look: suspend the godlike poking for a moment. I thought you'd make a clean end of it, at least, even if it was pretty dirty going in the middle – You wouldn't come to any harm: no one expected me to live.

'The scandal of five years ago will be nothing compared to what they'll raise in open court. You know damned well I'll be found guilty: nobody has any illusions about that.

502

But you've got the rest of your life to live, and what's more important, so has Mother and so has your wife. Do you want your sons to have that sort of nauseating exhibition cast up to them?'

'Don't get excited,' said Richard. 'Knowing Mariotta, I should never be perfectly sure that they *were* my sons anyway.'

'That's what I mean,' said the Master slowly. 'Your sense of values has broken down, and you won't face it. I had some sympathy – some – for this idiotic pursuit of yours: I was labelled cur, and in the end I had to bark. Not entirely your fault.

'But what the hell are you doing out of Edinburgh now? What reason had you to deprive Erskine of the support he had a right to expect at Flaw Valleys? What sort of a lead have you given anybody in the last six months? And now more intelligent, reasonable people are to be thrown into the circus so that you can continue to view your prejudices through a thick, green eyeglass. A long, fancy humiliation is to flatten your circle into conformity and your soul into grace. Well, it won't do, Richard.'

Lord Culter wore an expression of astonishment. 'I suppose that's the most eloquent protest I shall ever hear against professional justice. I've just told you. I'm not going to touch you.'

A smile touching his mouth, he saw Lymond's will defeated yet again by his weakness. His eyes closed, peremptory in exhaustion; and Richard flicked a pebble into the stream.

The heavy lids lifted.

Hospitality, Richard closed in. 'Have some fish?'

Lymond would not break. As one day and then another went by, Richard, insistently present and persistently gibing, began to find his own nerves betraying him, and sentence by sentence, Lymond fought back.

It was a tragic and annihilating war, in which intellect

503

fought naked with intellect, and the blows fell not upon the mind but upon the soul.

At times, the longing to kill became so overpowering that Richard had to blunder off, to get away from the sound of his brother's voice, his hands murderers at his sides. He knew, none better, what Lymond was driving him to do; and he guessed why. Indeed, the desperate savagery of these attacks gave him his only encouragement.

On the sixth day he became careless.

All week the weather had held. Dry stones were born in the stream and wagtails trembled on them; the grass was full of fledglings and flowers of disparate build.

On Saturday the dawn sky was poppied with high cloud and there was a welcome freshness in the air. Late in the afternoon, Richard found a rabbit in his traps and was cleaning it when he heard, very distantly, the sound of cantering hoofs. It was not coming near, and it seemed innocuous, but all the same he slipped through the stream to the next bay and laid a precautionary hand over Bryony's nose. She jerked disgustedly, her ears pricked, but stayed quiet until the sound died away. He gave her a clap on the back, checked her rope, and splashed around the grassy arm of the cliff.

Lymond was no longer propped up on rugs, where he had left him, but sat on a convenient boulder halfway between his bed and Richard's improvised kitchen. The bold light defined the untidy fair hair, the bruises and hollows of illness and the brilliant, heavy eyes: he looked high-strung to a shocking degree.

Curious and eager, Richard studied him; then his eyes travelled to the cooking stone and the rabbit. His knife had gone.

Lord Culter made no attempt to cross the clearing. Instead, hitching himself on the nearest ledge, he spoke mildly. 'Fine weather for travelling. The prickmadam chasing you?'

There was a little pause. 'No,' said Lymond. 'I was getting tired of the John-go-to-bed-at-noon era.'

'I find it quite pleasant,' said Richard. 'This peculiar

504

mental agility of yours has been no friend to you, has it? Without it, you might have survived, harmless, in a luke-warm limbo of drink and drugs and insipid women –'

'Do you want me to pursue the subject?' said Lymond. 'I don't think I can bring myself to pant all over your morals, or lack of them.'

'I wondered,' said Richard idly, 'now that you have leisure to think again, what you are missing most. You've no money, of course; and that has been very important to you. And you must, of course, miss the illusion of command. The ant milking the aphid. How pathetic: those simple men and broken criminals hailing you as their mighty Lar: how easy and exciting to gain ascendancy over them, to play at inverted Robin Hood, and become besotted with the vicarious thrill of defying nations. . . . You got a lot of attention that way . . .'

Impaled shrikewise on his boulder, Lymond had no reserves of strength to make the half-crippled journey back to couch and clear thought. Knowing, surely, that the last, bowelless assault was upon him, he spoke under his breath. 'Nay, brother,' said Lymond, '*I wyll not daunce.*'

Richard's voice, too, was soft. 'And the love of young boys, of course: you must miss that. Someone to relax with, in a gracious way, to twist and indoctrinate and shatter with the wild, delightful mutability of your moods. You must miss Will Scott. And your women.'

Lymond spoke without dropping his eyes. 'Suppose we leave out the women.'

'Christian Stewart, for example?'

'Suppose we leave out Christian Stewart and everything to do with her?' It was so quiet that his breathing was quite audible.

'Wouldn't you like it,' said Richard, 'if she were here with us now? A kindhearted girl, Christian: she wouldn't mind. She would help, without asking questions. She was used to that – a little too trusting, one would say, but after all, in God's world, we must trust somebody?' His gaze never left Lymond: inexorable, ruthless, dissecting, hygienic as burin or scalpel. And there was a change in his brother's face: the fissure; the first break.

A great pain of joy seized Richard's heart. My God: my God, was it coming . . . ? 'Yes,' he said calmly, and got up. 'A little adulatory company would be pleasant. That fellow who promised you all his gold, Turkey something: he tried to help you as well, and died, poor fellow. Blaming Will Scott for it, I'm told. Would you like his support now? I'm afraid you'll never enjoy his cottage in Appin . . .'

The level denunciation gave the words a power that rolled like the thunder of Götterdämmerung through the meadow. And Lymond cried out, 'Stop it, Richard!' and at last, violently swaying, forced himself to his feet.

Culter watched him; watched the hands groping at the cliff face behind for support; watched the death of all the characteristic, cultivated graces and spoke again, quite close now, a stony and judging shadow.

'Or if you hadn't killed her, would you be comforted by Eloise?'

Lymond made no sound.

'The only daughter, and the finest child. The most vivid, the most eager, the most intelligent. By now, cherished by her own lover, with her own children in her arms. Once, late at night when you were away, she told me . . .'

'*No!*' said Lymond. '*Oh, damn you, no.*'

'No? You wanted her burned alive, and she was,' said Richard with a terrible impartiality. 'Why should you cringe over it now?'

The guard was down. There was the face he yearned to see: never again inscrutable; never again would he need to wonder what lay behind the smiling mouth and the delicate, malicious wit. Skull, flesh and muscle, every fluent line and practised shade of Lymond's face betrayed him explicitly, and Richard, swept into a major, a foreign dimension, was suddenly dumb.

Behind clenched hands, face to the rock, Lymond spoke at last.

'*Why?* I made one mistake. Who doesn't? But I despised men who accepted their fate. I shaped mine twenty times and had it broken twenty times in my hands. Of course it left me deformed and unserviceable, defective and dangerous to associate with.... But what in God's name has happened to charity? ... Self-interest guides me like the next man but not invariably; not all the time. I use compassion more than you do; I have loyalties and I keep by them; I serve honesty in a crooked way, but as best I can; and I don't plague my debtors or even make them aware of their debt.... Why is it so impossible to trust me?'

'You shut the door yourself.' Richard spoke harshly. Now that it had come he recoiled from it: recoiled as Lymond turned and baring his face to the light went on, his voice exhausted, dogged, unsteady.

'Why should you think so? Why assume me to be of such different stuff? We have the same blood, the same upbringing. what else is there, at the end of the day, that we can call our own? We're our father's prejudices and our swordmaster's dead men; our mother's palate and our nurse's habit of speech. We're the books unwritten by our tutor, and our groom's convictions and the courage of our first horse. I share all that. Five years – even five such as these – can't tear me drop by drop from your blood.'

Numb, appalled, Richard flung back, reflecting horror with horror: 'And who made you a murderer?'

With the last offering of his strength, Lymond answered. 'Pull your hands away, Richard. Get out: get free. I have enough to answer for. If I've shut one door, you have barred and locked all the others against yourself.'

'Do you think *my* life,' said Richard violently, 'is a matter for your tarnished and paltry conscience?'

There was a silence. Then the Master said at last, 'Why else should I say what I have done?'

'Because,' said Richard cruelly, 'you're afraid of the rope. Because I'm the first victim you've failed to enchant. Because you're wriggling as you made others wriggle, and broken piecemeal as you've dissected others. Because you're crumbling and disintegrating and whimpering beneath the gut-sucking evil on your back; and since there was no one else to whine to; no one alive to listen; no one to help, you dropped on your belly and crawled and writhed and crept whining to me!'

Because his eyes had never left Lymond's hands he saw the flash of steel, and was launched already as the Master snatched out the bright stolen blade. He grasped the driving elbow and wrist – 'No: not that way, you poor, canting bastard!' – and was pulled up short by the strength of the thrust.

Lymond didn't drop the knife. Instead he bore downward, drawing strength from the hysteria of necessity: with his body braced against rock he withstood Richard's tug, made a leverage with the locked arms and, without a word, silently and inhumanly forced the point down.

It was uncanny. Richard found it terrible: it froze his blood, the slow descent of his brother's arm, prevailing heavily and inexorably against Richard's whole weight; forcing the bright, two-edged blade inward, between the locked bodies.

He damned the passion which had made him wait, instead of seizing the weapon at once; he damned the possessed body and the bent head and the transcendent will guiding the knife. He exerted all the strength he had. Lymond said something, on a gasp, and then bent forward, using his dead weight to help him, and the knife moved again, duly, along the path he designed for it; and an astonishing light broke on Richard.

In that second, Lymond looked up. Blue eyes met grey, and Richard read in them a power and a determination that he suddenly knew were unassailable. Anger left him. He framed the word 'No' with his lips; read his rejection in the dedicated eyes, and with all his strength drove first his knee and then his foot through the stained bandaging and deep into the other's hurt body. The knife dropped like a discarded straw. Lymond screamed once with agony, and then screamed and screamed again.

Within a dumb and breathless nature the sound exploded, addressing the arbour from its banks and gradients; bouncing; sticky-fingerd; callowly mocking. Culter, white as paper, picked up the knife and backed.

Lymond had stopped the noise with his hands. The long, cramped fingers hid his face as he crouched, the breath sobbing in his lungs and the blood flamboyant through the crushed bandages, welling between his rigid elbows, soaking into the trampled grass.

'Francis!' Excoriated by the shuddering, raucous sound, Richard spoke harshly. 'I can't let you take your own life.'

Lymond took his hands from his face. The blood was everywhere now; his torment of grief public, uncaring. 'Must I plead?' He stopped in extremity, beaten, shaken by pulses, and then struggled on. 'You claim your right of execution. . . . May I not exercise mine? Could all the chains of Threave outweigh what I already bear, do you think? Or all the Tolbooth's pains be worse than this? . . . You can't relieve me of your weight, or help me, or free me . . . except in one way.'

Richard, his memory taken by the throat, was mute. With a bitter courage, Lymond raised his head.

'I beg you.'

I will bring him to you on his knees, and weeping, and begging aloud to be killed.

Richard, rising, turned on his heel and walked over the meadow without looking back. Around the next spur of cliff was Bryony. She blew softly at him, pleased to have company, and while he waited, he smoothed down her lustrous neck.

When he went back, the clearing was empty. It was no longer a sanctuary, he knew, but the antechamber to a solitary, a desperately wanted death.

* * *

Beneath the cocked blue sky of summer, in the jostling towns and highways, in the forts hissing with tar and hot iron, the friaries and keeps, the foreshores where salt timber rolled ashore and oxen sprayed sand into wainloads of coal and cables and cannon shot and powder; in granaries rustling with early threshing and the unlacing of tents and the graithing of blades and the polishing of gorgets; and the intent of three European nations fastened to these small acres between Berwick and the Forth – with all that, it occurred to nobody in all this busy month that history was being made.

It didn't enter the head of Sir James Wilford, captain of English-held Haddington, that in twenty-five years someone would call his defence the most brilliant of the century. He was aware only that he was just seventeen miles from Edinburgh, and had forty-odd more and only two lines of communication between himself and the Borders; and that he had to keep in heart and health and, if possible, a state of truce – not only English but Spaniards, Germans and Italians against the malefic glitter of French arms and the shiftless shuffle of the neighbourly Scot on his patellas.

It was not in the mind of Lord Grey, riding his bones loose between town and town, insifflating the precious troops and horses, the pikes and powder and footmen, the rolls and matches and demilances and oil and flour and money, the working tools and men, men, and more men into the feverish maw of the fort. Or to Wharton, angrily denuded of the men sent to Grey, guarding a weak city and studying, whally-eyed, the ambiguous movements of the western Scots.

To the French, dropping like canescent frost on the discreet slopes about Haddington it was a small, acute campaign ordered by His Most Christian Majesty out of a fine warm regard for Scotland and a need to spit in the Protector's other eye.

To the Germans, the Swiss, the Italians and the Spaniards who were paid in écus and knifed each other when drunk and fished in the thin streams and picked lice out of their pallets, it was money to take home or to gamble away, some easy love and some more difficult; and leisure for boasting. To the Scots it was pride and fright, a wish to break the will of England and a need to smoke the vermin from one's little shoots and to pay the price with a hauteur that might make surrender a virtue.

510

The price was plain, and the Crown was ready to pay it. The Crown made its move on the day that Tom Erskine, altered and withdrawn, came back to Edinburgh from Hexham. Messengers slipped unobtrusively back and forth; Villegagne quietly left Court, and one evening four galleys of the French fleet slipped anchor at dusk and moved with ductile grace out of the Firth of Forth. The alert flickered, as it was conditioned to do, from point to point down the east coast of England; the skiffs fled about the English great ships of war and the stiff sails lay heavy on the decks, and men in the rigging strained at the recalcitrant block and the sullen, bearded ropes.

In vain. The four ships never came. They lifted their airy linen before a southwest wind and sailed out across the dark North Sea; then with four peacocks' tails at their keels they lay over, gathering the wind from port, the boom hammering to starboard, and hissed on their way north. Then having sailed over the roof of Scotland, turned south again, on her western shore, making with mischievous triumph for Dumbarton, where the Queen of Scotland, if she so wished, could safely step aboard.

The Crown had given evidence of its good faith. The last word lay with the people; and on a brilliant, wind-filled Saturday in July, the Scottish Parliament met in the Abbey outside English-occupied Haddington and gave their consent to the marriage of the Queen's Grace their Sovereign Lady and the Dauphin of France – 'provided always that the King of France keep and defend this realm and the laws and liberties thereof as his own realm, lieges and laws of the same; and as has been kept in all kings' times of Scotland bypast.'

Will Scott was there. As soon as the procession had left and the aisles were clearing, he slipped out to the church-yard where Tom Erskine stood talking, the short fur blowing on his hat. The moment he was free, Scott caught his arm. 'Any news?'

Erskine, nervously rubbing his face, gave him a non-plussed stare. 'What? . . . Oh. No – there's no news of either of them.'

Scott said suddenly, 'I men Lady Douglas yesterday: George Douglas's wife. She said –'

He broke off as a peer, his black hat at a rakish angle, jabbed Erskine in the back. 'My God, old Slovenly Thomas interpreting: who'd have thought it? I said, if his French hasn't improved since the Rome embassy, I said, we're just as likely voting on a proposal to crown Archie Douglas. Eh? . . . See your friend Culter didn't turn up to this one either. What's the holdup, eh? Buried himself instead of his brother?'

Erskine said, 'Looking after his own affairs, I expect,' and detached himself. To Scott he said, 'What about Lady Douglas?'

The boy was watching their hilarious neighbour take himself off. 'It doesn't matter. But I thought you should know my father is going to try and trace them.'

'Buccleuch? Why not you?'

Scott flushed. 'I'm supposed to stay with the army. Probation, of a sort. It would only make trouble.' He lifted his eyes to Erskine's noncommittal face. 'Damn it: why did you leave them together?'

Someone brought Erskine's horse. He pinned the flapping foot mantle with his glove, put his foot in the stirrup and mounted. Gathering the reins, he looked down for a moment at Scott's upturned face. 'Because my name isn't Crawford,' he said sharply. 'Any more than yours is.'

* * *

It was the cavorting and immalleable wind, boiling through the rowans and sifting the junipers and baying eagerly through lutelike caves and chasms, that chivvied Lord Culter into proper thought again that night.

A snatch of spray touched his hand, and he lifted his head from his arms and was vaguely surprised by the darkness and the noise. He rolled to his knees and stood up, automatically anchoring rugs and collecting his scattered belongings. Moving stiffly he crossed to the neighbouring arbour and found and checked Bryony's tethering and pulled her reproachful forelock. It occurred to him,

512

the first positive thought in a wilderness of dead emotions, that there was nothing to stop him from going home.

The thought, staring at him, divided and became twenty. He hooked one arm over the mare's neck and defied them for thirty seconds before recognizing the childishness of the impulse. Facts. He was bred to respect them: what were they?

The graceless, the dissolute, the debauched, the insolent, the exquisite Lymond was obliterated. As he intended, he had broken his brother. He had, indeed, been more merciful than he had intended.

The wind buffeted his shirt. Home. A hundred and twenty miles with the double packs behind him; a cold house in Edinburgh; his mother's face. Midculter, and an estranged wife. Erskine, with a sharp and speculative gaze; Buccleuch's uninhibited stare. The Court, where he would already be under censure.

The mare's skin was warm; his fingers tightened on her rough mane. God, Francis had screamed.

Something unused and ritual at the back of Richard's conscious mind stirred, and he stared into the buffeting darkness, quickly denying it. He assembled a chain of thought about provisions, about his route home, and about an imminent issue of jacks for his men. He thought seriously about the water problem at Midculter and began to plan, in elaborate detail, a discussion with Gilbert about new spearheads. And all the time the stiff-jointed thing at the back of his mind was flexing its subconscious limbs and shaking its aged neck and rearing nearer and nearer his waking mind.

The wind sprang among the young trees: persecuted beyond reason an ash high above them lurched heaving to its feet and crashed beside Bryony and the mare leaped, whinnying and shaking under Richard's idle hand.

The block of sensation, held so insecurely in check, broke its bar and blundered into the forefront of his mind. It gripped him as he pulled down and soothed the mare, beyond proper analysis: man's infant fear of the irretrievable; a starved yearning for warmth; a childish speck of

513

uncluttered vision; a tight and tangled warp of reason and emotion become suddenly an obsessive compulsion.

Abandoning sense, revenge, and the role of complacent dempster and letting reason fly like a hag through the night wind, Richard Crawford struck off through the darkness, plunging over myrtle and bracken and torn boughs and boulders, between thorn and furze and blurred trees and low thickets, in the direction last taken by his brother.

* * *

Instinct, in belated command on this ultimate journey, had led Lymond into the shelter of the thickest undergrowth and the wildest bushes and the closest trees.

Using them as crutches he had gone farther than seemed humanly possible for a man in his state. Richard, after two fruitless attempts, set out a third time with a flaring brand from his fire, regardless of who might see it, and in the end found him, in a deep and unlikely forme at the foot of a meagre willow.

It was not a heroic picture. Bracken obscured it, with botched and scrabbling hands; the wind whined and ran blenching through the long grass, split by dim breakwaters of burdock and furze. Lymond himself lay in a tangled abandonment of blood and bruised greenery and torn cloth: unruly; filthy; and emphatically severed from society.

Culter rose, extinguished the light, and gathering the derelict hands, lifted his brother and carried him back to the camp.

He had worked once before, impatiently, to succour the Master. This time he brought his will to bear as well as his strength. By daylight a thin and stammering pulse was his reward. By afternoon he was able, temporarily, to let go and rest, his tired shoulders propped against the over-hang and his legs splayed before him in a yellow carpet of silverweed. He watched his brother.

A remarkable face. Like the sea, it promised monts et merveilles: you might resent its graces and yet long to unclose its secrets. He began to look forward to the moment – the graphic, revealing moment, when a man

514

opening his eyes on the lentils and salt, found himself greeting the living.

He was there when Lymond woke, and saw neither surprise nor relief, but a dissolving horror, altering the other's already altered face and fading in ineffectual recoil. Richard exclaimed then, and put out a hand; and Lymond flinched as if he had been struck.

Throughout the day, it continued. Throughout the day, Lymond lay motionless, the eyes opaque and open, the mind incurious, inanimate, unaware; except for the terror which sprang into being when Richard appeared.

By nightfall Richard knew that the only thing living within the other man was the memory of a fear. You choose to play God, and the Deity points out that the post is already adequately filled. During an outburst of besotted philanthropy he had redeemed Lymond, but Lymond quite simply was not prepared to be rescued; and least of all by his brother.

Lord Culter was a strong, an honest and a stubborn man. He made his decision, and laying a finger on the one thread anchoring Lymond to reality, proceeded to twist it into a rope.

He talked. As his brother lay, reflecting the vacant sun in his eyes, Richard moved about him, chopping wood, cooking, cleaning, tending with steady hands. Moving and working he talked about the Midculter of his childhood; about school lessons and games and books and sporting excitements; about visits to Edinburgh and Linlithgow and Stirling and his own days in Paris; about the land and their tenants; about nurses and tutors and servants and relatives they had both known.

The empty calyx he was attacking made infinitesimal efforts to avoid him; to refuse his services; to deny his proximity; but he persevered. Hatred was life; shame was life; humiliation was life; the trivial movements Lymond was making in his extremity were life.

Richard Crawford was a very stubborn man.

He went to bed that nght hoarse but refusing to be depressed, although the next day, confronted by the same eyes and the same rejection, he was sometimes very near to giving it up.

He was unused to sustained talking: his mind balked; topics forsook him. Recent events he had forbidden himself: everything to do with the Master's own adult life; all political and national affairs. That left only the half-forgotten, virgin tracts of their common childhood. He dug, obstinately, into those sealed mines and shuttered bondhousese and in doing so dragged out days and weeks of his life hitherto quite forgotten.

That he should mention his father at all was accidental: it was years since the second baron had died, and he had hardly thought of him since. And that was surprising too, considering the part he had played in his boyhood.

'I don't fancy,' said Richard, thinking aloud, 'that he was fond of children, or even of marriage, much. But he wanted us to reflect his own physical superiority – in hunting, riding, shooting, swordplay, swimming and all the rest of it. My God, I used to lie like a Gothamite fisherman sometimes about my scores. And yet' – he paused, hands locked around knees, eyes unseeing as he groped after a new idea – 'and yet it wasn't altogether a good thing. He hadn't any other interests, and couldn't tolerate anyone who had. I remember Mother once got a case of new books from the stationer's, and he burned . . .'

No. That was one incident better forgotten. At the back of his mind he could hear the two voices, his brother and his father, shouting at one another: or rather, his father shouting and Francis retorting, using the very twin of the voice, he suddenly realized, that Lymond had used to himself in an obscure wood near Annan.

Memory, once jogged, showed him other pictures. A born athlete, at ease with every kind of sport, Richard had been human enough to enjoy his father's delight in him. He was adolescent before he suspected that his younger brother was less of an effete brat than his father made out; that although he was aggressively scholarly he also moved like an acrobat. He had eloquence. He had charm.

516

He submerged himself and his filthy tongue in music and books, and Sybilla abetted him. Why?

The answer to that had been easy, too. Apple of the baron's alcoholic eye, Richard was cut out for a mockery, a figurehead, a substitute leaking straw inconspicuously at the joints and accepting the respectful plaudits of the tenants. The steeples were being cut down so that the chimney could aspire. And Francis, of the sardonic blue eye, was without doubt a party to it.

It was a bitter discovery, and one that he had never questioned till now. It had never struck him that his brother, seeing their father with a clearer eye than his, might purposefully have turned aside from all that he stood for; might have taken a satirical pleasure in avoiding their father's approval. With Sybilla and the brilliant, worldly shadow of their grandfather behind him, he could afford to go his own way uncaring, and allow Richard his arena. Was that what had happened?

Was it? He looked with sudden, searching eyes at Lymond. The hypersensitive face gave him no answer, but there was a change of some sort: the eyes no longer reflected the sky but were half hidden by his lashes, as though there existed a thought to conceal. Richard lifted the fresh bandages he had prepared and kneeling, unfastened the old ones. The Master's mouth tightened, but he didn't recoil.

Slowly, it came. As well as instinct, there was somewhere a fragment of conscious will: Lymond's eyes recorded what they saw; and he was listening. Richard, talking like a mechanical corncrake, knew that he was listening, and yet he refused to come openly into the living world. He was refusing to fight; refusing the goad even when now at the eleventh hour admitting its pricks. Having come so far, Culter took a risk. He leaned over, closed both hands on the light tissue and bone of the Master's shoulders, and shook him like a puppy.

'All right: listen!' said Richard. 'I'm scunnered at washing bandages. I'm sick of cooking; I'm tired of hunting;

517

I'm fed up washing your ears and combing your hair like a bloody nursery maid. Suppose you make the effort now.'

It brought him his answer. A frail and passionate anger flickered through the other man's eyes; and weakly but distinctly Lymond spoke. 'You can't force me to live.'

'No. But I can force you to think.'

'– No.'

'You fought for Christian Stewart's good name. Why won't you fight for your own?'

His brother's voice made a mockery of the words. 'My good name?'

'Or Mariotta's, then?'

The flicker of animation died. Lymond said helplessly, 'No! You won't get me to Edinburgh . . . even for that. I won't go; I can't . . . Oh, God! I can't, now.'

To his surprise, Richard found himself shouting. 'Edinburgh! Who mentioned Edinburgh? If I object to playing apothecary in private, I'm damned sure I'm not going to trip about with hot towels in public.'

Lymond said something, from which only the word 'trial' emerged clearly. Lord Culter used three adjectives to qualify the same word, and pronounced flatly: 'You're not going for trial. You'll travel to Leith, and from there get out of the country. All you have to do is to work at your renovation until you can trust your feet on either side of a horse.'

It was much too sudden, he saw, for a tired mind to grasp. Richard leaned forward, one hand on either side of his brother's young, irresolute face, and said slowly and clearly, 'Listen. You're not going to Edinburgh. You're not going to prison, or the gallows. I'm here to help you. You're going to be free.'

For the second time in a few days, Richard Crawford had made a momentous decision purely on impulse. It made him feel uneasy, the prey of dark and atavistic caprice. But on thinking it over, more or less all night, he found that he regretted nothing.

518

The odd thing was that Lymond believed him without question. The next day, although catastrophically weak, he replied slowly and sensibly to Richard's necessary questions. Moved for the first time to imagine how it felt to exchange an oblivion so passionately wanted for such an extremity of defencelessness, Culter dealt with him wisely.

As the days passed, his sense of time perished. Lymond, however spent, was never less than scrupulous, unaffected, undemanding. Avoiding only the recent past, they ranged in their talk over the widest fields. Richard was impressed by his brother's grasp of affairs. He was well-informed, not at the level of ambassadorial junketings and court levées, but as the product of shrewd observation over the battlefields and spyholds of half Europe.

He spoke without embarrassment of such episodes in his life, but with discretion. Once, when Richard, seizing on a point, began to develop it with uncharacteristic excitement, Lymond himself interrupted with an anecdote so helplessly funny as well as so ribald that Culter was surprised into a shout of laughter and forgot, until afterward, the original issue.

Later, staring up into the night sky, Culter said, 'If only you'd come to us after you left Lennox, instead of . . .' Instead of foundering in self-pity. He could hardly say that.

Lymond flushed. 'Instead of surviving to bellow like a barghest?' It was his only reference to the other night, and Richard was caught without a rejoinder, but after the briefest pause, Lymond himself went on. 'But I did come back. To my kinsmen I will truly, praying them to help me in my necessity. . . . I thought you knew. I came to Midculter from Dumbarton in '44 – fully au prodigal son, puffing excuses like smoke from a chimney head–' A trace of the old mockery sharpened the light voice.

'What happened?' asked Richard quickly.

'I was shown the door. By our honoured father. He tried to enforce the suggestion with a whip.'

There was a short silence. Then Culter said, 'He must

have told nobody. I wouldn't touch you: you know that. Until the – the Midculter affair.'

'I know, you damned fool,' said Lymond mildly. 'That's why I had to attack Midculter.'

Lord Culter sat up. After a moment he pushed a hand through his flat brown hair and said bluntly, 'What about the setting fire to the castle . . . ?'

'Green boughs. Good God, Richard: I've mastered the art of making timber burn better than that by this time.'

'And the silver?'

This time there was a little pause. Then Lymond said, 'You're going to be annoyed about that. She didn't tell you, I expect, because she knows what a filthy bad actor you are. Mother got it all back the next day.'

Richard's stare was embarrassingly concentrated. 'And Janet Beaton?'

'Oh. That,' said Lymond bitterly. 'That was because I had to drink the whole bloody night through to get enough courage to visit the castle at all. One more skirl and one of my pets was going to slit the lady's larynx for her. So I did something first. Unfortunately, I was too damned drunk to do it properly. That and the passage with Mariotta: the kind of lunatic blunders that always blemish the high romantic in grim reality. . . . Come, my friend, my brother most enteere; for thee I offered my blood in sacrifice; and all that. Except that it was Janet Beaton's blood.'

Richard said mildly, 'It wasn't anyone else's blood at Hexham,' and saw his brother redden again. 'The climax to a series of sordid private fights. Don't get excited. Erskine got the idea he was carrying out the Third Crusade, but all he carried out was me, the lord be thankit. God, I've whined for ten minutes. Bury me at Leibethra, where the nightingale sings.'

As Lymond grew stronger, his brother forced the pace of their discussions and once, out of an obscure train of thought, said, 'Francis. Did you ever tell Will Scott how old you actually are?'

Lymond looked blank. 'No. Should I?' and Richard grinned.

'Probably not. You appear to be immeasurable in his view, like God and the Devil.'

'A year with Will Scott would make a dayfly feel like Enoch,' said the Master. 'Whose side is he on now?'

'Yours, by all accounts,' said Richard dryly. 'Buccleuch got him accepted back at Court and Will has taken to advertising your peculiar talents from the four walls in a voice like a Gadwall duck.'

'Don't be deceived,' said Lymond with equal dryness. 'That's only remorse because he bit me and I didn't bite back. He'll settle in time into a decent, douce Buccleuch.'

If Richard thought it unlikely, after a year of Lymond's company, he said nothing; and was not to know that his brother was watching him. A moment later the Master said equably, 'Nobody's going to hold you to a promise that needs this amount of nursing, Richard. I don't want my life at the price of anyone's outraged instincts. It has a rudimentary value in that you were moved to preserve it, but don't let's labour the point.'

He was not, clearly, interested in a superficial reassurance; also, his reading was correct. If he produced facts a yard a day like a guinea-worm, Richard didn't want them. He had promised to free Lymond, and he had no desire to regret it. He said at length, 'My instincts are very accommodating.'

'All right, but remember, although you've bought the rights of fuel, feal and divot, I shan't be lying here like an upset sheep forever.'

Richard said, 'You think I'll discard in the perpendicular what I favour in the prone?'

'Not if you talk like that: you'll want an audience at any price.'

Culter laughed, and it was the end of that particular discussion.

But although Richard forgot it, Lymond apparently did not. Next day he put his theory to the test, dispassionately and with the kind of calculated resolution that still startled his brother. Richard knew nothing until he came back from his traps to find the clearing empty and his horse gone, and one of the saddlepacks with it.

One by one, his first conjectures were discarded. No one had captured Lymond: there was no trace of struggle, and only their own footprints and the tracks of one horse in the soft grass. Nor could it be some flamboyant gesture to relieve him of his decision: horseless, Richard had little chance of reaching Scotland alive.

He looked again at the tracks. They were very recent, and not hurried. Lymond was unable, of course, to ride fast. With sudden decision Culter stooped again, and snatching bow and quiver followed the mare's hoofmarks out of the clearing. They led him along the banks of the stream, then up a shallow cliff to open grass. He picked them up, running lightly, as they swung out in a wide circle, and alternately studied the ground and the gentle, tree-scattered slopes in front of him. There was no trace of Bryony there. Driving back every apoplectic emotion which might distract him, he concentrated on the ground.

The hoofprints brought him, in a gentle arc, back to his own clearing. He stopped when he realized it, breathing tightly and fast and waited, resting, his free hand smoothing back his hair. When he had control both of his breathing and of the curious conflict within himself, he went on.

Lymond, lying face down beside the gently cropping Bryony, turned his head and produced a sick, placating grin. Richard exploded.

'This bloody mania for juggling with other people's guts. You lunatic, if I'd overtaken you back there, I'd have killed you.'

'I thought,' said the Master pacifically, 'that it was time to get used to the saddle again. We ought to start north.'

'Quite. And that was only part of what you thought,' said Lord Culter. He tied up the mare and stalked back again with a cup of water, which he dumped at his brother's elbow. 'You like to be sure of your relationships – who doesn't? But no one else does it by making themselves into a clearing nut for other people's emotions. If my sentiments are in a muddle,' said Richard angrily, 'I damned well prefer them to stay in a muddle, without any interference from you.'

Propping himself on one elbow, Lymond lifted the cup, spilled it badly and set it down again without drinking. He said, 'It seems I can now stick on a horse. Therefore we can get back north, beginning tonight if possible. And since, as soon as we move into Scotland, my company will compromise you, we ought to have some issues clear.'

He stopped. Richard said nothing; and his brother went on grimly. 'You offered me a reprieve knowing only half the story. You mentioned Mariotta, and what I told you about her was true. You haven't mentioned Eloise.'

Richard sat down, removed the fallen cup, and set it straight. Then he said, 'Look. I don't share your passion for self-immolation. I don't want to hear about Eloise, and I don't want issues made any clearer than they now are. Whatever your conscience has on it, I intend to take you back to Scotland and see you aboard ship. If you can ride, we leave tonight.'

'God,' said Francis with amiable rudeness, between his hands. 'What price now the mighty Lar?'

A day later, with Lymond mounted and Richard walking at his side, the two men began the slow journey north.

* * *

Dinner in Lord Grey's house was served at two o'clock, and he had invited company: Sir Thomas Palmer, his fortifications expert from London, and Gideon Somerville and his young wife Kate.

Katherine, neat as a peach and spruce in grey satin, was not impressed by Berwick, by the meal, or by Willie Grey. With a thoughtful brown eye she watched the salt cellar whisking past her nose – 'There you are: Bowes, Brende and Palmer with the horse, leaving tonight and lying at Coldingham' – the ale jug: 'Holcroft with the foot, leaving tomorrow and joining the two of you with the horse at Pease Burn' – and the salt cellar again: 'Monday, early, Palmer makes contact with Haddington and they give cover while all of you put fresh men into the fort and come back.'

Some of the salt had spilt. Kate threw it over her left shoulder and remarked, 'How simple it sounds in English! Just imagine Sir James drawing diagrams on the walls to convey his orders in Haddington. A quick course of Udall would work wonders with this army.'

Gold wire twinkled. 'Why Udall?' asked Palmer.

'Or any other nimble Latinist you can think of. Don't you think they need a lingua franca, poor things?' said Kate. 'And if your two thousand Germans are coming by sea, and Lord Shrewsbury with eleven thousand Englishmen from all the shires are exchanging dialects at York, and the Swiss and the Spanish and the Germans want to communicate from Haddington, throwing in a few Italian engineers for luck, you'll have a dear little Babel all of your own.'

Lord Grey's face was gloomy. 'So will the Scots,' he said. 'By all accounts. If Henry sends forty thousand more Frenchmen and the King of Denmark throws in –'

'All the more reason for linguistic action. Buchanan against Eton. You've been to Haddington, Sir Thomas?' asked Kate.

Palmer grinned. 'We all went the day they held Parliament, and popped a good few bags of powder in while they were busy. Bowes took young Wharton under his wing: he did rather well. Between Lord Grey here and his father he was a bit low to begin with.'

'Incompetent young fellow,' said Grey vaguely; and remembered something. 'By the way, sincere apologies: Gideon having to bring you that girl who escaped. Nasty business, but unavoidable. Lady Lennox could do nothing with her, I believe.'

Katherine said, 'You never caught up with the other, did you? The man who killed the messenger at Hexham?' and Grey stared moodily at Palmer. 'That damned fool Wharton. The father's worse than the son. Five minutes after the shot he sends a man to collect the body – No body. The fellow had an accomplice. One? The kind of guard my Lord Wharton had on that church, he might have had ten.'

Palmer said cheerfully, 'Enterprising fellow. Was that the one who tweaked Ned Dudley's nose at Hume?' Warned by the silence that he had only half the story he added quickly, 'Look out for him if you like, my lord. Never know what you'll come across, jogging post back and forth through the country like this.'

'I should be obliged if you would,' said Lord Grey. 'But the task on hand is to get all these men safely into the fort at Haddington tomorrow. Monday the what? – the sixteenth. That's our job.'

The point was made. Sir Thomas, butter-tooth veiled, seized a pigeon and said no more until the end of the meal.

Afterward, Gideon took Kate up to the castle ramparts, and with the Tweed running tousled and low beneath them, they studied the green fields to the north, where Palmer's men would travel that night.

Gideon said, 'It's a dangerous subject, Kate. Better forget it. Whatever happened, we'll never know now.'

'It doesn't matter what happened,' said Kate. She turned and looked across the river where the grass, identical, flower-ridden and boisterous, was English grass.

She said angrily, 'I don't like this war. I don't like the cold-blooded scheming at the beginning and the carnage at the end and the grumbling and the jealousies and the pettishness in the middle. I hate the lack of gallantry and grace; the self-seeking; the destruction of valuable people and things. I believe in danger and endeavour as a form of tempering but I reject it if this is the only shape it can take.'

There was a brightness in the flat, clean plane between her short nose and the cornea and brown cheek. Gideon, who had hardly ever seen his wife in tears, was moved and disturbed, his intuitive mind groping for the reason and the right reply. He said, gripping her shoulders, 'Philippa will be all right. She'll learn. We can explain to her.'

Katherine turned instantly and impulsively and put her

525

own warm hands on Gideon's. 'Don't mind me. I want to put right the world's sorrows in a night, and it might take a night and a day. But three stout people like us can afford to bide our time.'

'If need be,' said Gideon. He looked tired, she thought; but he smiled at her. 'Trust me.'

* * *

That night, the fine mid-July weather broke at last; clouds piling spinel-red in the west surged over all the sky by morning and brought small showers, with a minor, tugging wind.

Palmer, cheerful red face under a perfectly polished helmet and enormous shoulders tucked into steel mesh, was not the man to bother if the skies spouted venom like Loki's serpent. He and Bowes made their scheduled rendezvous with the foot soldiers on Monday morning and marched north to Haddington. At Linton Bridge, five miles away, he sent word to Sir James Wilford, captain of Haddington, that a fresh army was waiting to relieve the English garrison.

Forty Spanish horsemen from the fort came back with Wilford's answer. It was too dangerous. Although he needed the men, he distrusted the present quiet, and advised Sir Thomas to postpone his plan.

Palmer read it, swore lightheartedly, and took the Spaniards with him to have a closer look at the French and Scottish camps. It continued to be quiet until they reached the slopes north of Haddington. Then, against the bald, uncompromising sky, Bowes spotted movement. The lilies of France, whipping in the wind, were pouring downhill toward them in the van of a hundred and fifty armed horsemen.

Peace and sylvan propriety exploded. Gamboa wheeled and shot off with the hackbutters to hold the French; Palmer and Bowes interweaving behind him got the horse and foot into position and stopped, halted by trumpets. Long-sighted, Palmer saw new colours flying toward him, this time from Haddington. His face crimsoned with delight.

'Ellerkar, by God! Ellerkar and damned nearly half a thousand light horse from the fort. . . . *Now* let's pick off the smirks with your goose feathers, boys!'

Ellerkar was not called on to charge. The French had no wish to argue with four hundred fresh horsemen. Disentangling at speed, they shot up the hill and out of sight, leaving the English and Spanish to greet each other, reform, and set off in jubilation for Haddington, led by Palmer and Bowes.

None of them reached it. The French simply waited behind the nearest hill until the tail of the force was riding past them, and then slid down and cut them off. Then, having taken some smart bites at Ellerkar, they retreated hastily but in order around the hill, with the whole combined English force at their heels. Sir Thomas, furious at the destruction in his rear, had almost closed with them when the cutting edge of the little manoeuvre became horribly clear.

Round the shoulder of the hill on which the French were retreating was a solid quadrant of French foot soldiers and hackbutters, patiently waiting; patently armoured in a ready-made aura of rude success.

Driven headlong by their own impetus, Palmer and Bowes skidded and smashed into this impenetrable front. The Spanish leader Gamboa, coming up behind, was drowned in the recoil. Holcroft's footmen, faced with nose-to-nose fighting against an opponent of the first quality, wavered, crumbled and fled. For half an hour the fighting continued, and then Palmer's men broke too.

There was nothing to be done. Pursued by Gallic language and Gallic joy, English and Spanish streamed from the valley of the Tyne, and the French horsemen hunted them all afternoon like a coursing. Behind them, the Protector's army left eight hundred English and Spanish dead or captured, the major part of their horse, and a Haddington not only lacking the new forces intended for it, but disastrously bled of Ellerkar, Gamboa and the horsemen who had issued to help.

Thus, read the subsequent dispatch to the Protector: *Thus with victory in our hand, this mischance has altered things. Our principal horsemen and chief footmen are consumed; our powder wasted. Wherefore it is not good to venture anything by land, except by a royal force.*

Eventually, the royal force did come. Like Palmer's, it was tough and enthusiastic. Unlike Palmer's, although it made mistakes, it was not routed. But neither did it prevail.

* * *

Sir Thomas Palmer, riding hard, nearly reached the bridge at East Linton. With three of his own men and a Spaniard at his heels, he had broken loose from two skirmishes, and it was just beginning to seem possible that he had shaken off pursuit, when out of the ground before him rose a small, wicked, steel-bound phalanx of horsemen.

They were Scots. He didn't know the emblem, but he could recognize defeat: he let them encircle the five of them and waited in silence as the leader trotted forward. Grey, healthy whiskers sprouted from a pugnacious, sweaty face. 'Dod,' said the victor, peering at Sir Thomas. 'Don't tell me: it's on the nether side of my back teeth. Palmer! Am I right?'

'You are, sir, dammit,' said Sir Thomas with a polite snarl.

The whiskers twitched. 'Just so. Man, you're a devil for getting yourself hud by the neb. Ye were nippit in France as well, were ye not?'

Sir Thomas got redder.

'And had to pay your own way out?'

Sir Thomas swore, politely.

'I'm Wat Scott of Buccleuch,' said his captor courteously. 'Just so's your friends'll know where to send the siller to. Man: you'll like Edinburgh. It's a fine town to be in jail in.'

Buccleuch detached half of his men to march Palmer

and his companions to Edinburgh, and continued his ride with the rest, whistling.

Sir Wat was pleased with life; so pleased that he ignored the signs of flight all about him, and wished luck to the horse bands, both French and Scottish, who appeared and vanished like flying ants all through the blustering afternoon. After a while, disturbances became less frequent, and he was alone with his own dozen men, crossing rough moorland with no cover and chastened by a small, chilly wind.

Ahead on his right, a bird rose suddenly, vivid black and white, piping above the rustle of foxtail and club rush, and a moment later he saw two horsemen treading slowly where it had been, their faces to the north. He stopped and watched.

One of the figures, cloaked and hooded, he could make nothing of. The other, coatless, solid, unmistakable, was Richard Crawford of Culter.

Buccleuch rode over circumspectly, leaving his men behind without explanation, and brushing a thoughtful hand through his·whiskers as he went. Culter turned, and deserting the other rider, trotted gently to meet him, his face brown and watchful above a dirty and ruinous white shirt. He spoke immediately they were within hearing. 'Well, Wat. Still intent on appearing at the wrong time in the right place.'

He sounded temperately amused, but Wat's experienced eye read the tilt of his right arm with accuracy. He cleared his throat. 'Glad to see you, my boy. Damned good job you all did at Hexham. Arran likes you again: that ought to make you cheery. They're going to make the fool a Duke: did ye hear?'

'No. Erskine got back, then?'

'Dod, aye. He said you were taking your own time at his back, but we were beginning to think they'd jumped on you. The plan went off fine: just fine.' He paused again. The second horse was cropping grass, hocks nearest, and the rider, head bent, was sitting badly.

Culter didn't move, so Wat said bluntly, 'Are ye for Edinburgh?'

Richard shook his head.

'Oh.' A curious look came over Buccleuch's face. He rubbed his nose, spat inelegantly and said, 'It's a sharp wind for July. I won't say you're wrong, either. That brat of mine's a fool, but he's not bad company now, at that.' He caught the guarded grey eye and cleared his throat again. 'Well. I'm for the south. I hope you have a quiet trip. There's a damned wheen of horsemen clipping about today. Some stramash up the way, I believe.'

'Thank you,' said Lord Culter, and hesitated. 'Your men . . . ?'

'None of their business. Dod, Sybilla will be desperate glad to see you.'

Richard said suddenly, 'Tell her . . .' and broke off and swore, angry alarm displacing the subdued and wary mask. Buccleuch, wheeling, had his own hand on his sword an instant later and then pushed it back, gesturing ferociously at Culter. 'Ride, man, ride!'

On the hill behind, a party of Scots came whooping toward them. A second later, and they called Culter's name. Richard, his horse already moving, twisted, saw the cock pennants and cursed again. 'The Cockburns of Skirling. Devil take it. Wat: can you hold them while we run?'

They were too close. Buccleuch saw Culter's choice only too clearly: either to hand over his companion, or to label himself accomplice by trying an ineffectual escape.

As once before, Buccleuch filled the notorious lungs, and bellowed.

Long before Richard reached him, Lymond turned and saw what was happening. He straightened and shook the hood from his face, exposing ruffled fair hair and Culter's stained jacket below. Then he gathered his horse and stampeded artlessly across the moor, regardless of the slick, united hoofbeats of Sir William Cockburn's troop overtaking, surrounding and closing in on him. He made no resistance.

Buccleuch, riding after with Culter, arrived to find himself the butt of a number of bad jokes and some friendly wrangling over whether he had forfeited his prisoner by allowing him to escape. Since Richard had relapsed into utter silence, Sir Wat dealt with it brusquely, neither admitting nor denying the credit Lymond seemed to have given him; and after a bit they stopped pestering him with questions and offered pleasantly enough to travel back to Edinburgh together.

After his own men had joined him, Buccleuch asked to look at the prisoner and was directed to the rear, where Lymond was lashed flat to a horse-stretcher. He was not conscious.

Sir Wat studied him in silence before making his way back to the Cockburn brothers. He jerked his head. 'What'll happen now?'

'Oh. Well, he's at the horn, isn't he? It'll be the Castle then, I dare say, for a week or two; and then a sweet short trial and a swing in New Bigging Street. Nothing surer than that.'

And so Richard, after all, escorted his younger brother to Edinburgh.

2 · ONE LOSS IS MADE GOOD

*'Quant compaignons s'en vont juer
Ils n'ont pointe tou dis essouper
Cras connins ne capons rostis
Fors le terme qu'ils ont argent . . .'*

It was so long since the Dowager had broken into song that Mariotta and her two guests were surprised. Janet grinned, and Agnes Herries, who was half asleep, blinked and said, 'Is it time yet?'

'Not quite,' said Sybilla. The smallest flush under the white skin was the only sign that she was excited: she was beautifully dressed and not at all frayed in manner as was Mariotta, who showed the effects of the three newsless weeks since Tom Erskine's return from Hexham.

531

At midnight, in their presence, Johnnie Bullo was to turn a pound of lead into gold. Of the four women, Janet Buccleuch was deeply interested in Sybillia's experiment. Propping her large green velvet slippers on a footstool, she said, 'Did the gypsy want a lot of gold off you for this? I hope you were careful.'

The Dowager raised candid eyes over the rims of her glasses. 'Of course, dear. But the gold will have reached him only ten minutes before we do, which is just' – glancing at her enormous German clock – 'about now. Shall we go?'

Mariotta, leaning over, touched Agnes Herries awake. She opened her eyes with a jerk, followed the others vaguely to the door, and then seized Mariotta in a vicelike grip. 'What if he raises the devil?'

Mariotta laughed, and withdrawing her arm, put it reassuringly around the bride's shoulders. 'What if he does? Sybilla would simply exchange recipes for sulphur ointment and give him a bone for the dog. Come along . . .'

Outside it was cool and very dark. A wisp of straw, rolling over the cobbles in the light wind, caught the beam from the doorway and scuttled, spider-fashion, into the night; nothing else moved. Sybilla shut the big doors and in the darkness they walked over to where the small window of Johnnie Bullo's laboratory glowed like a malign and bloodshot eye. The Dowager rapped on the pane; there was a pause; a stealthy rattle of heavy bolts, and the door to the laboratory swung open.

The heat buffeted their faces. The low, square building was lined with scarlet from the glow of the furnace, snoring hoarsely as the wind sucked at its funnel.

From floor to ceiling rose vessels and retorts and bottles, jars, pots and crucibles, matrasses and pelicans, balloons, serpents and mortars, aludels, funnels and beakers. The walls bobbed and winked and glimmered with vermilion eyes as if wattled with bloated and striking serpents, swaying with the flames.

There was a wooden bench, littered with tongs and iron filings and dirty dishes and knives and heaps of flour and sand for the lutes; and old athanors, unused; sundry pots, chipped and blackened, on the floor; and two different sizes of bellows hanging on nails beside an outburst of chalked inscriptions in some sign language firmly based on triangles. There was an old carpet on the stone floor and two wooden stools, beside which stood Johnnie.

Johnnie's eyeballs shone like red glass. His face, swarthy and flushed, was running with perspiration and his short, wiry frame writhed darkly over the bottles and knives, coiling and disappearing in the leaping red light. He bowed without speaking and indicated the stools. The Dowager sat quickly on one and Janet on the other, with the two girls standing behind. Johnnie waited until they were settled and then following his shadow to the door, shot the bolt. The furnace flared up.

'Let us begin,' said Johnnie and stood, in an odd, prayerful attitude by his bench, his brown, long-lashed eyes fiery and grave.

'Tonight we follow where only the greatest have led. Tonight we invoke the aid of those who have allowed us to penetrate to the Chamaman, the Tan, the great mystery. We honour Yeber-Abou-Moussah-Djafar-al-Sofi, the Master of Masters; Zosimus and Synesius; Trismegistus the Thrice Great; Olympiodorus, Philosopher to Petasius, King of Armenia; Nagarjuna who discovered distillation; and the blind Abu-Bakr-Muhammad-Ibn-Zakariyya-al-Razi himself.

'We ask them to lend power to our Stone, that the imperfect metal, the crude substance of Saturn, shall fall into corruption and in the flames of its passing generate the moisture of mercury and the smoke of sulphur until, refined, purified, perfected, the substance in our crucible will no longer have the attributes, the vices, the weakness of lead, but instead will be transmuted to perfect gold.'

He touched gently one of the bellied pots at his feet, swathed in cloths and with an iron clamp about its neck. 'The gold is here; the chains and coins given me by Lady Culter, already melted down and ready to begin the reaction which compels the transformation to begin. Here'

533

– he lifted a grey brick from the table – 'is a pound of lead. Will you test it for me?'

Janet took it from him and examined it closely. It passed from hand to hand and returned to Bullo, who held it so that they could all see quite clearly, and placed it in the retort. 'So. And now the Stone.'

He bent over his bench for a moment, and turned. In his tough brown palm lay a box, beautifully made in silver, with Arabic characters on the lid and a small mirror inset in the bottom. He opened it, holding it for them to see.

Inside, on a bed of white velvet, lay a dirty grey stone, flaked and powdery in texture and uneven in shape. Johnnie spoke gently. 'The Stone of the Wise. The Magisterium. The Universal Essence.' He lifted it delicately and, opening another, clean box on his desk, he scraped gently at the soft skin of the stone. A little white dust, flushed in the rosy light, slipped into the box, and Bullo replaced the stone, keeping the box of dust in his hand.

'My lady. What we are doing is not without danger – to me. You are quite safe. But I must ask you not to speak, and not to move, until the mystery is over.

'For myself, I confide my safety to the alchemists and the philosophers who watch us, and speak the words of the Emerald Table: *True it is, without falsehood: certain most true. That which is above is like to that which is below; and that which is below is like to that which is above, to accomplish the miracles of one thing. And as in all things whereby contemplation of one, so in all things arose from this one thing by a single act of adoption. The father therof is the Sun; the mother, the Moon. The wind carries it in its womb: the earth is the source thereof. It is the father of all works of wonder throughout the world. The power thereof is perfect. Thus thou wilt possess the brightness of the world, and all obscurity will fly far from thee . . .*'

With steady hands, he lifted the great jar and set it to its resting place over the fire. Next, withdrawing the clamp, he tilted the little box of powder so that its contents drifted within the neck of the crucible to join the metal inside.

For the space of a heartbeat there was silence.

Then with a waft and a roar, blue smoke lipped like cream from the mouth of the retort, folded, arched and rolled servilely through the hut. It thickened, dropping languid fingers to the floor and flattening itself against the wooden roof; it became dense, black and choking with the stink of sulphur; it yawned blindly in the senses and the fire, leaping as if freed of some monstrous birth, rent its thinnest layers with tongues of yellow and crimson.

Agnes screamed. Mariotta, after a single alarmed cry, held the girl tightly and stood still. Janet, gripping her stool, watched the Dowager until she could barely see her, close as she was, for the swirling fumes. They were enclosed, hot and foul and black as charcoal, they were defying panic when, sweet as a summer dawn, the smoke bloomed, and bright gold rising living from its roots flooded the dark curtain and turned it into the pure yellow of Easter sunshine.

The veil hung, fresh and precious for the space of ten seconds, and then, breaking like floss, melting, separating, sifting and dwindling through the air, it slowly vanished. Behind it, Johnnie Bullo appeared, a shadow, a monochrome, a flat and coloured impasto, and finally the vivid man, standing beside the furnace. In one hand was the clamp, and he was raising from the fire the heavy, blackened jar.

There was an iron plate on the floor in front of the Dowager. Bullo set the crucible there, and the heat from it made them draw back. They watched in silence as Johnnie stepped up, an iron bar in his hands. He swung it, and the neck of the jar broke at its base.

In silence he proffered the Dowager his tongs. She bent, groping within the crucible. The instrument gripped; she raised it and lowered what it held to the floor. It was a small block of dull metal, unmistakably gold. There was nothing else in the jar at all.

Words could not contain their triumph and amazement. The bottles and jars chattered and clinked and the walls wept tears of strange emotion. Where there had been a block of lead, there was a block of gold. The Stone of the Wise was powerful indeed.

When she could hear herself speak, the Dowager, scarlet with pleasure, was also urgently pressing. 'May we see it again? May we see the Stone again? Now we know it *is* the true Stone.'

She had been less than tactful, and he demurred at first; but both Mariotta nd Agnes added their voices, and finally he brought out the silver box. Sybilla opened it lovingly.

'Lift it,' said Janet. 'It is heavy?'

The Dowager inserted a delicate finger and thumb. 'Not very. So small, and so powerful. If one scraping does all this, what mightn't the whole Stone do?'

The white teeth flashed. Johnnie, royally confident, was in carefree mood. 'It would burn as the sun in your hand would burn, my lady. But you will wish to use it sparingly and make it last long.'

'Not particularly,' said Sybilla. She weighed the precious thing a moment in her hand, a calculating look in the blue eye, and then pitched it wholesale into the heart of the furnace.

Everybody screamed at once, and Johnnie's shout was the loudest of all.

The roar and belch of black smoke this time pounced on them like the black underbelly of the ancient Chaos himself, snarling and surging about them with inhuman venom. It grew dark: far darker than before. Their eyes became blind as the eyes of the dead and the unborn; their senses thickened and stifled beneath the blanket of sulphur and their skins grew heavy and clogged with the rushing filth. The furnace roared. The last thing Janet saw was Sybilla's head, like eidelweiss on some black, mirrored tarn. She took two strides and, embedding her powerful grasp in Sybilla's long sleeves, hung on. Then they were all lost to each other.

There was no yellow flare. The sightless nightmare engulfed them and the seconds passed, and then minutes, of black choler, livid and briefly guttering with the surge of the furnace. Light came reluctantly, clearing the blackness in misty circles, like clean water running white and graining over the blackened face of a drawing.

The floor became visible to them; then the stools; the lower part of the bench, and the five persons in the laboratory, three of them in much altered positions. Instead of commanding the furnace, Johnnie Bullo was standing hard by the door, looking out of the corners of his eyes at Sybilla. The Dowager had reseated herself and with Janet peering beside her, was poking energetically inside a large crucible, the twin of the one which stood shattered on the iron plate still in front of her.

'Such a useful thing, smoke,' said Sybilla. 'Now what have we here? Yes. I thought so.'

She plunged her arm inside the jar and lifted something out, displaying it to them all. 'One pound of lead, untouched. From the first crucible, stealthily hidden beneath the bench. Leading us to the second crucible, now broken, and containing one block of lead (at a guess) thinly coated with gold. Leading us to the further matter of my chains and coins which were supposed to be in the first jar but are (at a guess) inside the bench drawer instead. Yes, here they are.

'Dear me. Having supplied me with my coated brick and my Stone, Mr. Bullo meant I suppose to pocket the gold intended for the experiment and to stimulate a small regular income of gold with which to repeat his initial success. I do call that a little grasping, when I seemed to have housed and fed and paid him practically all winter. . . . I shouldn't try it, my dear man. The door wouldn't open for a very good reason: half my servants are outside with pikestaffs. Didn't you know that Dame Janet dabbled in alchemy too? She has been a most valued adviser.'

Standing against the door, Johnnie Bullo showed his teeth; and there was something of the occult still about his smile, although he was unarmed and rather dirty, as they all were, and his hair was curling over his eyes. 'At least, as you say, I had a winter's lodging for it,' he said impudently. The brown eyes were limpid. 'Have I made an error? I was under the impression you were buying my services.'

The blue eyes were equally seraphic. 'Your services proved a little expensive.'

He shrugged a little. 'I did all I could be expected to do, barring manufacture fresh time. You feel,' and he jerked his head toward the door, 'you have no further need of me?'

'On the contrary,' said Sybilla, and gathering her stained clothes carefully, she sat down again on her blackened stool. 'On the contrary: I wished it to be very clear to you that you need my good offices much more than I need yours. If these men outside take you to a sheriff with this tale, you'll hang.'

Romanies, having no use for confessions and excuses, likewise prefer to reach a crooked point quickly. Johnnie Bullo moved away from the door, strolled to the bench, turned, and regarded the Dowager with resignation and some misgiving.

'All right. What must I do?' he inquired.

* * *

On that same evening, as the small, gusty wind blew heather off the fuel stacks and straw from the roofs and goffered the gutter mud in the High Street, Lord Culter left Edinburgh for home.

It was five months since he had seen Midculter; five months since he had ridden around the estate, or seen to his fishings and his warrens and his peats. He had watched his stock coming to market outside the city walls; had met and corresponded with Gilbert over the shipments of wool and hides and the ordering of the farms and the affairs of his dependents; his wright and his mason, his tailor and amourer and falconer and carpenter and smith and gardeners; the men who supplied his oats, meal and barley, herded his pigs and sheep and cattle, grew his peas and beans, brewed his beer and bred his horses and cared for his wealth, infield and outfield.

He had missed the lambing and the finishing of his new

barns and outbuildings; the shearing; the new plantings he had decided on for the spring. For five months he had carried a sleepless sword and husbanded other, corrupt intentions.

Now he was going home. Against the red western sky the outline of the Pentland hills, each shape familiar to him, moved and fell behind him on his right. The road, climbing up into Lanarkshire, reached the high moors as the wind freshened. The sky above him, changing from turquoise to Chinese blue, drew over him the inconspicuous film of night. The horizon, lingering apple green before him, breathed out its colour scrupulously after the prostrate sun.

He had said to Buccleuch, and Dandy Hunter, seeing him off, 'I'll be at Midculter before morning'; and Buccleuch had pummelled him briskly on the shoulder and said, 'Good lad. I hope it comes right for you. Kittle cattle, women, kittle cattle: but it's wersh and wae without them.'

Bryony's hoofs drummed in sympathy. Kittle cattle: kittle cattle. Would it come right? God knew, thought Richard – and closed his thighs like iron on the mare.

Like a wet and turgid emergence from a pool, the night became peopled with figures. Someone spoke harshly; there was a rush of soft feet and a chinking of metal against buckles. Bryony plunged, and trickling, wirelike fingers over nose and bridle secured her and then tugged and twisted at Richard himself.

Culter, kicking with his spurred boot still in the stirrup, freed his right hand and laid it on his sword, cursing himself under his breath. It was always a bad road to travel alone: it meant riding fast and staying alert, and he had been doing neither. Hell. They still had Bryony fast. There were two of them – no, three. He saw the shadow of a cudgel just in time, ducked, cut and heard a scream as he dodged and cut again.

The hands began again, twisted in his belt and pulling his leathers. The saddle became loose and he knew the girth had been slit. He slashed at the dim faces, feeling the numbness of a blow on his arm; fighting to free his sword arm from the clinging hands. The saddle was swinging, bringing him down with it. Below him, the unseen men grunted and swore; then the blade was suddenly wrenched from his grip and they leaped at him, bringing him successfully down, driving with his fists, knees and elbows into the tangle of hard bodies and then on to the road.

There was a gleam of steel: a solitary, agonized, breathless moment in which the irony of the thing struck him like a cannon ball, and the circle of dark heads above him opened out like girasol to the sun. A brown pony, dark with perspiration, shot into the circle and decanted a thunderbolt: a dark figure which skirled and spat like a being demented.

The men about Lord Culter froze. The newcomer raged, in a language which was not English. The leader of the assassins answered, sullenly, in the same tongue and was treated to another shrivelling outburst. The other two, making an attempt to speak, were cut off by a storm of abuse. Under it, the three moved off sulkily, mounted and, without a word, disappeared as they had come into the darkness.

The owner of the brown pony remounted. Richard, shaking his head, rolled over, groped for and found his sword, and got to his feet. 'I trust,' said the rider in clear but sibilant English, 'that you are not hurt?' His expression, so far as it could be seen, was one of resignation rather than triumph.

Richard got back his breath. 'Not at all. I would be suitably grateful if I didn't know they were your men.'

'You have the Romany?' asked his rescuer, and there was a dim flash of white teeth. 'Or only a little? Then I must explain that they attacked you through no orders of mine. We are a wayward people, my lord.'

Richard flexed his arm thoughtfully, studying the immobile, spare figure. Vivid in his mind was the firelit room at Stirling, and the stained arrows on the table. He had unfastened his jacket and, pulling out one of the points, laced his broken girth with it. 'I believe I could put a name to you,' he said.

The white teeth flashed again. 'I hope you won't. My people tell me, when I come home, of the little commissions they are offered. I seldom interfere. If it were not that I am at the mercy of the shrewdest of your relatives . . .'

Richard straightened suddenly. 'My brother?'

The other was already wheeling his pony to the Edinburgh road; he laughed as he went and shook his head. 'No, no. Not at all. Devil take it, not at all.' The pony's hoofs, gently pattering, dropped into rhythm and faded, leaving the echo of wry laughter on the air.

Richard slowly gathered Bryony's reins and put his left hand on her neck. A half-smile lifted his mouth, so that for a moment he looked astonishingly like the Master.

'Mother! What now?' he said, and lifting himself into the saddle put the mare, fast, along the Midculter road.

* * *

Patrick opened the gates to Lord Culter long past midnight, with incoherent words of welcome. He sent his chamberlain back to bed without rousing the household, and taking a candle, went alone up the main staircase and along the dimly lit corridor to his wife's room.

There he hesitated. He had removed all traces of his adventure: he had no idea of posing as a brave but battered warrior. Was it equally unfair to take her unaware like this? He wished he had kept Patrick. He could have roused Mariotta's maid; have sent her in to ask if she would receive him. . . . And if she refused? What a scene for the women, that.

He pulled himself together. If she didn't want him she should say so, directly, to him. He hesitated only a moment longer, and then put out his hand and knocked.

Through a welter of necromantic, smoke-ridden dreams Mariotta became aware of the light tap. When after a moment it was repeated, she sat up, fencing with the supernatural, and called, 'Yes? who is it?' The answer took her by the throat.

Silence had fallen again. Her breathing had become erratic. Unable to talk with this chaos in her lungs she was quiet, trying to control the disorder.

'Mariotta?' He was speaking again, very low. 'May I come in?'

It didn't occur to her to refuse. She pulled a bedgown over her ruffled linen, gave a despairing thought to her hair, and called to him levelly. 'Come in if you wish.'

She was paralysed by the change in him; because she had expected time to have stood still for him, as it had done for her. He was brown-skinned and light-haired with the sun, the corner of his eyes seamed with white. He was thinner and harder, and his quietness had a quality of power and repose in it which was new to him.

Coming no nearer than the foot of the bed he said, 'I wakened you. I'm sorry. I couldn't leave until sunset, and I thought it might be better to speak now, in private.'

Mariotta's eyes were unchanging violet in the glimmer of the candle. 'What is there to say?'

You may know the devil by the inverted image in his eyes. The candle flame in her husband's showed her, sanely, herself twice over. He dropped abruptly on the low chest below her bed and taking the fringe of her coverlet in his fingers, twisted and plied it with his eyes on his hands.

He said, 'I was brought up to distrust talkers. A foolish thing which recoiled, naturally, on my own head. I was taught to judge people by their actions, and I do – and it works – except sometimes, when it matters most. I probably haven't learned much, but I've learned that people don't always say what they mean, for good reasons as well as bad.'

'People don't always say what they mean for no reason at all,' said Mariotta lightly. 'Especially feminine people.' She saw he was troubled by this vein and watched him, her chin cushioned on her updrawn knees. She went on in the same deceptive voice. 'But you accused me of being Lymond's lover before I claimed I was.'

The trouble in his eyes deepened as she brought out, irresponsibly, the difficult thing he had to discuss. He rolled the tortured fringe in his hands and she went on, before he could speak. 'You're trying to tell me you know there was nothing between us. But I think you must tell me how you know. You didn't believe me. Whom did you find to believe?'

It was hard, but she meant to be hard. She watched him as he groped painfully for an honest and lucid answer; trying with all his strength to satisfy her and win through to her without invoking the shadows of the last five months, and of the last three weeks. It couldn't be done, and she made it clear to him that he mustn't try. 'Richard? What have you done?'

He didn't look up, or call his brother by name. 'Nothing. He's alive. This isn't an act of expiation.'

'Did he tell you what passed between us?'

Richard's face was buried in his hands. 'Some of it.'

'He told you he had never laid hands on me?'

'Yes.'

'And you believed him?'

'Yes. I don't know. Not when he told me. But later on – I've had a long time to think.'

'And when he took me to Crawfordmuir?'

'It was an accident: he intended you to be taken straight home. He did what he could for you. I know about that.'

'Then either Will Scott or myself is a liar,' said Mariotta gently. 'Because Lymond told me face to face that he meant all the time to bring me to Crawfordmuir; that he took me there to dishonour you and disrupt the inheritance. It was to save myself and you that I escaped.'

Richard's hands dropped from his face, and his wife said, 'So which story will you favour this time? His or mine?'

There was a long silence. Then slowly Richard got up from the chest. He looked very tired. 'Are you sure . . . ?'

'He spoke very plainly indeed. Will Scott can tell you.'

Her husband walked to the window. Faintly, in the courtyard, the dying glow of Johnnie Bullo's embers searched through the open door, were cut off, gleamed and disappeared as it swung in the wind. Mariotta said, 'Well?' and he turned, making a gesture of despair. 'I have lived with him for three weeks. He's tormented, perverted, dangerous, ruthless, but – '

The candlelight lit her soot-black hair and the soft wool on her shoulders, as if a silver quill had embellished the air about her. Her face, resting on her knees, was shadowed and unreadable. 'But you believe him. It's another impasse then, isn't it, Richard?'

'I'm damned if it is,' said Lord Culter suddenly, and swung around. 'My dear: listen. We've been married less than a year. Because of circumstances and foolishness and my mistakes and short-comings we've been parted for nearly half that time. We've each in our own way been through a number of minor hells; and we've had a great loss. . . .

'A mistake is something you build on: it's the irritant that makes the pearl; the flaw that creates the geyser – but a mistake made twice is a folly. It's cost something in terms of thought and sacrifice and even suffering to bring us tonight to speak with each other. We have a moral duty at least not to toss it away.'

'And Lymond?'

Richard said steadily. 'You had no right to ask me that question, and no right to expect me to make that choice.'

'I knew you wouldn't make it,' she said. 'I knew if you had made it, even in your own mind, that Lymond would be dead. I was only – '

'– Frightening me for the good of my soul,' said Richard, and suddenly smiled. 'As Francis rejoices in doing. I've spoken to Will Scott too, you know. But won't you believe me? I've been frightened enough already.'

He was standing looking down at her. 'Perhaps you've married the wrong brother. And that would be a pity. Because Francis lives in a passionless vacuum and keeps his love for abstract things. And in the second place, I should never let you go.'

She had longed so much to hear it that she was beyond speech; but there was a quality in her face that drove him suddenly toward violence.

'I love you,' said Richard to his wife. 'You have dominion of life and death over me. I am asking nothing except to prove it without being turned away. Or' – his eyes on her lifted arms – 'being taken out of pity.'

Her outstretched hands did not waver, and the candle-light on her face found an expression unsought even in his dreams. He came carefully to her side, and knelt under her light touch.

'Out of *pity*?' said Mariotta. 'My dear fool, why am I fighting you and denying you and hurting you except that I am so afraid of you, and of myself; because I love you far too well for peace and gentle harmonies. . . .

'It's all right. My dear, it's all right. I am here: I love you: I will not leave you. None shall take it from us now.'

He had dropped head and shoulders to the bed, one hand gripping the silk and the other holding her out-stretched hand as if it were his hope of eternity. Mariotta brought her other arm to encircle his shoulders and comforted him.

* * *

Roused very early next morning by Tibet, in tears, Sybilla received her son in her room.

She had risen and put on a vast brocade bedgown. With its stiff silk puckered about her, she sat in her high chair like Demeter about to breakfast on Pelops, her face in shadow from the paling windows. Richard bent over and kissed her.

She surveyed him, silently absorbing the pleasing, tranquil assurance of him and the woollen robe he wore. Her own mouth relaxed, and she touched his cheek as he dropped to a stool at her feet and hugged his knees. 'You've made your peace. What odd children I have! I'm so glad,' she said.

'Could I have leave to stay, do you think?' asked Richard. 'What you've done about the steadings I hate to think. Salted all the sheep and given away the pigs and allowed the salmon to be poached . . . I didn't kill him.'

'I know. You wouldn't have kissed me, would you?' said Sybilla coolly.

Richard flushed. 'He's – Francis is in Edinburgh. Tom would tell you, he was badly hurt in England. Then he was taken – gave himself up – as we were coming north. I'd planned to get a ship for him and help him to leave.'

Some of the natural colour had returned to Sybilla's fine skin. She drew a finger down his cheek and said, 'That was remarkably well done, no matter what came of it. You won't regret it, either. What will they do?'

'The warrant is out for letters relaxing him from the horn. That lets them bring him to trial before Parliament. In two weeks' time, probably.' His eyes searched her face. 'There isn't much hope, you know. But to be honest, I don't think he greatly cares.'

For the first time, he saw a spark of fear in her eyes. 'Why? Because of Christian?'

'A number of things, I think . . .' He waited, and then said, 'Will you go and see him? Soon?'

'No. I should only weaken him now,' said Sybilla curtly. 'And in any case, I have a little travelling to do, and I must be back in good time.'

'Travelling?' Never in this world would he understand her.

'Yes, my darling,' said Sybilla. 'And someone, as Buccleuch would say, is going to loathe my guts before I've finished with them.'

4

BARING

Wherefore the nobles and the peples ben sette in
their proper places. . . .
They that ben sette on the other syde kepe the Quene.
And thus kepe they alle the strength and fermete
of the royaume.

1 · REMISS

That year, as in other years, death was not man's ultimate
terror and chief source of his disquiet. Death was cheap
and quick, indiscriminating and often friendly. You could
die in a day, from the pest. You could die in a second in
the innocent hub of a brawl. Children in thousands never
came to life, or lived only hours. You could die in battle,
and you could die at the minor instance of the law, for
cheating and stealing and concealing disease. Death was
better, often, than pain, mutilation of deformity; than starvation in banishment; than the intangible evils of sorcery
and enchantment. People died suddenly, from week to
week and month to month, and their disappearance had
to be accepted. Death was cheap and quick.

In time of siege and foreign occupation, the doom and
death of a traitor might go unnoticed. But many in Edinburgh lost fathers or brothers at Solway Moss, and had
heard Carrick Pursuivant at the Cross six years before
charging and warning the traitor to appear.

Twice they had summoned the absent Lymond to the
diet of his libel, and twice the record book had noted, *The
aforesaid being summoned did not appear.* For this contemptuous failure in his duty to his Sovereign and this rebellion

against the law of his country, sentence of fugitation was passed, making him rebel and outlaw.

Now, six years later, triumphant officialdom spoke. Francis Crawford of Lymond, Master of Culter, being in ward in Her Majesty's Castle of Edinburgh, was summoned to appear on the eighth day of the month of August in the year of Our Lord 1548, to answer charges of treason, of revealing and showing to our ancient enemies of England the secrets of the Queen; of treasonable intercommuning and rendering of aid and comfort to our said enemies; of murder, assault, abduction and robbery, and crimes against the Estate and Church as set forth in the indictment.

The news reached Will Scott where he hung about in a frenzy of inactivity in Edinburgh. He tried and failed to get access to the Castle. Buccleuch, already aware of the event, left his son alone and got back to the siege of Haddington. Richard, with a lot to do at Midculter and strong unwillingness to leave it, stayed with his wife and made quiet preparations to return before the eighth. Sybilla, having got rid of all her encumbrances, collected a small, well-armed retinue and left for parts unknown.

* * *

The Dowager reached Ballaggan on the first of August, carrying the date in her breast like an aposteme.

She was brought into the hall and made welcome, under the vacant survey of alabaster and murrhine. Crossing the little Turkey carpets which cost so much, Dandy Hunter took her to his study as she asked, and poured her wine and made her comfortable, without pressing her for news of either of her sons. She smiled at him very gently and took from her purse a little box, which she laid on the table between them. 'I came to return this,' she said.

Smiling, a little puzzled, he took it. His sleeves were caught with embroidered bands and the stuff of his jerkin, as fine as her own, was lined with tissue. Smiling at her again, he unwrapped, fastidiously, what lay inside the box;

and then, with the smile lingering forgotten on his lips, drew out and laid before him the contents.

It was a hexagonal brooch, set in ebony and diamonds and shaped like a heart set about with crystal plaques, each bearing an angel's head in onyx.

The silence stretched out. Then Sir Andrew stirred and lifted his eyes. 'But this isn't mine.'

'No?' said Sybilla. 'But Patey Liddell altered it for you: I saw it in his shop. Your mother might remember.'

Remembrance brightened his face. 'Ah!' he said. 'Now I have it. Yes, indeed – I bought it for Mother, and lost it again the same day.' He gave her a rueful smile. 'I'm sorry, but your son was the culprit. The brooch lay by the bed when he broke into the house, and when he had gone, it had vanished too. I'm afraid I was so angry and concerned about Mother that I dismissed it . . . I'd forgotten it altogether. Wherever did you find it?'

'But,' said Sybilla, 'you handed it to Patey *after* Francis's visit.'

'Patey must be mistaken.'

'*I'm* not mistaken,' retorted Sybilla serenely. 'I overheard you.' She paused, and then went on. 'I got it from Agnes Herries: did it puzzle you to find her wearing it? Before that, it belonged to Mariotta. They took the rest of the rubbish from her at Annan. It very nearly did what you meant it to do.'

He touched his head with his hand and sat back, smiling again. 'Wait a moment – what *I* wanted it to do? I'm sorry, but hasn't Mariotta explained? It was Lymond who sent her all the jewellery. Blame me if you like for not telling Richard, but your poor daughter-in-law put me in an appalling position. But I swear I did my best to persuade her to confide in Culter.'

'I'm sure you did,' said Sybilla placidly. 'With results we all know. Of course Mariotta thought they were from Francis: she was infatuated with the idea of him. That must have been a little disconcerting for you. But when she didn't automatically attribute them to you, you must have realized she wasn't, after all, going to fall into your arms as you planned she should. So you adapted your scheme accordingly and it worked quite well. Mariotta thought they came from Lymond, and that was enough to break her marriage and nearly to kill her.'

The thin-boned, high-nosed face was flushed with emotion. Dandy said quickly in a troubled voice, 'Lady Culter. You can't know what you're saying. Mariotta was young enough and troubled enough to turn to me. I couldn't deny her help.' He stood up suddenly, anxiety in his face. 'Is this how she is explaining it to Richard? To whitewash Lymond and put the blame on me?'

Sybilla, neatly swathed in gauze and laces, was the calm within the hurricane. She stretched out a slender hand and retrieving brooch and box, returned them to her purse. 'Mariotta still thinks the jewels came from Lymond,' she observed, fixing the distrait man with candid, cornflower eyes. 'But I think she ought to know that you have now tried to kill her husband four times.'

There was a little, breathless hush; and then Sir Andrew said, 'Good God, Lady Culter,' and sat down unbecomingly. 'But this is nonsense. Do you mean to accuse me of . . . ?'

He stared at her, breathing quickly, and then slapped one hand on his desk. 'No! No. I'm damed if I'm going to be scapegoat. I've a very soft spot for you all, Lady Culter, and for Mariotta especially, but I can't let you twist and pervert facts to get your beloved son off the gallows. Give some thought to my mother, at least. . . . The only person who has tried to kill Richard is his own brother.'

'Facts?' said Sybilla. 'At the Papingo Shoot Francis aimed twice: once to cut the cord and the second time to kill the bird. Then he dropped the bow and quiver and left the glove. You were the person first on the spot: you had alrady tried and failed to free yourself of Mariotta and Agnes.'

Sir Andrew's flush had paled. 'It's still nonsense,' he said steadily. 'You know I can't shoot. Everyone knows that.'

'You can't shoot at a Papingo target,' said Sybilla, 'but you are an excellent marksman on the flat. Everyone knows that, too.'

'It's Lymond's word, in that case, against mine. Do you suppose for a moment – '

'Oh, of course. You've no evidence against you,' she said, 'any more than you had when you led Richard and Agnes Herries over a part of the Nith notorious for its potholes. Happily, Richard is a very strong swimmer. And there were, I suppose, too many witnesses.'

'I pulled him out myself,' exclaimed Hunter. 'Lady Culter – '

'But the third and fourth times,' said the Dowager, 'there *was* evidence.'

She had effectively stopped his protest. He made a little gesture of resignation. 'You'd better tell me.'

'Do you need to be told? I had some simple tests made with the herbal drink you brought from your mother for Richard's use. They tell me Mariotta would have been a wealthy and marriageable widow very quickly if he had drunk it.'

He said quietly. 'Go on. And the fourth occasion?'

For the first time, Sybilla lost a little of her self-command. She said, 'Do you know, if you had succeeded then, I think you would have had to answer for it yourself to those same gypsy gentlemen and not to me today. He was on his way to Mariotta when they attacked him . . . but you knew that, of course. It must have seemed quite foolproof at last: Romanies can only be controlled by their King. Unluckily for you, their King at the moment is controlled by me. He learned of your commission and stopped it just in time. Richard isn't dead, Sir Andrew; and I have three men who will swear to having been paid by you to assassinate him.'

Hunter's manner didn't alter: only his eyes, meeting hers, were curiously bright and impersonal. He said carefully, 'You are evidently bribing whoever you can to save your son. Forgive me, but if you take this any further I shall have to take steps legally to protect myself.'

This time Sybilla herself got up, moving away from the table with a rustle of petticoats. She said over her shoulder, 'I haven't taken it any further – yet. But don't be misled. The fact that I am here doesn't mean there is the least uncertainty; the least hope for you. There isn't any. The only doubt is in my own mind and is because of your mother.'

'Mother!' said Hunter's voice, half aloud behind her.

There was the briefest pause, and then her quick brain, suddenly showing her his mind, made her twist around. His sword was already half lifted, light stuttering from the blade.

She said rapidly, 'I may look simple, but I'm not precisely moonstruck yet. If I don't come back, you won't even have a chance to hang, my friend.'

He continued to come. The sword, still half raised, was aimed almost casually at her heart, and his face was quite detached, like a dreamer's. She drew one quick breath and stood still, her hands open at her sides, her head a little tilted and her lips parted. He walked until he was so close to her that he had to meet her eyes; had to make the small decision that would force the point onward.

Something of the message of the steady blue eyes must have penetrated; something of her unexpected stillness surprised him into a moment's pause; and Sybilla said quietly in that instant, 'I have your charter chest at Midculter.'

She thought she had misjudged it. The sword point wavered and approached and his eyes remained flatly purposeful. Then they came alive again, startled and disbelieving; the sword dropped and he said – and had difficulty in saying – 'That isn't true. I keep my chest in the strongroom of this house. No one – '

'Your mother keeps her recipes there: remember? And I have a very talented Romany on my side, Sir Andrew. . . . You've had dealings with the English, haven't you, for a very long time? Your visits to the Ostrich put you in no danger – you were already well known in Carlisle. How else did you know Jonathan Crouch was George Douglas's prisoner? Why did Sir George trouble with you unless he had a fairly good idea you were in the same sweet trade as himself?'

She turned, and walking past where he stood frozen in mid-room, she paused by the window, looking out on the ochre and viridian and sage green of the dusty summer treetops.

'Such a mean, thieving little trade: a dealing in secrets; in hissings and winkings and the selling of men's bodies, back and forth. And even then, they didn't pay you well enough. Maybe they realized that you weren't greatly intimate at Court; that you only touched the edge of what they could already get from Glencairn and Douglas and Brunton and Ormiston and Cockburn and the rest. . . . So you turned your eyes on my family. Wealth; a pretty heiress; a family feud – who'd be surprised if it had fatal results? And the widow, in due time, would naturally turn to the gentle family friend. Or at the very worst, Francis was worth a thousand crowns to Wharton. . . .'

He said, 'You needn't elaborate. I know what I've done. You've told, then. The papers in that chest – '

'Not yet,' said Sybilla, and turned to meet his white face. 'The chest will be opened if I don't come back.'

Tremors were beginning to shake him. He sat again, abruptly, at the table, his eyes fixed on her like stones. 'What are you going to do?' Seeing the expression on her face he gave a sort of laugh and bit his lip, stilling the shaking. 'What do you suppose my wonderful brother would have done now?'

He was too helplessly self-centred, too rotten, for her to pity him now. She said abruptly, 'Your mother has a lot to answer for, but if you had the heart of a rabbit, you would have made a man's life for yourself and let her make the best of it.'

He had some pride left. He said, making no excuses, 'Mother knows nothing of this. It will kill her. What – what are you going to do?'

The cool blue eyes rested on his trembling hands. The Dowager said slowly, 'Your mother is a sick old woman,

553

and an unhappy one. I don't envy you the life you've led with her, but she need never have become the sort of person she is now.

'Never mind that. She's going to suffer, but not as much as she might have done. I should like to see you hanged. Because of you, I nearly lost every child I have left: I did lose my grandchild. But that would be an insult to all the magnificent, vicious criminals we already have living freely among us.

'You are not of that kind. You did what you did at second and third hand, as you could, and sweetened over with a glaze of hysterical necessity. Once the need is removed, you won't kill again. A reason for living may be hard to find, too: but that is your problem.'

She walked to the desk and drawing a paper in front of him, laid a pen beside it. 'I want one thing,' she said. 'And that is a statement exonerating Francis from the things you have done.' And as he hesitated, she said sharply, 'Come along! Beside the other things you have done, what do these matter?'

He looked at her with dull eyes, and then, bending, took up the pen and wrote. She read it, sealed it, and put it away. 'Yes. It won't save him, as you may guess . . . but it will perhaps undo a little of the damage. And now you'd better leave. I'm going to talk to your mother, and then leave for my home. The chest will be opened and its contents published within two days. By then,' said Sybilla, 'you should be out of this land.'

He raised his head vaguely, only half understanding. 'I may go?'

'Yes. And I wish you well of it,' she said, her eyes hard as sapphires.

She waited until she heard the sound of his horse on the cobbles, and then rising quietly, climbed the stair to his mother's room.

The terrier had died in the spring, overcome with fat and lack of air.

Since then, Dame Catherine had had no distractions: her son had hardly been at home, and even her books and her paintings and precious pieces of ivory and jade had begun to pall. Longing for company, she welcomed it by releasing the barbs of months of lonely self-torture. Sybilla, sitting quietly by the taffeta-spread bedside, near the heaped-up delicate pillows, listened to Catherine Hunter's spiced invective against her son, her servants, her surroundings, her illness and finally, as the icy flood reached its spring heights, against her Maker.

The Dowager's voice cut lightly through the flow. 'Why don't you get them to carry you downstairs?'

The black eyes sneered. 'That would be delightful,' said the old woman. 'Unfortunately, I am part paralysed, you know.'

'I don't wonder,' said Sybilla pleasantly. 'And if you never try to help yourself you'll be wholly paralysed soon, and you *will* enjoy that. I've brought you a litter. Two of my men are coming up in half an hour to lift you down.'

A tiny spark of alarm showed in the black eyes, but the grey, crumpled face remained contemptuous. 'Money has given you a fine, arrogant manner, Sybilla, but I should prefer you to keep it for Midculter. I hear your son has left his wife.'

'He hasn't, but you won't change the subject by being rude,' said the Dowager. 'There's a warm fire and a comfortable couch in the hall. You'll like it very much.'

'Sybilla, I am neither a child nor an imbecile. I dislike being humoured and I particularly dislike being managed. Because of my disability I am unable to leave this room. You can hardly expect me to undermine for your benefit the little health I have left me.'

The Dowager said coolly, 'There's no need to be frightened. Your surgeon has given me full permission.'

The black eyes snapped. 'The child is dead, I hear.'

'Yes.'

'Did your younger boy kill it, or did she get rid of it herself?'

'Neither. Don't be silly, Catherine. You don't really want me to go.'

'I didn't say I did. Don't be too clever, Sybilla.'

The Dowager said, 'The child was nobody's fault, if you really want to know. Mariotta and Richard are together and very happy. Francis is in ward in Edinburgh. He is to appear before Parliament in a week, and we hope very much he will be acquitted.'

The little figure on the pillows looked pityingly at Sybilla. 'Acquitted! My dear woman, even the Culters haven't quite enough money for that.'

'Then we shall have to use our beaux yeux,' said Sybilla placidly. 'Perhaps if I made appropriate advances to all Her Majesty's lords of the Session . . . Or do you think I should hardly get through them all in a week?'

The quality of the black stare was changing. There was a tiny silence, and then Lady Hunter said in her cutting voice, 'This is a little overdetermined, even for you, Sybilla. Something is wrong, I take it. Nobody visits me unless something is wrong.'

The Dowager didn't prevaricate. 'A little. It concerns Dandy.'

The thin lips compressed themselves. 'Of course. What stupidity has he committed now?'

Sybilla said, 'Any – stupidity he has committed, he did for your sake. You've been a very hard mistress to serve, Catherine.'

'The boy needs hardness,' said the old woman. Her breathing had quickened. 'Toughness. Other people run estates and make a success of them – get on at Court – become popular – bring home heiresses. My other son – '

'Dandy did his best for you,' said the Dowager. 'That's what I have to tell you. He felt he could never succeed in – orthodox – ways, so he tried some which were outside the law. Too far outside.'

'He's in trouble?'

'Serious trouble. If he's caught.'

'You came to warn him. Is that it?'

'Yes,' said Sybilla. 'That's it.'

There was a long pause. Then, with an effort, the invalid pulled herself up in bed and spoke in her normal voice. 'Well!' she snapped. 'I suppose he'd better get out of the country. Tell him to come here and I'll give him money. And he'd better not show his face here again until it's safe.' She did not ask what he had done.

Sybilla stretched out her two fine hands and took the small, limp, puffed one in them. 'He has money. He has gone,' she said. 'There was no time to see you. He sent you his love.'

The small hand lay inert in hers; the black eyes were without visible emotion. 'Inept!' said Dame Catherine. 'Disorganized, as usual. Good riddance. Now perhaps I can get a good paid factor to make the place profitable.'

Sybilla released her hand and rose. 'I'm sure you will. You'll enjoy arranging it. Now, here's the litter and your maid to help them move you. Slowly and carefully . . . and you'll do very well.'

Lady Hunter made no protest at all as, wrapping her in her own soft blankets, they transferred her gently from bed to litter, and laid pillows beneath her head. With a manservant carrying each end the invalid moved for the first time in years across the blue tiles of her bedroom and toward the open door. As they carried her, the sun caught the shimmering cap, the jewels and the bright black eyes and flashed for a moment, before the door closed behind her, on the tears lying silently in the bitter troughs and seams of her face.

* * *

At Midculter, Mariotta and Richard heard the story in silence. As Sybilla ended, her son drew a long breath and said, 'The charter chest. Is it really here?'

'Yes,' said the Dowger. There were circles under her eyes and her back, although she held it straight, was tired and aching. 'Johnnie Bullo got it for me. It has all the papers on Sir Andrew's transactions with Carlisle.'

Richard's eyes met hers. 'What are you going to do with them?'

'That is for you and Mariotta to decide. You are the person most injured by him. It's only fair you should take what redress you can.'

'I don't want revenge,' said Richard shortly. 'I only want to forget about it.'

'You don't want to publish them?'

'No. Only the paper that affects Francis.'

'Mariotta?'

The girl's eyes were fixed on Richard. 'Oh, no. No. It's as much my fault as his.'

'Rubbish child,' said Sybilla. 'But I'm glad, all the same. He's not worth it. We'll keep them as surety for his good conduct abroad, and I hope we never hear of him again.'

Richard suddenly dropped beside his mother and tilted her chin. 'I don't think you've told us everything. You had no right to attempt a thing like that on your own.'

'Attempt!' said Sybilla indignantly. 'It was a tour de force!'

They smiled at one another, and then the Dowager's expression changed. 'Only five days!' exclaimed his mother. 'How could I be hard on her?'

* * *

Only five days. Will Scott, sitting bleakly in his father's empty lodging, could think of nothing more to do. How could he rescue Lymond, even if he were well? Even if he were rescued, how could he force him again into this death within life?

Four days. Sybilla, Mariotta and Richard moved their household to Edinburgh, and a surprising number of their friends came visiting, with an echo of Lady Hunter's tart 'good riddance' on their lips.

Three days, and the Lord Justice General issued an order and let loose a thunderbolt. On the instructions of the Crown, he desired the prisoner, if his state permitted, to appear for questioning before a Judicial Committee of Parliament on the day before his trial.

Regardless of the tenor of their previous meeting, the

boy Scott burst in on Lord Culter with the news. The brisk red hair was wild.

'It isn't legal!' said Scott. 'They can't have an Assize without a jury, and it isn't a meeting of the Estates. They can't condemn him without a technical court: they can't!'

'They won't,' said Richard briefly. 'They won't pass sentence, but they'll examine, and make up their minds, and force the result through Parliament the day after. You ought to be able to guess why. Lymond knows too much. He could shatter half the Government at a public hearing.'

Scott brightened. 'He should insist on it. Either they let him off, or else–' At the expression on Culter's face he broke off. 'No.'

'No, indeed,' said Richard. 'I really can't think of any surer way of signing his own death warrant. . . . And does it matter, anyway? They'll be out of their minds if they don't condemn him.'

2 · THE QUEEN MOVES TO HER BEGINNING

Rumour of the hurried Assize had reached the streets by midday, and by two o'clock the Lawnmarket from the Butter Tron to St Giles was thick with people.

By midafternoon, a further rumour spread that the prisoner, taken out through the Castle postern, was already in the Tolbooth. As this became known there was a good deal of shouting, and someone with no religious intent started up the 109th Psalm: the grave words, used ceremonially at a degradation for treason, yammered on the wind up to St Giles' sunny crown:

Deus laudem meam ne tacueris. . . .'

Sybilla at her window in the High Street heard it and rattled on, without pausing, with what she was saying to Janet Buccleuch.

Inside the Tolbooth, the sun piped in through the coloured glass of the windows. The Assize was preparing, in a narrow room above the hall where Parliament would sit tomorrow. Twelve Assessors, drawn from each of the

Three Estates and embracing the President and half the Court of Sessions, sat on three sides of a long board at one end. In the centre presided the noble and potent lord Archibald, Earl of Argyll, Lord Justice-General; the Campbell arms on his chair and the Royal arms above it.

On either side of the room, the sun striped red and blue and green the papers littering the desks of the Clerks: short Crawford and big Foulis and Lauder of St Germains, Lord Advocate to the Queen's Grace and member of the Governor's Council, with his long blue chin and shrewd eyes and interminable black-hosed legs folded beneath his chair with the blunt-knuckled inconsequence of a roe deer.

The Lord Advocate had made a wager before starting with Jamie Foulis on whether Argyll was still on speaking terms with the President. He had won, and was watching the golden louis Jamie had thrown him spinning like a sequin against the black rafters when the Justiciar cleared his throat, making him take his eye off the coin so that it dropped unseen into the straw on the floor.

Lauder, catching the Clerk-Register's ecstatic grin across the room, snorted aloud and assumed his legal face. He was, although he gave little sign of it, one of the astutest lawyers in Scotland.

'. . . Gathering,' Argyll was saying, skipping briefly and almost unintelligibly through the routine, 'at the instance of Parliament . . . delated and defamed for . . . imprison his body and try and seek out the verity of the matter by examinations and inquisitions before the Justice . . . report to the Lords Commissioners of Parliament on this and on the indictment for subsequent crimes as follows . . .'

Henry Lauder scratched his head, running his eye over the gaily dressed twelve. Argyll. Glencairn and George Douglas, both notorious for their dealings with the English. Buccleuch. Herries, or John Maxwelll as he used to be. Gladstanes the judge and Keith, the Earl Marischal, of the same faction as Douglas and Glencairn. A couple of Abbots; Methven, Queen Margaret's withered widower;

560

Marjoribanks; Hugo Rig and the President of the Court of Session, Bishop Reid of Orkney with his deaf ear.

Lauder wondered if anyone had hinted to the prisoner about that deaf ear. It was responsible for more executions, whippings and tongue borings than even its owner realized. The junior clerks, usher, macers and witnesses filled the rest of the room: they were going to need some air son. He had taken the precaution of wearing his thinnest jerkin under his robes.

Lord Culter . . . the Scott boy . . . the Master of Erskine, without his father. That should be interesting: it was already interesting. One or two unknown faces, and some at the back he couldn't see. He ran a bony finger over his chin and felt his usual rueful irritation that the hair which surged so cheerfully on his face should colonize his crown so feebly.

There was a hum of voices and a shuffle of feet: the initial procedure was over. They had put a chair in the centre of the floor for the panel: he remembered hearing that the fellow had been shot. Francis Crawford of Lymond, Master of Culter. They had called him. The name reverberated through the rafters: Lymond . . . Lymond . . . Master . . . Master. The boy Scott jumped and the brother, Culter, moved also. The rest simply looked stoic.

Everybody stared at the door. Two guards came in, and someone fair, of a vague distinction who walked steadily through the benches to the clear space in the middle, declined the chair and turned to face the Tribunal.

And this was a surprise. Unobtrusive, beautiful clothes; fine hands; a burnished head with a long, firm mouth and heavy blue eyes, spaciously set. He had been ill all right: the signs were all there. But his face was beautifully controlled, giving nothing away.

The guards withdrew. Orkney cupped his left ear in his hand and then took it away again. The answers to Argyll's questions were professionally pitched; clear, pleasant and effortlessly audible.

Henry Lauder, Prosecutor for the Crown, guardian and

administrator for all its people of the laws which secure their tranquillity and welfare, sat back in his seat and gave an unlegal twitch of sheer pleasure. He was, he felt, going to enjoy his day.

* * *

'This is not a trial,' Argyll had announced. 'This is a preliminary examination conducted by us through Mr. Lauder, to lessen the burden on tomorrow's meeting of the Estates. A number of questions will be put to you, and your replies will be noted. You will be given every chance to put your point of view, and a report based on these proceedings will be drawn up and placed before Parliament. . . .'

In other words, Parliament is busy with weightier matters than treason. Beware, for you are being judged.

'. . . And so, as a result of these productions,' the Lord Advocate was saying, swaying gently to and fro on his heels, 'the above charges are dismissed. The Crown does not accuse you of the attempted murder of your brother, Richard Lord Culter, or of wilful and malicious fire-raising, robbery and attempted murder at your own home of Midculter, or' – he put out a bony finger and moved a paper in front of him – 'or of the abduction of your brother's wife and the slaughter of her child. These charges, as I have said, are not being pursued.'

Henry Lauder broke off, took away the spectacles resting on the bridge of his nose and said, 'You don't look very pleased about it. Do you understand what I am saying?'

'I was considering its legal implications,' said Crawford of Lymond, without raising his eyes.

The Lord Advocate sensed the grin on Foulis's face while schooling his own. Of course, he had no right to recapitulate, but he didn't expect to be told so.

He said, watching the prisoner under his lids, 'I am glad you are following us. I am aware that you have not been in good health since a misunderstanding with your . . . force in June. We have no wish to unman you. It is, I think, unique in our time to encounter a plea of innocence against such a formidable list of charges.' He glanced up, getting no response.

Argyll said, 'It's after two, Lauder. Let's get rid of the new charges first. Dealings with Wharton.' He addressed the prisoner direct. 'You're accused of consistently giving help and selling information to Lord Wharton, the English Warden. Notably . . . When, Lauder?'

Lauder said agreeably, 'We are informed that you were a member of Lord Wharton's force for a period in 1545, and that while there you acted under his orders in a number of raids and other activities directly detrimental to Scotland. Have you any answer?'

The sure voice said laconically, 'Yes: but no proof. I offered my services to Lord Wharton over a period of four months and won his confidence by taking part in three small raids. On the fourth, major raid I misled him so that the English force was seriously damaged. I left him the same night.'

'I am sure you were wise. As an experienced soldier and tactician the throwing away of a troop – even a deliberate throwing away – must have been an ordeal for you.'

'Not at all,' said the prisoner briefly. 'I had never commanded a force before.'

'Ah!' said Harry Lauder, who was perfectly aware of that fact.

' – But I've studied geography and I know my chess.'

'Indeed.' There was a rustle of amusement. 'Excellent qualifications in themselves, but . . .'

Lymond said mildly. 'The one shows you where to go, and the other what to do when you get there. A man so fortified would be unique in Scottish arms, don't you think?'

'Since, as you say, you have no proof,' said Lauder, 'we must leave it to Parliament to decide how far your overthrow was deliberate and how much of your motive was selfless, against the tenor of your general character and behaviour. You are further charged,' said Lauder mildly, 'with conspiring to lay misleading information about the intentions of the English army during the western invasion of September last year; of attacking a Scottish force under Lord Culter and the Master of Erskine, and of taking from their possession an English messenger bearing a valuable dispatch.'

He smiled up at the beams. 'Doubtless the – misunderstanding – of 1545 between yourself and Lord Wharton had by that time cleared up, that you took such pains to help his invasion, Mr. Crawford?'

'Until the present moment, my lord, there was no misunderstanding over what happened in 1545. Lord Wharton had placed the sum of a thousand crowns on my head.'

'And yet you passed freely enough in and out of England, we hear. You offered to spy for him if he appeared to reject you?'

'No.'

'What fee did you receive from him for the services you did render?'

'After 1545 I received no voluntary payment from Lord Wharton.'

The Bishop, leaning forward, missed the significant word. He tapped the copy of the indictment before him. 'That, Mr. Crawford, is untrue. According to several witnesses, you agreed to a suggestion by your brother that Lord Wharton was paying you.'

'I beg Your Grace's pardon. What I said, more precisely, is that my money came from Lord Wharton,' said the Master coolly. 'It did. I had just extracted it by force. Mr. Scott will perhaps confirm it if you wish.'

Scott was already on his feet, but Lauder conceded the point without calling on him. 'Very well. I am prepared to accept the fact that a personal enmity had been established between yourself and Lord Wharton for reasons we shall not specify. You were not however freeing his messenger from purely humanitarian reasons?'

'Not precisely. He was a very silly man,' said the Master reminiscently. 'I thought perhaps he would irritate the English less than he irritated me.'

'And for that profound reason you engineered a vicious

attack on your brother's force, from which he was only saved by Mr. Erskine?'

For the first time Lymond was momentarily silent. Then he said, 'I was not on good terms with my brother. To such an extent that he would disbelieve automatically any statement which came from me.'

'We are all familiar with the sensation,' said Lauder blandly. 'Go on.'

Lymond said evenly, 'I had earlier encountered the messenger and after reading his dispatch put him on the right road to reach Lord Wharton. When my men found him in Lord Culter's grasp he had destroyed his message and my brother was naturally bent on preventing him from delivering it verbally.'

'But you thought he should be permitted to do so?'

'Yes. Isn't it obvious? The message was from Lord Grey ordering Lennox and Wharton to retreat immediately.'

The whirl of ensuing comment gave Lauder time to savour annoyance. Gladstanes said, 'And did they? Does anyone know?' and someone called, 'Aye, Jock: my boy was in it. He told me the English pulled out of Annan that night, though the previous evening they'd every look of long roots.'

'In that case,' said the Lord Advocate, caressing his blue chin lovingly, 'why, I wonder, did Mr. Crawford tell his brother the English were coming north?'

'Because I knew he would assume the opposite and take his men south to attack,' said the Master promptly. 'Which he did. I believe they were chasing Wharton south of Annan all night.'

The Lord Justice-General cut across the hubbub. 'If we grant your enmity toward Wharton – and I see you are prepared to cite witnesses for this – I still think you have to answer the charge of serving the English on the West March – whether Wharton, Lennox or another – for your own ends,' he said. 'There are witnesses, it says here, to your activities during the invasion of six months ago, when you opened the way of escape for Lord Lennox while appropriating for yourself some of the cattle used as decoys.'

The face turned toward him was quite composed. 'Most of the English who could still move had escaped by that time. The cattle were not for my own use: I returned them to their original owners, an English family to whom a number of Scots besides myself owe a great deal. For my part in the raid, Baron Herries can speak better than I can.'

This time the noise took much longer to die down. When it did, John Maxwell leaned back in his carved chair and astonishingly raised his deep voice, the impersonal yellow eyes fixed on the panel.

'The plan for the cattle raid was Mr. Crawford's, made in a chance encounter when I was ignorant of his identity. I could take little active part. But he and his band drove all the livestock from the south side of the Border and succeeded in taking them to the right place at the appointed time in spite of very bad conditions: a quite remarkable feat of leadership. The Whartons detest him. The young one did his best to slit his throat a month or two later at Durisdeer.'

He stopped speaking as suddenly as he had begun and restored the front legs of his chair to the ground, ignoring the commotion on either side. First blood, miraculously, to the panel.

Licensed by the moment's suspended excitement, Lymond stirred, and moving back a little, sat down in the chair provided for him. Lord Culter, watching, leaned back suddenly in his own seat and the Lord Advocate, who missed nothing, ran his eye quickly over the remaining charges and caught Argyll's attention.

The Chief Justice thumped on the table. 'Quiet, gentlemen! We have a great deal to get through. . . . Mr. Crawford, your explanations so far have been plausible if not entirely, as you will admit, supported by tangible proof. We now wish to examine your relationship with Lord Grey de Wilton, the Lord Lieutenant of the English army in the north. On the occasion of Lord Grey's invasion of

Scotland on the twenty-first of April last, you were the author of a message, purporting to come from a member of your band, which had the result of bringing the Laird of Buccleuch and Lord Culter, with their respective forces, in dangerous proximity to the English army?'

'It brought them, as I thought, within easy reach of Lord Grey himself,' said Lymond briefly. 'The approach of Lord Grey's troops at the same time was unfortunate and unforeseen.'

'You claim,' said the Lord Advocate, 'that this was done purely to enable your brother, with whom you were not on good terms, and Sir Walter Scott, whose son you had corrupted – '

'Hud your tongue, ye sacco, socco, ferrum, dwellum legalizing cricket – '

'–whose son you had enticed from the family hearth, purely to enable these two men to make an advantageous capture?'

'Not at all. I had a transaction of my own to complete. I was hoping to do so under cover of the ensuing melée.'

'A transaction with Lord Grey?'

'So far as his abhorrence of me would admit. I wished to meet a member of the English force, for private reasons. I had induced Lord Grey to arrange the meeting by promising him Will Scott.'

'Thus Sir Walter, Lord Culter and Mr. Scott were all invited into this commodious trap by you at the instance of Lord Grey?' asked Lauder. 'In that case you certainly hoped to bring them within easy reach of the Lord Lieutenant.' Out of the corner of his eye he saw their lordships shuffling. He paid no attention, but kept his voice as unvarying as the panel's. The man was an actor all right. But so was Henry Lauder.'

Crawford of Lymond said, 'Mr. Scott was invited in such a fashion that he could not possibly arrive in time to be in danger. The message to Sir Walter and my brother was sent without Lord Grey's knowledge.' Someone at the table shifted, and Lauder turned instantly. 'Yes, Sir Wat?'

Buccleuch hesitated, looking across the hall at his son.

'That's likely to be right,' he said at length. 'At least, they ran like the hammers when they saw us coming.'

'And you followed, I gather, into the jaws of half the English army?'

Buccleuch said shrewdly, 'What's your argument? D'you think that after the showing-up he got at Hume Castle, Grey would stand by and allow the man to invite half the Scottish army to Heriot? I'm damned sure Grey didn't know Culter and I were coming.'

The Lord Advocate stretched his legs. 'Are you, Sir Wat? To my mind, all the signs point to an astonishing trust by Lord Grey in the Master of Culter. He made an appointment with him, we are told, without the support of more than a few armed men in a particularly deserted spot in the middle of enemy country. I fail to understand your reference to Hume Castle.'

The Earl Marischal stirred. 'Wat means the attack on Hume led by a Spaniard last October,' he said. 'They captured most of a supply train and wrecked half the fortifications. Mr. Crawford claims to have organized it.'

'Oh? Dear me, I see this is another point on which Mr. Scott is anxious to speak,' said Lauder. The redheaded boy, angrily on his feet, began, 'I can vouch . . .' and was smiled down by the Queen's Advocate.

'Later, Mr. Scott. It makes very little difference to the argument, you know. Lord Grey's animosity, on Mr. Crawford's own showing, was mainly directed against yourself and not against the Master of Culter. We have already proved that the Lord Lieutenant trusted him sufficiently – or was certain enough of his loyalty – to allow him prior information of Lord Grey's own movements.'

Scott was still on his feet. He said angrily, drowning Tom Erskine's voice, 'Grey didn't even keep his part of the bargain. He didn't even bring up the man the Master expected to meet.'

'Then there was a bargain,' said Lauder placidly. 'Mr. Erskine?'

Tom said quietly, 'I can vouch for Lord Grey's feelings toward the Master of Culter as demonstrated at Hexham.

There was no question of his being on any but the worst terms with both Wharton and Grey.'

Lauder looked unimpressed. 'We have already proved, surely, that this is a man who sells himself to the highest bidder. If Lord Grey indeed failed to pay him in whatever coin had been agreed for his betrayal at Heriot, it was inevitable, surely, that such a man should bite the hand which failed to feed him. It does not alter the fact that the message inviting Sir Wat and Lord Culter to Heriot was sent off before his encounter with Lord Grey, and there-fore before he could have known that Lord Grey was not keeping his side of the bargain.

'And remember,' the Lord Advocate added agreeably, 'that at that time both Lord Culter and Sir Walter were publicly committed to seize Mr. Crawford. You are being asked to believe that Crawford would first antagonize Lord Grey by failing to produce the person of Will Scott, and then risk immediate capture by his brother and Buccleuch. It does not seem very reasonable to me; and I note that Mr. Crawford himself has very little to say.'

'I'm sorry,' said Lymond. Passionless devil, thought Lauder. He isn't sorry. But then, neither am I. I'm trying to hang him, and he's trying to save his strength so that there won't have to be an adjournment before he's ready for it. . . .

Lymond said, 'I was carried away by the strange charm of your reasoning. The unhappy Lord Lieutenant seems to be credited with a fearful grudge against the Buccleuch family. I thought perhaps you had found a dark plot to seize his wife and junior attachments as well.'

The Queen's Advocate replied without looking up. 'But we have been assured that Mr. Scott could not possibly have arrived in time to come to any harm. If he will forgive me, he was presumably merely the bait for his father.'

'Non minime ex parte, Mr. Lauder. The boy would have been ten times simpler and ten times safer to capture as well as being a much more telling weapon. If we may separate the facts from the faculae we seem to have this.

'One, both before (at Hume) as I think I can prove, and

569

after (at Hexham) as Mr. Erskine has proved, Lord Grey and I were enemies. Two, by failing to keep his part of the bargain at Heriot, Lord Grey had clearly no plans for collaborating with me in the future. Three, some of your prisoners, whose names I shall give you, will tell you that the English army had no orders to support Lord Grey in his supposed ambush, and that the dispatch of a troop was an afterthought due to their suspicions of me.

'Four, as Sir Wat has already stated, the men left by Lord Grey made no effort to capture him or my brother, but fled before them. Five, far from being caught between two fires, I had hoped my promised interview would enable me to reinstate myself with my brother and his friends, in which case I had nothing to fear from them. And lastly, Sir George Douglas, who was detained by Lord Grey during one of his embassies to England at that time, was present at Heriot, and if he will do so, can vouch for the fact that the only bait in the trap was myself.'

Henry Lauder pushed a hand through his sparse hair. Open your mouth too far and someone will fill it with rubbish. He wondered briefly what hold the man had on Sir George to risk citing him as a witness, and cynically applauded the tactics. Everyone knew Douglas played on both sides. By preserving his fictitious character Lymond had made it easy for him to co-operate.

He did. After the briefest silence Sir George leaned back in his chair, ruby flashing, and said, 'That is quite true. Mr. Crawford was actually tied up as a prisoner all the time he was with Lord Grey. Bowes, who led the ambush, appeared to be genuinely startled by Buccleuch's appearance and might well have been captured but for the arrival of other troops.' He paused and added mildly, 'I can also confirm the attack on Hume. Mr. Crawford is a fluent Spanish speaker and was identified by Lord Grey in my presence as the leader of the raid.'

It was too risky to take him up on it. The Advocate to the Crown swallowed defeat gracefully. He bore no grudges: the exercise of his wits against a quick and able man was the finest excitement he knew. He said, 'Well,

Mr. Crawford: we must concede that you seem to have an answer for everything. It will be a pleasure to see what you make of the more serious charges on the list which of course we have still to deal with. In the meantime, I should like to hear about the matter of the Earl of Lennox.'

This time the accusation was simple. In 1544, prior to the Earl's defection to England, the Master of Culter had been on the friendliest terms with him, had stayed at Dumbarton and thus shared, it was alleged, in his treason. What had Mr. Crawford to say?

Time, precious and profligate, was wasting before their eyes.

The heat, girdered with tension, crept like wadding into the interstices of the brain and muffled the starving air. Lymond was sitting up and forward a little, elbows on the arms of his chair, with his hands clasped and his head bent. Richard, familiar with the small signs of fatigue, wondered how he managed to keep it out of his voice. He saw that Lauder was watching his brother narrowly.

In the clear, unemphatic voice he had used throughout, the Master said, 'In 1542 I became a prisoner in France, and from then until 1544 was employed on travaux forcés in the French galleys. In March, 1543, I rowed in the ship which took the Earl of Lennox from France to Scotland, and was seen there by him. In September of that year I was also on the galley which conveyed gold and arms from France for the Queen Dowager. I escaped and applied for protection to Lennox, who I had reason to believe was preparing to defect from his Scottish friends and would therefore receive me. As you know, he sold his loyalty to Henry of England in return for marriage with Margaret Douglas, and left Scotland for England in May of the following year, having appropriated for himself the gold delivered to his keeping from France.

'Between those dates I stayed with him as secretary and general amaneunsis, leaving rather suddenly with a good deal of information and a good part of the gold. I returned some of it by devious ways to Edinburgh; the rest I used as best I could in the Queen's interests. I also established and armed my own force until by our services elsewhere in Europe we became more than self-supporting. . . . I am conscious, of course, that there is no proof of these events, except that I can in some cases give you the dates on which part of the French money was returned.'

It was audacious, all right. The eyes of the room, like sucking fish, were flatly attached to him, building up eager pressures which slopped over as soon as he halted.

Buccleuch gave a yelp. 'Lennox's money! Dod, he's never been known by man to pook a penny before now. I'd like to have seen the colour of him when he found out.'

The Lord Advocate said, projecting his voice, 'This troop you mention is of course the subject of a civil crime action also raised against you on the grounds of robbery and extortion – '

'Protection,' corrected the Master. 'In these lawless times we private forces must help the State to ward its citizens where we can.'

Lauder said dryly, 'The forces in question seem to have mixed opinions on the subject; but that is by the way. Your motives throughout in your dealings with Lord Lennox were again, we are to take it, completely altruistic throughout?'

There was a faint smile in the experienced eyes. 'Only to a human and limited extent. If I hadn't cultivated Lord Lennox's company I should be rowing up and down the Irish Sea yet, instead of being presently charmed by your society.'

'I see,' said Henry Lauder. 'And by the same token: when you presented Lord Grey with a secret of some national importance about our shipping, you were merely ingratiating yourself with his lordship?'

Because all his attention was on Lymond, he missed George Douglas's faint movement. He had brought out, underhand, one of the vital issues, and his opponent was fully aware of it. Come along, my boy! said Mr. Lauder happily to himself. Fight me!

He did. This was not a matter of doubtful history, four

years old; but a question of treason freshly committed and subject to minute examination. The Hexham episode was eviscerated.

'. . . The dispatch was being taken to Lord Grey by a courier called Acheson. I knew nothing of it until it was shown to me on the way to Hexham.'

'Mr. Erskine? You can corroborate that? – Come along. Did Mr. Crawford know nothing of the dispatch?'

'He . . .'

'Will you speak up?'

'He denied it at first, but when we showed it to him – '

'Showed it to him? Where had you found it?'

'In his packroll.'

'And did he continue to protest his ignorance even then? . . . Well?'

'No.'

'He admitted it?'

'I think it's unlikely he knew about it. He prevented the message from being delivered at great personal risk.'

'Ah, yes,' said Henry Lauder. 'Ah, yes,' and stretched himself like a long, disjointed cat. 'We've all heard a great deal about the dramatic scenes at Hexham. How our friend escaped from his brother's thrashing; how he rejoined his ally Mr. Acheson and had the misfortune to be spurned by the English friends he was trying hard to conciliate. So, using a woman as his shield – it has a familiar ring, hasn't it? – he chose the discreeter part; a positive act which would bring him at last under the cloak of the Scottish side at least. He shot the courier in full view of Mr. Erskine and relied on Mr. Erskine's notoriously kind heart to extract him from the muddle. Unfortunately, he himself was attacked in the process – undoubtedly not part of the plan.'

Erskine said forcibly, 'He knew when he made the shot that he hadn't a chance.'

'He knew that if he didn't shoot, he hadn't got a chance, either,' said the Queen's Advocate placidly.

There was a brief silence. Bishop Reid said, 'Well, Mr. Crawford?'

Good. He was going to attempt it. Lymond said briefly, 'If I hadn't used the protection of an English lady, as Mr. Lauder so kindly mentions, the secret of the ships' departure would be a secret no longer. I haven't any evidence that Acheson's message was unknown to me. I can only refer you to some probabilities.'

Argyll said sharply, 'Go on!'

Lymond raised his eyes.

'Am I not an unlikely messenger? To anyone in English pay in Scotland I should be known as an enemy of Lord Grey and Lord Wharton and of the Earl of Lennox; and also the object of a ... well-publicized pursuit by my brother. And even if I were approached, would I risk it for a moment, my relationship with these three men being what it was?

'But the man Acheson was a carrier of dispatches by trade, and an unscrupulous one. We know from what Mr. Erskine has said that Mr. Acheson knew the contents of this message; knew that it was a matter of delivering more than two perfectly legitimate messages from Sir George.

'How did he know? There was no provision originally for Acheson to have a companion. The safe-conduct was widened by Sir George himself to admit me, in order to promote an exchange of prisoners. There was no question, naturally, of accusing Sir George of complicity in treason, therefore you have to believe either that, being provided with this innocent means of getting myself safely to England, I confided my dreadful secret to this perfect stranger; or that when I joined him Acheson was already carrying the dispatch, in which case he was unlikely, surely, to talk about it to me.'

Plausible again. The Lord Advocate saw the eyebrows raised around the table and heard the muttered exchanges.

Reid leaned forward. 'What then was the object of going to England? Oh: I recall. The Stewart girl.'

It was what Lauder was waiting for. He hurled his pen from him so far that it cracked on the oak, and flung up an arm like a semaphore to flatten his hair.

'So-o, Mr. Crawford. Your sole reason for going to

England, your lonely and chivalrous reason for giving yourself up, for flinging yourself on the mercy of these gentlemen who, as you have so laboriously proved, wished nothing better than to see you dead, was to arrange that the Lady Christian Stewart might go free?'

'Yes.'

At last. Now, by God, you're hating it, thought Lauder. And I'm going to thrash you until you hate me as well. And then, my lad, you're going to lose that cool temper and the Bishop had better look out. 'Yes,' he repeated aloud. 'This is the girl, young, blind, wealthy, in close touch with the Court, whom you encouraged to obtain secret information for you – '

'That is untrue.'

' – while posing as a mysterious and illicit lover?'

'Both these accusations are untrue. Confine your attacks to me, Mr. Lauder.' The controlled voice clashed with Buccleuch's: 'Dammit, we can't have that, Lauder. The girl was no light o' love.'

The Lord Advocate said sombrely, 'If you will listen, Sir Wat, you will hear that I am implying the reverse. I am saying that this was an honest, gentle and virtuous girl, a young girl of open and innocent years, betrothed to a fine man, who fell into the power of a practiced and powerful seducer, appearing to her in a guise both insinuating and irresistibly romantic.'

Buccleuch growled. 'She knew who he was. I don't see what bearing this has on the thing.'

'She claimed to know, finally, when she thought it would save him. Did you reveal your identity to her when you met, Mr. Crawford?'

'No,' said Lymond, and his hands closed.

'Why not?'

There was a pause. 'It relieved her of what I felt to be . . . too cruel a quandary. I didn't expect to see her again.'

'No quandary for a girl as upright as we know this one was, surely. Or do you mean she was already in love with you?'

'I mean nothing of the sort. We had been childhood neighbours, and she was a – kindly person.'

'I see. And having all these scruples, no doubt you went out of your way to avoid further meetings. Or did you see her again?' added Lauder suddenly.

There was another pause. Then the Master said evenly, 'Several times. Shall we save some tedious questions and answers? – After the first and second, the meetings were not unavoidable. I allowed her to help me with my private affairs although I knew that by doing so I should make her virtue suspect, at least, if it became known. It was through pursuing my affairs that she was captured at Dalkeith. It was directly because of that that she came into the power of the Countess of Lennox. These were unprincipled and unpardonable acts, and you can't possibly blame me as much as I blame myself.

'But in all of them, Lady Christian was the innocent and deceived party. She did nothing dishonest, even in her efforts to help me; and, unpleasing as it may seem to Mr. Lauder's active imagination, there was nothing but friendship between us. Under the circumstances no doubt you will find it ludicrous that I should cast myself into Lord Grey's lap simply to free her; but that was what I did.'

The Lord Advocate might have been annoyed at having his effects spoiled, but he gave not the slightest sign. 'It certainly has its suspicious side. Particularly when linked with the fact that Lady Christian died suddenly and violently immediately after you traced her to England.'

Erskine's voice said harshly, 'Wait a moment. Lady Christian died from a fall from her horse.'

Lauder said simply, 'How do you know?'

There was real anger in Erskine's brusque voice. 'I knew Chris better than any of you – I was to have married her – and if we weren't in a court of law I would shove down your damned throat the implication you've just been making. I saw Crawford of Lymond immediately after her death and heard what he said and saw how he acted. If

I'd thought for a moment that he'd killed her, I wouldn't have let Culter have the pleasure of fighting him.'

The Lord Advocate let this poignantly confident rebuttal wreak its own doom; and then said gently, 'What then are you suggesting? That Mr. Crawford went to her rescue after all in a fit of erratic gallantry?' and was much surprised to hear Sir George Douglas's smooth voice.

'Suppose, since they worry you, we dismiss the romantic gestures in favour of another fact? Mr. Crawford had been disappointed in his efforts to exculpate himself, as he thought, from the older crimes we have not yet discussed: he had just heard from me that the man who might do so was dead. He had already disbanded his force in expectation of a satisfactory meeting with this man and had suffered the considerable shock of being handed over to us by his own protégé. He might well, under the circumstances, have decided on a course of despair such as this.'

The Lord Advocate bowed without the least shade of irony. 'A point well made. Particularly as it puts before us another fact. Mr. Crawford, it appears, had just been cheated of his hopes of reinstating himself in our midst — by whatever means — as an honest, loyal and worthy servant of the Crown.

'What then remained, one might ask, but to fly to England; to get rid of this awkward girl, who was in England and who knew so much of his activities, and at the same time to present information which he might hope at least would buy him a little leniency from Lord Grey? If not, how was he worse off?' Lauder let his gaze rove over the twelve diverse faces, shining with warmth and concentration; shrewd; passive; perceptive; wary.

'You are not dealing with a simple man. The accusations against him are astonishing in their variety. We have dealt with all but the most serious, and it would take a bold man to say "This is true" and "This is untrue." His past connections with Lord Wharton were deliberate and innocent, he claims. There is no proof either way. His actions at Annan may have sprung from well-intentioned, if obscure motives. That again we shall never know.

'Whether for his own benefit or not, he appears to have given a certain amount of aid to the Crown during the famous cattle raid on the western march. In the same way he rendered us all a service at Hume – this time entirely for his own benefit. At Heriot he played a dangerous game – again for his own ends – in which his own brother and the Buccleuch family were pawns though it appears, generous ones, in the way they have spoken for him. His connection with the Earl of Lennox again is a matter unproven either way – guilty or innocent – but again material reward enters the picture, and it seems likely that what was done was done for this reason.

'We are left with Hexham, and what happened immediately before. So complex is the picture this time, so various the possibilities, that we can isolate the truth, it seems to me, in one way only.

'To know what was in his brain as he drew back that bow at Hexham we must look at the record of his actions in the past for his real ambitions, his real mind on issues moral and ethical and all those intangible things which dictate whether a man conducts his body for the profit of his body, or for the greater renown and comfort of his country, or in the service of his God.

'We have not found out these things this afternoon; and we shall not find them in those things I have mentioned. For this we must go further back, to the dreadful and deadly crimes of which Francis Crawford was accused six years ago, and for which he has still to answer. These are the matters I am proposing to bring before you now.'

A macer, hurrying from Lord Culter's side, bent and said something to Argyll. The Justiciar's voice said, 'What? Oh. . . . Certainly. No purpose in endangering–' And wriggling back his sleeves, the Earl whacked the table. 'Adjournment for an hour. Break off meantime, Mr. Lauder.'

The Lord Advocate followed his eyes, then turned back, bowed and sat down as Sir James Foulis appeared at his elbow. 'The old fool: it's been coming for half an hour. Hasn't he got eyes?' said Lauder comfortably. Through the curtain of officials and guards he could see that Lymond had lowered his head on crossed arms, exposing nothing but the nape of his neck and the admirable lace of his shirt.

The room was clangorous with conversation. Most of them, Committee and witnesses, were on their feet with a flopping and unpuckering of robes, a stretching and a crackling of paper. They gathered in half-prepared knots, mesmerized still by the rigours and tensions of the day, and unwilling to leave while the play was not yet done.

After less than two minutes Lymond gripped the arms of his chair, and then rose. The moment's collapse, Lauder guessed, had been a bitter humiliation: he had not yet regained any colour. Nevertheless he made a deep and impeccable bow to Argyll and walked out through the door without pausing.

'That,' said Henry Lauder, closing his spectacles and throwing his pen in the wastepaper basket, 'is a brain. If I were ten years younger and a lassie, I'd woo him myself.'

Foulis of Colinton caught Oxengang's eye and grinned; to Lauder he said, 'Well, he timed that little episode neatly enough.'

'*He* timed it?' The Lord Advocate, peeling off his soaking robe, was making for the cool air outside. '*He* timed it? Don't be a bloody fool, Jamie.'

Will Scott was among the last to move. As he made to get up, a heavy hand cuffed his head and he looked around and up to see his father.

'Are your teeth sewn up?' demanded Buccleuch. 'You've been busy enough chattering all around Edinburgh up till now.'

Will said resentfully, 'Lauder stopped me twice, but he won't again. I'll damn well . . .'

'Dod, d'ye need a dub and whistle? Bawl it out, man, and he canna stop ye.' He grinned reminiscently. 'Your man has George Douglas's measure, anyway. There's no proof one way, but thanks to Douglas there's no proof the other, either.'

Scott said grimly, 'Does it matter? They'll have him nailed down with the original indictment. All the evidence is on their side this time.'

Buccleuch grunted, observing his son's expression. 'I've seen Henry Lauder up to the oxters in evidence and still lose a case,' he said mendaciously. 'I'm off to the house for a dish of eggs. If you're staying with Culter, find out about that little mare of his. If I get some siller for this fellow Palmer I'll think about buying her after all.'

Scott had already nodded and moved away when the sense of this penetrated. 'Palmer?'

Buccleuch grinned. 'High and mighty Sir Thomas Palmer, the engineer. Did ye not know? I took him after the raid last month.'

'Where is he?'

'In the Castle with the rest of them. A wild lot, I'm told. Why?'

'Nothing,' said Scott, and made for the street so fast that he jammed himself in the doorway with his sword.

* * *

Big Tommy Palmer, former captain of the Old Man at Boulogne, former knight-porter of Calais, former overseer of petty customs, former gentleman-usher and popular companion of King Henry VIII, had been a prisoner of war once before, in France, and although financially unembarrassed by this second mishap was spiritually much discomfited and in need of cheering up.

At his request, he and a dozen of his own men had been put together in one medium-sized room in the Castle. They were all men of good standing and of reasonable value in cash, so the room was pleasant, with carved oak panelling, slightly chipped; a small-paned window looking sheer down the Castle rock into the loch, and a low, thick door with an adequate guard outside it.

Will Scott found it less easy than he had expected to get in. He finally managed it only with the help of Tom

Erskine, and then on the pretext of discussing with Palmer his father's plans for his ransom.

Since in fact he had nothing to discuss, the business aspect of his talk with Sir Thomas came to an early end, and Tom Erskine moved to go. But captivity by this time was boring Palmer; he was willing to go on talking, and Scott was in no hurry to leave.

They exchanged politely some of the current gossip of both courts and touched chastely and with mutual interest on the characters of some of the less powerful but more public figures in each. One or two of Palmer's companions joined in.

Erskine, aware that it was nearly time to make for the Tolbooth and taking only a detached interest in the talk, found the engineer rather likable: a man in his late fifties with grey beard and bright curling hair. Between hair and moustache the skin was red-brown with the sun; his much-wired front tooth sparkled like a trout rising in still water when he laughed, which was often.

Tom was so busy watching Palmer that he missed Scott's move to open his purse. When they brought a small table and put it between the two men, Erskine was surprised. He was more surprised too see Palmer gaze on it as a mother elephant on the prize of some interminable gestation.

On the table lay a small pack of playing cards. 'Hold me hand,' said Tommy Palmer. 'If you'd offered me the throne of China and Helen of Troy thrown in, I'd still choose the tarots. You'll not miss them?'

'Not at all. Glad to leave them,' said Scott politely. And to Erskine's astonishment he added, 'I'll start you off with a game, if you like,' and sat down to hearty expressions of Palmer's glee. Erskine tapped the boy on the arm. 'The time, Scott. We ought to be going.'

The carroty head turned vaguely. 'There's time for one game, surely. You go on if you want to. I'll follow.' He was already shuffling the cards. Tom eyed him sharply; and then, twitching up a chair, sat astride it, watching the play.

He had seen these tarots several times in Scott's possession since he had come to Edinburgh. They were gruesome, Gothic, and graced with a kind of lithless malevolence all their own. The four suits were commonplace enough: the artist had reserved his fantastic brushes for the figured cards. The Bateleur, the Empress, the Pope, l'Amoureux and le Pendu, Death and Fortitude, the Traitor, the Last Judgment itself, all shared a grotesque camaraderie of the paintpot.

He admired the set. He enjoyed tarocco himself, but he was uneasily aware that there was not, in fact, time for a game. He said again, 'Listen, Scott'; but the cards were already dealt and Will was hesitating over his discard. Erskine gave up, and resigned himself to waiting.

Scott played not one, but two games. He lost them both, but so narrowly that it was not until the last trick of the outplay that Palmer's evident brain and experience gave him the day. Both games were played in an atmosphere of jocular excitement, and Erskine gathered that to have opposed Palmer at all was something unusual; and to have run him so close something unique.

At the end of the second game, Palmer leaned back with a kind of anguished roar. 'Damn it, I don't know when I've had two better games. Why the pest must you go? I can't settle: you can't settle: it isn't fair to the game.'

Scott got up and stretched himslf, grinning. 'You've got troubles enough. You don't want to risk being beaten by me.'

'Beaten!' It was a chorus. Someone said, 'Hey, my boy. You're speaking of the best card player in England.'

'I still say beaten,' said Scott.

There was an unholy light in Thomas Palmer's eye. 'Is that a challenge?'

'Not particularly,' said Scott. 'Sine lucro friget ludus is a family motto. Not much point in playing for love.'

'Hell, we can do better than that,' said Palmer. Their packs were stuffed into an armory let into the panelling: he tossed out parcels until he came to the one he wanted.

Then he had another look and, bringing out a second roll, flung them both at Scott's feet.

'A change of good clothes there, and some money and a silver cup and a good pair of boots. And there's more still in the other: it's another man's stuff that belongs to me now. Will that do for a start?'

Scott drew out his own heavy purse and tossed it once in the air. 'I'm sure it will; but we're a gey practical nation. Will you open them both so that we can see?'

Palmer, unoffended, glinted the butter-tooth in his direction, and slit open the packs with Will's knife. In his own the contents were exactly as he had said. The other roll was less well-kept: the clothes were soiled and there was no money at all. Scott bent and turned over a long, narrow rectangle of folded paper, sealed with red wax. 'What's this? Deeds of ownership?'

Palmer, shuffling the tarots, glanced at it and shrugged. 'Sam didn't own a rabbit, poor devil. Perhaps a letter to his lady friend.'

Scott turned it over. There was an inscription on the other side, and he held it so that Erskine also could read. The neat writing said, *Haddington, June, 1548. Statement.* And underneath in a different writing, presumably Wilford's: *Samuel Harvey. Put with things for P.*

That was as far as they got before it was whipped from Scott's fingers.

'Interested?' asked Palmer in the same good-tempered voice. 'I thought there was something fishy in the air. Perhaps I'd better keep this.'

For a moment, Erskine thought that Scott would attack the big man. Instead he turned and, opening his purse, upended it on the table by the cards. The crowns rolled and clanked among the little nightmarish drawings and rose in a winking, lunar pile. 'I could easily get it by calling the guard,' said Will. 'But I'll buy it from you instead.'

Palmer grinned. 'I don't want to sell.'

The freckles marched cinnamonlike over Scott's pale face. 'Name your price.'

Sir Thomas Palmer got up, the folded papers still in

his hands. At the fireplace he turned, and still surveying them both quite pleasantly, broke the seal. 'Perhaps I should see first what all the fuss is about. After all, he was my cousin, you know.'

They waited as the pages flicked over. He went through them all, folded the papers and handed them with an inaudible remark to the Englishman, Frank, who was nearest. Then he returned to the table. 'You want these papers?'

'Yes,' said Scott shortly. 'It's a matter of life and death.'

'Jesus. Whose life? A Scotsman's?'

'. . . Yes.'

Palmer grinned more widely. 'That's all right: I'm not the vindictive sort. Sine lucro friget ludus, eh? You want this, you say. Then play me for it.'

'I'm offering you any price you ask,' said Scott.

'I don't want money.'

'Then I'll give you what you do want. Your freedom. Your immediate release, Sir Thomas, in exchange for these papers.'

Palmer sat down with a thump, still grinning. 'I like Edinburgh. I like the Castle. I like the company. I can get my freedom any time, for a little cash, and a damned bore it is, with Willie Grey in both ears and the Protector under my hat. Give me the man who can stretch me at tarocco and you can keep Berwick and every bumbling Northerner in it.'

Scott sat down himself rather suddenly. 'For God's sake, I'll play cards with you all night, if that's all you want. I'll play every day for a month without the sniff of a win. But not to gamble on this kind of stake. What do you take me for?'

The big man was shuffling the cards. 'A member of a practical nation. I don't want bad play and a sure win: I get enough of it. I don't want a game that's a duty or an imposition or a debt or any other damned, dreary penance. I don't like it and the tarots don't like it. Look at them!' With a flip of his thick fingers he sent the cards reeling across the polished wood, convulsed, mouthing and snarling. 'Nobody's going to fob them off with paltry wagers of three louis a game. They want flesh, do the tarots.'

Scott and Erskine were standing shoulder to shoulder. 'Get the guard,' said the boy without turning his head. 'Quickly. Christian Stewart was killed for these papers.'

Erskine didn't go for the guard: he took action. The dive he made for the fireplace was nearly quick enough, but not quite. By the time his outstretched hand had reached the man Frank, the papers were already curling in the smoke a foot above the little fire.

'Call the guard – or try that again – and Frank'll throw the whole thing in the fire,' said Palmer agreeably. He settled comfortably in his chair. 'God! I was bored. Come along, laddie. I've plenty of time. I'll play you tarocco, my boy, for all the money and every stitch each of us possesses in this room, and these papers go into the rest on my side last of all.'

There was a short silence. Then Scott said, 'Let me see the papers.'

'No.'

The boy bit his lip, staring at Palmer's cheerful face. 'It might take all night.'

The tooth winked and wagged. 'It might take a good deal longer. Are you in a hurry?' – and continued to wink as Scott argued. At the end of it he picked up the cards and started to ruffle them through his big hands. 'It's no concern of mine what you want them for. I've told you the conditions.' He looked up. 'Why're you worrying? You might win the lot in an hour.'

Scott sat down. In silence he untied and pulled off his jerkin and in silence he pushed up his shirt sleeves and laid his hands flat on the table. 'Very well,' he said flatly. 'For God's sake let's start.'

* * *

The hour of recess had, inevitably, nearly doubled before the Committee was harried together again; and even so, the interrogation had been under way for some time when Tom Erskine finally slid into his seat, passing on the way

585

a face he knew: Mylne, the Queen's surgeon. But Lymond seemed perfectly composed in his chair: the abuses to his body were perhaps visible, but not those to his intellect, which showed fresh and sinewy still under the sharp and thickening barbs from Lauder. The Lord Advocate was beginning to concentrate his attack: the darts glanced in the silence and were returned, with unfailing felicity.

Erskine said in Lord Culter's ear, 'What's happening?' and Richard replied without taking his eyes from the high table. 'He's got Orkney on the raw, the fool. The nearer the Committee gets to Eloise, the harder he's hitting them. They don't like it, and it isn't doing him any good. . . . Where've you been?'

Erskine said uninformatively, 'At the Castle,' and glanced at the top table. Buccleuch's face was turned toward him and the black circle of the mouth shaped the words 'Where's Will?'

Having no desire to answer that either, Tom stabbed a finger several times in the air due west, and as Sir Wat continued to look expressively at him, mouthed the word 'Later' and turned overtly to the centre of the floor.

'You arrived in London,' the Queen's Counsel was saying, 'along with a thousand others taken prisoner in 1542 after the battle of Solway Moss. At that time, as we all know, the late Henry VIII of England had declared war on our King his nephew and was attempting to prove his title to Scotland by force. Unlike others of your own rank you were immediately given preferential treatment in being lodged in a private English house.'

'After three days in the Tower. Not very preferential.'

Lauder looked at his notes, 'We have that point quite clear. All but yourself were noblemen of the first rank, and all those with whom you say you had contact are now unfortunately bearing witness in higher courts than these. The Earl of Glencairn died last year; Lord Maxwell two years ago; Lord Fleming and Mr. Robert Erskine at Pinkiecleugh.'

'The nation's subsequent failures in the field,' said Lymond gently, 'are my misfortune, not my fault. Sir

George has already told you that I stayed at his brother's London house under no special concession.'

The Bishop of Orkney cleared his throat. 'And why, Mr. Crawford, did you not then return to Scotland ten days later as did the great majority of such boarded prisoners? Were your scruples such that even tongue in cheek you could not bring yourself to sign the necessary oath of allegiance to King Henry, as your compatriots did? Men of honour, it seems to me, must be prepared like them to sell that honour for their country's good. Why did you not sign?'

'I wasn't asked,' said Lymond, and a fleeting regret slipped through the pleasant voice. 'Only prelates and barons were thought to have sufficient tongue and sufficient cheek.'

Richard swore. It was Lord Herries who saved the situation with a brusque and bass inquiry. 'Since he's a younger son, there would be little point, surely, in asking Mr. Crawford to sign a bond to serve the King in Scotland?'

The Bishop said, breathing heavily, 'I disagree. He was, in sort, his brother's heir. If he were innocent he would have contrived, surely, to return on some pretext.'

'The thing reeks of ineptitude, doesn't it?' said Lymond. 'If I were a spy, it was shockingly careless of the English to capture me in the first place. And if I were a spy, my first thought would have been to return to Scotland as fast as I could. According to the Bishop, my treason lay in not promising to work secretly in Scotland against the Queen. If that's treason then let's make an end. I admit it.'

Lauder was undisturbed. 'You made King Henry no promise to serve him?'

'No.'

'You had in the past performed no service for him?'

'I had not.'

The Lord Advocate looked mildly regretful. 'And the presentation to Francis Crawford, Scottish gentleman, of the manor of Gardington, Bucks, was an elaborate ruse to make us believe you had done these things? King Henry must have thought you very important to us, Mr. Crawford. You did, I suppose, receive the deeds of this lordship and manor?'

'Yes. I did.'

'And can you suggest why, if it was not in gratitude for favours received?'

'Europe's most Christian Bachelor and I had nothing in common,' said Lymond. 'He had a fancy to control my tongue. And also to restrain his niece.'

'Ah, yes. The Lady Margaret Douglas, now the Countess of Lennox. Are we to take it that, seduced by your charms, the lady asked for Gardington as her dot?' George Douglas, he saw, was watching the prisoner like a predator.

'Not precisely. She is, shall we say, a person of violent but practical enthusiasms. She has already been imprisoned twice for endangering the succession, and one of her lovers, as you may recall, died in the Tower from a surfeit of Scottish heart and English briar. No. At a guess, she wanted . . . a new stimulus and a new experiment. And encouraged her uncle to leash me permanently by telling him what I had found out; and even perhaps some things I hadn't.'

Methven's silly voice cut through the tactful silence. 'And what had you found out?'

The Master's gaze neither looked at nor avoided Sir George. 'Something of his immediate plans, which later became common knowledge. I had access to rooms which should normally have been closed to me, and found them out by chance.'

'Bedrooms?' inquired the Queen's Counsel.

The veiled eyes lifted. 'Not every legal document is framed in a bedroom, my lord.' The Justice-Clerk laughed aloud.

'Well,' said Henry Lauder. 'You have an estate and a beautiful lady in prospect, and her wicked uncle allows you to enjoy neither. The gift of the estate has already made your fellow Scots suspicious; your return to Scotland is finally made impossible by spreading the news among your countrymen that you were responsible not only for the disaster of Solway Moss, but for a long career of previous spying and intrigue. . . . Why trouble with all this fearsome plotting. Mr. Crawford? If King Henry didn't like you, weren't there simpler and more obvious means of getting rid of you?'

Argyll, surprisingly, said, 'I can see the point of some of it. His Majesty learned just after our prisoners reached London that our King had died and Scotland was accordingly under a regency, and he was immediately bent on winning over as many leading Scots families as possible to his interests. Hence all the prisoners being taken from the Tower to better lodgings, and the offer to let the most important go free if they signed an oath of allegiance to England. It wasn't the time for the sudden murder of a prisoner of war in his hands – even a less important one.'

'Also,' said Lymond, continuing the argument with an unbounded scholarly detachment, 'he probably wanted to protect the real purveyor of secrets. If Edinburgh was becoming suspicious, he was calling off the hunt by making me scapegoat. Then, having discredited me at home and with the prisoners still remaining in London, he could dispose of me in safety.'

'And yet you survived?'

'I was taken to Calais and allowed to fall into the hands of the French. Perfectly simple.'

'And after that, the galleys?'

'Yes,' said Lymond with no trace of expression in his voice.

'Now we're coming to it,' said Buccleuch, and shifted his bulk in his seat. 'Lawyers! Dod, look at him: his een glinting like a coo with the yellows.'

The Lord Advocate's tone was mild and of a grave delicacy.

'How can we stay indifferent to such misfortune? We have before us a man unhappy and deceived; duped by the best brains of the kingdom; enticed by an immoral woman of royal birth; kidnapped; maltreated; shackled to the starving heathen at the galley oar and beaten through the seas for two undeserving summers.

'Look at him! Weak – from the knife of his own underling; but that has no bearing. Innocent – his admitted betrayal and corruption of this young, blind woman has clearly left no stain. Dismiss from your minds the robbing and thieving and murdering of those whom until recently he led – he is virtuous. Dismiss the ruthless plotting, the devious schemes for battle and gain which we have heard about this afternoon – he is simple and vulnerable. Think, last of all, of how he has conducted himself today; of the fluent and malicious tongue from which you, as lords of the highest court in the land, have not been exempt. Does it seem to you that this drunkard, this outlaw, this wastrel son of an ill-starred family, is the man of this pitiful history? Or do you think, as I do, that it is all a pack of lies?'

The echoes died. The Lord Advocate removed his spectacles, and spoke gently. 'But we are asked for proof. What proof have we? Nearly all the people concerned are dead. It is not the sort of transaction likely to leave a record; and those persons who still remember the event are in enemy country.

'But – we have one piece of evidence in writing. The notes which were picked up in Scotland and attributed to Mr. Crawford; the document he says was the work of an unknown English spy; and which was attributed to him, he says, to ensure his disgrace with us. If that is a forgery; if Mr. Crawford can prove that this paper is none of his; that it was compiled without his knowledge; then the case against him immediately loses its mainstay. Mr. Crawford!'

Like the face of many-eyed Indra, the corporate head of the Committee turned on the exposed chair. Douglas's lips were tight, his stare thoughtful; Herries wore a look of fastidious concern; Buccleuch was craning forward. Among the benches Lord Culter had made a tent of his hands, and his face was invisible.

The strain on the Master was sufficiently clear now. He sat still, a thin, deep line between his eyes, watching and anticipating Lauder as light might thrust and linger on a falling blade. Their eyes locked. 'Mr. Crawford,' said the advocate softly. 'This document before me was taken from the pocket of an English soldier after the raid which destroyed the convent of Lymond. It includes these words:

' "The convent is on my land six miles east of that, and we hid the gunpowder there just before being taken at Solway. If you go immediately, you should be able to reach it before it is discovered: no one else knows of its presence. There is an underground passage to the cellar where the powder is stored, reached in the following way. If it is difficult to move, I suggest you blow up the convent." '

There was a long silence. Culter did not look up and Erskine, beside him, folded his arms suddenly and gazed at the floor. The Lord Advocate said flatly, 'Mr. Crawford. Do you admit that these words are in your handwriting, and were written by you?'

The tyranny of pride and the tyranny of intelligence, however pitilessly forced, could not protect Lymond from this. His eyes, terribly, answered before his voice. 'Yes. They were.'

'Do you admit,' asked the lawyer, 'that the signature on the last page of this document is yours?'

'It is mine.'

A contraction passed over the Lord Advocate's face and was gone.

'I see. And,' said Henry Lauder with no levity at all in his voice, 'since the English did follow these directions, did find the passage and, when attacked, exploded the convent as you suggested – since these things happened, the deaths of four nuns and ten girls within the convent, including the death of Eloise Ann Crawford, your sister, are your responsibility?'

Flagging and infinite silence.

'Yes. I am responsible,' said Lymond, ashen to the roots of his sun-bleached hair.

* * *

The room in David's Tower was suffocatingly crowded;

591

chiefly because not only prisoners but all the guards off duty had mansged to squeeze in as well. The hottest man there was Frank, sitting by the fire with Samuel Harvey's statement hovering near the blaze.

If he had expired in a paste of perspiration, nobody would have noticed. The colletic stare of guards and Englishmen alike was on the sweating, subsaltive hands and on the grinning tarots: the impious Papess, the lascivious Lover, the jeering Fool. The two baggage rolls still lay on the floor, but their contents had changed: beside Palmer's chair lay some of Scott's money, and some of Palmer's minor possessions lay at Scott's hand. Both men were in shirt sleeves.

In the evening light, Will's face was the paler of the two. The older man was playing with a careless, sure hand: leading, luring, discarding with persistent ingenuity, and had caught Scott out badly several times. None the less Scott won, not once but reasonably often; and when he lost, it was not by an irretrievable margin.

He had a healthy respect by that time for Palmer's card playing. Watching him seated opposite, massive and smooth as a tree. Scott recognized also his toughness, and grew more and more afraid that through sheer fatigue he himself would stop thinking clearly. As if to drive home the point, Palmer tapped an elemental finger on the table between them. 'And the Fool, Mr Scott. Fool and three Kings: fifteen points – that right? Yes. And my game, I think.'

He was right, and the grin he exchanged with his audience did nothing to help. 'Mine, boys! Any more beer, while I choose me prize? That's a good belt, Mr Scott?'

Scott's chest tightened. Until one or other of them had nothing more to barter ... that was the length of the game; and they were so evenly matched that their damned belongings might be passing to and fro for weeks – unless he succumbed and lost all. And the stipulation was that Samuel Harvey's papers were to be Palmer's final stake.

The thought of it sickened him with wrath and frustration. AFter all they'd gone through – after what the

Dowager had suffered – after Christian's death – after the fool he had made of himself twenty times over – no one should present this prize under his nose and snatch it back like a toy from a kitten. He stopped shuffling and flung down the cards with a crack. 'My deal.'

Palmer winked. 'He thinks he's going to win this one.'

'I'm going to win them all,' said Will Scott. 'I'm going to have the nails out of your boots before I've done with you, and if you've any pins holding up your breeks you'd best watch them, because I'll have them skint off the superior Sassenach down o' ye before another day dawns.'

And he began to deal.

* * *

'So here,' said the Lord Advocate, 'is the truth at last. I cannot say I expected it. Your confession does you credit, Mr. Crawford. *Quum infirmi sumus, optimi sumus*, I see.' Lauder was aware, blissfully, beyond doubt, of the success of his onslaught. He was within Lymond's guard, and the passport was the name of Lymond's sister.

So he quoted Latin and Lymond, breaking painfully from his numb cataphract, retaliated. 'The credit is entirely yours. *Quod purpura non potest, saccus potest*, Mr. Lauder. But I prefer my truth flat and not concamerate, even with the most dulcet spring of famous rhetoric in spate beneath. The notes were mine. But they were written for Scots, not Englishmen to read. Not for a manor or a woman or the combined keys of Tucker and Schertz's treasure houses, in spite of your character reading, would I – '

'Harm a woman?' suggested the lawyer gently.

Buccleuch's grunt reached them all. 'You can be a damned fool over women without wanting to blow up fourteen lassies.'

Lauder said, 'Mr. Crawford's tamperings with Christian Stewart were more than those of a damned fool, I should have thought. She also died, remember.'

Argyll contributed. 'In any case, Sir Walter, the information about the convent in this document was prefaced

593

by three pages of detailed news about Scottish plans and some explicit references to previous reports to the English Privy Council. It is clearly absurd to imply that any of this was intended for Scotland and not for England.'

'I have been trying,' said Lymond with a deep breath, 'to explain. The first three pages of that letter are a forgery, based no doubt on the genuine spy's report sent to Henry. The letter about the gunpowder is real enough. I hid the powder in my sister's convent when it was partly wrecked and abandoned after an earlier raid. The man who helped me was killed at Solway: no one else knew of it, and it looked as if I might be kept in London for some time.

'I knew the Government needed the powder, and I was nervous in case the nuns might come to harm if they returned. So I wrote a letter in London and had it taken to the Master of Erskine who was being released to go back to Scotland. I was allowed no personal contact with other prisoners.'

At the high table. Buccleuch's eyes met those of Tom Erskine. He said, 'Robert died at Pinkie.'

'In any case, he never received it,' said Lymond quietly. 'I discovered that later. It was intercepted, the superscription cut off and the whole made a tailpiece of the other report, which was rewritten in my kind of hand. The next raiding party to cross the Border located the convent, was surprised into igniting the powder, and took care to leave behind the paper incriminating me.'

Sir Wat said, 'Ye gomerel: if that's right, why the devil didn't you watch that first letter? You could guess what'd happen to it in the wrong hands, even if you didn't know the lassies had gone back?'

'The thought isn't new to me,' said Lymond, his voice empty of expression. 'I took all the precautions I could at the time.'

'But not enough.'

'Obviously. If you're anxious to analyse my feelings on that occasion,' said Lymond with sudden savagery, 'you can measure them against my lapses from temperance according to the gospel of Mr. Lauder.'

'Bloody fool,' said Buccleuch briefly. 'Wait a bit, Henry. If the report was in two hands there should be some difference in the writing, eh?'

But the advocate shook his head and, getting up, stretched across to the Committee's table. 'Look for yourselves.'

The paper crackled as it passed from hand to hand: the sun, much lower, was climbing up one wall, forcing Erskine to shield his eyes against the heraldic dazzle of it. Culter sat without moving, his eyes on his hands.

From the benches opposite, Mylne suddenly got up, and crossing to the prisoner's side, bent and spoke. The Master shook his head just as Lauder sat down, the restored paper in his hands, and observed them. 'Well, doctor?'

The elderly figure straightened. 'If ye want to hang him, ye'd best watch your step.'

'Would you like a rest, Mr. Crawford? You mustn't swoon.'

Buccleuch growled. 'I wouldna say yes to a drink of water on the lip of Gehenna, put like that. Lauder's on top and he knows it. Look at him! He's a mouth like the smirk on a pig.'

The smile was certainly there, widening at Lymond's sardonic reply. 'So near the climax? I can surely hold together for the peroration, Mr. Lauder.' And the surgeon, shrugged away, disappeared.

The Lord Advocate waited for the rustle of adjustment to die down, and then stood up.

'There is no need, I think, to prolong this inquiry much further. We have heard Mr. Crawford's explanation of what happened in London, and in Lymond, in 1542: we have seen that there is no obvious difference in the handwriting in any part of the document which he claims is only partly his: we have heard him acknowledge responsibility for the appalling and cold-blooded crime whose results we know.

'On the one side, we have an explanation of these events which, if dreadful in its violence and its story of degeneration, is both straightforward and likely, and is supported both by documentary evidence and by part of the proofs supplied by Mr. Crawford himself. On the other, there is the history of what must appear an incredible twist of fate, which placed the defendant helpless at the mercy of powerful forces in London.

'We are asked to believe that he incurred the sympathetic interest of one of the highest ladies of the land, but that she could do nothing to help him: that while fervently supporting the Scottish cause he was feckless enough to allow a dangerous secret to fall into enemy hands: that there existed, as there exists in romances, some terrible English plot of which he happened to gain knowledge. Do all these things seem likely?'

The pause was for effect, but Gledstanes, meticulous and canny, broke in. 'It doesn't seem to me to be incontrovertible that the two halves of this letter are in the same hand. Also the suggestion about blowing up the convent seems gratuitous, if intended for English readers. Seems unnecessary and argues a callousness I find hard to believe. Particularly since – assuming he was a spy – the man surely expected when he wrote it to be sent back to Scotland in due course.'

Bishop Reid barely waited for him to end. 'The answer to that surely lies as Lauder has already said in proof of character. The man's led a life of abandon and profligacy – he hasn't denied it. There's the blind girl. The sister-in-law. The Scott boy–' He paused as Sir Walter shot up and was pressed down again by a neighbour. 'A young boy who, we know, vacillated wildly in his attitude to his new protector. Disgust – or self-disgust – at one point, as we know, forced him to take the honourable course. His affections, it seems, have since altered again. We do not know what happened in the year he was with the panel, but one can hardly wonder at these signs of an extreme and unhealthy emotional instability. I for one would have found it hard to place any reliance on his support of Mr Crawford, and I am glad to see he is not here this afternoon to perjure himself.'

It was beyond human strength to restrain Buccleuch any longer. 'Perjure himself!' roared Sir Wat. 'Unhealthy emotions! Self-disgust! Are you calling my son a debauchee?'

'I merely pointed out – '

'That boy,' bellowed Sir Wat, 'was a shilpit, shiftless, shilly-shallying gomerel before he met up with Francis Crawford. And now, by God – he still maybe makes up his mind three times in the time a normal man would do it once, but I'd sooner have him back of me in an argument or a fight than any finnicking ninny that stayed at home and got wed at St Cuthbert's before he stopped talking like the squeak off a tumbler!'

'I don't deny,' said the Bishop loudly, 'that your son is now an exceedingly efficient fighting man: witness his unprecedented attack on yourself. I am only seeking to prove – '

'It seems to me you were only seeking to prove six other things as well,' said Sir Wat threateningly. 'And all of them damned insulting.'

' – In any case,' said Henry Lauder quickly, 'the point is made. We may be forgiven for believing that associations natural and unnatural come easily to Mr. Crawford. And that brings us, distasteful as it may be, to a popular report very widely current in the months after the disaster at Lymond. I must remind you, Sir Wat, that Mr. Crawford may have had reasons – very cogent reasons of his own – for encouraging and even inciting the attack on the convent.'

The violence with which Lymond propelled himself to his feet was such that his monumental chair rocked behind him. In the flicker of an eye he must have seen his brother half-rise in the same moment, and must have guessed what lay behind the furious anxiety in the grey eyes, and behind the avid expectancy of the Tribunal.

Lauder, waiting, breathed thanks for the instant's pause before the attack. A storm of emotion might have coalesced all the liking and sympathy which existed already for Lord Culter, and the less than neutral curiosity of people like Herries and Buccleuch. But this fellow fought with his head, not his heart, and the Tribunal would never warm to him. Henry Lauder was not a cynic: he was simply very good indeed at his job.

But Lymond addressed the Committee and not the Queen's Advocate when he began to speak. The carrying, escharotic voice was thick with sheer cold fury for half a dozen words, and then he had it controlled.

'I see this idea is not new to you. Some lawyers believe that dirt will do as well as evidence any day; but Mr. Lauder, all heat and no light, like hell-fire, is not like that. He is simply provocative; without of course making concessions to the feelings of either the laird of Buccleuch or of other members of my family.'

Lymond paused, and his voice, rock-steady, dropped a little. 'Like Mr. Lauder, I have played on this stage before. I know the value of the stagger, the swoon, the vein swollen with ire and outrage. Mr. Lauder was a little afraid of all these; but instead he counted on me to wreck your amour propre as you had wrecked mine, with sad results for my case.

'That is why you heard the accusation you heard just now, grafted skilfully to the Bishop's preceding statements about Will Scott of Buccleuch.' He paused.

'There is no foundation whatever for either suggestion. Will Scott is a normal, lively youngster: he left me when he did because he thought I was planning to give him up to the English, among other misconceptions. If you discount his father's denial, you might also remember his moderation in the Tribunal today. Sir Walter is not a man to hide his feelings. My sister . . .'

His voice roughened suddenly. 'Who will speak for her? The rest of my family, perhaps: will you believe them? Who makes it necessary to speak for her; for either of these young people? Are you so short of rods that you must despoil young trees: so short of stones that you need to walk the very graveyards for them . . . ?

'My lords, my Lord Advocate: I suggest that you have surely material enough before you now to suggest a verdict to you; that nothing more of value can come from this inquiry; and particularly nothing of value from the path Mr. Lauder would have you tread. I do beg you to remember that I, and I alone, am the person whose acts you are judging today.'

He sat down, leaving behind him the uneasy silence of those who have watched a keg of gunpowder explode without a sound. Tom Erskine said in a whisper. 'God Almighty!' glanced once at Culter's face and wiped his own brow. Lauder rose.

'Are you withdrawing from further questioning, Mr. Crawford?'

'I am not. But – '

'But you would like us to close this inquiry for the sake of your health,' said the advocate comfortably, and watched out of the corner of his eye a note passing hurriedly to the top table. Buccleuch, crumpling it in his hand, said, 'I don't much fancy the line the questioning has been taking either, Lauder; but – by his Grace's leave – I don't think we should close the business without hearing Will again. I understand the damned limmer's got stuck somewhere, but he ought to be here at any moment.'

Argyll consulted his immediate neighbours and leaned forward. 'We are satisfied to leave our preliminary investigation at this point, Mr. Lauder. I cannot imagine, Sir Walter, that your son will have anything of great moment to add to what we know, but if he appears before these proceedings are finished we shall of course admit his evidence, although we cannot, I think, prolong this diet to wait for him. First, we should like you, my Lord Advocate, to gather together the facts which have been revealed so far and correlate them for us. Then, if he so wishes the prisoner may speak.'

Erskine sprang to his feet. 'My lords, I beg you not to close without hearing Mr. Scott. There is evidence of the first importance involved.'

'What?' said Reid. His ear was cupped in his hand and his face hot and irritable. 'It is irregular to speak now, Mr. Erskine. Sit down.'

Argyll was more patient. 'You have knowledge of this evidence?'

'Only that it may be vital.'

'You have no idea what it is?'

Erskine flushed. 'No. But – '

The Justiciar's voice was final. 'In that case, I am afraid you must abide by my decision. If it arrives before this Assize ends, we shall admit it. Mr. Lauder – ' He paused. 'Mr. Erskine, you may sit down.'

Tom said briefly, 'I was to give evidence in support of the prisoner's actions at Hexham. May I do so now?'

Argyll's tolerance this time was not so evident. He leaned forward. 'We know what happened there, Mr. Erskine, and accept that you can confirm it. We don't need to know any more at present, I believe. Now, Mr. Lauder?'

The Lord Advocate was amused and intrigued – intrigued to such an extent that he took a hand in the game. He said, 'There is one further thing, my lord, which we might have clear. We have heard no comment from Lord Culter for or against his brother. Although we all realize the matter is painful to him, he might be able to throw some light on the unhappy affair at the convent.'

Argyll began, 'I think we have heard enough – ' and paused as the lawyer's face became concerned.

Lauder said, 'It was Lord Culter who spared himself least in the past year in running his brother to earth, and who in fact brought him back in the end. Should we not ask him to give us his reasons?'

It was a justifiable slip; and it happened so late that the Crown suffered less than it might have done. The Justiciar waved a cursory hand, and Lord Culter rose, purposeful and solid as Ebenezer. 'It is true that I spent many weeks pursuing my brother,' he began, and Lauder, already warned by his voice, swore quietly under his breath. 'I did so under a complete misapprehension,' said Richard calmly. 'I believe him innocent of the charges against him; and I want to say that when intercepted – '

'Don't labour the point, Richard.' It was the defendant's voice, quick and caustic.

' – When intercepted, I was about to help my brother leave the country.'

Sensation. Lymond gave a curious grimace and stayed quiet; the Lord Justice-General sat up. 'You realize, Lord Culter, that if this man is found guilty you have made yourself an accomplice to his crimes?'

Richard said briefly. 'He is not guilty.'

The Lord Advocate was looking at him very hard. 'Your lordship has thoroughly surprised us. I do not propose to question you about your sister, but I must ask this: as to the other accusations on this sheet – do you have any proof that they are false?'

Culter stirred uneasily. Lymond's malicious voice spoke before he could open his mouth. 'No, he hasn't. I'm sorry to disperse the gentle and evangelical light, but even Richard can't achieve a complete volteface as quickly as that. All this whitewashing is intended, I gather, to protect my sister's reputation: that's all.'

The Lord Advocate said nothing; he simply lay back in his chair, the blue chin dropped on his chest, and stared thoughtfully a Lymond, who stared thoughtfully back. It was Argyll who said, 'We really must have this clear. Do I understand Lord Culter is romancing? That he didn't help you to escape?'

'Imagination reels,' said Lymond, 'before the improbable delights of such an event. No. He was bringing me here to have me hanged, having just failed to kill me in formal combat in England. Mr. Erskine will confirm.'

Mr. Erskine, in a dour voice, confirmed, without looking at Culter, who was on his feet and choked with protests. 'I think,' said the panel kindly, 'that you should sit down. It makes no odds now, you know.' And after a moment, Richard did so.

An odd silence had fallen. It was late: long past time for the evening meal. They were exhausted with argument and heat and concentration and the concealed ravages of fear.

No darts had been thrown; no mines exploded; no reputations peeled of their tactful patches and splints. All was righteousness and decorum; and the rich, pliant voice of the Lord Advocate, beginning in the stillness and unreeling delicately the case against Francis Crawford.

He was clever enough not to brush again through the harsh Orcadian pastures of Bishop Reid's imagining. He kept to his indictment – kept concisely and damningly to its severities, and made no appeal to the heart: the time for that was past. Instead, he bent his mind to weaving a fabric of steel: a case so massive, so intellectually secure, so lockfast that no man, however fluent and however gifted, should break it. Of these bright phrases, forged and concatenated, would emerge the gyves which tomorrow would snap into place. He ended very calmly.

'And so I present to you a trespasser of a kind which the law in its grace and impartiality has scarcely knowledge to deal with: a man who has plunged his kindred men into untimely death; has rent blood and limb from them; has forced apart mother and son and scythed sheer to the stubble a meadow of children, for a handful of tainted and murderous coins. A man who, nourished in this generous womb, can turn upon his mother land and hack her, deface her and betray her, deny her and spit upon her as an empty waste, a name upon a map, a race of strangers and a source of wanton exercise and plunder.

'Such a man is Crawford of Lymond: such a man this land may pray never to see again in the difficult ways of her history. I say: busy yourself no longer about him, for he is better condemned, and most harshly dead.'

The silence of his careful making followed him and lay upon the Tribunal for a stricken and pulsing space. Then at the long table Argyll moved, and the twelve Assessors stirred and sighed.

Erskine, lifting his stunned head, saw that Richard's eyes were wide and full on his brother; but Lymond looked at nobody, the queer cornflower gaze concentrated in space. The Lord Justice-General began to speak, and had to clear his throat.

'We have heard and understood you, Mr. Lauder, and have been well served by your skill and your clarity in this most distressing task today. The panel has also heard you. We now invite him to address us in his own defence on the charges so preferred against him. Mr. Crawford.'

From Lymond's pale hair to his finger tips no uncomprehending muscle moved. 'I have nothing to add,' he said.

In the crowded room the atmosphere tightened as if he had shouted. 'Nothing?' exclaimed Argyll. 'You are accused of treason, sir: you have heard the gravest accusations and the gravest doubts expressed about your evidence. Have you no excuse?'

Bare of irony, Lymond's eyes left the Justiciar and rested on his own immobile and flatly crossed hands. 'The margin is so small,' he said, 'between life and no life, fact and lie, treason and patriotism, civilization and savagery . . . If Mr. Lauder can see it, he is lucky; if you can comprehend it you have a better right to judge than I have to plead. I have nothing to add.'

'If you can't tell the difference between loyalty and treason, Mr. Crawford,' said the Bishop, 'then you are certainly safer hanged.'

The Master's eyes studied him. 'Why, can you?'

'As long,' said Orkney broadly, 'as I know the difference between right and wrong.'

'Yes. The position is very similar. Patriotism,' said Lymond, 'like honesty is a luxury with a very high face value which is quickly pricing itself out of the spiritual market altogether.'

'Feeling for one's country,' said the Lord Advocate softly, 'is not usually considered as a freestanding riddle in ethics. . . .'

The easy voice lifted the comment and the topic, and carried them to deeper waters. 'No. It is an emotion as well, and of course the emotion comes first. A child's home and the ways of its life are sacrosanct, perfect, inviolate to the child. Add age; add security; add experience. In time we all admit our relatives and our neighbours, our fellow townsmen and even, perhaps, at last our fellow nationals to the threshold of tolerance. But the man living one inch beyond the boundary is an inveterate foe.'

He laced his long fingers and raised them, his gaze resting on the exposed palms. 'Patriotism is a fine hothouse for maggots. It breeds intolerance; it forces a spindle-legged, spurious riot of colour. . . . A man of only moderate powers enjoys the special sanction of purpose, the sense of ceremony; the echo of mysterious, lost and royal things; a trace of the broad, plain childish virtues of myth and legend and ballad. He wants advancement – what simpler way is there? He's tired of the little seasons and looks for movement and change and an edge of peril and excitement; he enjoys the flowering of small talents lost in the dry courses of daily life. For all these reasons, men at least once in their lives move the finger which will take them to battle for their country. . . .

'Patriotism,' said Lymond again. 'It's an opulent word, a mighty key to a royal Cloud-Cuckoo-Land. Patriotism; loyalty; a true conviction that of all the troubled and striving world, the soil of one's fathers is noblest and best. A celestial competition for the best breed of man; a vehicle for shedding boredom and exercising surplus power or surplus talents or surplus money; an immature and bigoted intolerance which becomes the coin of barter in the markets of power – '

Into the silence, the Master spoke gently. 'These are not patriots but martyrs, dying in cheerful self-interest as the Christians died in the pleasant conviction of grace, leaving their example by chance to brood beneath the water and rise, miraculously, to refresh the centuries. The cry is raised: Our land is glorious under the sun. I have a need to believe it, they say. It is a virtue to believe it; and therefore I shall wring from this unassuming clod a passion and a power and a selflessness that otherwise would be laid unquickened in the grave.'

With the unfettered freedom of his voice, with the disciplined and friendly ardours of his mind, he made it plain where he was leading them.

'And who shall say they are wrong?' said Lymond. 'There are those who will always cleave to the living country, and who with their uprooted imaginations might well make of it an instrument for good. Is it quite beyond us in this land? Is there no one who will take up this priceless thing and say, Here is a nation, with such a soul; with such talents; with these failings and this native worth? In what fashion can this one people be brought to live in full vigour and serenity, and who, in their compassion and wisdom, will take it and lead it into the path?'

For two, for three, for four seconds, the silence continued. Then Lauder, an expression of pure joy on his face, let out a long sigh; Argyll himself drew a deep breath, and Erskine, dragging his eyes from the quiet chair, found Richard staring at his brother with the privacies of his stubborn spirit exposed, unheeding, on his face.

For a mighty moment Argyll faced Lymond, conjecture and curiosity and a certain sharp respect informing the pallid Campbell features. Then he said, 'I understand that you have said something you felt required saying at this time, and that you are not moved to argue and dispute over the complexities of the personal charges which have been put before us today. I am not sure that you are wrong; but this is not the place nor the time to reply to you, nor am I sure that I or any man present could do so – ' He paused.

'We have been shown the public interpretation of a remarkable case: a series of events borne forcibly to their close by a strong and unusual personality. Mr. Lauder has given us one reading of its character. He would, I think, be the first to admit that he has not, patently, shown us the whole man and that, whatever the true reading may be, Mr. Crawford, we may know that it is not simple, or obvious, or in any way commonplace.

'We have listened to the evidence most carefully. Most of the charges referring to crimes since 1542 are to my mind much weakened by what we have heard, and would be difficult to sustain. The original accusation however still stands, and the evidence has in no way been shaken by any argument of proof offered by the panel.

'We shall consider these things, however, and tomorrow this court will make its recommendation to the Three Estates, before whom you shall appear. It is this decision you must fear and face, and I warn you now to prepare yourself for it.'

It was as near a warning of doom as the Assize could achieve. Lymond was already standing to receive it, and there was no doubt that he understood what he was being told: the stamp of the day's assault lay in the very bones of his face. He bowed once, to the Assessors, and again, surprisingly, to the benches which held Erskine and his brother; then, flanked by his guards, he moved quietly to the door.

Neither Lauder nor the judges, nor the silent ranks of the witnesses remembered Will Scott.

* * *

A pretence of quiet had fallen on the night.

About the basin of the Tyne, small fire ringed Haddington: the boots of men clicked on the walls of the besieged town and padded in the trenches outside; and the unobtrusive gnawing of pick and mattock betrayed the pioneers still at work.

The river wound its way dimly to the coast; and the estuary, flat and moon-bright, with small ships black as buttons on its surface, lay at the bottom of the sky and rolled in the east-by-east wind which with spare and racking fingers was withdrawing the coasts from the English fleet.

Edinburgh, grimly warded, lay inside her walls, bedevilled by the shadows of her hills, her crag and tail a black and fishy emblem above the apologetic stench of the Nor' Loch. The moon copied on the cobbles the profile of all the new, high houses: the thatched gables and uncertain slates and the dancetté roofs; and the gutters ran in and out of the shadows like pied and silvery eels.

As always, there were lights at the ports; and tonight

there were lights as well at Holyrood, and at Mary of Guise's palace on Castle Hill. Farther down the slope another candle shone in an upper window at the Tolbooth: behind it Lymond lay, drugged into sleep, with a guard outside his locked door until the night should pass and Parliament meet to pronounce his doom. In the Culters' house in the High Street his family also waited, and the tapers burned all night.

They burned also at the Castle, where light and heat reeled in mortal embrace in the prisoners' room. The ceiling, low and plastered, pressed down the strata of exhausted air, stale with old beer and sweating bodies. There was no room left to stand and no air to inhale, but the light beat down on a swaying corymb of heads, and shone on necks craning with a nervous, avid tension like beasts at a water hole.

At the centre sat Will Scott and Sir Thomas Palmer, half-naked: sunburnt thews glistening under multiple lights and sweat slithering down the tough cord of their spines.

For maybe an hour now, Palmer's string of jocularities and pithy memoirs had stopped, and he was breathing hoarsely into the cards, eyes intent and chin set in three trim folds against his chest. Beside his chair, topped by a bundle of clothes, lay a good half of Scott's belongings. Beside Scott, kicked into a disorderly tangle by the eager feet of the onlookers, was every article presently owned by Tommy Palmer except one: his cousin's statement.

Scott was too tired to think. Often before he had played the night through, ending wild-eyed and unshaven and ravenously hungry and going on to perform prodigies of nuisance-making in his father's wake. But against Palmer he needed more than a flair: he needed nerve and watchfulness and weblike concentration, with an instinct for bluff, and an inspiration to know when to call it.

He ignored the chaffing of his enthusiastic audience; he refused to be upset by the games he lost and by Palmer's unworried bonhomie. He played on doggedly with his red hair sticking in cowlicks to his brow and stared at the

607

tarots until they glimmered in his eyeballs like invitation
cards to hell. He knew that it was dark, that the inquiry
was over and, from Erskine standing now at his side, that
it had gone against Lymond. He had no idea of the time.

Palmer was preparing his sequences. He did it slowly,
as if the feel of the cards gave him pleasure. 'My pretty
atous,' he said, and admired them, his broad fingers
sprawled across the painted backs.

Scott looked at his own hand, and the tarots' sleek,
Egyptian heads with ancient divination in their eyes stared
back, warming their painted hands at a world of flesh. His
feet were on le chemin royal de la vie and the thin travest-
ies in his hands this time were real: the traitor and the
hanged man, death and the fool. Their avid fingers were
real, and the scent of an evil nostalgia. He closed the cards
abruptly and held them closed until his brain cleared.

He had a good hand, but not a first-class one; and he
suspected Palmer's was better. There was one way he
might improve on it: by calling on luck. He had the World
and the Bateleur in his hand. He could challenge Palmer
for the Fool; if he didn't have it, his two tarrochi nobili
would bring him five points extra and almost certainly the
game. It had to. Each article redeemed by Palmer cost
him another game to win it back. If he lost this game he
had to play a minimum of two more and win both. And
he doubted if he had a reserve of mental energy for even
one.

It was very quiet. Scott looked at the cards again.
Palmer, breathing heavily, had the beginning of a smile
compressing his stubbled chins.

'Qui ne l'a,' said Scott, and Palmer's gaze, arrested,
narrowed and shot to meet his. 'Qui ne l'a? Well? Have
you got one?'

Palmer scratched his nose. He grunted, and the silence
moved down on the bruised and foundered men like a
wine press.

For as long as he dared, Palmer tested Scott's nerve.
Then slowly he shook his big head. 'No. Damn it to hell:
I have not.'

Will moved his hands very slowly: red hands like Buccle-uch's. The tarots, throttled and limp, dropped to their places on the table: sullen; maudlin; sulkily protesting the laughterless starvation of a paper world. There was a moment's pause, then Palmer moved, and his tarots ran like butter from corner to corner of the table.

It was a losing hand. 'My game, I think,' said Will Scott. The welter of congratulations, of back-slapping and draughts of flat beer and mounting noise hardly penetrated his brain; even when Palmer himself, after upending a pint of ale over his own head and shoulders with thunder-ous curses, broke into an equal percussion of laughter and embraced him like a son. Scott sat like a marmorean and gently smiling Buddha, the disputed paper safely clutched in his hand, and when he could be heard, spoke mildly. 'You can have back all your other stuff if you like. This is all I wanted.'

Surging up, Palmer elbowed his way forcefully to the window and stood with his back to it, flexing his beefy shoulders till the muscles flowed. 'What a game. God! What a game. I've played in every county in England and up and down France and in and out of Clinton's boats, but I've never met the man who could read my mind like you did. Never. I sat like a bloody plant and you read me as if my brains were thumbing signals from my ears. Where'd you pick it up?'

Scott was hauling on his shirt. 'I was taught,' he said invisibly, 'by . . .'

'Palmer swept up a fistful of linen and jerked. 'What?'

Like the rising sun, Scott's hand reappeared, still talk-ing. 'I was taught by a fellow called Jonathan Crouch.'

Sir Thomas's arms dropped like felled boughs. 'An Englishman?'

'Yes.

'With a wife called Ellen and a tongue with the perishing shakes?'

'Yes.'

'I taught that man to play tarocco!' yelled Sir Thomas.

'Yes, I know,' said Will Scott.

An hour later he was in Lymond's room.

The Master was difficult to waken. Under the boy's insistent fingers he stirred at length, and his weighted lids lifted a little. After a moment he recognized him and said 'Scott!' in a voice thickened with opiates. Then his eye caught a movement behind the boy and he turned his head. '. . . And Mr. Lauder too, I see.'

The laywer, his clothes rumpled and his hair on end, bowed and shut the door on inquisitive guards. Scott didn't look around. Instead, he held out the paper with Samuel Harvey's statement, the superscription lit by the bedside tallow. 'It's Samuel Harvey's confession,' the boy said. 'He made it to Christian at Haddington when he was dying, and it was taken down by their priest. It frees you from every taint of treason.'

The Master's fingers touched the folded papers, lingering on the broken seal, and delicately flattened them. Scott, watching his downcast eyes, visualized the pages as he had seen them an hour ago, when before his witnesses he had studied his prize.

> . . . summoned from the princess Mary's household and taken before the King. Essential to mislead the enemy as to the identity of the spy . . . Convenient presence of the Scotchman Crawford . . . Letter to his friends in Scotland already purloined . . . Forgery affixed and taken north with me . . .

And the last sentences.

> I learned afterwards that, ironically enough, the spy for whom all this trouble was taken died on his next visit to London. Of the others implicated, I have given my word not to mention them, and I do not see that I need do so, since it does not affect the substance of what happened. I am not ashamed of what I did: I obeyed orders in a justifiable act against the enemy.

Although he had reached the last page, the Master did not immediately look up. Scott was glad when at length he spoke. 'So she did get her proofs.'

'No one knows what went wrong,' said the boy. 'Either she was given the unwritten sheets franked and folded by mistake, or it was a deliberate deception: perhaps Harvey came to regret what he had done. The priest doesn't know.'

Lymond turned his head, searching the bright, sea-blue eyes under the gaudy thatch. 'And you: where did you get it?'

'Sir Thomas Palmer is Harvey's cousin. I found that out from Lady Douglas after she was released from Haddington. She told me as well that they were keeping Harvey's belongings for Palmer when he next came north.'

'. . . And?'

'And when he did come north, Father captured him,' said Scott, assailed with unforeseen embarrassments. 'Palmer's at the Castle now, and they also have the friar who wrote it out – I found that out later. I made them all witness the contents too, so that they could . . .'

'Your young catachumen played tarocco all night with Palmer to get possession of it,' said the Lord Advocate's most sumptuous voice. He had found a chair and was lying back in it, grinning benevolently at the ceiling. 'By God, I wish you'd take me in hand for six months in that troop of yours. Anyone who can beat Buskin's brother – '

'Not my doing: we imported a trainer for that,' said Lymond gravely, his skin faltering between red and white, his eyes brilliant. 'I don't think we could teach you much, Mr. Lauder.'

The legal gaze, leaving the rafters, swooped down to the pillows. 'Who stole your letter, Mr. Crawford? That damned Douglas woman, I take it.' He paused. 'You were very gentle with our friends today.'

Lymond's thoughts were clearly a thousand – a hundred – miles away. 'Our friends . . . ?'

Wiser than Scott, Henry Lauder ignored the boy's scowl and talked on. 'The Douglases. The Earl of Angus undertook, I believe, to set the crown of Scotland on Henry VIII's head by midsummer of that year. There was also talk of a secret bond signed by both Sir George and his brother in London, promising all their help to make Scotland Henry's. The King wouldn't want that noised abroad at the time.'

'No.' Lymond's hands still lay on the folded pages of the confession. He lifted the packet, a speculative, balancing finger at each end, and said, 'Nothing about the Douglases is news any more. The unpleasant truth is that, being a long-sighted family, they will attach themselves to the winning side, and not necessarily to the side that pays them most.

'When Douglas goes to Berwick as spokesman for the Scottish court, when he comes to Edinburgh sworn to promote the English marriage, both the Protector and Arran know very well he is putting his own words to the song he was taught. Perhaps even words which appear to be his own are sometimes not. These are stormy petrels: they show where the heavy seas are coming from and are to that extent useful. Their transactions shelter under sham diplomacy and they can truly be influenced in one way only, by personal shame. The side which succumbs to the temptation to strip the Douglases naked will lose them, and the considerable power of their men with them. Grey knew that: that is why he handled Sir George so tenderly in spite of the Protector and Wharton.'

Scott said defensively, 'My father also got permission to negotiate with the English. To protect his own interests.'

The Lord Advocate smiled involuntarily. 'Buccleuch has been driven to doing a lot of queer things to protect his own interests, but no one would ever confuse him with the Douglases. Mr. Crawford is right. The undiscriminating vulture is not our real danger: open scandal would simply drive him into profitless exile again, and would be of no possible advantage to us. Neither should we fear our sturdy patriots who, like your father, are busy with their loyalties in queer and crooked ways. Our danger lies with the men who want to take this country by trunk and limb and wreak it into such a shape that it will fit them and their children for hose and jerkin in their old age.'

'Some of them are sincere,' said Lymond.

'I know: and such men will wreck us yet. Preserve us above all from the honest clod and the ambitious fanatic.'

'There doesn't seem to be a bewilderment of types left to choose from.'

'The Culters, for example?'

Scott caught up Lauder with angry eyes. 'This ill-starred family with a wastrel son?'

The lawyer smiled. 'My business is with words, my boy; and the best ones grow like mushrooms on a good bedding-down of law. Your friend used some fairly choice expressions himself. . . . I admire your gift for commanding loyalty in spite of your tongue, Mr. Crawford. What will you do now?'

'I was going to ask you the same thing,' said Lymond; and it was clear that he had used the breathing space Lauder had given him to good effect.

The Lord Advocate rose. 'I think there are some people who should be shown this statement, and without much more delay,' he said. 'If you'll trust me with it.'

Lymond's voice saying 'Of course,' clashed with Scott's 'No!' His hands lingered a moment longer on the papers, then he ran finger and thumb along the fold and held the document out. Lauder took it.

'I should advise you to dress, if you can. Mr. Scott will help, perhaps. It may be necessary to send for you.'

The door shut behind him. Lymond said, his long mouth twitching at the sight of Scott's face, 'You must trust *somebody*, Will . . . in spite of any repeated advice to the contrary you may hear.'

Scott muttered, avoiding his eyes, 'You must have thought me the qualified king of the simple-minded.'

'If I did, I should never have allowed you to join me. Your father said as much to the Tribunal today – God, yesterday; and I can endorse it.'

'In spite of my hellish mistakes?'

'I was thinking of tonight. You made no mistake with that.'

With an enslaved eagerness, Scott asked the question

613

Lauder had put in vain. 'What will you do now?' But Lymond, stretching, caught him by the arm and forced him into a chair beside him.

'Wait a moment. It is gradually forcing itself on my consciousness that I am not to be divided into four pieces tomorrow. No appointment with Apollyon. You appear to have made a decision about my life far more arbitrary than any I made about yours.'

Scott's voice was uncertain. 'I owed you that much, at least.'

'You didn't owe me anything,' said the Master. 'There's an unnatural conspiracy to keep me alive, that's all. I hope to God you don't regret it. I hope to God *I* don't regret it. How the hell did you manage to thrash Palmer at cards?'

Delight rose within Scott's soul. Not expecting Lymond to say more, and not knowing that he dared not say more, the young Buccleuch explained, while the Master dressed.

* * *

The Culter's house in Bruce's Close had a red roof and a motto over every window, but inside it was comfortable and convenient, with two separate bedrooms and a parlour with a wide, light window above the garden for Sybilla's sewing.

At midnight the Dowager ordered her son and daughter-in-law to bed, promising firmly to retire. But she sat on at her window, a still shadow on the bright square of rosebushes outside, and every separate nerve in her body trembled and ached.

For five days Sybilla had launched herself and all her bountiful possession – her brains, her charm and her money – in a single-minded bombardment of authority. Her friends and contemporaries of church and nobility, the suitors of the Court of Session, the powerful of both sexes at Court, had all felt the impact of the Dowager's fear, and many of them tried to help because she was Sybilla, and people would lend her a needle to cobble the moon to her gates if she asked for it.

To no avail. From the start she had known that nothing

614

could save this son's life for her: the law recognized proof, and there was no proof. On his return from the Committee Richard had been made to repeat again and again the pattern of question and answer. They had thrashed the case out, the three of them, until they were exhausted; and she had sent her son and Mariotta to bed.

She moved, and the dark roses shivered. There was an Ewe had three lambs, and one of them was black. What of it? Sheep are commonly white: does that make white unassailable, any more than the pure light of the sun before the prism? How may a breed freshen except under mutation? How improve its whiteness except by admitting a rogue cobalt to its candid meadows? . . . Not that the misery had been lived through quite in vain. In all her life she had never heard Richard speak as, distressed and vehement, he had spoken to them that evening.

Sybilla looked out of the dark window. To the east, Moultrie's Hill and the Dow Craig, with Greenside on its farther slopes; where for nine hours she had once sat and watched Davie Lindsay mock the Three Estates before the Three Estates and the Crown before the Crown. That was a tolerance fast slipping from them.

The Lang Gait and Gabriel's road, unlit; and few and distant lights from Broughton and Silver Mills and Kirk-braehead and Canon Mills. Below, her garden plunged and rolled to the turgid waters of the loch, and the tall lands on either side shifted their shadows with the shifting moon.

There was an Ewe had three lambs; and one of them was black. The one was hanged, the other drowned; the third was lost, and never found. . . . Sybilla's hands closed hard on each other.

It was then that Tom Erskine, riding lightly and alone, came sweeping to the door.

Half an hour went by. In Mary de Guise's palace the tapers took fire from room to room, as the Queen Dowager moved with her maids to the audience chamber, turning her head as she walked to speak to Richard, on her right, and Henry Lauder, behind her.

They stood beside her as she settled on the dais. The Lord Chancellor was already there, his clothes wrinkled and dusty as the Queen's; and Argyll came in quickly, bowed, and sat with Huntly and Erskine and the secretaries along the wall of the short, elaborate room.

It was very hot, and the lights rebuffed their tired eyes. Because of the hour and the perpetual, malignant circumstance of crisis, the Queen demanded no ceremony. She spoke a little longer to the Lord Advocate, and next to Argyll; and then one of the secretaries answered her nod by opening the door. The Queen Dowager sat and watched Lord Culter, and Henry Lauder watched the Queen.

Richard smiled. Crawford of Lymond, standing just inside the doorway, smiled back, bowed, and remained where he was, in himself a novelty and a force to the considering gaze lifted to him. Chin sunk on her chains, starched gauze thinly shadowing the bridge of her nose, the Queen moved a hand and watched the man advance to her chair. She said, in her heavily accented English, 'I was curious.'

The Master replied in his own rapid French. 'It is I, Madame, who am curious, or I should not have manufactured myself a silly predicament.'

'The Justiciar cannot follow you,' observed Mary de Guise. 'We shall speak in English, in which he cannot follow me. There is no precedent, Mr. Crawford, for addressing a man who has been done an injustice by the State. We had, I thought, reached the safe haven of corruption where we need never fear to misjudge anybody. I am astounded to find myself wrong.'

A nasty one. Too shrewd by far to answer, Lymond only inclined his fair head: he had the knack of seeming to have been delivered in his garments, observed Lauder, irritably aware of sitting on rucked linen and surrounded by half-awake and unvaleted statesmen.

The matronly, autocratic voice continued. 'Through

Will Scott of Kincurd, we have had constant information of your providing about enemy movements and enemy affairs. We know now that we owe to you other gifts of money and of secrets over the years, and that we have had ignorantly the use of your talents and your abilities at Hume and at Heriot, at Carlisle and Dumbarton. All these services performed beneath the edge of our sword and below the heel of our boot: performed with vigour and wit and independence.

'You have amazed me, Mr. Crawford. You see in me a misery of rage which should compensate you a little for your suffering. Bequeathed a shabby and ransacked armoury, I have thrown away tempered steel. My God, M. le maître, you have done us an injury: you should have held us by the neck and shouted your wrongs into our lungs. What redress can language give you? A polite apology, and Mr. Lauder's regrets?'

'Modified regrets,' said the Lord Advocate. 'I love Mr Crawford like a son, but I wouldn't have missed that examination.'

'If you mislay your notes,' said Lymond, 'you will find them engraved on my liver. La reine douairière is generous. My impression is that I made several mistakes for every one of the State's. The thing is best forgotten.'

'My dear Mr. Crawford,' said the Queen Dowager. 'How can I forget, when my daughter recites scurrilous poetry, and holds you still dear to her heart . . . ?'

Huntly moved. Mary of Guise folded her hands without looking at him, but a fibre entered her voice which was not there before, and her gaze hardened over them all.

'I am aware,' she said, 'that to most of you – to most of the people who fight for me and against me, and for and against the Protector – the royal line is a certificate of birth, and a circlet of metal; a pawn astray on her own board and more used to domination and a ruthless handling than the weakest of her subjects.

'To me, it is a little girl, fresh and warm, holding surprises and knowledge and happy years in her palms. When armed invaders come and men die and are captured and plot and betray, she is still a small girl, crying because she has wakened in the night.' Her eyes dropped for a moment to her hands and her lip trembled for a moment, and then became firm.

'By all your efforts this year you have kept the Scottish crown safe from capture – yes, of course. What I remember, I, is that you have won me a year of my daughter's company.

'The last year, perhaps. She is safe. You, sir, with courage, kept the secret that allowed her ships to sail. Yesterday the wind moved from the south: autumn is coming, and a colder season perhaps than we have known yet. Yesterday my daughter set sail from Dumbarton: with Lord Livingstone and Lord Erskine, with her brother, with Fleming, Beaton, Seaton and Livingstone and Lady Fleming, she set sail for France, to live there and, in time, to marry the Dauphin.

'. . . Some will say, we should have admitted England, this importunate bridegroom; and kept unspilled blood and whole hearths for our dowry. I think not. I hope that we are choosing wisdom as well as pride, and a long peace as well as a quick harbour.'

'And England?' It was Lord Culter's voice.

'The King of France has taken this kingdom in perpetual shelter. He will demand of England peace between our three nations; and that all enmity between England and Scotland should cease.'

Outside, dawn had come, pale and wind-torn, with stars set tardily in its brightness. In the yellow glare of the lights, Lymond's gaze had turned to his brother. 'So they lose, after all,' he said. 'All the King's knights. Lord Grey and Lord Wharton, Lennox and Somerset, Wilford and Dudley, Sir George Douglas, Angus and Drumlanrig. Such plotting and striving and discomfort and distress; so much gold spent; so many peoples moved across the face of Europe to comfort us. It's a sad thing to woo with cannon and to lose.'

Mary de Guise had her mind as well as her eyes bent

618

on the intent, fair face below her. 'I wonder, are you with me?' she said.

The guarded eyes lifted instantly. 'Yes . . . I think so. There is a divine solution, but we are only human, and Scots at that. Which means we dote on every complexity.'

'And what award shall we give you,' said Mary de Guise gravely, 'for all you have done for us? Apart from the unqualified love of my daughter?'

Lymond's charming smile entered his blue eyes as he stood, experienced and passive, before her. 'I have no other desires, and can imagine none.'

'No?' said the Queen Dowager, and rising, swept Francis Crawford out of the room, ignoring her statesmen stumbling in surprise to their feet; leaving Richard faintly smiling and Lauder cursing with determination. 'No other desires? Au contraire. There are some that I shall expect to find out and one, assuredly, that I know,' said the Queen with decision; and opened a door.

In a lifetime of empty rooms, this was another.

Then there was a whisper of silk, a perfume half remembered, a humane, quizzical, intuitive presence; and a wild relief that deluged the tired and passionate mind.

Sybilla was there. She saw her son's eyes, and flung open her arms.